BINDING
OF
SILVER

To my sisters—

Thanks for being the earliest fans of my stories, long before publication days! From late-night laughter, book talk, and marathon Doctor Who sessions to supporting one another through trials and tears, your sisterhood has always been a gift. I'm blessed to share life with you!

SERIES READING ORDER

For the optimal reading experience, the *Blood of the Fae* series should be read in sequential order, starting with *Whispers in the Waters*—although you can start with *Tattoo of Crimson*, if desired.

Primary books:
    Whispers in the Waters (prequel)
    Tattoo of Crimson
    Ruins of Bone
    Binding of Silver
    Mirror of Argent (coming fall 2025)

Additional works:
    Jewel of Blood (free for newsletter subscribers)
    *Relic of Light**
    *Signs in the Stars**

*Should be read after *Ruins of Bone*.

These shorter works aren't necessary to enjoy the series, but allow you to dig deeper into the characters and world, if you so choose.

CHAPTER 1

Our earliest written records tell how high fae have ever sought to snare mortals, their reasons as varied as their pursuits are cruel. One might desire to craft an expendable monster, another to bind an unwilling thrall to his bidding, a third simply to entertain herself with a new plaything. Whatever the motive, when a fae claimed a mortal, it meant nothing but suffering for the unfortunate individual now imprisoned to an immortal will.

Our lore said no escape existed for those bound, only torment, and the eventual release of death. But I refused to accept that as truth.

Because now . . . now the fae had *Ainslie*.

The elm had revealed her enthralled departure, but where had her bargain-holder taken her? My grip on the bark tightened, its rough ridges digging into my skin, splinter-shards of pain racing up my arms. What sort of torture did this fae mean to inflict? What horrors had she endured already?

Risha fluttered to my side, her wings bright. "What did you see?"

"My sister. She was taken by fae."

Risha's vivid blues dimmed to indigo and gray. Since she'd

just lost her hatch-sister Asrina, she'd understand my fears. If Ainslie ended up like Asrina—how could I endure it?

She'd been so determined to ignore her binding mark, to pretend it meant nothing of consequence. I should have pressed her harder, should have spoken to Riven regardless of her wishes, should have done something, anything, to keep her safe.

Jade pressed herself against my legs, her warmth a comfort I did not deserve. *Much as you might desire it, you cannot dictate the choices of others.*

Yet I kept so much from her. If I'd spoken sooner, told her of my own experiences with fae, perhaps she would have listened and let me ask Riven for help.

Perhaps. Perhaps not. Jade chuffed. *Dwelling on regrets benefits no one. What do you intend to do now?*

Seek her. Could I use the trees along the lane to trace her path? A sharp gust of wind carried traces of salt from the sea, stinging my eyes and tightening my throat. I had to try.

The snapdragons' protective song surged across my senses, the thrum of the goldhearts deep and steady beneath. They bolstered me as I abandoned the garden of Willowere and hurried down the hill toward the curve in the lane, where the perspective of the elm vanished.

Trees arched over the bend in the road, their laced boughs casting dappled shadows that contrasted with the golden morning light. A gnarled, sea-swept oak lowered its branches toward me, offering aid, and I braced myself against its sturdy frame. This time images of Ainslie surfaced even faster.

Still moving as one caught in a dream—or nightmare—Ainslie abandoned the lane. She entered the forest, heedless of the thorns that snagged her gown, even her flesh. The moonlight played over her binding mark and caught on a bead of blood that dripped down her arm...

The oak had witnessed no more.

So I abandoned the shelter it offered, the strength it lent my unsteady limbs, and plunged into the forest of beech and ash that lined the road. Scarlet tuft mushrooms poked fiery heads from among the bracken, their bright melodies urging me toward a small clearing. Had she passed here?

I seized the smooth, silvery trunk of a beech.

She wandered toward her fate as if she were led by an invisible chain, at last stumbling to a halt in a small clearing. Even more luminous than the silvery moon, even brighter than her binding mark, the light of a passing prism flared. Without hesitation, she marched up to it.

And stepped through.

Oh, please, no.

Bile rose in my throat, burning and bitter. I wrenched away from the beech, stumbling over the wreckage of its fallen comrade and staggering to a halt in the clearing. The boles of the trees cast deep shadows across scattered scarlet tufts and filmy-ferns. No trace remained of the passing that had claimed her, but what I'd witnessed was indisputable.

I'd lost Ainslie to the Otherworld.

The ash above me shuddered, as if my pain became its own, and the filmy-fern murmured low whispers of comfort.

What now? I didn't have the power to open a passing. Only by traveling to a Crossing—which would take weeks—could I access the Otherworld, and even then, how could I hope to trace Ainslie without a starting point?

I couldn't, not on my own. But Riven had left me a means of contacting him. Could he help without overstepping the bounds laid by his king? I'd no way to justify this request, nothing to offer in exchange for his help, so I must trust the friendship we'd begun to form. For Ainslie, I would ask.

I turned to Risha, who hovered in a shaft of sunlight that pierced the clearing, its glinting light too reminiscent of the passing for comfort. Asrina had welcomed generous compliments, but Risha was bolder, less gentle in nature. Would she welcome flowery remarks or believe them condescension? All I could see, all I could think of was Ainslie—best to keep it simple. With difficulty, I steadied my voice. "Bright one, will you go for Riven? Please tell him that Ainslie has vanished into the Otherworld. Ask . . . ask if he'll come."

"As you wish." Her light brightened, then she vanished in a swirl of silver-laced blue.

Jade prowled the clearing. *No fae left scent here.*

It seems they didn't need to come; perhaps they simply used the bargain to compel her through the passing.

An echo of the sensation I'd experienced when Lord West impaled me with working-woven stone ghosted my shoulder. He'd taken pleasure in inflicting pain whenever he could—and whoever claimed Ainslie likely shared his malice. I rubbed my arm, seeking to drive away the spectral pain. Ainslie would have no defense, bound as she was in bargain. Even if we found her, it could be too late.

No. That was unlikely, since fae liked to toy with their prey. Was her bargain-holder hurting her, even now? Breath ragged, I collapsed on a fallen beech trunk.

Soft and distant, I heard Ada call my name. She must have finished in the cottage and come in search of me. Though I'd rather pluck thistles barehanded than tell her Ainslie's fate, I forced myself to abandon the clearing. I couldn't allow her to think I'd vanished also.

When I joined her in the lane, Ada seized my arm, her face as pale as a paperwhite. "I examined her belongings, and nothing is missing, not even a pair of shoes. Oh, Jessa, I can only think—what if someone took her against her will? I cannot fathom how, but if she left without any of her belongings, without so much as a word to me, to any of us . . . what other explanation could there be?"

"Her binding mark."

Ada turned paler still, even her lips taking on an uncanny pallor. "After all this time?"

How could I add another shock to the one she already endured by explaining the reason for my confidence? I faltered. "I cannot think immortal beings see time in the same way we do. If the moment has come that she must fulfill the terms of her bargain . . ."

"Then it's worse than I imagined." She paced the lane, her arms wrapped about her chest. "If you're right, what can we do? Mr. Burke! Should we go for Mr. Burke? Ainslie said he was exceedingly helpful when Lord West abducted you and—"

"He's already left for Avons." How I wished he'd remained . . . but not as much as I desired Riven's presence. He'd know what to do, how to find her. I fought the urge to join Ada in pacing the rutted road. Where was Risha? It was taking far too long.

"If not Mr. Burke, perhaps another stratesman?"

"If they learn Ainslie has a binding mark, they're more likely to call in the Vigil and confine her to an Institution than come to her aid." The notion tightened my shoulders. "Nor do I think them capable of assisting with high fae."

"Then what?" Ada shivered like a willow caught in a storm. "We just abandon her to whatever dreadful fate the fae have in store?"

I wrapped my arm around Ada, and she leaned against me, her frame feeling more fragile than before our visit to Withern. Only a few days ago she'd almost died of basilisk venom, and this certainly wouldn't help her recover. However improper, she needed a place to rest, and I helped her onto a broad, flat rock alongside the lane, hoping we'd encounter no passersby. "There's someone who might be able to help, an expert in fae bindings. If we have any hope of getting her back, we'll have to find out who has taken her and why."

Under ordinary circumstances, that meant we'd have no hope whatsoever. Fae did not relinquish their prizes readily. But I did not mean to surrender her, whatever the cost of her retrieval.

Ada clenched her hands in her lap. "Then you must go at once to ask for assistance. I can make excuses for your absence with Aunt Caris, only please hurry."

"I don't want you walking back to the cottage alone."

"I won't be the cause of a delay." She struggled to her feet. "I'll be fine if we just find Ainslie."

If we did not—no, I refused to consider it. Riven would come, and we *would* find her. Ada soon vanished down the lane, and Jade leapt atop the stone she had abandoned.

Risha should have returned by now.

If Jade felt it too . . . Something sank inside me. *Perhaps I presumed too much, asking Riven to come. He might have refused, and she might not want to tell me.*

I don't think you presumed, not given the terms on which you parted. I'm more concerned that someone might have had a vested interest in preventing her from reaching Riven.

My mouth went as dry as an unwatered garden. Had I sent her into some sort of snare? If I was responsible for the death of another sun sylph . . .

I deliberately inhaled the sweet-grass scent of Jade's fur, pressing back my fears. If I succumbed to panic, I'd never find Ainslie. I needed to *think*, not sit idle, conjuring dire fates for Ainslie and Risha. While I waited for Riven, I'd seek answers among the trees. Perhaps some trace of the passing would linger in their recall, maybe even some sign of the one who held her binding.

Time slipped away as I connected with one tree after another, attempting to pull forth any hint of the Other force that had claimed Ainslie. The world about me began to fade, yet I gained nothing except the same heart-wrenching tale chronicled from different perspectives, some clearer, others more nebulous and harder to bring into view.

I returned to the edge of the clearing, where I collapsed on a fallen tree trunk that had carved a space amid a tangle of sea buckthorn. My fingers were chafed and begrimed from gripping rough bark; my shoulders ached with tension, and my temples throbbed. My efforts weren't enough. *I* wasn't enough, not with the limited understanding I had of fae nature and my own affinities.

You'd not condemn another so harshly. Jade rumbled low in her chest. *I'll not allow you to speak so of yourself.*

But if I cannot find a way to her, if Riven cannot come—

He will.

Yet would his arrival come too late for Ainslie? The tangle of thorns rustled about me, their spike-sharp songs piercing. I could do nothing for Ainslie while trapped in the mortal world—and by the time I reached a Crossing, she might well be dead. What then?

I lifted my gaze.

In the distance, Kilmere loomed. Though dark against the clouding sky, its power no longer threatened. Before it recognized me as its mistress, it had opened a passing to thrust me from its borders. Could I encourage it to do so again? If I asked, would it open a way into the Otherworld? Even if it did, where would I request to go, with all the vastness of the courts open to me? I'd no notion of who might have claimed Ainslie, of where she might be found. It would be an act of desperation, not one founded in any true hope of discovering her location. It might come to that in the end, but not yet. Perhaps if I examined her belongings, I could find something Ada had missed—

A familiar lightning-charge sensation built about me, then a gleaming passing rippled the air. With a flare of blue light, Risha appeared, and relief flooded me. Then Riven strode through, a storm surging about him, the pressure in the air strong enough to steal my breath. I staggered back beneath the raw power pouring from him. Only the faintest hint of glamour veiled it, and none concealed the black spatters of blood across his hands and face. In places it had soaked through the jerkin he wore, and the sharp scents of death and pain rent the air around him, as jagged as the shards of light that lingered after the passing.

My stomach hollowed, and the distant roar of the sea pulsed in my ears. Instinctively, I moved toward him. "Riven, what— you're covered in blood."

He lifted a shoulder. "If it troubles you, I can make it vanish."

"That's not what I meant." Even as I spoke, he drew in shimmering strands of light, the storm charge sensation of power abating as he pulled it inward. I shook my head. "I don't want you to glamour away the truth. If you're hurt, I want to help."

A glint of gold appeared in his eyes, a light in the darkness. "I'm fine."

Yet I scent fae blood amid the other.

Which meant he *was* injured, however much he preferred to keep it concealed. My breath tangled in my chest. "What happened?"

"Dark wyvern." He scrubbed a dark blotch from the hilt of a dagger at his side. "It's of little consequence."

Little consequence? Through all Kilmere had brought against us, he'd sustained no injury. Just how brutal had this battle been?

Dark wyvern bear great enmity toward the Court of Gold. Jade regarded him steadily. *Risha says there were many.*

A strong sea wind swept through the trees, tugging my hair loose and whipping it about my face, chilling my skin. I'd taken for granted Riven's indomitable nature, but matters could have gone differently. If he'd not emerged the victor . . . I felt as though a sea breaker crashed over me, threatening to pull me under. "How did you come to encounter them?"

"It doesn't matter."

"It matters to me," I said softly.

His eyes lightened further, yet he made no reply.

Jade's tail twitched. *Risha says he's angered King Talon. Instead of sending some of the Valor along with Riven to deal with the matter as he ordinarily would, the king commanded him to face them alone.*

I drew in a sharp breath. *Why would he do that?*

It was a logical choice. The king cannot afford to be rid of his arbiter, nor can he appear to tolerate any hint of disloyalty. This provides a reminder his authority is not to be flouted. Though the Valor otherwise answer to the arbiter, they must heed the king's edict in this. And though the power of an arbiter is second only to the king's, Riven had to pay the required price.

It could have meant his life. The needlelike leaves of the buckthorn shivered. *What if it's my fault? If this is about what happened in the Court of Silver . . .*

Riven had said his king wouldn't be angry, but perhaps it caused more trouble than he'd admitted. I was cold deep within, so cold that even the brilliant sun failed to warm me.

His gaze sharpened, as though he could see through to my soul. "What's wrong? Risha said it was urgent."

So he'd come straight from his conflict with the wyvern without even taking a moment to glamour away the evidence, but oh—

My vision blurred, and I closed my eyes. No matter my fears for Riven, how could I have forgotten, even for a moment, what Ainslie suffered?

"Jessa." His voice came closer, softer. "What happened?"

"It's Ainslie." The evergreen song of the firs along the path bolstered my flagging strength, steadied my voice. "She disappeared last night, and I traced her to a passing in the forest just outside Willowere, where she vanished into the Otherworld."

He became very still. "Has she ever had dealings with fae before?"

"She . . . she has a binding mark."

Silence stretched; his jaw tightened. "How long?"

I spilled out the full tale—how we'd believed it a scar, how I'd recognized it as a binding mark when he'd made the first bargain with me what felt like an eternity ago, and how she'd refused to grant permission for me to speak of it to Riven or anyone else.

"I see stubbornness runs in the family." Little sparks of light licked the blood from Riven's skin, and glamour began to weave about him once more, concealing his fae nature. "If she's bound by bargain, even if I track her, there may be little we can do."

"But you can find her?"

"Yes. Unless she's vanished into another court. Then matters become more complicated."

"Do all your courts bear enmity toward each other?"

"We have rivals and allies and vassals, much as Byren does. If we're fortunate, she'll have been claimed by an ally court—though even that will present difficulties." His glamour complete, he stepped closer. "We shouldn't waste further time. Where did she disappear?"

"The forest just outside Willowere, in the clearing near where the road curves."

That was all he required. With a surge of power and rich golden light, he brought us through a passing to the place where she'd vanished. I gestured toward the clearing. "It was right between those—"

The words died in my throat. In the deep shade beneath the trees, something white fluttered, so diaphanous I first believed it a trick of the light. A faint rustle sounded from behind two towering ash, and the distant sensation of Other swept my skin. Riven kept still; silence fell between us.

Then a figure stepped from the shadows.

CHAPTER 2

Gossamer-like threads drifted about the figure, obscuring form and feature as it moved deeper into the clearing. Then, like mist burned away by the sun, the pale strands vanished.

And my heart stopped.

The figure—it was Ainslie.

I ran to her, pulled her close, but her skin was cold as stone, her body as unyielding. Her veins pulsed dark, as if living shadows raced through them. With unnatural strength, she shook off my hold and continued to march toward the lane.

The skin along my arms pebbled. She didn't see me, didn't hear me call her name. Her body was present, but her mind . . . Where had she gone?

Dimly, I sensed Jade drawing near, but I could not wrench my gaze from Ainslie's frame. Absent the spark of her personality, it had become a thing of horror.

Riven stepped in front of her and spoke a sharp command in the fae tongue. Like a marionette with its strings cut, she slumped, became motionless, her gaze distant and unseeing. Beneath her feet, the filmy-fern shuddered as it responded to an Otherworldly force swirling about her.

I choked down raw terror. "What's happened to her?"

"She's under a heavy compulsion." Riven sent golden coils of light spiraling over her skin. "By the looks of her veins, she's been subjected to shadowmancy."

"What does that mean?" Despite my best efforts, my voice quavered.

"That someone wanted to inflict pain without leaving physical damage. As a consequence for some infraction, perhaps."

My eyes burned. What had she endured in her absence? I clasped her hand, but her fingers remained limp in mine. The ferns brushed my legs, but their gentle murmurs brought no peace. "Can you bring her back to herself?"

"If you want her freedom, we shouldn't try. We should observe, see what we can learn."

Watch Ainslie forced to move like a mindless automaton, with no more self-awareness than a ghoul? What if that was why the fae had summoned her, to forever steal some vital part of her soul? I gripped tighter. "Very well."

"You need to release her."

I pressed my lips together to still a protest and forced myself to step back.

Then Riven addressed Ainslie once more. As if his words had cut a cord binding her, she shambled onward in her nightgown, her bare feet bruised and bleeding.

I braced myself on an alder, and its song became pained, as though it voiced the cry I could not. Riven closed the distance between us, the scent of sun-drenched forest drifting from him, warm and vital and grounding. "All is not lost. Not yet."

He wasn't one to give false hope—if anything, he could be counted on to deliver difficult truths. Which meant Ainslie *could* still be restored. I didn't trust my voice, so I simply nodded.

"Come."

With Jade draped over my shoulders, solid and comforting, and Risha lighting our way, Riven and I followed Ainslie.

She remained just out of sight of the lane, slipping from shadow to shadow beneath the trees, her features blank, her eyes fixed on something I could not see. When she neared Willowere and the sound of servants' voices drifted out, she hesitated, waiting motionless until they passed. Then she slipped to the back of the cottage, ascending the secondary stairs and traversing the corridor to her bedchamber.

"When she emerges from the compulsion, do you want her to know I'm here?" Riven asked, his voice low.

"I think she must." If she ever emerged from this enthrallment, it would be time for truth—however painful. As we ascended, the walls of the staircase seemed to close in about us, and I struggled to draw a full breath. I wouldn't think about how much a confession could shatter, not now.

Once inside her bedchamber, Ainslie withdrew a fresh gown from the clothes press, then vanished behind the dressing screen, emerging a few moments later properly dressed. She fetched a brush and worked it through her tangled hair. A scattering of leaves and twigs fell to the floor; she took no note.

Her eyes remained vacant, eerily reminiscent of the ghouls. Where was Ainslie, the true Ainslie? I checked a plea for Riven to intervene. He was right—if we were to understand, we must let this play out.

She swept her hair into tidy coils, then pulled stockings over her injured feet—shoes too, which must have hurt. Yet she never flinched, only continued to move in a languid, dreamlike fashion.

Riven stood in the far corner of the room. Light spilled through the windows and played over the sharp planes of his face, heightened the focused intent with which he regarded Ainslie. Could he perceive any hint of the workings woven about her?

From the folds of her discarded nightgown, Ainslie drew a small vial containing some sort of floral-scented salve that she smoothed over the scratches on her arm. Almost at once, they vanished. Yet she applied it nowhere else.

My hands tightened, the nails digging into my skin. This fae had supplied her with a healing salve, but evidently commanded her to use it only on visible marks, which meant her other injuries would continue to cause pain. The darkness of her veins had faded, giving her an ordinary appearance except for her blank gaze.

When she tucked the salve away, concealing it deep within the clothes press, a soft sigh escaped her. Some flicker of awareness returned to her eyes, and hope unfurled in my chest.

I stepped forward. "Ainslie?"

Slowly, she turned. A slight furrow marred her brow, but glorious life filled her face again. "Jessa? When did you come in? I didn't hear you knock."

How she'd returned to herself or why or what might yet come, none of it mattered, not now. I felt light as dandelion down drifting on a summer breeze. Whatever she'd suffered, she'd returned to us—and I pulled her to my chest with such ferocity that she gasped.

"What in the Crossings has come over you?" she asked.

Ada burst into the room. "I thought I heard—Ainslie!" Abandoning her usual grace, she hurled herself at her twin, and Ainslie staggered with the force of the impact. "We were so afraid. Where have you been?"

"What do you mean?" She clasped her arms to her chest as if bracing against some distant pain. "I've been right here."

Ada blanched. "No, Ainslie. I woke in the night to find you absent, and you were still gone when I rose this morning. We've been looking for you ever since—we feared the worst."

Though he'd not concealed his presence, neither glanced toward the sunlit corner where Riven stood. Their emotions consumed them, blinded them to all else, and I did not want them to express anything they'd regret before an audience. "Before we discuss the matter further—"

"There's nothing to discuss. You must be mistaken," Ainslie said. "I would remember . . ."

"Would you?" With a single smooth motion, Riven moved toward the center of the room.

They startled. Ainslie gave a quiet gasp, and Ada fluttered toward the door, as if she contemplated sounding an alarm.

Untroubled by their responses, Riven wove a concealment glamour about the bedchamber. "What do you recall about the past several hours?"

Ainslie turned to me. "Jessa, why is he here?"

"I asked for his help when you went missing. We found you in the woods, no more than half an hour ago," I said softly. "You returned here and tidied your appearance. Only then did you notice my presence."

Ada pressed a hand to her mouth, shaking her head.

"That . . . it's impossible." But even as Ainslie spoke, her fingers sought the binding mark on her arm. Did it pain her, as mine once had?

I moved toward her. "Take off your shoes and stockings."

She glanced at Riven. "It's not proper."

"We're beyond that now."

"I don't see what that will—" Her breath caught, and uncertainty clouded her usually bright eyes. "My feet hurt."

"I know." How I wished I could spare her this. "You need to understand the truth."

Her eyes slid shut; her features shadowed. Then she sank into the small chair by the hearth, undoing shoes and stockings alike.

In the bright afternoon sun, the myriad cuts and scratches along the pale skin of her feet appeared all the worse, some dark and discolored, others bright and oozing. When she lifted her gaze, the fear in it wrenched my heart.

"What happened? Why can't I remember?"

Ada sank down beside Ainslie, folding her in an embrace. Then she glanced up at Riven. "Lord Riven, we're very grateful for your assistance in finding Ainslie, but this is a private matter, and besides, you cannot be found in our bedchamber. Aunt Caris would—"

His gaze sharpened. "Do you want Ainslie safe?"

"Of course."

"Then you'll allow me to remain."

Ainslie surged to her feet, flinching when they touched the floor. "How can you possibly help?"

"By examining your binding mark and seeking the fae who forged it." Despite the emotional charge to the room, his voice remained as calm as if he proposed a stroll in the park.

Ainslie whirled toward me, stricken. "You told him about the bargain? You said you wouldn't tell anyone—you gave your word."

"And *you* said if something changed I could seek help on your behalf. Surely your disappearance counts." If she vanished again, if the fae tampered with her once more, would she be lost forever? I clenched my hands in the folds of my skirts. "If anyone can help us, it's Riven. He's the expert in binding marks I mentioned."

Her brows drew tight. "And what precisely has given him knowledge about binding marks?"

How could I possibly answer that, without betraying secrets that were not my own? "I—"

"Not now, Ainslie," Ada said. "We thought we'd lost you for good, and we still could in an instant, if the fae who holds your bargain summons you once more. Given the circumstances, we must accept Lord Riven's offer."

"At what risk? I can't—"

"Let him examine the mark." Ada rarely spoke with such resolution, yet Ainslie remained undaunted.

"Not without some explanation from Jessa. I know we agreed to wait till you recovered, but now that she's brought him here, it can wait no longer."

Ada looked from Ainslie—whose heightened color betrayed her inner turmoil—to Riven, who remained unmoved, despite the implicit insult. Then she caught her lower lip between her teeth. "Jessa, could we speak alone?"

"I'll answer all your questions, but not now. We can't afford a delay." If Riven left with matters unstable in his court, he might not be able to return until it was too late for Ainslie. "It won't take long."

Ainslie blew out an impatient breath. "If you won't send him away, then we will have this out with him present, however unfitting."

What must Riven think of all this? Most fae would have abandoned the matter already, but then, most fae would never have come. Uncomfortable warmth pricked up my neck. "Ainslie, please."

She shook her head. "How can you expect us to blindly accept this so-called help? You haven't been yourself in some time, and much of the change coincided with his arrival in your life."

"That's not—"

She lifted her chin. "Is he holding something over you? Forcing you to do his bidding? Is that why he's here now, why you won't send him away?"

Wait . . . they suspected *Riven* of underhanded dealings? Had they guessed at his fae nature? If they had, would he allow them to retain that knowledge? My legs weakened, and I sank into the chair Ainslie had vacated. "No, it's nothing like that."

"What then?" she demanded. "How can you say his presence here, his knowledge of the binding mark, presents no risk?"

Riven stirred at last, his eyes glinting dangerously. "You know your sister less well than you imagine, if you believe she'd bring danger to your door."

Ainslie's eyes sparked. "Who are you to speak of Jessa that way, when—"

Ada rested a hand on her arm, cutting short whatever she intended to say.

"Let her speak." Though Riven's face revealed no trace of emotion, pressure built in the air. "If you wish to make an accusation, then do so."

"Very well." Ainslie straightened, and I recognized resolve writ on her face—she'd been pressed almost beyond bearing, and she'd not surrender without the truth, however dangerous such a confrontation would be, if Riven bore us ill will. "Do you represent the Vigil? Have you forced Jessa to collect information for you? To allow you access to Kilmere?"

"No."

She appeared taken aback by the flat denial. Before she could level further accusation, I shook my head. "You thought I'd allow the Vigil an opportunity to hurt our family?"

That stung more than the thorns that had torn my flesh earlier. Yet at least they'd not realized he was fae—were not at risk of their memory of this conversation being glamoured away.

Not yet.

"Not by choice." Ada interposed herself between us, ever seeking to mediate. "We weren't certain what to think at first. It was clear Lord West and Lord Riven had some sort of animosity toward each other and that you were greatly troubled. We thought perhaps when Lord West pressured you to sell Kilmere, you turned to what you believed the lesser evil, and then found yourself trapped. We believed you were trying to protect us and endangering yourself in the process. That your recent fear of the Vigil was because . . . Lord Riven . . . he'd hurt you in some way."

Riven kept silent, watching me, dagger-sharp shards of light flaring about him. And I sank back, the chair spindles digging into my spine. He allowed me space to deal with the situation as I desired, without attempting to glamour away question or accusation, yet how could I even begin to address all the issues they'd raised? Some part of their theorizing held truth. I *had* sought to protect them, but the rest . . . it was a convoluted mess. I pressed my fingers against my aching temples.

It seemed they believed the story that Mr. Burke had spread about Riven rescuing me after I'd been abducted by Lord West, but they gave him no credit for it. Instead, they took it as further evidence that he sought to use me for his own ends against a rival.

"Jessa?" Ada stepped closer.

Beyond the window glass, the gold runners murmured

restively, as if they shared my sense of a coming reckoning. I'd withheld the truth, so they'd conjured dangerous theories. Now I must pay the price. "He's not Vigil."

"And yet we've found no trace of his family line or his holdings. If the Vigil has not hidden his background, then who has?" Ainslie asked.

They'd investigated him? What would Riven make of that? I didn't dare look at him. Instead, I reached for Jade, drawing her to my chest to shield me from what must come.

Perhaps the truth will not be as bad as you fear.

Yet the pressure in the air strengthened. Had Riven lost patience altogether? He'd come to lend aid and instead found himself accused of all sorts of underhanded dealings. He'd be justified in abandoning us to our troubles.

Instead he spoke with quiet authority, glamour shading his voice. "My past is no concern of yours. I'm here only to offer aid."

He meant to ease their fears, to make them forget they'd ever worried—and under the circumstances, I couldn't protest. But it was time for me to carry through the resolve I'd made before the basilisk poisoned Ada. "Riven, I need to tell them."

He folded his arms across his chest, his shoulders tugging at the seams of his jacket. "You're willing to leave the outcome to chance?"

"I am." Though I felt as if sea-tangle snarled in my stomach, it must be done. If they distrusted Riven, they'd never accept his help—and we'd lose our best defense against this unknown fae. I pulled Jade closer, then turned to face my sisters, the knot in my stomach tightening. "There are things I should have told you long ago. Only I was afraid."

"Of whom?" Ainslie still eyed Riven warily.

"Of many things . . . what you would think if you knew the truth, how it would endanger you," I said.

Ada eased between me and Riven, as if she still believed him a threat. She thought well of almost everyone, and if she was still suspicious, then neither of them would believe anything I spoke in his presence. Everything I said could be deemed suspect, a product of some sort of coercion. I hadn't wanted him to leave, not given the risks to Ainslie; now, it seemed I had no choice.

I released a shaky breath. "Perhaps we'd best continue this conversation in private after all."

A sharp glance from Riven pierced the thin veil over my emotions and threatened to undo me. Then he moved toward the door with the languid grace customary to the fae, as if he'd not just endured a maelstrom of mortal emotion and accusation. "Then I'll take my leave."

"May I walk with you?" Difficult as this conversation had been, I'd a harder task ahead. Because without the truth of Riven's nature alongside my own, my tale would make little sense—and I refused to tell them Riven was fae without his permission. To do so would violate any trust built between us.

He inclined his head, and we retraced the path down the stairs and into the garden behind the house, where Riven wrapped us in glamour.

The scent of warm earth and honeysuckle swirled about us, yet it did nothing to impart calm. "That didn't go as I intended. I'd no notion . . . that is, I knew they'd worried about me, but they never hinted at their suspicions toward you. I didn't expect—"

"Their fears are natural, if misplaced. Your plan, however . . ." His jaw tightened. "You intend to tell them of your nature?"

A tendril of honeysuckle curled about my fingers, its thin filament as fragile as I felt. "Yes, and . . . I'd hoped to tell them of yours also."

His expression became forbidding, and I hurried on before he could issue a flat denial. "I know they'll ask who you are, if you're not Vigil, and so much of my story doesn't hold together without your identity. If I can't assuage their suspicions, then they'll never agree to let you help."

The silence stretched taut, and the honeysuckle woven about my fingers quivered. Why had I thought this a good idea? I asked him to expose a truth he didn't wish to reveal in order to give help he most likely preferred not to offer—all of which had the potential to cause trouble for him within his own court. It was hardly a compelling argument.

I released the sprig of honeysuckle, the small warmth it afforded vanishing. "I'm sorry, I shouldn't have asked. I appreciate that you came, but this isn't your problem to solve, and I shouldn't—"

"You'll have to bind them not to speak of it."

"You mean . . ."

"If you wish to tell them, they must be constrained by bargain. Bound to inform no one." His expression showed no hint of emotion, nothing to lend insight as to why he'd agreed to something decidedly *not* in his favor.

"I understand." However little I wished to hold my sisters in a bargain, it was a reasonable request. Yet as far as I was aware, the only time I'd forged a bargain before was when I'd tried to find a way to protect the inhabitants of Withern, when I'd believed my life might be required to remake Kilmere—and even then I'd been unsure of what I'd done. This statement from Riven confirmed another unsettling aspect of my fae abilities.

"Don't mistake my agreement for support." His eyes shadowed. "If you confess the truth, you may find them even less inclined to accept my aid—and yours."

The words hung between us before settling on my chest like a millstone. "Even so, they have a right to choose. I have to believe the precariousness of Ainslie's situation will outweigh the rest—that once she knows the truth, she'll see the sense in accepting help."

Yet it had taken me a great deal of time wrestling with the idea of my fae nature before I'd begun to accept it or anything to do with the Otherworld. Could I expect them to do the same in a matter of hours? Soon enough that we could keep Ainslie safe, if such a thing were possible?

"When fear governs, you'll find reason often departs," Riven said. "I'll return at nine tomorrow morning. If you've secured their agreement, I'll examine the binding mark. Keep Ainslie close until then."

He turned as if to go.

"Riven, wait." I took a half step toward him, and he shifted to face me once more.

"Thank you for coming. It means more than I can say, particularly given the circumstances." I'd never forget the image of him stained in blood, a reminder of the brutality of the Otherworld—and that though he might be immortal and powerful even by fae reckoning, he wasn't impervious to harm.

He didn't acknowledge my thanks, but nor did he protest it as he'd done in the past—perhaps he'd given it up as a useless endeavor. Something indecipherable flickered in his eyes. "If you need anything before morning, send Risha."

Then he vanished through a vivid passing, and when it faded, the world appeared washed of color, the rays of the mortal sun pale in comparison to the richness of fae-light.

I forced myself into motion, ascending the stairs as slowly as if I faced my own execution. What would Ada and Ainslie say when I revealed the truth?

CHAPTER 3

After a fraught ascent toward Kilmere, Ada, Ainslie, and I settled ourselves beneath the tree I'd drawn from the nisi seed, its white-gold branches forming a vault overhead. It offered both shelter and a measure of concealment, and the ridges where its trunk met the earth provided seats of sorts.

When I'd told Ada and Ainslie we required greater privacy than the grounds of Willowere offered, they'd followed without further question, even when I led them up the cliffside path toward Kilmere, a place I knew none would venture, certainly not without my awareness. They'd gone along with the suggestion I'd presented to Aunt Caris that Ainslie and I take Ada on a stroll to enjoy the healing sea air. Yet the weight of their expectations pressed heavier even than their questions.

For now, they waited, reserving judgment. But when I confessed . . .

I braced my back against the tree, and it whispered its name into the stillness—*queenswood*—even as the branches above shivered. In response to my emotions, perhaps? If it sought to provide a proper mirror, its limbs would lash the sky above us, seeking an avenue of escape . . . or perhaps the tree itself would shrink back into the ground, into the shelter of its seed-shell, where it couldn't be hurt.

Ainslie leaned forward. "I'm doing my utmost to be patient, but I can wait no longer. Please, just tell us. Whatever it is, it can be no worse than our worries."

"She's right." Ada reached out and gently touched my hand. "Whatever it is, we'll understand. And we'll face it together."

"I . . ." Words failed me. How could I begin? I removed my gloves, folding them carefully in my lap, so I might brace myself on the queenswood with no barrier between us. Its strength was a necessity for what must come. In the short time since I'd birthed it, the tree had drawn life to itself. The land beneath its boughs already bore clusters of fern and moss and woodland flowers, a glorious array that should have taken far longer to grow, a testament to the Other within it—and the Other within me.

This will grow no easier for the waiting. Whatever Riven thinks, I believe it's right to take them into your confidence. Jade stretched her bulky frame across my lap. *And if we're both wrong, you can always resort to glamour.*

Oh, Jade. You know I would not.

Then you must do your best to convince them of the truth, starting now.

I sank my fingers into the moss, and its resilient life thrummed up my arms. I'd intended to craft a careful explanation, to unfold my tale like a rose would its bloom, petal by petal until the whole was revealed. Instead, the words spilled from me. "I'm fae."

Utter silence.

I stole a glance to find my sisters motionless as statues. Then Ada said very cautiously, "Jessa, you've endured a great deal of strain in recent weeks—"

"In part it's because of this. You've asked for the truth, and I'll do my best to give it to you. Only please let me unfold it all before you ask questions."

They subsided, and this time, I did my best to order the

account, starting with the songs I'd heard from childhood and my belief I was fae-touched and moving to my encounter with the sprites in Milburn and the Crimson Tattoo Killer in Avons. Then I told them of the nature of Kilmere and its curse and even Lord West, along with how I'd bargained with a fae to help survive it all and how I'd finally recognized my own nature, though I omitted speculation on its source, so as not to wholly overwhelm.

When I'd finished, neither of them spoke.

The mosses darkened beneath my touch, and I snatched my hands back, waiting for them to say something, anything, not daring to look at their faces.

Then Ainslie sprang to her feet, pacing beneath the canopy of leaves. "How could you hide this?"

I shrank from the force of her anger. "I was just trying to—"

"I told you my fears about my binding mark and what it might mean for my feelings about Char—Mr. Redgrave and my future, and even then, you kept this from us. Did you trust us so little?"

I faltered. "It wasn't a matter of trust. You didn't want to tell Mr. Redgrave of your binding mark because of the impossible position it would put him in. I felt the same about you and Ada. Surely you must understand?"

"I understand that you left us at a disadvantage by keeping all this hidden, and you endangered yourself as well." Her arms folded tight across her chest. "We could have helped—unless you no longer wanted mortal assistance."

I flinched as though she'd struck me.

Ada drew a ragged breath, tears tracing silvery lines down her face. "Ainslie, don't say things you'll later regret."

If I must, I'd rather endure anger from Ainslie than the deep sorrow Ada displayed—but perhaps they were one and the same, one force gentle and the other tempestuous, but both springing from wounds I'd caused. My stomach knotted. "Perhaps I should . . . take a stroll, allow you time to talk and consider what I've said."

"Don't go." Ada reached out and clutched my hand, this time fiercely. "Don't you dare go."

And I clung to her in return. "I'm sorry I deceived you both. I was just . . . so afraid."

Ainslie's lips trembled. She collapsed next to me as the strength born of her anger—or the anger she'd forged to lend her strength—gave way. She clasped my other hand. "I'm afraid too. But surely we can face this best together?"

I could no longer restrain my own tears, and the three of us huddled together, the branches of the queenswood sweeping low to shelter us as we wept.

At last, Ada rummaged a handkerchief from the depths of her reticule and swiped at her face. "I knew something was wrong, and I should have pressed until you confided the truth— you should never have had to face this alone."

"It's in your nature to make peace, not to trouble the waters. And even if you'd tried to force the matter, there was much I didn't understand myself." I lifted my shoulders. "And there's much I still don't know."

"We thought perhaps if we investigated and came upon at least part of the truth ourselves, then you'd let us in, allow us to help. We considered so many theories about Lord Riven, about Kilmere, about how you've seemed troubled ever since you traveled to Milburn." Ada offered me a fresh handkerchief. "Not once did we imagine . . . this."

I swiped at my cheeks. "How could you have?"

"What of Lord Riven?" Ainslie shifted uncomfortably. "Does he know that you're fae?"

"He *is* fae," Ada said slowly. "Isn't he?"

Of the two of them, I'd thought Ainslie more likely to make the connection, but she was far from herself after her disappearance. I wasn't ready for this, not yet.

"I must have your word you'll not speak to anyone of what I have to say regarding Lord Riven." My chest tightened. "And . . . I'm afraid it will be binding."

"You mean a bargain." Ainslie's voice was flat. "You can forge bargains?"

"It seems so."

"And you'd force one between us?"

I shook my head. "It's not my choice, not even my preference, but if you wish me to speak further, then I'm obliged to require one."

They exchanged a glance, then nodded assent, but still Ainslie shuddered as the fine lines of binding wove about her unmarked arm, and Ada tensed.

Perhaps I should have pushed back when Riven insisted on a bargain, but he'd already done so much. I couldn't reasonably expect him to risk more, so I must simply endure the consequences. With an unsteady voice, I hurried on. "You're right, Riven is fae. He's the one I bargained with first, about Wyncourt, the one who kept me from stumbling into a far worse bargain in the Otherworld. To answer your earlier question, Ainslie, that's how he knows of binding marks and why he might be able to help us find the one who holds your bargain."

Ada twined her fingers around her handkerchief. "Despite what he is, you trust him?"

"I do," I said quietly. "He could have taken advantage of me on countless occasions, and he has not. I would never have escaped Lord West without him."

"But he's fae," Ainslie said.

"I am also."

"Perhaps you have fae blood, but that doesn't make you like *them*."

The song of the queenswood surged into my senses. After all that had passed between us this afternoon, even after the bargain, they didn't understand, not truly. And I would not have them feel I'd withheld anything, not now. So I reached for the queenswood, and it reached for me, two of its arched boughs swooping down to curve around us, a gentle arc of protection. "In some measure, it does. My abilities are unpracticed, but they are not natural to mortals, only to fae."

Ada studied the graceful branches, growing paler. "If you . . . if this is who you are, then what of Ainslie and me? How can it be that we do not share your nature . . . or do we?"

"If that were true, surely we would know." Ainslie knotted her hands in her lap. "Wouldn't we, Jessa? There would be some sign, as you experienced?"

"I cannot say for certain, but I believe so."

"But we're sisters. How can you be fae while we remain mortal?" Strain laced Ada's voice. "It holds no logic, unless the tales of changelings are true?"

If I suggested such tales held truth, would it free my sisters from any sense of obligation? Allow them to express their true sentiments on the matter?

Jade lifted her head to glare at me through slitted eyes.

I know. I won't stop now. I inhaled the Otherworldly fragrance of the queenswood leaves, a bright, living sort of scent, and forged onward. "I don't believe so. Fae can't easily have children on their own, therefore they desire them to the point that they'll use mortals to produce offspring. Having obtained children of their own, I cannot see any reason they'd abandon them in favor of mortals."

"Then what?"

"There are several possibilities, all of them less than pleasant. It may be that a fae forced Mother to bear me." The words tasted bitter on my tongue.

Ada inhaled sharply; Ainslie looked as though she'd like very much to vent her feelings on said fae.

"It might also be that an enemy of my . . . my kin in the Otherworld took me and forced me into this world, purging my memories."

Which meant I'd have no blood ties to any of my family, not even Ainslie and Ada.

Ainslie narrowed her eyes, as if she guessed my thoughts. "Even if that proves correct, you won't be rid of us so readily. We'll do everything we can to help uncover the truth, but whatever it is, I'm afraid you're stuck with us."

My breath hitched as Ada nodded her agreement. "But I would like to know what Lord Riven believes about your heritage."

"Circumstances haven't been favorable for lengthy conversation, but he indicated there were other prospects he couldn't yet eliminate." I worked to steady my voice. "I've begun to learn fae are bound regarding what they can reveal to those outside their court."

"Then it *is* still possible that we . . ." Ada drew a deep breath and began again. "If there was a bargain in place, one that forced Mother to . . . to carry children for a fae, it's possible that you weren't the only one."

The wind rustled in the leaves above us, and their undersides flashed silvery-white. "If that were the case, I cannot think why he would have left you with Mother. She might have hidden me at the end, but it would have been more difficult to keep multiple children concealed, unless he deliberately left you to be raised in the mortal world for a time."

"What if you weren't produced by bargain?" Tears glossed Ainslie's eyes, giving them the appearance of burnished ebony. "If you could conceal your nature so long, what if Father or Mother—"

"When I first began to suspect, I considered everything, including the possibility one of them was fae. For Father, I find no evidence. If he was fae, he'd have perceived Riven's nature and kept me from him. As for Mother, the fact she bore the three of us in rapid succession indicates otherwise, given the fact fae struggle to carry children at all." The faint fragrance of the sea teased my senses, as salt-tinged as the tears I wished I could release. "More than anything, I desire the truth, but there's still far too much unknown to eliminate any possibility."

"So we must live with uncertainty, at least for now." Ada lowered her gaze. "How did you endure it so long?"

"I had no choice."

Nor did they. Ada collapsed inward, and Ainslie lowered her head. I wrapped my arms around them both. I'd upended their world and called everything they'd known into question, even their own natures—and how I wished there had been another way.

For a time, we sat in silence, broken only by the distant crash of the sea against stone and the gentle murmurs of the queenswood above.

"Well." Ainslie straightened. "We did ask to know, but I must admit this is sufficient to cure me of curiosity—at least for a day or two."

Ada drew a shuddering breath, half-laugh, half-sob. "They do say be careful what you wish for."

The knot in my stomach unraveled. They'd received this far better than I ever dreamed—far better than I had.

Because they have you to anchor them and to interpret it for them—to tell them all will be well. Jade nuzzled my cheek.

Ever hopeful, Ada reached out as if to caress her, but Jade turned to glare at her.

They are your sisters, but that does not mean I shall permit their touch.

I don't expect you to, if it doesn't please you. I stroked between her ears.

I have made my sentiments plain, yet still they try.

Persistence runs in the family, it seems.

"I suppose next you'll tell us Jade is no ordinary cat." Ainslie forced a light tone.

If they knew, she could better protect them. "Well, now that you mention it . . ."

She laughed softly, then subsided. "Truly?"

I released Jade. *Will you?*

With pleasure. She sauntered to the edge of the queenswood canopy and shifted into true-form. Her immense body rippled with power, and the sun gleamed across the starflower patch on her chest. She was graceful, lethal, and unmistakably Other.

"That's . . . well . . ." Ada blinked. "I suppose I should be thankful she didn't snap my hand off when I tried to pet her."

"She wouldn't, not yours, at least. She only considers drawing blood when someone threatens one of us."

"And you know this how?" Ainslie asked.

"She can mindspeak."

Ainslie leaned back, surveying Jade, and Ada tapped her fingers against her lips. "Then Lord Bradford—all that was deliberate?"

"Yes."

She nodded gravely. "Jade, it seems I'm in your debt."

In response, Jade gave a low rumble. She condescended so far as to stalk toward Ada, lowering her face until her nose gently pressed against Ada's forehead. Then she shifted back into lesser-form and curled up in my lap.

You're not as indifferent to them as you pretend.

Jade just sniffed.

Ainslie looked around as though a karzel might peek out from behind the trunk of the tree. "Do you have any other surprises lying in wait?"

"Only one, but I'm not certain you'll be able to perceive her. I don't fully understand how sun sylph glamour works." I beckoned to Risha, who had been perched in the nook of a branch as we'd talked, her attention rapt. "Will you show yourself?"

The light about her shifted in pattern as she fluttered down to land amid a patch of primroses—the removal of her glamour, perhaps? She looked up at Ada and Ainslie as if taking their measure.

And Ainslie paled. "Oh."

"What is it?"

"I'd wondered why the light so often seemed to fall on you in a peculiar way, and I feared the binding mark had begun to influence my senses, so I tried to ignore it. But it was the sylph all along, wasn't it?"

"Since a few weeks after Ibbie died, yes—not Risha at first, but another." The confession brought with it an image of Asrina's broken form, and I swallowed against the pain.

Risha cushioned herself amid the primroses, her face

propped in her hands. She continued to survey us with an intent expression. Did she seek to understand mortal interactions? Or did she also think of Asrina—and mourn?

"If it wasn't the binding mark influencing her senses, then . . . perhaps this is a sign we share your nature?" Ada spoke so low I could scarcely catch the words.

"Perhaps." I still couldn't fathom how Mother would have kept all of us hidden or how Ada and Ainslie could have fae blood without showing an affinity for Other. Nevertheless, a tiny seed of hope sprouted. Perhaps I wasn't alone in this after all.

As though Ada hadn't spoken, Ainslie turned to survey Risha. "She looks as though we're a novelty to her."

"I suppose we are. The way of mortals differs from fae." I shifted slightly. "Which is why you need to let Riven examine the mark and tell us what he can of it."

Ainslie shuddered slightly. "I know you trust him, but all you've just said of high fae—how can we be sure?"

"In our position, we must take whatever help is offered," Ada said. "The risk of inaction is far greater than whatever debt we might incur by asking Lord Riven for assistance."

"I suppose you're right." Her lips drew tight. "Very well, I'm willing."

Yet her reluctance was clear. This wouldn't be an easy process for her, perhaps not for any of us. "He intends to return tomorrow morning," I said.

"You were so sure I'd agree?"

"Rather, I hoped you would. While we wait, stay with me or Ada at all times. We don't want you vanishing again."

"I quite agree." Ada looped her free arm around Ainslie. "But what if she disappears during the night?"

"We'll all sleep together, and Jade will alert us if Ainslie stirs."

"Then it seems we have a plan." Though she spoke in a tone of cheerful determination, her features remained tight with worry, a sentiment I shared.

My fears, along with the fatigue of spent emotion, weighed

my limbs, and I wished nothing more than to remain here the rest of the day, allowing the queenswood to sing soothing melodies, its strength becoming my own . . . yet Aunt Caris would surely send someone in search of us if we delayed much longer. I stumbled to my feet, pins and needles pricking my legs from my long immobility.

Together, we made a slow descent down the cliffside path and back to Willowere. When we slipped into the cottage, I intended to make an escape to the quiet of my bedchamber.

Instead, Mrs. Warren stumped into the entry, barring our way. "Your aunts wish to see you at once in the drawing room."

"Thank you, Mrs. Warren." Ada swept down the corridor toward the drawing room with her customary grace, but a slight downturn to her shoulders revealed the lingering strain.

When we entered the drawing room, Aunt Caris looked up from her needlework. "There you are, my dears. I told Melisina I didn't think you'd be long—gracious, what's happened?"

Aunt Melisina frowned at us. "You look dreadful, all three of you. Are you taking ill?"

However abrasive she might sound, the concern in her eyes appeared genuine. Ada hesitated, and I stepped forward. "I suppose we ventured a bit too far for comfort this afternoon."

Aunt Melisina shut her book with a snap. "This has been a trying time for everyone, and none of you should be traipsing across the countryside, least of all Ada. She's only just recovered and must conserve her strength for the trip home."

"Melisina is right." Aunt Caris set aside her needlework to regard Ada. "You should go to bed at once, my dear."

"I'm not that done in. A few hours of quiet will see me quite restored."

"If you're certain." Aunt Caris turned to me and Ainslie. "What of you?"

"We shall spend a quiet afternoon also," Ainslie murmured.

"I suppose that will do." Aunt Caris drew a vibrant green thread through her embroidery. "But I shall see that something particularly nourishing is prepared for dinner."

"As matters are in hand, I shall take my leave." Aunt Melisina rose, her skirts rustling. "I depart Withern for Avons this afternoon."

After a moment's hesitation, I followed her from the room. If she returned to Avons, she'd face Uncle Milton, and I had to be certain my actions hadn't caused undue trouble.

She halted at the cottage door. "What is it, child?"

"Will . . . will Uncle Milton be satisfied with how matters turned out with Ada?"

Her features impassive, she secured her hat. "He'll have to be. Lord Bradford has removed himself."

I wanted to ask if he'd make trouble for her, yet couldn't force out the words in the face of her forbidding demeanor. "Safe travels, then."

Her eyes softened slightly. "For my part, I am satisfied. Goodbye, Jessa."

Then she marched out the door, leaving me in blessed solitude. The soft murmurs of Aunt Caris's voice drifted from the drawing room, her gentle tones soothing as she spoke to Ada and Ainslie. If she'd any idea what had transpired today . . .

My fingers tightened around the brass doorknob. My sisters had extended more understanding than I'd dared dream, their own experiences perhaps paving the way. Yet I could not expect as much elsewhere.

When should I speak? When should I remain silent? It had been easier to keep the whole matter concealed from everyone; now I struggled to discern the way forward.

Yet none of it mattered compared to seeing Ainslie freed. If Riven could not trace the fae responsible—no, that worry would be for later.

I shut the door, blocking out the uneasy murmur of the willows.

Tomorrow would tell.

CHAPTER 4

As I'd promised Aunt Caris, we passed a quiet afternoon. Ainslie pored over the gazettes that Mr. Redgrave had provided her, Ada worked on her correspondence, and I immersed myself in my sketchbook. I started by drawing the filmy-fern and other plants found in the clearing where Ainslie had disappeared, but each time my attention wandered, my pencil shaped her binding mark.

At last, I abandoned the attempt altogether. After dinner, I escaped into the gardens, which twilight had washed in shades of lilac and rose. Once the sun set, we'd be another hour closer to morning—and hopefully to answers. I sank down among a patch of snapdragons and let their fierce melodies wash over me, pressing back my fatigue until Dreda appeared, her white muslin spectral in the gathering dusk. Though Aunt Caris had meant her as a chaperone, she'd become a friend, and I welcomed her presence.

"There you are." She moved toward me. "May I join you?"

"Of course." I stood and brushed bits of dried leaf from my skirts. Whatever her purpose, I sensed distance from the cottage would be preferable. "Would you like to take a turn about the lake?"

"That would be lovely."

Together, we walked along the crushed-shell path, which crunched softly beneath our boots. "Is there anything wrong?"

"I'd hoped you'd tell me." Dreda stooped beneath a willow limb. "If you'll forgive my saying so, you've not looked yourself all day, nor your sisters either. Your aunt believes you've overfatigued yourselves, what with the abduction and poisoning and all."

"And you disagree?"

"I suppose it could be nothing more than ordinary fatigue." She fidgeted with the lace on her sleeve. "But I wondered, that is, I hoped that if anything Other had returned to trouble you, you'd tell me. There might be little enough I could do, but I don't want you to feel you must endure it alone."

"I'm . . . very grateful." Only what could I say? My pace quickened slightly. "To the best of my knowledge, now that Lord West is gone, no high fae seeks to harm me."

But Ainslie, on the other hand . . .

Perhaps Dreda sensed the avoidance in my words. After all, I'd not issued a flat denial regarding Other, and she knew of my intention to thwart its spread. In any case, her shoulders dropped slightly. "I understand if you don't want to take me into your confidence—"

"It's not that." I halted at the edge of the lake, where the gentle waves lapped at the shore. "I have no lack of faith in you. Rather I seek to avoid breaking a confidence and dragging you into unnecessary danger."

"It's a funny thing, but danger doesn't frighten me as it used to. Bad things come, I know, but after Lord West, it occurred to me I might spend my whole life in fear and miss out on living all the while." She dragged her boot through the pebbles at the shoreline, leaving a furrow that filled with water. "I don't want to live in fear anymore, but to understand and have courage as you do. I've been thinking a great deal about all that's happened— about the fae. And I hoped you'd know . . . how many fae are there in Byren?"

"I couldn't begin to say."

"But you have some notion?"

When had she become so determined? Perhaps thwarting the will of Lord West had built her confidence. For my part, I wanted to sink into the lake. "I feel that more Otherkind seek to prey upon our world than we understand. Yet not all fae bear the same ill intent as Lord West or even the dread-aught that afflicted you."

Her chin dipped slightly. "What makes you so certain?"

"Because I have seen some treat mortals with kindness." Unable to remain still, I returned to the trail about the lake, and Dreda kept pace alongside. "I met a nisi at Denby Hall, and in some way, it worked to protect the household there, just as our tales tell, though I suspect it could turn malicious if not provided recompense for its service." Mother had said so, and now all her stories had taken on new significance. "After all, fae work by bargains, spoken and unspoken. But this one appeared to genuinely care for Denby Hall and its inhabitants."

"It heartens me to hear it." A smile crinkled her freckled cheeks. "Perhaps if nisi and mortals can get on, we might find our way with other fae someday."

Oh, how I wished it could be so, but nisi had little power compared to most Otherkind—a peaceful arrangement bene-fited them. But the rest . . .

We'd made a full circuit of the lake now, and the first stars glimmered overhead, peering at us through gathering clouds. "Perhaps we should go in?"

"If we don't, your aunt will send one of the servants to fetch us before long." She hesitated, then said, "Thank you, Miss Jessa."

"For what?"

"Allowing me to speak so freely."

"I hope you always will." However uncomfortable it might make me.

She nodded as though satisfied, but I felt far less so. All I'd said about fae she'd taken to heart, requiring no proof—yet even as I offered reassurances, I concealed my fae blood from her. How would she feel if she knew the truth? Would everything we'd shared become tainted? All my words about Other suspect?

As we approached the cottage, I choked down the urge to confess. Every person who knew the truth increased the risk of it slipping out—and if it were made public, there'd be no safe place for me in Byren, perhaps nowhere in this world.

If the Vigil found out—no, I wouldn't think of it. Instead, I removed my boots and day dress and changed into my nightgown. Ada and Ainslie already occupied the bed, so I slipped in next to Ainslie and pulled the covers over my head.

Yet what my conscious mind rejected, my sleeping mind embraced. Within my dreams, Otherkind and Vigil alike sought to wrench me from those I loved. In the dead of night, I woke, my heart thrumming, perspiration slicking my skin.

Though I tried to shift positions with care, Ainslie gave a low, pained murmur, clutching at me. I pulled her close. If I meant to keep these dreams from becoming truth, I needed to find her bargain-holder—and swiftly.

Morning dawned with a heavy stickiness, and the clouds that had gathered during the night hung low and oppressive. If they'd only burst, perhaps we'd get some relief, but they showed no sign of doing so; rather, they clustered thick on the horizon, and the attendant pressure made my head throb.

I descended the stairs to meet Ada and Ainslie. They'd risen before me, but they appeared to feel little better than I did. Though they were as immaculate as usual in cool muslins, both lacked their ordinary radiance. In silence, we entered the dining room, where Aunt Caris waited. Though the pale blues and greens of the room ordinarily had a calming influence, I found I couldn't settle. Would Ainslie cooperate with Riven when it came time to examine the binding, or did her fear of fae run too deep?

As Aunt Caris poured out the tea, Ainslie entered a bright conversation with her on the connections cultivated since our arrival in Withern and those we might expect to retain after our return to Avons. Yet shadows under her eyes hinted at the turmoil within, and Ada's serene exterior had a brittleness about it, as though the slightest jolt could shatter her composure.

When the clock chimed, signaling fifteen minutes till nine, Ada jumped, and Ainslie nearly dropped her honey cake. With a small silver spoon, I stirred some sea-blossom honey—a gift from the Denby family—into my tea. "Aunt Caris, would you object if we spent some time in the gardens this morning?"

"Of course not, my dear. I don't mean to pay farewell calls until tomorrow afternoon, and Mrs. Warren can assist me with any necessary preparations for departure in the meantime."

I sipped my tea, and the Other in the honey sparked against my tongue. "Have you given our notice to Lord Denby?"

"Yes, my dear, and he's been most gracious, offering several of his staff to assist our preparations. He's even said we're welcome to return at any time."

A remarkable change in sentiments, but then, the breaking of the curse had brought freedom to his family. "I'm glad to hear it."

"I didn't think so at one time, but staying has proven worth the while." A smile softened the gentle curves of Aunt Caris's face further. "Now go, enjoy yourselves while you may."

Whatever awaited, it would be anything but pleasurable. Still, we mustered our best smiles and murmured assent, then left the cottage. As we walked toward the copse, Ainslie turned toward me. "What does Lord Riven mean to do?"

"He'll examine the binding mark, but beyond that I cannot say—only that he'll help as much as he can." A familiar sun-and-storm sensation washed over my senses. "We should hurry. He's waiting for us now."

Yet Ainslie slowed as we neared the copse. Riven awaited within, his arms folded, and I slipped between the alders to join him, then glanced back to find that neither Ada nor Ainslie had entered the grove. They hesitated just on the edge, beneath the sweeping boughs of the trees. What did they imagine might happen? If Ainslie changed her mind . . . My chest tightened. "Will you come?"

As though my words broke a spell holding them captive, they edged into the shadows beneath the trees.

Riven surveyed Ainslie, his expressionless features forbidding. "Now that you understand the situation, do you want your binding mark examined?"

Her hands tightened, fisting at her sides. "As I've no mind to spend my life enthralled, yes."

"Then you'll permit me to seek the truth?"

The brown of her eyes darkened, appearing almost black in the dim light beneath the trees. Yet she nodded.

Rapid as the race of gold runner vines, tendrils of unease spiraled down my spine. He'd used such terms before, when he'd intended to compel Lord Blackburn and Mrs. Ellsworth to speak. What did he have in mind for Ainslie? And how would she receive it?

"I suggest we go out on the lake so we're not disturbed." With that, Riven strode past us.

Ada turned to me. "If Aunt Caris happens to take note that we're with Lord Riven . . ."

Riven glanced over his shoulder. "She won't."

Though Ada looked as if she wanted to issue further protest, she fell in after Ainslie and me as we followed Riven toward the lake, his concealment glamour wrapped firmly about us. If they couldn't see or sense it, perhaps that negated my theory that they could share my fae nature.

But it wasn't time to think about that now, only to attend to Ainslie.

Riven chose the larger of the two boats that rested at the shore, launching it with ease. Even so, it was a bit too small for comfort, with Riven and I pressed together on one bench, not touching but close enough that his body warmed mine.

His glamour now concealed the whole craft from view.

Ainslie and Ada huddled across from us, and Jade perched upright on the bottom of the boat, her nose twitching in distaste. *So many perfectly lovely locations to choose from, and we just had to go out on the water.*

Well, it does ensure we won't be interrupted.

Risha hovered near Jade, quiet but alert. As for Riven, though he rowed through the water with ease, his attention was fixed on Ainslie. Ripples of light passed over her skin, and she gave a slight gasp.

Ada clasped her hand. "What is it?"

"I just . . . I thought I felt . . ." She gripped the bench. "It's nothing."

Could she sense the current of Other power Riven sent through her body? If so, what did that mean?

Riven let the oars rest and leaned back, to all appearances relaxed, except for the intensity of his gaze. "The fae who made this binding doesn't belong to my court. While said fae could technically belong to any court, the affinity that sealed the bargain runs strong in the Courts of Silver and Dusk, and it's after their style."

"Is the Court of Dusk also a rival?"

"No. They're more of a vassal court, smaller and less significant. They wished to avoid the Court of Silver annexing them, so they made a bargain with my court for protection," he said. "They still maintain their independence, but they pay a tribute. Unlike the Court of Silver, the Court of Dusk isn't closed to me, but matters must be handled with care in order to preserve the treaty between us."

He might have to tread with care, but could I enter the Court of Dusk without attracting undue attention? And if I gained entrance, could I hope to survive such an incursion? In order to investigate, I'd have to move within fae society—and I'd no notion of how to do so. Nor even where to begin searching. Somehow we must narrow the matter down further. "There's something else. Her binding mark has changed over time. Can that tell us anything?"

"There are several reasons a binding mark might change." He gestured toward the jagged elements along the edge that looked rather like thorns emerging from the beautiful swirled vines of the mark. "This pattern suggests she's fought the binding, and it was enforced."

"Could that be why she was taken?"

"It's possible." Riven focused once more on Ainslie. "Tell me what you recall, from the beginning."

Though nothing changed in his demeanor, power laced his words. I clutched the side of the boat, its rough edges digging into my gloves.

The tale Ainslie had given me once before tumbled from her entirely unrestrained—the account of the old woman in the park, her agreement to help, and the block in her memories. When Riven pressed regarding her disappearance, her whole body shuddered, but she could offer nothing. If these gaps in recall remained, even beneath a compulsion for truth, what options did we possess?

Ainslie slumped inward.

And the slightest hint of a frown tightened Riven's features. "She truly doesn't remember, which means I can obtain no more without entering the mindscape, an inadvisable course. We had remarkable good fortune with Tibbons, and though you could provide a far stronger anchor to Ainslie than you did him, this bargain is far more deeply rooted. We're unlikely to have such a favorable outcome."

To uncover the truth only to have Ainslie forever broken was an unthinkable cost, if any other path remained. "I cannot imagine the fae in question left a clear trace of their identity, even in the mindscape."

"At best, we'd get only hints. They might direct us in some measure, but not to a sufficient extent to justify the risks."

"Then perhaps we could—"

Ainslie sat upright so abruptly that the boat rocked, and riotous color flooded her cheeks. "Since it's no secret what fae think of mortals, I'm not surprised that Lord Riven seeks to decide my future without consulting me, but I never expected it of you, Jessa. Has embracing your fae nature already changed you so much?"

Her words sliced like a dagger into my chest, and I wrapped my arms around myself in a vain attempt to ward off the pain. Was she right? Had I become insensitive and unfeeling? A low rumble emanated from Jade, and my gaze dropped to the sun-bleached wood at the bottom of the boat.

"If I'd decided to determine your fate, you'd not see it coming nor remember it happened." Riven's voice emerged silky smooth—and dangerously low. "Fortunately for you, your sister, who retains very mortal sensibilities, opposes such tactics."

Though the lake remained calm, the atmosphere felt storm-tossed. How could I set things to rights? Ainslie had offered no insult to him, yet he'd appeared to take it personally.

Jade's tail twitched. *But she did insult you.*

She's upset, and she's not wrong. I shouldn't have spoken about her as if she wasn't there.

Ainslie tightened her grip on Ada's hand, and Ada looked from one to the other of us, her features strained, but neither spoke.

Riven filled the silence. "Why do you expect to have a voice in matters you don't understand?"

"Because it's my life we're discussing." Her words emerged uncharacteristically soft and uncertain.

"Not anymore. You are bound to another, and unless Jessa manages to free you, there will be no release." His tone remained emotionless and unyielding.

I'd experienced his blunt delivery of truth more than once, but after I'd had some acquaintance with him. While nothing he'd said was false, it did nothing to engender trust in Ada and Ainslie—and everything to heighten their sense that fae were dangerous and frightening.

But if I pointed out the effect of his words, doubtless he'd only say they *should* fear fae. Should be wary of everything Other. Because in all likelihood they were mortal, and even if not, they—we—were vulnerable. I pressed my hands to my temples. "Perhaps we should just—"

Yet Riven remained focused on Ainslie. "If you still want help, it will be on my terms. Understood?"

Ainslie shook her head. "I cannot enter another bargain."

"Nor do I require it."

"Then what do you want in exchange for your help?"

"That's between me and Jessa."

"Whatever debt is owed isn't hers to pay. I won't let her become bound on my behalf."

"Not even if she's tainted by fae blood?"

She turned away from him, her eyes locking on me. "I'm sorry, Jessa. That's never what I meant to suggest."

Wordless, I reached out and placed my hand upon hers. She might not have intended to hurt me, but her remark reflected unguarded truth. It came from somewhere deep inside her—a place where all mortals feared fae. I swallowed my pain, tucking it within. "So am I. We should not have spoken as if you weren't present."

She drew a deep breath, as if gathering her frayed emotions, then folded her hands, donning her usual poise like a garment. "Lord Riven, I beg your pardon as well. I appreciate and accept the assistance you've offered."

"Then know I will share what I can, but you'll have to accept there are many things I cannot speak of." His words came gentler now, yet there was no yield in them.

"It seems I must." A small wave lapped at the boat, but she remained still. "What do you intend?"

"There's only one option—find the fae who holds your binding and persuade him or her to release you."

"But why would my bargain-holder ever agree?"

"We'll have to make an offer more compelling than whatever they intend to use you for," I said.

"But first we must find the fae in question, and it won't be a simple matter." A small spark of light played about his fingers.

"And if she disappears again in the meantime?" Ada spoke in a voice scarcely above a whisper.

"I can trace her, but if she enters another court, it's likely I'll have to abandon the trail. Which means she'll remain out of reach, her captor hidden." After a brief silence, he continued, "There is a more certain alternative, however."

"Then whatever it is, surely we should take it." Ada grasped Ainslie's hand, as if she might vanish even now.

"I doubt Ainslie will share your sentiments."

"What is it you propose?" she asked.

"That I place a working on you, one that will allow me to perceive your location at all times."

"On Ainslie?" I tilted my head. "I don't understand."

"Workings can be wrought on living souls, just as they are on elemental objects. It's a more difficult process, but once placed, they're near impossible for anyone but the caster to remove." Riven rested his hands on his legs. "If the fae is strong enough, they might be able to detect its presence. But even if they do, they'll not risk removing it and damaging what they perceive to be their . . . property."

Ainslie shifted away, as much as she could in the limited confines of the boat. "And if I don't wish to have a working placed upon me?"

"I'll not force it on you, if that's what you're asking," he said. "But if you don't accept it, then much time will be wasted trying to trace you—time that will cost you a great deal."

Her lips trembled slightly. "And how do I know that you intend to use it only to track me and not ensnare me further?"

"You don't."

Her shoulders drew in, and her hand closed over the binding mark. It had caused her so much pain already that it was no wonder she didn't want fae power in any form to touch her body. Ada looked from Riven to Ainslie, her features strained, her eyes wide and dark.

The sun glinted off the water, painfully bright, a reminder that already the hours trickled away, and I shielded my face. "Let him place the working, Ainslie. Would you rather remain vulnerable to fae proven to have no mercy?"

She shivered. "It just . . . it's too much."

"I know. But let Lord Riven help."

"Very well." She released Ada's hand. "I accept your offer, Lord Riven."

At once, glorious coils of light spun about her, forming sigils that settled over her skin. They traced down her neck, then vanished as if they'd melted into her flesh. She exhaled, the sound ragged. "Is that all?"

"Yes. If you're taken to the Otherworld again, I'll know at once where you've gone." Riven claimed the oars once more and brought us swiftly back to shore. "Now, I require a word with Jessa. Alone."

Ada looked of a mind to argue, so I stepped forward to cut her off. "I'll rejoin you here shortly."

Riven set off at a rapid clip, but when we rounded the curve of the lake, he slowed his pace. "The working will allow me to track her, but it cannot protect her from the bargain. No one can. The priority of finding the bargain-holder remains, so I suggest you keep a close watch for any unusual actions that might betray the terms of her binding."

"I will." But I wasn't content to wait until the fae forced his bidding on her again—there had to be some way to *act*. If the Court of Silver or the Court of Dusk held answers . . . "Will you tell me more about the Court of Dusk?"

"No."

I stumbled slightly over the pebbled ground. "Why not?"

"Because you shouldn't waste time thinking about investigating there."

"How did you—"

"I know you'd do anything to set Ainslie free, but you have no idea the risk you'd take. This is no expedition into the wilderness, as when you traversed the Ecvan. You'd need to enter the court proper, and though your nature is fae, you cannot pass for one—not yet." His jaw tightened. "You have no court ties, no protection to claim. Couple that with your mortal appearance and lack of experience with affinities—they'd spy you out at once, and you'd not survive the experience. Your death will do Ainslie no good. In fact, it would remove her one chance of survival."

My stomach hollowed. "You paint a very grim picture."

"Not grim. Accurate." He lifted a branch so I could pass beneath it. "You cannot avoid the Otherworld forever, but the time is not now."

Jade chuffed. *It is so.*

My skirt snagged on a fallen tree, and I tugged it loose. "I concede your point, but you must grant that I need some way to investigate the Otherworldly side of this problem. I can't simply wait for her bargain-holder to strike again, when she may not come through unscathed next time."

He shrugged. "I intend to put inquiries in motion."

I stopped short. "Riven, I can't ask you to—"

"You didn't ask; I offered."

I didn't know what to say. We'd taken strides toward friendship, but this was a tremendous burden for anyone to shoulder. Why would he make such an offer? At best, involvement would gain him an enemy in the form of whichever fae had claimed Ainslie. At worst . . . what might the consequences in his own court be? His king was already displeased. How could Riven justify further involvement in mortal affairs, when this time it didn't link to the interests of his own court? And what would be the repercussions if he simply acted of his own accord?

He remained impossibly still. "Do you fear incurring a debt?"

I lifted my gaze to meet his. "No, it's only . . . it hardly seems fair to pull you deeper into a situation that will bring only trouble."

The green of his eyes brightened to a springtime hue. "If it makes you feel better, consider it professional curiosity. If you recall, I have interest in exploring what might be changing the interactions between our worlds. I believe this bargain could connect."

My breath caught. "Are you at liberty to say how?"

"Bargains are typically more limited in scope, and they don't often allow the mortal to remain in this world. That Ainslie has suggests there's a larger scheme at work."

"I see." A new vista of alarming possibilities unfurled before me. If this had anything at all to do with the eroding protections between our world and the oncoming tide of Other . . .

"There's one more thing. After I arrange matters, I intend to set up establishment in Avons as I did in Withern. If we're going to investigate your heritage along with Ainslie's bargain, it will be far simpler if I can call on you openly."

"I agree, but what reason will you give for your return to Avons?"

"Your aunt already believes me a potential suitor." The green of his eyes took on hints of gold—amusement? "I suggest we embrace that as the reason for my reestablishment in Avons and calling at your home. Unless I'm mistaken, it's the only reason that will satisfy mortal convention."

I twined my hands in my skirts. "You won't mind her remarks? She can be rather . . . persistent in her matchmaking attempts."

He lifted a shoulder. "It's of no consequence. But I require one thing in exchange."

Jade's ears pricked forward, and Risha's light brightened.

"What is it?"

"Your word that you won't enter the Otherworld without telling me." He started forward again, and I followed. "The situation is precarious enough without a deviation from the plan."

"Of course." It was a small enough concession compared to the aid he offered. His involvement meant I wouldn't have to look after Ainslie with my own resources alone—it would give her a far better chance of surviving this. It was easier to accept assistance on her behalf than my own, but even so, what might it cost him? "But I feel as though I've done nothing but drag you into one trouble after another."

"You do seem to attract difficulty." One corner of his mouth lifted. "It keeps life interesting."

"Interesting." I sighed. "That's one word for it. But what of the expectations of your king?"

"Those are for me to manage." We'd nearly completed a circuit of the lake. Riven nodded toward Ada and Ainslie. "You should go to them. I'll join you in Avons when I can."

As I strode toward my sisters, the power of the passing swept across my skin, and then the sense of his presence faded.

Ada hurried to my side. "Are matters well?"

"As well as they can be. Riven has offered to make some inquiries in the Otherworld, then join us in Avons."

A slight flicker of alarm crossed her face. Riven had allowed them only the slightest glimpse of fae nature and power, and yet they feared him. I could not blame them, but how long before their discomfort with Other caused them to fear what *I* might become?

CHAPTER 5

The following day allowed me little time to contemplate my fears for the future or Ainslie's predicament, as we were swept into a bustle of preparation for departure. Midafternoon, Dreda rapped at the door of my bedchamber, a letter clasped in one hand. I braced myself for anything—up to and including questions about my own nature.

"Miss Jessa, I know it's inconvenient timing, but I've received a letter from my sister-in-law. She, ah . . . requests my immediate return to her household." The fine lines about her mouth deepened. "She's had a bad attack of nerves and requires assistance until her strength is restored."

"And you wish to go?"

The letter shuddered in her grasp, the fluttering page revealing a script written in a heavy, ornate hand, with numerous sentences vigorously underscored. Never mind that I could not make out the words, it appeared less an invitation than a summons.

"I believe I should visit, at least for a short time." Her lashes lowered, brushing her freckled cheeks. "I don't wish to neglect my duties with you, but I thought perhaps when you depart Withern, I could travel to her and stay for a week or so, certainly no more than a fortnight. But I don't want to lose my position or disappoint your aunt."

"We won't require a chaperone while traveling, not with Aunt Caris accompanying us. And above all, Aunt Caris understands duty to family. I'm certain she'll grant her permission."

"Then I shall go speak to her at once." Yet she lingered in the doorway.

From what she'd shared before, her family wasn't particularly warm or affectionate. Was that the reason behind her reluctance? Or was it that she hadn't seen them since her so-called fae-touch? I crossed the room and pressed her free hand gently. "We will miss you—and you'll always have a home with us, if I've any say in the matter."

"That's very kind of you."

"It's not kindness, but truth. You've kept my secrets and honored every bit of trust I've ever given." I turned away to rummage in my basket, withdrawing an unused sketchbook and bound set of pencils and extending them toward her. "I wanted to take you shopping for supplies of your own, but while you travel you may have opportunity to practice. When you return to Avons, we will outfit you properly, but meanwhile, you can use these."

She bobbed her head, a slight smile tilting her mouth. "I'd like that. Don't know as I'll develop any true skill, but I'll enjoy the attempt. Now I'd best delay no longer speaking to Miss Caldwell." She tucked the letter beneath her arm and hurried down the corridor.

I finished filling a valise, then wended my way past servants gathering trunks and removing bed linens. Some part of me wished to escape Willowere and return to Kilmere in order to examine it properly now that it was no longer hostile. Who knew when I'd have the opportunity again? Yet I'd promised Aunt Caris I'd join her to pay farewell calls—and she'd not readily release me.

It was half past two; she'd be waiting. I hurried down the stairs to join her and my sisters in the entry, but before we could set off on our rounds, Mr. Redgrave and Elodie arrived. Aunt Caris whisked us all to the drawing room, and we soon fell into easy conversation, Elodie as effusive as ever and Mr. Redgrave attentive to Ainslie even as he conversed with Aunt Caris.

While Mrs. Warren delivered the tea things, Elodie leaned toward me, a smile dancing in her eyes. "I don't imagine it will be long before our paths cross once more. Strangely, Charles feels compelled to visit Avons soon. Our aunt Hester has long since desired that we stay with her for a time, and it seems he feels we must accept her kind invitation."

"You would be most welcome." Whatever my reservations, it was the proper thing to say.

Aunt Caris, who'd caught our exchange, engaged Elodie on the matter of her aunt, mentioning her previous encounters with the Avons-dwelling Redgraves. Doubtless she intended to allow Mr. Redgrave and Ainslie the chance for uninterrupted conversation, which he seized at once.

With the rest of us occupied, he seated himself next to Ainslie. From the leather folio tucked under his arm, he withdrew a thick sheaf of paper. "The 'Pickforth Proposal,' as promised."

Despite the circumstances, her eyes lit up. "Oh, wonderful. However did you get it so quickly?"

"I have my ways." A quick smile creased his face. "After you read it, I'd like to know your thoughts on the latest maneuver of the Alchemist's Guild. My uncle says the 'Pickforth Proposal' gives an accurate summation of the issues at stake."

That was all it took for them to begin a political dialogue. Fortunately, Elodie kept Aunt Caris engaged, and she took no note of the improper turn to their conversation. As for me, I watched them surreptitiously.

With the arrival of the Redgraves, Ainslie had become her usual charming self—her repartees swift as ever, her countenance as sparkling. And yet, Mr. Redgrave regarded her with a furrow seaming his brow. He'd never shown anything but delight in her presence, which must mean he'd noticed the subtle air of vulnerability about her—evident in the occasional downturn of her lashes and slight shadow to her smile. When her hand stole to the binding mark, concealed beneath the sleeve of her gown, his gaze followed the motion.

And the furrow deepened.

Blight and rot, why did he have to be so attentive? No outsider should have noted a change in Ainslie, not when she concealed her emotions with such skill. At least propriety forbade him from asking personal questions, though they must have burned on his tongue.

"Don't you agree?"

I became aware that Elodie and Aunt Caris looked at me expectantly, waiting for an answer—and I'd no notion what Elodie had asked. "I apologize, I'm afraid I was wool-gathering."

Aunt Caris sighed, but Elodie only laughed, a soft silvery sound. "I've been known to do the same at times. Preparation for travel does leave one so very distracted. I only mentioned that the gardens here at Willowere are among the most charming I've seen in the region. They appear to have flourished exception-ally these past few weeks, don't you agree?"

I nearly dropped my teacup. Was that an innocent remark or a veiled accusation? I'd spent a great deal of time in the gardens —had my affinity influenced their growth? The roses *had* bloomed with uncommon profusion, and the beds of snap-dragons and gold runners grew with wild abandon. "I do, and I shall be sorry to leave them behind. Though I spend consider-able time in our garden at Avons, it's much smaller in size."

"Then you must certainly call on Aunt Hester after your return to the city." Elodie lifted a queen's cake from the pastry tray. "She's not much for out-of-door gardens, but her collection of indoor plants—they're nothing short of glorious. Do say you will."

"It's very kind. I'd be delighted." Rather, I would if it was a simple invitation. But if she had some sort of test in store . . . The tea took on a bitter taste, and I returned my cup to the table.

"Of course, you'd all be most welcome." The earnestness in her tone belied any sort of underhanded scheme. "I'm certain Charles would like all of you to become better acquainted with our family."

Aunt Caris beamed. "Nothing would give us greater pleasure."

Across the room, Mr. Redgrave leaned toward Ainslie and spoke something low enough that I could not hear.

Ainslie drew back slightly. "I'm quite well, thank you."

A moment later, he stood. "I'm certain you have much to occupy you, so we will take our leave."

Elodie rose as well and moved to his side. "Please take care as you travel, and write to me upon your return to Avons."

By suggesting I write, she kept open the lines of communication between Ainslie and Mr. Redgrave, who could not properly correspond with each other. Yet her warning to take care . . . was there anything more to it? "Certainly, I shall let you know of our safe arrival. But do we have more reason than usual to exercise caution?"

"Forgive me, I did not mean to cause alarm. It's only that the tales of the missing have me imagining all sorts of dangers."

Ainslie recoiled. "The . . . missing?"

"It seems a number of the gentry have vanished without a trace, though the seclusion of Withern made the news slower to reach us." Was it my imagination, or did Mr. Redgrave study me as he spoke? "It's raised quite a bit of alarm with the authorities, apparently."

I felt as though he'd jabbed me in the stomach with his walking stick, rather than tucking it beneath his arm. If others had gone missing, what did that mean? "Does anyone have a theory about what's become of them?"

Aunt Caris pressed her lace handkerchief to her lips. "My dear, I scarcely think that's for us to discuss. As long as Mr. Redgrave feels there's no great risk to our traveling?"

"I'm certain you'll be safe. It's not travelers who have disappeared."

She relaxed. "You see, all will be well. Doubtless before we return to Avons, the authorities will have sorted the matter."

I'd no such certainty. Nevertheless, I joined in the farewells and then allowed Aunt Caris to shepherd me out the door along with Ada and Ainslie for a round of calls. Fortunately, our other visits were far less fraught, yet weariness seeped into my bones, and I welcomed nightfall with relief.

As we prepared to retire, Ada turned to Ainslie. "What did Mr. Redgrave say to you, just before they left this afternoon?"

So she'd attended closely to them as well. I pulled on my dressing gown.

"Only that . . . if anything ever troubled me, he hoped I'd not hesitate to tell him." Her eyes shimmered with tears in the gaslight. "I felt like the worst sort of liar, assuring him I was fine."

An ache formed beneath my breastbone. "Oh, Ainslie."

"I wanted to tell him, so very badly, but all I could think was that if I took him into my confidence, he'd be obliged to report to the Vigil or jeopardize his own future and that of his family. It would be entirely unfair to place that burden on him." The words spilled from her unchecked. "Jessa, you were right when you said I should have understood—it *is* an impossible choice, and I feel like a dreadful sister for condemning you for your own decisions. I am truly sorry—for what I said when you told us and what I said in the boat. I just feel so . . . so powerless to fight against this binding. I hate it, and sometimes, well . . . it's easier to be angry than afraid. I hope you'll forgive me."

"Of course I do." I climbed into bed alongside her. "And I understand your sentiments entirely."

"I want to do what's right, but I don't know what that is." She bit her lip. "I think . . . I fear I must discourage his attentions. Even if we manage to break the bargain, there's the prospect of fae blood. What gentleman could possibly accept such a connection to the Otherworld?"

Ada pulled her close. "Perhaps you shouldn't act in haste. All this might come to naught, and a future with him may yet be possible."

Jade clambered onto my lap, and I pulled her to my chest as a weighty silence filled the room. Any future between them depended on far more than Ainslie—it required understanding of what the Redgrave family concealed in turn.

If Mr. Redgrave possessed some tie to the Otherworld—as a Collector or something else altogether—then perhaps he'd be inclined toward sympathy. Yet if the Redgraves were merely a venerated family with a bent toward unconventional interests . . . well, they'd be more interested in protecting their future than anything else, which meant Ainslie would be an easy sacrifice.

"Do you agree with Ada?" Ainslie asked at last.

"You cannot enter any sort of agreement with him holding all this secret, but I also think you should give it time." I stroked the soft fur between Jade's ears. "Time for us to discover the truth about Mother and the fae and your binding, and then decide what must be done."

And, of equal importance, time to uncover the truth about the Redgraves themselves.

WHEN WE LEFT Willowere early the next morning, a regret pinched uncomfortably at my middle. I hadn't expected to feel anything but relief upon our removal from Withern-at-Sea, yet duty and perhaps something more bound me to Kilmere—I'd become its mistress and I must understand what it had become in its remaking. What secrets might it still hold, beyond just the dawn-dagger concealed in its depths?

Kilmere aside, I'd welcome a chance to return and enjoy the peace and beauty of the sea in a way that had been impossible when Lord West threatened, a notion which remained equally unfathomable in face of the current danger to Ainslie. Would Avons hold the answers we sought? It did represent possible avenues of investigation, and with the ease fae possessed of passing from one location to another, Riven might well be waiting in Avons when we returned, which would allow us to move forward without delay.

His comment about Ainslie's bargain possibly representing some greater plot had only cemented my resolve to learn more of the Forgotten War and whatever other information about fae remained hidden in our past. There must be something concealed that could help mortals, else why would the fae monarchs bind their subjects from speaking of it?

Jade, if I belonged to a court, would I have access to information on the Forgotten War and the rules that govern relations between fae and mortals?

You'd gain that knowledge, yes, yet you'd also share our geas—and the inability to communicate anything to help. A shudder passed over her frame, and she fell silent.

Even were it otherwise, how could I ever consider joining fae society? Embracing their ways? No, if I meant to understand the situation, I must use whatever resources I could find in the mortal world. If I could gain entrance to the Antiquary Society, perhaps I could use its records and the knowledge of its members to attempt to piece together a more accurate picture of the Dark Era I'd seen hinted at once before.

Would Thea still be willing to offer her aid? When I returned to Avons, I'd seek her to inquire. I owed Lord Blackburn a call as well—or at least the information that I'd returned to town, since it wasn't proper to call directly on him, chaperoned or not.

In the seat across from me, Ainslie and Ada carried out a spirited exchange, Aunt Caris chiming in with an occasional soft remark. Risha watched them with evident interest, the blue of her wings a bright hue. The familiarity of their exchange tempted me to forget that with each day, each hour, the odds of Ainslie being summoned back to the Otherworld increased.

I pressed down the fear threatening to grow as fast as silver creeper. Dwelling on it would do Ainslie no good, so I withdrew my sketchbook from my basket. If I meant to secure admittance to the Antiquary Society, then I'd require more than a good word from Thea. They'd expect a compelling paper, as well as references. If I included some illustrations of Kilmere, perhaps it would spark their interest without betraying its fae origin.

What could be studied without giving too much away? The apothecary, perhaps? I'd have to remove the poisons, of course, or conceal them, before I ever considered allowing anyone else to examine the ruin.

I began to sketch the friezes, their twining blossoms and serpentine forms scrolling across the page and the sensation of Other pricking along my fingertips. Wait, what was that in the border of the frieze? I should know; I'd just drawn it, and yet . . . I bent to examine it more closely.

Where it arched above a doorway, a distinctive collection of runes spiraled about a rising sun, its rays shot through with stars. It appeared almost like a crest or seal. I let my pencil rest. Though I'd not noticed it when we traversed Kilmere, some deeper part of me must have attended to the details.

Did this symbol represent the coalition of fae who'd crafted the ruin? Perhaps an emblem of their court? Something about it unsettled me—both its appearance on the page without my conscious recall and the ominous nature of the lines themselves.

I snapped the book shut.

Better to think of other things, perhaps—like finding the truth about Mother. Riven had offered to assist with that investigation also, and with the weight of it now oppressing Ada and Ainslie alongside me, uncovering those secrets was more important than ever.

Aunt Caris had promised to provide me her correspondence with Mother, which might shed some light on the past. And given what Aunt Melisina had told me about the night Mother died, it was possible the nature of her death itself could hold answers. No one had ever informed us what happened—Father had never given the slightest indication of whether she'd been attacked and injured or stricken down by some ailment or affliction. Any time I'd attempted to broach the matter, I'd been met with hushed silence and the suggestion it was improper to discuss. Which had left me nothing to fill the void of information but the unpleasant rumors that the low spirits she'd suffered in the weeks before we lost her in some way led to her death . . .

Aunt Melisina was the only one who'd been forthright about the night of Mother's death—and that only under considerable provocation. There was a chance she could provide more insight, if I asked the right questions. It wouldn't be pleasant, but it must be done.

Thornhaven too might reveal something; however, Father had remained steadfast in forbidding our return there, and I could ill afford the time away. For now, I'd conduct what research I could within Avons.

Thoughts of the investigative lines that must be explored so consumed me that it took Aunt Caris patting my arm before I realized the carriage had halted for the night and she waited for me to disembark. I murmured an apology and descended into the courtyard of the Bluebell Inn, a small trim building of aged stone.

Once inside, the innkeeper escorted us to a private dining room, where his wife provided a simple but pleasing meal. Since it was a small establishment and already mostly full, Ada, Ainslie, and I would share a single, larger bedchamber, with Aunt Caris occupying a tiny one across the hall.

Citing a wish to take the air before the sun set, Ainslie and Ada left for a stroll, while Aunt Caris went to make arrangements for the morning. With relief, I embraced the relative solitude of the bedchamber, though with Jade and Risha as companions, I was never truly alone.

Risha fluttered about the room, her light falling across the worn rug and the well-pressed but faded curtains. "Mortal waystations are so dull."

"I suppose so—most serve only the needs of a bed for the night and food for fuel, with little consideration given to beauty."

A pulse of indigo flared along the edges of her wings—

disdain for the notion? "No fae homes are drab, even the smallest ones. At least mortals themselves are quite interesting."

"Interesting?"

"They indulge in *much* emotion."

"So Riven has informed me." I tilted my head to regard her. I shouldn't have expected Risha to share a similar personality to Asrina, no more than one mortal sibling might another, but her outspokenness still startled me. Though her speech had its occasional quirks, she was far more articulate and bolder of expression.

"Much emotion means no fear of caring for others." A speculative flicker of light sparked about her.

"I wouldn't say it means I'm unafraid, but rather I'm aware love is worth the price that at times must be paid."

She eyed me in a contemplative fashion, but whatever she meant to say was cut off when Ada returned, Ainslie on her heels.

Ada sank wearily onto one of the two beds in the room, and it creaked even beneath her slight weight. "I shall be quite glad to return to the comforts of home. Though Withern was charming, I've had enough travel for some time to come."

"I don't know that we'll find Avons entirely comfortable." Ainslie tugged the cord holding back the drapes, and they fell to cover the windows. "I wanted to stroll to the mercantile so I could see if the gazettes had any new information about the missing individuals. It seems authorities have attempted to pass it off as a ransom grab or suggested it might be the Emstead protesters seeking to enact their resentments against those of greater privilege—but neither fit the situation entirely."

"Is there any suspicion Other might be involved?"

"None of the articles suggested as much; perhaps no such thought has entered the minds of the public. It *is* rather a leap if one knows nothing about how Otherkind have encroached, and it seems most believe it to be political or economical in nature, rather than Otherworldly. But I received a letter from Lovell just before we left. He wants to start working on a P. Smith article with me as soon as we return to Avons, and he's been talking with the families as much as he can without arousing suspicion, at least those located in Avons. But he's gained little insight. Still, he feels something is being concealed." She turned from the windows to face us. "And he's right, of course."

"Do you think the situation is Other in nature?" Ada asked.

"I don't know. I'm afraid when I was reading of the missing, my own situation consumed my thoughts." She shook her head. "How heartless does that make me?"

"Not heartless. Just afraid," I said.

"I'm more than weary of fear." Her chin lifted, and her dark curls spilled back from her face. "I'll do what I can to help Lovell with this article when we return, and perhaps in so doing, I'll provoke some reaction from my binding. If not, then at least . . . at least I might spare others my fate."

Her voice wobbled a bit on the last words. However bold a face she put on it, these fears would not be laid so easily to rest —for they reflected not vain imagination but the reality of the danger that stalked her.

The candles on the mantel burned low—evidently, they could not afford to install gas—so I kindled the thick pillar situated alongside the bed, its warm light driving back the shadows. How I wished I could so easily dispel the terrors cast by Ainslie's bargain-holder.

CHAPTER 6

On the final leg of our journey, one of our horses pulled up lame, and getting a replacement delayed us, so it was long past dark when we arrived home. Since Father hadn't known which day to expect us, he'd already retired.

We tumbled into our own beds with relief, and I entered at once into deep, dreamless sleep, until the familiar song of the oak greeted me the next morning. As its protective melody washed over me, something within settled. Though it paled in comparison to the beautiful grounds of Willowere, I'd missed my garden here. Aside from the trees that predated our arrival, I'd set nearly every plant in its place.

I pulled back the curtains and swung open the window panes. The rich scent of summer rose mingled with the soft, soothing fragrances of lavender and sun-warmed grass. Their lively melodies swirled about the room, beckoning me. Since I must wait until society began properly stirring to conduct any investigation, I might as well respond.

I hurriedly donned a dress and laced up my leather boots, then crept down the stairs to avoid disturbing my slumbering family. Yet as I secured the door behind me, the ivy thrilled a warning note. The gardens had altered in my absence—and worse, I wasn't alone. Any sense I'd had of returning to a haven withered as fast as an unwatered blossom in scorching sun.

The fur at Jade's ruff rose. *I don't recognize the scent. Not Other, yet not a mortal of your house. And there's something else also —rabbits?*

What in the Crossings? I inched toward the fountain, which blocked my view of what lay beyond. Jade stalked in front of me, and Risha hovered at my shoulder. Some part of me reached for the ivy, and its evergreen strength swirled about me, its vines rustling as if they prepared to strike—no, not yet.

When I rounded the fountain, I stopped short. It wasn't a threat, but a gangling boy who took no notice of our arrival—his attention remained fixed on a small flock of sparrows scattered across the shrubbery.

Ordinarily when Jade prowled the garden, not a single bird dared venture in, but this time, they didn't attend to her. Their bright black eyes locked on him, their cheery chirrups almost a conversation.

He extended his hand, and several of them fluttered up to perch on his palm and wrist.

Who was he? And what gave him such a knack with animals? He seemed to feel every confidence to roam the gardens, as though he belonged here. Beyond him, near the mews, was a small structure that held rabbits, one that hadn't been there before. Was it his? Nothing about this made any sense whatsoever.

Jade regarded him, and the fur at her neck lifted slightly. *There is something about him I cannot place.*

Then we should find out what we can.

I concur. She rumbled low, and the sparrows startled into flight. *But tread with care.*

The boy's head snapped around, his shaggy black hair falling across his eyes. When he saw us, his jaw hardened and his lips twisted into a scowl. He gave no sign of penitence for being caught in trespass nor trepidation at what I might think of his presence or his actions. Then again, I did not possess an intimidating appearance.

I stepped closer. "I think perhaps you might be lost."

"Not lost. I work here."

He worked *here*? When had that come to pass? He volunteered nothing more, just stood with his black eyes glittering beneath thick brows. Had I not just witnessed his gentleness with the sparrows, I would have found him entirely disagreeable. As it was, he presented a puzzle in need of a solution.

"I'm Jessa Caldwell. This is my home." For some reason, the final word stuck in my throat. "How have you come to find employment here?"

"Mr. Caldwell offered me a job." His bony shoulders hunched inward. "Best be about it."

"Wait, please. Where did you meet my father?"

"In Shepherd's Bush."

Shepherd's Bush? What in the Crossings had possessed Father to travel there? "What was his business?"

"Came for the star signs, he said." The boy jabbed the toe of his boot against a hassock of tufted grass, clearly ill at ease.

If Father had sought to witness some astronomical event, then his sudden trip didn't surprise me. And if I wanted to know more, I'd best ask Father, not this boy, whoever he might be.

He stole a peek at Jade, then he slowly extended a hand toward her. When she regarded him with wary scorn, his brows raised. Had he expected her to welcome his attentions, much like the sparrows?

He shuffled back. "May I go, miss?"

"Yes, of course." Yet a weight rested on me as I watched him vanish into the mews.

He reminded me of an untended sapling, all scraggly limbs and unkept edges, in need of both time and attention. Aunt Caris would have taken note of such a thing and been moved, perhaps, but it was unlike Father. Just as it was unlike him to hire any household staff, particularly such an unusual member. What could have motivated him?

Only one person can answer.

Yes, if he will. As soon as we broke the fast, I'd see what he was willing to share about his unexpected decision to hire the boy.

If Jade sensed something strange about him, might it be that he bore some sort of ward? If so, could he have been planted here to report to the Vigil? No, that was a ridiculous stretch—I was allowing my fears to unduly influence my thoughts. Still, I couldn't afford to ignore a new peculiarity cropping up within our own household.

It was early yet, and most likely everyone else still slept, so I busied myself for a time within the glasshouse, watering and removing any dead or withered leaves. The sprightly songs of the sweet orange were undergirded by the steadfast, sap-quickened melody of the heartnut seedling guarding the door. Yet none of the gentle touches of the plants housed within brought peace to my soul.

When the sun refracted light across the far wall, I straightened, wishing for the lovely sea breezes of Withern. Without them, stifling heat pervaded the air, even at this relatively early hour. I wiped perspiration from my brow. Small wonder most fled Avons as summer advanced, seeking the relative cool of the countryside.

The sun climbed in the sky, its height indicating it was time to join the others and see what I could learn about the boy in the garden. After a quick scrub of my dirt-stained hands, I entered the dining room, where Aunt Caris and my sisters already gathered to break the fast. Father was conspicuously absent.

When the meal neared its end and he'd still not appeared, I asked, "Have you seen Father this morning, Aunt Caris?"

"No, my dear, I'm afraid not."

From the doorway, Holden cleared his throat. "He went out first thing, Miss Jessa."

"Did he say where?"

He sniffed slightly. "He did not. Nor has he of late."

Evidently, Holden was discomposed by the irregularities of the household. Perhaps he knew something more of the boy I'd met. "I came across a lad in the garden. He said Father hired him?"

Holden stiffened. "He did, indeed."

Aunt Caris paused in the middle of spreading butter on a yeast roll. "Whatever for?"

"I could not say, Miss Caldwell. He requested I find some task for him. Yet the boy—Dryden—is uncouth and difficult, altogether unsuited for a life in service. He's even convinced Mr. Caldwell to set up a small rabbitry near the mews, an object fit only for a farmstead." His mouth twisted slightly. "His creatures have dared creep into the house at times. Perhaps in some rustic locale, he might do. But certainly not here in Avons."

It was unlike Holden to speak so freely. He must be troubled indeed to unburden himself in such a fashion.

"Oh dear." Aunt Caris sighed. "I suppose I shall have to speak to Alden. Perhaps, if he's bent on offering a position to the boy, he might be willing to transfer him to Caldwell House instead."

Holden unbent enough to nod. "Very good, Miss Caldwell."

I looked up at him. "Has Father taken any particular interest in his presence here?"

"Not that I am aware. He didn't even remain to see how he got on, but hared off once more shortly after he'd returned from Shepherd's Bush, this time with Lord Blackburn." With that, he stalked from the room.

Lord Blackburn? I'd not known he and Father shared enough relationship to undertake a trip together. What had Father fallen into?

"Poor Holden. The boy must have truly gotten under his skin." Aunt Caris glanced at me. "Was he so dreadful a child?"

"More . . . odd than dreadful. I can see why Holden feels he does not fit in the household, yet I'm certain Father must have a reason for placing him here."

"Well, I shall speak to Alden when he returns," Aunt Caris

said. "Meanwhile, I must set everything to rights here. Somehow travel always seems to leave things at odds and ends."

Ada sipped her tea. "Shall I help you?"

"I'd welcome your assistance, my dear." The soft morning sun caught in Aunt Caris's red-gold hair and softened the deepening lines about her eyes.

How many of those had been caused by the events of the past few months?

"I told Lovell I'd ride out with him this morning, but I shall be quite at your disposal this afternoon." Ainslie spoke with determined brightness.

If she and Lovell intended to depart early, more than likely they sought to gather information on those gone missing. I took a sausage and passed it to Jade. "If you wish, I'll sort through the correspondence. I saw quite the stack in the morning room."

She beamed at us. "Thank you both. With your help, we shall soon be quite settled in."

"There's one other thing—I'd like to call on Mrs. Darrington this afternoon."

"I see." Her smile faded. "With Dreda gone, you'd best bring Lianne, but do take care. She can do nothing more than ensure observation of the proprieties, and I'd not have you come to harm."

After my abduction and Ada's poisoning, I couldn't blame her for her fears—particularly not when the dangers were more real than she knew. "Of course. I'll be careful."

Before she could press further, Lovell breezed into the room. He brushed a kiss across Aunt Caris's cheek and cast a smile upon the rest of us. "Why so gloomy?" Though his voice was light, he surveyed us, his gaze lingering on Ada. "No lingering effects from the poison, I trust?"

"No, Dr. Fulton was pleased with my progress, and I feel nearly myself again." Ada motioned to the chair next to her. "Won't you join us before you spirit Ainslie away?"

"I'll never turn down an opportunity for Estine's renowned

pastries." He took the offered seat and snatched a honey cake from the tray. "Not to mention the excellent company."

When Gaile entered with a question for Aunt Caris, Ainslie took advantage of the distraction to lean toward Lovell. "Your letter was a tremendous help in ridding Ada of Lord Bradford." Some of the sparkle returned to her eyes. "You would have enjoyed witnessing his defeat, I believe."

"I dashed well would have." He scrubbed his hand across his jaw. "I should have intervened sooner."

"You couldn't have known what he was truly about," Ada said softly.

Aunt Caris rose. "Forgive me, my dears. It seems there are several urgent household matters to attend. Lovell, I trust you'll see Ainslie back safe?"

"On my honor." When she departed, he glanced at me. "Didn't want to disturb Aunt Caris, not when she's already got the wind up after Withern, but a Vigilist paid a call on Father and me a few days ago. Asked all sorts of questions about you and Uncle Alden."

My stomach tightened. "Did he give a name?"

"Ludne." Lovell snagged another pastry. "Naturally, I fobbed him off, but I'd the sense he's lying in wait for your return. What's given him such an interest?"

"We had an altercation over Kilmere, and I came off the better." How long did I have before he received word I'd returned and sought me out once more? He was unlikely to delay. I twisted the linen napkin in my lap. "I don't suppose he's accustomed to that."

Lovell's eyes shaded darker. "Well, I don't like it. He seems the sort to cause no end of trouble."

"I agree." Ada set down her teacup. "Does Father know?"

"Not yet. Wanted to talk to Jess first to find out what was behind it, but I mean to tell him."

Ainslie's lips tightened. "Surely there must be someone with whom we can lodge a complaint. His position shouldn't be used to further a personal grudge."

Yet he'd reason to be suspicious, even if his own enmity fueled his deeds. And Ainslie knew it.

Before I could reply, Holden appeared with the tense set of his shoulders that always spoke displeasure. "Miss Jessa, Mr. Ludne of the Vigil has called. He demands an audience. Alone."

Unless he had some sort of watch on our home, he could not have come so swiftly, the very morning after our return, the very moment Lovell issued his warning. A tide of heat scorched my chest. Mr. Ludne had no right to interfere with my family so, to spy upon our household. Yet doubtless he expected me to heed his dictates, careless of my reputation—perhaps he even hoped to damage it.

"Oh, Jessa," Ada said. "Surely you won't go."

"She dashed well won't." Lovell shoved back his chair. "I'll manage the fellow."

"Wait, please." I stood as well, catching Lovell's arm. "He could cause more trouble if his wishes aren't heeded. Let him feel he has the upper hand for now. It might make it easier to determine his purpose and the lengths to which he's willing to go to attain it."

Lovell frowned. "I should at least go with you, Jess."

"I don't want you made a target as well. Please, trust me to manage him."

At last, he gave a slow nod. Ada began a protest, but Ainslie restrained her. And Holden cleared his throat. "Miss Caldwell would not approve."

"Nevertheless, you're not to tell her, for now. I'll speak with her or Father afterward." As soon as the words left my mouth, I wished I could take them back, for despite my best efforts, a hint of glamour had seeped into my voice.

In response, Holden blinked slightly. "As you wish, Miss Jessa."

I clenched my hands together. I needed to better understand how to control glamour, how to keep it from influencing others when my emotions ran high. He'd not deserved the exertion of my will above his own, however small the matter. Fortunately, neither Lovell nor my sisters appeared to notice anything amiss.

You'll learn in time. Save your energy for Ludne. Jade's tail twitched. *Unless you want me to manage him.*

Don't tempt me.

In no positive frame of mind, I marched into the drawing room, Jade keeping stride and Risha bringing up the rear. She remained near the doorway, perhaps troubled by his ward-stone.

Mr. Ludne fidgeted with something on the mantel, turning toward me as I entered the room. In Withern, adversarial lines had already been drawn between us; it was no use donning the pretense of a naive young lady once more. Nor did I find myself inclined to do so. I offered a crisp nod. "Mr. Ludne. I cannot say I am pleased to see you."

"I scarcely expected you would be. Those with something to hide rarely appreciate the attention of the Vigil." His winterberry eyes held more than a touch of frost. "How far does the rot spread within your family, I wonder?"

My pulse roared in my ears. Could he know of Ainslie? No, surely if he had evidence of her bargain he'd have fetched us both to a Vigil House by now. "That's a rather remarkable state-ment. What do you mean by it?"

"I mean that I had an illuminating conversation with a colleague upon my return to Avons."

"About what?" In this proximity, his ward-stone tightened my chest unpleasantly.

"Your father. Surely you don't expect me to believe you know nothing of his unnatural interests."

Father? I'd thought this was about Kilmere, with Father an unfortunate casualty of my actions. But this? What had happened between them? I clutched the back of a chair. "My father lives a quiet life, attending to his studies and academic societies. I assure you there's nothing unnatural about that."

"I thought you might disclaim all knowledge. Just as you did about Kilmere." A laugh rasped from him, dry and humorless. "Consider yourself warned—even powerful friends cannot protect you forever. You'd best consider how to mend your ways."

He tipped his hat and strode from the room. Choking back an angry retort, I followed, determined to make sure he left the house without harassing anyone else. Of all the times to have drawn the focused attention of the Vigil—how could we properly delve into the matter of Ainslie's binding with Mr. Ludne and his compatriots lurking about?

When we reached the entry, Holden was nowhere to be seen —so much the better. Mr. Ludne wrapped long fingers about his iron-headed cane. "I'll be watching you, Miss Caldwell."

Without a word of acknowledgment, I shut the door firmly behind him. It would have felt better to slam it.

Jade growled softly. *Better yet if you'd allowed me to sink my teeth into him.*

Risha's blue light flared like a sunbeam. "Should like to see him keep watch after I burn his eyes out."

Her vehemence startled me. Despite the gravity of the situation, my curiosity sparked. "Can you do that?"

Nothing about the ephemeral beauty of the sylphs suggested they were prone to violence. But they were Other.

"Sun sylph flames accomplish many things." Her wings burned white. "Shall I? It would take but a moment."

I edged back. "No, I never meant to suggest—of course not."

"Why not? He *is* your enemy."

"It seems he's determined to make himself one, but . . . he has no defense against such an attack. It wouldn't be honorable."

"He has no mercy toward you."

I agree—there's nothing honorable about him.

"Perhaps not, but I don't think burning his eyes out is the solution." Nor had I expected Risha to be quite so bloodthirsty. "Though I appreciate your willingness to help."

Her wings dipped, and she dropped low. Did my refusal to act disappoint her? Before I could press as to what troubled her, Father charged into the room, his face set, his eyes kindled with rare awareness. "Where is he?"

I drew a ragged breath, seeking composure. "Who?"

"The Vigilist." Unusual color flooded Father's face. "Holden said one made so bold as to come here and demand an audience with you."

So that's where Holden had been. The slight glamour had kept him from speaking to Aunt Caris, but he must have addressed Father as soon as he'd returned. I tucked my trembling hands into the folds of my gown—if I appeared upset, Father might well pursue Mr. Ludne. "He's already departed."

Father smoothed an invisible wrinkle from his jacket. "Good. If he returns, you're not to see him, but send for me at once."

"He's not the sort to accept a denial of his demands."

"Then he shall have to become one." Father appeared unusually resolute. "I'll instruct Holden accordingly. He's to say you're not at home if the Vigil calls again. What did the man want?"

"He was angry over being denied access to Kilmere, and he seeks evidence to use against our family. It's difficult to say whether he genuinely believes we've done wrong or if it's simply a matter of vengeance." I shifted slightly. "He suggested you had a run-in with another Vigilist recently?"

"It was nothing of consequence." He tugged at his cravat. "But as it happens, there's something else I'd like to talk to you about. Will you come to the study?"

I trailed Father into his domain, one nearly as comfortable to me as my garden, thanks to the quiet hours I'd spent here reading or helping him organize his papers and correspondence. He took a chair beside the hearth, and I settled into the one opposite. If he intended to press about Kilmere, it would be difficult to keep the truth concealed.

He cleared his throat. "I believe you've struck up a friendship with Mrs. Thea Darrington?"

"Yes. I didn't know you were acquainted." I inhaled the scents of parchment and leather and ink. They were familiar; this side of Father was decidedly not.

"We met recently in Lord Blackburn's home."

Thea and Lord Blackburn? I'd not known they were acquainted either, though most of those with wealth or title in Avons knew each other, even if only in a passing way.

"How did you come to meet her?" Father's gaze remained fixed on the empty hearth.

He'd never had the slightest interest in society or the relationships we cultivated. Why did he press for information now? I leaned forward, and the cushion crackled beneath me. "She was a friend of Ibbie's."

"Did she, ah . . . ever speak to you about Otherworldly concerns?"

I tensed, unease shivering down my spine. Did he know or suspect something? "We discussed her belief in a curse on Kilmere. I'd not expected her to hold such views."

He wrenched his gaze from the hearth, studying me as though I might have taken some mortal wound. "And now that you've examined Kilmere, do you believe her theory correct?"

"Not as such." Given it wasn't a true curse, but rather a bargain that had doomed the inhabitants of Kilmere. I needed to change the subject, before we trod into even more unchancy waters. If I pressed him on an uncomfortable matter, he'd likely withdraw altogether—Father could be counted on to take the path of least emotional resistance. "Still, I'm glad to be home. However, I was surprised to find a boy in the garden this morning. Dryden?"

"Ah . . . yes." He shoved his spectacles upward.

"He said you found him in Shepherd's Bush. Why bring him to Avons?"

"He . . . well, he seemed in need of a place, and he did me a good turn, so I thought I'd offer him a position here."

The words left Father in a rush. I tilted my head. Was he covering something he did not wish us to know? "What brought you to Shepherd's Bush?"

He waved a hand. "Just some star charting."

"And that's why you ran afoul of the Vigilist?"

"Vigilists ever seek to meddle. You know as much."

I did. Just as I now felt sure something of an Other nature had happened in Shepherd's Bush. Because Vigilists most often sought to meddle wherever they believed Otherworldly connections existed. Yet whatever Father had encountered, he'd clearly no intention of revealing it. Brambles of unease tangled in my stomach. "But if—"

"It's best you steer clear of them altogether." He fumbled for the stack of gazettes on the side table, retreating from the conversation. "Just leave them to me."

With that, he lifted a paper, effectively ending the conversation. I sat for a moment, staring at the orderly lines of type across the back of the gazette. What had prompted Father's questions about Thea? And what had drawn the attention of the Vigil? Pressing the point now might lead him to turn the uncomfortable questions toward me. Perhaps I could gain answers elsewhere. Holden might offer some insight, or if all else failed, I could seek Dryden again.

Yet if Jade's suspicions were correct, that held its own risks. I slowly descended the stairs, halting outside the drawing room. Something about the visit from Mr. Ludne troubled me. While he might have come simply to taunt or intimidate me, surely it would have better suited his ends to lurk in the shadows collecting evidence until the time came to strike. So why show his hand now?

Perhaps he sought to distract you.

It's possible. Or he simply believed he could frighten me into giving up information, but after Withern, that feels unlikely.

I rehearsed the visit in my mind, halting at the very beginning. There'd been something odd about the way he'd stood at the mantel, his movements furtive. I returned to the room, where his sharp, repellent scent still lingered. Yet there was something else also, something I'd not noticed during the heat of our conversation—a pinprick sensation of Other that strengthened as I crossed to the mantel.

I bent to examine its underside.

There.

Amid the carved vines and flowers nested a small polished stone that didn't belong. I skimmed my fingers across it, and the sensation of Other intensified, rushing up my arms. I plucked it loose.

And Jade bristled. *A listening stone.*

What's that?

Listening stones run in veins through the Echo Mountains—thus the name. They're coveted even among the fae. To function properly, they must be paired by fae workings. The possessor of the other linked stones can hear all that transpires in the vicinity of the first.

My hand tightened about the stone, and it seemed to sear my palm. *Why would a Vigilist possess a fae-worked object? Aside from its value, how could he have possibly obtained it?*

This was a far cry from the alchemists sending Collectors for scraps of flora and fauna to use in their devices. If fae valued these stones, they'd keep them close, not allow them to slip into the hands of mortals.

The prospects are troubling.

Yes. It appears he's more resourceful than I believed. And it seemed what I'd always feared was coming to pass—the Vigil was hunting me, and at the worst possible time. *We can at least see that this attempt fails.*

With the stone tucked into the folds of my gown, I slipped back into the garden. If it carried a fae working, I suspected that to destroy it would require use of an affinity.

I glanced around the garden to ensure none of the servants —nor any of my family—lurked nearby. All remained quiet, so I collected a hand shovel from the glasshouse and then knelt beneath the oak. Its protective nature would make it easier to bend to my intended purpose. I dug a small hole, as if I intended to plant a seed, then dropped the stone in the ground, burying it until only the faintest trace of Other prickled along my skin.

Then I opened more fully to the song of the oak, and a deeper connection formed without effort. My eyes slid shut as the sensation of roots unfurling beneath the ground burgeoned within my belly. My purpose became its purpose, and its roots twisted from their quest within the earth to reach for the stone.

They surged about it, shattering it into tiny fragments faster than the blink of an eye—and without an element to contain them, the workings unraveled.

It was done.

Unsteady, I pressed to my feet. The ground roiled as the roots returned to their proper places, but not enough that anyone would take note, not unless they stood nearby.

Jade's rumbled warning at last pierced the haze brought on by the use of my affinity. Oh—oh no.

I turned and met a black-eyed gaze.

Dryden.

CHAPTER 7

I dusted my hands, attempting to pretend that nothing out of the ordinary had occurred. And Dryden shuffled past me, his face expressionless and his arms laden with coal for the kitchen fire. A small gray rabbit followed in his footsteps, as if drawn by invisible thread, and together they vanished into the house.

Even several hours later, I couldn't begin to guess if he'd noticed anything amiss. Certainly, his face had betrayed nothing —and yet, how could he not have taken note? He'd been so close, at the end.

Theories about how much he'd seen and what he might say —even a chance remark could betray me—proliferated like weeds within my mind, making it difficult to concentrate on the pile of letters that needed sorting. My hand instinctively went to where the protective pendant Mr. Heard had given me once rested. How unfortunate I couldn't obtain a ward to protect me from the Vigil.

Jade stretched out her limbs, sprawling across the surface of the table and nearly knocking over the stacks of mail I'd set in order—general invitations in one pile and personal correspondence sorted by individual. *I shall be your ward.*

I don't know about a ward, but you could certainly be a deterrent. In true-form, she'd terrify all but high fae. *What do you make of Dryden?*

I don't like mysteries that I cannot decipher. For now, he is one.

I shared her sentiment. I couldn't make peace with his presence here, particularly when it coincided with the Vigil's interest in my family, but nor could I think of a reason to have him dismissed, not when Father believed he owed him a favor. And if he *was* just an innocent bystander, who happened to witness something I'd very much rather he'd not have, I couldn't justify snatching away his livelihood.

Perhaps Aunt Caris had the right idea—if he was transplanted to Caldwell House, it would be better for us all. I slit open the last envelope, an invitation from Aunt Gillian to a house party a month hence. Would Aunt Caris wish to remove us from Avons? Almost certainly, if given the chance. Society was sparse this time of year, and she'd already expressed her unease about the missing individuals.

I rubbed my temples. Perhaps Aunt Caris could be swayed by the presence of Riven and Mr. Redgrave, when they came. Her desire to matchmake overruled much else and might well prove a safeguard. The clock chimed the hour, and I sprang to my feet. At last, I could reasonably call on Thea. Yet I hesitated in the doorway; Risha didn't flutter alongside as she ordinarily did, but remained huddled on the windowsill, holding herself distant from us. "Risha, is something wrong?"

Wings dull, she shook her head.

If she did not wish to confide in me, I wouldn't press, not yet.

Jade lifted her head. *Whatever troubles her, she knows her duty. When you leave, she'll follow.*

Still, I wish she'd speak. I tugged on my hat and gloves and hurried to fetch Lianne, who gladly agreed to accompany me—she'd enjoy the change of scenery, or so she said.

With Lianne at my side and Jade draped over my shoulders, her bulk warm and comforting, I descended to the waiting carriage, Risha dragging along behind, her coloring still a dull, splotchy blue.

My shoulders dropped. Had my refusal to accept her aid with Mr. Ludne violated some sort of fae convention? Even if it had, I'd scarcely expect this response. When Riven returned, perhaps he'd have some insight. I settled into the carriage and peered out the window. I'd give a great deal for him to be here now . . .

The driver secured the door behind us and then clambered into his seat and flicked the reins. As we traversed the cobbled streets, Lianne inquired about Withern, her enthusiasm brimming over at the notion of exploring the sea. I did my best to describe the sights to her, wondering all the while how I might persuade her to allow me a private audience with Thea when we arrived at Crestridge Court.

However selfish it might be, I hoped Dreda would return soon. Her willingness to "conspire," as she'd called it—to choose deliberate blindness when required and allow me liberty to conduct unladylike business—made these sorts of situations far easier. I dared not expect the same from Lianne.

I'd not had time to procure a new novel to absorb her attention, but perhaps Jade might help. *After we greet Thea, could you act as if you need to go out of doors? I know it's beneath your dignity, but it would provide an excuse to remove Lianne—I'd ask her to take you.*

Oh, I don't mind leading Lianne on a merry chase. Her tail quivered. *It will be quite entertaining, far more so than sitting in the drawing room while you take tea.*

With that, we descended from the carriage. This time, the butler admitted us without question, his birch-slender frame bending in a slight bow before returning to its customary rigidity. At his request, I followed him into Thea's private study, where she sat on a camelback sofa finishing dictation of a letter to a tall brunette—Miss Everby, perhaps?

Thea offered me a brisk nod, her eyes bright. "Miss Caldwell, this is my assistant, Miss Everby."

"I'm pleased to meet you, Miss Everby." She murmured a similar pleasantry in return. We'd corresponded before, when she'd written to tell me of Thea's illness. I turned to Thea. "I trust you've made a full recovery."

"Indeed, I have." She straightened her small frame. "And I cannot tell you how pleased I am that you've called."

"How very gracious."

She shook her head, and her milkweed-floss hair wisped about her face. "On the contrary. I'm not at all gracious of speech. If I didn't truly enjoy your company, I would have instructed Forester to tell you I wasn't at home. As it happens, I heard you'd returned to Avons, and I meant to give you another day to settle in before I visited. I'm quite pleased I shall not have to wait. Events have taken a rather unexpected turn of late, and I hope you might have answers to offer."

What events might she mean? Had she looked further into Kilmere, thinking to lend aid? Unease pricked down my spine. The time had come to enlist Jade in removing Lianne from the situation.

But before I could act, Thea nodded toward Lianne. "I've a mind for fresh air. Your maid can remain with Miss Everby while the two of us take a drive to Benhem Park."

"That sounds lovely."

But not nearly so entertaining as your original plan.

I stifled a smile. With Lianne entrusted to the capable Miss Everby, I followed Thea into her ornate open carriage. It was the expected sort of vehicle for driving in the park, an activity done more to see and be seen than anything else, but it meant we'd have no opportunity to speak until we arrived at our destination.

What did she mean to ask? She was shrewd, and she'd already guessed too much about the nature of Kilmere for comfort. Could she intend to press the matter? Whatever her questions, they'd be difficult to evade, and I didn't want to lie—it was possible I *couldn't*, given my fae nature . . .

We passed the ride in silence, and when we arrived at

Benhem Park, she motioned to the driver. "Very good, Thomas. We shall stroll now."

Blessedly, Benhem was rather quiet at this hour, though Thea had given nods of acknowledgment to several acquaintances as we'd traversed into the park proper. Everything within was kept in well-maintained order. Upright beds of irises remained neatly enclosed in stone borders with perfectly trimmed boxwood clustered behind, crisp dahlias occupied orderly rows, and even the roses had been pruned into rigid shape. A murmur of longing swept over me, a desire to grow gloriously free. *Not now.*

After I climbed from the carriage, I turned and offered a hand to Thea. She sighed slightly, but accepted it. "I cannot recommend growing old, but when one considers the alternative, well, it must be embraced with thanks."

As I'd seen what felt like far too much death of late, I had to agree. I slowed my pace to match hers, and we entered a shadow-dappled lane lined with laburnum. Their brilliant golden flowers formed a cheery arch above our heads, their appearance warm and welcoming even as their songs whispered of death. Like the Otherworld itself, they'd lure one in with beauty, but if consumed, they'd be lethal. I fought the urge to quicken my steps.

Thea leaned heavily on her walking stick as we ambled down the path. "Perhaps you wonder why I've taken all this trouble?"

"I assume it is because you do not want our conversation overheard." The sweet, woodsy scent of the laburnum filled my senses, a reminder to tread with care.

"Precisely. One cannot be too careful. I trust Miss Everby implicitly, but others might let a careless word slip—or take alarm at the nature of our conversation."

"As it happens, the privacy suits me as well." Time to test the waters. "I received an unpleasant visit this morning from Vigilist Ludne."

Her grip on her walking stick tightened, the bones of her hand standing out stark against age-thinned skin. "What did he want?"

"To bring all sorts of vague accusations and threats." I pressed aside the offer of assistance from the laburnum. "I believe he's angry because I refused to turn Kilmere over to the Vigil."

Her eyes snapped. "They sought to make a claim?"

"Only a dispensation from the king stopped them from seizing it."

"Well done." She gave a satisfied nod. "How I'd have liked to see their faces the moment they learned they'd been thwarted."

From her reaction, it seemed clear that Thea didn't welcome the idea of Vigil interference, but that didn't mean that I could entrust her with the true nature of Kilmere. If I checked her questions with answers beforehand, perhaps she'd be satisfied. "In any case, it allowed me the opportunity to examine Kilmere properly. I'd like to share my findings with the Antiquary Society."

"You mean to speak openly of what you discovered there?" A note of surprise laced her voice.

I shrugged. "I all but promised to inform the society of what I observed. Given the Vigil interest, I don't feel prepared to open it for excavation, yet I'd like to honor Ibbie by sharing what I can—and putting to rest any rumors of the curse."

"You still believe the tales only rumors, then?"

"Not rumors, precisely." I offered a careful account of the venomous snake, the suffering it caused, and its death, as well as how the Magistry and the Vigil had declared the area devoid of any other such predators. "I expect we'll see no further deaths."

"How very remarkable." She halted, studying my face as though she sought something hidden within.

And I fought the urge to shift beneath her scrutiny. Did she guess how much I'd amended my account?

Then her gaze softened. "Ibbie would certainly be pleased if Kilmere were to become a place of peace and research, the stain of its so-called curse removed, even more so if you were to join the Antiquary Society. Is that still your intent?"

"It is."

"Then I'm prepared to vouch for you and review your application, if you desire. I know the sorts of things they want to see, and I'll make sure they place no unnecessary obstacles to your membership. After a recent debacle when our president admitted a charlatan, he has no grounds to deny you, provided you follow proper procedure."

"I'd be deeply grateful for your assistance."

"Then we're in accord. Which leads me to why I brought you here." Our path opened to a large clearing where stone benches surrounded a fountain. A few people meandered along the far side, but the vigorous cascade of water would muffle our conversation from any listening ears. Thea sank onto one of the stone benches. "Won't you join me?"

I settled alongside her, and she nodded approval. "Now to business. I did intend to address Kilmere and the society with you, but there's more. I've recently become better acquainted with Lord Blackburn, and he informed me that you gave him evidence on a war that's been forgotten, also that you requested his views on Otherworldly matters. It suggested to me that you know more than you shared with him. Do you?"

She'd chosen an unavoidably direct approach. The cold of the stone beneath me seeped through my gown. "If I . . . held unconventional views about the intersection of the Otherworld and our own, I'd be most unwise to speak of them."

"Quite so." She leaned closer, as if she sought to draw the truth from me. "Yet Lord Blackburn and I have been examining some new evidence about the relationship between our worlds. I'd like to know what you make of it."

No doubt she sought to spark my curiosity, perhaps even draw forth questions by which I'd betray the knowledge I held. I could afford no such missteps, yet I needed to know what she and Lord Blackburn had discovered—as well as what they planned to do about it.

Distant voices filtered through the trees. And I made my choice. "What sort of evidence?"

"Among other things, an unusual artifact we're in temporary

possession of. It belongs to one Cyril Redgrave, but he's been absent from Avons, so we cannot yet restore it to him."

The burble of the fountain receded before the sudden rush in my ears. A mysterious artifact belonging to a Redgrave? If it had Other origins, it would suggest a great deal about the family's practices. I smoothed the folds of my skirt. "Perhaps you and Lord Blackburn would consider attending an informal dinner party at Wyncourt? I'd very much like to examine the artifact, and it would allow sufficient time to do so without raising questions." I couldn't justify springing a dinner, however small, on Ibbie's staff without any warning. How soon could they prepare? "Perhaps the day after tomorrow?"

Her lips firmed. "This is a sensitive matter. With the Vigil already nosing about, we must take care."

"Danvers and Mrs. Peters will ensure our privacy. You know how Ibbie trusted them." And I trusted Wyncourt. Though I understood little of its inner workings, I believed I could coax it to cloak our words. And if not . . . "They kept secrets for Ibbie, and I believe they'd do no less in this matter."

"True enough." She gave a decisive nod. "I'll take care of extending the invitations, so all is proper, and I'll bring Miss Everby, so you'll need no chaperone."

"Thank you."

"You're quite welcome. But Jessa—I do hope you're prepared to be forthright when next we talk." She tugged her lace shawl around her shoulders, then fixed me with an unyielding gaze. "Discretion has great value—the proper allies, even greater. Ibbie trusted me. I hope in time, you will as well."

If I could have sunk beneath the hedge of lilac, I would have done so. She knew I'd skirted the truth about Kilmere and all the rest—which meant our dinner party would be difficult at best.

How much did she and Lord Blackburn already know or guess? Could I trust them with the truth, even in part? Or would it result in disaster?

CHAPTER 8

After we left Crestridge Court, I hesitated. Wyncourt beckoned, promising a haven from the tumult that had ensued since our return to Avons. Perhaps I could afford to indulge in a short visit—certainly, plans for a dinner party offered just cause. I leaned forward, calling out instruction to the driver, then offering a brief explanation to Lianne before we climbed into the carriage. Once inside, I scribbled a note to Aunt Caris on one of the pages of my sketchbook. When we reached Wyncourt, I'd send it to her via the footman so she'd not worry about the delay.

My confession that I needed to speak with Mrs. Peters in no way stretched the truth, for I'd rely on her knowledge and expertise in the matter of the dinner. Ada and Ainslie had spent time with our aunts planning all sorts of events, whereas I'd been little involved in such things. For the dinner to unfold properly, I would need to throw myself on Mrs. Peters's mercy. It wasn't as if Lord Blackburn and Thea would expect a society affair—only the exposure of uncomfortable truths. Yet I wanted it to be pleasing, in honor of Ibbie and the hospitality she'd always offered.

As we neared Wyncourt, the demesne reached out and

wrapped its vibrant presence about me, its strength promising protection against any assault. When I crossed its threshold, the air, fragrant with the sweet spice of goldhearts, stirred gently, and the tension knotted in my muscles since my confrontation with Mr. Ludne began to unravel. Certainly, I wanted to explore its secrets as soon as was wise, starting with the hidden room in its depths—an endeavor which would require Riven—but for now, I'd content myself with its presence.

Danvers wore his usual welcoming smile. "I'm delighted you've returned, Miss Caldwell. I've been wanting to consult you and had just begun to contemplate speaking with your trustees or seeking your father for your Withern address."

"Why? Has something gone wrong?" With the reassuring warmth of Wyncourt settling over me, it was difficult to believe anything was seriously amiss.

Jade prowled ahead of me, her tail twitching slightly. Yet her body remained relaxed. *Whatever troubles him, I sense no intruder.*

"It is perhaps not too great a matter, but it's my desire that you find satisfaction in the way we manage Wyncourt, as Lady Dromley once did." He steepled his hands, a precise gesture. "She always took pleasure in her orderly garden, but I'm afraid it's rather fallen to ruin. Our gardener tendered his resignation shortly after your last visit, as have the two we engaged after him. They appear to have fallen prey to the sorts of fears that plagued the servants after Lady Dromley passed."

I peered past Danvers, seeking some hint of the demesne's mood. Why would Wyncourt wish to drive away the gardeners? Light filtered through the enormous windows, gleaming off the white marble stairs beyond and illumining the statues in their sheltered nooks. Certainly, all appeared in order. "And you've seen no evidence that their tales reflect reality?"

"None whatever. It's possible they simply wearied of the work and fell back on a convenient excuse so as not to blacken their reputations. It is unfortunate, because the garden has become overgrown at an alarming rate." His brow furrowed. "I'll confess, I never paid much attention to it, but it does seem to have . . . changed."

"Perhaps I could assess the matter for myself?" The air about me warmed slightly, as if Wyncourt approved. "I'll seek you out before I leave."

"Very good, Miss Caldwell."

"Oh, one more thing." I drew my sketchbook from under my arm and tore out the note for Aunt Caris. "Will you see this gets to my aunt Caris?"

"Of course." He gave a slight bow, then stepped aside.

Though I skimmed my fingers discreetly across the wall as I traveled down the corridor, I sensed no alarm from Wyncourt, only delight. I quickened my steps, escaping out the back door and into the gardens. As befitting the size of the house, the garden was many times larger than the one behind our Avons home. Instead of the rather rigid formal design that had constrained the grounds before, a sprawl of lavish life unfolded before me, walls of foliage offering a sheltered haven which no outside eyes could pierce. A small brook that hadn't existed before now meandered along the stone wall at the farthest corner, its mossy banks lined with water hawthorn and wind-flower. Somehow, Wyncourt had diverted the power woven through it into the garden to produce this breathtaking retreat, shaded and cool despite the summer sun. Perhaps to Danvers it appeared disordered, yet every plant existed in harmony, one with another, every line of the garden thrumming with life. I breathed in the rich fragrances of sun-warmed greenery and bright blossoms. Why had Wyncourt rearranged the grounds? Did demesnes ordinarily do such things?

Jade sniffed. *I've heard of such changes after an inheritance.*

Whatever the reason, it was magnificent, and yet I could only imagine how unnerving it would have been for the gardeners to find the very terrain changing, if not before their eyes, then when they returned to their labors from one day to the next. Perhaps Wyncourt cared nothing for that—or perhaps it had influenced their perception as it pleased. Certainly,

Kilmere had the power to do such things. Was Wyncourt any different? Regardless, I sensed a certain pride, and with such refuge generously offered me, I couldn't bring myself to worry about the implications. I supposed if I had to justify the sudden changes to outsiders, the suggestion we'd employed alchemical methods could make a convenient excuse. Only why had Wyncourt gone to such lengths?

I think it wishes you to make your home here. Jade stretched out in a patch of sunlight. *A demesne greatly desires the presence of its master or mistress. It strengthens you, but you also strengthen it.*

I sank into the bed of moss. *But how could it achieve such a feat?*

It was designed to respond to the wishes of its owner, and it appears it understands you well.

I see. I glanced back at the demesne. "Can you conceal us?"

The air warmed, and the slightest hum, like the distant buzz of bee wings, filled the space about us as Wyncourt extended its workings. By connecting with the gold runners now woven up its walls and around its windows, I could more readily perceive the power woven within and all the silvery sigils and runes that made up its workings. The longer I examined them, the clearer their details became. This process of immersing myself within the intricacies of the workings tucked beyond mortal perception brought a sort of peace deep within my soul. Though I could not interpret the sigiled language, it conveyed a sense of Wyncourt's stalwart presence.

My eyes slid shut as my fingers wove into the moss beneath me. The sun caressed my skin, and the sprightly songs of the windflower mingled with the babble of the brook to quiet my soul. Above and beyond and through it all, Wyncourt wove into my awareness. In time, a sense stole over me that Wyncourt and I drew breath together, ever slower and more steady.

Was this part of what it meant to be fae? This sense of connection, the sensation that I was becoming truly alive, truly myself? Time slipped from me, and when I opened my eyes again, I felt the sort of quickening energy that follows the awakening from deep and undisturbed slumber. A brilliant profusion of blossoms had sprung up at my feet, not born of my will, but rather another offering from Wyncourt.

With the plants as a bridge between us, I didn't need physical contact with the structure for it to impress on my mind images of me settling into the demesne, becoming its mistress in a proper way, and exploring its secrets, a sort of warm, wistful invitation.

"I can't dwell here, not yet." But perhaps one day, when we'd freed Ainslie, when I came of age by mortal convention, I *could* make a home here. "But I'd like nothing more."

Though I'd not planned the words, they slipped out, and the flowers tinged pink, as though with pleasure. Perhaps the offering would satisfy Wyncourt for now. I glanced up at the sun which filtered at a low angle through the trees.

Though I'd sent the footman to tell Aunt Caris of my detour, if I delayed much longer, I'd miss family dinner and worry her unnecessarily—and I still must speak with Mrs. Peters before I departed. I pressed to my feet and went in search of her, locating her in the housekeeper's room, along with Danvers.

He cleared his throat. "Ah, Miss Caldwell. I confess I'd begun to wonder if something had gone amiss. I trust you did not find any signs that the peculiar tales were true?"

"I cannot speak to that, but I find the current state of the gardens pleasing."

His brow raised. "You do?"

"Indeed. However, I understand we must have a gardener." I brushed a bit of moss from my skirt. Although Wyncourt was perfectly capable of managing the space, we must appear to have someone tending it. Perhaps I could speak with Sister Margery and ask her to recommend someone who wouldn't be troubled by oddities. If she did not know, the Brothers might. And I could instruct Wyncourt to exercise more care. "I will send you possible candidates for the position."

"Very good." Genuine relief rang in his voice. "Did you desire anything else while you're here?"

"Actually, yes. I hoped to have a small dinner party here—Lord Blackburn, Mrs. Darrington, Miss Everby, and myself."

Mrs. Peters's hazel eyes gleamed. "That would be a welcome event. Did you have a request as to the meal?"

Bless her—she didn't question why I wanted to host a dinner party, nor, if so, why I'd planned it outside my family's home. I settled into the chair across from her. "I assume you know the preferences of Lord Blackburn and Mrs. Darrington?"

They would have dined with Ibbie before, though perhaps not together.

"Yes, Miss Caldwell."

"Then I'm content to leave the matter in your hands, if you're willing to see to all that's proper."

"Of course." Her lips curved upward. "It will do us good to have an event to prepare for again. I don't want to see the staff grow complacent, nor lazy either. And Lady Dromley, she'd be glad to see the place alive again."

"I believe you're right." A soft gust of air swirled about my skirts. Could they feel it? Would they notice the oddities? They certainly appeared unperturbed, and it seemed Wyncourt approved of my plans. Though Ibbie couldn't have known all the facets of its nature, I could well imagine her delight over the transformation of Wyncourt and the specters of Edward's reign being driven out. I pressed to my feet, Wyncourt's strength becoming my own. Surely, if the demesne could be so liberated, then Ainslie could as well.

BACK INSIDE THE CARRIAGE, Lianne chatted cheerily about the pleasant staff at Wyncourt. She'd always been a good-natured soul, but today she seemed in a particularly elevated mood. A love interest, perhaps? Or the simple joy of an outing? I let her words wash over me, her good spirits bolstering my own—until we returned home and I noted the gate to the garden stood ajar. Perhaps once I would have dismissed it as the act of a careless servant, but now, with the Vigil nosing about . . . it bore investigating. I halted on the footwalk. "Lianne, I think I'll spend some time in the gardens. You may inform Aunt Caris we've returned."

"Of course, miss." With a bounce in her step, she made her way into the house.

And I approached the high stone wall bordering the garden. I nudged the iron gate with my foot to send it swinging wide, but even the brief contact sent an ice-shard of pain up my leg. It seemed in one thing the Vigil was correct—those with fae blood did not respond favorably to iron.

I hurried past the gate and around the back corner of the house, watchful for any sign of an intruder. Jade stalked in front of me, prepared to strike if needed. And above my head, maple limbs swept toward a distant nook, as if gesturing toward something.

There.

Tucked into the shadows, in one of the few places that couldn't be viewed from any window in the house, stood a familiar figure. The tension in my shoulders released as I hurried forward. "Mr. Burke? Whatever are you doing here?"

"Gambling that a peculiarity in your gardens would draw your attention." A rueful smile creased his face. "If you'd been much longer, I'd have had to try again another day."

"But why conceal yourself in the gardens?"

"Because I received a frosty reception at your front door. I was informed by your butler that unless I came with a direct order from the Magister himself, I'd not be admitted."

It couldn't have been at Aunt Caris's instruction—whatever her sentiments about stratesmen in general, she'd been grateful for the help Mr. Burke had offered in Withern—so Holden must have acted on Father's orders. It seemed he was taking this notion of our protection very seriously. "I'm sorry. I'll speak to Father and let him know that you've proven yourself a friend. When he learns you helped Ada—"

"His sentiments may remain unchanged. Many don't feel a

stratesman is an acceptable visitor." He appeared untroubled by the fact. "It's perhaps more surprising that my calls have been tolerated until now. I could have pressed the point, but I'd prefer the Magister not take note of this call—and he would, if your father chose to voice a complaint."

Given the situation, I wished more than ever that I'd mastered some sort of concealment glamour. Could I, if I was not full fae? Never mind that, Mr. Burke wouldn't have come without cause, and learning it was worth the risk to my reputation. "Has something gone wrong?"

A sudden smile flashed across his face. "What in our acquaintance could have given you that notion?"

Jade chuffed.

And I laughed softly. "I cannot think."

"Tell me, has Riven returned to the . . . ah, his true home?"

"For now."

"That's unfortunate."

"I would have expected you to rejoice in the prospect."

"Given that I counseled you against any contact with his kind?" Mr. Burke shook his head. "I know better than to think you'll heed my advice on the matter, and at the moment, I could use his knowledge."

Which meant the trouble was Other in nature. As if in response to the sudden quickening of alarm in my veins, the verbena behind me shuddered. "What is it that concerns you enough to seek Riven?"

"It's a case." He scrubbed a hand along the back of his neck. "Doubtless you've heard about our missing persons situation."

"A little." If it hadn't been for Ainslie's binding mark, I might have investigated further—as it was, there'd been no time. The verbena brushed my skirts, its bright citrus scent seeking to dispel fear. "Do you think Otherkind are involved?"

"There's no evidence of it. The Magister has put forth another theory, one which I'm expected to operate under."

"But you're not satisfied with his explanation."

"Not in the least." His gaze sharpened. "I'd hoped for the

perspective of someone who understands the nature of the Other problem we face."

The clatter of carriages from the street beyond drifted over the garden wall. "I cannot pretend to possess the understanding of Other affairs that Riven does, but if you'd like to discuss the matter, I'll share any knowledge I'm able to."

"You're a civilian, and if it became known that you were privy to confidential information . . ." He drew a hand over his jaw. His usual circumspection and adherence to regulation must be warring with his need to gain information to help the missing. "Our regulations have always helped maintain justice and order. It seems that's no longer the case. Not given the threat fae offer."

Would he count me as a threat, if he knew the truth? I pressed my hands into the folds of my skirt. "If you choose to share, know that I'll keep it in confidence."

Amusement softened his features. "I've no doubt of it. You've proven you'd rather die than divulge a secret."

"That's putting it a bit strongly, perhaps."

"Really? Then I suppose you'd care to tell me the extent of your arrangements with Riven?"

"Well, I . . ."

"I thought not." He remained silent for a moment, then he exhaled. "Regardless, perhaps you can be viewed as a consultant. We use them from time to time, and I can't think of any mortal with more knowledge of Other aside from the Vigil, and they're not inclined to share that knowledge."

Jade sprawled beneath a gardenia, the white on her chest glowing to match its blossoms. *And I don't believe they have as much understanding as they claim. Certainly their actions give no such indication.*

As though he'd given himself permission, he continued. "Shortly after my return to Avons, I was brought into the investigation of the missing individuals. It seems that my actions on the cases of the Crimson Tattoo Killer and Kilmere, along with a few others, have drawn the attention of my superiors. In the matters of the killer and the curse, I can claim no credit—but unfortunately, I also cannot explain why."

He sounded nettled by what he seemed to view as undeserved acclaim. Yet his commitment to justice—whatever the cost—had helped in protecting Kilmere from Vigil interference and keeping an innocent man from being condemned. And whatever other cases he'd handled had been on his own merit alone. I started to protest, but he'd already moved on.

"Despite their approval of the 'results attained by my unorthodox approach,' they don't wish to consider any unnatural explanation for these disappearances." He paced the sheltered nook that concealed us from prying eyes. "With an utter lack of logic, they somehow hope I'll conjure an ordinary answer for these inexplicable events."

"How very vexing." I'd not heard him express himself so freely before, which meant he must be frustrated indeed—and how could he not be, when those meant to keep Byren safe insisted on turning a blind eye toward the truth? "What makes you suspect Other involvement?"

"The fact that there's so little reason for these individuals to disappear. Among the impoverished, people vanish with alarming regularity. We do what we can, but they're often untraceable—or they eventually turn up dead." He stopped abruptly, his body rigid. "We've never seen anything like this among the well-to-do before, nor were the individuals in question afflicted by misfortune or melancholy. In fact, in most instances, the missing were reported to be in unusually good spirits leading up to their disappearance."

A fact that I imagined none of the gazettes had reported. "Are the missing from Avons alone?"

"No, several other regions have experienced similar disappearances—no trace of foul play, not the slightest sign of disturbance to any of the scenes."

"I see." In the distance, a dove called softly, the peaceful sound at odds with the sinking sensation within. If the fae in question hadn't released Ainslie for purposes unknown, she would have fit perfectly among these missing individuals.

"As you can imagine, there's a great deal of pressure to solve this quickly—and return the missing unharmed." His shoulders lowered slightly, as if he'd taken the full weight of it upon himself. Perhaps he had.

Yet if the missing had been claimed by fae, it was far more likely they'd never be seen again. I brushed my fingers across the verbena, and its sprightly song swirled about me. "What theory have your superiors adopted?"

"At first, they discussed the notion of abduction for ransom, but when no demands materialized, it was discarded. Some wanted to blame the Emstead protesters—but though they grumble, they've never resorted to violence in their demands for better working conditions, nor do I think they have the coordination to carry out a plot of this nature. It was a sop tossed out to appease the public. The current theory is that the missing are victims of alchemy gone wrong."

Of course—the wealthy had access to alchemical devices those of lower means could not afford, and the alchemists would make desirable scapegoats for the king. I frowned. "And they believe what? That their devices are killing them and destroying the bodies? Translating them elsewhere? Driving them mad so they lose themselves?"

Tension radiated from him. "They'll accept any of the above —and I've heard even more outlandish thoughts."

"Have they found any evidence to support this claim?"

"Very little. All of the missing were wealthy enough to have alchemical devices in their household, yet none exceptional." A welcome gust of wind stirred the still air in our shadowed alcove, rustling among the branches above. "It's conceivable but impossible to prove."

Absently, I swiped at the dirt collected in the seams of the stone wall alongside us. "Was anything strange found in their households?"

"How do you define strange? Everything about the collecting

habits of the wealthy is odd—from wards to statuettes to snuff boxes, even illicit substances. The list could go on, but nothing tied one household to another, at least among the residences I examined." His lips tightened. "But then, we're hampered by the fact we cannot travel as readily as the fae, and no one stratesman has visited every home."

"Even if you had, it seems unlikely that any trace—or Other object—would have been left behind."

His kestrel-sharp gaze fixed on me. "You have any theories?"

I did—and they choked me. I brushed the dirt from my gloves. "What if . . . what if these individuals had bargained with the fae? Perhaps even bargained away *themselves*, unknowing?"

He rocked back, brushing a hedge rose. "You think high fae presence so prevalent in Byren?"

"Perhaps. In the end, with Uros . . . he tried to distract me by offering a bargain." I chose my words with care. "He spoke of Other invading our world, said if I left him alive, he'd prey on the fae and thus stand between our world and the coming destruction. At the time, I thought it another one of his lies, but now . . ."

He swore, then swiftly begged pardon. "Even if this bargain theory is correct, we'd have no way of proving it."

"We might. Fae bargains leave a mark."

His eyes narrowed. "What kind of mark?"

However little I desired it, I must tell him, if he was to protect the vulnerable—and then I must warn Ainslie to conceal her binding mark at all costs. Or perhaps Riven would conceal it for her upon his return, as he once had mine. I fought the urge to ask Risha to seek him, instead opening my reticule and with-drawing a notebook no larger than the palm of my hand. I sketched the binding mark Riven had left on me when we bargained for Wyncourt. "This is an example."

"And you know this how?"

I pressed the pencil harder into the page, tracing the final lines. "I've bargained with Riven before."

"You said he wasn't coercing you."

"He isn't—not now."

"But he did once? And you take no exception to the fact?"

How could I possibly explain the whole? I snapped the sketchbook shut. "I didn't say that, but we're losing sight of our main end."

"You're right." Though his eyes had darkened to a stormy gray, he nodded. "I can work with this, inquire if those close to the missing noticed any new scars or marks on their bodies. Ladies' maids or valets are likely to know, even if family members don't."

His dispassionate commentary returned him to the role of stratesman—one who excelled at his job. If perceptible-to-mortals evidence of the binding marks existed, I felt certain he'd uncover it. Still, some part of me felt obligated to involve myself, to attempt to move in places less accessible to stratesmen, to use what Other senses I possessed to seek any possible fae involvement in these disappearances.

Mr. Burke watched me closely, as if he too expected something more. Yet Mr. Ludne also watched and waited, his intent malevolent, and Ainslie was vulnerable right now. I couldn't afford to attract attention to my family by visiting the households of the missing, even less so by using my affinities, not when it might endanger them. Perhaps there might be a way to help without exposing my entire family to the wrath of the Vigil, but for now, I'd wait and see if Mr. Burke uncovered a link to the Otherworld or fae bargains before risking my family further. "Will you tell me what you find?"

He inclined his head slightly—relieved? Or disappointed? "I believe I owe you that much. Whatever comes of it, this is a better line of inquiry than I've had for many days."

"Thank you." I glanced toward the house to make sure all remained quiet, then back to Mr. Burke. "While you're here, there's a more . . . personal matter I hoped to discuss."

"What is it?" His full attention concentrated on me in a disconcerting way.

"Have you ever heard rumor of any connection between the Redgrave family and anything . . . unusual?"

"You're concerned with Mr. Redgrave's interest in Ainslie?" His brows lifted. "It seemed genuine to me."

"I don't doubt his sincerity. But he was unusually knowledgeable in certain areas most gentlemen aren't. He recognized the oddity of the injury Lord West inflicted on me at once."

"I noticed that, but if he has a passion for weapons and sport, then a knowledge of how to treat injuries is a logical extension. I'm familiar with the family, but until we met in Withern, I'd never crossed paths with them, nor have I ever heard any unsavory rumors about them."

"I haven't either." The verbena brushed my hand, its leaves slightly rough, but the gesture nevertheless reassuring. I couldn't confide the whole in Mr. Burke, but I also wanted him aware and watchful. "Yet he and Elodie both had an unusual amount of interest in Kilmere. I'll admit everything odd I noticed about them could easily be explained away, but since he's professing interest in Ainslie, I just . . . I want to be sure."

"I'll poke about a bit, see if anything stands out." He lifted his hand, as if to offer a gesture of reassurance, then let it drop to his side. "Try not to worry."

Excellent counsel, if only I could take it—if only there weren't so very many things to worry *about.*

CHAPTER 9

L ate that night, when all was still, when the lights were snuffed out and the moon poured silver-bright through my windows, a faint rustle pulled me from the edge of sleep. I peered into the room, seeking the source.

It was Risha.

Ordinarily, she slept on the windowsill, absorbing whatever light spilled through the glass. Yet now she'd abandoned her post, fluttering over to my bedside table, where she perched for a moment, the droop of her wings forlorn. Then she launched into the air, shimmering with ethereal light as she drifted down to rest on the bed. "What do you consider just punishment for disloyalty?"

All notion of sleep fled. I pressed upright. "What do you mean?"

"Sylphs are to act only in the interests of those they serve, else it endangers the fae whose messages they carry."

Beside me, Jade tensed, and I twined my fingers in her fur. "And you've . . . acted in other interests? Or desire to do so?"

She offered a swift, jerking nod.

My stomach knotted. "It isn't my place to mete out some

sort of punishment, but if you feel you cannot remain whole-heartedly in my service, then I will release you."

"No!" Brilliant light flared from her. "More than anything, I want to stay."

"Then will you tell me of these other interests?"

"Sylph matters. Not high fae." Her tiny shoulders dropped. "We're not meant to have such concerns, only to serve without question."

I tilted my head to study her. "So when you spoke of disloyalty, you did not mean you'd disclosed my affairs to someone who meant me ill?"

Her light flared. "No! I would never."

"Then why do you fear? I'd hoped . . . that is, when you first came, you seemed to trust me."

"Trusted enough to serve, yes. It's what sylphs do, what's required of us." Her light muted. "For more, it is difficult. I think you are what Asrina believed . . ."

"But?"

"You do not just *ask* high fae for help. Not when they can kill if angered. We serve high fae, not the other way around."

The stark pain in her words stole my breath. "Have you seen such things?"

Her frame shuddered as she nodded. "Many times."

Jade stretched out across the bed. *Most high fae ensure so-called loyalty by instilling fear.*

Chilled despite the bedcovers, I fetched my dressing gown and wrapped it tightly about myself before rejoining her in bed. "Does this have anything to do with what happened with Mr. Ludne earlier?"

"I thought if I performed some extra service, you might be willing to hear my request. But you did not favor the idea." A muted blue shivered across her wings. "I made things worse."

"Not at all. You and I don't have to deal in the fashion fae and sylphs ordinarily do." Whatever that might be. I lowered my voice. "Surely you already know that not all high fae are uncaring. Asrina said Riven dealt fairly with your flight, that he looked after you."

"Yes, yes. But still Lord Arbiter would not approve of my request."

"Will you tell me and allow me to decide for myself?"

"You know we must serve bond-terms to high fae. It is our sworn agreement from generations past." She took a quivering breath. "There's another sylph, from a nearby flight. Kiran. We had a desire for bonding, but he had to serve his term first. Lord Arbiter cannot be seen to enlist all flights, so I suggested another fae Kiran might serve. I thought she'd be a safe one. She seemed so."

"What happened?"

"She sent him to collect youngling sylphs for bait." Risha shuddered. "He refused, and she withheld light till he nearly died. Kept him alive to use as an example to other sun sylphs who might think to rebel. Torments him still."

"Oh, Risha."

"My hatch-brother sent message this morning. Kiran grows weak, does not have much time left. I don't want to lose him too."

Small wonder gloom had hung over her all day. "And you believe I can help?"

"You could purchase his freedom, then his term of service would belong to you." She clasped her hands to her chest. "Isn't there something you could find for him to do?"

"Of course, but, Risha—I cannot travel into your world like other fae do. I understand very little of my own affinities, certainly not enough to create a passing."

"Sylph could carry messages on your behalf. It's common."

Everything in me wanted to agree, yet I forced myself to reason—I couldn't afford to plunge into dangers unknown right now. "Wouldn't it appear strange if I was willing to pay for a particular sylph when it sounds like I could gain the service of others for free?"

Jade's eyes glowed bright. *I suspect that's why Riven wouldn't approve. Your intervention could attract attention of the sort you can't afford.*

She might be right, and yet . . . I tugged the bedquilt closer about me. "Under ordinary circumstances, is there any reason a fae might make such a request, much less offer something of value in support of it?"

Risha looked as though she wanted to swear *yes*, but in the end, she collapsed on the bed, misery etched into every line of her body. "No."

She had nowhere else to go. How could I turn her away? She'd extended trust, overcoming her fear of appearing disloyal to act in the interests of her love rather than serving as a mindless automaton, as most fae evidently expected. There must be some path forward. I reached toward her, touching her arm gently. "What if you tell her that I wish to use him in an experiment?"

Her head lifted. "An . . . experiment?"

Is it wise? Jade's ears pricked forward.

Only time will tell. But how can I condemn the one she loves?

Jade huffed. *Quite easily. You are far too reckless with your own safety.*

If all goes well, there will be no danger. I turned to Risha. "We don't have to tell her the nature of the experiment, only that a trouble-maker would be particularly suited for it."

She hesitated. "What sort of experiment?"

"Let us say, between ourselves only, one of the change that comes with being given the chance to choose for oneself. If Kiran wishes employment, I'll offer it. If not, he may return to his flight. But, please, try not to name me."

She dipped and brushed a wing across my hand. "I owe you thanks, my lady."

"I'm not a lady—"

"You are *my* lady." Bright silver swirled through the blue of her light as her chin lifted. "My hatch-brother, he will come for the funds and the message. Yes?"

"That will suit. What amount do you think will be required?"

"An experiment would interest her more than the sum, I think."

"Good, because I don't keep large quantities on hand." Nor did I possess them. But I had drawn money from Ibbie's estate to cover the expenses of traveling to Kilmere. I could give what remained to Risha and hope it would be enough—though it would be recognizable as mortal money, which could pose a problem.

Have it changed for gold coin. Jade shifted to rest her head on my lap. *Mortal gold makes its way into the Otherworld often enough.*

Father kept a strongbox in his study, and I thought he'd exchange it for me without too many questions—I'd see to it first thing in the morning. "You are close to your hatch-brother?"

She nodded. "Most hatch-siblings are."

"Riven has told me that in the Otherworld, families are not bound by affection, rather they're structures of power. What makes it different for sylphs?"

"High fae have strength enough that they need not rely on anyone. Sun sylphs, all sylphs, know we need each other. That our bonds make the hard times endurable."

"I see. In that, perhaps, we are alike."

Her eyes widened slightly. "Do not let high fae hear you saying you have any likeness to low."

A sigh escaped me. "I—"

"Jessa!" Ada surged through the door, pale in her ivory dressing gown, her curls tumbling down her back. "Something's wrong with Ainslie. I locked her in the room to try to prevent her from disappearing, but I don't want to leave her long. I can't rouse her."

I dashed down the stairs, stumbling on the bottom step and jarring my ankle. Locking the door would do no good if a passing opened in her bedchamber—oh, there was so much yet to explain to my sisters.

Jade kept pace, and Risha's blue flame lit the way. Ada fumbled with the key in the lock, and together we tumbled into the room.

Ainslie writhed on the bed, moaning softly. Perspiration gathered at her hairline, and her binding mark gleamed bright. I clasped her hand, but she did not respond. "Ainslie, can you hear me?"

Tears spilled down Ada's face. "I tried to rouse her, shook her, called her name, but she showed no sign of acknowledgment. She's caught in some unnatural torment."

I glanced at Risha. "Please ask Riven to come at once, if he can."

In a brilliant flare, she vanished. Ada grew paler still but made no protest. Nothing mattered except sparing Ainslie.

I touched her binding mark—it burned like flame. Was this the cause of her suffering? Once before, my own binding mark had pricked with pain, when I'd considered going against its terms, but this . . . I dropped my fingers to her wrist, where her pulse raged. How much more could she take?

The power of passing surged into the room, heralding Riven's arrival. The welcome scent of sun-drenched forest traveled with him, sweeping away the stench of sweat and pain. With a glance, he took in the situation, then strode to Ainslie's side and bent over her body—yet he sent no light along her frame. Why?

"She's being influenced by the liminal realm." His jaw was tight. "Best guess, she can no longer discern dream from reality, therefore she can't begin to free herself from its grip."

My stomach tightened. The nightmare I'd experienced under the influence of Lord West's liminal affinity had felt so real that I'd unconsciously summoned plants to my defense. How much did Ainslie suffer, caught in terrors from which she couldn't escape? "What does that mean?"

"Her dream could kill her, if it pleases the fae who holds her binding to plant sufficiently dangerous ideas. Her body struggles beneath the strain already."

Ada sank into a chair, burying her face in her hands. And I stood rooted in place like a frost-mired tree. "There must be something we can do."

"Any attempt to enter the actual mindscape will make her more vulnerable. At best, I can plant suggestions of my own about her, things that might help her free herself."

Did that mean he also possessed liminal abilities? He'd never spoken of it, but then, he divulged little of a personal nature and —never mind that now. I wrapped my arms around my middle. "Are there risks?"

"Always. If the fae in question watches this liminal space, he or she will know I've involved myself. And the infusion of more power into the situation could tip her over the edge."

Ainslie thrashed against some unseen threat, her binding mark flaring. If he didn't act, we might lose her here and now.

Ada lifted her face, the gaslight playing over the tear traces on her cheeks. "She can't take this much longer. I think we must try, whatever the risk."

Riven glanced at me, and I nodded slowly.

Then he rested his hand on Ainslie's forehead. Strands of light wove about her face, then traveled down her body, and the lines of pain began to smooth.

Jade wove between my ankles, and I lifted her, clutching her close to my chest. *If she cannot wake . . .*

She shares your stubbornness, and she has Riven to help her, both points in her favor. I believe she'll rouse.

I buried my face in her fur. *I pray you're right.*

Remember, kit-isne *always are.*

With her confidence to bolster my own, her warmth seeping into my cold skin, we kept vigil as Riven stood over Ainslie for what felt like an eternity. At last, he withdrew his hand.

And still we waited, silent and motionless. The mantel clock chimed a single bell-like tone. As if the ordinary sound had broken her enchantment, Ainslie's eyelids fluttered.

Then opened.

Her gaze fell first upon Riven, and all color washed from her face. She scrambled back, clutching the bedquilt to her chest. "You. Why are you here?"

Riven's features shuttered, and he stepped away from the bed, while I hurried forward to clasp Ainslie's hand. "He's here to help. You were caught in a fae-influenced terror. Do you remember?"

She was shivering now, the heat of her torment turned to ice, her fingers frigid to the touch. "I remember something. A terrible maze. It went on without end, and the things inside . . ." Her breath rasped. "I don't . . . I can't recall any more."

I looked back at Riven. "How can we protect her from such assaults?"

"You can't." He was expressionless now. "Yet I've altered the working on her to signal if liminal power surges around her again. Next time, I'll know at once."

Ainslie didn't appear reassured; she still watched him much as one might a monster materialized from under her bed. Despite the help he'd offered, it seemed she saw him only as a representation of the realm she feared.

Perhaps he realized it, because he distanced himself further. The shadows in the corner of the room fell over his face. "I don't expect further trouble tonight. I arrived in Avons late this evening, and I intended to call on you tomorrow. We'll look into the matter further then."

Whatever Ainslie might feel, I wanted to plead for him to stay, to discuss the matter now. Yet Ainslie needed care and comfort—and we all required sleep. So I simply nodded and murmured my thanks, which Ada echoed.

Then Riven vanished, taking much of the light in the room with him. I removed my dressing gown and climbed into bed alongside Ainslie, Ada anchoring her other side. We'd sleep much as we had after my own liminal nightmare, but mine had been meant to manipulate—Ainslie's had felt crueler, intended only to torment.

And it might have killed her.

Even now, she shivered, unable to warm herself, shadows dark as bruises lurking beneath her eyes. If we couldn't find the holder of her bargain soon . . . it might be too late.

When I woke midmorning, Ainslie and Ada still slept, but Ainslie's features were drawn tight, as if some pain still remained. Fear rooted deeper in my chest.

Had Riven uncovered anything of use in the Otherworld? Any evidence we might use to find her bargain-holder? I'd take even the smallest clue, and I was determined to find one. With care, I eased away from Ainslie. Since we were to pretend he was an ordinary caller, Riven would most likely wait until afternoon to visit, which meant it would be hours yet until we spoke. If I simply sat about and waited for word, worry would drive me mad.

At my side, Jade stirred. *What do you mean to do?*

Put the time to the best use I can by attempting to determine if a link exists between the missing individuals and Ainslie's bargain. Were it not for the fact that the Vigil watched me, waiting for some scrap of evidence to condemn us all, I'd succumb to the temptation to call upon the families of the missing and search directly for any signs of connection.

Yet it could betray far too much. I required a more discreet approach while I awaited the report from Mr. Burke, and I could think of only one that might serve. *We should call on Sister Margery again. Perhaps she's heard rumors, maybe even spoken with the missing or their families.*

They may well have sought comfort from the Cloister in their loss, and it seems Sisters see and hear much. But will she speak of what she knows?

If she thinks I mean to help, she might. I meant to speak with her about a possible gardener, anyway. *If I don't find her receptive, I can always fall back on that. And most importantly, no one can object to a visit to the Cloister, not even Mr. Ludne.* I slipped from the bed, careful not to disturb Ainslie. Jade leapt down as well, with a soundless, graceful motion.

I tugged on my clothes. Before I could visit the Cloister, I must seek Father and give Risha the means to purchase Kiran's freedom.

A slight growl came from Jade. *I still object.*

I know how she feels, therefore I cannot ignore her plight, not when I can offer assistance. I knelt alongside Jade. *If you were the one enslaved and mistreated, I'd beg someone, anyone, to help me free you. And you'd do no less for me.*

If you were taken, I'd tear your captors limb from limb.

If I was taken, I hope you'd make the best strategic decision to get me back unharmed and keep yourself safe in the process. And if high fae were involved, a direct attack would be unwise. But since I don't ever intend to be separated from you, we needn't worry about that.

Perhaps not, but you should *worry more about the danger you keep exposing yourself to.* She turned away and began licking a paw.

Oh, Jade, don't be angry.

She peered back over her shoulder. *I don't want you to help, but if you did not, I suppose you'd not be you.*

That was the best concession I was likely to get. I gathered her in my arms and stroked her chin. A soft purr suggested that even if we did not agree, harmony existed between us once more.

With Jade clasped close, I descended the stairs. Through the window at the base of the steps, my eye caught on a figure in the garden—Lianne. She talked to someone whose back remained toward the glass. Perhaps my suspicion of a secret love had been correct. If so, it was improper for her to steal out to meet him, but just as society expected ladies to make excellent matches, they also expected servants to dedicate their lives to their household, rather than pursue marriage and family, however much they might desire them. Most servants would have to leave their positions if they ended up marrying. I didn't blame her for wanting to keep the matter secret until she was sure.

Which meant I should allow her some privacy. I ducked back from the window and went in search of Father, whom I found in his study, so deeply immersed in his charts that he murmured agreement to my request to change the money without even glancing up. In short order, I'd acquired the gold and surrendered it to Risha's hatch-brother. He departed, tugging the funds behind him in some sort of web crafted of light. If all went well, Risha would have good news before long.

Aunt Caris looked up when I entered the dining room, and after greeting her, I put forth my request. "Aunt Caris, I'd wondered if you'd accompany me to the Kelforth Cloister this morning?"

"Of course, my dear." She poured out a cup of tea and offered it to me. "Did you want to attend the midweek oratory service?"

I accepted it, the warmth welcome. "Actually, I'd hoped to speak with Sister Margery."

"She's a kind soul, or so I've heard. Small wonder you feel the need for comfort and counsel, after all that happened in Withern." Aunt Caris patted my hand. "We shall go together, and I'll attend the service while you speak with the Sister."

"Thank you." There was something to be said for choosing

the path of least resistance, on the rare occasions it was possible —if only all my troubles could be so easily solved.

Aunt Caris maintained a light conversation during the meal and through our ride, fortunately expecting little in terms of reply. When we halted in front of the Kelforth Cloister, it appeared utterly unchanged, its gentle curves and arched domes as inviting as ever, its sun-warmed gardens drenching the air with rich floral fragrances—lavender and lily, lilac and rose. Evidently Risha approved of its beauty, for her wings glowed bright and she fluttered about, examining everything while we passed through the courtyard and ascended to the immense central door.

Once inside the pillared-and-arched entry, Aunt Caris departed to the oratory chamber, and I asked the attendant for Sister Margery. Without any further questions, he whisked me to the private room where we'd shared an audience before. Sister Margery stood to welcome me. "I'm glad to see you again, Miss Caldwell. Will you sit?"

I took an armchair across from hers.

She offered a soft smile, which pulled at the half-moon scar near her right eye. "I think often of you and Dreda. How does she fare?"

"Quite well. She's become a friend, and I'm grateful to know her."

"Then I'm filled with joy for you both." Sister Margery regarded me steadily. "Yet I cannot help but think you came here with a purpose in mind."

She was right, yet it was difficult to begin. Perhaps I might start with a simpler matter. "As a matter of fact, since Dreda has been such an excellent fit for our household, I'd wondered if you might have a recommendation of someone who needs a position as a gardener. Someone of a rather . . . unshakable disposition. They must serve at Wyncourt, and evidently, rumors still persist about odd happenings after Lady Dromley's death."

"I shall inquire among the Brothers. I have a prospect in mind, but they'd be best suited to know."

"Thank you." I clutched Jade to my chest. "There's one thing more . . . do you know . . . that is, I was hoping I'd still be permitted access to the Cloister library. After what happened last time, I wasn't sure."

"Ah yes, the Vigilist. Many tongues were set wagging by his desecration of our halls. It's been many decades since we were forced to accept an unwanted guest."

"Does that mean I'm banned in the future?"

"Not at all. It wasn't your fault. Though if you believe it likely to happen again, we might ask you to refrain from visiting for a time."

"I certainly hope it won't, but honesty compels me to say I'm unsure. It seems I've earned the enmity of the Vigil—or at least of Mr. Ludne, the one who intruded before." And if he'd gone so far as to somehow acquire a fae listening stone, what other steps might he take?

"Then you are in need of our aid, and we'll gladly grant it." She shifted, her gown rustling slightly, the soft fragrance of violet wafting from its folds. "But will you tell me why you've truly come?"

Despite her gentle appearance, she perceived a great deal—and I could put this off no longer. "In your position, you speak to many and hear things others do not. Without breaking confidence, can you tell me if you were acquainted with any of those who have gone missing?"

Her hand went to the emblem of her order emblazoned on her gown. "Will you tell me why you wish to know?"

"Only that it is my aim to help." Anyone could say that, but I hoped she'd believe I meant it.

"I do not like to be a spreader of information, even that which is not confidential. But I think perhaps the situation warrants it," she said slowly. "I did know one of the missing. An individual beset by ennui, perhaps the result of never having wanted for anything. She was always chasing some new excitement to lift her spirits—the most outrageous fashions, extravagant jewels, newest dances and the like."

"And did you notice any change in her before she went missing?"

"Only that she seemed to have found some new zeal for life." Her honey-gold eyes held a thoughtful look. "She said she owed a great deal to a new friend. I'd wondered if perhaps she had fallen for someone, but she did not take me into her confidence as to details—and if she had, I could not share them."

A new friend? Could it have been a fae who'd bound her in bargain? Or was I imagining only what I wished to see? I'd come in hopes of finding some possible link between Ainslie and the missing, something that might make her bargain-holder easier to trace. But unlike the others who'd vanished, Ainslie had never experienced an unnatural elevation of spirits—quite the contrary. Perhaps I sought a connection where none existed, but . . . I had to be sure. "You never noticed any unusual marks on her arms?"

"Indeed not." She leaned forward slightly. "Do you fear something unnatural in these disappearances?"

I swallowed hard. "I confess that I do."

Something flickered beneath her serene exterior. "I have felt the same, then wondered if I was simply prejudiced by my time spent watching over those afflicted by fae."

"Do you still feel it's right to conceal the fae-touched you encounter from the Vigil? To keep it secret that more and more have fallen to this affliction?"

"If we make their presence known, it's doubtful we can protect them from the Vigil. Yet if we continue to hide them, we further the notion all remains as it ever was, with the Vigil protecting Byren from Otherworldly assault." A sigh escaped her, one signaling deep weariness. "Which is the lesser evil? I cannot say, and in the absence of greater wisdom, I will heed the head of our order, who says we owe mercy to the afflicted above all else."

I couldn't argue with that.

"Yet it seems we mostly stand watch as they sink into decline." Lines furrowed about her eyes. "We make their days as peaceful as we can, and we try to keep them in pleasant, home-like rooms, with liberty to move about. But there's so little we can do."

Another Sister appeared in the doorway, making a small motion with her hand, and Sister Margery stood. "I regret I must go, but if you learn anything that might be of help or you wish to speak of the matter further, I trust you'll return?"

"Of course."

After Sister Margery took her leave, I walked to the oratory chamber. The service had just concluded, and Aunt Caris soon joined me. In short order, we'd situated ourselves in the carriage, Jade ensconced in my lap and Aunt Caris across.

"Did your talk with Sister Margery lift your spirits, my dear?"

"Not as much as I'd hoped, but she was very kind, and I'm glad we spoke."

"Perhaps Ainslie would benefit from a visit to the Cloister as well. I've noticed she's not been quite herself since our departure from Withern." Aunt Caris plucked the lace lining the throat of her gown. "Do you think she might be missing Mr. Redgrave? Their acquaintance has been rather short, but the attachment appears genuine on both sides."

"I agree about the attachment, but Ainslie isn't one to pine over a separation of a few weeks." She'd too much zeal for life to fall into a decline over a suitor's absence. An Otherworldly threat that could claim her life any moment, on the other hand . . .

"Perhaps you're right. In any case, I shall call on Hester Redgrave this week—it can do no harm to deepen the acquaintance while we wait for Mr. Redgrave to arrive in Avons." Aunt Caris's hand dropped to her lap. "But today we must remain at home to receive callers. Will you join us?"

Despite the hopeful lilt to her words, she appeared to expect I'd offer an excuse. If I hadn't known Riven intended to be among them, I might have sought one. Instead, I nodded.

Her red-gold brows lifted. "Truly?"

"Truly—and if you wish, I'll accompany you to call on Hester Redgrave as well."

She beamed at me. "That would be lovely, my dear."

With that, we retreated into silence, Aunt Caris satisfied and I rather less so. How long could we continue to withhold the truth from her? Yet if we confessed it . . . how much would it destroy?

CHAPTER 11

However much I wished it, Riven wasn't our first caller; instead it was Mrs. Winters, who breezed in brimming with the latest gossip. Fortunately, she didn't expect much engagement from me. Under certain circumstances, a reputation for lack of social polish *could* stand one in good stead—I could simply smile and nod and confine my remarks to a polite comment or two, then busy myself with my sketchbook and listen without anyone worrying over my well-being. Ainslie, on the contrary, must appear her ordinary sparkling self, whatever she felt.

Much to her credit, she did. Never mind that her smile was a touch overbright or her eyes a bit shadowed—to any callers that might come, she'd appear fully herself, vibrant and lovely. And yet the shape of her binding mark took shape beneath my charcoals, dark and ominous. Swiftly, I flipped to a blank page, but even then, the creamy expanse seemed to bear an imprint of her hidden suffering.

"We mean to withdraw to Dormer Hall for the summer." Mrs. Winters unfurled a lace fan and waved it before her face. "I'm certain I don't know what things are coming to in Avons, if we must worry about being kidnapped from our very homes, but I don't intend to stay and find out."

"You believe the missing were kidnapped?" Ainslie asked.

"What else could account for such disappearances?" She lowered the fan. "I only hope they've been taken for ransom, and not some darker purpose." Then she flushed, as if recalling the impropriety of such conversation, and rattled on. "But of course, that's for the authorities to worry about. I have the most charming midsummer house party, and I'd welcome any one of you to join."

As she shared all the details of her party plans, I considered her social slip. It was telling that the disappearances preyed upon minds enough that even someone like Mrs. Winters forgot propriety. How much longer would the people of Byren accept a natural explanation for such peculiarities?

I sketched a strand of ivy about the page's border. The authorities were determined to only consider natural—or alchemical—explanations. But could I condemn their close-mindedness while I considered the supernatural to the exclusion of all else? Could they be right about some alchemical connection? Simply because I found it unlikely didn't mean I should eliminate it altogether. I pressed my charcoal harder. There were equal flaws with the theory that fae had claimed the missing directly. For instance, why would they have taken only those from well-to-do families? What advantage could it possibly give?

Unless . . . could some among the impoverished have vanished as well, their disappearances unreported or counted as ordinary for their station? My charcoal bled dark on the page, swirling from the ivy into the maw of a monster.

Perhaps Mr. Burke had already considered that angle and investigated. Oh, I'd so much to inquire about. Though he'd scarcely had enough time to uncover any new evidence, I wrestled with the temptation to take a hack down to the Magistry and seek him out. But Riven meant to come, and my questions for him were even more pressing.

A sudden flare of silver-blue light washed over my paper. Risha fluttered up from her perch on the windowsill.

She wishes you to know it worked, and she owes you eternal thanks. Jade's eyes narrowed. *If you ask me, she owes a great deal more for the risk taken.*

Let her know I'm most pleased. Indeed, after Ainslie's torment last night, any hint of good news was a welcome balm.

Mrs. Winters stood to depart, and I collected myself long enough to offer a farewell. When she bustled from the room, Father appeared in the doorway. We all blinked at him.

"Alden . . . you do know we expect more callers this afternoon?" Aunt Caris asked.

"Holden informed me." And still, he took up the chair next to mine. "I have realized I'm acquainted with very few of those who call here. I thought perhaps it was time to remedy that."

"Oh." Aunt Caris surveyed him as if a stranger had taken his place, then her face curved in gentle lines. "What an excellent idea."

Ada and Ainslie exchanged a suspicious glance, and I eyed Father above my sketchbook. Aunt Caris had tried to get him involved in society affairs for years without success. What was behind his sudden change of heart? I turned to another clean page, one without mark or monster, as Holden ushered in the Havers family, possessed of a bevy of daughters, the eldest of whom immediately engaged with Ada on the newest composition by a musician they evidently both enjoyed.

Through the flurry of activity that followed, Father stayed the course. And as the Havers departed, the familiar sensation of Riven's presence washed over my senses—he was here at last. He filled the doorway behind Holden, and despite the cloak of glamour he wore, the warm, vibrant sensation of Other filled the space between us.

Holden gave a small bow, then stepped out of the doorway. "Lord Riven and Mrs. Birch."

As Holden moved aside, he revealed the presence of a tiny

wizened woman. A light glamour concealed her sharp ears and the unusually fine structure of her bones. To mortal eyes, she'd appear like a prim elderly lady with cottonwood-fluff hair and a stooped-willow frame. What was she? And why had Riven brought her?

Riven beckoned her forward. "Miss Caldwell, please allow me to introduce Mrs. Birch. She's been associated with my family for a considerable time and has come to stay in Avons briefly."

"A pleasure to meet you, Mrs. Birch." Aunt Caris beamed at her—perhaps considering any connection of Riven's a desirable acquaintance—and gestured to the open seating. "Please, join us."

Mrs. Birch took a chair at the edge of the room, where she occupied herself with something that would have resembled tatting, were it not for the threads of Other power woven through it—fortunately beyond the perception of the rest of the room. Her bright eyes surveyed the chamber with interest. "Thank you for the welcome."

In turn, Riven situated himself between me and Aunt Caris, and she offered him one of her warmest smiles. "I'd not realized you were in town, Lord Riven."

"I hadn't planned to visit Avons again, but I found I couldn't stay away." His gaze rested on me as he spoke, his words laced with significance.

Though it was mere pretense, I struggled to keep warmth from flooding my face. Ada glanced between us, her brow slightly furrowed. But of course, Aunt Caris suspected nothing. She believed all three of us remarkable enough to catch the eye of any gentleman, and few things brought her greater joy than the prospect of a good match.

Therefore, she practically radiated delight, beaming up at him. "Though things do slow in Avons over the summer months, it still has its charms—and we're very pleased to have your company."

Father looked from Aunt Caris to Riven as if bewildered, toying with his wedding ring all the while.

Riven nodded at it. "That's a well-wrought piece. Where did you obtain it?"

"From my late wife. It was . . . we purchased each other wedding bands."

"Do you know the name of the craftsman who forged it?"

The silky smoothness of Riven's voice put me on alert. I set aside my sketchbook. What did he perceive about the ring? I bent my attention toward it, and for a moment, I thought I sensed the pricking of Other down my spine—but perhaps it was only my imagination. Because if it had some Other nature, surely I would have noticed before now.

Father shook his head. "Kensa wanted it to be a surprise."

"How unfortunate. If you'd known, perhaps I could have commissioned him for a piece. True craftsmen are rare." Then he turned his natural fae charm on Aunt Caris, conversing with her about Avons in summer and requesting her recommendations on the best places about town, drawing in Mrs. Birch, Father, and my sisters at appropriate intervals. He acted the part of a mortal gentleman to perfection, and though Ada and Ainslie still regarded him warily, Aunt Caris practically glowed.

After a quarter hour or so, Riven turned back to Father. "If you're agreeable, I'd like to take Miss Jessa to the park. Mrs. Birch has graciously offered to serve as chaperone, so your plans for the afternoon might not be disrupted. And I've brought my open carriage."

Father glanced at Aunt Caris, who offered a slight nod, her eyes gleaming with approval. He tugged at his cravat. "Ah, of course."

With that, Riven swept me from the room, along with Mrs. Birch. Evidently, now that he'd decided to embrace the charade of mortal courtship, he intended to do it thoroughly—while still allowing us the privacy needed for open discussion. In short order, we were situated in the carriage, Mrs. Birch in the smaller seat behind us, where ostensibly she could observe all our actions. I glanced back at her. Though the glamour Riven had woven about us would keep our conversation from her, to those we passed we'd appear a properly courting couple escorted by a demure elderly chaperone. Her own small glamours continued to obscure the sharpness of her ears and wideness of her eyes, as well as the threads of power woven through her working. To craft it, she used a device that looked like a tatting shuttle, whether to better anchor the glamour or because it was a tool required by low fae to craft their workings, I could not be sure.

"Who is she?"

"An oalan—they're tree dwellers. Her family has dwelt within my holdings for centuries, and she leapt at the opportunity to explore this world, though she cannot long be away from our own."

I couldn't imagine Riven bringing a potential threat into our home; still, the notion of another fae aware of my existence and my family left me slightly unsettled. "She won't speak of anything she's learned, will she?"

"Oalan are bound to those within whose holdings they dwell. Even if someone should try to press her for information, she'd be physically unable to give it, as it would breach the contract between us." He flicked the reins. "I knew you'd prefer to avoid the unnecessary use of glamour and that your aunt wouldn't countenance our riding out together without a chaperone. With Dreda gone, Birch's presence offered another path. Perhaps I should have warned you first."

"If you're confident of her loyalty, I've no reason to doubt it." He'd gone to great lengths to protect my family and satisfy convention, and the realization warmed me. "Thank you. She's satisfied even Aunt Caris, and that's no small feat, given her worries of late."

He shrugged. "It was simple enough to arrange."

Perhaps, and yet . . . The sweet scent of jasmine permeated the air around us as we neared the park, and for a moment, I allowed myself to imagine we'd not convened to discuss all the pressing troubles, but rather to simply enjoy the brilliant afternoon in each other's company. Then the carriage rattled over the cobblestones, drawing me back to myself. I took a deep breath as an oddity occurred to me. "You knew of Dreda's absence?"

"Risha makes use of light messages between sylphs to inform me of any substantive household changes. Would you rather she not?"

"No, given the circumstances, I'm glad of it." Yet she'd not told me. What else did she keep concealed? I tucked the thought away to consider another time. "There's something else I wondered . . . that is, you seemed to take note of Father's ring. Should I be concerned about it?"

"Cautious, at least. It's of fae-make."

"Then why have I never noticed anything Other about it?"

"You're accustomed to seeing it on your father and familiar with the workings on it—they're subtle and deeply hidden. It's not surprising that you felt nothing." Glamour shimmered in the air about us. "There's no malice woven in it—rather, workings of protection. When considering the question of your heritage, its presence is noteworthy."

I sank back against the leather seat. If Mother had truly given it to him, what did that mean? Had she sought to protect him from affliction by fae? If so, how could she have come to possess such a relic? Later, I'd think about it later. "And Ainslie— did you find anything while you were gone?"

"Not yet. Lures have been set, but of necessity they must remain subtle. To avoid betraying one's hand requires patience."

Which meant time that Ainslie might not have. An ache took up residence beneath my breastbone. "Perhaps there's another connection we might explore. Mr. Burke informed me that other mortals have gone missing." I summed up for him what I'd learned. "There are significant differences between Ainslie's condition and the situation of the others gone missing, yet it's difficult to believe they're wholly unrelated."

"Have a care you don't forge a connection just because you

want one to exist." His hands tightened slightly about the reins. "The state of things between our worlds . . . it's possible that these situations are linked, but equally possible they are not."

"I see." The ache within grew, rooting downward. "At least . . . can you tell me how you helped Ainslie? If something like that happens again, could I offer aid?"

"It's unclear, since our knowledge of your affinities remains limited. If she were to undergo another such attack, you'd need a liminal affinity to offer the suggestions she might use to free herself. Even then, she must retain enough control of her mind to craft an escape."

"Then you do possess a liminal affinity?"

He nodded.

"Do most high fae?"

"Less than a quarter." Riven navigated us into the park and down a tree-lined avenue. "Which means her ordeal gained us something. The fact that her bargain-holder possesses a higher-order liminal affinity will narrow down our search."

It was a small scrap of evidence, but better than none. Above us, the leaves rustled soft sympathies. "Not soon enough. Last night, we could have lost her. If another such attack comes on her or the fae summons her . . ."

"Jessa." Riven tucked the carriage in an alcove beneath two spreading yew, wrapping it with glamour, then turned to face me, his eyes dark. "You need to prepare yourself for an unfavorable outcome."

The rustling strengthened into a near roar that matched the one in my veins. "What are you saying?"

"That this bargain has deep roots. It's complicated, which suggests it's part of a greater scheme." He drew the glamour tighter about us. "We have little to go on. She may not last as long as it takes us to find the bargain-holder."

Even before he'd finished, I was shaking my head. "She's strong; she can resist—"

"Her will to resist is part of the problem. It's causing her to fight the terms of the bargain, and she's suffering as a result. It may prove too much for her."

Images filled my mind: Ibbie, her life drained by Uros; Asrina, her body crushed by Lord West; and the victims of Kilmere, their slow, agonizing deaths by basilisk venom. I clenched my hands in my lap—if Other claimed Ainslie too, how could I endure it? "I can't lose her."

There must be a way out. I refused to consider otherwise, even for a moment. Jade rumbled low and climbed into my lap, but her presence brought no peace. In the back, Mrs. Birch continued her ceaseless tatting.

Riven drew his hand across his jaw. "Even if we find this fae, he or she cannot be forced to release Ainslie from the bargain, only offered a more compelling one. Furthermore, the terms may dictate that the bargain must pass to another fae in the form of an inheritance, which means even the bargain-holder's death won't free her."

I hoped I'd never become so desperate and unfeeling as to suggest murder, but to know Ainslie could remain bound in life or death, that the matter depended entirely on finding proper leverage and persuading this unknown fae to release her . . .

Jade regarded me with unblinking eyes. *It's why Riven thinks you must prepare.*

You cannot agree with him.

I think it is better to cling to hope than otherwise. Yet her gaze lowered.

The tightness in my chest made it difficult to draw breath. "The bargain-holder must have some vulnerability—or something they want enough to release Ainslie, if I can just provide it to them. Everyone desires *something.*"

"Yet not all desires are possible to fulfill. What if they wanted you to become a supplier of mortals? Would you consent?"

Overhead, the tightly woven yew branches blotted out the sun. "I couldn't. But it might not come to something like that, and . . . and I must try."

He remained silent.

I pulled Jade closer. "Your cautions—do they mean you intend to give up?"

If I must, I'd seek to break Ainslie's binding alone. Yet I knew what it felt like to oppose a high fae on my own, and I'd no desire to repeat the experience.

"No. Nor do I counsel surrender. But you must understand the gravity of the situation and master your emotions so you can look at the matter objectively." His eyes were dark as the yew above. "Best case, we find the fae responsible before he or she destroys Ainslie. If we do, you'll have to conceal your true feelings. If you reveal how much you want the bargain broken, you'll lose any opportunity for negotiation."

Could I manage to bury my feelings? To treat with the fae in question as if Ainslie didn't matter? A sudden gust of wind swept over the carriage, tugging my hair, stinging my face. Somehow, I must.

"Meanwhile, you'd do well to explore and strengthen your abilities," he said. "As you've observed, fae have codes as rigid as mortals. Yet they don't resemble yours. In this world, it would be considered improper for a man to match his strength against a woman—correct?"

I nodded.

"That's not true of mine. Power is everything, and it doesn't matter whether a lord or lady wields it—only who is stronger." Riven braced a leg against the footboard and leaned back, his gaze intent. "It remains to be seen where this investigation will lead—you should be prepared for all ends."

"What do you mean?"

"That there's no downside in becoming more skilled with your affinities."

What end did he foresee? Clearly he didn't mean to divulge anything more, but his point stood on its own. However exploring my affinities might frighten me—particularly the prospect of becoming lost in them, or worse yet, witnessed in such a state—this was something I *could* do. Yet there was so much about my fae nature I didn't understand. "If I'm only half fae, will that limit the strength of whatever affinities I possess?"

He sat upright. "Half fae? What do you mean?"

"If my theory is correct, and Mother was forced to bear a child for a fae lord, then . . . wouldn't that make me half fae?"

"There is no half fae, whether a mortal carried the child or not. I assumed you understood that, or I would have clarified sooner. If you choose to embrace your fae nature, you won't remain mortal in any way."

Suddenly, I recalled his remark when I'd first entered the Otherworld and narrowly escaped Mocvar's clutches: *Fae have trouble bearing young. Mortals are fertile, and their joint offspring will be full-blood fae, if they so choose.* I'd been so consumed by the coming confrontation with Uros that I'd not once considered his words further, not even when I'd wondered if fae blood meant I'd share their immortality. The answer pierced like the blade of a knife.

Embracing my fae nature meant I'd watch all those I loved die, in the end. How could I endure loss after loss and remain whole? Would I become what I feared, after decades and centuries of pain? The boughs above my head blurred, and I lowered my gaze. *Did you know about this?*

I assumed fae had some way to ensure mortal breeders did not diminish their power or dilute fae blood, but no—I was not aware. Jade nestled closer. *But I'm afraid I didn't attend to what Riven said then either. I was in no clear frame of mind after our separation.*

I inhaled, and the scent of earth and shadow filled my lungs. Perhaps Riven was mistaken somehow. "If it is as you say, and no diminishment of my fae heritage comes with mortal blood, then why . . . why do I appear mortal? I possess neither the beauty nor grace of full fae."

That earned me a sharp glance. Then Riven pulled a small mirror from his fae pocket, the back scrolled silver. Just how much did he store there? He handed it to me. "Look into this and stop willing yourself to hide—to appear ordinary so that none take note."

I couldn't deny that as long as I could remember, I'd striven to blend in with society, though I so often fell short. But . . . could that possibly lead to using glamour unaware? Reluctantly, I looked into the mirror. My own familiar eyes looked back, their blue darker than usual, my gaze strained. Afraid.

I didn't want to see what I might become, to behold an alteration in my own features like that which I'd seen in Riven or Lord West when the veil of their glamours lifted. With a shiver, I turned away.

The lines of his jaw tightened. "You've embraced the glamour so deeply that it has become part of you. There may be more to it than that—it may be the result of a working placed upon you by someone who wished to keep you hidden. Regardless, it will take a great act of will to cast it off. Are you ready to stop hiding?"

I wasn't hiding. Was I? I turned away from my reflection. I had accepted my fae nature, or so I'd thought, but some part of me clearly still sought to cling to the familiar. Because I might be fae, but I couldn't bear to forsake all I knew and loved, to earn their rejection by becoming wholly Other . . .

Wait.

Riven had said there was a choice involved. How could that be? I turned the mirror over, so its reflective surface faced my lap. "If there's a choice, does that mean it's possible to reject my fae blood?"

"Yes. You could renounce your affinities, become fully mortal." His words were clipped. "When mortal-born fae children reach majority, they embrace their fae nature, sever their mortality forever. I don't know any who've made the opposite choice, but it's possible."

He'd gone cold and emotionless, the planes of his face drawn sharp. Was it an offense to ask about such things? Never mind that—I must know, and Riven was the only one who could possibly provide answers.

And the information changed everything, not about my own choices, but something altogether different—Mother. Perhaps I'd been mistaken all this time; perhaps it had never been about a fae lord forcing Mother into a bargain. What if, instead, Mother had been a fae who'd forsaken her affinities? I'd considered the notion of Mother as fae before—Ada and Ainslie had even raised the question—but I'd always considered it an impossibility since she'd borne three children in rapid succession when most fae struggled to conceive at all. "Can any high fae—not just those with mortal blood—choose to reject their affinities?"

"For a fae with mortal blood, both elements are true facets of their nature, albeit ones that cannot exist together long-term." His voice remained utterly devoid of emotion. "But a fae who never had mortal blood to begin with—such a choice would mean they'd become something they were never intended to, much like the humans seeking immortality who ended up with corrupt forms."

"But might diminished fae appear mortal, rather than monstrous, like a ghoul or wight?"

"I think it likely they would," he said slowly. "But to surrender one's affinities would be in your mortal terms like giving up one's soul—unthinkable."

"But if one did, they could still pass on their fae nature?"

Something flickered in his gaze, and his grip on the reins relaxed. "You're thinking of your mother."

I nodded. "I cannot imagine why she would have done so, but it's a prospect I can no longer ignore."

Even as I spoke, a knife-twist sensation pierced my middle. If she'd been fae, that meant she'd deceived Father, deliberately hidden the truth of our natures from us, and . . . no, I wouldn't think about that now.

A low and mournful song resounded from the yew, and I closed my ears to it. I needed the facts; I could process the pain they brought afterward. "If she gave up her affinities and embraced mortality, could she still have children with fae blood?"

"In theory, yes. Even powerless and soulless, she should still reproduce after her original kind." He shook his head. "But it would have been a drastic step. You have not yet embraced one nature or the other. To forsake your affinities as one between would be painful enough—beyond that, it's an agonizing process."

Even for me, the notion of severing my connection to botanical life, to all of Other I'd begun to see and sense, felt akin to seizing a sword and hacking off a limb. If I'd never had any share in a mortal nature, how much more insupportable would the idea seem? I buried my face in Jade's fur. "If fae don't ordinarily forsake their affinities, how do you know what the process is like?"

"Because there's one circumstance in which they will—the moments before death. If they've sustained a mortal injury or wearied of life to the point they choose to depart for the Final Haven, then most will leave their affinities, if they can." He lifted a shoulder. "This choice creates our greatest objects of power—they're forged by the direct transfer of one or more affinities into elemental material, resulting in an object of incredible strength."

"Like the dawn-dagger Lord West sought?" I shuddered at the notion of somehow wielding a dead fae's affinities.

"That one is different. It's a relic of the Dracai, particularly coveted since not many exist among our people."

"I see." Never mind the dawn-dagger now—I'd left it in safety, at least. But Mother . . . I pressed gloved fingers to my pounding temples. If forsaking one's fae nature came at such a cost, why would she ever have made such a choice? Perhaps I was still mistaken, and yet, with this new information, everything made more sense—Mother's attachment to Thornhaven, her desire for proximity to Aelfgard Crossing, Father's ring, even her tales of high fae . . .

Which was worse—to know I'd been conceived by force or that Mother had deceived Father and the rest of our family? Emotions tangled like thorny vines within. Though I'd rather crawl through a patch of bog briar than cause further pain, I'd have to tell Ada and Ainslie of this possibility—because if my new theory was correct, they shared my fae nature.

The oratory bells rang out over the city. However unsettling the truth, somewhere in our past rested answers that might bring understanding to our present, perhaps even help free Ainslie. I would cling to that hope—and pray it was not in vain.

CHAPTER 12

After our discussion of Mother, Riven allowed me to subside into silence. Perhaps he sensed how close my emotions rested to the surface. In any case, the most pressing questions about Mother and my past, and more importantly, the fae who threatened Ainslie at present, he could not answer. Even so, his presence and the steady calm he emanated brought comfort.

Back at the row house, he secured the horses and we ascended the steps, Risha hovering at my shoulder and Jade padding alongside. Mrs. Birch remained stationed in the carriage, tatting away. Holden opened the door, and a rush of Other swept over me, pricking sharp discomfort down my spine.

Jade bristled, but Riven remained unruffled. Whatever it was must not present an immediate threat—but then, Riven never appeared ruffled, no matter how great the danger.

A dark, enchanting melody charged the air, a strong, astringent scent alongside it. I spun, seeking the source.

There.

A breathtaking plant had taken up residence on the scrolled entry table. Silver limned its purple-black leaves, and its branches coiled upward like serpents ready to strike. As if in response to an unseen wind, they rustled—and the pricking discomfort intensified.

It didn't belong in our world.

Light from Riven spiraled across its surface, and his eyes narrowed, even as its song strengthened, the militant notes speaking of conquest and subjugation.

"Holden, where did this come from?"

"Dryden accepted it from a caller and brought it to me." He eyed it dubiously. "I did not know if it was meant to be kept withindoors or out, so I left it here for you to do with as you pleased. It was addressed to you."

I looked closer. A missive with my name inked in a purple-black that matched the leaves was nestled amid the reptant branches. I fought the urge to recoil. "I see. I don't want to trail dirt through the house—I'll just take it down the footwalk and into the garden."

I turned to Riven, hoping he'd follow. "Thank you for a lovely stroll."

He offered the expected pleasantries in return, then took his leave—or rather, he feigned departure by driving the carriage with Mrs. Birch to some unknown locale, perhaps through a passing, then returning to wait at the base of the stairs, glamour wrapped about him. I lifted the silver pot and followed, instinctively reaching for the inner life of the plant as I descended. Pain stabbed my chest, and I stifled a gasp.

"What is it?"

"It doesn't respond to me, not like the others do. It seems almost as if it wants to inflict harm."

"Perhaps it does. It may answer to another."

What did that even mean? Sharp, hostile notes emanated from it, striking at me, and small thorns emerged bristling from the vines. I held it farther from my body. "Do you know what it is?"

"Nightspire." Shards of light flared about him. "The choice to send it is in itself a message, whatever the note may say."

A rumble emanated from Jade. *If it means harm, we should destroy it.*

Not yet. It may be important. I reached for the familiar melodies of the oak and ivy, filling my ears with them to block the clamor of the nightspire. I wasn't wholly successful but at least muffled it to a tolerable level.

I quickened my steps, hurrying into the glasshouse. As Riven secured the door behind us, I plucked the note from the branch. When I opened it, fae words spiraled about the page, forming a maze. "Risha . . . bright one, would you mind?"

A hint of purple crept into her blue light, and she fluttered to perch on my shoulder. Riven closed the distance between us so he could examine the note at the same time.

I didn't face this alone—I had Riven and Jade, even Risha— and yet my pulse drummed unsteadily at the base of my throat. Though I wanted to close my eyes and pretend it didn't exist, I forced myself to look as Risha's light translated the words into a form I could understand.

Some prefer to claim any possible advantage, but I believe in fair play. It keeps things interesting. With that in mind, I've decided to give you a gift. And a warning. Your sister belongs to me. If she serves as promised, she will live. If she tries to break her binding, she will die. Advise her well—and stop interfering, lest the terrors of her nights become the reality of her days.

The message fluttered from my lifeless fingers, and Riven caught it, the living scents of sun and forest swirling about me as he did.

"It seems Ainslie's bargain relates to an ongoing task." Despite my best efforts, my voice emerged strained. "Does our observation keep her from fulfilling its terms? Is that why she suffered so last night?"

"It's possible. The erasure of her memories suggests a desire for secrecy."

"Then do you advise we stop watching her?"

"I advise that you tell her you must, so she'll believe herself unobserved. Then she can work to keep the bargain in good faith." He folded the letter, tucked it beneath the pot. "I'll set another sylph to watch her."

Risha landed on a sprig of sweet orange, her slight frame insufficient to bend the branch. "Kiran will. He wishes to serve my lady."

"Yet he is bound to Lady Cela."

Was Riven so aware of everything that transpired within his court, or had Risha raised Kiran's plight to him in the past?

She gave a tiny shake of her head. "Not anymore."

"And how, exactly, did that come to pass?"

"She released him."

Sudden pressure swirled in the air. "Might you be omitting some important fact about this sudden liberty?"

Risha faltered, her wings drooping. "My lady offered her help."

Though his expression never shifted, the pressure intensified. "At your request?"

If she'd been Asrina, she would have tucked herself against me, but she was Risha. Besides which, no matter his displeasure, Riven wouldn't harm her. Still, I could spare her interrogation. I stroked the sweet orange, and one of its limbs shifted to conceal her. "She informed me of his plight, and it seemed a small way to offer aid."

"Did she warn you of the risks?"

"After a fashion. She suggested that you would not approve."

"She was right." A hint of a frown tightened his eyes. "Those unaware of your true nature will perceive you as a mortal with no protection, as Lord West did. Those who understand your fae nature could easily learn you're not allied to any court, and therefore unprotected. And you have limited knowledge of your affinities. By any account, your position is precarious. It's unwise to draw any further attention to yourself."

Though his words unsettled, I lifted my chin. "Unwise or no, I couldn't leave him to die."

"She shouldn't have put you in that position." He turned to Risha, whose light shimmered through the sheltering leaves of the sweet orange. "I brought you here to help Jessa, not take advantage of her good nature."

"I *will* help." She darted out and up. "And Kiran will help; he wants to discharge debt."

"As I've said, it's not a debt—"

"Very well." Riven toyed with a spark of light. "Since it is done, see that he does."

"Yes, yes. It will be."

I looked at the note again. "If the bargain-holder knows I'm investigating, somehow he must have been watching me along with Ainslie." Though we didn't know if it was a fae lord or lady, it was easier to think of the shadowy figure as male—easier to refer to him as such also.

"Yes. He knows more about your family than is safe—yet it could offer an advantage. I might be able to trace him through the delivery of the plant." A spear of light pierced the pot containing the nightspire, and its vines lashed out. "We should start with the boy who received it."

If we could somehow trace the fae . . . Hope bubbled up, despite the difficulty of the situation. "His name is Dryden, and he's often about the gardens."

Too often for my comfort.

"He must be the one near the mews, then." With that, Riven strode out of the glasshouse, drawing a glamour about himself that would conceal him from mortal eyes—a nod to the conventions that bound me.

Now didn't seem the time to inquire which of his affinities gave him that knowledge of Dryden's location, so I simply followed him to the rabbitry, where Dryden was delivering fresh water and kitchen scraps. I stepped forward, and Dryden straightened, his thick brows lowering and his eyes wary.

"Good day, Dryden." A small gray rabbit sniffed at my

shoes, then scampered back beneath his feet. "I understand you accepted the delivery of a plant this afternoon. What brought you to the door?"

"Heard a knock. Couldn't see the gaffer, so thought I should answer. Was a toff there, he gave me the plant—said it was for you."

The gaffer was Holden, I assumed. Fortunately, he'd not heard that term used for his person. "Can you tell me what the gentleman who delivered it looked like?"

"Tall, light hair, brown eyes." He lifted the rabbit and stowed back in the hutch. "More young than not."

Unease pebbled my skin. His description could fit Charles Redgrave, though to my knowledge the Redgraves hadn't yet arrived in Avons. It could also fit a number of other gentlemen; I'd best not make any leaps in logic. I tucked my hands in my skirts. "If you happen to see him again, please fetch me at once."

He offered a slight nod, then set his back toward me, determinedly scrubbing out a water bowl.

Riven watched him a moment, then walked back toward the glasshouse. I trailed him, refraining from speech until his glamour wrapped about me as well. "What do you think?"

"He shows no signs of being under fae influence. I doubt the responsible fae would have undertaken so mundane an errand anyway. Even if he did not view the task as beneath him, he might have acted so from caution. Or because he did observe and take note of my presence when I interfered with Ainslie."

We entered the glasshouse, and Riven lounged on the bench, at ease despite the ominous rustle from the nightspire. I remained too unsettled to join him. "What then?"

"If I locate the messenger and he interacted with the fae recently enough, I can gain a trace, and we may have the identity we seek. What I find—or don't find—will prove telling."

As was the choice to send the nightspire. This fae toyed with me as surely as Lord West had done, only this time, whoever it was had far greater leverage, since Ainslie was already bound. Perhaps the bargain-holder had overstepped and would reveal himself through this so-called gift . . . or perhaps we simply played into his hands. The sweet orange brushed my shoulder, its bright notes urging me to hope. "While you do, I'll examine the nightspire further."

"Be careful. By nature, it's designed for assault, and someone has also woven numerous workings into it—it may seek to examine you as you examine it. Destruction would be the safest course."

I took a step back. I'd never considered plants weapons, despite having wielded them in such fashion on occasion. But those instances had been for protection, not surveillance and attack. Even so . . . "If you remove it, we'll lose any chance to learn more of who sent it. If I can read it, then perhaps I'll catch a glimpse of the fae—or the location it originated from."

Riven lifted a shoulder. "True. The reward may be worth the risk, temporarily at least. I suggest you learn what you can. Then destroy it."

It went against the grain to think of destroying something so alive and aware, and perhaps Riven recognized my hesitation, for shards of light, sharp as blades, swirled about him. "Think of it as some particularly pestilent weed that will prey on all in its path, if that makes it easier."

The nightspire's song shivered down my spine, harsh and discordant—as if it knew what we discussed and sought to resist. "Will it be safe to leave it here?"

"I wouldn't recommend leaving it unchecked. I'll place some workings on the glasshouse that will keep it contained until you've learned what you can."

"Thank you."

After Riven swathed the glasshouse in gleaming gold workings, which vanished into its transparent panes, he stepped through a passing.

Jade leapt onto the table where I'd stowed the nightspire. *I shall keep watch as you try to read it.*

Good. I approached the nightspire. Among its leaves, workings shimmered, runes and spirals of deepest purple and silver mingling, as barbed as the thorns that sprouted from its stems. It bristled with hostility, yet I reached forward and—

"There you are, Jess." Lovell strode through the glasshouse door, dark hair flopping across his brow.

I startled and stepped in front of the nightspire. It was ridiculous, perhaps, to imagine it lashing out at him, yet an eager, hungry note had crept into its song.

Unaware, he continued, "I must have missed you the first time. I was beginning to think Aunt Caris was right. Holden told her you were in the gardens, but when she didn't see you out the window, she feared some evildoer had spirited you off. Can't say I blame her, with all that's happened of late."

"As you see, I'm quite fine." I dredged up a half-smile. "I just wanted to spend some time in the gardens."

"Time's up, I'm afraid." He offered his arm. "I gave my word I'd restore you to Aunt Caris."

"Well, we can't have you break it." If I protested, it would draw unwanted attention to my actions, so I'd accept the reprieve for now. As we departed, I stole a glance over my shoulder.

Tucked into its silver pot, the nightspire almost managed to appear innocuous—if one could not perceive its Other nature, it might well have found a dwelling in a mortal home, celebrated for its unique beauty. What then? I secured the door tightly behind us, shutting out its insidious whispers.

As we strolled toward the house, Lovell said, "Mr. Redgrave and his sister called shortly after you left. Miss Redgrave seemed particularly sorry to have missed you."

I stumbled over a stone. The Redgraves were here, and worse, they'd called upon my family not long after the Otherworldly plant arrived, which meant they *could* have had some part in its delivery, however little credence I wished to give the notion. Surely Mr. Redgrave would have been more subtle as to the timing, were he involved—unless he had no choice. My breath quickened.

"When I realized Ainslie returned his interest, I dug about to see what I could learn about the fellow. I haven't found a single unsavory rumor about him. He doesn't dally, doesn't gamble, appears dedicated to his family." Lovell steadied me. "A relief, after Lord Bradford."

I murmured agreement. Yet learning of his good character didn't address any of my deeper concerns. I couldn't leap to conclusions based on such scant evidence, nor could I afford to wait any longer to understand what connection the Redgraves held to the Otherworld—if any.

Tomorrow evening, I'd examine the evidence from Thea and Lord Blackburn when we gathered for dinner, but it might not be conclusive. Lost in thought, I settled onto the scrolled couch in the drawing room, the low conversation between Aunt Caris and my sisters receding into the background. The public genealogical records held at the library should hold information on their family background, but if I wanted more detailed information, then I should undoubtedly apply to Aunt Melisina. Whatever my sentiments toward her, no one could deny she knew—or knew *of*—every family of importance in Byren. Though the conversation might be less than pleasant, I couldn't ignore her as a source, particularly when she might also hold answers about Mother.

At once, I became aware silence had fallen. Aunt Caris was looking at me, her embroidery lowered to her lap. "Well, what do you think, my dear? Shall we invite Lord Riven?"

I sank back into the cushions. "I . . ."

Even as Jade began to repeat the conversation into my mind, Ada came to the rescue. "I think he'd make an excellent addition to the dinner party, as he's already acquainted with the Redgraves."

A dinner party with the Redgraves and Riven? Since I was meant to appear to accept Riven's attentions, I nodded. "That would be lovely."

Jade chuffed. *Interesting, to say the least.*

Father wandered in with a book tucked under his arm just as

Aunt Caris patted Lovell's hand. "You shall come too, of course. And extend an invitation to your mother."

His usual look of lively good humor faded. "If Mother means to come, perhaps I should not."

"My dear boy, why would you say such a thing?"

"We've had a rather sharp difference in views. Your party will be more harmonious without my participation."

I sat upright. I'd not realized how deep the strain between Aunt Melisina and Lovell ran. Was the divide over what had happened with Ada or something else altogether?

"Oh, Lovell." Ada set aside her letter. "Surely for one night you can make peace?"

"Is that what you want?"

"Of course it is."

"Then I'll do my best." However, the set of his jaw suggested the notion was anything but pleasing.

"We all have disagreements from time to time, but it's best not to dwell on them—to put all unpleasantness in the past and leave it there." Aunt Caris lifted her embroidery. "Ada, shall I invite anyone on your behalf?"

"No, thank you." Ada folded the letter and tucked it away. "I've had enough of possible suitors for a time. Lovell can be my escort for dinner."

He flashed her a smile. "Gladly."

With determined good cheer, Aunt Caris turned to Ainslie. "Whatever else may have happened, I cannot help but think it's a good sign that the Redgraves traveled to Avons with such haste. It may not be long before Mr. Redgrave declares his intentions."

Ainslie flinched slightly. "I don't think we can go quite that far—we've not been acquainted for long."

"If the match suits all involved, a long acquaintance isn't necessary."

"Perhaps that's so." Yet Ainslie lowered her head, the inner conflict over all she withheld from him evident. Were it not for her secrets, I imagined she'd be all joy at the prospect of a future with Mr. Redgrave.

Some part of me welcomed her caution, because what could be attributed to a desire to further the relationship—the motive I *wished* to assign Mr. Redgrave's actions—could equally be a sign he was entangled with fae in dangerous ways, perhaps compelled to stay near us. I stood, determined to seize the opportunity offered. "Perhaps I could carry the invitation to Aunt Melisina, if Lovell does not mean to return home right now. I'd like to go to the library to fetch a few books, so it would be a simple matter to call on my way."

Lovell gave a decisive nod. "Excellent notion, Jess."

"My dear, surely it can wait until tomorrow." Aunt Caris rummaged in her basket for her embroidery scissors. "It's less than an hour until dinner, and I cannot expect Estine to hold it at such late notice."

"I don't mind a cold meal later, truly." After the events of the day, my appetite had vanished. "And I'm certain Aunt Melisina will wish to clear her schedule so as not to miss the dinner party."

She snipped a thread. "Perhaps Lovell could inform her later this evening—"

Though he didn't know my purpose, he leapt to support my endeavor. "Afraid I can't carry the invitation today. Going out to Pelham's, won't be home tonight."

"Well, I suppose I shall accompany you then, my dear." Aunt Caris released a soft sigh. "Lianne has a great deal to get done this evening, and it's not properly her job to act as chaperone. I must say, I do hope Dreda returns soon."

As did I. "I don't want to trouble you—"

"I'll go." Father set down his book and blinked up at us. "I want to fetch a copy of *Fotham's Treatises*."

Aunt Caris hesitated. She tried not to gainsay him regarding our care, yet she must know as well as I did that he might forget all about me when he entered the stacks.

Best not give her opportunity for protest. "Thank you, Father. I'll collect my things."

Aunt Caris gave a slight shake of her head. "I'll tell Estine to keep something back for you both."

"No need to trouble her. I'll prepare something simple for Father and myself when we return." If Estine would let me. She had strong ideas about who was to set foot in her kitchen and when.

"As you wish." She clasped my hand. "Only . . . do have a care."

I squeezed her hand in return. "Of course."

CHAPTER 13

Though Father carried his leather folio and two clothbound books with him, when we entered the carriage, he set them aside to survey me, his expression uncommonly grave. "I'm glad to have an opportunity to speak with you alone. There's something I've needed to ask, but I didn't want to chance being overheard—the others taking alarm."

My shoulders tensed. What now?

He pushed his spectacles upward, then scrubbed his hands along the legs of his trousers. "Perhaps you will find this question strange, but I have reason to . . . that is . . . Have you ever encountered . . . fae?"

Jade's ears pricked.

And my pulse quickened, every beat sending fae blood racing through my body. I had encountered fae, yes, but so had he—in me. How could I possibly answer such a question? Confess the deceit? I pressed a hand to my churning stomach. "Why do you ask? Do you think we've reason to fear?"

He ran a finger beneath his cravat, as if it had suddenly grown too tight. "Not long ago, I took a trip."

"To Shepherd's Bush?"

"Not that one. I . . . Well, Lord Blackburn and I traveled to Ashford, and there we encountered a Mr. Heard. It seems . . . He said he recognized our family name and asked if I shared any connection with you."

What else had Mr. Heard told him? And why had Father traveled to an edgetown? What had brought Mr. Heard into his path? I swallowed against rising queasiness. If he pressed, far too much could come spilling out. "Mr. Heard was once good enough to advise me on a difficult situation in Milburn. Aunt Caris isn't aware of this, but I encountered water sprites there, and he gave me counsel on how to remain safe in dealing with them."

Father went pale. "You took no harm? You were not . . . fae-touched?"

His words pierced my heart like thorns. If he knew the truth, would he treat me with the same fear he did the mere mention of the sprites? I lowered my gaze to my lap. "No fae-touch. They were negotiated with, and I emerged safe."

"Then it seems I owe Heard more than I thought." Father absently traced the spine of his book. "He means to come to Avons soon, he told me. Perhaps I'll invite him to stay with us."

Blight and rot. I couldn't reasonably discourage it, but Mr. Heard knew far too much about the Otherworld to make a comfortable guest. I shifted. "How did you make his acquaintance?"

"We wished to consult a loremaster, and he was the only one in the area. It was nothing." The hurried clip of his words suggested otherwise.

What had he encountered? Glamour swelled within me, along with the desire to learn the truth, and I choked it down. Father lifted his book, concealing his face, and I lost the moment. Better that than my glamour escaping again without my consent.

Yet Father and Lord Blackburn had encountered Otherkind in some fashion—I'd no doubt of it. Even in ordinary times, one might expect such dangers near a Crossing, and these were far from ordinary times. Was that what had given Father a new determination to involve himself in our affairs? If so, the timing couldn't be worse.

Well, it could *be.* Jade stretched across my lap.

Perhaps—but if he means to watch me closely, it will impede my actions even further. How much longer could I continue to maintain this pretense?

Jade regarded Father, her eyes glowing. *If he does, then we shall have to arrange some distractions.*

I looked out the window, but the rows of houses blocked any view of the sky. What would happen if I confessed to Father? My suspicions of Mother would come out, and he'd be shattered . . .

Our driver halted the carriage in front of Aunt Melisina's house, breaking into my thoughts. Father didn't look up from his book. "I'll wait here while you complete your call."

"It shouldn't take too long." However else Father had changed, mercifully his desire to avoid Aunt Melisina remained. I climbed down from the carriage and hurried to her door.

In short order, her butler whisked me into the house. He cast a dubious glance at Jade, but did not attempt to remove her.

Wise of him. She prowled alongside me as we entered the morning room, and Risha bobbed just above, taking in her surroundings with evident interest.

Aunt Melisina looked up from the stack of invitations she was addressing and raised a brow. "You need new gloves."

Evidently, the tart observation was the only greeting I'd receive. I glanced down. Sure enough, a streak of dirt had stained one of my gloves, likely from when I'd carried the night-spire. I brushed at it, but only succeeded in smudging it further. "You're right. I was . . . distracted."

Her mouth pinched. I could only imagine what effort it was taking to refrain from commenting on the rest of my appearance. Ordinarily, I attempted to tidy myself before calling on her; this time I'd been far too caught up in recent events. At once, I perceived every small fault in my attire, from the slightly out-of-kilter angle of my hat to the small scuffs on my leather boots.

Yet she didn't provide further admonishment on my less-than-perfect appearance. Instead, she waved a hand toward a delicate chair with an arched back. "I shall take you and your sisters shopping soon, and you can choose whatever you like."

Ordinarily, her generosity came with the stipulation that she dictate every decision—though since her taste was impeccable, it wasn't altogether a bad thing. Perhaps she *did* seek to change. I settled into the seat. "Thank you, Aunt Melisina."

"You're welcome." She set down her pen. "But I'm certain you didn't come to discuss your attire. What has brought you?"

I nodded. "An invitation. Aunt Caris intends to host a dinner."

"Whom does she mean to invite?"

"Mr. and Miss Redgrave and Lord Riven. Lovell has also agreed to come."

"He has?" She busied herself rummaging in the drawer of her secretary. "Does he know Caris invited me?"

Had her lips trembled slightly? I inclined my head. It seemed they'd had a greater falling out than I'd imagined. "Yes, he was there while the plans were being discussed."

"In that case, I accept." She pulled a blotter from the drawer, any trace of vulnerability disappearing—perhaps I'd simply imagined it. "It would be better for the numbers if Caris arranged to invite someone suitable for Ada. I shall speak to her first thing in the morning."

"Ada has already declined any such arrangements." I folded my hands in my lap so the streak of dirt was concealed. "Perhaps it's best to leave the matter this time."

The lines about her mouth firmed, and I expected her to chastise me for my audacity. Instead, a sigh gusted from her. "Perhaps it *is* a bit soon to consider another suitor. Though what Mr. Redgrave and Lord Riven will think of our uneven numbers, I cannot say. Perhaps we might invite someone likely to appeal to Miss Redgrave—then Lovell can escort Ada, if she has no desire for other companionship."

"I don't think they'll mind."

"The Redgraves are among the oldest established families in Byren. Whatever their own eccentricities, they'll not be accustomed to overlooking them in others." She set down the blotter with a bit more force than needed. "I suppose we must make the best of it and hope Mr. Redgrave will be too besotted with Ainslie to take note."

I sat up straighter. She'd provided me the perfect opportunity to inquire about the Redgraves. "What do you know about their family?"

"Before the Sainsbury line of monarchs, they used to be much in favor with the royal family and served as their most trusted advisors. Naturally the first Sainsbury king did not wish to keep the advisors of the monarch he'd deposed, so they no longer served the crown. One might have expected their family to fade into obscurity afterward, but they weathered the change in succession unscathed." She stacked the invitations in precise order. "Naturally, they did not keep in such close confidence with the new king, but they maintained and even expanded their holdings. Furthermore, they kept the respect with which they'd been generally regarded. They're fiercely clannish, to the point that they demand the unheard of—that men who marry into the family take the Redgrave name."

Strange. Jade leapt into my lap, drawing a frown from Aunt Melisina.

Yes. It went beyond eccentric and far into unconventional. Yet somehow, it hadn't tarnished their good name. Perhaps the influence they wielded as one of the oldest families in Byren shielded them. But what could possibly motivate such a dictate? Family pride was a stretch. Fae cared about names . . . but nothing else about the Redgraves suggested any sort of fae nature. If they'd shown any sign of it, Riven would have said as much. Besides which, they bore wards and appeared susceptible to glamour. Still, did it signify some strong connection to the Otherworld?

"Should Ainslie wed into the clan, I fear we'd scarcely ever see her. Yet the advantages of such a match far outweigh such sentimental considerations." She smoothed the front of her gown. "Mr. Redgrave will inherit his uncle's title and seat in the Assemblage of Lords due to the tragic death of his cousin."

I shifted Jade in my arms. "What happened to his cousin?"

"It seems on some sort of family hunting trip, this cousin—the only son of his uncle—was killed, along with Mr. Redgrave's father and another of their companions." She shook her head. "Quite tragic, really."

A hunting accident? The fragrance of the tall jasmine in the corner strengthened, yet its sweetness couldn't sweep away the bitter taste in my mouth. Many gentlemen favored the thrill of the hunt, and accidents certainly occurred from time to time, but three fatalities in one expedition? It seemed excessive.

But not if they'd ventured near a Crossing or even into the Otherworld. Did this prove they were Collectors? I still couldn't fathom what would motivate a family like the Redgraves to engage in such a speculative venture—unless they'd only kept their fortune and power by turning to the Otherworld to regain what they'd lost in the change of kingship . . .

"Jessa!" Aunt Melisina spoke sharply. "Have you listened to a word I've said?"

"Forgive me, I was distracted by considering what they've suffered. Elodie—that is, Miss Redgrave—told me of the loss of her father, but I hadn't realized just how difficult the circumstances of his death were."

"Life holds a great deal of pain." Perhaps her tart tone covered her own. "But by all accounts, they've managed well enough. And if Ainslie marries Mr. Redgrave, we shall all have cause to rejoice."

I fidgeted slightly. As far as visits with Aunt Melisina went, this one had unfolded well. If I brought up Mother as I'd intended, would it all fall apart? Never mind that—if I was to address the matter with Ada and Ainslie, I needed as much evidence as possible. "There's one more thing I was wondering."

"Really, Jessa, your habit of unending questions is something you must check."

"It's about Mother."

She stilled. "I see."

"You were forthright with me before, and I very much appreciated your honesty. But I'll admit it's raised questions for me, and I don't want to trouble Father—or speak of it to Aunt Caris, where he might overhear."

"Very well, I will answer what I can."

There was no easy way to ask, so I took a deep breath and plunged in. "How did she die?"

"You don't know?" She turned away slightly, leaving only her profile visible. "Well, I suppose it's not too surprising. It wasn't an appropriate topic for children, and I imagine it's been too difficult for Alden to discuss since. Not that it would have helped if he had. The physician was never able to determine the cause of her death—she had no evident injuries or maladies— which gave rise to rumors that you've doubtless heard. His suggestion was that she'd had a weak heart or some otherwise hidden condition, and she'd sustained some sort of shock, out of doors and alone at night as she was. But it was all speculation."

Somehow, I didn't think the explanation was so simple, not when Father had said that Mother feared for our safety before she died. Was it her connection to the Otherworld that frightened her? That caused her death? The thought of her facing Other alone, without any affinities to defend herself . . . My throat tightened. "What do you know of her family?"

"Only that she preferred not to speak of them. When it came time for wedding invitations, she refused to acknowledge any relatives." Aunt Melisina drew herself straight as a pole yew. "My parents believed her without family, but she never outright said they'd died. I always wondered if perhaps there'd been some great estrangement. But then, if they'd lived, nothing would have explained her independence of circumstance."

Except a fae heritage. "What did she tell you of her past?"

"Only that her family didn't hail from Byren. She gave their name as Floran."

"I've never heard of the Floran family."

Her eyes clouded slightly. "They have ancient and prosperous holdings."

"In Byren?"

"Some distance away."

It wasn't like Aunt Melisina to be vague. Did residual glamour influence her, after all these years? Had Mother introduced herself to the whole Caldwell family with glamour and deceit? I'd envisioned her the victim of fae manipulation, but it seemed *she'd* schemed instead, seeking to snare Father for her own ends.

The spindles of the chair dug into my spine. No—that wasn't right. She'd loved him; she must have loved him, else all my memories were false. I rubbed my temples. Nothing made sense. If she'd had access to glamour, which she'd used to integrate herself into the Caldwell family, then she could not have forsaken her fae nature. But if she'd not forsaken her fae nature, then how had she carried three children in so short a span?

"I don't think it wise to dwell too much on the matter." Was that concern in her eyes? Certainly, her expression held none of its customary hauteur. "You have your whole life ahead—it will do no good if you become mired in the past."

"I assure you this has done no harm. It helps me feel I understand her a bit more."

"Well, see that you don't allow yourself to become maudlin. It's unbecoming in a young lady." The crisp words erased any trace of emotion I'd sensed. She cast a glance at the window. "It's growing late. Will you stay for dinner?"

"Thank you, but I can't stay. Father's waiting for me."

She shook her head. "Only Alden would remain in the carriage to read rather than avail himself of the comforts of the drawing room. Tell Caris I shall do all in my power to further the connection between Ainslie and Mr. Redgrave, and she's to let me know if she changes her mind and wishes to add to the party."

"I will."

"And one more thing. I intend to summer in the Stanford family home. If you and your sisters and Caris wish to join me, I'd be happy to host a house party and include the Redgraves."

"I'll be sure to tell her." Which of the growing number of invitations would Aunt Caris deem most desirable? I could only hope the presence of Riven and Mr. Redgrave would tip the scales toward staying in Avons.

After bidding her farewell, I joined Father in the carriage. This time, he didn't even glance up, so I signaled to the driver to take us onward. When we arrived at the library, Father wandered off to the sciences, while I made my way toward the gazettes archive. Though Aunt Melisina had offered a good deal of information, I didn't want to pass up a chance to learn more.

I paged through recent gazettes. For the most part, any mention of the Redgrave family occurred in society events, usually ones in which they were praised. I moved to the marriage records and found confirmation of Aunt Melisina's statement that the men who wed into the family took on the Redgrave name. What had motivated such a flouting of convention?

Jade settled on my feet. *It must be tied up in whatever secrets they hold. If what I've seen of the Redgrave siblings is any indication, they're not the sort to act without purpose.*

I agree. From a wide drawer, I pulled out the political papers. Aunt Melisina had said Cenhelm Redgrave served in the Assemblage of Lords. Perhaps his service records could provide insight. I skimmed the pages as swiftly as I could, trying to gain a sense of the family structure. It appeared Cenhelm was the elder brother of Cyril Redgrave and had taken over the family seat in the Assemblage of Lords at the request of his father, Derian, who now kept himself largely at the family estate. Cenhelm appeared to attend nearly every session, but from the notes available to the public, he refrained from commenting when asked to weigh in on Lord Blackburn's proposed reforms, though on most other subjects he was outspoken. Was it because he had a vested interest in Otherworldly matters, one he did not wish to betray?

I straightened, rubbing my stiff neck. This was like trying to find a jewel lost in the detritus of a forest floor. Unless the sun caught it just right, it would be near impossible. I returned the papers to their places. Time ran short, and there was one thing more I wished to investigate before we left—Mother's so-called family name.

Yet however many lineage records I paged through, I could find no reference to a Floran family, nor even to her appearance among the society of Byren before her marriage to Father. That should have drawn speculation in the gossip column, yet the only mentions of their engagement and wedding were glowing —also odd. Mechanically, I replaced the records.

You're reacting very little to these revelations.

At Jade's gentle words, my eyes suddenly stung. I swallowed hard. *If I think too much about what it might mean—that she might never have cared for us all, except for her own purposes—then I shall react far too much. I need to keep my mind clear, for Ainslie's sake, if nothing else.*

She regarded me steadily. *Perhaps.*

My shoulders bowed inward. Despite all she'd withheld, what I wanted most was to feel Mother's arms about me again, her summer-rose scent surrounding me, her lilting voice calling me golden one. Surely it hadn't all been a lie.

Or had Mother glamoured even our memories? Perhaps she'd never forsaken her fae nature. Perhaps there was some other way she'd been able to conceive us—by dwelling in the mortal world or taking a mortal husband or . . . something, anything else. Was it her doing that a glamour had concealed my fae looks —perhaps even my affinities? Because I'd not begun to experience them until after she'd died.

The relentless silence of the reading room became oppressive, and the page before me blurred. No, not now. I yanked a handkerchief from my reticule and swiped at my face, locking my emotions deep in my chest.

All that mattered now was finding the truth—and I owed Ada and Ainslie what I'd discovered so far. Father appeared, and I snapped the record book shut, perhaps a bit too abruptly.

"Did you find what you needed?" he asked.

I nodded. "There's nothing else for me here."

I followed him from the library, my pace slow. With each step, sorrow battered at my chest, fighting to free itself, pressure building relentlessly. With a shudder, I wrapped my arms about myself and hurried over the threshold.

A sudden sense of Other swept over me, cool and refreshing as the waters of a lake on a warm summer day, and somehow, slightly familiar. I'd sensed this once before, outside Hampton House after Lord West attacked—but it had not been Lord West. What then?

The fur on Jade's neck rose, and I halted so abruptly, she almost collided with me. However soothing the sensation, I could not trust it without more knowledge. What if it were a lure for some trap? "Father, wait!"

He stopped partway down the steps. "Did you forget something?"

"I—" As suddenly as the sensation had come, it vanished. Though the songs of the mottled plane trees lining the streets surged over me, they whispered not of danger but of sturdy confidence. Would they sense Other, if it still lingered?

Perhaps we should ask Riven to come.

He's tracing the nightspire. If something Other remained, perhaps it would be worth pulling him away—but whatever it is has vanished. And above all, I needed Ainslie safe.

Jade sniffed the air. *Then we should return home as swiftly as we may.*

Father still waited on the steps.

"I . . . It's nothing. We should go."

CHAPTER 14

Though I remained wary and alert, our return trip was blessedly uneventful, and home soon welcomed us. No matter how I protested, Estine insisted on preparing dinner trays for me and Father, and weary of thought and conversation alike, I took mine to my room.

Just as I finished the meal, a male sun sylph materialized next to Risha, his light dim. Thick golden hair fell about his face, and dark umbers and muted crimsons played across his wings, which were slightly ragged—a sign of the abuses he'd endured?

Risha's light flared bright enough to consume them both, and rapid patterns flickered and swirled between them, some sort of communication I could not follow. I turned away to allow them privacy, collecting my dinner dishes onto the tray Estine had provided while I waited for their moment of reunion to pass.

When Risha's light faded, Kiran flew toward me. He halted a handbreadth from my face. "I am here to serve."

This close, I could perceive the weary lines set in his face, and it tugged my heart. "You and Risha have only just been reunited. Do you want to be separated so soon?"

"I wish to repay debt."

I sighed softly. "Did Risha explain you're under no obligation?"

"She explained. I remain." The umber tones of his light deepened, shot through with threads of gold.

In a way, Risha and Kiran were very alike. Small wonder they were drawn to each other. "Then I accept with gratitude. My sisters are twins and bear a strong resemblance to one another, but Ainslie has a binding mark. She's the one who requires watching, but she's not to know you're present."

He nodded, and we made our way toward Ada and Ainslie's bedchamber, one they'd always shared by choice. Risha and Kiran flew in perfect harmony, and their joy—evident in the vibrant, multihued light swirling about us—brought a measure of comfort. At least one thing had gone right. Even Jade no longer appeared disgruntled when she regarded them.

She cast a look over her shoulder. *Appearances can deceive, you know.*

I stifled a smile. *I'm well aware—also aware that you're softer of heart than you claim.*

She rumbled low as I gave a soft knock against the polished wood door.

"Come in," Ada called.

I twisted the brass knob, revealing a familiar sight. The two of them leaned against the headboard of the large four-postered bed that anchored the room, Ada reading a collection of poetry and Ainslie writing. They often spent time in such quiet activities before retiring, and the peace of the scene wrenched at my heart. How could I upset this fragile tranquility?

Kiran fluttered to rest beside Ainslie, Risha at his side. Their light mingled, spilling across the bed linens, a tangible sign of Other overlaying the mundane and mortal, a reminder that I had no choice.

Ada looked up from her book, then shut it at once and set it aside. "What's wrong, Jessa?"

Were my feelings so obvious? I settled onto the edge of the

bed and buried my cold fingers beneath the tumbled blankets. "I received a disturbing message today from the fae who holds your binding mark."

Ainslie sat bolt upright, the papers dropping to her lap. "What . . . how?"

I told them of the Otherworldly plant and the message, and Ainslie's lips whitened at the edges, folding into a tight line, while Ada clutched her hand as if she might be snatched away this very instant.

"Riven means to trace the nightspire, and in the morning, I'll seek any information I might gather from it." Venturing down in the dark to confront the threatening power behind the plant seemed unwise at best.

"And then what?" Ada asked.

"It depends a great deal on what we find." If we uncovered the identity of the bargain-holder, it would change everything. I braced my back against one of the carved bedposts. "In light of this message, Riven suggested that we stop keeping watch over Ainslie. If she's never left alone, it may inadvertently force her to break the terms of her bargain."

Ainslie collected her scattered papers and stacked them with precision. "Given the contents of the note, his reasoning seems sound. I agree."

Ada shook her head. "Oh, Ainslie—"

"It's nothing to worry about." She lifted her chin. "I shall go about life with neither more nor less than my usual level of companionship while Jessa and Lord Riven see if they can force this fae to reveal himself."

Ada lowered her head, her dark curls spilling down to conceal her face—clearly, she was upset with the proposal. Later, I'd tell her about Kiran; for now, I'd best distract her. "There's something else. I talked to Aunt Melisina today about Mother."

With that, the whole of my speculation on our parentage came tumbling out, along with my conversation with Riven about fae blood. When I finished, neither of them moved or spoke.

After a time, Ada rubbed her hands along her arms, her silk shawl rustling slightly. "I cannot think . . . If it's true, why would Mother deceive us so? *How* could she through all those years?"

"I don't know. And I may be mistaken." Some part of me hoped I was, hoped that my memories of closeness and connection were not wholly false. "Still, we must seek what evidence we can gather. Have either of you ever sensed anything Other? Experienced anything out of the ordinary?"

"I don't think so—certainly nothing like what you've described," Ada said softly. "But there have been a few moments when I've . . . we've wondered."

I caught Jade in my arms. What did it mean that they'd not shared my experiences? Did it negate the possibility of fae blood? Regardless, now was not the time to press, not when Ainslie looked only a moment away from shattering.

She released a shuddering breath. "It's not what I wanted to hear, but perhaps there's a bright spot in it all."

"What can you possibly mean?" Ada's eyes shimmered with unshed tears. "If Mother lied to Father, if she . . . if we are . . . what bright spot can there possibly be?"

"I have no answers about the past, about what Mother might have done or intended." Ainslie hugged the bedquilt to her body. "I speak rather of what Lord Riven said—that whatever has been forced upon us by birth, we don't have to remain fae, become as they are. If we choose, we can still live ordinary lives, still wed and have families without worrying about the fate we'll visit upon them."

Any thought of confessing that I didn't intend to forsake my fae nature altogether—that I hoped to somehow remain within this world yet still retain my affinities—withered within. How could I, when Ainslie viewed Other with such animosity? I pulled my knees to my chest, displacing Jade. If she did not understand, what hope did I have that anyone else would?

"Is this about Mr. Redgrave?" Ada asked.

Ainslie traced the embroidery of her nightgown with her

finger. "You must think I'm ridiculous to hope there's still a way we could share a future. It's only that I . . ."

"You care for him a great deal."

"Yes. And it frightens me sometimes, the enormity of these feelings. It should take time to . . . to fall in love properly."

"I don't think there's a proper way to fall in love, nor that it always requires time." Ainslie had ever rushed headlong into life, her passion lending her a sparkling vibrancy that drew others wherever she went—why should her romance be any different? I shifted, rustling the linens. "We don't even know for certain this theory about Mother is correct. But even if it is, and you choose to forsake your fae nature, complications remain."

"The bargain." Her shoulders collapsed inward. "You're right. Which is why I've resolved to confess the truth to Mr. Redgrave."

"And if he means to tell the Vigil?" Strain filled Ada's voice.

"I don't believe he will." Yet the pallor of her face made the shadows beneath her eyes appear starker. "I've thought about it a great deal since our earlier discussion—ending things with me would provide equal protection for him and his family. If he feels he must act, I believe he cares enough to choose that course rather than turning me over."

"You could end things with him and avoid the risk altogether," Ada whispered.

"And hurt him without cause?" Ainslie shook her head. "None of this is his fault. He's shown me nothing but kindness."

Yet a secret, once shared, was no longer safe. In the sharing, the burden might lessen—or it might multiply. If Mr. Redgrave had some connection to the Otherworld, it might make him inclined to accept Ainslie's own ties—or he might be ensnared in a way that threatened her. I needed to buy time to uncover the truth. "If you're willing, I think you should wait until after they join us for dinner. It will avoid the risk of unanswerable questions from our aunts if all does not go as you hope."

She nodded slowly. "Very well. But no longer—I cannot endure it hanging over my head."

Clearly, she was as determined to confess as to shed her fae nature. Perhaps I should shift the subject before she reconsidered. "When we were out, Father asked me if I'd ever encountered fae."

"Oh, Jessa! What did you say?" Ada asked.

"Very little. I cannot imagine telling him about Mother, not before we're certain. If we're wrong—and I've been wrong about such things before—then he will suffer a great deal for nothing."

Ainslie held my gaze. "And if you're right?"

I looked away, unable to bear speaking the truth: it would surely crush him.

CHAPTER 15

Though I'd fallen into bed bone weary after my conversation with Ada and Ainslie the night before, I woke with the first hint of sun gleaming through branches of the old oak, very aware that Riven remained absent. Did he still seek the source of the nightspire? Or had some trouble occurred within his court?

If so, he'd doubtless keep it to himself. I cast aside the bedquilt. If I could collect information from the nightspire while he was gone and the rest of the household slumbered, perhaps we could make quicker progress when he returned. Glancing out the window, I dressed hurriedly.

Risha darted upward from her perch on the sill, and Jade stretched out to her full length before leaping from the bed and sauntering to my side. I tucked the basket with my sketching and gardening supplies over one arm, then together the three of us made our descent.

Though it was summer, the early morning air held a slight chill. I peered out one of the front windows. Pale folds of mist billowed over the cobbled streets and swirled about the gaslights, which had extinguished with the first light of day. Small puddles remained from a middle-of-the-night shower.

Jade pressed her nose to the glass. *It's still far too damp for my taste.*

You could remain inside.

And let you venture out alone? She chuffed. *Not likely, given the way trouble follows you.*

Aside from the nightspire, I don't think malevolent Otherkind are lurking in the garden, but I'll concede your point. I'd certainly rather have your company. I lifted Jade and cradled her close to my chest. As we approached the back door, harsh notes assaulted me, discord among the harmonious melodies that had always made the garden a haven. I wrenched open the door, then stopped short.

Oh no.

The nightspire was no longer in the greenhouse, nor contained in its pot. Rather, it had taken up occupation of the bed alongside and more, rooting through the garden, charging toward the door. Its song had an edge of triumph, that of a conqueror who'd successfully staked a claim. In its quest for control, it had upended and consumed lavender, calendula, and peony, leaving a gaping hole in the melodies of my garden.

On one side, the ever-vigilant oak hemmed in its spread; on the other, ivy twined through it, attempting to slow its progress, yet both were losing the battle against its Other nature. Cottony wisps of fear brushed the back of my neck. Who had removed the plant from the protections of the glasshouse? Skirting the nightspire, I touched the rough bark of the oak, seeking the one responsible.

There.

Ainslie glided through the garden, once more barefoot and bareheaded, slumber still in her eyes. Moonlight bathed her blank features. She entered the glasshouse and emerged with the nightspire cradled in her arms. One spiked vine stroked the side of her neck, drawing small beads of blood.

Even so, she did not flinch, did not show any sign of awareness, only glided effortlessly onward, placing the nightspire in the garden bed, then vanishing back into the dark house.

Shuddering, I released my hold on the oak. Had the presence of the nightspire made her more vulnerable to the bidding of the fae? Or was it simply part of her bargain to do as she was commanded, whatever the task? The haunting call of a mourning dove echoed in the distance, reverberating in my chest.

What now? As I deliberated, a new vine darted from the nightspire, spiraling down the path toward me.

Jade stalked forward, growling low, and it coiled upright as she approached, its purple-black leaves gleaming in the morning sun.

Wait. I swallowed hard. To constrain the nightspire, to alter its course, would require an open use of my affinities—in a dangerously conspicuous place—but little choice remained.

Still, before I attempted to change its course I must understand what compelled it—and if I could, who controlled it. I marched down the crushed-stone path toward the grove of nightspire. When I approached, another thorn-spiked vine uncoiled from beneath the leaves. Before I could pull back, it twisted around my wrist, digging into my skin, drawing droplets of blood. I gasped.

An eager shiver rustled the leaves of the plant.

Jade charged forward.

Not yet! Stay back.

Its hungry song burned through muscle and sinew; the power behind it staggered me. The vine tightened about my flesh, thorns digging deep, as if they quested not only for blood but also for something deeper, something hidden within my very soul.

With my free hand, I grasped for the strands of ivy. They rushed toward me, swirling with green-gold vigor, their determined nature rising to meet the Other that surged through my veins.

Jade whirled to Risha. *Go for Riven.*

"No, wait—"

But Risha had already vanished.

And I could spare no further thought for anything but the nightspire. As I poured power into the ivy, it became thicker and stronger than its natural form, and it charged into the nightspire, the vines roiling together in an unruly mass.

They tangled together, the workings on the nightspire glinting silver-bright. A tide of heat swept over me, and the nightspire released its grip, writhing under the assault.

In the end, the ivy—limned with green-gold power—formed an impenetrable barrier for the nightspire. Yet even those without eyes to see the Other power surging through both plants couldn't look at this tangle of botanical life that had appeared overnight and imagine it a natural occurrence.

Never mind that for now, this interloper had taken something—now it must give in return. Bright and burning and glorious, Other swirled within me, and I opened my senses further, resting my fingers upon a nightspire leaf and bending all my thoughts toward perceiving its origin.

Something else pressed back, something far greater and more powerful than I. It stung my fingers, brought a taste to my tongue like that of burnt leaves. Yet I refused to release my hold, and through the fog shrouding my senses, a single image formed —a garden unlike any I'd ever seen, a magnificent expanse stretched beneath a starlit sky.

Then the connection severed.

When I wrenched away, Riven leaned against the oak, waiting. How long had he been watching? "When did you come?"

"As soon as Risha appeared, though it seems her alarm was unwarranted. I saw no reason to interfere when you had the situation under control, only to conceal your actions." He eyed my wrist, which still dripped blood, and then lifted a brow at the unruly ivy-and-nightspire tangle. "How did it escape?"

"Ainslie." I clasped my stinging wrist to my middle. "It seems the bargain compelled her, though she appeared unaware."

With my uninjured hand, I pulled the amelior salve from my basket and fumbled with the lid. Riven plucked it from my grasp, twisted it open, and took my hand, smoothing the salve over the marks left by the thorns, his touch warm and confident.

Other sparked against my skin and raced up my arm. The salve had never felt so before—had he infused it with greater power?

Jade watched us, eyes gleaming. *Naturally, that must be the case.*

The hint of amusement in her tone managed to convey a wholly different impression. If not Other, then . . . Discomfited, I stepped back slightly. "Did you . . . ah, trace the source of the nightspire?"

"Only back to its source in your world." As if nothing of consequence had passed between us, he released my hand and resealed the jar, returning it to me. "A solicitor—thoroughly glamoured—delivered it as a commission for a client he could scarcely recall. He could only describe her as an old woman, said this client instructed him to keep it one week, then deliver it to Miss Jessa Caldwell at 68 Camden Row."

An old woman. Like the one Ainslie recalled seeing when she'd made the bargain. Did she hold Ainslie's bargain, or was she simply the pawn of a more powerful high fae? I stowed the jar in the basket, glad for a chance to conceal my face for a moment. "Why a week?"

"So all signs of her passing between worlds would be faint enough to make her identity impossible to discern."

"That means she knows you're involved."

"Either that or she's exceptionally cautious. Given the letter, I think it's most likely she knows. Regardless, her attention to detail will make matters more difficult—she's anything but sloppy and arrogant."

Unlike Lord West, whose pride had driven him to underestimate what a mortal might do. This fae wasn't just watching us in a cursory way. Through some arcane means, she'd studied and observed, and now it seemed she *knew* us. I traced the mostly healed marks left by the nightspire. Even while keeping herself at a safe distance, she'd proven to have a long reach.

At least this information indicated that the arrival of the Redgraves had nothing to do with the appearance of the night-spire. I'd take whatever silver lining I could find. I surveyed the jumbled mess before me. "I cannot leave the garden this way. It will raise too many questions. Do you think the time has come to destroy the nightspire?"

And, if it had . . . could I?

"When it was contained in its pot, I could have simply taken it away. Now that it has staked its claim in the soil and grown many times stronger, things are not so simple. You must confront the workings placed on it, which have rooted through your garden." He wasn't volunteering to help, which meant he intended me to see this through—and I supposed it was wise, since there remained a small chance the bargain-holder was unaware of his presence. "If you intend to destroy it, you'll need to consider how you might approach it without drawing unwanted attention."

He was right—this wouldn't be the task of a moment, but rather a complicated unraveling, which would leave me vulnerable, even assuming I could succeed.

"For now, I suggest containment and glamour. We may want to learn more from it later."

Could I manage that much? Perhaps, since I knew this garden, knew the curve of every bough and blossom, the structure and song of every plant. Riven didn't propose a glamour of a destructive sort, but rather one that suggested that what should be still *was*.

I allowed Other to swell within once more—but perhaps I shouldn't think of this fully alive sensation as *Other* when by nature it belonged to me. In my mind's eye, the garden unfolded before me as it had been before the nightspire wrought destruction, only with new shades of green-gold vibrancy in its lines and colors, and I willed that image to remain.

When I released my hold on the power within, it did. Riven gave a nod of approval. "As you have no gardener here to meddle, this should satisfy."

I angled away from the glamour, unwilling to think too long on what I'd done. "Earlier, when I tried to read the nightspire, I saw something."

He looked at me, intent. "What?"

"It was a magnificent garden." I fumbled for my sketchbook and then sank down on the bench to draw the exact image I'd seen. When I passed the sketchbook to him, his jaw tightened.

"You recognize it."

"Yes." His gaze met mine. "It's the royal garden of the Court of Dusk."

"The royal garden?" That boded poorly. "Does that mean their monarch is involved?"

"Not necessarily. But it does provide a clear link between this scheme and the Court of Dusk. It further indicates that those behind this bargain hold considerable power, which will make obtaining leverage more difficult." He lifted a shoulder. "Inter-court relations are touchy at the best of times—and this is not. We'll have to tread with care."

Tread with care? Ainslie was becoming a pale shadow of her usually bright self. How long did we have before she faded altogether? Everything in me yearned to depart at once for the Court of Dusk, to somehow uproot the nightspire and force it to take me to its place of origin—but then what? In the royal gardens I'd be surrounded by plants who obeyed the commands of masters far stronger than I. And my presence would surely not go unheeded. Finding myself imprisoned in some Otherworldly dungeon for intruding on palace grounds would only endanger Ainslie further, so I tamped down the desire. "Is there any circumstance that would allow us to search for more information within the court?"

"There's an angle that may allow an official visit, and I'm already exploring it."

His words lifted some of the weight from my shoulders. Despite his claim of professional interest in the matter, I could perceive far more risk in this situation than reward for him, yet I couldn't bring myself to protest, not when his involvement gave Ainslie a far better chance of survival. "Thank you."

"There's something else you must consider." He surveyed the nightspire, his eyes darkening. "When you first tangled with Damir, he investigated you. It's how he uncovered your part in Uros's death, which he believed marked you as an unprotected mortal. If he discovered it, others might also—he might have outright informed his son. Then there's the matter of your involvement in his death and the remaking of Kilmere. If you set yourself against another prominent fae, you risk exposure. And once the truth escapes, it will draw a great deal of unwanted attention. Perhaps it already has."

"What do you mean?"

"If the current theory about your mother is correct, it's possible someone used knowledge of your nature—and that of your sisters—to craft this bargain and use Other more freely against you. At the least, if you weren't dwelling here, in this home, this fae would never have bothered to send the nightspire."

Which now threatened the gardens and house. Could it somehow influence the mortal inhabitants? The valerian at my feet shuddered, its heart-shaped leaves quivering. "But when Ainslie was marked, I knew nothing of my nature. Nor did she understand hers."

"That doesn't matter. It's what someone else might have known—or could yet find out. Even if her bargain was a coincidence, your presence in their lives acts as a beacon to attract Other."

Jade bristled. *You've protected them.*

But I was *the cause of their danger.* My healing wrist throbbed, thorn-sharp pain creeping toward my heart. Uros had threatened Lovell to entertain himself with me, Lord West had glamoured Aunt Caris and others in my family when I'd refused to surrender to him, and Kilmere had nearly consumed Dreda, Mr. Burke, and Elodie—what might come next?

Riven still watched the nightspire, his face turned from me, and a spark of light flared between his fingers. "It's long past time you considered the risk of your continued involvement with those you call your family. Fae and mortal relations never end well for mortals. How much does their survival matter to you?"

"How could you ask such a question?" If he'd seized a knife and plunged it into my chest, it would have hurt far less. "You know I'd do anything to keep them safe."

"Even cut all ties?"

I stumbled back. When we'd remade Kilmere, and I'd spoken of my fears of losing my family, he said I'd face difficult choices, but I never dreamt he'd meant *this*. "You're saying I must either forsake my fae nature or—"

"Given that you've forfeited all protection from Other, I'd never counsel abandoning your fae nature. It would leave you in an even more vulnerable position." He folded his arms across his chest, his demeanor forbidding. "Detaching from mortal relations is the only logical step. It's protection for them and for you."

"And then I would just . . . what? Abandon Byren altogether for the Otherworld?"

He gave no reply, only inclined his head, a motion which drove the breath from my lungs. Even if immortality meant one day I must lose my family—a choking thought—I'd assumed I'd have them many years yet, that I could remain where all was familiar and safe. The knife blade dug deeper. "I can't just leave. This—*they* are my home."

"Then you must accept the price—and the fact that it's unlikely you'll be the one to pay it." Abruptly, he spun to face me, something wild and fae bleeding into his features. "Your presence in their lives will continue to attract the attention of Other, and they are defenseless. Do you think you can protect them forever?"

No.

I knew I could not.

Particularly not without Riven's assistance. I'd been fortunate in my dealings with Lord West, but even that had been far too close for comfort. I'd had one small advantage—he'd believed I was mortal. Without that, matters might have gone differently. I could not expect that every time I faced a more powerful fae the outcome would settle in my favor. The bitter scent of the night-spire filled the air, tightening my throat. "But Ainslie is already bound. I can't leave her alone to face this fae."

It was a fragile defense, but the only one I could summon against his cold logic. My pulse stuttered, unsteady and uncertain. *You don't agree, surely?*

Jade's tail lashed the ground. *I withhold judgment.*

She'd always expressed her opinions freely before. Did that mean she believed Riven was right, but did not wish to hurt me?

"I don't suggest you leave her to her fate, rather that when this situation resolves—one way or another—you remove yourself from their lives." His voice remained devoid of emotion, his expression unyielding. "For your sake, I hope your sisters share your blood and will choose the same path. But either way, you must resolve to act."

I shook my head. "Whether I remain involved in their lives or not, conflict is coming—"

"And you will draw it to them. They'll be used as leverage to control you, much as Damir used Ada in the end, when he finally realized your true sentiments. You cannot forever rely on the blindness of fae in matters of emotion." The lines of his face sharpened, his words cut like shards of diamond. "And you cannot be seen to care, if you want them to remain safe. As it stands, you're a danger to them."

Blindly, I grasped for the oak, its rough bark scraping my skin, its protective song sweeping around me—but it could not shield my heart from this overwhelming pain. And I could not show it, not now. Only try to grasp for some defense. Why did he press the matter with such urgency? Unless he knew something I did not . . . My breath shuddered.

If Riven believed fae sharing connections with mortals such a danger, then why had he concerned himself in my affairs . . .

Oh. He'd suspected long before I had that I was fae. My lips trembled. "If you'd not believed I had fae blood—if you were certain I was only mortal—would you have severed all connection after Uros died?"

"I would have had no other choice." Very little glamour veiled his features now—they were sharp and beautiful and Other, limned with brilliant light. "No more than you will, in the end. Do you want to know your family was destroyed because of you? To watch it happen—or find the aftermath—and know you failed to save them?"

Hot, angry words burned on my lips, and my eyes stung. No, no tears, not now. Shaking, I turned away. I didn't want to accept his perspective held any truth, yet how could I argue otherwise? If I brought down the wrath of the Otherworld upon them, if they did not survive the encounter—how could I possibly live with that?

A sprig of ivy spiraled across my foot, and the oak tried to comfort with its gentle songs, but oh, the familiar gestures only wrenched my heart. If Riven was right, even these beloved homely plants would have to be abandoned.

He took a half step toward me. "Jessa—"

"Just stop. Please stop."

With that, I fled.

CHAPTER 16

I stumbled into the house and past a gaping Gaile, darted up the stairs and into my bedchamber, where I flung the bolt on the door and buried myself beneath the covers. The thick blankets stifled me, constricting my limbs, and yet I was so cold, so very cold. I did not want them, but could not cast them off, could not think of what must be done . . .

Jade curled up on my chest, for once wordless, and nuzzled my chin. A dull pressure built behind my eyes, then traveled down to settle in my chest. From beyond the glass, the oak still reached for me, its protective melodies swirling through the bedchamber, but even stronger echoed the memory of Riven's voice: *you're a danger to them.* My throat tightened.

Forsake my fae nature.

Or abandon those I loved.

It was an impossible choice. How could I accept those as the only options? My eyes slid shut, blotting the room from view. *Kit-isne are always right, or so you say. What do you counsel?*

For a long time, only the steadiness of her breathing anchored me. Then at last she answered. *I have no counsel. Not about this. Whatever choice you make, you'll have to live with it for a lifetime. It must be yours alone.*

Yet if I chose wrong, or perhaps even if I chose rightly, everyone I loved would suffer. Adrift in a sea of sorrow and confusion, I clutched Jade close.

Some time later, Aunt Caris knocked on the door, then rattled the knob. "Jessa, are you well? You never joined us for breakfast, and Gaile said you looked very poorly. Have you taken ill?"

I pressed upright and pushed back the covers. How could I endure the thought of never seeing Aunt Caris again? Of one day walking away from them all, letting them believe me dead? I did not think I possessed the courage. On leaden limbs, I crossed the room to open the door.

"My dear, you look dreadful." She pressed a gentle hand to my forehead—how often had she made such a motion, tending to one of us girls? "You're a bit warm too."

"I'm not ill." Not in body, at least. How could I explain the turmoil within? I must offer something or she'd continue to press. "I'm just . . . conflicted. I can't stop thinking—what if things had gone differently in Withern and we'd not emerged unscathed?"

What if we did not, this time?

She clucked softly. "Your injury and abduction and Ada's poisoning—they were dreadful things by any standard. I thought perhaps the emotions of it would surface at some point, and there's no shame in it. Perhaps a cup of tea would help?"

"Perhaps."

In short order, she sent for tea, repinned my disheveled curls, and smoothed the wrinkles from my gown. Though I let her cluck and fuss over me, every kindness only twisted the pain in my soul deeper, the sensation sharp as nightspire thorns. What must I do?

She poured a steaming cup of tea and spooned in a generous measure of sugar, then handed the concoction to me. "There, my dear. I know it's been a trying time, but it's all over now."

The grassy, floral notes of the chamomile-and-lavender tea

turned flat and slightly bitter, yet I managed to paste on a smile. "Thank you, Aunt Caris."

Before she could reply, Holden materialized in the doorway. "Miss Redgrave is here for the young misses."

"So early? I suppose she still observes Withern calling hours." Aunt Caris glanced at me. "Ada and Ainslie went for a drive with Lovell. Do you wish to receive her? If not, I can make your excuses."

I couldn't afford to decline any opportunity to learn more about the Redgraves, however frayed my emotions. I set down my cup. "Since she may become family one day, it seems wise to accept the call."

Aunt Caris beamed at me. "I quite agree."

But even if Ainslie wed Mr. Redgrave, I might not be there to witness—

Stop. I couldn't keep thinking about it, or I'd never maintain composure long enough to conduct an ordinary conversation. Until Ainslie was free, there was no question—I would remain with my family. Beyond that, I could not consider.

As we approached the morning room, Risha halted abruptly. With effort, I avoided glancing over my shoulder.

Jade's ears twitched. *It's the ward—Elodie wears a strong one today. Risha can come no closer.*

What about you?

It's not pleasant, but I've endured far worse.

I hesitated just outside the door. *Why don't you remain in the entry? You can still keep watch, but there's no need for you to suffer.*

Very well. With a low rumble, she settled just inside the morning room, leaving me to advance toward Elodie and the bone-chilling discomfort of the ward alone.

Elodie sprang up to greet me, fresh and radiant in a pale muslin gown. "I know it's unforgivably early to call in Avons, but Charles suggested you're not the sort to lie about all morning, and I'd hoped to catch you before you went out calling. You don't mind, do you?"

"Not at all, but I'm afraid you've already missed Ada and Ainslie."

Gaile brought in a refreshment tray with pastries and a chilled pitcher of orgeat lemonade as Elodie gave the slightest lift of her shoulders. "Missing them will only give me an excuse to call again soon, and I must say I don't mind. It's a pleasure not to have to sit on ceremony, isn't it?"

"Indeed." Despite my fears about the Redgraves, Elodie's bright and seemingly open nature drew me. Any lady who carried—and effectively wielded—a parasol sword wouldn't be alarmed by my own unladylike tendencies. My fae nature, on the other hand . . . I settled onto the chair across from her. "You mentioned your intention to stay with your aunt Hester? Does she share a household with Cyril Redgrave?"

"No—Aunt Hester is properly our great-aunt, though that would be a cumbersome title, so we simply call her Aunt Hester. She's Uncle Cyril's aunt, in fact." Her brilliant blue eyes widened slightly. "But I did not know you were acquainted with him."

"I'm not. A friend mentioned his name in connection with the Antiquary Society. She wished to meet him to discuss a matter of society business, and when I heard his name, I wondered how all the members of your family are related." I offered her a glass of lemonade, its cool touch welcome.

"It *is* a great deal to keep track of. I sometimes get lost in the family tree myself." She laughed softly, accepting the glass. "Are you a member of the society?"

"Not yet, though I'd like to join. I've gathered they have a stringent admission process and prefer not to welcome ladies into their midst. But Mrs. Darrington has offered to provide a recommendation for me."

"Then I shall introduce you to Uncle Cyril. I believe he'd second her suggestion, if you prove yourself to him. He values knowledge, wherever it may be found." Her gaze fixed on the fountain that burbled across the room. "He'll return to Avons this weekend. Shall we plan to call then?"

"Yes, I'd be very grateful for an introduction."

"I'm the grateful one. Avons is rather quiet this time of year, and Charles is much preoccupied these days—I'm certain you can guess why." Light danced in her blue eyes. "Aside from Aunt Hester and Charles, most of the family isn't residing in Avons at present, and I'm afraid I'm not the sort to sit about with no one to talk to. I'd simply wither away. In absence of a good ball or party, one must find something to do."

The arch expression which adorned her final remark suggested that she'd added it because it was the expected thing— after all, it was eminently suitable for a young lady to yearn for the social swirl that might provide a husband, far less for her to look for some other purpose. I sipped my own lemonade, the faint orange and almond notes mingling with the lemon on my tongue. "If you were altogether unable to move in society, what would you choose to occupy your time?"

It was an entirely inappropriate question. Calls were for light conversation—meaningless topics such as the weather or the latest fashion or gossip about mutual acquaintances.

Elodie blinked, as though taken aback, then she said thoughtfully, "If all social events ceased, then I expect I'd simply busy myself with family affairs."

I inclined my head. Family affairs? Something about the way she'd spoken suggested more than participating in mundane household tasks. "This involvement with family matters gives you a sense of purpose then?"

Elodie colored slightly. "Perhaps purpose isn't quite the right word, but I'm pleased to help my aunt at Redgrave Hall, of course. She and Uncle Cenhelm have been very generous in providing a home after Father died." She hurried on. "How fortunate that it need never come to such a fate. I do not think I'd welcome an eternity of household management, though anything would be preferable to boredom."

Though most young ladies were expected to know how to oversee servants and run a home, I did not think she was refer- ring to such responsibilities. I'd no opportunity to press further, since she leaned toward me. "But do tell me about Lord Riven.

I've heard he's come to Avons. Do you still maintain he has no interest in anything beyond friendship?"

"He has business here."

"And is that all?"

Warmth crept into my face. If our charade was to be believable, I shouldn't demur too much. "I suppose time will tell."

She offered an approving nod. "It's always wise to hedge one's bets until a declaration has been made."

I choked slightly on my tea.

Unconcerned, she rattled on. "But that's neither here nor there. Since it's just the two of us, I must confess it's not only for the pleasure of a social call that I've come. As we traveled to Avons, Charles was telling me all about Wyncourt, and I'd dearly love to see the antiquary collection Lady Dromley possessed. I'm no expert—I've only an amateur-level knowledge—but I find such things intriguing. Do say you'll allow me to visit."

How could I justify a denial while continuing to cultivate the relationship? But perhaps I didn't need to. Her reaction to Wyncourt might be telling. "I'd welcome a visit—Ibbie loved nothing more than sharing her collection with interested individuals."

She fairly glowed. "Excellent. I don't suppose you've the time now?"

I set down my glass. "As it happens, I need to speak with the housekeeper today, so now would be perfect."

Though Mrs. Peters had written of her preparations for the dinner party and her proposed menu, I'd prefer to speak with her in person before we gathered this evening, and Aunt Caris was unlikely to object to an excursion with Miss Redgrave, given it furthered the connection between our families. "Just allow me to inform my aunt."

"Of course. If you've no objection, I've come in one of Aunt Hester's carriages—we could take it to Wyncourt."

"That will suit very well."

Only it did not. Once we were in the enclosed carriage, her ward sent a crawling sensation across my skin and stirred a queasiness in my stomach. How mortifying it would be if I cast up my accounts in the silk-upholstered interior.

"Are you quite well?" Elodie asked.

She leaned toward me, and I fought the urge to shrink away. "I've a touch of motion sickness, perhaps."

I took refuge in the *perhaps*, though I knew full well the source of my affliction—the ward-pendant dangling about her neck. I kept Jade as far from Elodie as possible, but even so, her ears were pressed back, betraying her discomfort. Risha hadn't even entered the carriage, but kept pace from outside.

Are you well?

Well enough. Your presence protects me, since you absorb the greater part of its energy.

At least something of value came from my discomfort—I felt as though I was about to crawl out of my skin. The carriage itself must be warded also. Had Elodie brought me here as some sort of test?

Never mind that. If I must endure these sensations, I meant to gain something from the situation as well. I nodded to the chain about her neck. "That's a remarkable ward-pendant. Does your family have connections with the Magistry or Vigil to allow you to procure it?"

She lifted a golden brow. "You believe my family would cultivate such low connections?"

"I intended no insult." I clasped my hands in my lap so they did not travel to my temples. Oh, I wished I could flee this infernal carriage and the oppressive ward-pendant, both of which muddied my thoughts. "I only meant I did not think such wards were readily available."

Her lips remained tight. "With sufficient funds, one can purchase nearly anything from the alchemists. My uncle procured it for me—all sorts of curiosities intrigue him, and he's of a generous nature."

"Of course. I meant no offense, truly."

She gave a little lift of her shoulders, then a sudden smile broke through. "I should not have leapt at you like a prodded wyvern. If there's anything you should know about us Redgraves it's that we take aspersions on our family name far too seriously. I suppose I'm in no way immune, however much I should like to think that I am."

"Then we need consider it no more."

"Gracious, I hope we won't." She tilted her head. "But I must say—not many recognize this as a ward-pendant. May I ask how you did?"

"I saw Mr. Burke with a similar one before, and he informed me of its nature."

"Ah yes. Your family's acquaintance with him is rather unusual, is it not?"

"Not so very unusual, given he helped us when the Crimson Tattoo Killer stalked Avons." I hesitated, but I needed to assuage any suspicion she held, so I continued. "May I trust you to keep a confidence?"

"Of course," she murmured. For a moment, keen intelligence flickered in her eyes, before the society mask she ordinarily wore—one of wide-eyed innocence and radiant smiles—dropped back into place.

Perhaps we were more alike than I wished to consider. In any case, her reaction would prove telling—and it would be better for my endeavors if she believed I trusted her. "This isn't widely known, and I don't suppose my family wishes it to be so, but my cousin Lovell was marked, in the end."

She gave a soft gasp. "Oh, how dreadful."

"It was . . . beyond words." Even now, the memory brought a sick churning to my already unsettled stomach. I pressed a hand to my middle. "Fortunately, the killer was apprehended before he could claim Lovell's life—yet the assistance Mr. Burke offered during that time, and then later in Withern, has made him rather a friend of the family."

"Yes, I see how it might." She unfurled the fan at her wrist and waved it slowly before her face. "I cannot imagine how terrible it would have been if you'd lost your cousin in addition to Lady Dromley."

"Nor can I."

Her gaze lowered to the pattern swirled across the silken seat. "I don't suppose one ever fully recovers from such losses."

Was she thinking of her father and her cousin, claimed at once by "accident"? Despite the danger she and her brother might pose, sympathy tugged at my heart. But whatever emotion she experienced vanished as the carriage pulled to a halt.

"Oh, is that Wyncourt? I'd heard it was of remarkable design, and in this case rumor does not outstrip reality."

In truth, the reality far exceeded any rumor that might have spread about it, for Wyncourt was a fae demesne tucked into the mortal world. Even now, it beckoned me, its honey-colored sovstone and white granite warm and inviting. Yet when we crossed the threshold, Wyncourt bristled, the air about us throbbing with pressure—and dropping several degrees. What in the Crossings?

Oh.

The ward-pendant.

A low, angry groan sounded through the house, the sort of sound a structure made when it was assaulted by a gale-force wind. Only in this case, I suspected the gale was about to come from Wyncourt, meant to eliminate what it viewed as a threatening intruder.

Elodie had gone slightly pale, and she clasped her pendant in one hand. Could she sense the Other nature of Wyncourt?

Regardless, this would never do. I whirled about. "Danvers, won't you take Miss Redgrave to the gallery? She's very interested in Lady Dromley's collections, and I thought it would be a good place to start." If I must treat with Wyncourt, I required privacy. "I'll join you both in a moment—I must fetch something from Ibbie's study."

Danvers gave a solemn nod. "If you'll come this way, Miss Redgrave?"

She followed him while I hurried into the study and shut the door. I rested my hands lightly on Wyncourt's walls, and its outrage spilled through our connection. "If her ward causes you any discomfort, I apologize. It's necessary that she remain here, just for a short time, to avoid future complications."

The wall shuddered beneath my touch.

"Perhaps I can make it up to you later?"

The air warmed slightly, and Wyncourt once again filled my mind with images of me making a home within its walls, returning to its heart and becoming acquainted with its secrets, a notion that appealed. This incident confirmed I needed to better understand the demesne and all it kept hidden, including the room at its heart—preferably before I continued to bring in guests. The ward-pendant had provoked hostility. What else might? I traced my fingers along the wall. "I'm afraid I'm still obliged otherwise, but I'll return this evening for a dinner party, and then I'll come again as soon as I can to explore whatever it is you want me to see."

The air warmed further, as if with approval. Then, as it had done before, Wyncourt funneled sound to me.

"Danvers, how long did you work for Lady Dromley?"

It was Elodie's voice. Evidently, Wyncourt wished me to hear her conversation.

"Since I was quite young," he said.

"In all that time, did you notice anything unusual about Wyncourt?"

"Never, miss." His words emerged stiff—and wholly false. "Wyncourt has always been an excellent place to work, and Lady Dromley was the best of mistresses."

That was true, at least. Danvers and Mrs. Peters were so loyal to Ibbie that they'd concealed her strange rune-painting and the other peculiarities of the place, even from stratesmen, so I couldn't fathom he'd confess them to Elodie. But it seemed that she had a purpose here beyond examining antiquities.

A little gust of air puffed at my neck. Agreement from Wyncourt, perhaps?

My shoulders dropped. It wasn't a surprise; nevertheless, I wished it wasn't true. Now it was my job to ensure she learned nothing of Wyncourt's true nature—and given the Other power surging through it, that might prove difficult.

"I'm certain she was. Everyone speaks highly of Lady Dromley, and Wyncourt exceeds my expectations," Elodie said. "Do you intend to remain in service to Miss Jessa?"

"Indeed, miss. Lady Dromley would have wished it."

"Still, it must be quite a change."

It was time I intervened, before she began pressing him for information about me. I seized the statuette that Nikol had once tossed through the air—a fine example of the early Sainsbury period, according to Ibbie—and hurried toward the gallery. But by the time I arrived, it was occupied by Danvers alone. He was bent low, as if in search of something.

I halted abruptly. "Where's Miss Redgrave?"

"She believes she lost one of her wards along the way and said if I'd search the gallery, she'd retrace her steps and see if she could find it." He tutted quietly. "Such things are valuable, and I'd not have it said one of the servants snatched it—nor would one do such a thing."

"I'm certain you're correct." I straightened. "I'll seek Miss Redgrave and attend the matter."

With Wyncourt's assistance, I soon found Elodie in what I'd dubbed Ibbie's map corridor, for she'd lined the whole thing with carefully preserved and framed works of long-dead cartographers. Elodie stared closely at a map of the little-occupied Morwern region, her mouth moving slightly as she parsed out the words.

Words written in runic script.

How much knowledge did Elodie conceal? And what harm might it do? Our meeting with her uncle could not come soon enough—one way or another, I must provoke them into revealing the truth, before it was too late.

CHAPTER 17

As we approached Elodie, a slight ripple altered the air about Risha and Jade, as if Wyncourt had folded some sort of protection around them to insulate from the pain her wards might inflict. "Did you find your missing ward?"

She started, her hand flying to her chest. "Oh! Yes, I have all my wards. I'm afraid I became a bit distracted—Lady Dromley has so many enchanting collections, don't you agree?"

"Quite. In fact, I thought you might have interest in this statuette. It was a piece Ibbie favored."

Elodie bent her head over it, exclaiming over the exquisite detail, then we moved room to room, examining those of the displays I hoped would not further any untoward schemes. When the nearest clock chimed, I seized the excuse. "Oh, it's growing late. I'm afraid I must return home to prepare for another engagement."

"You've been most gracious to allow for this unexpected visit." She smiled brightly. "I must confess, I'd very much enjoy a return. Lady Dromley collected such beauties that it would take considerable time to appreciate them in full."

I murmured something noncommittal and swept her toward the door. When we emerged from Wyncourt, the sun beat down upon us, its heat radiating from the cobbled stones of the street and the stone dwellings. The air held an unpleasant stickiness, yet I would have lingered for hours rather than return to that dreadful carriage.

Still, I forced myself to follow Elodie, and she filled our ride back to Camden Row with lively commentary on Ibbie's collection. Fortunately, since I struggled even to draw a full breath, she didn't require me to fill in many gaps—nor did she appear to take note of my distress. I greeted our return home with relief, scarcely managing pleasantries before making my escape.

As I ascended the stairs to the house, Aunt Caris appeared in the window and then as swiftly vanished. The moment I walked in the door, she popped her head out of the drawing room. "We've been waiting for you, my dear. Won't you join us?"

Despite my weariness, I could scarcely say no. When I crossed the threshold, Aunt Melisina beckoned me imperiously onward. "Ah, Jessa. A most pleasing development has occurred."

I settled onto the sofa across from my sisters, the cushiony pillows enveloping me. Good news would be more than welcome at this juncture. "What is it?"

"Lord Riven called in your absence, and he seemed most disappointed to find you out. He showed every pleasing and proper sentiment for a suitor, and I think you're well on your way toward securing a match." Her gaze rested on me with something close to approbation.

Aunt Caris beamed. "With proper management of the situation, perhaps matters might soon be settled."

Words failed me. I'd not expected their schemes to extend this far—not this swiftly, at least. Ada ducked her head to conceal a smile, while a hint of concern puckered Ainslie's brow. Yet neither of them knew how strained matters were between Riven and me, nor that I'd fled our last encounter. I twined my fingers through Jade's thick fur, and she nuzzled my hand. "I think perhaps you make too much of it."

"I don't believe in young ladies having overinflated opinions of themselves, but there's such a thing as too much modesty as well." Aunt Melisina fanned her face, stirring the otherwise still air. "It's evident his interest is sincere."

Or that a mingling of fae glamour and charm allowed it to appear so.

"All that's required now is a bit of encouragement, which I have offered," she said.

I straightened, the cushions rustling behind me. "What sort of encouragement?"

"Merely a nudge toward the time required for a gentleman to make a decision. I pointed out that Telford's has begun offering iced creams, and it would make for a delightful outing, given the heat. I suggested that, if he wished, I would be pleased to serve as chaperone."

Warmth swept across my face. "Aunt Melisina, that seems like rather too much encouragement."

She waved a hand. "He welcomed the notion, so it's all settled. You're to go out tomorrow afternoon."

To have to put on a show of courtship beneath Aunt Melisina's attentive gaze, to pretend all was well between us . . . how could I possibly succeed?

She furled her fan and rested it on her lap, surveying me. "You don't seem pleased. I was given to understand from Caris that you enjoyed his company."

That she took time to consider my feelings was a marked change. Nor could I claim I found Riven an unwelcome companion. Or could I, if I tried? I attempted to test the matter by voicing a flat denial, and my chest tightened, the words dying on my tongue. Evidently, the belief fae could not lie was fact, not fiction. My pulse quickened. "I do find him pleasing company, but—"

"Good. Then you may trust I know what I'm about." She gave a decided nod. "In truth, I couldn't have chosen better myself. His consequence will elevate the whole family, and he appears enamored enough not to be concerned with some of your . . . more unusual interests. It's quite satisfactory."

How could I object, when my own confession had revealed

an unsettling truth: whatever the tension between us, I still preferred his company to that of any other man of my acquaintance. If I let slip that revelation, they'd make far too much of it, so instead, I sank deeper into the cushions. With the best of intentions, Aunt Melisina had neatly outmaneuvered me.

Aunt Caris leaned forward to pat my hand. "I quite agree. Lord Riven is most suitable, and we'd be remiss if we did not support the match."

As I couldn't explain the true situation, I simply murmured acquiescence.

Then Ainslie took pity on me and launched into a tale of an acquaintance's recent engagement, complete with all the details of the upcoming nuptials, which distracted both of my aunts and threaded the conversation with laughter.

I snuggled Jade close. Whatever difficulties had come before, whatever challenges and threats might lurk ahead, I pressed from my mind, allowing the light conversation to wash over me. These ordinary moments, filled with love and life, were what I fought to secure for Ainslie—and my whole family. I'd savor them while I could.

When the mantel clock chimed the hour, I excused myself and hurried upstairs to complete my toilette for the dinner party. I removed my day gown, then Lianne bustled into my bedchamber to help me dress. With her dark eyes sparkling, she looked more like a poppy than ever, and as she worked, she hummed softly.

"You seem in good spirits."

"Yes, miss. It's my day off tomorrow, and I mean to spend some time with a friend."

A friend? Or a new love? Thanks to Mr. Burke's reports, her good spirits left me vaguely unsettled, despite the evidence that she had a budding romance. But it wasn't my business to inquire, so I just nodded. "I hope you have a lovely time."

Her lips curved upward. "I certainly shall." She pinned some starflowers to my upswept hair, then stepped back. "Do you need anything else, miss?"

"I think I can manage now—thank you." When she left, I regarded myself in the mirror. Even features, dark curls, deep blue eyes—an altogether mortal appearance. How could it be glamour? Though I sought it, no waver at the edges betrayed illusion . . .

The door opened, and I startled, whirling from the glass as Ada and Ainslie entered.

Ainslie perched on the edge of the bed. "Will you give a full account of whatever you learn tonight?"

"Of course." I fumbled with the clasp of my necklace. "There's one thing before I go—do you remember anything about last night?"

She flinched slightly. "Only going to bed as usual. What happened?"

"I'd left the nightspire in the glasshouse, where Riven wove workings to prevent its spread." I secured the clasp, then turned to face her. "You . . . carried it out into the garden proper."

"You're certain?" Her voice was low, haunted.

"Yes. You'll both need to be careful. It's established a hold in the garden now." I glanced at Kiran, who occupied the windowsill next to Risha. Why hadn't he said anything of her nighttime excursion?

She slumped against the bedpost, and Ada rubbed small circles on her back. "Why would her bargain compel her to such an act?"

"I wish I knew." I rummaged in the drawer for my gloves. "Perhaps only to torment us. Fae like displays of power. But with each act, your bargain-holder takes a risk of exposing her intent. We will figure this out."

I'd accept nothing less. As they left, I caught Ada's wrist. She lingered long enough for me to inform her that Kiran kept watch over Ainslie, and a sigh of relief escaped her. "That's something, at least."

Though I still could not account for his missing report.

After we exchanged farewells, I turned to Risha. "Why didn't Kiran mention Ainslie's nighttime visit to the garden?"

Her wings pulsed, and light swirled in a rhythmic pattern about her, as if she received one of the light messages she'd referenced earlier. "She was at home, safe. He did not know it was not right. All ways of mortals seem strange. Shall he report all her doings at home?"

"I suppose not. Only if someone approaches her or she leaves the grounds unplanned—or he sees any sign of Other about her."

She nodded assent, and then I left the room, thoughts of what the evening would hold—what would be revealed and what I must reveal in turn—chasing me as doggedly as my own shadow. As I walked out the door, I snatched up a letter waiting on the entry table that bore my name in a confident scrawl I recognized as Mr. Burke's hand. Once inside the carriage, I broke the seal.

Miss Caldwell,

No signs yet of the evidence we discussed. I'm chasing down a new theory. If it proves viable, I'll attempt to call so we might review the matter.

With regard,
Mr. Burke

It was carefully worded so as not to arouse suspicion, the missive vague enough that it might have referred to any Magisterial matter. He'd taken further care not to affix his name to the outside and draw attention to the fact he'd written to me, all efforts I appreciated. Still, I'd hoped he'd find some clear connection between the cases . . .

I leaned my head back against the seat, and Jade climbed into my lap, her resonant purr soothing me as we made our way back to Wyncourt. Some part of me wished Riven were attending the dinner tonight, but doubtless he'd disapprove of mortals convening to discuss Otherworldly affairs, just as he'd disapproved of my connection with my family. Even were that not so somehow, the way matters had ended between us—oh, it was bound to be uncomfortable when next we talked.

I buried my face in Jade's fur and remained that way the rest of the ride to Wyncourt. When the driver halted the carriage, I descended at once, ready to escape my oppressive thoughts, never mind what must come next. And I wasn't the only one to have arrived—Thea and Miss Everby climbed down the stairs of their own carriage. I hurried forward to greet them. "Thank you for coming."

"Think nothing of it." Thea clutched Miss Everby's hand and made a laborious ascent of the stairs leading to the door. She halted at the top. "I only hope you'll feel as grateful when you find out what I've done."

Danvers opened the door, but I remained rooted in place. "And what is it you've done?"

"I've interfered a great deal." Her cornflower-blue gaze shadowed. "For the best, I hope."

Danvers attempted to appear impassive, but even the best of butlers must experience curiosity at such a statement. I felt only dread. The faint scent of goldhearts emanated from the open door, attempting to drive back the fouler scents of the streets— but all of it mingled to churn in my stomach as a carriage bearing the Blackburn crest approached.

In short order, Lord Blackburn descended, age-weathered yet commanding as ever, followed by another figure, one dreadfully familiar.

Father.

I stumbled back, bracing myself against the sun-warmed banister. "You invited my father?"

She clutched her ivory-handled walking stick. "I did."

"You had no right." A sudden, strong desire swelled within me—glamour them all, make them forget we'd ever agreed to meet, flee and hide before Father could realize how deeply I'd become embroiled with the Otherworld . . . If he attempted to forbid further involvement, then I'd have to choose—and I wasn't ready.

Not yet.

Perhaps not ever.

Nor could I use glamour in such a base way. What then? I pressed a hand to my temple. I could make my excuses, say I was feeling poorly—certainly true—and they must carry on without me. No, that would not answer. Father would certainly demand an explanation later. A sense of mounting power built in the air around me, as if Wyncourt contemplated my defense. What might it do, if provoked? Once again, I rued the little time I'd been able to spend here.

Father marched up the stairs. He rarely showed signs of anger, but now he glared at Thea. "Mrs. Darrington, you told me we were to convene to gain answers about—"

He glanced at Danvers with an expression of chagrin, as though suddenly aware that he'd not only offered no greeting to me or anyone else, but he'd nearly revealed affairs best kept secret before a little-known-to-him servant.

I straightened, drawing myself up to my full, insubstantial height. "Thank you, Danvers. We'll be in shortly."

Fortunately, Danvers recognized this as a request that he withdraw and vanished into the depths of the house.

Father lowered his voice. "Why are we at Wyncourt? And why is my daughter here?"

Though many ladies would have quailed, Thea remained unmoved. "Both you and Jessa have important knowledge, and it seemed sensible to have you both present at once, that we could all gain a fuller picture of what's taking place."

"Blackburn, you agreed to this?" Father's words held a distinct edge.

The craggy lines of Lord Blackburn's face deepened. "I'll admit I had my reservations about the affair. But Mrs. Darrington and I discussed the matter. Given what's at stake, it seemed necessary."

"He means it appears the two of you are equally determined to avoid exposing your dealings to one another, but we believe if we join our resources, we will get much further."

An evening breeze swirled about us, tugging at the lace on her cap and her milkweed-floss hair. However small and fragile Thea might appear, clearly she didn't intend to yield. And she'd upended everything. No matter what happened this evening, things could never return to the way they were. Father would have questions impossible to answer and . . . "I think we should discuss this withindoors."

Lord Blackburn nodded and offered his arm to Thea, while Miss Everby fell in behind.

But Father didn't move, just looked at me as though I'd transformed into something Other before his eyes. "I asked you what you knew of fae. If you'd encountered them. You gave every indication you knew nothing."

My breath caught. "It seems we've both withheld information." With that, I hurried past him into the house.

The others awaited us in the entry, and Danvers materialized from somewhere deep within Wyncourt.

"Excuse me a moment, I need to have a word with Mrs. Peters about the extra guest. Danvers will see that you're seated." I moved away, but Thea followed, trailing me into the corridor, her steps unsteady. I could have outpaced her, but I slowed. Whatever my feelings, it would be unfair to take advantage of my youth to leave her behind. We halted beyond earshot of the others, beneath a painting of Inish burial cairns.

Thea's breathing came slightly labored. "I just wanted you to know that I've already addressed Mrs. Peters. It seemed unfair to surprise her."

"But not to surprise me?" The cairns glared down at us. "In your lifetime, you've ventured where few ladies are welcome. Given that, I would have thought you'd be inclined to recognize the difficulties this situation presents."

She leaned heavily on her cane. "You're not one to shrink from a few difficulties—"

"By our laws, I'm not yet of age. My father could forbid my involvement in any of this if he pleased." And since I'd no intention of heeding such instruction, what sort of trouble might follow?

"I've had the opportunity to get to know him in recent weeks. He's not that sort of man."

I'd grant that Father wasn't ordinarily the dictatorial sort— far from it—but if he feared for my life, what then? "Would you be pleased with such interference in your own affairs? To be treated as incapable of making your own decisions?"

"It wasn't my intent to meddle." She looked past me, her gaze distant, as if she perceived things long gone. When she spoke at last, her voice was whisper soft. "Through the years, I've lost more of those I loved than I care to count. If this matter of the Otherworld threatens Byren, as it appears, then I feel bound to protect all I can, though it may be little enough—and to put to work any resource in my sphere to do so."

How could I condemn her when I shared her sentiments? Only why did she have to involve *Father*? What did he know?

Using her walking stick as leverage, she straightened. "Nevertheless, you're right—I should have asked your permission before involving your father in your affairs. Or at the least informed you that we could not continue to converse otherwise. I hope in time you'll forgive me."

"I understand why you acted as you did. I just . . . I just need a moment."

"Take whatever time you require. I'll stave off the gentlemen." She retreated toward the dining room.

And I withdrew to the study where I could speak to Wyncourt without being overheard. I rested my forehead against a cool windowpane, seeking calm. "Can you keep our conversations this evening from reaching the servants?"

The air warmed in a way becoming familiar as an affirmative.

"Thank you," I murmured. The goldhearts perched on Ibbie's desk sparked bright with Other, washing over my senses. I moved from the window to stroke their petals, their honey-spice fragrance permeating the air about me, familiar and reassuring.

What now?

I could still make excuses and withdraw, but I'd wanted mortals to understand the danger, and this gathering represented the best chance of that. Lord Blackburn had the ear of the king, he and Thea both had wealth enough to support such a quest, and evidently, Father possessed knowledge that he'd kept hidden. Pulling back now would mean abandoning my own chance for answers. And my best opportunity to protect my family, perhaps. Because if Father was here, he'd become more deeply involved in Other affairs than I ever dreamt. No, the only way was to move forward—and accept what loss might come.

With Jade at my side, I glided into the dining room, where everyone sipped at their wine. Father looked at me, then just as swiftly away, while everyone else pretended not to notice the tension.

As soon as I sat, Danvers motioned for the first course. Thea and Lord Blackburn maintained a light conversation, drawing in Miss Everby from time to time. Of course, we'd not examine the relic until we'd retired from the table—the meal was a facade to cover our true purpose.

I swirled my spoon through the white soup. Though Ibbie had an excellent cook, every bite tasted like ash, and I soon abandoned all attempts to eat, allowing the chatter to swirl about me until Lord Blackburn raised the matter of the missing persons.

A frown tugged at Thea's lips. "What does the Assemblage of Lords have to say about this recent spate of disappearances?"

"A good deal, but none of it particularly insightful. It's clear neither Vigil nor Magistry know how to manage situations where Otherkind might be involved." His grip on his fork tightened. "Which is why the people of Byren deserve the truth."

I rested my hands in my lap. "Do you have evidence that might provide a link between the Otherworld and the recent disappearances?"

"I don't, which means I might be mistaken. But what other explanation is there? They've found no proof of natural causes, despite the resources being thrown at the problem. I knew one of the missing, a melancholy sort." Lord Blackburn lifted his knife. "He seemed different before he vanished. Happier. But also not quite himself. He kept fingering something in his pocket whenever we spoke. It was unusual behavior for him."

"Could you get a glimpse of what he held?"

"A hint of something ivory, no more." His prominent brows lowered. "Might have been nothing besides a new snuff box; he was always a fanatic about the stuff. Could be that I want evidence so badly, I'm imagining what does not exist."

"If the authorities did not keep on burying the evidence that *does* exist, perhaps one would not experience such temptation," Thea muttered. "Still, we must remain open to all theories."

I leaned back in my chair. If some Otherworldly object was involved in the disappearances, then perhaps they did *not* link to Ainslie's binding mark? Was this the theory Mr. Burke pursued? Had he uncovered some new evidence to support it? I chafed at the convention that forbade me from seeking him to ask.

At last, the final course was removed, and we withdrew to the drawing room. I'd no intention of waiting for Father or Lord Blackburn to press me for information or lead the conversation down undesirable paths, yet I could not find the words to begin. After a basilisk, an auvok, a fae lord, and a cursed ruin, how could a simple conversation feel so terrifying?

Father sat in silence, a familiar folio in his lap—his star charts, no doubt—and Miss Everby excused herself, saying she'd withdraw to the study to catch up on correspondence, with my permission, which I granted. Then I could delay no longer. "Thea, you indicated you and Lord Blackburn had found an Otherworldly artifact?"

"Indeed, we did." She gave me an account of a would-be thief and the object he'd attempted to pilfer. "He managed to hand off some documents to his employer, whom we were not able to apprehend, but we found this."

She motioned to Lord Blackburn, who opened a leather satchel and withdrew a permanent fae-light of the sort that had hung on the walls of Kilmere, but this one was resplendent with rich shades of gold and bronze. Darker flecks swirled within, hues far more saturated than those belonging to our world. If any doubt remained about the Redgraves having an Other-worldly connection, the fae-light erased it. A shard of pain lodged in my chest. "This belonged to Cyril Redgrave?"

"It came from his private collection, housed in the Antiquary Society." Lord Blackburn set the orb on the table, and its rich light bathed the room, sharpening the prominent crag of his nose and driving back the shadows.

Wyncourt warmed with approval—no doubt it preferred this to the gaslights Edward had installed. But like the listening stone Mr. Ludne had possessed, this wasn't the sort of item a Collector might be expected to procure. What did that say about the Redgraves? "Have you corresponded with him about it?"

With evident difficulty, Thea wrenched her gaze from the fae-light. "Lord Blackburn and I called and were informed he was away from Avons. His butler refused to speculate on when he might return nor give us an address where he might be reached, so for now, we're doing our best to keep it safe."

I lifted the fae-light, and when I cradled it in my hands, Other washed over me, cool as river water on a summer day, and the light seemed almost to brighten.

Jade raised her head. *It's responding to you.*

I hastily set the orb back on the table. "As it happens, I'm acquainted with Miss Redgrave, and she informed me he's returning this weekend. We've made plans to call on him, since she said that he might vouch for my membership to the Antiquary Society."

"Excellent. I'd thought I might have to request a favor from another member, but this is better by far." Thea gave a decisive nod. "Since Mr. Redgrave and I have no personal acquaintance, I cannot be accused of undue influence."

Lord Blackburn cleared his throat. "Back to the matter at hand—we should return the relic to him at once."

"Perhaps . . . would you consider allowing me to return it?"

"What if the thief returns? Tries to assault you and steal it on the way? No, it's out of the question," Lord Blackburn said.

Father looked up from the stack of star charts in his lap. "Quite so."

I couldn't announce that Jade in true-form would make short work of any assailant, nor that if the thief was mortal, I could protect myself even without her. I *could* point out that the chance of such an assault was statistically almost zero, a point that Father should appreciate, but I suspected that I'd require a more persuasive argument. I straightened. "Perhaps Miss Redgrave would consent to introduce you and Thea when she and I call. You cannot state your purpose to the butler, nor does it seem wise to write something that could be intercepted. Her introduction would assure you are received, even if you cannot declare your intent."

"Yet to speak of the relic with Miss Redgrave present would only draw her into danger," Lord Blackburn said.

"Perhaps, but I have reason to believe that at least some of the Redgraves know a great deal about the Otherworld. I think understanding how many of them do would be helpful."

Father blinked. "But Mr. Redgrave—the young Mr. Redgrave—Caris tells me he courts Ainslie."

"Yes, and his intentions appear serious, which is why I want to know if he has any connection to Other matters."

Father just shook his head, clutching at the arms of the chair as though they were a lifeline to keep him from sinking into treacherous waters.

Meanwhile, Risha perched next to me, her head swiveling from one party to the other with evident interest—perhaps mesmerized by mortals' so-called overindulgence in emotion.

"You'd not wanted to come with us before, Caldwell. Does this change things?" Lord Blackburn said.

"Only if young Redgrave is involved." Father straightened his cuffs so they sat at precise angles, seeming to collect himself in the process. "If we descend en masse, Cyril Redgrave may turn us away. Better if you inform me, then I will address the young man, if I must."

Lord Blackburn slowly nodded. "Very well, then. Miss Caldwell, if you think Miss Redgrave would be amenable to your plan, we shall proceed."

"I'll send along a message by footman this evening to confirm."

"Good." Then his lips firmed. "I must say, you do not seem much alarmed by the discovery of this relic in Avons, Miss Caldwell."

Perhaps I should have feigned unsettledness. The fae-light flickered, swirling with darker shades, as if taunting me with the reminder that we were alike—except *I* was far more likely to provoke fear in mortals, if the truth were known. I looked away. "Alarm won't provide protection against fae."

The air chilled about me—a sign of displeasure? The last thing I needed was to offend my own demesne. I reached out and brushed my hand against the wall, in an attempt to reassure.

Thea rapped her walking stick on the floor. "Hear, hear. Fear will accomplish nothing. We must act."

"What course of action do you pursue?" I asked.

Lord Blackburn lifted the fae-light and tucked it back into his satchel. "We seek sufficient evidence to make a case to the king about the incursion of the Otherworld into Byren—and the dangers inherent to our citizens—in the hope it will prompt him to act for our protection before it's too late."

"Ignorance is always a danger, and right now most are wholly unaware that our protections fail," Thea said.

"To be frank, I'd begun to think everyone was unaware." If they could truly gain the ear of the king, would it spare Byren? Or was it already too late? Never mind, the attempt must be made. "Views on the relationship between the Otherworld and our own are so deeply entrenched that you'll have to provide proof that cannot be denied—more than just this fae-light."

Thea rested her hands in her lap. "I believe you could help with that, if you chose. Am I correct?"

Father ceased shuffling through his star charts and peered at me through his spectacles, the lines about his eyes carved deep.

"Caldwell, you object?" Lord Blackburn asked.

Thea gave an impatient shake of her head.

And Father stood, the papers on his lap scattering across the floor. "It's just . . . I cannot—"

Then he turned and stumbled from the room.

A frown deepened the creases in Lord Blackburn's face. "I told you he'd not take it well, Mrs. Darrington. No man likes to think of endangering his family."

"No woman does either," she said tartly. "But must we ignore the best resource at our disposal? Blind ourselves to the truth?"

"Better to be blind than stubborn as a karzel."

Her eyes flashed, and I pressed to my feet. "Excuse me. I must seek my father."

Once the sounds of their heated discussion faded, I trailed my fingers along the wall. Wyncourt's gentle presence wrapped around me, carrying an impression of Father standing in the library. I wavered, tempted to turn and hide myself in the heart of Wyncourt, where it was peaceful and cool.

Jade chuffed. *Better to have it over with.*

I suppose. With Jade draped over my shoulders like a stole, her confidence bolstering my own, I entered the library. Only one gas lamp had been lit, and it flickered unsteadily, casting eerie shadows in the corners. Father stood next to the shelves, staring sightless at the rows of books, muttering something under his breath.

"Father? Will you . . . tell me what's wrong?"

"What's wrong?" He paced the room. "I've always sought to protect you and your sisters from whatever claimed your mother. Yet instead I find you couldn't trust me with the truth—and I've only my own failings to blame for whatever danger you face."

"You haven't failed."

"No?" A gust of air escaped him. "You should have been able to come to me if you had concerns about the Otherworld or anything else. I may not be a brilliant man, but it's clear even to me that you've collected a great deal of knowledge about the Otherworld. That relic didn't surprise you in the least. You called it a fae-light, which suggests you've seen such things before. Mrs. Darrington tried to tell me, but I didn't want to believe it was true."

"You have your fears. I have my own," I whispered. "Perhaps we can figure them out together."

"How? I can't lose you like I lost your mother." He faltered to a stop in the shadows cast by the lamp. "Whatever you know about the Otherworld, however it has entangled you, I cannot allow your continued involvement."

"I understand you want to keep us safe, but I'm involved in ways that are . . . impossible to change."

"The Vigil already holds concerns about our family. Any hint that you're curious about Otherworldly affairs could give them the leverage they need to claim us." He scrubbed his hands along his trousers. "I haven't been forthright either. You asked about Vigilist Felton and my travels, and . . . there's much I withheld."

"Will you tell me now?" The words tasted sour in my mouth. How could I ask what I wasn't willing to offer?

He nodded. "I was seeking evidence."

"Evidence of what?"

"That something Otherworldly claimed your mother's life."

Wordless, I sank into the nearest chair.

He hovered above me, tugging at his cravat. "Jessa, perhaps I shouldn't have . . ."

"How long have you believed Other had some role in her death?" My voice sounded stilted and distant even to my own ears.

"Since she died." His eyes dulled. "That night, the stars were all wrong—the constellations misplaced, color and hue changed. Over time, I linked these aberrations to Other incursion."

All his attention to star charting and studying the heavens —instead of attending to his family, as he'd done when Mother lived—all his efforts had been to seek the cause of her death, to keep us from harm. I closed in on myself, wrapping my arms about my chest, and Jade climbed on the arm of my chair, her breath warm against my cheek. Somehow, I managed to collect my ragged emotions. "What of Vigilist Felton?"

"He seized the evidence I'd gathered about the signs in the stars marking passage of the Otherworld into our own." He shook his head. "I still don't understand how it is possible, but the proof is clear, even within Avons itself."

Did that mean passings left a trace, the momentary opening between worlds allowing one to bleed into the other? I'd never paid attention, never once looked upward during a passing, but no other explanation made sense. "Perhaps we don't need the stolen evidence."

"What do you mean?"

"Perhaps simply swaying public opinion will suffice. The word of a gentleman and a lord—"

"No." His voice was hoarse. "The Vigil has made it clear—if I speak on this openly, they will come after us. And it won't end well."

Heat swirled through my torso. "Then we shall find other evidence they cannot snatch away, allies they cannot silence."

"It's too dangerous for you to resist them."

"Father, if Other has come for us, then no one will remain untouched. Otherkind will not have mercy if we choose to hide —rather, they will take advantage of our weakness and lack of knowledge. The Vigil is little different." I leaned forward. "This way, we have a chance to set the terms."

"Perhaps—or perhaps you'll place only yourself in the path of destruction. Blackburn lost his family to Otherkind, and it nearly ruined him." He adjusted his spectacles. "I don't have his fortitude. I cannot face the prospect of such a loss."

"Then let's make sure it doesn't happen."

He fell silent for several long minutes. "You've always been like your mother. When she took an idea in her mind, there was no dissuading her." His gaze became unfocused—did he remember Mother, even now? "I don't suppose there's any dissuading you either."

"There's not."

"Then we carry on." He hesitated. "But, Jessa, don't take any unnecessary risks."

I murmured agreement—any risks I must take would be wholly necessary—then together, we left the library and returned to the drawing room. The air still fairly snapped between Thea and Lord Blackburn, his bearing as rigid as a pencil tree and her face as flushed as a coral rose.

Thea inclined her head toward us. "Are matters settled between you?"

"For now, but I was wondering . . . how did the three of you come to investigate together?"

Thea offered a succinct account of how their paths had intersected, starting with the relic, moving through Father's travels to Shepherd's Bush and his Other encounter there, and culminating in a trip to Ashford in search of the truth about the deaths of Lord Blackburn's family.

All these years, and he'd finally found the answers he sought. "So the Vigil deliberately concealed the truth? You're certain?"

"Quite. Coupled with their seizure of Caldwell's evidence, it seems clear they've operated in this mode for some time, perhaps to save face or preserve their power—or perhaps because they believe they're genuinely keeping Byren from the panic that would ensue if it became known their protections failed." His eyes burned like embers in his face. "Miss Caldwell, if you have knowledge, now is the time to share it. What did you find in Kilmere? Did you learn anything there to suggest the Vigil's interest was warranted?"

"I did." I shifted toward Thea. "I must beg your forgiveness for not being forthright earlier. I know you sensed it then, but the park seemed neither the time nor place to discuss the true nature of Kilmere."

She tightened her shawl about her shoulders. "Under the circumstances, I can't condemn caution. What did you learn?"

"The ruins did conceal a serpent, as I said, but it was no ordinary snake." I fixed my gaze on the windows, nightfall making their surfaces black and reflective. "It was a basilisk, and it killed those who broke a fae bargain made generations prior. The slow, painful death it caused gave rise to the legend of the curse—there was an archive hidden in the depths of Kilmere that recounted the details."

A collective inhale marked this revelation. Then Lord Blackburn drew himself up. "This record. Could you present it to the king?"

"I'm afraid it would be difficult. It was written in the fae tongue. I had assistance in translation, but given the lengths the Vigil has gone to conceal other evidence, they could easily discredit it by saying the translation was false, if they wished. Not many could gainsay them."

"What of the body of the basilisk?"

"It was destroyed."

He grimaced. "So we're back where we started, with knowledge and no way to prove it."

"What of the ruin itself?" Thea clutched the arm of her chair, leaning forward. "Do signs of fae occupation remain? Perhaps if you allowed select members of the Antiquary Society access, and they formed their own conjectures and began to publish their findings, it could pave the way for the truth."

"They would discover much to bewilder them, but without any framework of understanding, I don't believe they'd identify it as a fae ruin."

Lord Blackburn downed a gulp of wine. "How could a fae ruin and a bargain of this nature pass from memory?"

"I believe it relates to the Forgotten War—and all that has vanished from our knowledge of that era—but I cannot prove it."

"Ah, yes. Lord Blackburn and I have worked together on dating the materials we do have—the logbook and the letters and several other items in his collection." Thea leaned into the chair cushions. "It seems conclusive that they issue back to the era in which Kilmere was constructed, so it would follow."

"Could this sway the king?" Father asked.

"It's evidence of past interaction between our world and the Other, yet not proof positive that it's happening now." I shifted Jade on my lap.

"Still, if we can understand what happened then, it will instruct us on what happens now." An eager light kindled in Thea's eyes. "Then perhaps we shall trace our proof."

Lord Blackburn shook his head. "Ever the antiquarian."

"Thea may be biased, but surely if we understand the Forgotten War, what happened then, and what has changed, it will tell us a great deal." Wyncourt creaked gently at my words—agreement or contemplation?

"Then I suppose we must hope that Redgrave will be forthcoming about where and how he acquired this relic, and if there are any more such devices." Lord Blackburn glanced at Father. "Caldwell, your star theories could also lead to more hard evidence. You can't be all places at once. Perhaps we could set some men to assist?"

Father shuffled through his charts, unearthing what appeared to be several letters beneath. "I could send them to investigate the reports I receive and document their findings. Then I could follow up on the most promising."

I tensed. However hypocritical it made me, I didn't like the idea of Father venturing near passings, not when he'd no protection. Yet he was determined to take the risk, so I swallowed my fear.

Thea looked at me in the way Ibbie used to, with a sort of maternal perceptiveness. "What is it you mean to do?"

My throat tightened. "Continue to learn what I can. I have a feeling that evidence won't be as hard to come by as we might wish."

"I don't know whether to hope you're correct or pray that you're not." She grasped her walking stick. "Shall we send a summons to convene here once more when any of us find something worth sharing?"

Though I voiced my agreement with the others, unease cratered my stomach. I'd held back far more than I'd divulged, and still I felt uncomfortably exposed. Had I said too much or far too little? If Riven were here, he'd say I'd shared a great deal more than I should, yet much of what I'd withheld intimately concerned Father.

And I was left with the unpleasant question: was I trying to spare Father the pain of the truth—or myself?

When I arrived home, the song of the nightspire drifted from the garden into the footwalk, laced with a sort of savage joy that sent shards of ice down my spine. Despite the late hour, I changed course at once. I rounded the house, passing through the discomfiting iron gate into the garden proper, and the glow of the gaslights faded, leaving only the moon to illumine my way. The scents of rose and lavender hung heavy in the air, along with the faint trace of something more acrid and unpleasant. What?

Jade sniffed. *It's blood.*

From where?

Among the nightspire.

A swift connection with the ivy assured me that the nightspire hadn't left its bounds, so what had happened? I hurried down the path and found Dryden staring at the glamoured section of the garden, the moonlight cold on his face. He didn't move, didn't acknowledge my presence in any way. The muscles of my back tightened. Had the glamour somehow mesmerized him? I edged forward. "Dryden, is something wrong?"

He startled, then lowered his gaze, shaking his head.

"If there's something troubling you, you're at liberty to speak."

"No trouble. None at all." Yet his hand crept to his chest, as if something pained him.

"In that case, perhaps you should retire. Morning will come early." And I wanted to examine the nightspire.

He scuffed at the ground with a boot. Whatever he claimed, something *was* troubling him. At last, he looked up. "If you find a rabbit, a small gray one . . . will you send for me? She's gone missing."

At once, my stomach twisted. The cruel notes thrilled in my ears, and I peered through the glamour. She was there. She'd worked her way through the cage of ivy, perhaps beckoned by the nightspire. The thorns had shredded her flesh, and her lifeless form remained snared within.

I pressed my fingers to my lips, swallowing a swell of nausea. Dryden had loved this rabbit, and Other had claimed it. Other that *I'd* brought into the garden. Other that I'd contained, but not fully enough to protect the most vulnerable. All I could do was nod—perhaps once he left, I could fetch her body and give him closure.

When he disappeared, I stepped over to the cage of ivy, strengthening it, bidding it to keep out all living things, no matter how small. In so doing, I found several other small creatures snared within the nightspire—lured by its song?—their deaths taunting me.

Yet if I tried to uproot Other from the garden, there would be nothing discreet about it. The power woven into the nightspire would surely put up a fight. And what if removing it triggered something worse? I would wait and take counsel in the morning—when my mind wasn't muddied with emotion and exhaustion.

For now, I'd simply seek to free the rabbit. If her body remained hidden, Dryden would always wonder, and he deserved the chance to mourn his pet properly. I sent the ivy weaving among the nightspire, pressing back its hold, green and gold weaving among the sparking dusky purple, my surroundings fading as the songs of the plants swelled to drown all else. When my awareness returned, the rabbit rested at my feet.

Choking back instinctive revulsion, I gently lifted the broken form and set it near the fountain, well out of the imprisoned nightspire's grasp. Then I slipped into the glasshouse, with Risha bobbing alongside and Jade following as a rear guard. Once inside, I collapsed on a bench, staring down at my gloved hands.

A small splotch darkened one finger, a trace of blood that testified to loss. I drew one unsteady breath, then another. I'd cried far too often of late; I refused to indulge again.

Yet it was too much, all of it. I curled up on the bench, forgoing proper posture, since there was no one to witness. How often must I fail to meet expectations? Dryden's sorrow mingled with Father's disappointment and Aunt Caris's fear and all the pains I'd caused or failed to prevent. I tucked my hand beneath my skirt so the bloodstain no longer glared at me.

I couldn't pour all this out to my sisters, couldn't burden them when they struggled with their own fears. What then? I inhaled the fragrance of sweet orange, which drove back the coppery scent of blood. Riven always listened, even when we disagreed. Perhaps if we made peace, it would lift some of this dreadful weight. "Bright one, will you go for Riven?"

At once, Risha fluttered upward.

"Wait."

She halted midair, her wings sparking bright.

I shouldn't ask him to come, not for this—or should I? The thought of having to speak with him next under Aunt Melisina's chaperonage, of feigning courtship with nothing resolved between us, decided the matter. "Just make sure not to trouble him if he's busy—or sleeping. And tell him it's not urgent, that he's only to come if it's no bother."

Jade chuffed softly. *I think you should add several more disclaimers, just in case.*

Oh, be quiet. This is difficult enough as it is. Why would he even want to come, after I ran out on our last conversation?

Excellent question. Jade's eyes glowed bright in the blackness. *I believe he will. But why? It's an interesting conundrum.*

Risha's light flared even brighter. "I will carry out my errand with pleasure. Some sylphs aid assignations often, but this is my first."

"It's not an assignation." At least not in the manner her tone implied. "He's fae and . . ."

So was I.

"Just . . . please don't imply anything of the sort."

The tiniest gleam entered Risha's eyes. "So I shall not say you've missed him a great deal and desire his company?"

Her summation of the situation held too much truth for comfort. I sat upright, nearly knocking over the potted camellia behind me. "No. In fact, don't say anything. Just—I'll give you a note."

Though I'd hoped in time Risha would grow more comfortable with me, I'd never dreamt she concealed such a mischievous streak. I drew a piece of paper from my sketchbook, its ivory surface glowing soft in the moonlight. What could I possibly say? I'd keep it simple, make amends if I could.

Riven,

Whatever our differences in perspective, I know you meant only to help by bringing up the matter of my family. I'm sorry I did not fully hear you out.

Jessa

With any good fortune, he'd be occupied on some matter of business and Risha could leave the message and go, and I could hope that the missive would smooth over any remaining tension —however unsatisfying it would be compared to his compan-ionship. "Perhaps it's best if you leave this where he'll see it in the morning, bright one?"

"Yes, yes. I shall heed your desires." With that, Risha snatched up the note and fluttered away.

Jade stretched out on the bench alongside me. *You could have an "assignation," as Risha calls it, you know. Could marry one day, now that you understand the truth of your nature.*

But what mortal would accept it?

I wasn't suggesting you wed a mortal. I'd not see you suffer the heartbreak of his eventual death.

Of course. Since I was fae, why *would* I marry a mortal? Except for the fact I desired to remain in this world, stay close to my family . . .

Did Jade's comment suggest she agreed with Riven that I must prepare myself to sever ties with the mortal world? Everyone had an expectation of what I must do—and of necessity I would disappoint some. Perhaps all of them. The camellia drooped, as if my grief became its own. I removed my stained gloves and caressed its glossy leaves. I should go inside, and yet despite the presence of the nightspire, the garden offered some haven.

I closed my eyes and sank into the gentle song of the camellia until a wave of sun-drenched power nearly knocked me over. What had Risha done?

With the light of passing still swirling about him, Riven strode forward. Then he stopped, assessing me. "Risha was emphatic that you did not want to see me. Yet your note suggested otherwise. Which is it?"

"It wasn't that I didn't want to see you . . ." Warmth crept up my chest. I had desired it, far more than I *should*. "I simply meant . . . I told her I didn't want to trouble you at this hour for a matter that wasn't urgent."

He raised a brow. "You also informed her that you were not interested in an assignation?"

"I didn't say that." The heat rose to flood my face. "That is, I did, but I didn't mean . . ."

A faint flicker of amusement lit his features. "I wasn't sure we were speaking at all, let alone having not-assignations. But I wasn't sleeping, so it was easy enough to come now. There's less chance of interruption at this hour."

"I—thank you." I hesitated. "I should not have run out on our last conversation."

He lounged against the wall of the glasshouse, his bearing relaxed, his gaze intent. "I didn't expect you'd receive that without emotion."

Suddenly, a few tears spilled over. If he'd been angry about what transpired, it would have been far easier to restrain them. He handed me a silk handkerchief, rich with the scents of fir and sunlight, and I swiped at my cheeks.

"What happened?"

The events of the past day poured from me with dangerous ease. At last, I straightened, checking the flow. "You must be more than weary of hearing my woes. I didn't intend to say all that."

"I'm given to understand that unburdening one's soul to one's friends is a convention of this world."

"That's true." The camellia gently brushed my neck. "But ordinarily, it goes both ways. You never speak of what troubles you."

"Perhaps nothing does."

It wasn't a denial, rather a deflection. Fae did not divulge emotion, but I no longer believed him incapable of it. So why did he refuse to reveal anything of a deeper nature? I leaned forward. "Is that true?"

He shrugged. "Fae don't unburden their souls."

"Why not?"

"Because divulging unnecessary information offers weapons to potential foes. Gives others leverage they should not possess."

I rocked back. "You think I would use something you say against you?"

"I didn't say that. Only that it's a dangerous habit to adopt."

"Yet you've not advised me to stop."

"Would you listen?"

"If you told me you did not want to hear, of course I

would." Suddenly chilled, I rubbed my hands along my exposed arms. "I don't want to impose."

His eyes warmed, hints of gold surfacing. "You're not."

Outside the glasshouse, a rustle sounded, and I tensed. What now?

A moment later, Ada called softly, "Jessa? Are you there?"

What was she doing in the garden at this hour? Though she knew Riven's true nature, I didn't feel inclined to try to explain his presence. Evidently, he shared my view, for he'd already moved back in the glasshouse and concealed himself with glamour.

I swung open the door. "I'm here."

She hurried in, the soft light of the oil lamp she carried spilling over her face and turning her ivory gown to a soft cream.

"What happened? Is it Ainslie again?"

"No, she's sleeping." Her lips trembled, and she collapsed to the bench.

"What is it, then?"

"Oh, Jessa, I'm so very selfish."

"I cannot imagine a world where that's true." I sank down beside her.

"But it is. Ainslie suffers from the most dreadful of afflictions, and all I can think about is that when she's freed, I'll lose her." Her eyes flooded. "It's ridiculous. I should only be concerning myself with undoing her bargain—and of course, that *is* what I want beyond all else—but this evening while you were out, Mr. Redgrave called. She loves him, I know she does. And if the best of all possible scenarios unfolds, and he can accept the truth of her past once she's freed from her bargain, then she'll still leave us. Her first allegiance will be to him, as it should be . . . . and nothing will ever be the same. I don't know how I can even think such dreadful, self-absorbed things, but I can't seem to stop."

Doubtless it was easier to consider the possibility of losing Ainslie to Mr. Redgrave—and a happy future—than to think about her bargain-holder claiming her life. It didn't escape me that she'd said *when* Ainslie was freed, though that wasn't a given. Though our sense of loss when Ainslie wed would be real, how much of this turmoil sprang from her mind attempting to ward off greater fears? I wrapped my arm around her, and she nestled her head into my shoulder.

"The two of you have been halves of a whole since birth." Their bond had pained me more than once, since I'd yearned for someone to understand me in the same way. "Of course it hurts to consider her absence, and it's not self-absorbed to mourn that loss. Yet I cannot think her love for you will diminish, only change."

As did everything else around us. How would Ada feel if she knew I must consider leaving? I glanced up. Through the swirl of glamour, Riven remained completely still, but something in his expression suggested that whatever his counsel, he was not so detached as he claimed—even from mortal affairs.

She sniffed. "At least, now that we've no secrets, I don't have to worry about you disappearing again without a word."

I tensed.

And her head lifted. "I don't, do I?"

The slats of the bench dug into my side. "I've no intention of leaving without notice."

"Good." The lamplight reflected off the walls of the glasshouse, brightening her face. "You don't need to keep carrying things on your own, now that we know the truth."

She said as much, yet would she ever understand my reluctance to abandon my affinities? If I chose my fae nature, I might have to abandon my family, disappoint all their expectations. But if I did not . . . I straightened. "If Ainslie wakes and finds you gone, she'll be worried."

Her eyes widened. "You're right. I'll return at once. Are you coming?"

"Not yet, but soon."

She stood, gently brushing an escaped curl from my face. "You shouldn't sit here in the dark. I'll leave you the lamp."

When she vanished, Riven released the glamour. But before

he could speak, the song of the nightspire swelled stronger, throbbing in my temples. Upon the canvas of my mind it emblazoned an image of Ainslie impaled on its thorns. And I stifled a gasp.

"Jessa?"

I became aware that I'd sprung to my feet. "It's the night-spire. Tonight, it seized and killed Dryden's pet rabbit, and despite the barrier holding it back, its song is strengthening. Then I had an image of Ainslie snared—could it force such an impression into my mind?"

"A liminal working could, and it bears many."

"I see." Until I'd encountered the nightspire, it had never occurred to me the multitude of ways a plant could be used as an offensive weapon.

Riven glanced toward the shadows beyond the glasshouse walls. "Do you want it destroyed?"

Unlike when he'd intervened with Ainslie, this wasn't an issue with immediate life-or-death consequences—save for the poor rabbit that had already been claimed. If there was a chance the bargain-holder remained unaware of Riven's involvement, I did not want to give up that small advantage. "Do you believe my workings will hold for now?"

"Yes. If it could have broken them, it would have done far more than claim a rabbit. But you'll have to keep a close watch for any sign it's getting stronger and act if it presents a threat."

"Very well. We will wait and hope it does not." Only time would tell if the choice was wisdom or folly. I drew a breath laced with the soft fragrances of camellia and princess-of-the-night. "There's one more thing. Aunt Melisina informed me that she . . . strongly suggested an outing to Telford's tomorrow. Whatever pretense we must present my family, I hope you know you're not obliged to satisfy her demands."

The light of the lamp played across his features, softening their sharp planes. "I wouldn't have agreed if I felt it an incon-venience."

"Still, Aunt Melisina will expect . . . that is, she believes you're sincere."

He inclined his head. "That is the idea behind a charade, is it not?"

"Of course, but . . ." I glanced down, fidgeting with the silk handkerchief. Just how far did he intend to play along? When I'd agreed that this pretense of courtship was the logical choice, I never dreamed it would force the rise of so many discomfiting emotions.

He assessed me. "If the idea makes you uncomfortable, I can make my excuses to your aunt."

Oh, I was being ridiculous. I straightened. "If it's no trouble to you, then I'm willing."

The light of passing began to flare about him. "Good. Then I'll call tomorrow."

Why did I feel a flutter of anticipation at the words? This was no different than the countless other occasions we'd explored Avons or elsewhere together. Aside from the expectations of my family.

After the passing faded, Jade eyed me. *What of your expectations and desires?*

I brushed some fallen petals from the bench alongside me. *Regarding what?*

Your own future. The prospect of a true relationship, at some point.

How could I consider what I desired, with everything so uncertain? The gentle songs of the garden washed over me. I had to admit she was right about one thing—now that I understood myself as fae, rather than afflicted with fae-touch, a future that included love and marriage wasn't an impossible prospect, as I'd once believed. Even so, the matter held endless layers of complication.

As we've established, I cannot marry a mortal, and if I considered a future with a fae lord, what then? Would it force me to abandon this world altogether? I could not endure that fate. I stared into the darkness beyond the glasshouse walls. *Besides, there's no reason to suppose I would be a desirable match by fae standards, whatever they are—I'm far more a liability than anything else, with no court to call my own and little understanding of my abilities. In any case, my attention should be on Ainslie and her survival, not far-distant hypotheticals.*

For now, perhaps. But such things cannot be ignored forever.

As I could find no fitting response, I collected the lamp Ada had left, and we emerged into the night.

CHAPTER 19

Though I'd retired late, I woke early the following morning. Despite my insistence to Jade that any notion of future relationships must be pressed from my mind, her words returned to me upon waking, leaving me absurdly unsettled. I did my best to keep the thoughts from reaching her and prevent them from distracting me from the matters at hand, snatching up my simplest gown and dressing as swiftly as possible before hurrying down toward the garden to check the nightspire. I stopped only long enough to dispatch Ives with a note for Elodie, something I'd neglected to carry through the night before, as the nightspire incident had distracted me. In the message, I asked if she'd be willing to have Thea and Lord Blackburn accompany us on the morrow, offering my apologies for the late notice. Hopefully, her good nature would incline her to accept the request.

When I emerged into the cool, brilliant morning, I found Dryden bent over a tiny grave. Part of me wanted to flee from his grief, but the other part felt bound to honor it—and own my part in it. I moved closer. "I take it you found your rabbit."

"Aye."

The strip of exposed earth condemned my missteps. "I . . . I'm very sorry."

His eyes lowered, but he only shrugged. "Strong take the weak. It's the way of things."

"Not always."

"When's it not true?" Suddenly, he lifted a blazing black gaze. "Those that have power force what they want, and who's to say otherwise?"

"Sometimes those with strength use it to protect, as I heard you did, in Shepherd's Bush with the wolpertinger."

"Got no strength, not enough to do what needs doing." He swiped at his eyes, then stalked off into the house.

My shoulders slumped. As far as I knew, he'd no one in the world except for the animals he doted upon. While some might dismiss the death of a rabbit, he appeared to feel it as keenly as I would the loss of Jade.

The nightspire rustled, all dusky purple and thorned, its bloodthirsty song mocking me—shaming me for my fears of revealing my fae nature, of upsetting expectations, of making a mistake due to ignorance. I frowned at it. Its song had strengthened yet again, though no external change had taken place. And yet . . .

With quick steps I made my way over to the oak, whose roots reached wide in the garden, and I touched its rough bark, drawing an image in my mind of the nightspire. At once, it poured into me an angry, pained sort of melody and a vivid impression of dark purple roots tangling far underground, relentlessly questing toward the house. When Riven had examined it last night, it had made no advance. How had it come so far in just a few hours? Had the blood taken fueled it? Or did it merely respond to new instruction?

Never mind that—clearly the time for caution had gone. I didn't know what would happen if the roots reached the house, nor did I want to find out. The fae who bid it was stronger than I, no doubt, her workings powerful enough that I might not be able to unmake them, but this was *my* garden, and the plant an interloper in it. Surely that gave me some advantage?

I turned to Risha. "Bright one, will you keep watch? Make sure no one enters the garden?"

When she nodded, I stroked Jade's head. *You too. If anyone stirs—even within the house—I want to know.*

I would try to conceal my actions with glamour, yet I knew so very little about it, I couldn't be sure it would work. Still, I must make the attempt. I fixed in my mind an image of the garden as it should be—at peace and unmarred—and projected it outward, then stepped toward the nightspire, sensing its roots spread through much of the garden. To remove it would require coordinating many plants beyond my physical reach—something I'd never done. Yet I refused to fail in this.

I sank down to the earth, rooting my fingers into the moss beneath the oak, feeling the vibrancy of every living thing that belonged in the garden thrumming in and around and through me, strong and exuberant.

Below their melodies throbbed the deep, dark malice of the nightspire. Already it had strangled the roots of some of the smaller plants, and even now, it advanced to assault others beneath the earth. A bitter purplish scent filled my lungs, and my heart beat a rapid tattoo in my chest.

Some sort of dreadful awareness emanated from root and vine. It watched. No, someone else watched through its workings—the bargain-holder? Could she do such a thing? Or did my fear drive me to vain imagination?

Never mind, if I withdrew now, I'd be conceding defeat. With effort, I tuned out the militant notes of the nightspire, attending instead to the deep, resonant song of the oak, the cool, quiet hum of the lavender, the vibrant, pricking pulse of the rose. Beneath the soil, these and more surged forward.

Strong.

Determined.

Ready to uproot what did not belong.

The nightspire twisted and spiraled like a serpent, but its roots could gain no further hold in the garden. Glorious filaments of light filled the earth beneath and around it, carried by the roots of my plants, the connection so deep that it nearly burst my chest.

The earth shuddered beneath my hands, one final massive heave, and then stillness, quiet. I couldn't move, couldn't even open my eyes; I simply collapsed onto the mossy expanse, soft seta caressing my face.

Perhaps I'd done as I feared and played into the hands of the one who sent the nightspire, showing her more than was wise. But I could not regret it.

With effort, I pressed upright, then staggered over to the fountain and collapsed on the stone ledge. My breath caught at the disorder before me. While all my plants had returned to their proper positions, exposed soil sliced in jagged swaths across the garden, everywhere the nightspire roots had been wrenched from the ground. Its vines still writhed angrily, seeking some purchase. Though it had been momentarily vanquished, it wasn't enough—it must be destroyed.

I shuddered at the thought. How?

Risha hovered at the edge of the fountain, her light sparkling off its waters. She'd once offered to burn out Mr. Ludne's eyes— what more could her flame do? "Bright one, could your fire consume the nightspire without spreading to destroy the garden or anything else?"

"Yes."

"Then please, will you?"

A fierce glee lit her face. "Yes, yes!"

Searing light poured from her, as potent as a sunbeam condensed through a microlens, and the nightspire burst into flame. Somehow, she concentrated only on the individual roots and shoots of nightspire, her flame not hurting as much as a blade of grass below, an act that defied the logic of this world.

Yet it wasn't exactly inconspicuous. I did my best to use the brightness of the morning and the glamour of the garden to shield the truth from the outside world.

When the nightspire was finally consumed, some of the tension knotted within released, leaving me indescribably weary. I pushed off the stone ledge and collapsed on the bench in the glasshouse, falling into a sort of half-waking, half-sleeping state as the sweet orange and camellia murmured low in my ears.

When I finally made my way withindoors, I found Holden ushering Dreda into the house. Her usual hesitancy of demeanor had disappeared; she carried herself with a more upright posture, her hazel eyes sparking with determination.

"Dreda!" I pulled her into an embrace, and as I did, a pricking sensation of Other swept over me. My words of welcome died in my throat.

"I'm glad I found you first of the family, and I hope you don't mind my lack of notice. I figured by the time I sent word, I could be here and without the expense of the post, but Miss Jessa, I must speak to you in private." She drew back, clutching her valise. "Something happened while I—"

Aunt Caris bustled into the corridor. "Miss Twells! I thought I heard your voice! We couldn't be more delighted to have you home. You've been sorely missed."

Color rose to her cheeks, washing out her freckles. "I'm glad to be back."

I was thankful for her presence as well, only what had happened to her? As Aunt Caris plied Dreda with questions about her journey, I studied her for any signs of harm. The sleeves of her gown concealed any possible binding mark, and I could perceive no glamour about her.

Yet she kept her bag firmly at her side, when it would have been more sensible to rest it on the floor. When she'd first come to stay, she'd clung to her valise in a similar fashion, but that time she'd emanated no sensation of Other. Did she conceal something within it? Some fae artifact, perhaps? I couldn't fathom how she could have stumbled across such a thing, but neither could I dismiss the possibility.

"Let me send for Ives." Aunt Caris offered her a warm smile. "Are you hungry? You must be—the food served at inns often leaves much to be desired."

"That's very kind, Miss Caldwell, but I don't need anything just yet. And there's no sense in troubling Ives—I can fetch this to my room and freshen up a bit while I'm at it." Dreda clutched her valise a bit closer, as though prepared to defend her claim.

She rarely gainsaid anyone; she was more likely to accept a meal she didn't want than to proclaim a lack of hunger. Did that mean she was determined to claim a moment of privacy to talk? If not, I certainly was. "I'll come with you."

Aunt Caris gave an approving smile, then patted Dreda on the shoulder. "You're to take all the time you need today to recuperate from your travels. Though I must say, I'm glad you've returned. With Mr. Redgrave in earnest about Ainslie, and Lord Riven pursuing his suit of Jessa, we could use your assistance."

Dreda murmured a reply, and I followed her up the stairs, refraining from endless speculation with difficulty. As we approached her bedchamber, I said, "I share Aunt Caris's sentiments—I'm quite glad you're with us once more."

"As am I." She secured the door behind us. "I can think of nothing more pleasant than to be about an interesting task again."

"Was your stay with your family so very difficult?"

Her gaze lowered. "More so than I'd hoped. But what of Lord Riven? Your aunt seems pleased."

"Both of them are." Before she could press further, I said, "But I'd like to hear more of your trip."

She hesitated, slowly removing her hat and gloves. Though I wanted answers, some things couldn't be rushed.

Jade hopped up on the bed and began grooming herself. *Sometimes the governances preventing me from peering into minds at will are very tiresome.*

Patience never hurt anyone. Unbidden, my thoughts drifted back to Riven. I'd give a good deal to know what he was truly thinking when he'd agreed to Aunt Melisina's scheme.

Finally, Dreda collapsed into a chair, a soft sigh escaping her. "My sister-in-law—Hildie—I believe she expected me to abandon my position with your household to tend her. She was most displeased when I refused."

"Did you want to stay?"

"She is the sort that . . . doesn't make life easy." Her fingers tightened on the handles of her valise. "I . . . I worried that it was my duty to remain with them, only they don't need me, not truly. They have the funds to retain servants, just difficulty keeping them. Do you think me very dreadful that I did not want to stay?"

"On the contrary, I respect your courage in choosing your course." *Particularly when I wavered in regard to my own.*

"I've seen you stand up for what you believe you're responsible for time and again, Miss Jessa, and it gave me courage. I know it's a small thing, but I gave my word I'd act as chaperone so you could do as you must, and I don't mean to go back on it." Dreda set the valise on the table alongside her. "All the same, I hope you'll still have me after you hear what happened."

I closed the distance between us. "Dreda, compared to confrontations with high fae, whatever you must confess can't be so very dreadful."

"I wish I could believe that. I know above all you want to keep your family safe, yet I . . . I did not know what else to do."

My pulse quickened. "What is it you've done?"

"I've brought a nisi to live here."

Oh.

Jade stopped licking her fur mid-stroke. *How very unexpected.*

I breathed out. *Yet it could have been far worse.* I supposed it was more my fault than hers, since I'd filled her mind with tales of the nisi's kindly nature . . . and it *did* explain the death grip on her valise. "Have you stowed it in your bag, by chance?"

"I have. You see, she traveled beside me glamoured, but I thought you might be able to see her when others could not, like you did the creature that afflicted me, and I didn't want you to take fright before I could explain." Her grip on the handles tightened. "So she agreed to enter my bag until I told you the whole tale, and I hope you'll consider letting her stay, because I've given my word. I know I had no right to do so, since this isn't my home, not truly, but I couldn't just leave her and—"

"Why don't you draw a breath and start from the beginning."

She settled back in the chair, regaining composure. "It all started with Hildie. She's prone to attacks of nerves, during which things are very . . . difficult for her."

And everyone around her, unless I missed my guess. As the spinster in the family, Dreda was expected to cater to the whims of her family members—which was doubtless why her refusal to remain angered them.

"That's why I felt obliged to go." She swallowed hard. "When I arrived, I found Hildie in a near-hysterical state, and it seemed to me more than her usual complaints. She was convinced that something unnatural was happening in the household, though my brother gave her accounts no credit. When I found out Hildie had removed the household fountain for interfering with her view of the lake, I thought about what you said—that nisi turn malicious if slighted. And removing the fountain seemed a sight worse than giving no payment. So I set myself to search for any nisi, and after a time, I found Morwen. I thought she might want jewels and such, like the one at Denby Hall, but thankfully she only wanted songs. I've spent many an hour singing lullabies to fractious children, so it seemed a simple enough request to fulfill."

"And how did you come to bring it here?"

"Hildie would never admit to her existence, much less consider restoring the fountain. So I thought it best to bring her where she could be treated well. I hoped she'd protect this home and leave my family in peace." An anxious look hollowed her face. "But if I've done wrong . . ."

"On the contrary—I'll welcome any protections that might

be offered, however small." I stepped closer to the table. "Can I meet her?"

Dreda unlatched the valise, and the faint scents of cinnamon and clove drifted from within. "Morwen, you can come out."

"No." A muffled voice emerged from the bag.

I bent over the valise. "I give you my word you are safe and welcome here."

A small head popped above the edge. Unlike the nisi I'd met in Denby Hall, this one possessed wiry spouts of pinkish hair. Her features were a bit softer than the one I'd met before, but her eyes were just as enormous, her ears every bit as long and triangular. No bangles adorned her limbs; instead she was draped in an assortment of vividly colored fabrics that produced a rather dazzling effect. She surveyed Risha and Jade, then frowned at Dreda. "Did not tell me—"

Quiet, small one. Jade's voice resounded forcefully. *Your mortal is ignorant of our presence, and you shall not tell her, unless you wish this household utterly overset.*

The nisi's eyes widened slightly.

Correct. Jade must be responding to whatever reply the nisi had made. *She does not know of my mistress's true nature either. But you will find my mistress fair in her dealings and this home a haven to you. You may hold your silence and stay—or go—as you choose.*

After a moment, the nisi gave a quick nod. "Here will be my home."

"We're pleased to welcome you." I studied the small fae as she perched on the edge of the table, swinging her legs. "I believe it is common for nisi to remain concealed in mortal households?"

Morwen gave a vigorous nod.

"Will you permit me to inform my sisters of your presence also? My eldest sister makes beautiful music."

She clapped her hands in childlike glee. "Meet them now?"

"Of course." I nodded and hurried to fetch them, lifting Jade into my arms as I left the room. *Thank you for intervening.*

She nudged my chin. *You could not very well address her before Dreda.*

My stomach twisted. *No, I could not.*

I found Ada at the pianoforte, Ainslie turning the music for her. I collected them both, informing them of the situation as we ascended the stairs.

Ada shook her head. "After this, I believe we shall be impervious to surprise."

However uncertain she'd appeared at first, upon introduction, Ada cooed over Morwen, who appeared to bask in the attention. In short order, she informed Ada that she would dwell next to her bedchamber—but that this house needed a great deal of setting in order, and she must be about it at once.

With that, she darted from the room, glamour woven tight about her.

"Well." Ainslie appeared slightly dazed. "It seems we're destined to invite Other into our lives at every turn."

Dreda's gaze darted swiftly between us, but she made no inquiry.

"Perhaps if they were all as small and darling as that one, we should not mind." Ada turned to Dreda. "If you're not too weary, would you like to accompany me to the milliner this afternoon? I'm to pick up a hat, and I'll see if I can get some silk scraps for Morwen as well. She seems like she'd enjoy them."

"I'd like that, if only I can freshen up first." Dreda scrubbed at a smudge on her skirt. "Miss Jessa, Miss Ainslie, will you accompany us?"

I shook my head. "Lord Riven means to call for me this afternoon."

"Then do you require my accompaniment?"

"No, Aunt Melisina intends to chaperone herself." I brushed a small scrap of colored fabric left by the nisi from the table's surface. "Though I confess I'd rather your company, you should go with Ada. And Ainslie?"

"I . . . I think I'll remain behind this time." Ainslie looked far paler than her wont, as if someone had taken a watercolor wash to her features. "I'd like to catch up on my correspondence."

The lines about Dreda's eyes crinkled with concern. "That's not like you, Miss Ainslie. Do you feel quite well?"

"Just a bit fatigued." She flashed a bright smile. "A quiet afternoon will restore me."

Yet her words sounded forced, and a pang of doubt pierced my soul. How much longer could she endure?

As the appointed hour for Riven's arrival drew near, I made a concerted effort to press my fears over Ainslie's plight from my mind—indeed, as I dressed, she insisted I do so, just as she'd insisted I required her assistance to prepare. And despite the fact the outing was meant to further a pretense, an unexpected eagerness blossomed in me as she helped me with my hair.

"You have not kept much company with gentlemen, not in the way society holds ordinary. You cannot count solving mysteries with Lord Riven and Mr. Burke, not for this." She tucked a jeweled comb into my curls, then stepped back, considering. "If you intend to convince Aunt Melisina your interest in Lord Riven is genuine, then you mustn't appear worried and distracted. He should absorb all your attention."

"But—"

She shook her head. "I'm more thankful than I can say for all you're doing on my behalf, yet even you cannot force a new avenue of investigation to open. And your worry won't ensure my safety, however much we might wish it." Her gaze met mine in the mirror. "I'll be here when you return, and I expect a full report."

I studied her closely in the reflective glass. "You will be careful?"

"Of course. I'll keep company with Aunt Caris. If we're right that the bargain won't force me to betray myself before others, then I should be fine." She adjusted the comb, then rummaged in my clothes press, examining possible hats. "With Lord Riven . . . It *is* just pretense, isn't it?"

"Why do you ask?"

"Because Aunt Melisina was right, he gave a most convincing display—just the right amount of interest, without any overeagerness." Her hand tightened around the brush. "He wouldn't try to . . . force you into anything?"

The note of fear in her voice tugged at my heart. Riven represented Other, and to Ainslie, everything Other symbolized danger. I turned to face her. "Of course not. Fae charm can be very persuasive, but in this case, it serves our cause. We'd agreed upon this charade before we left Withern as a way to justify his involvement in our lives as we try to find your bargain-holder. There's no coercion involved."

"It was bad enough that Lord Bradford determined he'd have Ada, regardless of her feelings in the matter, but if someone like Lord Riven made such a choice—how could we stop him?" Her shoulders drew inward. "I suppose I cannot help but worry, since you're undertaking all this on my behalf."

"Ainslie, I promise there's no pressure nor anything unto-ward taking place." I caught her hand and gave it a small squeeze. "You need have no fears on that score."

She handed me a hat. "Then you should make up your mind to enjoy the afternoon. There's a reason Telford's is a favorite for courting couples, and you can content yourself that you're convincing our aunts of the necessity of keeping Lord Riven involved in your life."

Which was of no small importance. Their approval made everything easier and removed the need for undue glamour. I wrapped her in a fierce hug and felt her shudder slightly.

"If you don't go down you'll be late." She pulled away, a true dimpled smile flashing across her face. "Aunt Melisina may be softening, but still, it's best to avoid stirring her wrath."

I laughed. "Truer words were never spoken."

Arm in arm, we descended the stairs, Jade and Risha alongside us, Kiran hovering near Ainslie's shoulder. Once we entered the drawing room, both my aunts began to offer a long list of instructions and cautions, until I began to feel certain I would make some dreadful misstep. I shook my head. It was ridiculous to feel nervous about this. Whatever my aunts might think, Riven didn't expect me to act the part of a proper young lady as the society of Byren dictated. He never had. If we could face auvok and curses and ancient fae strongholds together, then iced creams at Telford's should be of no concern.

You seem to be trying terribly hard to convince yourself.

I lifted Jade into my arms, her bulk a shield. *Well, Ainslie is right. I'm not accustomed to this sort of thing.*

We'd be on public display and under private scrutiny, a fact which weighed on my mind so much that when Riven stepped into the room I found myself irrationally flushing. That clearly pleased *both* my aunts and made me want to sink into the floor. Yet soon, the sunlit warmth of his presence drove back any uncertainty, and when his brilliant eyes met mine, glints of golden amusement lurking in their depths, worry fled and anticipation took its place. Ainslie had told me to resolve to enjoy the afternoon, but it appeared that would happen on its own.

Aunt Melisina soon saw us ensconced in the carriage. She situated herself at my right side, while Jade perched on my left and Riven sat across from us. Before his charm, Aunt Melisina soon appeared more at ease than I'd ever seen her, even conversing unguarded about her hopes for Lovell. Watching him interact with her, no one would suppose he was fae. As ever, he showed an uncanny understanding of mortal convention, even drawing a laugh from her.

Our carriage slowed as we pulled into a busy square. In short order, our driver stopped beneath a row of towering maples whose shade offered welcome relief from the summer heat. Carriages filled the row, and waiters dashed to and fro from the old arched building across the street that housed Telford's Confectionary, taking orders and then returning to fulfill them. One stopped alongside our carriage, his frame as thin as a river reed. Only a slight beading of sweat along his brow betrayed the exertion he put forth in the heat. In a rapid patter, he recited a list of the myriad flavors and types of confections Telford's offered.

I requested bayberry iced cream and Riven maple, while Aunt Melisina declined any refreshment at all. Once we ordered, he departed, and Aunt Melisina glanced down the row, then pressed to her feet. "Ah, I see Lady Aftwell. I take it you won't mind if I join her?"

Without waiting for a reply, she gestured to our driver, who opened the carriage door and assisted her down. Then he retreated to a small square at the end of the maples, where all the drivers appeared to be lounging in the shade, chatting among themselves as they waited for their employers to require them once more.

After all her lectures on propriety, why would she deliberately leave us alone? A glance down the row confirmed it was not at all out of the ordinary way. Most of the carriages held couples seated across from each other. Because everyone was situated in the open—and in such proximity to others—couples could speak with relative privacy yet raise no question of anything untoward. Any attempt at intimacy, at crossing the gap from one side of the carriage to the other, would be witnessed by dozens. It satisfied convention and allowed deepening of relationship all at once.

And I wouldn't be surprised if Aunt Melisina had planned this with Lady Aftwell. She wasn't one to leave things to chance. Nor could I complain, for Riven and I could now speak freely. Any hint of lingering discomfort with public scrutiny vanished as the sweet melodies of the maples mingled with the hum of conversation arising from nearby carriages. I smiled across at him. "Thank you for your patience with Aunt Melisina—and all our odd mortal conventions."

"I wouldn't have missed this." His mouth tilted upward. "When else would I have the opportunity of being known as a suitor worth scheming to catch?" A small laugh escaped me, and his eyes brightened. "I'll credit mortals with this: they're never boring."

Before I could reply, our waiter brought the iced creams, presenting them with a small bow. The colorful ices were mounded high above the sculpted cups of frosted glass, and a small sprig of mint adorned the top of mine, while a stick of cinnamon was tucked into the side of Riven's.

I lifted the engraved silver spoon and took a tentative taste. The sweet-tart flavor exploded on my tongue, its coolness refreshing. Ainslie was right—this was delightful. How had I never come here? "Does your court enjoy such confections?"

"Those with water affinities at times turn them to crafting elaborate ice creations, each one more elaborate than the last." He glanced across the street at Telford's. "But this sort of public service would never occur."

I swirled my spoon through the pink cream. "Then there are no inns or public eateries?"

"Given that most rely on their ability to create passings, or on passing prisms to make up for the lack of affinity required to do so, there's not the same need. Nor is it difficult to construct a temporary habitation if required."

I tilted my head. "And that would be preferred to accepting lodging with another?"

"It would be preferred to incurring an implicit debt. There are ways around that, of course. Rules of hospitality come into play. Yet it's often simpler to avoid the complication."

A sudden desire to understand everything about the world my blood tied me to surged to the surface, nearly stealing my breath. The geas kept him from speaking a great deal about the courts, but perhaps not about more personal matters. "Surely there must be something about the Otherworld that's not unduly complicated or fraught with danger. Something you enjoy?"

He rested his glass on one leg. "We're not meant to indulge in mundane pleasures, certainly not in the ready way mortals do."

"But surely one cannot face an immortal life without some prospect of joy in living?"

His face shadowed. "One is permitted to take joy in amassing power and outmaneuvering others, in what you manage to gain—in bargains and debts owed you."

"And is that how you feel?"

"No." A small spark played across the frosted glass, chasing away the shadows our discussion of the Otherworld had brought. A sudden smile lit his features. "You wish to know of something uncomplicated? Twice a year, there's a confluence of lights within the Court of Gold, and the demesne of the king was designed to capture the beauty of the display. There are quiet places from which it can be enjoyed without the demands of court. Perhaps someday, I'll have the opportunity to show you."

Though small, this was more a glimpse into his personal world than he'd offered before, and I leaned forward. "I would like that."

A small ruckus started at the end of the row, jolting me back to awareness of the outer world. A little brown dog darted between the feet of the standing horses, and a young boy pelted after it. He called for it to stop, but it paid no heed.

Bright coils of light unfurled from Riven, snaring the dog. The harness he made wasn't evident to any of the mortals, but it gently restrained the pup long enough for the boy to catch up. He snatched it up, alternately scolding and lavishing love on the miscreant, his relief evident. The harness of light melted away, and the two of them departed, Riven watching over them with a slight softness to his features as they vanished from view.

Though this kindness remained hidden from the public eye, he'd allowed me to witness it—without attempting to justify it as a necessary intervention. Perhaps something in the peacefulness of the afternoon had lowered his guard as well as my own. Though I felt certain he could come up with an excuse, if I pressed.

I didn't want to draw attention to it, so I allowed my gaze to drift down the street. Sun filtered through the gas lamps, far more brilliant than the flame that would be kindled at night. Oh —the fae-light. How had I neglected to mention it before? I turned back to Riven. "I meant to tell you sooner. I'll be calling on Cyril Redgrave tomorrow to find out what he knows about the fae-light Lord Blackburn and Thea discovered."

"I'd like a report afterward, if you're willing."

"You don't mean to come?" I'd thought perhaps he would accompany us, concealed by glamour, as he'd done before in Withern.

He shook his head. "I have some bait to lay within my own world, and I've already delayed overlong. I intend to leave as soon as you return home."

"Does this concern your arbiter affairs or Ainslie?"

"Both."

Despite the heat of the afternoon sun, a sudden chill shivered across my skin. My fingers tightened about the glass. "Then be careful, please."

"I always am." The warmth in his voice drove back the chill. "Besides, I have no choice but to return. It wouldn't do to disappoint your aunts."

"Indeed not. I wouldn't put it past them to hunt you down, if you vanished." Though I couldn't restrain a smile at the outrageous notion, I was unable to shake the odd sinking of spirits his impending departure brought. I traced the spiraled pattern on my glass. Some part of me wished to forget what must come and linger here a great deal longer. Before I could sort out my conflicted emotions, a waiter appeared to take our empty glasses, Aunt Melisina on his heels. Our driver returned to his post to assist her up into the carriage, and her presence at my side inhibited any further conversation.

"Ah, Lord and Lady Worell." She gave them a nod in

greeting as they passed. "They were the match of the season last year. I mean to host them soon, and I shall introduce you, Jessa—and you as well, Lord Riven, if you wish."

"I regret to say I must remove from Avons for a short time on business. Perhaps introductions could be made on another occasion."

It would have been strictly polite to express pleasure in the prospect, yet fae could not offer a direct untruth. And I could not blame him for not desiring the acquaintance. They'd halted their carriage nearby, and as Lord Worell addressed his wife in a sharp undertone, she shrank back, her lips trembling. Then, as if nothing were amiss, he claimed her arm and swept her onward toward the nearest shop.

"She doesn't look very happy." I'd allowed myself to adopt my usual ease in Riven's presence, and the words slipped out without thought.

Aunt Melisina frowned slightly. "The matter of their marriage was arranged to everyone's satisfaction."

"Yet does she feel any love for him—or even respect?" Watching them together, I struggled to believe it, though appearances could deceive.

"She took vows to do so." Aunt Melisina unfurled her fan. "I'm sure you'd never suggest she should break them."

"A vow is a serious thing. Perhaps she should have been given a greater choice before making one." I stole a glance at Lady Worell's lowered face as they passed, her demeanor as retiring as a violet. "If she's bound in an unhappy marriage, then she has my sympathy."

"Decisions cannot be made on sentiment," Aunt Melisina said tartly. Then she turned to Riven. "You may be certain Jessa understands what marriage vows require."

"I did not dream otherwise. I'm aware of how seriously she takes the giving of her word." The beams of sunlight peering through the maple limbs seemed to settle upon Riven. "And I find her compassion charming."

Jade regarded him with evident approval, while I battled the sweep of warmth up my neck.

As for Aunt Melisina, she visibly relaxed, perhaps satisfied that I'd not spoiled matters. "Well, it must be admitted that a tender heart makes a woman an excellent mother."

Jade chuffed, and I fought the urge to bury my face in my hands.

A smile tugged at the corners of his mouth. "Doubtless you're correct."

As we departed the confectionary—thankfully without any additional comments about my suitability as a wife or mother—Aunt Melisina steered the conversation to Riven's family and connections. He deftly offered answers that appeared to say much while offering very little. Yet they left Aunt Melisina satisfied, and indeed, fairly glowing as we entered the house.

"You comported yourself very well. He even appears to find your eccentricities pleasing." She handed her parasol to Holden. "It was an afternoon well spent."

Despite my pressing concerns for Ainslie, as well as the reality that I must soon attempt to unearth the Redgraves' secrets without Riven—and without betraying my own—I couldn't help but agree.

CHAPTER 21

At breakfast the next day, Holden brought me a missive from Elodie confirming our plans to call on her uncle in the afternoon, and her willingness to perform introductions for Thea and Lord Blackburn. I asked Holden to send word to both other parties, then tucked the letter into my lap and swirled my spoon across the surface of the blackberry fool that had been set before me.

Though sweet and refreshing, it turned tasteless on my tongue. What would our conversation with the elder Mr. Redgrave reveal? I managed to maintain a pretense of enjoyment until the meal concluded, then I excused myself and passed the next few hours restoring order to the garden before Lord Blackburn and Thea arrived to fetch me. They passed the ride speculating on how he'd come to acquire the fae-light, but I kept quiet, my own thoughts focused on the possible outcomes of this encounter—and how they might impact Ainslie.

As the oratory bells chimed the hour, we halted in front of his home. Elodie emerged from her own carriage to greet us, then swept us through the door.

My imagination had conjured some sort of imposing warded figure, yet the gentleman who greeted us was perfectly ordinary.

He looked of an age with Father, and he shared the fair good looks that marked the Redgrave family. He stepped forward with an affable smile and welcomed Elodie with a kiss to her cheek. "Who have you brought me, niece?"

As she performed the introductions, I catalogued the interior of the home. I'd been concerned for Risha, yet it appeared free of wards, except for the one Elodie wore. Nevertheless, something left me ill at ease. It seemed more like a lifeless replica of a home than a true one. Though Mr. Redgrave was an antiquarian, not a single artifact was on display. Nondescript art adorned the walls and beige-and-white rugs the floors, nothing that betrayed any sense of the owner's personality or interests.

As he escorted us to the library, the lack of personal touch became more noticeable still—nary a family portrait was to be seen and all the books were of the most common sort, ones that you might find anywhere. The house contained nothing to hint at any sort of interest or passion, nor even the wealth and standing the Redgrave family possessed.

Risha fluttered near my shoulder, examining the scrolled wallpaper, while Jade prowled about the corners of the room. *I agree it's odd. When something is so very ordinary, that in itself signifies something extraordinary.*

I sighed. *Or perhaps the only extraordinary thing is our suspicious natures.*

Once seated, Elodie nodded toward me. "Jessa means to seek admittance to the Antiquary Society, and I told her you might be willing to help. And Lord Blackburn and Mrs. Darrington have a matter of society business to discuss."

"I'm always delighted to further the society in any way I can." A polished smile crossed his face, neither too broad nor too restrained—it was as seemingly ordinary as the rest of him. "What drives your interest, Miss Caldwell?"

I recited my history with Lady Dromley and my desire to honor her wishes with Kilmere, and he gave a nod. "That's laudable. I'd like very much to know what you've learned of Kilmere, and I'm sure others in the society would as well."

In case an offering needed to be made, I'd brought my sketchbook with my drawings of the frieze and the apothecary, and I extended it toward him. "It's far too much to sum up now, but perhaps you'd like to see some images from the time I spent exploring what appears to be an apothecary within the ruin."

He studied the drawings. "The detail in these is remarkable. No wonder Lady Dromley praised your artistic skills. If you allow me to review your paper before you submit it, I'd be pleased to endorse you, providing I find it satisfactory." He glanced at Thea. "I assume that's your intent also?"

She inclined her head. "The society would gain a great deal from the addition of such a bright new member, not to mention access to the ruins at Kilmere."

"I quite agree." His brow furrowed slightly. "And I understand why you've come, but Lord Blackburn, I did not believe you had any connection with the society."

"I don't, not as such," Lord Blackburn said. "However, an alarming incident recently took place there, the details of which both Mrs. Darrington and Miss Caldwell have been privy to."

Mr. Redgrave gave a light laugh. "I'm all agog to learn what could have brought together such an unlikely assemblage."

The lines in Lord Blackburn's face deepened as he drew forth the fae-light from his leather satchel. Its radiance transformed the room, drawing vibrant colors from the ordinary, everyday objects that surrounded us. A hush fell as everyone gazed upon it, except me—I watched the others.

Elodie sat motionless, save for her hand clenching about the arm of her chair. Then she looked to her uncle.

A slight flicker of emotion crossed his face, but no sooner did it appear than he thoroughly erased it. "Well, this is a surprise. I didn't know the society had begun to allow members access to each other's belongings."

"They have not." Thea jabbed her walking stick toward the fae-light. "Rather, a thief stole this, along with some papers from one of your chests. We apprehended him after the fact. I'm afraid whoever hired him absconded with your documents, but we managed to recover this. Given he succeeded once in breaking into the society, we thought it best to hold on to the artifact until we could restore it directly into your keeping."

"A thief at the society? How very odd." He lifted the fae-light and crossed over to his desk. "I'm much indebted to you for its safe return."

He tucked the fae-light into the desk drawer, and Risha darted in after it, just clearing the drawer before it closed, confining her in its depths. My muscles tensed.

Jade padded over and curled up at my feet. *She knows what she's about, though sun sylphs do not usually display such initiative.*

What could she be after? I fought the urge to cross to the desk and free her. She would not have gone in without a way out, surely.

"One does find oneself becoming sentimental about one's discoveries, and I would have mourned the loss of any part of my collection." Mr. Redgrave returned to his seat. "That a thief could successfully target the society marks a deplorable lack of security. I shall have to speak to our president to see if it may be remedied."

Thea inclined her head. "While I agree our security measures could use improvement, the thief didn't target the society—he spent considerable time seeking a discreet way to access your chest in particular."

"Can you think of any reason the thief would have sought your chest specifically?" Lord Blackburn asked.

"None whatever." Sun streamed through the windows behind Mr. Redgrave, briefly obscuring his face. "There are members of far greater standing than I, Mrs. Darrington among them, whose hoards possess greater treasures. Are you certain you're not mistaken?"

He was far too glib for someone who'd had a fae artifact nearly stolen. Did he hope to conceal its importance by acting as if he cared little about it?

Thea rapped her walking stick on the floor. "Quite certain,

young man. I spoke to the thief myself to verify the matter. We'd rather hoped you could speak to his reasons."

"I see. I'll confess I'm at a loss." He beckoned to a servant who stood in the doorway with a tray. "Perhaps we can speculate together over a pot of tea. At the least, we can consider security stratagems to prevent any other such assaults on our society."

Over tea, he kept up a steady stream of conversation about reform in the Antiquary Society and all sorts of ancillary matters. On the surface of it, he seemed almost a banal sort, smooth-spoken and easy-going, determined not to be ruffled by such an inconsequential matter as theft. Yet any attempt made by Lord Blackburn to return to discussion of the fae-light he deflected. Without appearing to do so, he was holding the conversation to the course he desired—and Elodie helped him with her light and cheery patter.

Lord Blackburn's demeanor was growing imperious, his jaw tight and his eyes dark above his crag of a nose. If he grew too impatient, he might well press the matter in such a way as to cause a breach—Elodie had said the Redgraves were very sensitive to insult. That would certainly prevent us acquiring the information we desired. I stared into my cup, the scents of bergamot and lavender swirling up from its surface.

I couldn't leave here without answers, which meant I needed to provide some sort of jolt to shake him from his complacency, without causing him to cast us out. A gentleman would take a challenge from a lady far more readily than from another man. Yet I couldn't stop with simple provocation—I must give a lure if I hoped to draw him out. At the next lull, I set aside my teacup. "Mr. Redgrave, I must return to one of your earlier remarks."

He arched a light brow. "Which one?"

"You said you were at a loss as to the purpose of the thief, but I think you know or guess exactly what he was about."

Now both his brows lifted. "Are you calling me a liar?" He spoke mildly, yet no doubt he expected the words to force a retreat—for me to claim I'd misspoken and cover over the matter with the polite niceties of society.

"Not at all. I think you act with discretion, that perhaps you fear the truth being known, as I have." I should not come off too bold. Perhaps I'd overdone it already—it was growing markedly harder to hide behind the demeanor of a young society lady. I faltered, lowering my voice. "I hope you'll forgive my boldness and take no insult. It's just that I'd hoped so very much you'd wish to discuss what Mrs. Darrington and Lord Blackburn found. Because . . . this is not the first such artifact I've encountered."

My confession fairly electrified the room. Elodie sloshed tea over the edge of her cup, and Mr. Redgrave's affable mask slipped ever so slightly, revealing a flash of interest impossible to conceal. Lord Blackburn glowered, but a slight smile lit Thea's face—evidently, she did not mind that I'd not yet confided this information in our mortal coalition. She'd said before she loved a good rout; perhaps she hoped I'd carry one off.

Mr. Redgrave's eyes remained bright. "How very remarkable. And where did you come across another such artifact, Miss Caldwell?"

"I . . . It came to me near a Crossing, and it seemed so peculiar, I thought it must be Other in nature." I chose my words with care, and evidently, the basic facts satisfied the requirement for strict truth. I twisted my fingers in the simple necklace I wore. "Please, Mr. Redgrave, won't you tell us what you know? I've been in agony wondering."

So I had, though not for the reasons he would suppose.

At last, he gave a heavy sigh, with the air of one who makes a great concession. "You're right about the Other nature of this relic. I did not intend to speak of it, as I did not want to drag anyone else into any sort of Otherworldly affair and the attendant dangers. You'll forgive my caution, I hope."

Lord Blackburn harrumphed. "Your reservations are understandable. Can't go broadcasting these affairs. But if there is some traffic of Other into our world, we want to stop it before it destroys us all—there must be some exchange of knowledge, if we're to succeed."

If they were somehow Collectors, they'd not take kindly to such a notion. I tilted my head, studying Mr. Redgrave.

He nodded gravely. "It seems we share a purpose. I want nothing more than to keep Otherworldly threats from those I love."

It was a carefully worded reply, one that neither confirmed nor denied his involvement with the Otherworld. Now that I'd provoked a revelation, I'd subside into the background and wait for the matter to play out. When Elodie settled back in her chair, her gaze sharp and speculative, I realized with a start she meant to do the same.

Mr. Redgrave turned back to me. "If we're being forthright, I'd like to understand more. You say you just stumbled upon an Otherworldly artifact. Did it radiate light, as the one in my keeping?"

I'd not said I'd stumbled upon it, but if he believed it, so much the better. "It was shaped like a pendant, much smaller and less luminous." I shrugged as if bewildered. "One does not quite know what to do with such things."

"You could have gone to the Vigil."

I widened my eyes. "It seemed a very frightening prospect. My aunt would have said it's no place for a young lady."

"Quite so."

"I meant to keep it safe, but one day it . . . shattered."

He leaned forward. "Did you save the remnants?"

I shook my head. "The liquid inside it appeared of a caustic nature, so I took care to avoid it."

"A shame. Perhaps it could have told us something. But the Other has a way of corrupting all it touches, so perhaps it's for the best. You're very fortunate to have come off unharmed."

"Indeed." My throat tightened as if Lord West's hands closed about it once more—if it hadn't been for the sacrifice of the pendant, I *wouldn't* have come out unharmed. "Did you discover this . . . orb near a Crossing also?"

He spread his hands. "It was brought to me by someone who knows I collect oddities. I don't believe the man knew its nature, and I could get no clear account of its discovery from him—other than that he'd traveled the Northern Reaches. Given the incoherency of his account, I fear the fellow was fae-touched, but that's a matter for the Vigil to sort out."

A frost-like sensation burned down my back. If he had any sort of alliance with the Vigil, that made him a danger. What if he reported to them that I'd once possessed a fae object? It could be what Mr. Ludne needed to press charges. I didn't have to force breathiness into my voice. "And they didn't seize his discovery?"

"They permitted me to keep it so that I might seek its source." His gaze drifted back to the desk. "I'm well-warded, so the object could have no influence over me, and of course, I agreed to report my findings."

I clenched my hands tightly in my lap. That meant he worked *with* the Vigil in some measure. If that were true, my theory about the Redgraves acting as Collectors no longer held water.

Jade's eyes slitted. *He could be lying about the entire thing, crafting a tale that suits the conventions of your world.*

True. If Riven were here, he'd know . . . *Do you believe he is?*

I think he holds back a great deal. He wants your knowledge as you want his, so both of you dance around the truth.

"If others knew of the existence of the orb, perhaps that explains the actions of our thief," Thea said.

"It's possible. Though the Vigil isn't prone to leaking information, at least not to my knowledge. But who's to know?" His gaze drifted back to the desk. "I'd like very much to speak with this thief, see if I can get anything more out of him."

"I'll arrange the matter." Lord Blackburn eyed him. "Would you be willing to let us know anything you discover about the nature of the artifact?"

"Indeed—though I fear it intends to give up very little. I've had no success thus far." He stood. "I don't wish to be an ungracious host, but I have another engagement at half past four, so I'm afraid I must depart soon."

What else was there to do but go? Clearly, he didn't mean to divulge any more, and we could not stay after such a dismissal. Only . . . *What about Risha?*

Jade's ears pricked. *She says she needs you to find an excuse to open the drawer.*

Wonderful.

"Mr. Redgrave?" I asked. "I know you're pressed for time, but might we look at the orb once more? Just to be sure it has not altered nor shattered, as my pendant did?"

"It's never changed, not in any of my observations." He hesitated, looking between Elodie and me. "I suppose it cannot hurt." He unlocked the drawer and drew it forth. Its light flared bright, and he nearly dropped it. "By the Crossings, that's odd."

Thea hobbled forward. "Has it ever done that before?"

"Indeed not." He frowned, surveying it closely.

While the elders clustered around the fae-light, discussing the matter, Elodie's gaze traveled toward me, lingering for an uncomfortable moment before she hurried to her uncle's side, exclaiming over the peculiarity of its altered state. Meanwhile, Risha escaped to perch on my shoulder, her light flaring with intricate patterns that suggested urgency. What had she discovered?

I needed to get her alone, at once.

CHAPTER 22

With difficulty, I endured the carriage ride home, deflecting questions from Lord Blackburn about the fae pendant and my earlier lack of disclosure by claiming that since the item no longer remained in my possession, I'd not thought it worth mentioning. When he pressed, I pressed back, asking if he'd divulged everything he knew or suspected about these Otherworldly affairs.

Thea chuckled softly. "She has you there. I recall a certain reluctance to share details from Ashford?"

Lord Blackburn grumbled, but subsided into disgruntled silence. At last, we halted in front of my house, and I hurried up the stairs, only to be waylaid by my sisters as soon as I crossed the threshold.

Ainslie arched a brow at me. "Well?"

"Let's retire to my bedchamber, so I can freshen up, and I'll tell you what I know." They readily embraced the excuse to gain privacy, and together, we ascended the stairs. Once inside, I secured the door behind us. "I promise I will give you an account, but first, I must speak with Risha." I turned toward her. "What did you learn, bright one? Why did you go into the desk?"

"Thought he might keep secrets inside." She blazed bright. "He had many, many letters. They all spoke of one thing—Other. I thought you would wish for more information. Did I do wrong?"

"No, I'm glad you acted when you had a chance. Was there evidence he dealt in Otherworldly items, like a Collector might?"

"No." She perched on the potted ivy. "The letters were reports. Like sylphs might carry in my world. Only here all is written down, a dangerous choice, because anyone might come along and see. Like I did."

"And what did you see?"

"First letter talked of a third selkie sighting rumored along the North Sea, with a chart of reported movements. Another talked of a hag near Ashford. One was from someone called the First, telling Cyril to go to the Fens Crossing."

The First? Where had I heard that term before . . .

Wait.

A sudden sour taste flooded my mouth. I leapt up and rummaged in the bedside table, seeking the book Ibbie had located on the Vigil, the last gift she'd given me before the killer had claimed her life.

"What is it, Jessa?" Ainslie hurried to my side, Ada hovering just behind her.

Wordless, I thumbed through the pages until I came to the passage my memory had conjured.

There.

Long ago, the First of Vigil had been one Sir Redgrave, and the Redgraves served in this capacity until the Sainsbury line of monarchs ascended to power. The new king had appointed Lord Everstone as the new First. I rocked back. *This* was how they'd advised the old line of kings—only the knowledge of the old Vigil and their involvement must have been lost along with the details of the Forgotten War. Which meant now . . .

My pulse beat ragged at the base of my throat, and I clutched for Jade.

Ada crept closer. "Jessa?"

I sank onto the edge of the bed, Jade clasped in my arms. Why hadn't I remembered sooner? Why hadn't I pressed harder into the nagging sense of familiarity I'd experienced when I first heard the Redgrave name in Withern?

Jade nudged my chin. *You had quite a few other things on your mind, both then and when you first read this book.*

Still, if I'd remembered sooner—

You could not have acted without evidence.

And now, it was imperative we acquired some.

"You have to tell us what's wrong." Ada folded her arms across her chest and spoke with uncharacteristic sternness.

"Mr. Redgrave made comments today suggesting he's on good terms with the Vigil—and this book proves that the Redgrave family were part of the original Vigil. In fact, one of their members once served as First."

Ainslie's breath caught. "You're certain?"

I handed her the book.

She and Ada pored over the pages, then Ada collapsed next to me. "You truly believe they still have Vigil ties?"

"The letters Risha found suggest it's possible, not to mention the fae-light . . ." As would all the other oddities I'd noted about the family, but voicing how long I'd held suspicions would only distract from the matter at hand.

"But the Vigil isn't known to collect such objects," Ainslie said.

"How can we say what they truly do? They take care to keep their methods hidden. And Mr. Ludne possessed a listening stone." I rested my head on Jade's, seeking comfort. "Who's to say they don't hoard whatever Otherworldly artifacts they come across?"

Ainslie paced in front of the hearth. "It seems more likely they'd condemn them as a danger to us all."

"Even if they did, they could justify keeping the items locked away, brought out only for study. They took the wolpertinger Father found, and we know they have a history of seizing anything connected with Other." I rubbed my temples. Did this concern Mr. Cyril Redgrave alone, or were the Redgrave siblings also involved? I couldn't fathom them working with someone like Mr. Ludne. Surely I was letting my fears get the best of me.

The ivy swayed tempestuously, spilling over the bounds of its pot, and Risha took to the air. Ada and Ainslie both shot me glances of alarm, and I drew a slow, steady breath, seeking calm. Perhaps I was mistaken. In any case, I must gain control of my emotions. I braced my back against the bedpost. "They could still be Collectors. Perhaps they took the knowledge of the Otherworld they gained during their time in the Vigil and turned to Collecting to support their fortunes, and that's why they made it through unscathed. Perhaps they act to stay in the Vigil's good graces so as to procure information."

"But when alchemy was forgotten, what gain could there have been in preserving the knowledge? How could they have remembered, when others forgot?" Ainslie asked.

"I . . . I don't know."

Her chin dropped, and she tucked her arms about herself. "If Mr. Redgrave is truly involved, what does that mean?"

Ada crossed the room to pull Ainslie into an embrace. "Even if some of his family has ties to Vigil affairs, Mr. Redgrave may be wholly unconnected. And if the other explanation is true, then perhaps he'll be more understanding of your situation."

"But Ainslie cannot possibly confess until we know one way or the other. We need the truth, or we could stumble further into danger—we cannot leave this to chance any longer."

"Then what do you suggest?"

"That we take a calculated risk." Beyond the window glass, the sky had grown steel-gray, somber and sunless. "I propose we call on Hester Redgrave today—and hope that Elodie has not yet returned from paying her own calls. If she has, we'll just carry on the best we can."

"But what excuse can we give, since you have just seen her this afternoon?"

"I can say that I felt most troubled by our meeting with her uncle and act as though I require reassurance." The meeting had troubled me, yet the notion of such a pretense turned my stomach. But what else could we do? I couldn't ask outright and expect to receive the truth.

"And if we go, what then?" Ainslie straightened. "We cannot skulk about, looking into drawers and poking into cupboards, hoping some secret will spill out."

"Elodie told me her aunt has a great fondness for indoor plants, so nothing could be more natural than to ask for a tour. Ada, if you can manage, you'll pretend to grow faint and need care, and Ainslie, you can raise a fuss over her—it will buy me time to connect to the plants while she's distracted. I might be able to find what we need."

"I'll do it." Ada gave an uncertain nod. "But Jessa, what if they realize what we're about?"

"Then I suppose there will be trouble. Perhaps a great deal of it."

LESS THAN AN HOUR LATER, we arrived at Hester Redgrave's house—and the bone-chilling sensation of oppressive wards swept over me, halting me at the base of the stairs. Verbena and Saint-John's-wort spilled over the edge of large planters on either side of the door, bristling and snapping at me, and ward runes were engraved on the stone lintel and doorstep. The elder Mr. Redgrave's home had possessed no such protections, further suggesting we'd been ushered into some sort of staged environment, not his true dwelling, wherever it might be.

Yet that was of no consequence compared to the problem at hand. I'd already felt as though wyvern writhed in my stomach —now my whole body shook with the urge to turn back. *Can we even enter?*

They will keep out Risha, but wards cannot bar high fae altogether—only make things very unpleasant.

Wonderful. I clutched the stone banister, and the cold bled through my gloves. *Tell Risha to remain as close as she can without doing any harm to herself.*

I'd hoped to enlist her to stand watch when I attempted to connect to the plants; now I'd be forced to rely on Jade alone. Sharp staccato notes sparked from the Saint-John's-wort, and if it could have lashed out, it surely would have. How could I shield us?

Never mind, I couldn't dawdle on the doorstep any longer. Ainslie already prodded my back, waiting for me to move. I opened my senses, ignoring the painful throb at the base of my neck and the way the world seemed to tilt about me as I ascended the stairs.

White poplars stood out silver against the leaden sky, their star-bright song pouring into my soul—it would do. I pulled it toward me and Jade, as if the notes themselves were tangible things that could wrap around us, their sprightly strength becoming our own. And some of the pain ebbed.

It wasn't perfect, but it would have to do.

Ada knocked, and the butler greeted us graciously. As I'd hoped, Elodie and Mr. Redgrave remained absent, but their butler willingly ushered us in to meet Mrs. Hester Redgrave, who was at-home to call for the afternoon. She put me in mind of a blooming foxglove, upright in posture and vibrant in color, her appearance everything charming and refined.

She hurried toward us, her arms extended in welcome, the sun catching on the white strands woven into her golden hair. "What a delightful surprise! Elodie and Charles will be so disappointed to have missed you, but please, do come take tea with me. If you find the weather overwarm, we have chilled cordial water and lemonade as well."

She radiated goodwill, and it was difficult to believe she conducted any sort of nefarious scheme. Yet if she was truly like said foxglove, her pleasing appearance concealed deadly danger within. I shook off the fancy and sat back, giving my sisters the lead. As poised as usual in these sorts of settings, they exchanged social niceties with Mrs. Redgrave, discussing mutual acquaintances and recent society events and encouraging the easy flow of conversation.

After I made a pretense of indulging in the refreshments—in reality I struggled to swallow a single bite and slipped what I could to Jade—I inclined my head toward the orchid on the mantel. "That's a lovely specimen. I hope you won't find it too forward, but Elodie told me of your collection of houseplants. Would you mind giving me a tour?"

"Ah, you're the one who enjoys gardening." She offered a bright smile, one reminiscent of Elodie—the Redgrave family ties ran strong in more ways than one. "Nothing would give me greater pleasure than showing off my collection. I'm afraid I often bore my family droning on about my newest specimens, so I'd welcome a fellow enthusiast. Perhaps we might start in the conservatory?"

As we trailed her down the hall, she asked, "Have you toured the new display at the Botanic Gardens? I think they've outdone themselves this year."

"I did have the pleasure of a brief tour—and I'd like to return to soak it all in more thoroughly."

She nodded. "It's become my favorite place to steal away to when I'm otherwise unoccupied, which sadly, is rarer than I'd like."

Was it possible she knew something about the Other plants on display? Redgrave family portraits stared down at me from the walls; nevertheless, I collected my courage to ask. "I noticed one particularly remarkable display, filled with plants I'd never encountered before. Do you know who provided them?"

Her steps faltered for the briefest of moments, then she swept onward. "I believe the donor wishes to remain anonymous."

"I understand, but if you happen to know the individual, perhaps you could pass on a message? I would dearly love an introduction and a chance to learn more about the remarkable exhibit."

"I'll see what I can do." She fixed another bright smile on her face, then began to rattle on about her favorite species of orchid.

Had *she* been the mystery donor? Or someone else in the Redgrave clan? If they possessed fae artifacts, why not Other-worldly plants?

As we crossed into the conservatory, Ada pressed a hand to her temple—she looked far paler than one simply feigning to be unwell. We'd agreed she was to pretend to feel faint when we found ourselves among the plants, but this seemed something more—were the wards impacting her? Could I somehow extend my protections to surround her?

Mrs. Redgrave gestured to a rare cultivar of jasmine, detailing the story of how she'd acquired it. Before she could finish, Ada stumbled against her.

"Forgive me, Mrs. Redgrave. I . . . I feel rather dizzy."

"Heavens, you look quite pale. We can't have you fainting." She clasped Ada's hand. "Come, we'll find you some smelling salts."

"I'll go with you." It would look odd if I didn't volunteer to attend my own sister.

Ainslie shook her head. "No need to bother. I can see to Ada, with Mrs. Redgrave's assistance. You enjoy the displays."

"Yes, by all means," Mrs. Redgrave said. "I'll return as soon as I can."

With that, they departed, Ainslie supporting Ada. When they vanished, I exhaled. So far, matters had gone well enough, but how long would our fortune hold?

Dire images of discovery and apprehension proliferated in my mind as abundantly as the array of plants before me. No—I could not indulge in such fears. I must focus on what we'd come here to do. I closed my eyes and inhaled the spice-sweet fragrances permeating the air.

Would the conservatory hold what I needed? Likely not. It wasn't a place to conduct any sort of private conversation, open as it was to the rest of the house. What then? I wouldn't have long, so I needed to make a swift decision.

I opened my senses wide, pressing back the near-crippling wave of pain from the wards at the entrances of the house. A strong, perseverant song emanated from an abutilon on the floor above, the clarity in its notes promising vivid detail when I requested recall.

Most of the row houses in Avons had a similar layout, and if my senses guided me correctly, it was located in an area likely to be some sort of library or study. I hurried from the conservatory and ascended the stairs.

There.

The notes thrilled from behind double doors. I twisted the brass handles, and they gave beneath my touch, revealing a library with a large desk situated in the center of the far wall, flanked by windows with cushioned seats beneath. On a brighter day, they would have flooded the room with sunlight, but now a sort of dusky dullness hung over the space. I spared only a glance at the contents of the floor-to-ceiling bookshelves on the wall across, my attention locked on the abutilon, which perched on the desk.

As I brushed its soft, velvety leaves, the faint fragrance of its bell-shaped flowers washed over me, and I pulled the younger Mr. Redgrave and Elodie to the forefront of my mind.

Images flashed and ordered themselves . . .

Mr. Redgrave sat at the desk, a leather folio resting before him, his features drawn and weary. Then Elodie entered the room and collapsed onto the window seat nearest to him. "How did you find Ainslie?"

"I don't know. Something troubles her, but she won't confide in me, and I have no right to press."

"And you still wish to continue your suit, even with the . . . uncertainties surrounding Jessa?"

A rueful smile played about his lips. "I'm afraid it's rather late to withdraw."

"Nor do I want you to, not truly. It's just . . . how can we carry on? It feels dreadful to deceive them so."

"I know. I've never felt more like a cad when carrying out my

duty." His jaw tightened. "My only comfort is in so doing, we may clear them all."

"Do you truly think so?"

"Rather, I hope." He lifted a thick stack of paper from the folio. "If it was anyone but Jessa that we'd collected this much evidence on, we would have gone to Uncle Cenhelm long ago. Yet I feel there's something we're missing—it seems difficult to believe she's a danger. I know he'll say my judgment is compromised, and perhaps it is. I cannot pretend to think clearly when it comes to Ainslie. And anything that hurts her sister will hurt her also."

"Oh, Charles. I'm sorry that it has come to this." Elodie moved to his side and rested a hand on his shoulder. "How long can we reasonably wait?"

"A few days, perhaps."

A storm of emotion severed my connection with the abutilon and jolted me back into the library proper. I couldn't move, couldn't lift my hand to attempt to reforge the bond, could scarcely even breathe.

This wasn't what I'd expected; it was far worse. Whatever the Redgrave family business, Mr. Redgrave and Elodie were intimately involved and they'd investigated *me*.

The rush in my ears obscured even the sprightly notes of the abutilon, which reached out to caress my cheek. I should look for the file, should see what information he'd gathered, try to understand what he knew and what he sought, what he meant to turn over to his uncle. Yet I remained rooted in place.

Jade's fur bristled. *Someone's nearby—it smells like Elodie. Areth's fire take these wards. I should have noticed sooner.*

I practically ran to the door and flung it open, hoping to make it back down to the conservatory before she found me. Instead, we nearly collided in the landing.

Her eyes widened. "Jessa? What are you doing here?"

CHAPTER 23

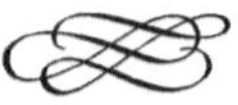

Asmile or a carefree expression, perhaps those would quiet her suspicions, but I could manage neither, drowning as I was in a vast ocean of fear. My hold on the protections about us slipped, and the stomach-churning sensation of the wards swept over me. I pressed my lips together to choke down a swell of nausea.

"Jessa?" Elodie took a step closer. "Aunt Hester told me you were in the conservatory, but I couldn't find you. What brought you here?"

"I suppose I was carried away by her collection, it's truly remarkable. I hope you'll forgive me for wandering. Your aunt gave me permission to look around, and the abutilon caught my attention—one doesn't often see them in Avons, and I've always been fond of their flowers, they're so very unique." Rambling, I was rambling far too much, and nothing I said held together.

Her gaze traveled past my shoulder. "But she always keeps the library doors closed."

A polite way of saying she suspected me of deceit. Under the circumstances, how could she not? If she told her brother, would they go to the Vigil at once? I clutched the banister to stay upright. "Does she? Perhaps someone forgot."

The rush in my ears nearly drowned the sound of my own voice. I needed to pull myself together—and quickly. The determined notes of the abutilon marched about me, and I drew its essence into myself, the constancy of its nature steadying my pulse.

"Aunt Hester keeps no careless servants." A frown pinched Elodie's features.

She didn't believe me, and who would? She might allow me to smooth over the matter and save face to adhere to social convention, but she'd doubtless act as soon as she could. And if she drew the Vigil in, Ada and Ainslie would be caught up in the whole affair—and Ainslie's binding mark would assure her condemnation.

Glamour welled up within me, an invitation to blot this event from her memory and be done with it—to ensure safety for myself and my sisters. No, I could not. I drew deeper from the abutilon, from the jasmine below, the white poplar beyond the glass, a swirl of power to match the charge of emotion within, to hold back the glamour. "I'm afraid I can offer no other explanation, and I certainly cannot answer for the movements of your aunt's household. Perhaps it's for the best that we forget the matter and return to the conservatory. I wouldn't want to keep your aunt waiting."

"Yes." Her face softened, and her words took on a dreamy quality. "It's for the best. Can't keep Aunt Hester waiting."

Oh no. I pressed trembling fingers to my lips. I'd decided I would not, so . . . how had I glamoured her? Had the power I'd drawn to myself undermined my resolve? Would fae affinities always twist themselves to harm mortals, no matter the intended purpose? My chest tightened.

I wanted to beg forgiveness for violating her will; I wanted to condemn her for collecting information to turn over to—who? The Vigil, most likely.

The conflicting emotions rose hot and acrid in my throat. And with the sudden swell, the bite of the wards sharpened, making me feel as though I'd rather leap from the window than endure their sting another moment.

Unaware, Elodie descended the stairs, talking of the time her aunt had sent her uncle on a two-week trip just to collect an unusual nerine cultivar.

Halfway down, I halted abruptly. Wait, could my glamour have truly been so strong despite the wards? Despite my intention otherwise? What if she'd simply feigned being glamoured but meant to go to Mr. Redgrave at once? Was it all a test?

My pulse leapt, but I forced myself onward. I could do nothing about it now. She had been susceptible to glamour before, when Riven had done it. Perhaps that meant I was safe— for the time being. But even if that were true, how long remained before they reported to their uncle Cenhelm? Was he their chief connection to the Vigil? If they'd grown up living in his home, was he a father figure to them?

I trailed Elodie back into the conservatory, which we found empty. "They must be in the drawing room," she said.

In short order, we rejoined the others. Through lips gone numb, I murmured compliments to Mrs. Redgrave about her conservatory collection while Elodie gaily exchanged sallies with Ainslie about the deplorable trend for excessive feathering on hats. She exhibited no signs of suspicion or residual glamour. Across from them, Ada sipped at a cup of tea, still ashen.

I declined the additional refreshments Mrs. Redgrave offered —we had to go, and quickly. "You've been most gracious, but we've taken up enough of your time. Perhaps we could call again, and I could bring you a specimen from my greenhouse."

Mrs. Redgrave smiled. "Certainly. We'd be delighted to have you. I've told Charles and Elodie that they're to treat my house as their own as long as they're in Avons. Any friends of theirs are always more than welcome."

"You're very gracious." But was any of it sincere? Or was it simply a snare?

"Wait." Elodie tilted her head. "You never said what brought you this afternoon."

"Matters with your uncle were weighing on my mind. I thought perhaps we could discuss things further." I inclined my head toward Ada. "But Ada still does not look like herself, so I suppose it shall have to wait."

"Of course. As Aunt Hester said, we'd welcome you any time."

Somehow, after interminable farewells, we extracted ourselves from the house—though I half-expected a squadron of Vigilists to spring from the cellar and drag us back inside. When we entered the carriage, I collapsed against the leather seat. And both my sisters turned to me at once.

"What did you discover?" Ainslie demanded.

With Jade nestled at my side, I faltered through the conversation I'd overheard about the file and their investigation on me.

Ada inhaled sharply. "Oh, Jessa."

"How could he? He pretended to . . . And all along . . ." Bright color surged into Ainslie's face, and her eyes glittered. "There's only one thing to do. Cut ties at once. I'll send him a note saying I don't ever want to see him again."

"But Ainslie—"

"I mean it, Jessa." Her voice shook. "I was blind enough to believe his attentions sincere, and my indulgence in sentiment has endangered you—perhaps all of us. If he reports to the Vigil what he's observed . . . I refuse to hand him more evidence. When I think I nearly told him about my binding mark . . ."

Wordless, I clasped her hand, and it trembled beneath mine. She'd trusted Mr. Redgrave, dreamed of a future with him—and now this? How much more could she endure?

Given what I'd witnessed, I didn't think his attentions a sham, but did it matter, in the end?

If they went to the Vigil, then any choice about my future would be taken from me. I could no longer remain in the mortal world, not unless I wished to live confined to an Institution. But nor could I leave my family to their fate. What then? "Cutting ties might not be enough. I fear my excursion into the library may have provoked them to more urgent action."

"Then what shall we do?" Ada's eyes were wide and dark with distress.

"I don't know, not yet." The carriage jostled over uneven stone, and I pressed a hand to my churning stomach, a vain attempt to calm the storm within. If only Riven had not gone to the Otherworld. He'd not indicated his business would take long, so for just a moment I allowed myself to hope that he'd return before the day's end.

"We could . . . perhaps . . ." Ada clutched at Ainslie, who clung to her in turn.

My ideas were scarcely more formed than hers. Aside from erasing their memories and claiming the evidence, thereby utterly and wholly violating their wills, I could think of no way to change their resolve.

A tense, choking silence fell. I needed to clear my mind of emotion, to steal away alone and *think*. Wyncourt beckoned, its peaceful, untouched heart promising refuge—no, I could not afford to be so far from my sisters, not with matters so volatile.

We ascended the stairs to our front door, but Holden didn't appear to open it with his usual promptness. We waited one moment, two. And my mouth went dry.

Of course we were more than capable of opening a door, but Holden never neglected his duties. What had happened in our absence? Surely the Redgraves could not have already summoned the Vigil?

I shoved open the door and half-ran down the corridor, only vaguely aware of Ainslie sweeping up the stairs with Ada in pursuit. Where was everyone?

Your father and Holden are near the servants' stairs.

I changed course. What was Father doing at the head of the servants' stairs? I rounded the corner to find him and Holden engaged in grave conversation.

Father appeared harried, and he peered at me above the rim of his spectacles. "Ah, Jessa. It's good you're home. Caris is in a state, the whole household is."

The distant chime of the clock seemed overloud, ringing into the unnatural stillness. "What's happened?"

"Your lady's maid—she's disappeared."

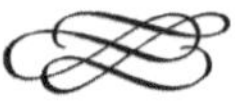

CHAPTER 24

The final chime of the clock faded, and still I stood unmoving. It hadn't been the Redgraves or the Vigil, but . . . Lianne.

My hands clenched. She wasn't wealthy, didn't fit the profile of those who'd vanished over the past weeks, but her spirits *had* been unusually elevated. I'd attributed it to a budding romance, but no matter her station, I should have seriously considered the prospect of her being a target, should have heeded the vague unease it had sparked in me.

Yet I'd sensed nothing of Other about her or the household, nothing to rouse such suspicions. What did that mean?

Jade stalked the corridor, sniffing at the head of the stairs. *I don't smell any unfamiliar people, Other or mortal—though depending on when she vanished, any scents could have dissipated.*

"How long has she been gone?" My voice emerged as unsteady as I felt.

Holden cleared his throat. "I took the liberty of releasing her from her duties after dinner yesterday so she could rest. She said she wasn't feeling herself, nor did she look it—she was flushed, almost appeared feverish. I did not want to chance illness spreading through the household, so I told her not to return to her duties until she'd recovered. When no one had seen her all day, I sent Gaile to attend her. That wasn't long ago, perhaps a quarter hour, at most. Gaile found the room empty. Her bed hadn't been slept in, and her belongings were untouched."

I felt as though I'd braced for a frontal attack and someone had stolen behind me, dealing an unexpected blow that took my breath away. A muffled sob drifted from the morning room—Gaile, perhaps?—followed by soft words of comfort from Dreda. Where was Aunt Caris? Perhaps she'd gone belowstairs to reassure the other staff?

If Riven were here, he could examine the scene for traces of Other—perhaps this justified a request that he search for evidence as soon as he was at liberty to do so.

Jade, will you ask Risha to go?

It is done.

Risha swiftly vanished, while Jade leapt onto the windowsill and perched there, her eyes aglow.

Father ran a hand across his jaw. "What's the name of that stratesman, the one who called here before? Holden can't recall."

Holden recalled everything, so this lack of forthrightness must signify that he disapproved of summoning a stratesman on behalf of a missing maid. "Mr. Burke—and I think we should send for him at once. I'm certain he'll give his best efforts to seeking Lianne."

"Like as not, she's eloped or something equally foolhardy." Holden stiffened. "She's been flighty enough of late."

"If she wants to make a home somewhere else, we certainly shan't stop her." Father shoved up his spectacles. "Still, we should be sure she's safe. Send Ives to fetch this Mr. Burke, please."

Whatever his sentiments, Holden nodded gravely and departed.

"Did you notice anything unusual about your maid lately? Any signs she might have contemplated seeking another position?" Father asked.

"Well—"

Aunt Caris fluttered up the stairs, clutching her handkerchief in one hand. "All the servants are in turmoil—they think Lianne is among the missing. Oh, Alden, do you think it could be true?"

He shrank back from the raw emotion she displayed. "That's for the authorities to determine."

"First the events in Withern, now Lianne disappearing from her very bedchamber—how are we to ever feel safe again?" Aunt Caris's usual radiance had vanished; her whole body drooped like a flower in dire need of refreshment.

I moved to her side. "We'll ask Mr. Burke what he advises. I'm certain he'd not leave us in a dangerous situation."

She shuddered. "Were I prone to superstition, I'd wonder if the curse of Kilmere followed us here."

"No curse remains. Certainly not one that has chased after us." Unless one counted my own presence as a curse that brought danger to those I loved. My body went cold.

"Of course, you're right, my dear." She dabbed her eyes with her handkerchief. "I don't know what's come over me. I suppose I feel that everywhere we turn, danger appears alongside."

Father shifted his weight from one foot to the other, as if he considered flight. "I'll see to the matter, Caris. You needn't worry."

I lost the thread of the conversation as Risha materialized next to me.

One of Jade's ears flicked toward her. *She says Riven will call, so he can investigate openly.*

A distant knock at the door summoned Holden, and he reappeared a moment later to announce Lord Riven.

But Riven didn't wait, just entered the space with a relaxed, easy stride, a tangible air of calm about him. And the knot within me began to unravel.

"Lord Riven, what a pleasure to see you again." At once, Aunt Caris transformed into a proper hostess. "Forgive us for the irregular reception, but we're all at odds. One of our maids has gone missing."

"So I understand from your butler." He inclined his head.

"While you await the stratesman, perhaps you'd like me to examine her room? Any information we can provide will make his job easier and see your household more quickly set to rights."

Such was the innate charm of fae that neither she or Father appeared to consider why Riven had arrived at this precise time, nor why he'd want to involve himself.

Father exhaled, his relief evident. "Excellent notion."

He stepped back, and I led the way to her bedchamber. The simple, narrow room was as neat and orderly as Lianne herself had been. Clean whitewashed walls were brightened by splashes of color from the embroidered bedquilt and braided rug. Her brush and comb sat in straight lines on the small washstand alongside the bed. Though I steeled myself to look through her belongings, no missing clothes, shoes, or personal items revealed themselves. If she'd eloped or even sought another position, she would have taken her things.

A pricking sense of Other emanated from Riven, hinting he explored the scene with his Other senses. How I wished I could speak freely with him—about the Redgraves and the Vigil and Lianne. Instead, the unspoken words pooled in my throat, choking me.

I kept quiet and listened as Father asked grave questions and Riven gave answers that said little but sounded very reassuring. A moment later, Mr. Burke appeared in the doorway, escorted by Aunt Caris.

He stopped short when he saw Riven. "Lord Riven. Why am I not surprised to find you here?"

"Because you've developed more sense than most."

Most mortals. The unspoken word hung in the air, drifting by Father, who blinked at the two of them.

Mr. Burke turned to address Father. "Mr. Caldwell, I received the message about your maid. Have you uncovered any further evidence?"

"We'd hoped to find something here, but . . ." He spread his hands.

Riven stepped forward. "There's nothing missing, no sign of

any forced entrance, nor of any but members of the household having passed through here."

Mr. Burke would understand the extent of what that meant—there had been no incursion of Other to spirit her away.

"I see." His gaze rested on me, assessing. He had questions of his own, no doubt, since when we last spoke, I'd told him Riven had returned to the Otherworld.

I shut the washstand drawer firmly. "Her bedchamber may hold no evidence, but I think it significant that she's been in excellent spirits of late. I thought perhaps she was falling in love, even saw her with someone in the gardens early one morning, though I couldn't make out any details about the gentleman with whom she spoke."

"That doesn't bode well." Mr. Burke stepped over to the pegs that held her work garments. "I'll need to examine the room myself and speak to the rest of the staff."

"Oh, must you?" Aunt Caris took a half step into the room. "They're already in great distress."

"If your maid was taken against her will, then I must gather any evidence I can."

Aunt Caris's hand fluttered to her throat. "Is that what you believe?"

"It's too soon to know, but I assure you I'll look for her as I would my own kin."

"Thank you, Mr. Burke. We're most grateful for your aid—and your discretion."

"Of course."

The narrow room was becoming confining, but I ducked around Father to address Mr. Burke. "Might Lord Riven and I assist with the questioning?"

"My dear! That's hardly appropriate—"

Mr. Burke turned to her. "If you are willing to allow your niece to assist, a familiar face from your household would make the process smoother, particularly when it comes to the maids. I'd like you to stay with the servants we're not questioning and ensure they don't exchange stories among themselves—it's best if I can receive accounts untainted by the memories of others."

"Well . . . of course, we must do all we can to find poor Lianne." She hesitated in the doorway. "But see that you conduct the interviews in the drawing room with the door open."

"As you wish."

Since we didn't employ a large number of servants, it didn't take long to interview them. Riven sat back, allowing Mr. Burke the lead, yet his intent gaze suggested that he sifted their words for truth. All agreed Lianne had been in an excellent frame of mind these past few weeks and had shown no signs of dissatisfaction in her position—quite the opposite, in fact.

Only Gaile nodded when I mentioned a possible love interest. "Yes, miss, I know she met a few times with a young man, but she wouldn't tell me much about him. She liked to keep things close. I thought perhaps she was waiting to see if his interest proved true, so as she wouldn't lose her position with no cause."

None of them had noticed any physical mark or alteration in Lianne, no matter how we pressed—not even an insignificant burn, scratch, or scar. As Gaile and Lianne often assisted one another with their toilettes, the evidence seemed fairly conclusive.

With the drawing room finally cleared, Riven leaned forward. "None of them withheld the truth. They've told what they know, and they exhibit no sign of altered memories."

Mr. Burke scrubbed a hand over his face. "Their reports are in keeping with those I've questioned in other households. No one observed a single sign indicative of a binding mark."

I sank back in my chair. Did that mean we weren't dealing with an Otherworldly problem after all? Or had the bargain-holder simply taken more care to conceal the marks? Somehow, all of this must connect—the Redgraves, the Vigil, the disappearances. Or did I merely *want* it to be so, in order to bring the chaos around me into some sort of logical whole and thereby control its outcome?

Mr. Burke straightened. "I have another theory—"

Aunt Caris bustled into the room. "Lord Riven, Mr. Burke, I must claim Jessa. I trust you've gotten all you require?"

Blight and rot. I clenched my hands in the folds of my skirt. Why did she press for proprieties at such a time?

Mr. Burke and Riven both stood.

"I have what I need for now, but you can expect to see me again soon," Mr. Burke said.

Riven offered a small bow. "I trust you'll excuse me as well, Miss Caldwell, Miss Jessa. I don't want to keep you longer than necessary during such a distressing time."

Which meant I'd have to wait for information, wait to speak of all the things pressing on me. Doubtless, Riven meant to trace Lianne's trail, and who knew how long that would take?

When they departed, I turned to Aunt Caris. "Did you need assistance?"

"No, my dear, but it wasn't fitting for you to remain once the servants had gone."

I'd opened my mouth to reply when Holden came to inform Aunt Caris that Gaile was on the verge of giving her notice, as the events of the day had overset her. She hurried from the room after him. The interruption had been a mercy perhaps, for my response would have been less than gracious—and however inconvenient her strictures, Aunt Caris didn't deserve anger. However, if I didn't escape the stifling confines of the house soon, I might not retain the control I desired.

As I moved from the drawing room, past the large windows that looked over the footwalk and Camden Row beyond, a figure caught my eye. I stood in the shadow of the curtain and peered out. It was Mr. Redgrave. He ascended the stairs, then hesitated in front of the door before descending once more. I'd never witnessed any hint of indecision in him. What had brought him to such a pass? Had Ainslie already written something in haste? If so, he must have come as soon as he'd received her message.

He remained standing at the base of the stairs, head lowered. And I made my decision, hurrying toward the front door and catching an unwary Dreda by the hand along the way, so as to give rise to no gossip. I murmured a promise to explain everything later, if only she'd come. Then we hastened onward. Somehow, I had to pretend I'd happened upon an ordinary caller, not the gentleman who'd so deeply wounded my sister and who might mean to cause further damage still.

Jade gave a soft rumble. *It would be more satisfying to pin him down and demand answers than to pander to convention.*

Perhaps, but then we'd lose any plausible deniability that remains. Not to mention any chance of mending matters.

You still think that's possible?

I stepped through the door. *I don't know. But for Ainslie, I wish to try.*

Risha's light softened, and she came to rest on my shoulder, the gentle sweep of her wings warming where they touched. Her unexpected support bolstered me, and I descended the stairs, resisting the oppressive pressure of his wards. "Mr. Redgrave. What a surprise to find you here. Won't you come in?"

The sunlight filtering through the poplars revealed lines of strain etched across his face. "Ah, Miss Caldwell, that's very kind, but I think I'd best not. I came in haste after I received a letter from Miss Ainslie, but on second thought, I don't wish to trouble her. She made her sentiments quite plain." He half-pivoted, then turned back toward me. "Only—do you know how I have offended her?"

"I cannot speak for Ainslie," I said softly.

"And she's made it clear she never wishes to see me again." His brown eyes darkened, and his shoulders seemed to hollow. "Aunt Hester said she passed a pleasant visit with the three of you. I'd hoped . . ." He straightened, gripping his walking stick. "It's of no consequence. I'll respect her wishes and plague her no more. But please tell her if she ever changes her mind or wishes to discuss what's wrong and how I might make amends, she has only to send word."

Whatever his ties to the Vigil, I sensed his sincerity in this. He respected her enough to honor her request, though it clearly caused him pain. This choice, coupled with the exchange I'd witnessed between him and Elodie—did it mean he truly loved her? I lowered my head. How had we all become entangled in such a mess? It would have been far easier to deal with the Redgraves if they were wholly villainous. "I'll tell her."

"That's very good of you." He offered another bow, then hesitated once more on the footwalk. He looked as if he wanted to say something more, but in the end, he simply shook his head and departed, leaving me cold and weary.

"Well." Dreda released a soft sigh. "You know why she won't see him, don't you, Miss Jessa?"

"I do, and I fear it won't be an easy hurdle to cross." I watched the empty doorway, seeing again the look in his eyes. Was it even possible to change the situation? Should I take the risk to try?

Dreda moved to stand by my side. "You'll see a way, if there's one to be found."

"I'll do my best—meanwhile, she'll need all the support we can offer." Because if she had to endure much more . . .

"I know she prefers to keep active. I'll offer to go out with her on the morrow."

"Thank you." When Dreda vanished back into the depths of the house, I lingered beneath the poplars. I needed to speak with Ainslie, to find out what she'd said to Mr. Redgrave in her letter and inform her of his visit, but I required some time to collect myself first. With Jade and Risha at my side, I slipped around the house and into the garden, where I sank down into the soft mossy expanse beneath the oak. Jade curled up in my lap, her presence warm and consoling. Yet she refrained from speaking into my mind—perhaps she knew that one more input would entirely overwhelm me.

Lianne was lost, Ainslie bound to an unknown fae, vulnerable and heartbroken, and the Vigil sought me, perhaps all of us. How much of it was my fault? Perhaps Riven had been right. My presence here had endangered my family, drawn the interest of both fae and mortal enemies. I braced against the oak, and its bark dug into my back.

Despite my attempts to be discreet so far, I'd betrayed far too much to those who watched me. I'd hesitated to involve myself in the missing persons investigation because of Mr. Ludne, yet all along, the Redgraves had presented a far greater danger, because we'd allowed them so close. All the Vigil needed were the smallest scraps of suspicion to construct their accusations, and they'd assembled much more.

How long before they used their information?

My eyes slid shut.

I'd attempted to straddle the line between worlds, satisfying the conventions of neither, and where had it gotten me? For all my cautions, I'd been exposed in some measure. And now I must act, before the Redgraves did.

But how? The low notes of the oak thrummed in my chest as I considered what I knew of them. They had Vigil ties; they were accomplished in the arts of espionage and deception. They'd investigated me and found evidence they'd been reluctant to use, though they'd had ample opportunity.

Despite all that, I couldn't regard them as enemies. The exchange between Mr. Redgrave and Elodie revealed by the abutilon might well have been a discussion between my sisters and me, their affection for one another and their resolve for duty shining through their words and expressions. And Mr. Redgrave had always treated Ainslie with respect—as a person and an equal, not only a woman who'd caught his eye. She might believe his affection false, but after seeing him today, I disagreed. Still, whatever his feelings, if he'd resolved to protect Avons from Otherworldly threats—and he believed me to represent one such danger—he'd have to act.

Which brought me full circle. I couldn't consider the other pressing problems until I'd remedied this situation and the immediate danger the Redgraves posed. My head throbbed. I knew the fae solution: glamour answers from them, then sweep away all recall of our interactions and claim the records while brother and sister remained in a fuddled haze, before moving on to others of the clan, if needed.

The pounding in my temples intensified. Whatever they'd done, I refused to violate them so. I knew what it was to feel helpless before fae, and to become that threat, to wrench away memories without care for the damage I might cause—I could not.

Yet only one alternative presented itself . . .

I'd have to offer up the truth.

The whole truth.

I'd rather root out a blackthorn hedge by hand than become so vulnerable. Yet aside from force, it was the only way I could maneuver them to keep this secret—and hold them to their word. By exposing myself to their censure, I just might be able to protect us from true harm.

I buried my face in Jade's fur, her sweet-grass scent filling my senses. Then she tensed. *Burke approaches.*

A moment later, he rounded the corner of the house. "Miss Caldwell? Is something amiss?"

"Mr. Burke." I scrambled to my feet, blinking rapidly. "I didn't expect you back so soon."

"I wanted to examine the gardens to see if I could find any trace of trespass here. I'd intended to look for a chance to speak with you about what's been uncovered." His steel-gray eyes softened. "But I didn't expect to find you in such distress. Is this about your maid?"

His kindness raked across my soul, as sharp as firethorn spikes. I'd deceived him, much as the Redgraves had deceived me. What would he say if he knew? I pressed a hand to my chest. "I feel as though I've failed her."

And so many others as well.

He closed the distance between us, standing far closer than

was proper. "Is that all? Now that Riven has involved himself, I'd wondered . . . I trust this time you'd tell me if—"

As if the mention of his name summoned him, the brilliant array of a passing opened, and Riven strode through. His jaw tightened as he surveyed us. "Causing trouble, Burke?"

"Rather, attempting to alleviate it."

"It doesn't look that way."

"He's done nothing. It's . . ." I couldn't divulge the situation with the Redgraves in front of Mr. Burke, so I simply shook my head. "It's of no consequence compared to finding Lianne."

Riven arched a brow, but did not press. Instead, he wove a concealment glamour about us, then turned to Mr. Burke. "I trust you found something, since you returned in such haste."

Mr. Burke touched his ward. Did it respond in some way to the working of glamour? Or could ordinary mortals in some way sense the change in atmosphere? "As I told Jessa, I returned to examine the gardens as well as discuss current theories. But since you're here, I'd like to know why you've chosen to involve yourself. What does it gain the fae to assist in this matter?"

"I have an understanding with Jessa."

Mr. Burke's brows slashed downward. "And what price have you demanded for your assistance this time?"

"My dealings with her are no concern of yours."

I shrank back further. Despite the fact they'd worked together to bring down both Lord West and Uros, Mr. Burke distrusted Riven's motives simply because he was fae—as I'd done for so long. If the truth became known, would he view me in the same light?

"Anything that impacts the safety of mortals in Avons concerns me," Mr. Burke said.

Sharp shards of light gathered about Riven. "If that's your concern, I suggest you worry about those in imminent peril. Lianne has gone to the Otherworld."

The confirmation tightened my chest. Whatever the risks, I could no longer hold this investigation at a distance for fear of exposure. To find those missing—if they could be found—I couldn't rely on mortal senses alone, couldn't abide by mortal proprieties in full. And yet, knowing the Redgraves and the Vigil kept watch . . .

"What did you find?" Mr. Burke was far too committed a stratesman to ignore a lead in favor of continuing a personal argument.

"I traced her to Shepherd's Bush, where she vanished through a passing prism."

"Where did it lead?"

"It had been removed by the time I arrived. Only traces of its energy remained. She could have come out anywhere."

"Then she's truly gone." I wrapped my arms about myself, wishing for the warmth of a shawl despite the radiant afternoon sun.

"For now. Likely for good. The fae who claimed her either can't create passings or used the prism to further obscure his or her identity." The light about him dissipated. "Aside from the passing prism, nothing Other intersected with her path along the way."

I struggled to form a logical follow-up question, my thoughts as beleaguered as roots slogging through waterlogged clay—in this case, the clay being the blighted emotions that slowed any attempt to process the situation.

Mr. Burke frowned. "If Otherkind didn't coerce her, then why would she have gone? Are you able to say with certainty no Otherworldly creature crossed her path?"

"Yes."

Spikes of speedwell swayed in the breeze, brushing my skirt, and I skimmed my fingers across their tops. "Then surely that suggests a bargain? What else could have lured her there, if no fae were present?"

"There are other possibilities." The set of his shoulders suggested he'd not speak of them. "It's best to keep an open mind at this juncture."

"I intended to share one such possibility before your aunt interrupted earlier." Mr. Burke cast a glance toward the house, as if Aunt Caris might materialize to spirit me away once more. "A number of the missing individuals met with Collectors in the weeks prior to their disappearance, a fact that went unnoticed until I began revisiting the households to gather information about possible binding marks. In questioning them afresh, I discovered the connection."

"Then perhaps the man I saw with Lianne wasn't a suitor, but a Collector. What if the Collectors are the ones bound by bargain, and they must deliver mortals to the passing prisms to be handed over to the Otherworld?"

We both looked at Riven.

He gave a curt nod. "It's not beyond the realm of possibility —certainly more likely than all the missing bearing bargains."

"Or could the Collectors have brought something back with them?" Absently, I twined together speedwell stems, pressing back emotion to better assess the situation. "Something that exerted influence over the missing, compelling them to seek these prisms?"

"While the households were searched for signs of a break-in, different stratesmen visited each scene." Mr. Burke tapped his fingers against his leg, as if considering. "If there were some small object common to them, it could have been overlooked— or could have been an item kept on the individual and therefore brought back to the Otherworld to be used again."

"Which makes it exceedingly difficult to prove or disprove." I released the speedwell to sway in the wind once more. If this were in fact some scheme of the Collectors—something they sold on a black market of sorts—then the matter became more one of mortal greed than fae hostility, though I imagined the fae would take advantage of any opportunity presented. "There's one fault with that theory. Even if she met with a Collector, Lianne wouldn't have had the funds to purchase Otherworldly items, unlike the others who have disappeared."

Mr. Burke shook his head. "Not all payment must be monetary."

Oh.

A knot snarled in my chest. Would she have felt driven to such lengths?

"Regardless, the next logical step is to speak with these Collectors," Riven said.

Mr. Burke straightened. "Agreed. I'll go after I leave here."

"You think they'd welcome a stratesman with open arms?" Skepticism bled into Riven's voice.

"I think they'd fare better with a stratesman than with fae."

I stepped between them. "In this case, I think neither of you would inspire anyone to make confidences, unless Riven means to glamour the body of Collectors entire. May I suggest another course?"

Mr. Burke nodded.

"Mrs. Darrington has offered her assistance before, and I believe she might be of help in this matter."

"How so?" he said.

"She's wealthy and known to be eccentric—she's the ideal victim for this sort of scheme, since she appears a vulnerable mark."

His eyes narrowed. "And why would she want to undertake such an endeavor?"

I folded my hands, tucking them in my skirt. "Because she recently confided in me concerns about the Otherworld invading our own."

"Did she?" Mr. Burke shook his head. "If even the elderly ladies of Avons are developing suspicions, then it seems the Magistry's schemes for secrecy are failing in earnest. Be that as it may, I hardly think it's a good idea to allow the two of you to approach the Collectors on your own, with no means of gaining assistance should the matter provoke a hostile reaction."

"They might turn us away, but I can't imagine they'd openly act against us." And if they did, I wasn't defenseless.

"I shouldn't even consider it, but I can't deny the Collectors will become tight-lipped the moment they suspect official Magistry business." He hesitated a moment. "If Lord Riven agrees to keep clear of the Collectors, then I'll agree."

Riven shrugged. "For now, I see no need for my involvement."

"Then it's settled." I forced a bright smile. "I'll speak with Mrs. Darrington, and meanwhile, I'll see if our own servants know anything about Collectors."

"While Jessa pursues the Collector angle, I intend to visit the households of the missing. If anything Other remains, it should be easy enough to uncover."

Riven's tone practically dared Mr. Burke to protest—and unless I missed my guess, he greatly desired to do so. Yet people were vanishing into the Otherworld, so how could he? As far as Mr. Burke knew, Riven was the only one of our party who could detect the presence of Other, and it was an avenue we couldn't allow to go unexplored.

His jaw tightened, and then finally he said, "I assume you'd not have to interact with the inhabitants to determine this?"

"Correct."

"Then go."

"I wasn't asking your permission, merely stating my intention."

"Oh, I'm well aware." Mr. Burke's lips tilted upward slightly. "But you could at least let me pretend to grant it—pretend I retain some shred of control over what's supposed to be my investigation—rather than have to face the fact that I've allowed myself to be pulled into unorthodox shenanigans that would result in my immediate dismissal if the truth came to light."

"Don't worry." Though Riven's tone remained dry, amusement lit his eyes. "You're far too useful in your current position for me to allow your dismissal. I'd intervene on your behalf before it got that far."

"Just when I thought things couldn't get worse, I find I was mistaken," Mr. Burke muttered.

I laughed softly, some of the tension of the day lifting from my shoulders. "I find that assumption a dangerous one."

"That's why we have a pact among stratesmen never to comment on how well things are going—nor conversely, to ask if matters can get any worse. Either are sure to usher in a string of unprecedented catastrophes." His words held a wry twist. "Evidently, that holds true for thoughts also."

Riven shook his head, but his lips lifted slightly. "Mortal superstitions never cease to take surprising turns."

I raised a brow. "You mean to suggest fae hold no superstitious beliefs?"

"We're not much for superstition. That requires acknowledging things might lie outside one's control." His dry tone conveyed equal mockery for his own kind.

"An impossibility, of course." Mr. Burke didn't manage to fully stifle his smile. "Given that our superstitions are mostly about Otherfolk, I'd hate to consider what yours might be, if you indulged in them."

"Perhaps this is one case where ignorance is preferred," I said. Was it wrong to indulge in lighthearted conversation on the heels of Lianne's disappearance? On the face of it, it did not seem to honor her, and yet the relaxed exchange had cleared my thoughts and strengthened my resolve, reminding me I didn't face the situation alone—that Mr. Burke and Riven would help in any way they could.

Though things had taken a turn for the worse, we knew more than we had before. And however fragile the threads of evidence we'd uncovered, we had new lines of investigation to pursue, at least as it concerned the missing. And perhaps delving further into this fae activity in Avons would shed some light on Ainslie's situation as well—certainly, I'd hold to that hope, even without possessing evidence to support it. As for the Redgraves . . . well, I had a plan, however discomfiting.

"Will you keep me informed?" Mr. Burke's question drew me back to the conversation.

"About anything of note," Riven said.

I glanced back at the house. "If that's settled, we should be about our business. Aunt Caris will likely seek me soon—she's been uneasy since the events in Withern, and this situation hasn't helped. Perhaps you could call again in another day or two, Mr. Burke? I will find a way to send word if there's anything requiring your attention sooner."

"Very well." He gave a nod and took the path back toward the footwalk.

Though Riven followed Mr. Burke to the gate, he glanced back over his shoulder. He might make a pretense of departure, but his expression made it clear—he wasn't done with our conversation.

The tension that had lifted crashed back onto my shoulders. What did he mean to say?

CHAPTER 25

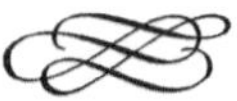

Once Mr. Burke departed, Riven returned, covering the ground with a loose, easy stride. When his glamour wrapped around us once more, he asked, "What transpired with Redgrave?"

I tilted my head. "How did you—oh, you mean Mr. Cyril Redgrave?"

"I did. But now I'd like to know what you thought I meant."

I hesitated. I'd wanted nothing more than to discuss the matter with him, but now I found myself reluctant to hear his proposed solution, which was likely to be very fae in nature . . . I certainly couldn't fathom that he'd favor my plan, and yet, I still wanted his counsel.

I shook myself. When had I become so irresolute? The oak swayed gently overhead. "Well, I—"

In the distance, the door creaked open, and Ainslie surged into the garden, Ada gliding behind her.

"Jessa?" Ada called.

Would it be more alarming if I did not reveal myself—or if I appeared abruptly? They halted midway down the path.

"She must be here," Ainslie said. "We've searched the whole house. Where else could she have gone?"

"What if she was taken too?" Alarm rang in Ada's voice.

I looked at Riven. "Please release the glamour."

The threads of light dissipated at once, allowing them to perceive us beneath the oak.

Ainslie started, and Ada leapt back. "Have you . . . were you here all along?"

"Yes, and it's best if we remain concealed so as not to draw attention." I extended my hands, beckoning them to join us.

Reluctantly, they moved forward, huddling close to each other as Riven rewove the glamour.

Ainslie rubbed her hands along her arms. "Lord Riven, I beg your pardon, but we have unfinished business."

"Carry on." The gleam in his eyes suggested he did not intend to take the hint and remove himself.

That meant any chance of presenting the facts—and my plan —in a well-ordered fashion had vanished, because if the expression on Ainslie's face was any indication, she did not mean to wait.

"Very well." She spun to face me. "Dreda let slip that Char —Mr. Redgrave called, but she would say no more. I sent him a message telling him I wished to sever any connection between us, and I could not possibly have been plainer, so I cannot fathom what brought him, nor can I wait any longer to know. What did he say?"

The world beyond the glamour shimmered. "That if you ever change your mind and want to tell him what's gone amiss and how he can make amends, you only have to send word. Otherwise, he will respect your wishes and stay away."

"And . . . you believe him sincere?" Her voice broke.

"I do."

"But how can we truly know, when all this time he pretended . . ." She pulled in an unsteady breath. "Oh, this is absurd. I should be able to let it go—it's not as if we had an understanding."

"But you cared for him a great deal. And though he kept secrets, I believe his feelings for you were—are genuine."

"My feelings don't matter, nor do his. Not when he means to harm you."

The air suddenly snapped with pressure, a storm-swirl of Other filling the space about us. "What precisely does Redgrave mean to do?"

I offered the most concise summation I could. With every word, Ainslie withdrew further into herself, while Ada watched, worry evident in her gaze.

Riven's expression gave no hint of his thoughts. "How do you intend to manage this threat?"

"That's what I've been trying to figure out." I fidgeted with a loose thread on my glove. "I'm convinced they mean well and regret their obligation to collect information on me."

"Regret will not spare you your justice system." Riven's brows slashed down. "Unless you are prepared to sever ties with this world and abandon the missing to their own devices."

Ainslie's breath caught.

And Ada stumbled back slightly. "Oh, Jessa, you're not—"

"No. I'm not." And Riven knew as much, but doubtless he'd wanted me to say it, to make me consider what I risked.

His jaw tightened slightly. "Then you intend to remove their memories?"

I shook my head. "They believe they're protecting Byren. Should they suffer for it?"

"Are you willing to accept the consequences if they do not?"

"I am." I lifted my chin, though I trembled inwardly.

"Then what do you intend?"

"To tell them the truth of my nature."

"You would hand your enemy a weapon?" His voice held an edge now.

"What if they don't have to be enemies? If I can mend matters, I have to try."

"You're not the one who has broken them."

"Nevertheless, I'm the only one who currently sees both sides." I spread my hands. "I don't plan to throw caution to the wind and just hand them the information. They'll have to agree to silence first."

"Ah. You propose a bargain and geas?" The storm-swirl faded slightly. "It could still go sideways if they balk."

"That's a risk I'm willing to take."

Ainslie's lips were pressed together tightly, as if to hold back her emotions, and Ada clenched her hands at her sides. I would have rather not had this conversation in front of my sisters, but they did have the right to know.

Ada stepped closer. "But perhaps Lord Riven's reservations are valid. If you return to call on them, you'll be at their mercy. What if they try to take you to the Vigil at once?"

Riven shook his head. "When I spoke of risks, I didn't intend to suggest Jessa isn't capable of managing them if they mean physical harm. It's just that they could make it very difficult for her to remain in this world, if she cannot convince them to agree to a bargain and she refuses to claim their memories."

"You don't have to do this for me, Jessa." Ainslie's shoulders drew inward. "I don't like to think of anyone having their memories taken, but if you somehow think you must mend matters because of my feelings for Mr. Redgrave—I don't want to lose you. That matters more."

"It's not that alone. I'm doing this because I feel it's right."

"Then perhaps one of us should go with you," Ada said.

"I don't want you dragged deeper into this. As it stands now, I don't think they suspect either of you, and there's no sense risking us all."

Her lips tilted downward. "But you shouldn't have to face them alone."

"I agree. And I intend to accompany her." Riven turned to me. "If you'll accept my company."

"I'd welcome it." The notes lilting overhead echoed my relief. Since he could discern truth from lie, his presence would be invaluable. And despite what I'd said to my sisters, I'd no desire to face the Redgraves alone.

"Lord Riven, you know my sentiments about Other. It has not been kind to me." Ainslie's fingers stole to her binding mark. "Still, I'm glad you're going with Jessa. Please . . . don't let them hurt her."

"I won't." His voice was low, reassuring.

And she visibly relaxed. "Good. And Jessa, I expect to hear everything that passes between you and the Redgraves. Promise you won't hold anything back to spare my feelings?"

"You shall know the whole," I said. "But it will have to wait until tomorrow—we can't reasonably call at this hour, but I believe Elodie has set a precedent to allow morning calls, however unconventional they are for Avons."

She sighed. "It will make for a long night of wondering."

And she didn't need anything else to weary her. In the diffused light that shone through the glamour, her binding mark seemed to glow and her skin appeared almost translucent. I gripped her hand, and its fine bones rested closer to the surface of the skin than usual. My heart twisted. "Why don't you ask Estine for some heart's ease tea? I have a jar in my compounding room."

"I'm not in danger of the vapors." A tart note crept into her voice.

"I didn't mean to suggest you were, but rest would do us all good. And . . . I'd like a word with Riven alone."

Ada's gaze rested on him for a moment, then returned to me. "I quite agree. Come, Ainslie, we can pester Estine like old times. I'm sure I smelled scones earlier."

"Oh, very well."

With that, they stepped beyond the glamour, leaving us in silence.

Riven surveyed the garden. "I see you removed the nightspire."

"It was encroaching beneath the ground, and I feared it would breach the house from below." Even now, the echo of its melody seemed to prick against my skin. "But I think I revealed more than I intended to whomever sent it."

"Perhaps it was meant to provoke that response." His shoulders lifted. "But if it sought to cross its bounds, you'd no choice."

I traced the mottled pattern of the lichen on the oak's bark. "Sometimes I feel as if I'm beginning to understand how to use some tiny part of my affinities, like with the nightspire. Other times, I feel I know nothing. With Elodie, when all this happened, I resolved I wouldn't glamour her, and then . . . somehow I did."

The pale green of the lichen and gray-brown of the bark blurred together. Why was I confessing this now?

"What happened before you glamoured her?"

I recounted the scene, nausea swirling within as I recalled her face.

Riven nodded, as if I'd said what he expected. "You were drawing in power to deflect the wards—likely more than you knew. Your desire to protect your sisters almost certainly overruled your conscious decision, your affinities responding to your deeper desire."

I shuddered. "But . . . that means it could happen again, any time my emotions are heightened."

"Yes. It is one of the things fae are first taught to govern, lest they betray more than they intend of their emotional state."

"Could . . . could you teach me?"

"No, not now." He scrubbed a hand across the back of his neck. "I have already spoken more freely of such things than is technically permissible. Instruction comes within a court. Never outside it."

Did that mean if I chose to remain in this world, I'd forever fumble to understand my affinities? Whatever the case, I couldn't expect him to violate the laws of his court. I dropped my hands to my sides. "I understand."

But I did not understand where I belonged, nor how to meet the expectations of all those I loved. I was not fae enough to satisfy the Otherworld, nor mortal enough to satisfy my own—

and right now, both threatened not only me, but also my family. Above all else, I must keep them safe.

If my plans failed . . . No, I could not think it. I had chosen a course, and I would hold to it, whatever the cost.

I woke on the floor in front of the hearth, tangled with Jade in true-form, morning sunlight slanting over us. Wait, what had happened? How had I . . .

Oh. Slowly, my thoughts ordered themselves and recall returned. I'd requested this arrangement after a sequence of nightmares—full of the Vigil and the Redgraves and nightspire consuming Ainslie. In the small hours of the night, I'd reached for her. *Jade?*

Mm. Her sleepiness had spilled over into my mind.

Would . . . would you shift into true-form?

The sleepy sensation vanished. *Do you believe there's a threat?*

No, it's just . . . . At Kilmere, after everything that had happened with Lord West, when I'd rested with her in true-form, I'd felt wholly safe—and I craved that feeling again. *Your true-form is so snuggly. And comforting.*

Comforting? She snorted. *I think you mean fierce and intim-idating.*

That too, but also . . . warm and snuggly.

A rumble sounded low in her chest. *No kit-isne has ever been known as snuggly.*

Despite her protest, she shifted, standing next to the bed,

her head lowered to touch mine. As we'd no longer fit in the bed together, I snatched a quilt and we lay in front of the hearth, her body cradling mine. With the rich sweet-grass scent of her fur hanging over me and her warmth surrounding me, I'd drifted into dreamless slumber at last.

Yet now, footsteps approached the bedroom. If we were found like this . . . I scrambled to my feet, and Jade shifted just as Aunt Caris marched into the room, her face pinched. "Jessa, I've had a most distressing account from Holden."

She only used my actual name when she was truly upset. Mind racing, I clutched the blanket to my chest. "About what?"

"Your conduct."

Risha flared bright, drifting over from the windowsill to perch on my shoulder, and Jade's tail twitched.

What had Holden told her? I'd been altogether too careless of my reputation of late, which meant he could cast blame upon me on any number of accounts, and I could not fathom which he'd chosen.

"He says you received Mr. Burke in the garden alone and unannounced—he looked out the window and saw you talking."

He must have seen us before Riven arrived to glamour the scene. "That is true, but it wasn't planned."

"Do you think that matters in the least?" Aunt Caris pulled in a quick breath. "If Holden saw you, someone else might have done so also. And he said you stood far closer than was proper—anyone might have mistaken it for some sort of assignation."

The embroidered flowers on the quilt rasped against my arms as I pulled it close. "We've walked through Avons together before."

"You must see that a chaperoned stroll in a public place is an altogether different affair."

"He was here about the case, nothing more."

Her hand sliced downward. "It doesn't matter. I forbid you to speak with him again, under any circumstance. However grateful I am for the help he's offered in the past, clearly he has no consideration for the damage he might do your reputation."

Never had mortal conventions chafed quite so strongly. "Aunt Caris, I will do my utmost to avoid drawing censure, but I cannot agree to avoid Mr. Burke altogether. Lianne has vanished, most likely into a situation of great danger. Some things supersede propriety."

"The Magistry will manage her case, and if needs must, Mr. Burke can interview you or the others in our household with a proper chaperone present." She spoke as if that settled the matter.

And in other times, I would have conceded—or smoothed the situation over with some noncommittal reply. This time warmth bloomed in my chest, and I found I could not. "I understand your concerns, but you must believe I know what I'm about—"

"How can you know? You're unfamiliar with the ways of gentlemen, and I'll not see you come to ruin."

"Aunt Caris, Mr. Burke isn't the sort of man to ruin a lady—"

"You can't know that!" Her voice cracked. "You cannot possibly know what lies within his heart, not upon so short an acquaintance. Perhaps never. A dalliance does no damage to a gentleman, but it can ruin a lady forever. It may be unjust, but it's true."

"Perhaps so, but I'm no longer a child." My hands tightened in the folds of the quilt. "You must trust me to make this choice."

"I once thought the same—that I knew and could choose." The bloom vanished from her cheeks, leaving her pale and worn. "And I was wrong. I'll not see you pay the price I did—I would give anything to keep you from such pain, even have you hate me."

"Aunt Caris, I could never hate you."

"You have no idea what I've done!"

I'd never heard her lift her voice, betray any sign of unladylike emotion. What she'd done . . . She spoke of her secret, held close all this time. I stepped closer. "I would if you told me. Why should you carry this alone?"

"Perhaps, after all, confession must be part of my penance." She stood still and colorless, her fingers creeping toward her locket. "Very well. I will tell you. When I was young, I fell deeply in love with a dashing lord. He was of a good family, and I thought he—I believed he returned my feelings. He said he did. He claimed his family had set store by a match of greater fortune than I possessed, but that his heart and devotion belonged to me." The words tumbled faster from her, gathering force like a stream spilling down a mountainside. "He suggested an elopement, saying that his family would then be forced to accept me afterward. I could think of nothing but a future with him, so I agreed. After all, however upset Mother and Father would be with such an irregular event, their sentiments would vanish before the prospect of such an excellent match."

Risha leaned forward, her attention rapt on the mortal drama, while I dared not speak, lest Aunt Caris change her mind about taking me into her confidence.

"I secured permission to visit a friend of mine—to stay a month or two, as she'd invited me often enough before, only I never told her. It was a cover for our elopement. After what he called our honeymoon, I found myself with child."

A child? I checked my instinctive exclamation. Of all the things I'd dreamt, I'd never imagined this. What had befallen our unknown cousin?

She drew a shuddering breath. "When I told him, saying surely now we should return to our families and share the joyful news, he informed me that there was no marriage, that the ceremony and documents—all were a sham. It was only a game to him, I suppose."

The warmth that had kindled in my chest earlier burst into flame. Aunt Caris loved with deep devotion, and he'd twisted that to his own advantage, treating her no better than refuse.

"If it became known I carried a child . . . that I'd allowed Lord—that I'd allowed him to ruin me, I could never have appeared in society again. The child's future would have been even bleaker, his illegitimacy a taint impossible to overcome." Her voice wavered. "I knew what I must do, but I couldn't find the courage to confess to my parents, so I went instead to Gillian. She was already wed, with two little ones of her own, and I thought . . . I hoped she'd help me. She spoke no word of condemnation, but I could see her shock and disappointment. And why shouldn't she feel so? If I'd only been more wary, if I'd insisted on a proper wedding instead of allowing myself to be blinded by love—"

"The condemnation isn't yours to bear." The only blame went to the one who'd used her so cruelly. The melody of the oak swirled about me, its notes low and protective, and I reached out and clasped her hand.

She clutched it as if it were the only thing keeping her from drowning. "Gillian arranged for me to travel to the far north and stay with Melle's family. That was long before she dwelt in Milburn."

Melle. Of course that was where she fit—the old friend who'd summoned us with her letters that could have incriminated Aunt Caris. An illegitimate child surfacing would have blighted our prospects, which mattered to her above all. But what an unbearable burden to carry alone. If only she'd spoken sooner.

"She and I became fast friends, and she provided tremendous support through the months I resided with them. The circumstances of my son's conception didn't seem to trouble her at all, and she helped me find courage to endure the moment I surrendered him." With her free hand, she grasped the locket at her neck. "I have a bit of his hair here, the only thing of his I kept. Melle and I maintained a correspondence for some years afterward, in which I spoke freely. Perhaps it was a great folly, but she was the only one who understood. She was there that dreadful moment when my son . . . when I had to part with him forever, when he went to a family that could give him a life far better than any I could offer."

"Oh, Aunt Caris. I'm so very sorry." How had she endured such a loss? The absence of a child . . . Could one ever recover? I tightened my grip on her hand. "And that is what she held over you to get you to come to Milburn?"

"Yes, my dear. Yet if I'd not been so naive, she'd have had nothing to hold over me, nothing with which to threaten ruin to those I loved." Aunt Caris's eyes glistened with unshed tears. "A lady cannot be too careful."

"I understand." Yet perhaps not the lesson she intended. If the innocent had to bear the pain of wrongs done against them, then somehow our world must change. "But surely you must see none of this changes how I view you. You were not at fault."

"You should not be so forgiving, not of actions that were . . . folly at best." She shook her head. "I trust you'll not speak of this to anyone, not even your sisters? Aside from Melle, only Gillian knows."

"If that is what you desire, I'll respect it. But those who love you will think none the worse of you for the truth."

She shuddered. "If Melisina ever found out—"

I squeezed her hand. "Your secret is safe with me."

"Thank you, my dear." She straightened. "I know you've not understood why I insist on the proprieties even when they seem such a great inconvenience, but they're also a protection."

Certainly, I better fathomed why she clung to society's conventions with such fervor. How much had she suffered, mourning for her child? How much had her child lost for not ever knowing her? If ever a woman was made to be a wife and mother, it was Aunt Caris, with her generous, nurturing nature. I studied the full lines of her face. "Have you ever considered seeking your son?"

Her son, our cousin. What would it mean if we found him? Would he desire kinship or shun the connection?

"Of course I've thought of it, my dear. How could I not?" Her shoulders slumped. "But I gave up my right to disrupt his life when I surrendered him to a new family. And if it ever became known—well, I have the three of you girls to consider."

My eyes burned. "We want your happiness also. If someday you change your mind—"

"No, I am resolved. I'll do what's right in this." Aunt Caris swiped at her cheeks and smoothed the front of her gown. "But I must admit, it feels good to speak of it, after all this time. Gillian never does. I think she prefers to forget it happened."

"Such things are not easily forgotten. If you ever want to talk of him, then I'm always willing to listen." I'd experienced a similar relief after my confession to my sisters, a lifting of the burden brought by truth, even when it could not change the circumstances. The least I could do was offer the same.

"Thank you, my dear." A soft sigh escaped her. "Now, I really must go speak with Estine. The staff is still overset by Lianne's disappearance. Perhaps we should postpone our dinner party, if you don't think the Redgraves and Lord Riven would take offense."

"Given the circumstances, they're sure to understand. I'd intended to call on the Redgraves this morning anyway. I'll take Dreda and carry the news."

"Thank you, my dear. But hadn't you better wait for afternoon?"

"They don't mind morning calls, or so Elodie has informed me."

Aunt Caris nodded. "And Lord Riven?"

"I believe he means to call again soon. I'll inform him also—you have enough to manage."

She gave my cheek a gentle kiss, a sealing of the new connection between us. "Very good."

Well. Jade stared after her retreating back. *Mortal affairs are peculiar ones.*

Yes. I'd considered the prospect of a lost love, but this is far worse —it's love betrayed and loss endured alone.

Jade stretched, her nails flashing sharp. *It is unfortunate that she withheld the name of her erstwhile suitor from her confession. We could make quite an impression, calling on this lord together.*

Despite the circumstances, a small smile tugged at my lips.

Whatever she claimed, Jade's protectiveness was extending from me to the rest of my family. *Since that would only cause more trouble, perhaps it's for the best we don't know. At least in some way the confession seems to have lightened Aunt Caris's load.*

I dressed swiftly—and simply, since I couldn't manage any elaborate styling of my unruly hair without Lianne—then I sought Dreda in her bedchamber.

She admitted me, a sketchbook tucked under one arm, and offered a cheery greeting, which I returned.

I hovered on the threshold. "I might be able to mend things between Mr. Redgrave and Ainslie, but I must speak to Mr. Redgrave and his sister in private. Will you accompany me as chaperone but then leave me to speak with him and Elodie alone?"

"I'd be glad to." She tucked away the sketchbook. "Though I hope your aunt does not learn of it."

"If she does, I'll make sure you receive no blame." I hesitated in the doorway. "While we're there, will you keep your ears open? I'd like to know what you hear and any impressions you have of the Redgrave household."

Her hazel eyes warmed. "Of course, Miss Jessa."

With that, I could put it off no longer.

It was time.

CHAPTER 27

Once again, I waited on the Redgraves' doorstep, but this time, Riven stood close enough that the light of his glamour spilled over me and the intense Other about him warmed my skin. His presence pushed back the influence of the wards, yet he remained concealed from mortal eyes. Unless things went dreadfully wrong, they'd never know he accompanied me—the situation was fraught enough without introducing another participant, whose presence I could not possibly explain.

On my left, Dreda remained unaware of Riven, her eyes bright and curious as she regarded the rune-wards scripted on the lintel.

I knocked, and a moment later, the butler opened the door. "Good morning, Miss Caldwell."

"I'm here to see Miss Redgrave."

"Is she expecting you?"

"No, but you may tell her I've come to speak about Miss Ainslie." It was true enough, in its way.

He invited us into the entry, then vanished into the depths of the house. We stood beneath a large medallion that unfurled across the ceiling, an elaborate gas chandelier in the center its only concession to modernity. Closer inspection revealed small runic wards woven through the swirled pattern of the medallion. My chest tightened, and I wrenched my gaze away.

Beneath arched panels set at intervals about the entry sat exotic plants in tall marble planters. I attended to their lively songs in a vain attempt to steady my ragged pulse.

Why had I thought this was a good idea?

Before I could reconsider, the butler returned. "This way, Miss Caldwell, if you please."

He ushered us into the drawing room, where Mr. Redgrave and Elodie sat on chairs beneath a large oil painting of the Fens. They both stood to greet me.

Elodie offered a gentle handclasp. "I hope you don't mind, but I asked my brother to join us. He's been quite worried about Ainslie. If it troubles you, he shall, of course, leave to grant us privacy."

Was it only because of Ainslie that Mr. Redgrave had come? Or because he did not want to risk Elodie speaking to me alone? A swell of queasiness surged through my body, one I couldn't blame on the wards this time, since Riven's power still swirled about me. "I'm glad you did. Truthfully, I'd hoped to talk with you together."

Riven took up a post near the windows, where the sunlight mingled with his glamour, and Dreda waited quietly at my side. I nodded toward her. "Since this is a private matter, Miss Twells has offered to withdraw, if there's a place she might wait at her leisure."

"Certainly." Mr. Redgrave offered her a small bow, a sign of respect not required by society—and one more point in his favor. "If you'll come this way, we have a conservatory that you might enjoy exploring."

Dreda nodded. "That would be nice."

As he escorted her from the room, Elodie gestured to the tea tray that sat on the scalloped table next to her. "Will you take some refreshment?"

My stomach knotted further. If I accepted, I feared it would only come back up. "Thank you, but no."

Silence stretched between us. Perhaps I should have accepted, if only to give myself something to do while I waited. I didn't have the wherewithal for small talk—and it appeared, for once, Elodie didn't either.

Jade leapt into my lap. *You may hold me, if you wish.*

I pulled her close as I could, my body icy despite the warmth she offered. Once Mr. Redgrave returned, I drew myself upright. I'd long considered which approach offered the best chance of swaying them; now I seized upon it. "I've come because there's a chance you can mend matters with Ainslie, if you care to do so."

"I want nothing more." Mr. Redgrave ran a hand through his hair, disarraying its usual perfection. "Will you tell me what's gone wrong?"

"Yes, but first you both must swear never to communicate anything we discuss today to another living soul, aside from Ada or Ainslie. You must not speak of it in open terms even between yourselves and certainly never write it down." If I wanted protection, I couldn't avoid the odd choice of wording, nor apparently the touch of glamour that unconsciously colored my voice—not a compulsion to accept, but rather one that urged them not to consider the peculiarities too deeply. I pressed my lips together tightly, resisting the urge to look at Riven.

"Of course." Mr. Redgrave leaned forward. "You can trust our discretion."

But his word alone wasn't enough. "Do you agree also, Elodie?"

She glanced at Mr. Redgrave. "I do."

Power passed between us, a vivid and living thing. Was that all? Had I created a geas? This time, I risked a glance at Riven.

He gave a slight nod.

I drew a deep breath, then plunged in. "When we came to call on your aunt, I discovered that you had a file detailing an investigation you'd conducted on me."

Elodie set down her cup so abruptly that tea sloshed over the edge.

Mr. Redgrave tensed. "There must be some mistake—"

"There's no mistake." I wrestled to steady my voice. Never mind how I felt, I needed to appear calm. "When Ainslie learned of it, she felt she needed to cut ties. I suggested we have a conversation to clear the air before any final decisions were made—on either side. I mean to be forthright with you, and I'd like the same courtesy in return, else we'll never reach any understanding."

Mr. Redgrave rubbed his jaw. "Then ask what you will."

I'd expected they'd demand a confession from me first, but I'd gladly take the reprieve. I inhaled the fragrance of jasmine that emanated from the pot on the mantel. "Did you come to Withern to investigate me?"

"We were sent at first to find out the truth about the curse, but it soon became apparent you collected oddities about you." Elodie spoke very softly. "It was our duty to find out more, but we—neither of us wished to do so."

"Your duty to whom? The Vigil?"

They both started.

"Sir Redgrave once served as First. Do you continue the tradition?"

"Not many know our ancestors founded the Vigil." Mr. Redgrave spoke slowly, stalling perhaps.

"I came by the knowledge recently and then found that a great deal made more sense—but not everything. Do you still serve?"

Elodie's chin lifted. "No Redgrave serves in the Vigil as you know it; rather, our family makes up the true Vigil. I realize it sounds ludicrous, and I cannot explain further, only to say it is a charge we carry. The ones who have since claimed the name of the Vigil—the Everstone Vigilists—seek their own power, for the most part. Even those who mean well are unable to provide true protection, because they've no notion of the truth about what happened . . . before, nor anything since."

A tingle went down my spine. "And what *did* happen before?"

"It's . . . I . . ." The color left her face, and her voice became choked. She pressed one palm against her chest, as if to alleviate some inner pain.

Mr. Redgrave rested a hand on her arm. "You know it's useless to try to speak, Elodie."

Useless?

How could that be, unless . . .

Unless they were already under a geas. That must be it. And if the geas concerned something that happened long ago—could it possibly be the Forgotten War? Or some of our past dealings with the Otherworld? If so, how had they come by the knowledge? "Is your whole family bound to keep the truths you know secret?"

He gave a terse nod. Evidently even that caused pain, for he winced. What did they know?

Jade perched upright on my lap. *Perhaps a great deal, if someone bothered to inflict a geas.*

Mr. Redgrave held my gaze, a challenge in his eyes. "You promised truth, but it seems to me you've instead asked a great deal while offering very little."

My heart thrummed against my stays. I should make my statement at once and have done with it, and yet . . . "What do you want to know?"

"What truly happened at Kilmere? What is the curse?" Elodie asked.

"Kilmere is a fae stronghold constructed in the mortal world, and its curse was a bargain made centuries ago that bound the descendants of Withern's original inhabitants to its dark purpose, on pain of death by basilisk venom." I was getting better at this explanation; it was starting to rattle from my tongue. Certainly it came far more readily than the confession: *I am fae.*

"That's . . . remarkably forthright." Some of the tension left her shoulders. "Thank you."

But Mr. Redgrave remained guarded, his features shuttered. "And how do you know this?"

My muscles coiled tight. "Because I have seen its workings and changed them. It no longer poses a threat to the inhabitants of Withern."

Elodie's lips drew into a tight line.

And Mr. Redgrave frowned. "You realize those are the sort of . . . mad remarks the fae-touched make."

"Charles, surely she's not—"

"I agree, she appears of sound mind." His jaw set. "So do you have any explanation to offer, Miss Caldwell?"

"I'm not fae-touched, though I did believe it of myself for most of my life."

"How very dreadful. What changed?" Elodie asked.

"I discovered the truth, but you may be . . . disinclined to believe it."

"We've heard and seen a great many peculiar things." Any trace of the society lady was gone; her expression was open and sincere. "And we'd like to understand."

Faint and bell-like, the melody of the abutilon that had started this all drifted down to me. It was determined, courageous. I would be also. I met her gaze, though I'd far rather have studied the floor. "I'm fae."

Her lips parted, and she recoiled, her hand instinctively flying to the ward at her neck.

Slowly, Mr. Redgrave shook his head. "Miss Caldwell . . ."

If I wasn't glamoured to a mortal appearance, perhaps it would be easier to sway them. Since I'd no notion how to shed it, I reached for the jasmine on the mantel, and its vines surged forth, spiraling over the chair in which I sat. "I promised the truth, and that's what I've given."

Elodie's fingers went white about the ward, and Mr. Redgrave's hand drifted to the dagger at his side. Riven shifted, the slightest charge filtering into the air.

Elodie stared at me, her eyes wide and dark. "If this is true, as it seems, how can you have only just discovered your nature?"

"I don't have an easy answer for that, but I believed I was mortal my entire life, until things started happening that I could not explain."

"A changeling then?" Mr. Redgrave's voice deepened.

"There's much I don't yet understand—"

"The source of your blood doesn't matter." His hands fisted. "Given your confession, you understand it's my duty to take you in? I have a sworn charge to protect Byren from Other, in whatever form it may take."

The pressure in the air increased, and I breathed deep of the jasmine, its rich scent quieting the riotous surge of my pulse. "I understand you must protect Byren, but I'm no danger to it."

"Your very nature makes you a threat."

In this moment, I felt incredibly vulnerable, and yet, by virtue of my blood, they feared *me*. "If that were true, then why would I come to treat with you, rather than strip you of your memories?"

Elodie regarded me warily. "Have you meddled with our memories before? Glamoured us to your bidding? Glamoured me to feel . . . to feel as though you could be a friend?"

"I've never taken memories from you." Although Riven had, after Kilmere assaulted her. "Nor did I ever glamour a friendship between us. Whatever connection we experienced sprang from common interests and a shared desire to protect those we love."

I could have left it at that, attempted to distract and omit my use of glamour—but I had promised the truth, and instinct told me this was not time to withhold. "But yesterday, I did glamour you when you found me after I discovered the file in the library. I was so afraid—and I thought you would ask impossible questions. I didn't know how to respond."

"You're fae." Her grip on the ward tightened further. "What have you to fear?"

"Stronger fae. The enemies I've made helping mortals. The Vigil harming those I love." My voice shook. "You don't understand. I may be fae, but I know very little of the Otherworld, though I'm learning more each day, and the mortal world . . . If it knew the truth, I wouldn't be able to make a home here, not as myself. I'm caught somewhere . . . between, and I don't know what my future holds."

"Then why trust us with this?" Mr. Redgrave folded his arms across his chest. "Why not continue to glamour us or strip us of memories or whatever it is you fae do?"

"Because I don't want to hurt either of you." The jasmine curled up to caress my cheek—oh, I must make it stop, must cease to remind them how Other I was. "If things can be repaired between you and Ainslie, I want to see it happen, if only for her sake. She believes your pursuit of her was only a pretense by which to observe me, and it's hurt her deeply."

Mr. Redgrave looked as though I'd stolen a dagger and plunged it into his chest. "That's not true."

I gently brushed the jasmine away. "But you can see how it looks? How it must feel?"

"I can. Unfortunately." He braced his arms on his legs. "Ainslie . . . does she know of your nature?"

"Only recently, but yes."

"And your intent to speak with us?"

I nodded.

Mr. Redgrave blew out a breath. "I appreciate your honesty. But even if I deviate so far from my vows as to allow you your liberty, I will still be obligated to tell our First. He'll want an audience with you. If you can assure him of all you've said, then perhaps this can be put to rest."

I didn't bother to correct his assumption that he could take me by force—or perhaps it was not an assumption, but rather resignation that he must try or die in the attempt. Something inside me withered at the notion. "You will find that you cannot speak of this to your First. You gave your word, after all."

Mr. Redgrave shot to his feet. "You mean you've bound us? You expect us to believe your goodwill after that?"

Riven no longer lounged against the wall—he too had pushed upright, the light about him sharpening.

"I presented the terms clearly. You can only resent them if you intend to break your word." I'd come so far; I'd take one step further. "Yet if you truly desire to betray your vow, I'm sure in time you'll find a way to make the truth known. Is that your nature? I did not think so, but tell me. Was I wrong to trust you?"

Elodie flinched. "We believe in keeping our word."

"Yet we've also been presented with ample proof that fae cannot be trusted, their bargains even less so. You expect a great deal." The words wrenched from Charles, and he passed a hand over his eyes. "My father . . ."

Cold crept over my flesh. "He was killed by Otherkind, wasn't he?"

"Yes. I was there, hidden. It was . . . not a way anyone should have to die."

"I'm so very sorry." If Other had in fact claimed Mother also, then we shared a loss, despite our different heritages. The weight of remembered grief, of fears new and old, ushered in a heavy silence.

Even Jade didn't move.

At last, Elodie stirred, the sunlight that caught in her golden hair making her appear more ethereal than ever. "In a way, perhaps this new geas is a good thing."

Mr. Redgrave spun to face her. "How so?"

"We don't have to wrestle between conflicting duties and desires." She lifted slim hands. "The truth is, Jessa, we should have turned over the information we'd gathered on you some time ago, but neither of us could convince ourselves you posed a threat. I suppose that makes us fools, given the power you possess, but if what you say is true—"

"I vow to you that I would no more see fae exploit mortals than you would."

Elodie turned to regard her brother. "Charles?"

He collapsed back into his chair. "Maybe you're right."

Since we'd made grudging peace, perhaps I could gain a bit

more information before I made a strategic removal. "Your uncle Cyril, when he referred to the Vigil . . ."

"He spoke of our family," Elodie said.

"And why do you call the other Vigil, the one we all know, the Everstone Vigil?"

"Because the king handed over authority of the Vigil to Lord Everstone centuries ago, despite the fact that he did not have the knowledge to keep Byren safe." A breath gusted from her. "It was a political maneuver designed to consolidate his power, and we could offer no explanation to prevent it. Some of our kin remained within the Everstone Vigil or worked in cooperation with them in order to monitor their activities—while the rest of us simply continued carrying out our duties. How could we not, given the . . . the situation? But please, don't ask any more."

"I appreciate that you've shared what you can." I restored the jasmine to its proper pot.

Both of them did their best not to attend to the unnatural rustle.

"About Ainslie . . ." Mr. Redgrave leaned forward. "Do you think she desires an explanation from me? Or would she prefer I left her alone?"

"I cannot answer for her, but I will ask." And now I must leave, before I shattered beneath the pressure of maintaining my composure. We exchanged stilted goodbyes, then I went to collect Dreda.

I wouldn't soon forget their expressions when I'd made my confession. Through long centuries, their family had remained devoted to their cause—and certain of the threat fae posed. Could they ever truly accept that I meant no harm? They'd withheld judgment, and I should be thankful for that small mercy. But what if they'd merely concealed their true sentiments? Withdrawn to plan some sort of strategic attack? Riven would know if they'd been truthful or not, and I meant to ask at the earliest opportunity.

But either way, some part of me couldn't help but wonder— if I'd not bound them in bargain first, what might have come?

What might still?

Gaining protection from the immediate threat of the Vigil was one thing, but if I meant to investigate the missing properly, I risked exposure on a far larger scale.

Even so, I was no longer willing to turn back.

CHAPTER 28

When we stepped out of the Redgrave household, Riven vanished, and the residual power of the wards cut sharp across my skin. I hurried down the stairs. I half-hoped he'd withdrawn with the intention of "stumbling upon" us before we returned home, though we'd discussed nothing of the sort, so I suggested to Dreda that we take a brief walk in the park we'd passed to allow for the opportunity.

He did not take advantage of it.

What did that mean? He didn't ordinarily leave so abruptly. Had something gone wrong in the Otherworld? The song of the lilac hedge tugged at my attention, but I pushed it away. The explanation might be far simpler. Perhaps he just didn't feel the need to discuss the matter further. He'd ensured my safety, as he promised Ainslie, and no immediate threat remained.

Or was it that he wearied of the entire affair? I could not blame him if so; for a fae, this must be a tedious maelstrom of mortal emotions and conventions.

After we'd strolled in silence for a time, Dreda glanced at me. "You wanted to know my impressions of the household?"

"Indeed. Were you able to learn anything?"

She tucked a stray strand of hair beneath her hat and

nodded. "I stayed in the conservatory a bit, then ventured out to explore. I took care to catch my finger on a thorn, tearing my glove, so I should have an excuse if anyone noticed that I wandered."

Though I'd never have guessed it at our first meeting, it seemed Dreda had a knack for espionage.

"On the surface of it, the household was run well. Everywhere I went, servants were about their tasks, and everything was in order, belowstairs and above. I was about to return to the conservatory when I saw a man come in through the servants' entrance, bleeding from the shoulder. He was whisked abovestairs to Mrs. Redgrave, and from the sound of things, she tended his injuries with the skill of a trained herbalist." She caught her lip between her teeth. "Perhaps I should not have listened in, but I knew you'd not have asked me to learn what I could if it wasn't important. So I did. I heard them speaking of a boggart sighting in Avons, and it seems that's how the man came by his injury. Mrs. Redgrave said someone must be sent to contain it, but she seemed worried that their efforts were not enough to manage all the reports they received. How is it they know all this, Miss Jessa?"

We turned down a gently winding path. "It seems they've made a practice of fighting the Otherworld."

If the Redgraves noted such a substantive increase in Other . . . how much vaster was it than I perceived? I was only able to attend to the most pressing matters one at a time, but they'd built a network in their large, close-knit family, which meant they were able to filter vast quantities of information from across Byren.

"Then . . . they could be allies?" Her eyes brightened.

"That remains to be seen." How much should I tell her? Surely her assistance had earned her some insight into our plans. "Lord Blackburn wants to take evidence of Otherworldly matters to the king in order to compel him to reveal the truth. It seems the Redgraves could lend a great deal of credence to his arguments, if they chose to do so."

"Will they?"

"I cannot say, not yet." My thoughts raced down a new trail. It was possible they could also assist with the missing persons investigation—I imagined it must have drawn their attention. Dared I ask when we were on such tenuous ground? Even if I did, they might not be able to speak of whatever they knew.

My skirt snagged on a branch, and I bid its release. What precisely were the terms of their former binding? I rehearsed our conversation in my mind once more. Elodie had said that when the king replaced Sir Redgrave with Lord Everstone, they'd not been able to tell him why it presented a danger. Did that mean the geas had extended across generations? Was it possible for a family to be so bound? A gust of wind scudded clouds across the sun, and I shivered.

Jade pressed close against my legs. *Regrettably, yes. And it would make sense. If their knowledge extends as far back as the Forgotten War, their geas must also.*

Then they must have abandoned the notion of working with others and resigned themselves to total secrecy. Could they ever be persuaded to a joint endeavor?

It was a question Jade could not possibly answer, so she padded along in silence.

And I became aware that I'd utterly failed to carry my end of the conversation with Dreda. "I'm sorry, I'm just considering all you've said. I didn't intend that you should take such risks, but I'm appreciative of all you learned."

"I don't think anyone took note of me." She fidgeted with the button on her glove. "It's the advantage of being a spinster chaperone: no one really attends to you."

I studied her closely. No hint of wistfulness laced her words, but rather a certain satisfaction—as though she derived pleasure in taking a disadvantage and turning it into opportunity. "And you've used it well."

Dreda tilted her head to survey the open expanse of the park, which was dotted by figures riding or walking. "Are we . . . meeting someone?"

"It seems not." I wavered a moment, then turned back toward the park entrance. I could delay no longer; it would be cruel to keep Ainslie waiting for no purpose. "I suppose we should return home now."

We entered the carriage, which was waiting for us outside the park, and passed the ride in reflective silence. As soon as we walked through the door, Ainslie dispatched Holden to tell the driver to wait.

Then she swooped upon me. "Ada and I have decided we should take the carriage to Enderly, as it would be a shame to remain cooped up indoors on such a lovely day. Will you join us?"

Though she'd worded it as an invitation, it was clearly a summons—it seemed she wanted the opportunity to speak uninterrupted. And after Holden's report to Aunt Caris, I'd begun to feel more wary of speaking where we might be overheard. I nodded. "That's an excellent notion. Enderly should be enchanting this time of year."

Unlike most parks in Avons, Enderly wasn't favored by society—it was wilder and more remote, which meant odds were favorable we'd not encounter anyone and could conduct our business in peace.

Yet all peace fled the moment I stepped back out of doors. When we entered the street, Other pricked over my skin, the same cool sensation I'd experienced leaving the library with Father. It strengthened into an unmistakable fae-presence—not sun and storm like Riven, nor shadow and starlight like Nikol, but something altogether different, more like a brisk wind that traveled down from the mountains, carrying hints of fragrant pine and ever-shifting possibilities.

Ainslie and Ada continued toward the carriage, but Jade bristled, and I braced myself against the white poplar planted at the edge of the footwalk, seeking some sign of the intruder, now or before.

Nothing.

Jade, what do you sense?

A fae scent I do not recognize—but I do not think the individual is fully present, at least not now. It's too faint.

Indeed, even as we spoke, the sensation faded, leaving me unsteady on my feet. What was this? The bargain-holder taunting us?

Somehow I did not think so.

The workings within the nightspire had felt entirely different, all rich and dusky and redolent with old power. I released my hold on the tree. If I'd drawn the attention of some other fae . . . No, I wouldn't allow fear to sink its strangling roots deeper.

Whatever I'd sensed, it didn't seem to signal an imminent attack. So I'd consult Riven when he returned, and for now, I'd attend to my sisters. Ainslie wouldn't wait much longer—already she beckoned me from the carriage.

I joined them, and as we traveled, Risha and Kiran communicated in their peculiar language of light, the joy in their expressions the only thing that was comprehensible. In some small measure, it lifted the weight sitting on my heart. By unspoken agreement, we addressed none of the issues until we'd sequestered ourselves on a quiet hilltop blanketed with a glorious array of wildflowers. Where the hill spilled downward, a line of trees marked the beginning of the forest, but any lurker within would be well out of earshot. With the soft floral songs whispering about me, I unfolded the story. Not a single cloud marred the perfect blue sky, but as I spoke a gloom nevertheless descended.

At the last, Ada drew back beneath the shade of her parasol. "I suppose that's the best we could have hoped for your meeting. And . . . they do mean well."

"Does it matter?" Ainslie's cheeks flushed. "They almost caused irreparable harm. If they'd shared this information with their Vigil, then surely those in charge would have found a way to come for Jessa."

Was it anger or hurt that caused her to condemn them? Better not to press when she was so unsettled, but attend to the facts. I brushed some fallen petals from my skirt. "We cannot wholly discard that possibility, even now. They will hold their peace, but Cyril Redgrave now knows I've interacted with a fae artifact before."

"Surely that alone isn't reason for them to condemn you?" Ada asked.

"Perhaps not to condemn, but certainly sufficient to rouse suspicion. If he begins asking Elodie and Mr. Redgrave questions they cannot answer, then he may begin to suspect a geas . . . particularly if they want him to do so." If they meant to cover for me, I suspected they'd find a way—but I remained uncertain of their deeper desires.

Ada turned to Ainslie. "In any case, it's clear you must at least talk to Mr. Redgrave, tell him about the binding mark and whatever it is you feel about his actions. Then if you cannot move past the things you've kept from one another, at least you will have tried."

"I'm not certain I should be trusted to do so. I fear my judgment is compromised, that because of my feelings I'll be inclined to give him the benefit of the doubt, and then he'll . . . he'll betray us to the Vigil after all."

So that was the reason she'd been quick to criticize their actions—not anger, not even hurt, but because the inclinations of her heart were to trust him. "With the choice to trust there's always a risk, but do you want to spend the rest of your life wondering what might have happened if you'd just opened your heart?"

"No. You're right; I must try." Her voice was little more than a whisper. "Meantime, there's one more thing—it's the reason I suggested Enderly. I felt we needed privacy for more than just the matter of the Redgraves."

My breath caught, and at my side, the Queen Anne's lace stood at attention.

A slight frown clouded Ada's face. "What's happened? Is . . . is it the binding?"

"No, but I've started having a dream. It's come the past few nights, each time the same." Ainslie tilted her parasol so it concealed her eyes. "I wake, but it returns the moment I fall asleep. And every time it's frightened me, though on the face of things, it isn't so very dreadful. It's just felt so . . . real."

"What was the dream?" I asked.

"It starts with Mother sitting in the attic at home—our row house in Avons, not Caldwell House—and writing in a book. Even that's peculiar, since she didn't like to spend time in Avons. In the dream, it's always been night, but around Mother, the room is flooded with light. She has no lamp nor candle, it's just . . . light. After she finishes writing, she opens the wall beneath one of the windows and puts the book inside. Then she looks straight at me and says, 'If I die, find it.'" Ainslie shuddered, her parasol dipping lower. "Each time—oh, it feels like losing her all over again."

I swallowed a tight knot of grief. If I'd guessed right, and Mother had forsaken her fae nature, then she shouldn't have been able to craft such a dream, which sounded tinged with liminal power. Had I been mistaken? And what did the dream signify?

"I didn't want to consider that it held truth, but once the notion crossed my mind, I couldn't shake it." Her words emerged faltering and unsteady. "I needed to prove to myself it was only a dream, so I went up to the attic this morning."

Lacy fronds brushed my skirt. "What did you find?"

Her face pale, Ainslie rummaged in her reticule and withdrew a small leather-bound book. "This."

"Oh, Ainslie." Ada wrapped her arm about Ainslie's shoulders. "You shouldn't have gone alone."

"I know you already fear for my state of mind." Her voice dropped low. "I couldn't bear either of you thinking I'd taken leave of my senses altogether."

I understood that fear all too well. I squeezed her hand. "This has nothing to do with you descending into any sort of madness. Clearly, it was a dream meant to find you, though I cannot think why now."

Ada gave a sharp gasp. "Oh! Morwen said something I couldn't comprehend the other day, as she often does. She said a dream was caught in the attic, and it should have been released long ago, that any self-respecting nisi would have seen to it promptly while attending the house. When I asked her what she meant, she said that the dream had gone where it ought, and she'd no more to say about it."

If Morwen was responsible for the release of the dream, what other things might we expect to come to pass, now that a nisi occupied the house? Mother had never told us the precise duties nisi performed, only that they were considered keepers of the home, and if they were cared for well, the home would prosper. Clearly, there was more involved.

"Does that mean Mother . . . or someone left it for one of us, somehow?" Ainslie asked. "Did she think Jessa would engage a nisi, if she learned to exercise fae affinities? Or did one used to dwell here, back when Mother was alive?"

If that were true, she might have meant us to have this information much earlier in life. Our only hope of answers would be within its pages. "What does it say?"

"I can't read it." Ainslie extended the book toward me. "Perhaps you'll be able to?"

Inside, fae words marched across the creamy pages in an elegant script, each one like a drop of cold rain falling on my skin, leaving behind an uncomfortable chill. "It's definitely Mother's hand, but in the fae language. If we needed any further confirmation of her identity, this offers it."

The dream also suggested she knew she might die, and she wanted us to have this for some reason. The chill worked its way inward. Was it that we might understand our natures? Or whatever threat she fled?

"Then we certainly share her nature." Ada looked down, her shoulders drawing in. "I know it was the likeliest explanation, but this . . ."

"It changes nothing for me, in the end." Ainslie's delicate jaw firmed. "My dealings with Other have caused nothing but pain, so my path seems clear. I intend to forsake my fae nature and become mortal, as Mother must have done."

I reached for her. "Ainslie, just consider—"

"I've done nothing but think about this, and I am resolved."

"Will you at least accept counsel not to act on your resolution until we've freed you from your binding?" I didn't know if her fae nature offered her any protection, but it could, and forsaking it prematurely seemed unwise.

At last, she gave a nod. "I suppose it would be prudent."

"Whatever comes in the future, Mother wanted us to have this book." Ada traced the cover of the slim volume with a gloved finger. "She must have believed we'd be able to read it somehow."

I looked at Risha. "Bright one, will you help?"

She fluttered over. "Yes, yes. I wish to see what your mother said. She must have been a most unusual fae."

Soft blue light spilled across the pages, and the words resolved themselves into a familiar language, but they still made no sense. "I understand the words now, but—they're some sort of code."

Mother had always been fond of codes and ciphers, and she'd delighted in leaving all sorts of encrypted messages for us to unravel. Only this appeared like none she'd used before.

Ainslie slumped. "Of course it is."

Since Mother was fae, the layers of subterfuge made sense. They were known for favoring puzzles, mysteries, and mazes.

Jade sniffed at the book. *It helps the centuries not become unbearably tedious.*

I pressed that unpleasant notion from my mind and bent to examine the script more closely. *Thornhaven* leapt out at me from several places on the page. Otherwise, the contents appeared as though they could have been selected at random from a dictionary. This would take time and attention to decipher.

My spine pricked as a breeze stirred the trees at the edge of the forest. I shut the book with a snap. "Perhaps we'd better examine this further at home."

"No, we can't go. We have to wait." Ainslie's gaze locked on the tree line, and her features suffused with delicate color. "Don't you see it?"

However much I strained, I could spy nothing except the gentle sway of tree limbs in the breeze. Yet a sense of dusky-rich power gathered in the air.

Jade put her body between us and the wood line, and Risha hovered just above her head. Still, Ainslie's attention remained locked on . . . something. Whatever she beheld, I could not see.

Nor can I. Jade's tail bristled. *Which suggests it's not truly here.*

Not here—oh. If that were true, then this was a liminal suggestion reaching for Ainslie, persuading her of its reality. Riven had said liminal power strengthened in the times and spaces between, as within dreams. What did it mean that it seized her while she was awake? How could such a thing be?

Ada clutched Ainslie's arm. "What is it?"

Her pupils dilated so the blackness nearly swallowed up the brown of her eyes. "Please, don't . . ."

Then she collapsed.

CHAPTER 29

My surroundings faded as I bent over Ainslie. Her pulse raced, her breathing faltered, and she showed no signs of awareness, no connection to the world around her. Surely this intrusion of Other would signal Riven, given the working he'd placed on her. But how long would it take him to come?

How long did she have?

Ada removed Ainslie's gloves and chafed her hands, but she did not stir. "What should we do?"

Before I could answer, Ainslie sat up, then struck out at Ada with a wild blow that landed on her chin. Ada stumbled back. And Jade bristled, springing between them.

Snatching a fallen stick from the ground, Ainslie scrambled to her feet. Her eyes were wide and staring, yet seemed to register nothing of reality.

Frantic, she swung the branch like one who sought to drive back a foe, nearly catching my side—she would have, had Jade not tugged me back. Despite the sun beating down on us, I went cold. Jade's size increased slightly, as if she contemplated a shift to true-form.

Not yet.

The song of a nearby clematis surged into my senses. Instinctively, I seized upon it, and one of its vines shot into the air between us, thickening rapidly, prepared to bind and defend—no. I snagged it in my hand. Ada hadn't noticed; her attention remained locked on Ainslie, on the shadow cast in front of her, one that did not match her body.

What was happening?

Could something from the liminal realm be brought into our own? Never mind that. She needed something to pull her from her trance—and I did not know how to wield plants so, nor did I know if I'd any other affinities which might work in such a fashion.

She shouted something incomprehensible as she lashed out again with the branch. Silvery tears fell from her eyes, darkening her bodice where they landed.

Somehow, I had to stop this. I reached for her—and the light of a passing drenched us, warming the air, driving back the cold touch of fear.

Riven stepped through, stalking toward Ainslie, golden coils unfolding from his hands. The shadows vanished.

And just before his light touched her, Ainslie blinked and stumbled back, awareness returning to her gaze. Coincidence? Or had her bargain-holder designed this as a test to see how we would respond? If Riven would come—and how swiftly?

Jade settled back on her haunches. *Whatever else it may be, I don't think it coincidence.*

Ainslie released the stick and pressed her hands to her head, moaning softly.

"This came on her while she was awake?" The coils of light softened, dancing across Ainslie's skin before vanishing into the ether. What had he perceived?

I struggled to regain my voice. "She thought she saw something in the forest, and then . . . she lost herself entirely."

"But there were . . . I saw . . ." Ainslie shook her head, her lashes still damp. "Was none of it real?"

"Whatever you perceived bled through from the liminal

realm. It was not reality, though it was well on its way to becoming so." The light vanished, and he regarded her, expressionless. "It may be that your bargain-holder seeks to remind you of the stakes if you fail."

The qualifier attached to his remark suggested he'd another theory, one of which he didn't intend to speak.

Ainslie cupped a hand over her mouth, her fingers trembling, and Ada moved to her side. A bruise had already begun to discolor her face where Ainslie had struck her.

"If the fae holding her bargain judges she's failed to uphold her end . . . what then?" Ada whispered.

"She will die—and it will be a death to serve as a warning to any who would consider trying to break their bonds."

Ada bowed her head, resting it against Ainslie. For her part, Ainslie stood still as a statue, unspeaking.

Riven surveyed the tree line. "As that's not happened, we must conclude that she is keeping her end of the bargain, however much she wrestles against it."

Perhaps for now, but how long before the fae holding her bargain went too far and we could not bring Ainslie back? A skylark chirruped overhead, its cheery sound jarring. Surely the world about us should bear some reflection of the shock we'd just endured.

The sound seemed to stir Ainslie from her stupor. Slowly, she straightened. "Lord Riven, you spoke before of entering the mindscape. I don't know what that means, but if it offers any chance of finding the one who holds my bargain—"

"At best, it would reveal the nature of the bargain, but not the identity of its keeper." His tone remained even. "And it would likely shatter your mind forever."

"It seems she means to do so anyway. That she takes pleasure in . . . in making me doubt my sanity." Her eyes glistened.

For a moment, I thought I perceived some emotion flicker across Riven's face, but he said nothing, only waited, impassive.

And Ainslie continued. "I went back to the park one day, with Lovell, in hopes it would remind me of something, but it's all this dreadful void. Perhaps if you could force the memory, we'd gain something from it. If . . . if I'm doomed anyway, at least I could rest knowing that I'd spare someone else this fate."

"You can't just give up, Ainslie. We have time yet." I spun to face Riven. "There must be some way we can protect her while we seek the one who holds her bargain. What about Wyncourt?"

"It cannot serve as a safeguard against the influence of the bargain. But it may possibly protect against this sort of torment, as long as she remains within its walls. Certainly, under your orders, it would keep out any fae influence that might seek to exert control over other members of your family."

"Then perhaps we should—"

"What reason could we give to relocate our family? To uproot from our home?" Ainslie shook her head, her dark curls tumbling about her face. "Even if Father agreed, society would certainly look askance. Do we want to draw further attention to ourselves?"

At this juncture, that could undo all our efforts. Pressure gathered at my temples. "Perhaps we should just mention it to Father. See how it's received."

But even if he agreed and we surmounted all the other obstacles, could I truly suggest a move when I did not know what lurked behind the arched door at its heart?

Riven still watched Ainslie. "In absence of external protections, you should consider what resources you can bring to bear. If you're able to access any of the affinities that belong to you by virtue of your blood, it will give you some means to resist these attacks. Can you?"

"I'm not like Jessa. I . . . When I was a child, there were times I thought I felt things out of the ordinary way, but I believed them mere fancies. Mother told me she would help, and she took me to see someone. Ada too." She brushed remnants of bark from her hands. "I don't remember exactly what happened, but afterward, I never experienced further peculiarities."

Despite her distrust of Riven, of everything fae, she'd confided in him far more than in us. Why hadn't she told me this before, when I'd asked about any encounter with Other? Had there been some edge of compulsion to his words, so subtle that I'd not felt it? Or was it simply that he was a person one did not readily deny or deceive?

Ada's hand flew to her mouth. "You're right. I always thought it a dream, because it was so very strange. Mother never spoke of it, and you didn't either, and Father didn't seem to know . . ."

"How old were you?"

"Nine, perhaps."

If that was when they'd started to experience the burgeoning signs of affinity, then perhaps Mother's passing had not triggered mine as I'd once thought. Perhaps it was simply a matter of maturation. And her death meant she'd not had a chance to interfere with mine. My throat tightened.

Jade wove about my ankles, her warmth reassuring.

"When I placed the working on you, I sensed another. It's conceivable that when your affinities started to emerge, your mother found a way to conceal them—even from you," Riven said. "Jessa attempted to place such a working on herself, though she lacked the experience to fully seal it—and eventually her own desires thwarted her."

My cage of thorns. That had been a working? My chest ached with the memory of its strictures. If Mother had not died when she did, would she have procured a true cage? One which would have fully locked away any trace of my fae nature? Was her loathing for her fae heritage so strong that she'd sought to eliminate any sign of it from us also? No matter how I looked at it, the situation made no sense.

And Riven. He'd withheld a great deal—and it stung.

"I can examine the working, if you desire. See if it can be removed. But I cannot say what the outcome will be." He might as well be offering her a choice between flavors of tea for all the inflection in his voice. "There's a chance she meant only to leave it in place until you became older and were able to choose for yourself which world you desired."

"Whatever she meant, I want no part of it." Ainslie's voice was almost fierce.

"And you?" Riven turned to Ada.

She studied the ground. "Perhaps, when we reach the other side of . . . all this. I don't think we need to introduce more variables to the situation."

Ainslie stumbled back and pinched her lips together, evidently as taken aback as I was.

Only Riven showed no surprise. He simply nodded.

Sudden restlessness seized me. I wanted to speak with him freely; I wanted answers. "I think we should examine the tree line."

His all-too-perceptive gaze seemed to strip away what little covering I managed for my tumultuous emotions. "Very well."

Ada looked from him to me, then she looped her arm through Ainslie's. "We'll stay here and rest."

Rather than protest, Ainslie leaned against Ada, her eyes sliding shut as we walked away, Jade keeping pace.

Riven remained silent until we reached the tree line. "There will be nothing to find aside from traces of liminal energy. But then, I imagine you knew that."

"I did. I—why didn't you tell me before that you'd sensed a working on Ainslie? That Ada might have one too?" I crunched through the dead leaves at the border between forest and field.

"How would it have helped the situation?" Riven lifted the branch of a low-hanging fir so I could pass under. "If I'd probed the nature of the working, it would have been unpleasant at best for Ainslie. Yet the most cursory of examinations revealed it does her no active harm. It does not carry any sort of compulsion nor any trace of the bargain-holder's affinities."

"Perhaps it wouldn't have changed the investigation but—"

"It would have distracted you, and it wasn't relevant at the time. You already knew Ainslie was bound, that Other influenced her life, and—"

"When it comes to my family, you can't just decide to withhold information because you don't deem it relevant. It all matters to me." Raw pain flooded my voice, the fear and uncertainty of the day surging to the surface. With effort, I choked it down. The truth was that he could do as he pleased. He didn't have to help with any of this; he could easily cut ties and walk away.

And then somehow I'd have to find a path forward amid an impossible maze of potential threats. The shadows of the forest fell heavy on me, and I shivered.

"I forget sometimes the mortal way of seeing things." Riven stopped, forcing me to turn and face him. "Everything I do—it requires withholding information, revealing it only when absolutely necessary and for strategic purpose. I regret that it caused you pain."

He might regret it, yet he'd likely continue to keep his own counsel. What else did he know or guess about me? My sisters? This bargain? He'd told me a great deal but clearly withheld even more—and I must choose to accept help or not, knowing his terms. I stumbled over a jagged stone. But did he truly trust me so little?

Jade leapt onto a low tree limb. *You feel he's withheld a great deal, and he has—far more than we can likely guess. At the same time, I've never seen any fae deal so freely with information as Riven has with you. Ordinarily, access to facts and even speculation are things to be bargained for—I don't think there's a lack of trust.*

Perhaps. Yet time and again, I'd exposed my deeper thoughts and feelings, while his remained behind a barrier. I halted beneath the spreading branches of an ash, pressing down my emotions—this wasn't time to indulge in them. "I shouldn't have spoken as I did. I'm thankful for your help, in whatever form it comes."

"Jessa." He shook his head slightly.

"It's fine." I wrapped my arms about myself and peered deeper into the forest. "The liminal realm . . . is it ever possible to trace fae through it?"

He remained quiet a long moment, watching me. Then at last, he spoke. "No fae came through, so there's nothing to trace.

The bargain-holder only shaped the power, she did not approach herself."

"So she risks nothing in these sorts of attacks." A squirrel scurried through the branches overhead, dislodging several withered leaves, which drifted down about us. "If we cannot trace her, even when she jabs at Ainslie like this . . . what hope do we have of ever finding her?"

"I've had a report from the Court of Dusk—a sylph signaled me as we departed the Redgraves. It's why I left when I did."

"And?"

"There's no gossip about noteworthy bargains, nor has anyone claimed more mortal thralls than usual—at least not openly. In this case, the absence of information is telling. It suggests the success of the plan hinges on its secrecy. It's likely to be unveiled when it's complete, a display of power."

"And then it might well be too late."

He didn't reply, which perhaps told me everything I needed to know. The murmurs of the forest rushed in my ears, drowning out all else. "Your earlier business in your world, that which you said might intersect with Ainslie . . . has it come to anything?"

"It is still developing. If we find the right thread to pull on— the right piece of information, however small—everything will unravel. We must continue to lay our plans."

But as yet, we'd no clear means by which to pursue her bargain-holder, only the very broadest of nets that Riven had cast—and which he refused to discuss. We'd also the small hope that the bargain-holder might intentionally betray herself as she dealt with Ainslie, though that dwindled as time passed.

When it came to the other missing, at least we had a path forward. Could that investigation offer any insight regarding Ainslie's plight? All we had were the slimmest of threads to follow, aberrations occurring concurrently, a hope they might intersect—because more data would give us more paths to follow. At least, it was something upon which I could *act*, rather than sit and watch her suffering.

"I sent messages this morning asking if Mr. Burke, Lord Blackburn, and Mrs. Darrington would meet at Wyncourt to discuss our approach to the Collectors. Perhaps it will reveal what we need." I turned back toward the grassy meadow. "Meanwhile, if . . . if an attack were to come on Ainslie again, and you could not come, would Wyncourt offer respite? If I cannot move my family, perhaps I can still take advantage of its protections."

"It's worth a try, though there are no guarantees. It depends very much on the nature of the assault."

I'd take any possible chance of helping above none, yet I must consider the risks posed by the mysteries in Wyncourt. I'd not thought it prudent to delve into the hidden room without Riven present; Wyncourt itself had warned me away once, but now . . . I twined my fingers around a sprig of climbing ivy. "You've done a great deal already, but if you don't have to return to the Otherworld at once, would you be willing to join me at Wyncourt today before I meet the others? Before I bring my family—or even additional guests—I'd rather understand what's in the hidden room."

He gave me a sharp look. "Which one?"

I told him what I'd found while acquainting myself with Wyncourt—the heart pulsing at its core and the mysterious arched doorway, woven with countless workings.

"Wyncourt was steadfast in refusing to open its deeper ways to me, and I'd no reason to force it. Still, it could not conceal the great power at its heart. You were wise to wait."

"What do you think is inside?"

"I think it's better to know than to speculate. Return your sisters home, and we'll meet in an hour."

It was far from being a solution to all that oppressed us, but at least it offered a place to start. Only, as I rejoined my sisters and surveyed Ainslie's drawn features, I found that a start did not feel anywhere near enough.

Her strength was dwindling.

CHAPTER 30

When I crossed the threshold of Wyncourt later that afternoon, Danvers offered a warm welcome. Yet it was nothing compared to the embrace of the manor itself, the warmth bathing my skin and the gentle fragrance of goldhearts wafting about me. They were too distant to smell by natural means, but Wyncourt funneled the sweet-spice fragrance to me, and it drove back fear and fatigue alike.

Stepping across the threshold felt like coming home. Was this why fae dwelt in demesnes? This sensation of unwavering affection was certainly a heady one.

"Do you desire refreshments now, Miss Caldwell?"

"Thank you, but I'll wait for the others. I thought I'd spend some time sorting Ibbie's affairs."

"Very good. Mrs. Peters has all in readiness for your guests, but you have only to let us know if you require anything more." With a small bow, he withdrew.

A familiar pricking of Other heralded Riven's arrival. He'd opened a passing somewhere upstairs, most likely in Ibbie's bedchamber. I hurried to meet him, Wyncourt bright and buoyant around me. Part of me couldn't believe it harbored danger—but it *had* been built by Lord West. And it wasn't so very long ago that the ghouls entrapped within its walls sought to kill me . . .

The dichotomy between its two natures troubled me sufficiently that the moment I'd secured the bedroom door, I said, "I don't understand. Edward . . . Lord West . . . was bent toward cruelty. If a demesne reflects the nature of its creator in some way, then why does Wyncourt feel so generous of spirit?"

Riven lounged against the mantel, apparently untroubled by the lack of proper greeting, but then, he wasn't one to stand on ceremony. "In the ordinary way, a demesne wishes to please and protect its master or mistress, therefore when it changes possession—a rare occurrence—inherent alterations will take place to accommodate the new owner. I imagine you were a particularly welcome one, after it rested fallow in mortal hands for a time. It would have greatly desired a fae mistress and made swift adjustments to accommodate."

I rested a hand on the wall, and the surface seemed to soften, as though I could bid it to change with the smallest of wishes or workings. So very different from Kilmere. Though it was sentient, the ruin hadn't been a true demesne, but rather a stronghold crafted by many, and even a change of ownership had in no way inclined it to cooperation. "Then its workings allow for such alterations?"

"Generally speaking, they do. However, this is a significant change, and I think there's more at work. Damir crafted Wyncourt to woo a wife—however deceptive his plan—and he would have wanted it to appear warm and welcoming. Some portion of this purpose would have bled into its workings from the very beginning, because it needed to appear as a haven for her. Furthermore, based on the records I accessed, he used not only mortal materials but mortal craftsmen to do a great deal of the work. Yes, he infused each element with his power, but Wyncourt forges Other and mortal together in a unique way, something more fluid and malleable than an ordinary demesne. Damir certainly did not foresee that it would adhere to mortal law and heed the declaration of his death in this realm, severing its connection to him and accepting you as mistress. But then, its creation was a gamble. It should not have worked, and yet here it stands."

It pleased me to think that Lord West had not prevailed in this, that Wyncourt would not stand testament to his cruelty, but offer haven to mortals instead. I pressed his memory from my mind, stretching my senses to encompass Wyncourt and the bright spark of life it held. "I wonder what else might unexpectedly work, if our worlds ever joined forces?"

"As long as mortals fear fae, and fae regard mortals as prey, we'll never know."

And what reason did either party have to change? From what I'd seen, mortals were justified in fearing fae—at least, most fae. And . . . why would fae ever change their views of mortals? What would it gain them, when they already had the upper hand?

Wearily, I crossed to the door to Edward's bedchamber, placing my hand in the blood lock. The door swung open. Though gloom and shadow lingered in his room, the scents of ancient stone, of decay and dust, had dissipated. Something fresh and green and lively swirled in its place, stirring amid the shadows, urging us onward.

Was it possible to remake this space altogether, to drive the specter of Lord West from the demesne entirely? Whether or not I could succeed, I believed Wyncourt would help me try, much as it had assisted me in unlocking the hidden compartment where Ibbie had stored the chronicle of her dealings with Kilmere. In another, more peaceful time, I'd have to explore it further.

For now, Jade and I crossed to the hidden staircase. With Riven following and Risha fluttering overhead, we descended to the chamber at the heart of Wyncourt. Lustrous fae-lights illumined the space, and the radiant starburst on the floor beckoned. As before, Wyncourt itself surged into my senses, living and aware, the vast layers of power woven into every stone and beam tugging me deeper . . .

No, I couldn't allow myself to be distracted. I could easily lose myself in its many workings, in the immersive layers of revelation it held, but our time was short. Whatever the hidden room held, we needed to uncover it before my guests arrived.

Riven paced the chamber, taking care not to step into the central starburst.

I edged back from it. "Should the star be avoided?"

"Not by you. It is the means by which you'll achieve the deepest connection with the demesne." He sent a spark of light along a spiraled working on the wall, which flickered back at him in a speculative way, as if one tested the other. "But if any other fae steps into it, it would be deemed a bid for control—a potential threat."

And I'd seen how Wyncourt responded in such cases. If it came to open conflict, I didn't doubt Riven would prevail—but it would be unpleasant for us all.

He moved toward the arched doorway. Silver-laced strands of black wove about the magnificent spiraled stars in an enchanting array. When I tried to pick out the threads of power that comprised the workings, they began to blur before my eyes, the room washing away and the stars shining bright as sunlit diamonds.

"It's a pocket world."

"A what?"

"A pocket world. When you mentioned a locked doorway in the heart, I thought it likely. It was known even between courts that Damir had an obsession with crafting them. It's why he was so determined to claim objects of power—he needed them as fuel for creation."

"But what *is* a pocket world?"

"You recall the pocket in which I stored the antidote?"

I nodded. I still desired one. What could be more practical than to keep a host of tools at one's disposal at all times?

"A pocket world is similar. The interior is much larger than the exterior, yet it's a living ecosystem rather than a storage container. A chamber such as this one may contain a surprisingly expansive world within."

"For what purpose?"

"It depends. For someone like Damir, it offers a chance to rule unrestrained over whatever happens within its confines."

A world in which Lord West reigned would be one of my nightmares brought to life. The stars blurred before my eyes.

Riven stepped closer, his warmth washing over me. "Pocket worlds can also serve as prisons. Some of these workings aim to keep the door sealed, which would only be the case if he sought to trap someone—or something—inside."

"Is there no means of escape once confined?"

"As a form of imprisonment, a pocket world is absolute. No trace of the soul contained can escape the bindings that form its seams, so there's no chance of the imprisoned one being located and rescued." Riven surveyed the workings. "If the imprisoned being possessed sufficient power, they might unravel the workings from the inside out, but then they'd be destroyed when the world shattered. It's an ingenious and unpleasant method of eliminating one's foes."

"Why not just kill them, then?"

"Fae are not known for their mercy." He shrugged. "A chance for true, meaningful revenge might be the work of centuries—and then unfold over countless more. Perpetual imprisonment is deemed more . . . satisfying than an instant death. Or even a slow one."

A metallic taste filled my mouth. Such beauty concealed such malice. "Is . . . is that a common purpose?"

"Not overly so—pocket worlds aren't common. Yet each court possesses at least one for the imprisonment of dangerous beings."

If Lord West had stashed ghouls in the chambers above, what might he house below? I could not fathom his pocket world containing something pleasant and peaceful. I took a step backward. "So either I leave it alone, its contents forever a mystery—or I unseal it and accept that I might unleash some dire evil on this world."

"If it contains some sort of evil, I'll end it before it escapes. Or you will." Nothing in his expression hinted the prospect troubled him. "But the choice remains yours."

"If I intend to trust Wyncourt to care for my family, then I cannot allow some hidden danger to remain." The threads gleamed brighter as I spoke. "Yet Wyncourt tried to keep me from opening this before. Why?"

"It foremost desires your safety. It may be more amenable to granting you access since you're now informed of the risks."

I moved into the center of the starburst, where the presence of Wyncourt swirled about me, its immense power stretching my awareness to conversations in distant chambers. With effort, I pulled my attention back to the here and now. "It's time for us to open the door."

A wash of icy air chilled me, yet Wyncourt made no move to check my progress, and the central star remained bright and clear. It seemed it did not mean to bar my way, only to suggest caution—an admonition I didn't require, not after all my dealings with Lord West.

I crossed the marble expanse, the night-sky door beckoning. Without a word, Jade shifted into true-form, her eyes glowing bright as the diamond-like stars etched into the frame.

Risha darted behind me.

And I pressed my hand to the latch of the door.

CHAPTER 31

The foundations of Wyncourt trembled, as if in warning. The door blazed white-hot, then melted away. And as the barrier fell, in the heartbeat before the power of Wyncourt charged forward into the void, a crimson-gold blast of Other, hostile and angry, blazed toward me. Like a flash of lightning, Riven's power surged to meet it, suspending then repelling the crimson tide.

Wyncourt, fierce and possessive, wrapped me with a sensation like rushing wind, tugging me back.

The green of Riven's eyes deepened, and all vestige of mortal glamour fell away, leaving only his fae features, wild and beautiful and entirely devoid of emotion. He spoke a word of command in the fae tongue.

And the assault ceased.

The frame of a woman materialized in the doorway, her hair vibrant gold, her eyes bright, and her form tall and stately. When she saw Riven, she stopped short. Her beautiful face lost its vivid coloring, and she released her hold on the power swirling about her, before dropping into a low curtsy. She addressed him softly in the fae tongue.

What is she saying?

Jade stalked forward. *She says, "Lord Arbiter, I beg your pardon. I believed you were Damir returned to torment me. I'd sworn to myself that I'd secure my liberty or force him to kill me in the attempt, if he ever visited again. I owe you a great debt for my liberation, and I trust you will overlook my assault."*

He offered an imperious nod. "I accept your apology. Yet you owe your debt to Lady Jessa. She secured your freedom, not I."

Her gaze swept my frame, and one perfect brow arched. Clearly, I did not meet with her approval. And why should I? Compared to her, I appeared small and insignificant. Nevertheless, she inclined her head ever so slightly, a motion that acknowledged the debt, yet also made clear that I was not worthy of greater attention.

She belongs to Riven's court?

The fur at Jade's neck bristled. *So it seems.*

"I do not sense Damir." Her voice rang out, clear and bell-like. "Where is that *ashna*? I shall deal with him once and for all."

"I'm afraid Jessa's already done that also."

Her eyes narrowed at his silky-smooth words. Once again, she assessed me, and this time her gaze lingered on Jade, who stood imposing at my back. "It seems I owe you a greater debt than I first believed."

I opened my mouth to disagree, but Riven shook his head slightly, and I changed course. "Damir was the sort to collect enemies. I'm pleased he no longer can."

"As am I. I hope you dealt him an excruciating death." She sauntered toward me, exercising the same care Riven had to avoid the central starburst. "Yet you are unfamiliar to me. Are you from his court?"

I sensed there was a right answer—and one wrong enough to endanger me. "I—"

"There will be time enough to develop your acquaintance later, if you desire. For now, we must turn our attention to the future. King Talon will be pleased by your recovery. However, I must counsel you to shelter with one of our allies rather than returning at once to court." Light spiraled lazily about Riven. "Perhaps you might visit the Court of Dusk? Our ambassador there would offer welcome—she understands the need for discretion."

"You think it necessary?"

He lifted a shoulder. "Someone betrayed you, else Damir would never have succeeded in spiriting you away. If you shelter elsewhere, I can consult with the king about how he desires to proceed."

Her lips curved in a malicious smile. "Very well. I shall go to the Court of Dusk, as you counsel—on the condition that I return in time to see the execution of justice. I have a very good idea of the culprit."

He lifted a shoulder. "It is your right. A summons will be given in due time."

She slipped into the fae tongue, a disconcerting choice. Riven had advised her to shelter in the Court of Dusk . . . why? Surely they had other allies. Did he seek an excuse to enter the court?

He's canny enough to make use of whatever situations present themselves.

A fact for which I was grateful, but I'd not realized the extent to which he engaged with fae political games.

Jade padded to stand alongside me. *He is their lord arbiter— and therefore at the center of these games, whether he favors them or not.*

Clearly, his role meant something that I couldn't even begin to understand. Mocvar had feared him, and though fae were notorious for concealing emotion, the lady had appeared petrified when she realized she'd wielded her power against him. But never mind that now. *What are they saying?*

She presses Riven regarding your nature and why he switched to the mortal tongue before.

Pressure gathered in my temples, and I fought the urge to rub them. I did not need to betray weakness.

Riven regarded her with a cold expression, and a sort of impassive scorn laced his response. Though not directed at me, I shivered nevertheless.

He's dismissed her bid for information and suggests she puts her energies toward staying alive. Jade paused, listening. *It seems she cannot open a passing, so Riven has offered to escort her to the ambassador's dwelling.*

Which gave him an opportunity to visit the Court of Dusk. Without a glance my direction, they vanished. She must have accepted his offer as her best course of action, and naturally, he could not stop to discuss it, but his disappearance left me out-of-kilter.

If some threat remained within the pocket world, it seemed I was to face it alone. I sank to the floor, my back to the wall. I'd thought myself prepared to open the chamber, but I'd proven far from it. I'd imagined we'd encounter potential dangers, yet I'd not expected instantaneous attack when we opened the door.

Nor, it seemed, had Wyncourt. It must have known the fae lady inhabited the space and posed a threat, thus the warning, but perhaps it could not sense her position within the hidden realm. Given how Riven had described pocket worlds, it seemed logical that the workings severed the two as long as the door remained locked.

In any case, I'd exercise more care in the future. Clearly, it would have been sensible to wrap the power of Wyncourt about me before opening the door, never mind that I didn't quite comprehend *how*. Riven had made it clear he could answer no further questions about the use of my affinities. Likely it was why he'd issued no warning, only stood ready to intervene if needed.

Perhaps I did not need to rely on my own knowledge, but rather on the goodwill of Wyncourt. I entered the central star and said softly, "Will you keep me safe, if I enter? Can your power accompany me?"

The star brightened, warming the air around me. In our previous conversations, it had darkened to convey a negative, so

I'd take that as a positive response. I filtered through the flood of images available until I landed on the mantel clock. I still had half an hour to explore before my guests arrived. I turned to Jade. *Shall we go?*

With Jade at my side and a sense of Wyncourt's pulsing life surrounding me, I entered a stunning nightscape. Silver and gold and blue and even pinkish stars sat low and enormous in the sky, casting cold radiance over strong, craggy land. Risha perched on my shoulder, surveying the scene.

The radiance of the stars served to cast the shadows more deeply—and they reached toward me hungrily, out of size for the features that cast them. Once more, a wind-like sensation gusted about me, driving them back.

In the shifting shades, I struggled to discern the bounds of this world. What else might Lord West have snared within? Near the entrance towered an unfamiliar sort of tree, its song as distant and detached as the stars themselves.

On the underside of its leaves, shimmering in a vaguely translucent way, tiny eggs clustered. I drew closer to inspect them.

And Jade gave a low rumble. *Don't touch them. They're the eggs of the reva moth—extremely toxic.*

Of course they are.

Rather than go deeper into the pocket realm, I turned my attention to the workings that crafted it. Though they continually slipped from focus, I was able to hold some in view long enough to gain familiarity with their structure. They sprawled across the expanse of sky and wove through every element within this self-contained world, spiked and starry runes that somehow chilled upon sight.

Risha shivered slightly. "The light in here, it is not pleasant. It does not give life or warmth as it should."

Could the pocket world be altered? Or did this, an entirely fae construct, contain too much of Lord West's nature? Certainly, it held the tang of cold stone and ancient metal, much like his presence had in life—and I found myself reluctant to explore further.

Can you scent anything else living inside?

Jade shook her shaggy head. *It seems he constructed this only as a prison. Perhaps he meant to add others in time.*

That meant, for now, no monsters lurked. And whatever came of it, I was glad I'd freed the lady. Riven had once said that few things hurt fae as much as being bound by the power of another. How much had she suffered during her time entrapped here?

As I touched the lintel of the door, an image of the mantel clock popped into my mind. It was time to go. I placed my hands on the lock, sealing the pocket world once more, then hurried up the hidden stairs and back into Ibbie's room. I stopped before the glass to check my appearance—oh. Small wonder the fae lady had looked askance at me, disheveled as I'd become. I tugged a cobweb from my curls and smoothed the wrinkles from my skirt. As long as one did not look *too* closely, I was presentable.

And just in time.

As I descended the stairs, Lord Blackburn's stentorian tones echoed from the sitting room. "I see you still uphold Lady Dromley's standards of hospitality."

"We certainly try, my lord."

I entered the room in time to see the pleased smile on Danvers's face. If the bounty of chilled beverages and other refreshments were any indication, Lord Blackburn had good reason to praise Wyncourt's hospitality. I swept toward him. "Lord Blackburn, it's so good of you to come."

Before we could exchange anything beyond pleasantries, Mrs. Darrington, Miss Everby, and Mr. Burke joined us. Father. I should have asked Father to attend also. I'd spent so long concealing my actions from him that it hadn't occurred to me to extend the invitation. He'd been gone a great deal the past few days—perhaps that would provide sufficient excuse—but I did owe him some sort of update on my activities, at least those of which pertained to our joint endeavors.

I situated myself in an armchair that allowed a good vantage to watch them all. "I asked you here to discuss the missing individuals. As you might have seen in the gazettes, our maid is now one of them."

"A shame. Poor girl," Thea said.

"I cannot resign myself to the fact that she's gone." I poured a glass of cordial water. "After talking the matter over with Mr. Burke, we've landed on a possible lead."

I nodded toward him, and he seamlessly picked up the thread of the possible Collector involvement, detailing our theory.

Lord Blackburn frowned at the queen cake in his hand. "That's why you asked us here?"

"If anyone has heard rumors of such activities, we thought it would be you. We'd hoped you'd have some knowledge of how they operate that might better inform our approach."

"I've wondered before about hidden dealings on their part, but I've no evidence of it." He stroked his chin, considering. "Strict rules govern their actions—how often each Collector can travel to the Otherworld and how long they can stay, what sorts of things they may bring back and so on. They're meant to provide a comprehensive report of all they collect on each expedition to the alchemists, who are obligated to present the report in full to the king. These are concessions the Assemblage of Lords agreed upon when they would not pass the bans I proposed. However, enforcing such rules is another matter altogether, as I've pointed out time and again. The Collectors could easily bring back more than they account for and sell them in a sort of black market, if desired. Why shouldn't they? The sort of man who'd undertake such an expedition in the first place is either desperate or lacking scruples or both."

"So you think it conceivable they've set up a black market?"

"Nothing more likely, to my mind. It's only a surprise it hasn't done traceable damage before now." The craggy lines of his face deepened. "However bleak this circumstance, evidence of illegal dealings by the Collectors would go a long way toward swaying the king and stopping such things in the future."

"Which also means it will be hard to come by." Thea straightened slowly. "If these individuals sell contraband items—and have for some time—then they're experienced with concealing their deeds."

"Which is why, despite his desire to question them directly, Mr. Burke has agreed to keep his distance from this part of the investigation." I placed my glass on the side table, then leaned forward. "Thea, I'd like to propose that we call on the Collectors with a legitimate request. Then, by hinting you desire more, we might draw the attention of those who have preyed upon individuals in your situation."

"I do rather fit the mark." A smile creased Thea's face, lightening her cornflower eyes. "It's an excellent notion."

"Unless they become violent." Lord Blackburn pursed his lips. "A simple request to fetch an antiquity or other valuable item would be in their legal purview. I could go, instead."

"You'd be a logical person to make the actual request, but you don't present nearly as vulnerable a target as we do." At least from an outside vantage. "Which is why we must go."

"There's no *must*." Mr. Burke stirred at last. "I'll concede this is most likely to be the effective approach, but I must be perfectly clear about the risks. Mrs. Darrington, Miss Caldwell has already been warned, but this expedition is not sanctioned by the Magistry. If you stir trouble, I'd be forced to disclaim knowledge of your purpose."

Thea blithely waved a hand. "As it happens, I love a good intrigue. It's nearly as satisfying as an open rout of one's foes—and worth any number of risks. When shall we call?"

"I suggest tomorrow afternoon. We don't want to waste further time."

"I quite agree," she said.

Lord Blackburn leaned back with a resigned air. "Will you at least let me send an escort with you?"

"The Collectors are savvy, they must be in order to survive." For appearance's sake, I took a pastry from the tray, though I'd rather concentrate on the business on hand than confectionary. "I think we'll be safer, and more likely to succeed, if we appear as ordinary as possible."

Though Lord Blackburn put up a few more protests, he seemed to accept the inevitability of the plan, and after a bit more cursory conversation, he and the others departed. I replaced my untouched pastry on the tray.

Even the soothing breath of Wyncourt could not dispel the weight of worry that descended upon me in their absence, the gathering pressure of all that remained unknown. Though dusk gathered, I didn't rise to light the lamps.

What now?

I should return home, yet I didn't want to leave. Just as I'd resigned myself to departure, light deluged the room, and Riven appeared. His features, now cloaked in mortal glamour once more, displayed no trace of emotion—yet some sort of imperceptible shadow seemed to hang over him.

I sprang to my feet. "Is everything all right?"

"Lady Avis is situated in the Court of Dusk." He took the chair opposite to the one I'd occupied, lounging back, the green of his eyes dark. "Her presence will be a small boon, while it lasts."

If by chance something *did* trouble him, perhaps I could gain some hint of it obliquely—or perhaps I imagined it all. I resettled myself. "How long ago did Lord West claim her?"

"Several decades. Given the circumstances, I'm not certain you recall, but I once mentioned Damir had acquired something my king valued."

"Lady Avis." I sank back. "I cannot imagine it was easy to spirit her away."

"No. She disappeared on a hunt in the Wilds. On the face of it, evidence suggested she'd ventured out alone and was overtaken by a swarm of dark wyvern. I found it suspicious, but I'd no evidence of any foul play. No trace of other high fae could be found in the vicinity." Small sparks of light drifted from his fingers, kindling the gas lamps and brightening the room. "But Damir wasn't content to allow his part to remain unknown. After a time, a few hints of his involvement trickled back to me—nothing actionable, of course. No evidence, only rumor and speculation. And one does not start wars on such a basis, particularly since the Wilds belong to no court. Venturing there has its risks, which must be accepted. When it became clear that Damir and potentially the Court of Silver were involved, the king ordered me to abandon the investigation for a time—to watch and wait for an opportunity to strike at Damir in some hidden way."

"But you knew—or thought—there was some betrayal from your own court that pulled her into the Wilds?"

Riven nodded. "Yet given how the Court of Silver was entangled in the affair, the king did not want it ferreted out—not then. The repercussions would have been inconvenient. Now, with Damir dead and Lady Avis able to give evidence that it was a personal vendetta, rather than an attack by the court, it's no longer so. Your king might decide to wait days or weeks for a plot to unfold before acting to end it, mine is content to wait decades and more to gain the upper hand."

I took a sip of now-tepid cordial water. "What is her relationship to the king?"

"She's his court weaver—and the strongest in centuries."

"Is that an important role?"

"The seamless weaving of workings into fabrics of all kinds is one much valued, and it gives the king certain advantages." His voice held little inflection. "Her position was temporarily filled with another, less skilled weaver. But even if Lady Avis hadn't been a valued member of the court, he'd have avenged her when the time was right. The king feels a certain . . . possessiveness toward those in his court, all fae monarchs do."

"I see."

"The king wishes to give her betrayer another day of liberty.

See how he reacts to the news of her return. It might prove illuminating." Yet as he spoke, his eyes shadowed further.

I twined my fingers in Jade's fur. Riven was arbiter for his court. Did that mean he'd have some involvement in the execution of justice? He remained silent, present yet unusually detached, the light sharpening the planes of his face and deepening the shadows behind him. Though fae weren't given to unburdening their souls, I had to at least ask. "Is there anything else you . . . want to discuss?"

"No."

I flinched at the curtness in his voice. Perhaps I'd misread the situation entirely, presumed far too much.

He stood in a single fluid motion. "Your family will be wondering at your absence. I'll call tomorrow, if I'm not required in my court."

With that, he departed, leaving me to the quiet of the demesne.

CHAPTER 32

As I descended the stairs the following morning, tempestuous melodies stormed out to greet me. I pursued them to the morning room, where Ada sat at the pianoforte, lost in her music, her emotions bleeding into every note.

My throat tightened. I took a seat near the window and picked up my sketchbook, scarcely attending to the path of my charcoals across the page—until I found myself looking into a shadowy version of Riven's face, his eyes dark and haunted.

I swiftly turned the page and chose a more appropriate subject—the garden beyond the window, all pools and puddles from an early morning shower. Small tendrils of mist rose as the sun beat upon the damp earth.

And my thoughts drifted back to Riven. Had I caused offense last night? It had been a simple question, and yet . . . fae preferred not to speak of emotion. Perhaps there had been none to discuss, and I'd chased something that did not exist. Why was I even thinking about it, with so many more pressing problems?

Jade leapt upon the arm of my chair, her whiskers tickling my ear. *If something does trouble Riven, it may reach for you also. It's not something to overlook entirely.*

I darkened the lines of the oak. *That's . . . not exactly encouraging.*

From somewhere behind me, Holden cleared his throat. I turned, and he handed me a small stack of letters from the morning post. Was it my imagination, or was his demeanor frostier than usual?

I studied the immobile set of his features—definitely frostier, no doubt because of the tale he'd carried to Aunt Caris. I stifled a sigh as I glanced over the letters.

Then I froze. An envelope illustrated with nightspire vines occupied the bottom of the stack, the stark spirals sparking dread.

I tore through the coiled vines. A scrap of paper fluttered out, bearing a spiraled maze of words:

> *Naughty girl. I warned you to stop interfering. Now the terrors of your sister's nights have begun to invade her days. How long will it take before she cannot tell one reality from another? It will be interesting to find out, don't you think?*

The melodies of the pianoforte faded before the roar in my ears, and I crumpled the letter.

Jade rumbled low. *If her bargain-holder would stop hiding behind letters and phantasms, then we might show her something of interest.*

But why would she? This way, she has every advantage.

I unfolded the missive. Whatever my instinct to discard it, perhaps it contained some evidence. I tucked it between the pages of my sketchbook. I should tell Ada and Ainslie—but I'd wait until the raw edge of emotion subsided. Ainslie, in particular, deserved my support, not my fear.

As I sat listening to the haunting music spilling from Ada, Morwen marched into the room. Her hair spiraled wilder than before, and her lips were pressed together in a tight line. She passed me and went straight to Ada, clambering atop the pianoforte. "Shaggy beast has drunk from my fountain!"

"A . . . shaggy beast?" Ada paused with her fingers still resting on the keys.

"Shaggy beast with great flappy jowls. One that accompanies shaggy boy. Has spoiled my water." She sniffed. "Are no baths for me now. Will not do, no indeed."

The shaggy boy must be Dryden, but a shaggy beast? Perhaps a dog? Dryden did seem to have a knack for collecting creatures.

Somehow, Ada kept her face from betraying amusement. "I'll see that the water is replaced and the fountain cleaned today."

"Yes, is good. You keep fountain clean. I keep away intruders."

Sketchbook in hand, I moved toward the pianoforte. "Have there been intruders of late?"

She nodded vigorously, her curls bobbing. "Man watches, two times. Hides, thinks no one sees. But I see always."

I clasped the sketchbook to my chest. Mr. Ludne, perhaps? But when I offered his description, a shake of her head sent her ribbons fluttering.

"Was more young, with hair like sunset."

"Fae or mortal?"

"Mortal." With that, Morwen vanished into the depths of the house.

Ada rippled her fingers across the keys, the notes sharp and discordant. "Who do you think she saw?"

"I wish I knew. Perhaps someone else belonging to the Vigil surveils us." Or someone sent by Ainslie's bargain-holder, perhaps? We still had no notion of how she watched us. Only it felt we were beginning to collect an alarming number of enemies. "Either way, we must have a care."

"It will be easier with Morwen to keep watch. I'm glad Dreda brought her." A soft progression of chords spilled from the pianoforte, punctuating her words. "Until now, everything Other has felt so threatening. But she's a homely, comforting sort of soul—if I don't consider that she has the power to upset the household if displeased."

"It seems she's taken to you."

"She says it's been long since one of her kind has been able to claim and care for a household and receive open acknowledgment."

Was that something else that had changed during the time of the Forgotten War? Another lost memory?

Ada removed her hands from the keys and placed them in her lap. "This arrangement seems to make her happy. She's taken to popping up at odd moments to tell me of household gossip. I'm not certain it pleases Ainslie, though."

"Anything that reminds her of Other must be difficult right now."

"Oh, Jessa." Ada's lips trembled. "She's trying, but—she's not herself. And I'm so afraid."

It wouldn't help matters to confess that I felt the same, so I simply slid onto the bench beside her and pulled her into a hug. We sat so until Aunt Caris bustled into the room.

"There you are, my dear. Lord Riven has come to call, and I've invited him to stay to tea. It's earlier than proper, but I suppose we can excuse that. He tells me he prefers to keep country hours."

He'd come, so perhaps that meant matters were not as unsettled as I feared. "You left him alone?"

"Oh, no, my dear. Alden is with him. They were having quite the conversation—it's been some time since I've seen Alden so animated."

And what turn might their conversation take? I hurried after Aunt Caris, but Holden intercepted us before we reached the drawing room.

"Miss Caldwell, the mantua-maker has arrived."

"Oh dear, this is what comes of callers arriving at the wrong hour. If only Lord Riven had waited until afternoon." Aunt Caris shifted from one foot to the other, looking as though she'd like to divide herself.

"Don't worry. With Father present, there can be no fear of impropriety. I'll go join them."

Still, she wavered. "If Alden gets distracted, you must be sure he doesn't wander off until Lord Riven departs."

"I will."

With that, she kissed my cheek and bustled after Holden. As I approached the drawing room, Father's voice rang out, discernible even through the closed door. "Caris has informed me that you're paying marked attention to Jessa."

Oh no. My eyes slid shut. Of all times for Father to listen to Aunt Caris's declarations of suitors . . .

"Has she?" A note of amusement laced Riven's voice.

"I have no wish to interfere, but I feel it my duty to ask— what are your intentions toward my daughter?"

If I'd possessed Risha's abilities, I would have gladly vanished into the ether. Why now? We were meant to make a pretense of Riven's interest, yes, but he'd surely not expected an interrogation from Father. Warmth flooded my chest.

From somewhere in the vicinity of my ear Risha whispered, "Does he know he speaks to the Lord Arbiter?"

I shook my head.

Jade gave a low rumble, almost a chuckle, and her amusement rippled over me.

"I assure you my interest is not a trifling one," Riven said. "I find Jessa . . . remarkable."

I shifted uncomfortably. Remarkable in what way? Remarkably difficult, most likely, considering the trouble I'd brought into his life.

"That's how I felt when I met her mother," Father said blithely, unaware of the shades of meaning Riven's words could hold. "One does not ignore such things."

Before the conversation could take a further turn for the worse, I pressed the door open with a bright smile. "Lord Riven, I'm delighted you've called."

"Are you?" The shadows of the day before had given way to gold flecks, which now danced in his eyes.

Did he know I'd overheard them? He must, since by some

means he was able to discern my presence. My cheeks warmed. "Of course."

"I've come to see if you'd like to stroll in the park." Riven inclined his head toward Father. "If your father has no objection."

Father pressed up from his chair. "None whatsoever."

"Just allow me to fetch Miss Twells to accompany us." While a man and woman might be permitted to stroll together in public, some semblance of chaperonage was usually expected on such occasions, particularly in Avons. And given Aunt Caris's distress over her own past and her worries for me, it seemed an important concession to grant, however much I chafed at the demands of convention.

Yet Riven gave a slight frown. "If you're certain it will not trouble her."

I halted in the doorway. We'd strolled in such fashion in Withern on several occasions, and a simple glamour had sufficed to conceal our conversation. Just what did he intend this time that he expected it to trouble her? Never mind that—if I turned back now, even Father would question it. "I'm sure she won't mind."

After I returned with Dreda, Riven ushered us out the door, and when we reached the footwalk, she immediately fell back to give us some privacy. I turned to him. "About what Father said—"

"He seeks only your good, and I am aware of your mortal conventions. Think no more of it."

Yet I undoubtedly would. One always remembered the mortifying moments at the most inconvenient times—they returned like spectres to haunt the nighttime hours. A soft sigh escaped. "I imagine you didn't come simply to take a stroll."

"You're correct." Whatever disturbance I'd thought I perceived the night before had disappeared—or been buried. He moved down the footwalk with a purposeful stride. "I spoke with Burke late last night. A lady in Clemford vanished. Like the others, she left no trace. Burke says she was known to have been melancholic for months before brightening into excellent spirits these past weeks."

Clemford—that wasn't terribly far, perhaps a half day's travel by horse. "Have you visited her house?"

"Not yet." A carriage rattled by, splattering the footwalk with mud, yet by some working Riven conjured, it didn't touch us. "It would be most effective if we went together, as we did with Dr. Fulton."

When we'd called on Dr. Fulton, Riven had accompanied me concealed by glamour and thereby gained access with the good doctor unaware. I nodded slowly. "That would allow me to speak with the household while you seek any trace of Other."

I'd no notion what sort of story I could conjure to explain my presence, but I'd think of something. "Does the lady have family?"

"She's widowed, and her nieces live with her."

The act of calling openly could signal my interest in the case to any who sought to observe, yet it wasn't a crime to go calling. "Does Mr. Burke know your intent?"

"I thought it better to withhold that information for now. What he doesn't know, he cannot be forced to give an account of."

A few remnant raindrops that lingered on the leaves above fell, dotting the muslin of my gown. "We should go soon. I'll have to return in a few hours—I'm to call on the Collectors with Mrs. Darrington. But Dreda . . ." I glanced back at her serene figure. "She covered for us once with Kilmere. Perhaps she'd be willing to do so again."

"You'd have to inform her this concerns Other matters to justify it."

"I know, but I believe she'll hold it in trust. She has before." I halted beneath a spreading oak, waiting for her to close the gap between us.

"Is anything the matter, Miss Jessa?" She eyed Riven a bit uncertainly as she spoke.

"Only that I must ask you a tremendous favor." I inhaled

the scent of sun-warmed leaves, the shadow of which provided little relief from the strengthening heat of the day. "Lord Riven must take me to investigate something concerning the missing."

Her hands tightened at her sides. "It's Other that's taken them, then?"

"It appears so." I drew a breath. "I cannot bring you—are you willing to let us go?"

A gleam brightened her hazel eyes. "You wish me to cover for your absence by remaining out until you return?"

"If you're willing." She'd expressed her readiness to conspire with me before, but was this too great a request?

"I'd be pleased to do so, as long as it places neither you nor your reputation in danger."

"Lord Riven will see to the safety of both."

She surveyed him. Before, she'd perceived more than I wished. After all she'd experienced, did any part of her guess at his nature? At last, she nodded. "Then I shall do my best to draw no notice."

Nor would she, because even as she spoke, Riven took advantage of the absence of passersby to weave glamours, one for her, the other for the two of us.

I squeezed her hand. "Thank you, Dreda."

"You're very welcome." With one final glance over her shoulder, she proceeded down the path.

When she vanished from sight, Riven opened a passing, its light and color and power swirling around us in a way that was both disorienting and exhilarating. We emerged in front of a small country estate, crafted in the old style, with gentle arches and curves. It lacked the usual bustle of such manors—no one tended the gardens, no callers visited, and the drapes at the front windows remained closed. Would they receive us?

With Riven glamoured alongside me, I knocked at the door, waited a few minutes, then tried again.

At last, a butler creaked it open. "The household is not receiving visitors."

I offered a serene smile. "Nevertheless, please ask Miss Chevon if she'll see me. I wish to discuss the matter of her aunt."

His lips pinched in a firm line, but he did as I asked, returning some minutes later. "She will see you."

His tone made his disapproval clear. Yet I'd gained access, and I'd not had to rely on glamour. That was something, at least. Once within the house, Riven broke off to conduct his own investigations, while Jade trotted alongside me, and Risha bobbed at my shoulder.

The butler ushered us into a rather gloomy drawing room, and Miss Chevon rose to greet me, her disheveled appearance revealing her distress. Her hair feathered out of its confines like strands of astilbe, the lace of her collar sat uneven, and she clutched a handkerchief. She hurried forward. "Oh please, do you know anything about my aunt?"

"I'm afraid I cannot tell you where she might be, yet I've come to see if I can offer assistance." I glanced at Jade, who prowled about the corners of the room. "What has the Magistry told you?"

"Very little. They say they cannot account for these disappearances, but that we must have hope." She crumpled her damp handkerchief, her features clouding further. "But I don't understand—how did you know my aunt?"

Given her state, a forthright approach seemed best. "I have no personal acquaintance with your aunt, but not long ago, someone close to me vanished unexpectedly. She was restored to us, but she does not recall what happened to her, and I still fear she may disappear again. I wish to see her safe—and as many others as I may—which is why I seek information, not as the authorities do, but as one who understands your pain."

"It seems a very strange occupation for a lady." Her voice broke. "And yet, I do understand. If it would bring my aunt back, I'd knock on the doors of a thousand strangers, however improper. She's been everything to us."

"Yet I understand she suffered from low spirits at times?"

"Every spring. My uncle passed away of an attack on his

heart three years ago, and the memory always pains her at that time of year and lingers through the summer." She twisted the handkerchief. "This time, she made a quicker recovery of spirits than was her wont, and Lydia and I, we thought it a good sign. She'd had new wardrobes drawn up for all of us and talked of all sorts of plans for the future in a way she'd never done before."

"Was there anything else unusual?"

"The stratesmen asked that too." She brushed an astilbe strand from her face. "They inquired about unsavory individuals or threatening notes or anything along those lines and kept insisting that there must have been something out of the ordinary. When we could recall nothing, they acted almost as if they suspected *us* of underhanded dealings. I cannot imagine . . . We would never . . ."

It sounded as though the stratesmen responsible for speaking with her had mismanaged the entire situation. In her distress, she needed coaxing, not command. "You cannot be expected to recall something that never happened. But perhaps the peculiarity wasn't something that seemed noteworthy at the time. You knew your aunt well. Aside from her plans for the future, was there anything she did that was unlike her, no matter how small or silly it may seem? Perhaps even an object she acquired?"

Her pale lashes fluttered downward—she'd thought of something. "Well, I don't see how this has any bearing on her disappearance, but among her new acquisitions there was one that did not quite seem to fit—a statuette that was quite ugly. Well, sometimes it seemed ugly. Other times, I found it oddly attractive." She shuddered slightly, her light pink muslin rustling. "I saw it in a box with a new hat she'd ordered, and when I asked about it, she said it caught her fancy. I cannot see how it would matter—the stratesmen didn't even want to hear about her ordering a new wardrobe to begin with, let alone peculiar statuettes."

But I most certainly did. "You never know what will turn out to have significance. What about it seemed strange?"

She faltered. "I don't know exactly. It just didn't *belong*, if you know what I mean."

"Can I see it?"

She nodded. "I'll take you to her bedchamber."

Jade returned to my side. *We have a problem.*

No sooner had she spoken than the butler glided into the room. "There's a stratesman here to see you, Miss Chevon. He says he's traveled from Avons and cannot wait."

That. It's Mr. Burke.

However tempting, I could scarcely climb through a window, and I refused to attempt to glamour Mr. Burke or anyone else, which meant I'd simply have to face the consequences.

My stomach tightened as he stepped through the door.

CHAPTER 33

Mr. Burke entered the room. "Miss Chevon, thank you for seeing me. I—" Then his gaze fell upon me, and his face became like stone. "Miss Caldwell."

"Mr. Burke. I didn't expect to meet you here."

"I'm sure you did not." His words emerged clipped, the presence of Miss Chevon forcing restraint. "I have official business to attend with Miss Chevon, so I must request you depart. Along with *any* other visitors."

Miss Chevon glanced between us, her confusion evident.

I straightened my shoulders and stepped forward. "Actually, Miss Chevon was just telling me of an unusual item her aunt acquired before her disappearance. I think it worth discussing further."

His kestrel-sharp gaze shifted to her. "You mentioned nothing of this to the stratesmen who visited before, Miss Chevon."

She fumbled with her handkerchief. "I . . . I did not think it important."

"But they did inquire about any recent changes?"

She shrank back. "Well, yes, but—"

"It's not for you to judge importance, only to provide the requested information."

Mr. Burke frowned, and Miss Chevon seemed to collapse inward, drawing away as if she'd like to flee.

I moved between the two of them. "Mr. Burke, may I consult with you a moment?"

He was tempted to deny me—I could read it in the set of his jaw—but at last, he gave a clipped nod. "Excuse us, Miss Chevon."

I followed Mr. Burke down the corridor and into an empty drawing room. Stiff satin curtains remained drawn over the windows, giving it an air of gloom. Once he pulled the door halfway shut, I said, "You're angry with me, not Miss Chevon, but you're frightening her all the same. You won't achieve anything that way, nor does she deserve the condemnation you heaped upon her."

"I'm not—" He stopped short, then exhaled slowly. "You're right. I owe her an apology. But I'd like answers as well. Where's Riven? You couldn't have arrived so swiftly without him. Nor known of Lady Chevon's disappearance."

"He's exploring the Other angle of the situation."

"I see. Apparently he deemed it necessary to embroil you openly in the case, hang any scandal it might cause. Why?"

"To avoid glamouring the inhabitants of the household, a decision I thought you'd support."

"I do." He scrubbed a hand across his jaw. "However, it cannot become known you're involved in this case. Mr. Ludne has been making a nuisance of himself these past few days. I fear if he finds you're involved with Magistry business, he'll use it against you. You shouldn't have come."

I'd known involving myself in the investigation held risks, but to hear it stated so bluntly . . . I swallowed a swell of bitterness. "I was aware of his enmity, but not that he'd broadcasted his sentiments to the Magistry and Vigil."

"He's exercising caution so he does not expose himself to any sort of libel suit, but he's dropped plenty of hints and asked a number of leading questions. Now that he's pulled others into the matter, his reputation is on the line. I fear he'll invent evidence before allowing it to drop."

Jade bristled, and Risha's light took on dark indigo tones, her indignation clear.

Mr. Burke drummed his fingers against his leg. "If he discovers this . . . I should never have involved you in the first place."

"You're not to blame for any grudge he holds. His choices are his own." Even so, the heavy gloom of the chamber pressed in on me. "I'll not deny I find it concerning, but I'm here now, so we might as well make the best of it. As for Miss Chevon, she was completely overset by the loss of her aunt and the presence of stratesmen in the home. She felt they suspected her or the servants of some wrongdoing—they kept haranguing her about how it was possible that no one could have noticed anything— and it seems to have shut her down altogether."

"Stratesman Gray had charge of the case, and he's like a troll at an afternoon tea even at the best of times." Mr. Burke shook his head. "Yet I can't consider myself blameless, given how I addressed her. I'd planned to approach her differently, and I shouldn't have allowed myself to be thrown off course."

"Given what's passed, will you consider allowing me to remain?" I tucked my cold hands in at my sides. "The risk can be no worse if I linger."

He inclined his head. "You're right. She's clearly more comfortable with another lady—and I assume you have no means of returning home."

"Not until Riven arrives."

"Then you might as well stay. I'd welcome your perspective on the matter."

That settled, we returned to Miss Chevon. She sat pleating and unpleating her skirt but leapt to her feet when we came back into the room.

When Mr. Burke approached her, all hint of the sharp stratesman vanished as he donned the more polished air of a gentleman, recalling his origins as the third son of a lord. He gave a slight bow. "Forgive my abruptness earlier, Miss Chevon. I know this is a trying time for you, and I'm certain you did your best to share what you could with my colleagues."

"Indeed, I did. I cannot think what we will do if you don't recover Aunt Agnes." Her eyes flooded again with tears. "We've had ever so many visitors, but not one of them expects she'll return—they'd rather take advantage of our plight."

"How so?" I asked softly.

"Oh, you know—the usual grist for the gossip mill. But there's one man who's made a particular nuisance of himself—he claims acquaintance with our aunt, but I've certainly never met him before."

I leaned forward. "Did he give a name?"

"Mr. Fuller. I cannot give a description, but our butler would know—he's sent Mr. Fuller away each time. Mr. Fuller said our aunt owed him a considerable sum, but she didn't believe in paying anything on credit, so I can only imagine he sought to profit by our loss. After his last visit, our butler suggested we stop receiving visitors altogether—but of course, when I thought you'd word of my aunt, I had to accept."

This Mr. Fuller could be a swindler . . . but what if Agnes had owed money for some Otherworldly artifact? Such things would come at great cost. It was possible she'd paid a sum up front, with the remainder to be delivered later.

Evidently, Mr. Burke had the same thought, for he strode to the doorway and summoned the butler. "Can you describe Mr. Fuller?"

"Of course. He was a man of middling height, of an age with you or a bit older. He had brown hair and eyes, and there was nothing out of the ordinary in his appearance except a scar on his left cheek."

It was difficult to believe this was the same butler who'd eyed me with suspicion. He seemed pleased to divulge any information he could to Mr. Burke. Being a member of the Magistry— and a man of authoritative bearing—had some advantages.

"What was your impression of him?" Mr. Burke asked.

"I disliked him at once. He had a sort of hungry look about him that boded no good." He sniffed. "He was no gentleman, no matter the finery with which he adorned himself. A decent man would never have sought to prey on the young ladies in their time of grief."

Mr. Burke and I exchanged glances. Was Mr. Fuller a Collector, perhaps? Furnished with his name and description, Thea and I could inquire later today.

Mr. Burke's lips tightened. "Did he claim a connection to the Collectors? Or did any of your lady's other callers?"

The butler grew stiff. "My lady did not consort with such riffraff."

"Then that will be all." After the butler left, Mr. Burke turned to Miss Chevon. "Now, if you don't mind, Miss Caldwell and I would like to see the statuette you mentioned."

"Are you certain?" She twisted her handkerchief, the lace spilling over her fingers. "It may not be of any consequence after all. I . . . I don't wish to waste your time."

"Whether or not it proves to have any bearing on the case, it will help me form a better picture of your aunt and her interests." He maintained a gentle, even tone, and she visibly relaxed.

"Oh, that is so. She kept it in her jewel chest, at least that's where I last saw it. If you'll just come with me, I'll show you to her bedchamber."

We ascended the stairs with her, and she opened the door to an elegantly appointed room. She withdrew a key from the dressing table drawer, then unlocked the jewel chest that sat on top. When she opened it, she stilled. "How very strange—it's no longer here."

Mr. Burke stepped forward. "Has anything else been taken?"

She sifted through the contents, then shook her head. "Everything else appears to be present."

It wasn't the evidence I'd hoped for; I'd wanted to find some hint of another bargain, some scrap of information that might suggest a connection to Ainslie's situation. This could help the missing, and I was grateful for that, but Ainslie . . .

Mr. Burke lifted the chest to inspect the lock, the jewels casting sparkles against the wall when the sunlight hit them. "There's no sign the case was tampered with." He returned it to the dressing table. "Can you give a description of the statuette?"

"It was ivory and small enough to fit in the palm of one's hand. It looked old and rather unattractive, but . . . well, it's difficult to describe."

Her bewilderment suggested the possibility of glamour resting on the object. "Is anything else missing from her bedchamber?"

"Only the clothes she wore that day—a green day dress, a matching reticule, and her slippers. Stratesman Gray had my sister and me look through all her garments and shoes. Nothing else had been taken."

Mr. Burke paced the room, stopping to examine the windows and rummaging in the clothes press, and Jade followed, sniffing about. If only Lady Chevon had kept some sort of plant indoors—perhaps I could have discreetly gained further insight. Yet the neatness of the room suggested there'd been no intrusion of any kind, so perhaps there simply wasn't evidence to be found. My gaze caught on two small side-by-side portraits, a lady and gentleman. "Is that your aunt and uncle?"

A sad smile tugged at her lips. "Yes. They loved each other dearly."

Mr. Burke circled back to my side. "Did your aunt mention any new acquaintance to you?"

"No, but as I told Miss Caldwell, she was very much anticipating the future. She'd even planned to go to Avons in the fall so we could enjoy the social season. I just know she wouldn't have left of her own accord."

His features settled into grim lines. "We will do everything in our power to find her."

"If you cannot—"

"Don't give up hope. It's not time for that yet." I gently pressed her hand.

"Thank you," she whispered. "If . . . if you don't need anything more from me, I'll return to my sister now."

Mr. Burke nodded. "We can see ourselves out."

Together, we descended the stairs. I didn't sense Riven anywhere nearby, so he must be tracing the path of the missing woman. I couldn't reasonably impose on Miss Chevon's hospitality any longer, so even though I'd no means of actually departing until Riven returned, I must give the appearance of doing so.

In the shadow of Mr. Burke's carriage, I halted. "There's a small copse just down the road. I'll wait for Riven there."

"I'm not abandoning you to wait on the edge of the road for some unknown amount of time. At least let me accompany you." Mr. Burke started down the lane without awaiting my assent. "Besides, I'd like a word with Riven."

I followed him down the lane. If he meant to confront Riven over his decision to visit the Chevon family, I'd rather be present. "You didn't guess he meant to come after your conversation?"

"Interrogation, more like." His hands tightened at his sides. "I can't say I'm surprised that he came, rather that he dragged you into the affair. Perhaps I shouldn't be, because before I told him about Lady Chevon, I managed to obtain a concession that he wouldn't barge in and glamour the household. In retrospect, I'm certain he only agreed because this was his plan all along. He could placate me and carry on as he'd always intended."

"You're probably right. Still, it's given us new insight. When Thea and I go to speak with the Collectors, we can ask after Mr. Fuller."

"And if it turns out the man wasn't a Collector, only an opportunist?"

"Then we're no worse off than we were before, perhaps better, because we know of the statuette."

"That may be true, but I dislike everything about this situation." His eyes took on a stormy hue. "I would offer you escort home, but that would only damage your reputation further."

"I still have plausible deniability. I was at home with my family and the servants this morning, and I'll return to go calling with Mrs. Darrington this afternoon. By mortal reckoning, there's no way to cover these distances with such speed. If someone claims I've been here, they'll have difficulty proving it."

"Never underestimate the power of a grudge."

Before I could reply, a swift surge of Other heralded Riven's arrival. I came very close to betraying myself by signaling his approach and only just subsided in time.

A moment later, Riven strode into the copse. He raised a brow at Mr. Burke. "You keep popping up."

"I could say the same about you," Mr. Burke said coolly.

"In a way, it's fortunate we're all here together. We can compare notes." I forced cheer into my voice—no sense in allowing an argument to break out. "What did you find, Riven?"

"Agnes disappeared in the same way Lianne did. But she went farther afield before she entered a passing. As before, it was removed after she traveled through, which leaves little to go on."

I rocked back slightly. "So despite the fact that Lianne was in service, unlike the others, it seems the same culprit is responsible for all the disappearances?"

"The evidence points that direction."

Suddenly weary, I leaned against the elm stationed behind me. "Mr. Burke and I learned something from Miss Chevon. Her aunt was in possession of a statuette that sounded Other in nature."

"There was nothing Other in the house. I checked."

"I know—we asked, and it was conveniently missing."

"Then we've learned all we can here, and it's time we returned to Avons."

"Not quite yet." Mr. Burke spun toward Riven. "I'd have a word with you."

"About what?"

"Jessa." A frown tightened Mr. Burke's features. "Next time

you act on information you've demanded from me, don't use her as your decoy, not unless you want the Institution to claim her."

"And why would they do that?" Riven's voice dropped dangerously low.

"Since the events at Kilmere, Ludne has sought evidence to use against her."

The light about Riven sharpened into glittering shards. "Jessa? You didn't tell me Ludne was trying to make trouble."

Though I wanted to claim it was nothing, the words stuck in my throat. "In all honesty, I forgot to mention it—there have been far more pressing matters."

"Then perhaps I should have a word with him."

I expected Mr. Burke to object to the implicit threat, but he kept quiet. The bark of the elm dug into my back, and I straightened. "According to Mr. Burke, he's spread his suspicions about—for him to suddenly drop the matter would only attract more attention. Unless you mean to glamour the entire Vigil?"

He said nothing. Surely he wouldn't . . . but I'd best make a clean breast of the entire affair. I pivoted toward Mr. Burke. "Have you heard of the use of listening devices, either by the Magistry or the Vigil?"

His brows raised. "It's not something that we possess the ability to do at the Magistry, at least not to my knowledge—I didn't know such things even existed."

"Did Ludne possess such an item?" Riven asked.

"Yes. I have reason to believe it was a . . . fae listening stone."

"He left this device in your home?" Mr. Burke asked.

"He did—but I destroyed it before he could overhear anything."

Riven folded his arms across his chest. "That is not something he could acquire by accident, nor something your alchemists could come close to replicating—at least not without fae instruction. I will be paying him a call."

"But—"

"He owes answers about the stone, at least. I'll grant that a sudden change of heart where you're concerned would only confirm to the Vigil that you do bear watching—a subtler approach might be required there. But I will have the truth as to the source of the stone. If it was gifted by fae, it can be for no good purpose."

Mr. Burke shifted. "Will you share what you find?"

"If I deem it relevant."

"In other words, no," Mr. Burke muttered.

I found myself entirely in sympathy with his sentiments. Riven's definition of what was relevant often felt more limited than I would prefer. I glanced at the sun, which had already crested the sky and begun to dip westward.

It was time to return—and confront the Collectors.

Our absence had been rather protracted for a simple stroll, but hopefully Dreda's presence would smooth over that departure from convention. As we retraced our steps toward home, the tearful expression of Miss Chevon returned to me. Though I'd offered reassurance, did we truly have hope of restoring her aunt to her?

"While I traced Agnes, I received word from my court." Riven lifted his voice over the clatter of a passing carriage. "After I call on Ludne, I must return to the Otherworld. It may be several days before I can come back to Avons."

"Is this about Lady Avis and her betrayer?"

"Among other things. I'd also like to move some final pieces into place to be used if needed." His long stride left me hurrying to keep up. "While I'm gone, you should practice your affinities. It would be best if you had someone to train you, but since that requires belonging to a court . . . just do as much as you can."

The hint of warning in his words left me unsettled, as did the prospect of his absence. Yet we'd arrived home, and no time remained for further conversation, save a brief mention of the letter sent by the bargain-holder that morning. Riven delivered me to my doorstep, and I slipped into the house to freshen up and snatch meat buns from the kitchen—one for me and one for Jade—before hastening to join Thea in her carriage.

She offered a birdlike nod in greeting, her eyes bright beneath her milkweed-floss hair. "I spent some time this morning speaking further with Lord Blackburn about the Collectors, so we might be as prepared as possible. He confirmed that the same regulations that bind Collectors to sell their goods only to the alchemists or directly to the king allow for them to conduct other lines of business when they're between excursions to the Otherworld. Evidently, since their ultimate goal is to become established in some safer line of trade, it's not uncommon for them to deal with matters of alternate business in what's known as the keeping chamber. I intend to request someone to help me fetch an antiquity, while hinting I have other interests. We shall see if anyone takes the bait."

"There's a new development that might help. Lady Chevon has gone missing, and she was known to have struggled with melancholy before a recent turn in spirits. Perhaps you could hint at suffering the same?"

She nodded slowly. "I like that. Few would question the notion of a woman in my situation enduring such a malady."

Though Thea didn't seem prone to melancholy, I'd no doubt she could sell the idea. "Lady Chevon also had a tie to a Mr. Fuller, who might be a Collector. Perhaps we can request him."

"That's simple enough—and if we find he isn't, I'll just inform them that I must have misheard the name." She adjusted her hat so it shadowed her features, giving her a greater air of fragility. "Meanwhile, I wanted to inform you in person—I've just had word that if you will submit your admittance paper within the next fortnight, you're to be granted provisional access to the Antiquary Society. I believe it's a result of Mr. Redgrave hinting at his support, perhaps also because our esteemed president hopes you'll make a misstep and thereby discredit me. However, it's all to our good. As long as I accompany you, you'll be permitted to access anything you want."

"Then perhaps we can go tomorrow—I should be able to

finalize the report on Kilmere this afternoon." If I could access the full records of the society, it meant I could more deeply examine the era of the Forgotten War and the history of the Redgrave family. There must be a way to circumvent their geas and gain the knowledge they held. The missing, even Ainslie's bargain, were only symptoms of a far greater problem—and the answers might well lie in our forgotten past.

"Very good. I'll come to collect you in the morning."

We halted in front of a tall sovstone building with clean lines and an imposing array of windows. The only thing that attested to its nature were the scripted rune-wards about the doors and windows; otherwise it had a perfectly ordinary appearance. In a motion now becoming familiar, I pulled the songs of the plane trees anchoring either side of the building toward myself and my companions, an act which alleviated the sting of the wards. When we crossed the threshold, we found ourselves in the central keeping chamber, which rather reminded me of a beekeeper's garden, alive and thrumming with activity.

As we crossed the polished wood floor, Mrs. Darrington leaned heavily on her cane. She tottered over to a tall table in the center of the room, where a doorkeeper occupied himself with a large ledger.

When she approached, he looked up. "Your business?"

"I was hoping . . . that is, I'd heard I might come here if I needed to employ someone for a dangerous task. I need an antiquity fetched from the Northern Reaches—at least, I should like to have it." Her voice held a slight quaver. "I was advised someone from the Collectors might be willing to undertake the trip while between expeditions."

"We may be able to help." He traced his fingers down a list of names. "Benson can't return to the Otherworld for another month. I'll send for him, and you can discuss arrangements."

I stepped closer. "Didn't you mention wishing to speak to a Mr. Fuller?"

"Yes, I believe that was the recommendation I received."

Thea blinked up at the doorkeeper. "It's most important I have someone I can trust, you understand."

"Fuller may have time. You can ask him yourself." He nodded toward the left. "He's the one by the hearth there."

Thea thanked him, and we moved toward the hearth. I'd no question this was the Mr. Fuller the butler had described—the scar on his cheek served as confirmation. As Thea and Mr. Fuller discussed their arrangement, I noticed a man with auburn hair and a bearing as straight as an ash tree watching us. He leaned against one of the pillars at the edge of the chamber, and though from time to time his gaze swept the room, it always returned to us.

The back of my neck prickled. Morwen had mentioned a man with hair like a sunset. It was perhaps a bit of a stretch to imagine the first individual with red-gold hair I encountered could be the one who'd surveilled our house . . . yet whatever his history, his current interest was clear.

I returned to the conversation in time to see Thea pass a wavering hand over her eyes. "If only my dear husband was still alive. I find it so difficult to manage these matters without him. I simply do not know if the acquisition of this antiquity is worth the risk. Perhaps you can advise me? I know you helped my friend Lady Chevon."

The scar on his cheek tightened. "I didn't know you were acquainted with her."

"I'm acquainted enough to know you helped her a great deal, at least, her spirits certainly improved of late." Her voice became wistful. "It must be lovely to have one's load so lightened."

"Some people need a bit of assistance to lift their spirits." A hint of eagerness shaded his voice. "There's no shame in it."

"If only my physician believed as you do . . ."

"It may be that I can help, if you're interested. But it will take a few days."

"If you could see your way to doing so, young man, I'd be

most in your debt." She offered an unsteady bob of her head for emphasis.

Perhaps Thea had missed her calling in life—she could certainly have occupied the stage, were it a remotely acceptable occupation for a lady.

"In the meantime, if you'd like to discuss an expedition to the Northern Reaches . . ."

His voice faded as I discreetly glanced at our watcher. He'd not moved from his post, nor bothered with discretion of his own. Perhaps he believed no lady would take note of his actions. *Jade, could you create a distraction so we might cross paths?*

Gladly. She prowled along the edge of the room, then when she drew near to our watcher, she broke into a run, scrambling over his boots as if in pursuit of a mouse.

"Jade!" I rushed after her. "Please forgive me. My cat can become quite enthusiastic when on the hunt."

"No harm done."

I snatched up Jade and cradled her to my chest, her bulk spilling over my arms. "Nevertheless, I must offer an apology."

"Accepted." He jabbed a hand toward Thea. "Is that your friend? The one speaking to Fuller?"

"Yes, she'd hoped to commission him to fetch an item for her." Perhaps I should venture a bit further. I lowered my voice. "Confidentially, I think she hopes he'll help her with a personal matter as well."

"Did he offer to do so?"

"He didn't make any promises, only suggested he might be able to lift her lowered spirits."

"If you'll accept advice, I'd keep her away from him. It won't end well."

"Thank you for the warning. I assure you I'll take care—she's dear to me." I clutched Jade closer. "But may I ask you what you know about Mr. Fuller's dealings?"

"There's little to be said. She will simply have to choose to heed the warning—or not." His brows lowered over hazel eyes, something in the expression almost familiar.

It prompted me to probe a bit further. "Forgive me, but have we met before?"

His features shuttered. "I'm afraid not."

He gave a small bow, then marched away, leaving me to wander back to the doorkeeper. "Who was the Collector I just spoke with?"

"Mr. Wells. He's one of our best. Should Mr. Fuller not have time to accept a commission, you might consider working with him."

"Thank you."

Something about our whole encounter—and Mr. Wells himself—left me unsettled. Thea soon completed her business and hobbled to my side. I offered my arm to help her into the carriage.

Once we were situated inside, her lips tilted into a smile. "That was quite satisfactory. He's all but promised a personal delivery of whatever he provided Lady Chevon in the next several days."

"You'll send for me when he does?"

"I'd never dream of making you miss the moment." Her eyes crinkled. "Though one should never count a bird in the bush, I believe we have him."

Did we have him—or did he have us? He'd certainly been ready to leap on the offered bait. And why had his fellow Collector deemed it necessary to issue a warning? The questions lingered for the rest of the day, plaguing me as I scribbled notes for my admittance paper. I'd just completed the final sketch and tucked away my portfolio when Lovell appeared in the doorway.

"Consider this an official summons," he said.

"Summons to what?"

"Fun and games."

"Lovell, I don't think—"

He held out a hand. "Even Aunt Caris has agreed to join in, and you can't sit here alone pondering the mysteries of the ages forever. Besides, I picked a puzzle game just for you."

I allowed him to tug me into the drawing room, where

evidently he'd already worked his wiles on Ada, Ainslie, and Aunt Caris, for they were smiling over the illustrated cards, and Ainslie appeared more at ease than she had in some time, as if the distraction had lifted a measure of her burden. So I attended to the lighthearted puzzle, each possible clue and hinted-at solution more ludicrous than the last, until laughter overcame us all. Finally, flush with satisfaction, we unraveled the final mystery, which gave us possession of the victory token.

Aunt Caris smoothed the lace at her throat. "Heavens, I don't know when I've enjoyed something quite so ridiculous."

Lovell sat back with a satisfied grin, and Ainslie began to restore the cards to their lacquered wood box. My breath caught at her relaxed and ready smile, the ease of her motions. For a moment, she'd appeared her old self—and I'd find a way to make sure she could return to herself for good.

When I retired to my bedchamber afterward, an unfamiliar sylph appeared. She flashed a rapid message to Risha, then vanished as Risha fluttered to my side. "Lord Arbiter says Ludne ignorant of true source. He believes he acquired the stone from a Collector, but the Collector does not exist. Means it was fae in the guise of Collector."

Fae posing as Collectors? I considered those I'd met today. I was certain neither of them had been fae, but what did it mean that one had infiltrated their number in the past? And why would fae have given Mr. Ludne the stone? Was it meant as a snare for him—or for mortals in general? Or . . . might there be a fae who wished to see me fall afoul of the Vigil? I could not fathom the purpose, unless it was to force me into the Otherworld, only I'd the sensation of swimming in a vast unknown ocean, with the coils of a net slowly tightening about me. I pulled the portfolio so tightly against my chest that the edges jabbed into my skin.

What didn't I see?

CHAPTER 35

After I dressed the following morning, I flung open the window to breathe in the fragrance of the gardens. From this vantage, the lines of disturbance left when I'd uprooted the nightspire held an uncanny pattern, almost like a labyrinth or maze spiraling toward the house. I lowered the window sash and spun away, blocking from view the reminder of the bargain-holder's power and the lines of fracture reaching toward us from all sides.

I didn't feel up to facing my family just yet, to pretending all was well. Perhaps instead I'd slip down to my compounding room before breaking the fast. It had been far too long since I'd indulged in the soothing rituals of crafting tinctures and salves.

When I passed my sisters' bedchamber, I caught a glimpse of Dreda examining Ainslie's new hat—she'd wholeheartedly embraced the mission of cheering her up—and of Morwen cooing over the selections of fabric Ada offered her. On the surface, it was an idyllic scene, yet even as I watched, Ainslie's hand stole to her binding mark and Ada's eyes shadowed.

I withdrew from the doorway and continued my descent. When I arrived belowstairs, several small rabbits in a variety of hues scampered into the corridor, followed closely by Dryden. I drew back into the shadows, willing myself to go unnoticed.

He was shirtless and his hair was damp, as though he'd been washing up. His chest bore furrowed scars, but they weren't ragged like one would obtain from an injury—rather, these were precise, almost surgical, positioned around his chest at even intervals. Who would have done such a thing?

With one rabbit in his arms and the others trailing behind, he spun on his heel. "You should know better," he muttered. "If they find you here, they'll make you go outside. And it might happen again."

I stepped forward. "Dryden, may I have a word?"

He jumped and the rabbits scattered. "I'm not proper, miss."

With that, he fled toward his quarters, his entourage of rabbits following, and the door shut on them all. I hesitated, words from the alchemical tome dancing before my vision once more. Could those scars signify such tampering?

There's only one way to find out. Jade stalked forward.

If he has been experimented on, he's unlikely to just confess. Still, I had to try. I waited a moment, then knocked on his door. "Are you decent yet?"

"No."

"Then please dress so we can speak."

A long silence followed. Finally the doorknob twisted and he stepped into the corridor, his gaze fixed on the floor.

"Forgive the intrusion, but your scars—how did you receive them?"

He scuffed a foot against the woven rug. "Don't affect my duties none."

"I understand." I wrapped my arms about myself. Unquestionably, this was a sensitive matter. I'd rather drop it, but ignorance could cause a great deal of harm. "Still, if you're willing, I'd like to know."

"Why? You want to gossip about the villager boy?"

"Of course not."

"Send me back, if you have to, but I don't got anything else to say."

"No one means to send you back—"

He slammed the door between us. A soft bark sounded from the depths of the chamber beyond. Just how many animals had he accumulated in there?

Jade sniffed the air. *I'd say ten or so. Yet I suspect he conceals far more than that.*

I can't justify pressing further—he doesn't answer to me. But perhaps it warrants another conversation with Father.

Her eyes glowed in the dim corridor. *I concur.*

I hesitated in the hallway, the shuffle of paws behind the door reminding me of just how unusual Dryden was. Though the compounding room beckoned, I no longer felt inclined to indulge in herb-craft, not when everywhere I turned evidence of Other—or possible Other—assailed me.

I changed course for the dining room. Perhaps Aunt Caris had learned something else of his past. She'd meant to convince Father to find him a position at Caldwell House, yet he remained here. What had Father told her by way of explanation?

The scents of savory and sweet mingled together, drawing me into the dining room, where I found neither Aunt Caris nor my sisters, but Lovell, with an enormous plate of food before him.

He raised a cup to me. "Good, you're awake. I've eaten nearly a whole platter of Estine's pastries waiting for someone to join me. I was about to give up hope."

I smiled at him. "It was good of you to make such a sacrifice."

"Someone has to do it." He patted his stomach.

And I laughed softly. "What brings you this morning?"

He stabbed a fork into a sausage. "I've been commissioned to invite all of you to a picnic that Mother has planned for Friday. She's given her word it's to be family only, no matchmaking endeavors involved."

"What inspired her to plan such an excursion?" While an

excellent hostess, Aunt Melisina ordinarily turned her skills to society events, not small family affairs.

"It seems she feels the lot of us have become altogether too dull—she wants Uncle Alden, Aunt Caris, and the three of you girls to attend."

"Do you mean to join us?"

"I intend to be sure Mother keeps her word, so it seems I must."

I poured a cup of tea, the fragrance of rose and elderflower wafting from the cup. "Things still are not well between you?"

"Not well? That's rather understating it."

"If it's about Ada, she's forgiven your mother—"

"Ada would forgive a horseman who deliberately trampled her down, if he asked nicely enough." Lovell sliced a thick piece of ham. "It's not just about Ada, however Mother mishandled her situation."

"What then?"

"Suppose you might as well know. Ainslie already guessed some of it when she first came to Avons." He exhaled, resting his fork on his plate. "There was a lady—Miss Worthing. After the death of her parents, she came to stay with her aunt and uncle, who lived near Stanford Hall. Her father was a merchant, so in Avons it's likely we'd never have struck up an acquaintance, but you know what it's like in the country."

He fell silent, and I waited for him to collect his thoughts. Risha perched on the back of the chair across from Lovell, her attention rapt on the unfolding drama. Fortunately, he didn't realize he had an interested audience.

"We were growing . . . better acquainted, and then Miss Worthing just left, without even a word to her aunt and uncle of where she meant to go." His jaw tightened. "While you were in Withern I learned that a few days before she disappeared, Mother told her if she ever kept company with me again, she'd see her ruined. If I'd had the sense to keep my distance or observe which way the wind blew with Mother, perhaps I could have prevented her receiving such treatment. As it stands, her friendship with me put her in harm's way." Regret laced his tone. "I'd like to make sure she landed on her feet, even if she wants nothing more to do with me. But I haven't been able to find her."

"I'm sorry, Lovell." For him to confess even a developing acquaintance suggested his feelings ran deep—ordinarily he was very particular about not giving attention to any one lady, so as not to suggest interest where it didn't exist. "Is there anything we can do to help?"

"Not now, perhaps not ever. When Mother returned to Avons, I confronted her about her actions. She said first infatuations come to little, and that in the end, I'd be thankful I was spared from such a poor match. You know how she is, never one to admit to wrong, whether she regrets her actions or not." He set down his glass with a thunk. "I informed her I dashed well wasn't—in rather stronger terms—and then she broke down. She told me she'd interfere no further in such matters, said she'd already resolved to allow for freedom of choice after what happened to Ada. Perhaps she will. I don't know. I never thought she'd go so far in the first place, so I doubt I can judge. I was half-tempted to engage myself to our serving maid, just to see if she'd hold her peace."

"That would hardly be fair to the maid in question."

"No, it wouldn't—she'd have to put up with a great deal." He gave a crooked sort of smile. "Don't take fright, I haven't abandoned all sense of decency and reason. But I can't continue to remain here in Avons. I've some new prospects to explore, and I intend to take up the search again. Perhaps I never should have let it lie. I won't be at peace until I know that Miss Worthing has found herself in a safe situation, not when I bear some responsibility for her flight. Of course, I could be mistaken about the cause of her departure, but if she believed Mother meant to ruin her reputation, she'd little other recourse."

I slipped a bit of ham to Jade. "I don't like to mention it, but is there any way she could be connected to the others who have gone missing?"

"Believe me, I've considered it. Considered just about everything. But this was more than a year ago, well before anyone else disappeared. Besides, she took her belongings. There was every evidence of a planned departure, only she didn't inform anyone of her intended destination."

Whatever her plans, society wasn't kind to young women on their own. She could have encountered all sorts of trouble. I reached over to clasp his hand. "You will write and keep us informed?"

"Of course. And if Mother meddles again, I want to know at once."

"She does love you, you know," I said softly.

He snatched up his fork again. "Let's not speak of her any longer. I'd rather know about Ainslie."

I bent down to pick up Jade and so conceal my face. "What about her?"

"Come now. You expect me to believe you haven't noticed how dispirited she seems?"

"A great deal weighs on her—but the specifics are for her to share."

"Which she refuses to do." He gestured with his free hand. "Been very touchy about the research for the article on the missing, too."

"What have you uncovered?"

"Dashed little. Nothing that makes sense of the situation, which makes me think someone has covered things up. Or perhaps there's some sort of unnatural explanation. Maybe the missing are succumbing to fae-touch and being removed for treatment, and it's being hidden to avoid scandal? When I proposed the theory to Ainslie, she suggested we drop the article altogether—but she's never been one to shrink back from exploring such ideas before."

Lovell was well-liked in society, and he might well have heard rumors that hadn't reached me. So I confessed, "I can't speak for Ainslie, but I agree there's more than meets the eye when it comes to the missing individuals."

"Then you've been looking into it also?" A faint note of surprise crept into his voice.

"I have, and I recently spoke to one of the family members of the missing. She mentioned something I found interesting—a peculiar statuette her aunt acquired before her disappearance, one that vanished when she did." I nibbled at a pastry without tasting it. "Have you noticed anyone among your acquaintance with an odd-looking ivory statuette?"

"No, but I'll certainly look out for it now. Is it some sort of alchemical device?"

"It's unclear, but I'd very much like to look at one and find out."

"As would I."

I brushed a pastry flake from my lap. "About the article . . . I think perhaps you should keep it to yourself for now. It's my understanding that the authorities are motivated to control what's said about the situation."

"You have this from your stratesman friend?"

"Yes, but please don't share it."

The clash of approaching voices and hurried footsteps cut off whatever reply he might have given.

"I've warned her, but she pays insufficient heed—so you must intervene," Aunt Caris said. Her relaxed good humor of the evening before had vanished. "It's all to the good if Lord Riven has a proper interest in her. He'd make an excellent match, and I'm in full favor of it. But he cannot be allowed to take her on an extended jaunt through Avons, even with a chaperone. Holden informed me this morning that they were gone for hours, and you didn't even bother to find out where he intended to take her. Such things may pass without exception in the countryside, but the gossips of Avons are always looking for an excuse to darken a reputation."

"Caris, she has a good head on her shoulders—"

"What difference does that make when it comes to affairs of the heart?" Her voice was strained. "Miss Twells assured me she found nothing improper in his behavior, but she should have insisted they return far earlier. And in the end, the responsibility is yours. If you don't attend to your daughters with more care, you may come to regret it."

"What are you suggesting?" Father sounded decidedly terser than usual. "I want nothing more than . . ."

His voice grew more distant, fading into a low rumble, as if he'd changed course—likely seeking to retreat toward his study, rather than break the fast in such contention.

Lovell gave a low whistle, and I wrapped my hands about my teacup, its warmth seeping into my cold fingers. We were fraying on every side, our secrets, our hidden pains fracturing us. If the truths emerged, would they shatter us altogether? Or could they in some way heal?

Lovell looked at me with an arched brow. "Is Lord Riven serious about his attentions?"

"It is . . . difficult to say."

"Do you want him to be?"

I nearly dropped the cup. What kind of question was that? "I find his company pleasant."

"That's a very careful reply." He assessed me. "Come, I told you about Miss Worthing."

"At this time, there's not much to tell—"

Aunt Caris stormed into the room, her color heightened. Evidently, she remained unsatisfied with the conclusion of her conversation with Father. When her gaze fell upon Lovell and me, she smoothed her hair before moving more sedately to her chair.

Lovell set himself to charm her, repeating the picnic invitation then regaling her with an anecdote of a horse race gone wrong, while I contemplated a discreet avenue of retreat.

Before I could make good my escape, Holden appeared in the doorway. "Mrs. Darrington has called, and I've installed her in the dining room."

I wasn't surprised that morning to her meant immediately after breakfast, but Aunt Caris threw up her hands. "Does no one in Avons adhere to convention these days, or is it simply that you've befriended every eccentric in town?"

Her tone stung. "I'm sure she doesn't mean to cause trouble —nor do I."

"Forgive me, my dear. I'm aware. I'm just not feeling like myself." Absently, she caressed her locket. "You cannot be held responsible for when Mrs. Darrington decides to call."

"But I do bear responsibility for worrying you." I hesitated, then continued. "I overheard part of what you said to Father."

She flushed. "That wasn't meant for your ears."

"Perhaps not, but I want you to know that I take your concerns seriously." How could she believe it without a full confession of my own? "I give you my word that I'll not be swayed into unconsidered action."

Lovell sat silent, watching the two of us.

And Aunt Caris folded her hands. "Yet you let him keep you out for hours."

What now? I couldn't promise not to act so again, if the situation warranted, nor did I wish to cause her further pain. "I don't believe we drew any notice, but I'll exercise greater care in the future."

If I could.

Then I added, "As for Mrs. Darrington, if you're not in the mood for company, I'll receive her myself."

"No, it won't do to offend her." She stood. "We shall see her together. Please send in refreshments, Holden."

Lovell excused himself and went in search of Ainslie, then Aunt Caris swept down the hall. Whatever turmoil churned within her, she welcomed Thea graciously. Though her lips folded tight when she learned Thea wanted to bring me to the Antiquary Society, she voiced no complaint. However much she disapproved of the society as a destination for ladies, she wouldn't snub Thea by expressing such a view.

In short order, Thea extricated us, and when we were situated in her carriage, she leaned forward. "What is it you hope to uncover at the society today?"

Though I wanted nothing more than to find the fae who held Ainslie's bargain—not to mention the one preying on the missing—I'd no direct angle of approach, nor did the society promise one, so I'd have to take an indirect path. I waved my fan before my face, using its lace panels to conceal. "I'd like to learn more of the history of the Redgrave family, perhaps also the Bretton line of kings."

"And so perhaps the Forgotten War, in a roundabout way?"

Her frail appearance concealed an exceedingly sharp mind—which could prove dangerous for what I wanted to keep hidden. Jade nuzzled my hand. "I know it's a bit far-fetched, but I'll take any scraps of evidence I can unearth."

"I concur with the approach. With the knowledge you possess, you may be able to make connections where others have not. And I think I have an idea of someone who might help—he spends most of his days within the society, so I expect we'll find him this morning."

Thea's carriage halted in front of the Antiquary Society. Slowly, we ascended the steps and made our way into the building.

When we entered, the doorkeeper's face creased into a wrinkled grin. "Mrs. Darrington and Miss Caldwell, what a pleasure to see you together."

Thea favored him with a smile in return. "Did you hear Miss Caldwell has been granted admittance to the society?"

His chestnut eyes twinkled at us. "With you on her side, I hardly expected a different outcome."

"She owes little to my intervention—she'd never have gotten this far without her case having some merit." Thea rested on her walking stick. "Still, some things are better done together."

We passed from the entry into the depths of the society, and I followed Thea as she approached a portly gentleman with long sideburns that drifted down his cheeks like bracken fern. He was bent over a shard of pottery, murmuring something indecipherable as he examined it. Thea cleared her throat—loudly—and at last he looked up.

"Mrs. Darrington, well met." His slightly unfocused gaze traveled to me. "And this must be Miss Caldwell. Our president was looking a bit sour this morning, and now I know why."

"Right and right again." She chuckled. "Miss Caldwell, this is Mr. Remson. Mr. Remson, I've brought Miss Caldwell to you because she wishes to hear more about the Bretton kings and how the Redgrave family served them."

"Ah, yes. It's an interesting history." He stroked his sideburns. "The first Redgrave whose name is linked with the Bretton family was named Ceolman, and his name was connected with King Aldred. Ceolman died without record as to the cause, and his body was never recovered for proper burial, though they raised a memorial at Redgrave Hall, where his descendants still celebrate the date of his birth each year."

"King Aldred. That should be of interest." Thea nodded toward me. "He reigned during the time we believe Kilmere to have been constructed."

As I didn't have the lineage of kings memorized, I appreciated the hint. "Is it known what led to the king taking on Ceolman as an advisor?"

"No. In fact, though we're certain later Redgraves advised the crown, the capacity in which Ceolman served is unclear. We know little of Aldred's rule—the record is quite spotty from that time. Lots of speculation, little information aside from the legends that high fae last entered Byren during his reign."

Legends I'd every reason to believe fact. "Is the lack of information unusual?"

"Not given the number of centuries that have passed. Some rulers have always been more well-documented than others." Mr. Remson shrugged. "Aldred wasn't a particularly noteworthy king, it seems. I mentioned him only because you were keen on the Redgrave connection, which flourished after his time. There are legends to suggest that Ceolman Redgrave died in some act of valor, after which the king chose to bestow various honors on his family—including several valuable land holdings. Difficult to say what the deed might have been."

Could it have been during the Forgotten War? Certainly valiant deeds must have been done . . . or perhaps simply desperate ones. I inhaled the scents of aged leather and ink that filled the chamber. "If you have anything in your collection about Ceolman, I'd like to read it."

"I can't say that I do, nor about King Aldred in particular. But I have a book on the Bretton kings, if you'd like to parse out what references you can."

"I would, thank you."

Once he'd handed me the thick volume, I tucked myself into an out-of-the-way nook, while he and Thea returned to the center table, debating the nuances of some obscure runic language inscribed on the pottery shard.

I paged through the tome, stopping at the entry about King Aldred's son. The writer mentioned a plague of fae-touched individuals that occurred during his reign and how the Vigil did their best to stem the tide and restore the afflicted.

I rested the book in my lap. Riven had said the greater the deviation from the truth caused by a glamour, the greater the chance of shattering minds. If the fae had removed great swaths of memory and knowledge from the people of Byren, then it must have broken at least some minds—which would explain the surge in those considered fae-touched.

But then how had the Redgraves escaped such a memory purge? Through a bargain? Why would the fae have ever agreed to allow any mortals to retain their memories?

I could conjure no reason yet, but I'd accept it as provisional fact, because it made everything that followed hold together. If the Redgraves had recalled the war and the near-destruction of Byren, then the formation of the Vigil for protection was a logical step.

I traced a finger down the page. While the theory seemed to hold together, without facts to back it up, it was only specula-tion. If I asked the Redgraves pointed questions about Ceolman, would they be able to give yes or no answers, or would even that press the bounds of their geas? Somehow, we needed to access what they'd locked away inside—

Like the shock of cold water on a hot summer day, Other burst over me, distinct yet familiar, the pine-scented breeze I'd encountered before filling the room. A shimmering net of power settled over us.

Jade's ears flattened against her head.

Risha hurled herself against it and was flung back at once—it wasn't just concealment, but also imprisonment. My pulse spiked.

And Risha shuddered. "I cannot go to Riven."

The note of fear in her voice tugged at my heart. Instinctively, I reached for her, pulling her close, and for the first time, she willingly sheltered at my side.

Jade growled as a fae lady stepped through the golden working, smaller in frame than any other I'd encountered, her eyes a bright gray and her hair dark. How much of her appearance was true and how much a powerful glamour shrouding her?

"Don't try to send the sylph to the Lord Arbiter." Her voice was low. "I must have a word with you in private. There's no reason for anyone to come to harm today. Will you grant me an audience?"

The note of pleading in her voice stilled me. It wasn't customary for fae. They commanded, they spoke with authority and confidence, even arrogance—they did not placate. Yet even her gentle demeanor could be a deceit. Certainly, she'd taken care to confine us before her approach.

Evidently Jade shared my concern, for she bristled, her shadow growing as if she contemplated a shift.

Not yet. We cannot hope to take her by direct assault, not when she already holds us captive. I hugged the book to my chest like a shield. "What is it you desire?"

"Just the chance to talk. I've long sought the right moment to approach you." Her gaze traced my features as though she sought something in them. "You've begun to understand your nature, to cease fearing all things Other. Your release of Lady

Avis made it clear the degree to which you've embraced your affinities, and I knew the time was now ripe."

I clasped the book tighter. I'd not once considered that by releasing Lady Avis, I might draw unwanted attention from the fae courts, but it was only logical. She held a position of power in the Court of Gold, and her return would attract notice. Further, she'd no reason to keep quiet about me. Though Riven had temporarily sequestered her in the Court of Dusk, he'd been obliged to inform his king of her newfound freedom. Would my decision bring a succession of high fae into our lives, endangering my family further? My stomach hollowed. "I've felt you before. How long have you watched me?"

"Quite some time." She glided closer. "I felt obliged to do so, given my relationship with your mother."

Like the wind through the treetops, a rushing sound filled my ears. She'd known Mother. What did that mean?

"I considered approaching you after Damir assaulted you, but you appeared to manage well enough—and I thought you might flee if another fae appeared just then. Still, I ensured he did not follow you to Wyncourt."

She could not lie; she must have done so. But why? Fae generally did not act from the goodness of their hearts. Still, if she'd known Mother . . .

Jade glared at the fae lady. *Have a care.*

Of course, Jade was right, yet the longing to understand more about Mother rose up so strong it nearly choked me. I straightened, probing at the edges of the working that snared us, seeking some connection to the plants beyond, yet I could find no seam or weakness in it, and abandoned the attempt. "What was the nature of your relationship with my mother?"

"You might say it was a . . . partnership."

"You might *say* it was or it was?"

"Excellent question. You're learning . . . and you will need to learn far more, in order to face what's to come." Her gray eyes seemed to grow more luminous. "I helped your mother when she wished to leave the Otherworld. But to divulge more without a bargain between us is a risk I refuse to take. I value my life, and I don't want word of my deeds getting back to the wrong people."

"Then . . . my mother was fae?"

"Yes, until she forsook her affinities. Then she became something we have no word for—not precisely mortal, but certainly not fae as we know it. Something lesser."

I felt as though I'd tumbled from a tree, all the breath driven from my lungs and the world tilting about me. She offered the answers I craved, and oh, I wanted to believe her sincere. But how could I trust my judgment when it came to Mother? This lady could not overtly lie, but she could seek to deceive. Somehow, I managed to speak, though my voice was unsteady. "If you're acting in good faith by sharing this, then remove your working and allow me to send Risha for Lord Riven."

"I will give you liberty to do as you choose, but if you send for the Lord Arbiter, I will not remain." The working grew more shadowed.

"Why not?"

"You know little of the ways of our courts, or you would not ask." Her features hardened. "Arbiters are to be feared. He can demand any truths he pleases, in the name of the king—and force them from me. If word returned to the king of how I assisted Kensa, it would not be safe for me. Those with less power must exercise more care."

Was she truly a weaker fae? All I'd learned suggested there was great variation in the strength and number of affinities between fae, and the strong preyed upon the weak, so her fear could be justified. I clutched the book tighter, its leather-and-ink scent grounding me. "What bargain do you require in exchange for the truth about my mother?"

"One which will ensure my safety, that is all. You must not reveal my identity or the source of your information to anyone —ever. You will not communicate anything about me. Your *kitisne* and the sylph will be bound to silence also." She tilted her head. "You of all people should understand wanting to avoid the wrong sort of attention."

I could. Did she guess I'd crafted a similar binding for the Redgraves? Mouth dry, I swallowed. "And . . . that is all?"

"As I said, I seek only my protection in this matter. Despite its value, I will offer information at no other cost."

"Why? What do you gain from it?"

"It's quite simple—revenge." Her perfect features hardened. "I have a score to settle. Several, in fact."

At last, there was a reason I could believe. But still . . .

"There's something I must know first." Her power felt very different from that of the bargain-holder, but I could not afford to leave the matter to chance. I lifted my chin. "Do you hold my sister's bargain?"

Her brow furrowed. "I do not. Why do you ask?"

"Because I seek the one who does. If you've been watching us, did you witness the one who bound her?"

Her expression softened slightly. "I wish I could say I had. You're the one I've watched most, since you attracted attention by entering the Otherworld. I understand your wariness, but now you must make a choice—either bargain, or I will depart and leave you in peace."

She represented my best opportunity of learning about Mother—how could I say no, when the cost was so very small? "Very well. I agree."

Though I knew it would come, it took effort not to flinch as her power etched a binding mark across my skin. I forced myself not to examine the gleaming threads—that could come later.

"Some years ago, Kensa came to me in distress, her true identity concealed." Her voice lowered. "I assume Kensa was not her actual name, but rather the one she chose for her flight. She didn't want anyone to know her true identity on the chance she might be traced. She would not share about her past or why she wished to forsake her very nature, and I did not press. It was not my business. We bargained, and I created a convincing illusion of her death, so she'd have liberty to enter the mortal world unimpeded."

Breathe, I must breathe—but that had become so very difficult. The book dropped to my lap. "Why did she want to flee?"

One brow arched. "As I said, I was not in her confidence— her reasons were not my business. Even so, I developed a vested interest in her situation. Most believe the forsaking of affinities a heresy, but I found her courage to pursue her own path intriguing, and I hoped for good things. The outcome was . . . most disappointing."

"Her death," I whispered.

"I did not say her death." Her full lips tightened. "What makes you so certain that was the outcome?"

Once again, the world tilted about me, a dizzying array of color and chaos. "What are you saying?"

"I merely ask if you saw her body yourself." Her scent, the one of shifting winds, swirled about us. "Though perhaps it would not matter what you saw or thought you saw. At that young age, you could not have seen through glamour."

"Do not toy with me." I choked out the words.

"I do not seek to toy with you. I have my own limitations on what I may speak, so I must do the best I can." Her voice lowered. "I merely mean to suggest that the only thing I believe would have induced your mother to leave was the protection of her children. She fled from something—she might have returned in order to hide you, to see you safe."

Like a root bursting from a seed, hope sprang to life in my heart. I couldn't fathom Mother would leave us without any sign or hint she still lived, yet if it were to protect us from the cruelty of the fae—it *was* possible. Beyond the working, the room blurred.

We have no evidence of the truth of this part of the account. She's taking great care not to state things outright.

Does that mean she's under a geas? Or she's hiding something?

Possibly both.

"Jessa? Where have you gone?" Thea's voice echoed in the distance, muffled as though underwater.

The lady drew back. "I must go."

"Will I see you again?" I clasped my hands in my lap to still their trembling.

"I will offer aid when I can. That's all I may promise."

With that, she stepped around a towering shelf and vanished, along with her working. But I remained rooted in place, my breath shallow and unsteady.

Could Mother truly be alive?

CHAPTER 36

That night, I fled from one dreamscape to another, always chased by images of Mother, at first pleasant, peaceful ones of her laughing and happy, but those soon faded, and her face became stained by tears, then by blood. The moon gleamed in her hair as she glided past a fountain . . .

The last drew me toward waking, my emotions tangled like rushes in a raging river, my pillow damp beneath me and the scents of sun and storm saturating the air.

Riven.

No, that wasn't right. I'd wanted to talk to him after I'd encountered the fae lady, wrestled with the desire to send Risha and rejected it, knowing he could not come—he was bound to serve his court. My head spinning, I struggled to cast off the remnants of my dreams, to discern between impression and reality, desire and truth.

And the scent of sun-warmed forest strengthened. I pressed upright, clutching the bedquilt to my chest, and my breath caught.

There.

In the corner beyond the windows, a familiar figure stood,

present yet also distant, even formidable in bearing. I didn't know how or why he'd come, but Riven *was* here.

"Forgive the disturbance." His voice rasped like stone against stone. "I shouldn't have come at this hour. I didn't mean to wake you."

And he wouldn't have done so without cause. My pulse beat a ragged rhythm, and I brushed the tangle of curls away from my face, seeking calm. "Is something wrong?"

"I just . . . meant to ensure you were well."

I braced against the headboard, staring into the gloom between us, wishing that something more than cloud-obscured moonlight and the faint glow from Risha would illumine his features and give insight into his thoughts. The proper thing to do would be to inform him I was perfectly fine and ask him to return in the morning. And yet, the utter lack of light about him, the distance he maintained, the roughness of his voice— something *was* wrong. He might not want to reveal it, yet he'd come for a reason, and I wasn't about to let him leave. "Turn around, please."

He complied, and I climbed out of bed, snagging my blue dressing gown from the bedside table and fastening it securely about my waist. It was a small concession to propriety, perhaps not even worth the bother, given my tumbled hair and bare feet. "I'm . . . more decent."

He turned to regard me, shadows obscuring his face. I reached for the gas lamp, but he shook his head, the motion almost indiscernible in the gloom. The moon strained at the edges of the dark cloud that confined it, casting only the slightest silvery light into the room. What did he fear I'd see in him?

Any direct inquiry into the state of his emotions he'd surely shut down, yet he'd come . . . and I must do *something*. Should I act as if this were an ordinary conversation? As if my own emotions weren't already in tumult, even before his unexpected appearance? I would try. I moved toward him, the floor cold against my feet. "I didn't expect you back so soon. Has your business concluded?"

"The traitor has been dealt with." His silk jacket rustled as he folded his arms across his chest. "My investigation confirmed Lady Avis's suspicion. The traitor allowed himself to be placed in a vulnerable position in relation to Damir—unfortunate, because he had a great deal of promise."

"And . . . what will happen to him?"

"He has already received the penalty for his deeds." No hint of emotion laced his voice now.

Jade shifted behind me. *The penalty for betraying the king is death. The arbiter executes justice.*

Oh.

The words felt like a knife twist in my gut. That meant what? Riven had done what was required of him, then . . . come here? My eyes burned. What must it feel like to carry out such a sentence?

Abruptly, the moon broke free of its cloud prison, casting cold silver light across the planes of Riven's face. "I should go. Everything else can wait."

On instinct, I caught his arm. "Please don't leave."

Tightly corded muscles betrayed his tension. He pulled free. "If you knew what I've done, you'd ask me to leave. Fae cherish a brutal sort of justice, one that mortals—that you—would not favor."

"Tell me then, and allow me to decide for myself." He might not readily speak of his emotions, but if I provoked him, perhaps something would shake loose. "Don't make assumptions about my feelings."

"You really want to know? Fine." His features became as unyielding as marble. "You recall that I said that the removal of affinities causes excruciating pain? You asked how I knew—it's by experience. Because I've inflicted that pain and worse. Those who willingly forsake their affinities only wish for death while it's happening. Those who have them severed do die, a slow, excruciating death." The words held a sharp edge, each one cutting deep. "That's why it's deemed the fitting penalty for traitors—their life and power given to the king they meant to betray. It's a death that leaves even the strongest begging for mercy."

The storm charge to the air sparked against my skin and tightened my chest, as though it meant to drive me back. I shivered but stood firm. "Then why doesn't the king execute this justice himself?"

"Because only an arbiter can forcibly sever affinities. Among other things, our ability to do so marks us for our role. We have the privilege of entering the minds of the condemned. Experiencing their terror. Witnessing their pain." The air fairly crackled now. "That is why arbiters should not indulge in sentiment. More than the rest, we cannot afford it."

I swallowed hard against the bitter taste that surged into my mouth. How could he endure it? Having to pretend before the court that he did not care about the suffering inflicted? Because he did, that much was clear.

Red-gold sparks of light flared about him, brilliant and angry in the dark. "Now, if your curiosity is satisfied, I'll go."

"Not yet."

Before reason could overtake instinct, I stepped forward and embraced him, just as I might one of my sisters in need of comfort—but the experience was not at all the same.

For the briefest moment his arms tightened about me, and all my senses surged with awareness of his presence, a flood of warmth spilling over my body, rich and golden and glorious— and altogether bewildering.

Then he stepped back, away from the spill of moonlight, his features swathed in shadow.

What did that mean? I shouldn't have been so forward, only it had felt right in the moment—in the face of his pain. Had I violated some fae standard? I'd certainly violated every mortal one. Heat flooded my face. "I'm sorry. I didn't mean—"

"You owe no apology." His voice held a slight unsteadiness,

and oh, I wished I could see his face. "But I should go, allow you to rest. I'll call properly tomorrow."

I could only nod. The brilliant light of passing washed over me, a heady rush of power that left the room feeling extraordinarily empty when it vanished. I collapsed on the edge of the bed. What had I done?

Jade padded to my side. *I wonder the same thing. Life with you is certainly never dull. I've never been quite so tempted to invade a mind as I was when Riven first appeared—and even more so when you embraced him.*

Jade!

Don't worry, I have more sense than to attempt breaching the thoughts of an arbiter, even were their mental walls penetrable. She wove between my ankles. *And most people have more sense than to come into physical contact with one.*

Is it so very dangerous?

Were you not listening when he described how he killed the traitor with a touch?

That wasn't an act of vengeance or anger, but of upholding the law as he's bound to do. You cannot imagine he desired it.

The glow of her eyes dimmed. *No, I rather think otherwise.*

Then why must he? Can't he just . . . cease being arbiter?

That's not how it works. The monarch and those who occupy the central positions of his government are chosen according to their affinities, and there's never more than one at a time with the unique combination required.

Why?

Some believe the court—the very land itself and the power it contains—makes the selection. Others say that the Infinite governs which affinities fall upon individual fae. She leapt upon the windowsill. *In the end, it doesn't matter. If a governmental fae abdicates his or her role, the court will begin to deteriorate, harming all who dwell within. Even those of us not high fae understand as much, though I cannot answer as to the details.*

So he has no choice but to assume this role and all it requires, lest worse befall him and his court?

Yes.

My eyes pricked. Why must the Otherworld be such a hard, unforgiving place? I leaned my forehead against the cool pane of the window, the light of the moon falling cold and comfortless across the garden beyond. Mother had fled the Otherworld, and its brutal justice and harsh demands provided yet another reminder why she might have made such a choice.

How would I feel if I was forced to wrench the life from someone who begged for mercy, no matter how dark or cruel their deeds? A bitter, burning sensation surged within. Small wonder Riven had counseled me not to indulge in emotion, because if one felt in that situation—what must it cost? More importantly, how did he endure it?

Perhaps that's part of the reason he came here afterward. Jade nestled at my side. *If I endured any trial, I'd certainly seek you first.*

I ran my fingers across her thick fur, smoothing the starflower patch. *Our connection makes you rather biased.*

Silence settled over us, then she snuggled deeper. *Other connections aside from the* kit-isne *bond also hold strength and offer comfort.*

Unbidden, the sensations of my embrace with Riven returned, and unfamiliar longing unfurled in my chest, as swift as the advance of wild rose. I stood abruptly, as if the motion might chase away the discomfiting emotions. *It's time we went back to bed. Morning will come soon.*

As you say.

Gentle amusement echoed in her words and settled over me, as comforting as the handwoven bedquilt that I drew around us. Yet warmer and more vibrant still, a lingering impression of golden, sun-kissed light teased my senses as I drifted toward sleep.

CHAPTER 37

The door creaked, and my eyes fluttered open as Ainslie bounded into the room. "You're still abed, Jessa? We searched the garden first, thinking you'd have been up hours ago."

Vivid sunlight blazed through the windows, and I blinked, struggling to dispel the lingering haze of emotion and order my thoughts. "I had . . . difficulty sleeping."

Ada murmured sympathy, while Ainslie dropped into bed next to me. "Well, rouse yourself. Mr. Redgrave sent me a note asking if I'd join him on a carriage ride this afternoon. He told me that he could wait, if I needed more time, but he'd like to discuss matters."

"What did you say?"

"I agreed." Her fingers skimmed along her binding mark. "Waiting won't make things any easier—it's better to face whatever must come."

I pulled the blankets close about my chest. I'd counseled Ainslie to speak further with Mr. Redgrave, because I'd wanted her to find happiness, wanted to believe it was still possible. But what if I'd been wrong to extend trust? What if he played a deeper game than I perceived?

Ainslie pulled her knees to her chest and leaned against the bedpost. "You don't look pleased. Do you disagree?"

"I suppose I just feel very aware of the precariousness of our position. It would be so easy for the Redgraves—or anyone else who uncovered our secrets—to make this world unsafe for us. And if it was, what then? I fear the Otherworld would hold far greater dangers." Riven's sharp-edged commentary on fae justice brought physical pain upon recall. With difficulty, I pressed back the discomfiting echoes. I did not owe my sisters those truths, but what about Mother?

I scrambled over the edge of the bed, snatching up a pale blue muslin gown, then stepped behind the dressing screen. I tugged off my nightgown—as Ainslie had said, best to get it over with. "I agreed to a geas yesterday, in exchange for information about Mother."

"You what?" Ainslie charged around the edge of the screen, followed by Ada.

So much for privacy.

Jade chuffed. *That was rather the equivalent of dropping a firecracker in their midst.*

Mechanically, Ada began to help with the buttons of my gown. "Why would you—"

"I won't be able to answer many questions. Just listen, and I will tell you everything I can." I drew a deep breath, then rattled off the tale, the haunted look in their eyes doubtless mirroring my own. In the recounting, more questions arose about the fae lady who'd sought me out. Since she knew about Lady Avis, did she belong to either the Court of Dusk or Gold? Or had she simply learned by observing me? Her court might provide a clue as to which one Mother had once belonged to . . . yet I could voice no such speculations to my sisters, not bound by the geas, so I wound down my tale.

"If she lives . . . oh, Jessa." Ada twisted the engraved sapphire ring Mother had left her. "It would make all this worth enduring."

Ainslie's eyes took on the glossy shade of polished ebony. "Is there any chance your source is actually telling the truth?"

"About this? I don't know, but the rest was straightforward enough." I brushed my skirts to smooth out any lingering wrinkles, a vain attempt to act as if the very notion didn't shake me to the deepest places. "When you're freed, we'll have to find out."

They exchanged a glance, heavy with the unspoken question—what if Ainslie was not? Nevertheless, they withdrew, and I descended the stairs. Before I was halfway down, an ethereal sensation of Other broke over me—not Riven, nor the lady from yesterday, nor any fae I recognized, but rather a sensation that darted about like a swift, difficult to pin down, much less discern its form.

Blight and rot. Did the whole of the Otherworld mean to descend upon us? I hurried down to the entry, where Holden ushered an elegant woman into the house—a fae lady. Something about her pricked my memory, and I chased the ghostly sensation through the chambers of my mind—oh. She was the one who'd spoken to Riven during the ball in Withern.

She glided down the hall as if she owned the house, in appearance like a gilded lily, elegant and stately, with hair and eyes of gold, her very presence a reminder that I'd been exposed, another sign of the damage done by my choice to release Lady Avis, of the incursion of Other I'd feared the moment the fae who claimed to know Mother revealed herself. Could I ever retreat back into hiding?

Twisted brambles of fear snarled in my chest, and I chased them back with a blaze of anger. It was far easier to embrace the sparking warmth within than confront the truth. Riven had been right. I was drawing Other inexorably toward those I loved.

Dark threads of indigo pulsed about Risha, and Jade glowered at the lady as I moved to meet her. "Why have you come?"

Holden edged between us, his eyes slightly glazed. "Ah, Miss Jessa. I was just going to fetch you. Lady Celeste has come to call."

He spoke as if this were a revelation. Clearly, he'd made no attempt to dissuade her from the early call, nor had he forced her to wait while he determined if I was at-home, as he ordinarily did with unfamiliar guests—which meant she'd imposed her will upon him. The sparks of warmth flared to full life.

"Lady Celeste." I offered a nod. "Perhaps you'd like to join me in the drawing room?"

She drifted toward me, the scents of alyssum and oleander wafting about her. "It will do."

"Will you need refreshments, Miss Jessa?" Holden asked.

"No, thank you. Lady Celeste won't be staying long."

"Very good." He slipped down the corridor and vanished from sight.

Her golden eyes hardened. "I have business to conduct, and I've no intention of departing until it's complete."

"Yet so often things do not go as we intend." If we dwelt in Wyncourt, I could evict her even now. Yet Holden had admitted her here, to a house that had no fae nature, that did not belong to me. Now I must make the best of a poor situation. "Please join me."

Side by side, we walked into the drawing room, and I took the chair nearest the window, where the life of the garden beyond surged over my senses. "What business brought you here?"

She tsked softly. "Such a hurry. Have your ties to the mortal world made so deep a mark?"

I rested my hands on the arms of the chair, poised to stand, to dismiss her altogether—if I could manage such a feat—for the thickening of the air about her suggested danger.

"A quiet one. How interesting." She settled into a chair with the grace I'd come to associate with high fae, shades of gold and ivory tinting her features. "I wanted to make your acquaintance at the ball in Withern, yet the Lord Arbiter did not seem to approve."

If Riven hadn't wanted me to meet her, what did that mean? It seemed more prudent to keep quiet and wait for her to reveal herself than leap into the conversational gap, so I held my tongue.

"I saw enough that night to know you seem very comfortable with our arbiter. Most do not feel so. Having one's emotions read as if an open book—it's a risky business. Few can afford such a disadvantage." Her lashes lowered. "What makes you think you can?"

This time, she did not move on, only watched and waited. If I ignored her, this interview might never come to an end. Beyond the glass, the oak pulsed in time with my heart, its steadiness reassuring. I'd offer a nonanswer and hope it satisfied. "I don't believe a perceptive nature a reason to cut ties."

"Ah, now I begin to see." The corners of her mouth curved upward. "You're ignorant of the truth, and he has taken advantage. Well, why not?"

I pressed my lips together. What did she mean? I dared not ask, lest I betray even more than I already had.

"I shall do you a favor, because it suits me to hinder his purpose, whatever it may be." An unnatural breeze spiraled from her, one that carried a distinct chill. "What you credit to a perceptive nature is in fact a blending of affinities, one that all arbiters carry. They read emotions as effortlessly as you draw breath. And I don't mean that figuratively. Whatever you feel becomes tangible to an arbiter, visible in an aura about you. Nothing can be hidden from them—it's why it's best to keep one's distance."

At the pane, ivy spiraled upward, swaying against the glass, its frenetic tap blending with the rush of my pulse. *Could this be true?*

I can find no twist in her words, nowhere she could layer in deception. Jade leapt into my lap, offering her bulk as a shield.

Yet you did not know.

High fae keep many matters close.

My stomach churned, but I tilted my head, as if nothing she'd said mattered, as if she'd not just upended all that had ever passed between me and Riven. "You've come all this way from the Otherworld just to discuss the Lord Arbiter and his dealings?"

"No indeed." Her face settled into lines of satisfaction. "I've come all this way to give him a message."

"If you seek him, why call on me?"

"It seems he can often be found where you are." She tapped a slim finger against her lips. "Why is that, I wonder?"

Jade's muscles tightened. *I should very much like to drive her from this house.*

So would I, yet we still know too little. Did Lady Celeste pretend to seek Riven in order to collect information for the king? She'd some reason for her presence beyond what she claimed, that much was certain. I stroked Jade's head, seeking her calm and my own. "You'd have to ask him."

"It seems I'm about to have that opportunity."

Even as she spoke, Riven's power surged into the room, strong as a summer tempest. He strode through the passing, sweeping her with a dismissive gaze. "Lady Celeste. You must have missed my company a great deal to venture so far from home."

Her features tightened. "Though some may prefer the court without an arbiter, our king disagrees. You weren't in the mortal home you've taken, so I took a chance on finding you here. Besides, I've been curious about your mortal since I first caught glimpse of her in Withern. Even more when the king informed me she's not in fact mortal, but some sort of dreadful mongrel— fae but raised by mortals, with all their flaws and follies."

Jade rumbled low, but I remained bound in place, as if by heavy frost. *This* was why she'd come. She wanted me to know I was exposed to her king; she wanted it to spark fear. To hurt.

And she hadn't failed.

Because if the king knew this much, he could only have learned it from Riven. The song of hawthorn in the far corner of the garden surged above the rest, sharp and barbed. Was this the "everything else" he'd said could wait?

Riven lounged back in his chair. "Then consider your

curiosity satisfied. You know it's my duty to investigate such aberrations."

I flinched. Was that truly his purpose? Had I been mistaken all along?

The scent of oleander emanating from Lady Celeste strengthened, as if it meant to poison the very air about us. Yet she merely inclined her head. "As you say."

"What is your message?"

"The king bids you attend the Harmony of Lights these next two days."

"For what purpose?" His tone was suggestive of boredom.

"He desires it. Must there be another purpose?"

"You may inform him I'll return before the first ceremony this evening."

His words were a clear dismissal, and she disappeared through the doorway. Evidently, she meant to leave in the ordinary way, whether or not she'd open a passing once beyond these walls.

The hawthorn still surged across my senses, desirous of my protection, yet its jagged notes sliced deep into my chest. I'd wanted nothing more than her departure, but it had left me alone with Riven.

Alone and exposed.

I pulled Jade closer. What now? He would see my panic and know something was wrong and . . .

His eyes narrowed. "What did she say?"

I just shook my head, my pulse thrumming beyond my control. How had I missed it before? "It's nothing. Perhaps later—"

"We need to talk. But not here." He stood.

I could deny him, but that would only prolong the inevitable, so I followed him to the morning room, where Ada sat at the pianoforte. When we entered the room, her song fell silent.

Riven stalked toward her. "Jessa and I will be gone for a time. Cover for her."

She drew back slightly, her face tightening. She looked over his shoulder at me. "Do you . . . wish to go, Jessa?"

If even Ada perceived my distress, then what did Riven discern? I'd like to run away, to lose myself in the gardens, to pull the ivy close until it formed an impenetrable lattice about me . . . But though I wanted nothing more than to hide, what I needed were answers—however painful. "Yes."

I didn't trust myself to voice more.

She inclined her head. "Then I will do all I can."

As stormy and tempestuous as lightning-shattered clouds, the passing closed about me, its currents of power pulling me from the familiarity of home to—where? Riven wouldn't take me to the Otherworld, would he?

When the light faded, I could breathe again. We weren't in the Otherworld, but rather deep in the forest of Enderly, not far from where Uros once opened a passing. My pulse drummed unsteadily at my temples. I needed time to consider what I would say, what I *should* say—and none remained. "Why have you brought me here?"

"Because there are matters we need to discuss without interruption." He assessed me, and it took everything in me not to step behind the nearest tree.

Undoubtedly, he could see that too. Yet he did not probe. Instead he spoke. "What Celeste said, about the king—"

Withering frosts take his king. I could choke down the hurt no longer. "Why didn't you tell me you could read my emotions?"

He stilled. "So that's what she was about."

"Was she telling the truth?"

His face became inscrutable, his eyes darker than the shadows beneath the firs. "Yes."

I stepped back, dried leaves crackling beneath my boots. I'd confided in him a great deal, and all the while he'd withheld so very much about his nature and affinities. Granted, he'd warned me in the beginning not to trust him, but he—I'd thought we—

I didn't want to think about it because then I would feel and he would see what I felt and—

Jade shifted into true-form, lowering her head to kiss my cheek. *Breathe, Jessa.*

I inhaled her sweet-grass scent, her steadiness becoming my own. Then I stepped from the shelter of her shadow. Riven was carefully *not* looking at me, his gaze fixed on the spread of a distant chestnut, the one that had once sheltered Uros.

What now?

From our first interaction, all that I felt had been exposed to him. And no matter how practiced I became at concealing my emotions from the world at large, I could hide nothing from him. Even now, if he looked, he would see all my uncertainties, all the fears churning within. I brushed my fingers across the whorled bark of the elder that stretched its branches overhead. All those times I'd thought him far too perceptive, he'd seen more than I ever guessed. "Did you think it just didn't matter?"

"No. I knew it did."

"Then all this time, you meant to entertain yourself with my ignorance—with the fact you could perceive everything I thought long before I confessed it?"

He rubbed a hand across the back of his neck. "Perceiving emotions isn't the same as reading thoughts, not even close. You've surprised me more times than I care to admit."

The spindled boughs of the elder brushed my shoulders, weaving themselves about me. "Then why didn't you tell me sooner?"

"Because I knew it would change things."

His words held a hint of vulnerability I'd never perceived in him before. The soft fragrance of the elderflowers filled the space between us. Why did it matter to him if things changed? If they fractured in some way? I might not understand, but it seemed this was as difficult for him as it was for me, in its way, a notion that left all my assumptions upended. I didn't want to see the situation from his vantage, to consider any parallels to my own

—to my fears of confessing my abilities to my family and the change in how they'd see me.

In a world where information was power, his ability to look beneath any mask, to perceive the true emotions buried deep would give him an immeasurable advantage. Small wonder high fae, accustomed to being invulnerable, would find the presence of an arbiter intolerable. Had he thought I would feel the same? *Did* I feel the same?

The leaves of the elder brushed against my face, its greening song whispering courage in my ears. Whatever advantage his abilities had given him in our dealings, he'd never turned it against me—quite the opposite. Why? From this vantage I could see only his profile, drawn sharp against the backdrop of the forest, and it offered no insight.

"Would you like me to leave?" The question came utterly devoid of emotion, and yet the offer . . .

I shook my head, and the elder branches shuddered. I needed time to process all that had just unfolded, yet I still required facts. Perhaps they could be a shield to in some way deflect emotion? "No, I just . . . It's fine. What did you need to discuss?"

Now he spun to face me, pinning me in place with a sharp glance. "You're not fine."

The shifting shadows on the forest floor blurred before my eyes. "Perhaps not, but it doesn't change the situation."

"The situation? You refer to the fact that we must deal together in some way. Or else you must manage the matter of Ainslie's bargain alone." His voice remained emotionless, and he no longer watched me. "There are alternatives. We could return to our former arrangement."

To working together by bargain, an arrangement fraught with uncertainty and distrust? It would limit contact between us, limit the exposure that I instinctively withdrew from, but . . . "That's not what I want. It would be useless to deny that I find this difficult. It will take me time to become accustomed to feeling so exposed, but I will."

The quiet between us stretched almost unbearably. Then at last he turned to me again, glints of gold lightening his eyes. "There's another alternative, if you're willing."

"What do you mean?"

"I can put a working on you that will hide your emotions—unless you choose to lift it."

My breath caught. "Have you done such a thing before?"

"No. Nor would my king appreciate the notion, as he relies on my readings of those in his court. But you have sworn no fealty. Which leaves me at liberty to offer." The light before him sharpened, casting shadows of leaf and bough behind. "However, I understand if you do not trust it."

Because if I agreed to a working, he could weave into it whatever he wished. But he wouldn't do that, I felt sure. He could have allowed the situation to continue to his advantage, but he'd offered a way out. I closed the distance between us. "I trust you, that has not changed. Place the working."

"It will take some time." His voice emerged low. He moved closer, until less than a handbreadth separated us, and his warmth became my own.

Light spiraled up my arms, then vanished as abruptly. "You made a bargain." He muttered something that sounded suspiciously like a fae curse. "Who approached you?"

"There was . . ." My chest seized as though strangled by ancient roots, the pain burrowing deep into my body. Only when I released all thoughts of the fae lady could I draw air once more.

His brows slashed downward. "You agreed to a geas? What else? Can you say?"

"The geas was the only condition of the bargain."

"What did you bargain for?"

"Information about my mother."

He drew a hand across his jaw. "Jessa—"

"I know it was a risk, but I couldn't turn down the chance to gain some answers. What she said—we were right, Mother *was* fae, and she did forsake her affinities." My throat closed as I contemplated telling him that the fae had helped Mother. "There was a suggestion that she might not be dead."

A small, rare flicker of surprise crossed his face. "If that's true, then we'll find out. Can you say anything more?"

I shook my head.

"Then I'll continue." The air between us filled with a rich glow, then, like drops of distilled sunlight, sigils spiraled across my skin, sparkling with life before they vanished, leaving only traces of warmth to brand the places they'd adorned. My sense of time and space vanished in favor of my Other senses, which absorbed the traces of his power. They became part of my very being, yet the notion wasn't unsettling as I'd expected, rather bright and comforting.

When the last of the sigils faded, Riven surveyed me. I'd nothing but his word to go on as to whether it had worked—yet he could not lie. "Can you perceive my emotions any longer?"

"No." Something unfamiliar shaded his expression.

"Then why are you looking at me like that?"

"Fae emotions are twisted. Stunted, perhaps, by long stifling. Yours were not. They were . . . arresting. It is strange to have them severed." The golden glow dimmed. "I'll adjust."

Would this concealment of my feelings make a difference in the end? How many years had he spent perceiving the emotions of fae and mortal alike, pairing them with expression and inflection? Remove one, and the other still remained. Yet it did not trouble me as it once had. He'd voluntarily disadvantaged himself, knowing that his king would not approve—the king. "You wanted to talk to me about your king?"

"Yes. After the situation with Lady Avis, I could no longer keep you concealed from him. He's demanded an . . . interview." Riven's jaw tightened. "I persuaded him to wait."

But perhaps he'd not been entirely sure the king would follow through, thus the middle-of-the-night visit to ensure I'd not come to harm? Suddenly chilled, I rubbed my hands along my arms. "Do you believe he truly will?"

"For a time. But he wants you to know he's watching. He

made that clear by sending Lady Celeste on an errand any sylph could have performed. Ordinarily she goes on only the most sensitive tasks. She was sent to shake things up."

"And report the outcome?"

"Naturally."

"But why would the king have any interest in me?"

"You and your sisters reflect something inexplicable. He cannot afford to overlook it, given the state of things between worlds. Nor can any fae monarch, though to my knowledge the rest remain unaware. Not to mention the fact you're responsible for the deaths of both Uros and Damir. These things draw notice."

"I see." The image of the fractured garden etched itself upon my mind once more. How long before it crumbled about me?

"There's something else. You're unaffiliated with any court. Unprotected. He'll look to claim you to his advantage. As I've mentioned before, it will be difficult if you remain unallied," Riven said. "It could be to your benefit to join his court—but make no mistake, it will also come at a cost."

The complete severing of ties to this world, no doubt. What else? Fealty to a fae monarch? I could imagine few things as terrifying. What might he require?

"Jessa." Riven stepped closer, his voice driving back my fears. "Nothing must be decided now. If needed, you can call in the debt owed you by Lady Avis. She has the standing to buy you more time with the king."

"And would she?"

"She'd have no choice, given the nature of her debt. She cannot keep you from the king forever, but much can change in a matter of weeks."

A matter of weeks had upended my whole life. I brushed the creamy elderflower back. "That's why you insisted she owed me for her release."

He lifted a shoulder. "I cannot be seen petitioning any favors on your behalf. Yet given her debt, no one would look askance if she did."

"Do you always think of the politics of a matter?"

"I have no choice. And if you are to survive the Otherworld, you must learn as well."

But I didn't want to survive the Otherworld, I wanted to protect the mortal world—and all I loved—from its encroachment. My chest squeezed unbearably tight. Everything in me yearned to return home, to the shelter of the safe and familiar, but how long before it became impossible?

Had I already become the danger I feared?

Riven returned me to the gardens, and we stood near the fountain, wrapped in glamour. He inclined his head toward the house. "Elodie is inside the house with Ada."

A soft sigh escaped me. I'd have liked to remain immured in the garden for several weeks—perhaps then the melodies of the plants would begin to soothe the turmoil within. Now it seemed I wasn't to have the luxury of even a few moments. "I suppose I must join them. I don't want to leave Ada alone with Elodie any longer than necessary, in case she tries to press matters."

He gave a slight nod. "I'll return when I can. Be careful."

With that, he vanished through a passing, and the concealment glamour evaporated along with him. As the last gleam of golden light faded, shadows began to pool beneath the eaves of the house. Nothing cast them; they simply formed, inky black, along the entire back wall. If Mr. Ludne still used the Vigil to keep watch on us—and I couldn't afford to believe he did not— would they notice this aberration? Or was it only evident to my Other senses?

Jade stalked toward the shades, and they winked from sight as swiftly as they'd appeared, their seeming awareness all too reminiscent of the shadows Lord West had wielded. I braced myself against the fountain, and its cool mist dampened the backs of my arms. Whatever it was had waited until Riven vanished to make its presence known. He was bound to the Harmony of Lights, whatever that might be, and the wishes of his king.

And I was bound here, at least until Ainslie was freed. If some high fae—perhaps the bargain-holder—wished to make it known that they kept me under observation, the message was abundantly clear. The best I could do was show no fear—and keep watch in turn.

When I entered the house, Holden met me with the hauteur he'd adopted of late, his demeanor making it clear he was aware that I skirted the edges of propriety and he disapproved. "Miss Jessa, will you be joining Miss Ada?"

"Joining her where?" I should at least maintain a pretense of ignorance.

"She's in the drawing room with Miss Redgrave. They've been visiting quite some time. Miss Redgrave asked after you upon her arrival, but Miss Ada said you were not to be disturbed."

"Thank you, Holden. I'll go to them at once." Yet my steps slowed as I approached. Nothing felt less desirable than another fraught conversation. I'd not even begun to process the ones that had come before. Yet apart from the issue of Ada's vulnerability, I had questions for Elodie, and I did not want to abandon the chance for answers.

When I entered the drawing room, they stood to greet me. Ada lifted her brows slightly, as though in inquiry, and I offered a small nod, hoping to reassure her.

Then I turned to Elodie. She stood still, her hands clasped before her. In our previous encounters, she had been nothing but confident, sparkling and possessed of immense social poise —now she offered a hesitant smile. "I'm pleased you could join us. Charles has taken Ainslie out, and I thought—hoped—we might have a chance to talk."

I sank into the nearest chair, struggling and failing to conjure a polite answer—I'd so very little left for the art of social pleasantry. At last, I abandoned the attempt. "I'd rather thought you'd prefer to avoid my company in the future."

She fiddled a bit with the necklace at her throat, and its simple lines caught my eye. She'd forsaken her ward-pendant in favor of a plain gold locket. What did that mean? Was it an effort to make peace?

"We—Charles and I—were not at our best when you shared your news. It was quite a shock."

"I understand," I murmured.

She studied me closely. "I believe you do. And I hope you also understand that we never meant to hurt you."

"I know you did what you thought best."

"Sometimes there is no best, only an attempt to choose the lesser of two ills." Sadness etched itself across her face. "And I confess I still struggle to see the path forward, since our silence in itself betrays another vow."

"Then has your brother come to cry off with Ainslie?"

She shook her head. "Nor do I want him to do so, despite the fact I see troubles ahead, particularly if—"

Her words cut off abruptly, and a sharp sensation twisted my chest, as if I felt the pain of the geas myself.

She continued, "If certain things prove true. Above all, I want to see Charles safe and well. I suspect that's a sentiment we share about our siblings."

Ada offered a gentle smile. "Indeed."

"More information might make that possible, might make Avons safer for all mortals," I said softly. "If I were to ask about your ancestor Ceolman, what might you be able to tell me?"

"You've been making inquiries." She hesitated, as if weighing her words. "He was a good man. A—very good man."

That was not what she'd meant to say the second time, I'd stake a great deal on it. "A man with a great deal of knowledge, perhaps?"

"Perhaps." Her clear eyes met mine. "I cannot say."

Then this line of inquiry would only pain her. "What of the missing? Can you speak of them?"

"Charles and I have no involvement in that matter—others in the family have taken that task, and we've heard little." Her features were composed now. "I'm not certain it would be wise at this point to draw attention to ourselves by inquiring, when we've not completed our own assignment."

Which was, of course, investigating me. I'd compelled them to hold their silence on that matter; I'd not attempt to force this one. Still, was it possible that the Redgrave family would ever share information openly? The geas wouldn't keep them from speaking about current investigations, unless I entirely misunderstood its nature. Either way, perhaps I dreamt of the impossible. Even Elodie remained guarded, unsure.

For that matter, so did I.

"Would you ever be willing to talk to my family in the future?" She leaned forward, a note of pleading in her voice. "Tell them what you've told us?"

I swallowed against the tightness in my chest. "Can you assure me of how such news would be received?"

"I wish I could." Her eyes lowered. "But I cannot answer for the rest."

Which meant for now we must continue as we'd started, with layers of secrecy shrouding every conversation and every deed. "Then perhaps we'd best take each day as it comes."

Certainly, each held enough trouble.

"Come now, these are grim topics for such a lovely afternoon." With that, Ada shifted the conversation to a discussion of mutual acquaintances and who meant to stay in Avons and which house parties the Redgraves might betake themselves to later in the season. Elodie matched her lightness, the two of them conducting the charade of an ordinary call, a pretense which became necessity when Aunt Caris joined us.

Not long after she appeared, Mr. Redgrave and Ainslie entered the room, the distance between them erased. Though she released his arm when they crossed the threshold of the room, he remained close to her, his gaze caressing her face—the rest of us might as well not exist. As for Ainslie, she looked more herself than she had since her disappearance. Some of the old light had returned to her eyes, and her smile held a note of true joy—so it must have gone well.

After the Redgraves took their leave, the three of us slipped to the garden to take the air, and Ada spun to Ainslie. "Don't leave us in suspense. What did he say?"

"A great deal. He apologized for his deceptions, and I did for mine—perhaps it was easier for us to forgive each other when we had similar motives for concealment." A pensive expression crossed her face. "Still, I hope to never have such a difficult conversation again. It is far easier not to care at all than to have to confess how very deeply someone has hurt you, and then hurt them with your own revelations in turn."

Ada wrapped an arm about Ainslie and pulled her close. "I'm so very glad you're talking again and that you've both forgiven what has come before."

"I won't deny that it still troubles me that he collected information on Jessa, but I understand. The way forward won't be simple, yet somehow he wishes to walk it with me, fae entanglements and all. We covered much, but even so, we will have a great deal more to discuss."

"But you will be discussing it?" I asked.

"Yes. We will." Ainslie extended a hand to pull me close. "And I don't think it would have happened if you hadn't told him of your nature and bridged the gap between us, so thank you."

The three of us embraced beneath the oak, its branches spreading over us, swaying gently as if in approval. Its song and the warmth of my sisters pressed back the fears that had assailed me since Lady Celeste appeared, allowing a small ember of hope to burn once more. Perhaps, just perhaps, things were not as bleak as I'd thought them.

Could we find a place in this world after all?

CHAPTER 39

As the purple-and-gold dawn unfurled, I clung to the small hope from the day before with fierce determination. Surely the brilliant morning boded well for the family picnic planned this afternoon—and perhaps this would be the day I'd lay hold of the information required to keep them safe. We'd cast plenty of lures; we only needed one to return a shred of evidence, a thread that could be followed to some clear conclusion.

I joined the family at breakfast, and lively chatter flowed between my sisters, Dreda, and Aunt Caris across the table. Only Jade remained unusually quiet, almost subdued.

I stroked her head. *Is something bothering you?*

The air smells . . . wrong.

Wrong how?

I don't know. Her eyes glowed in the morning light. *And that's what troubles me.*

From the doorway, Holden cleared his throat. "A message for you, Miss Jessa."

My pulse picked up as I accepted the thick ivory envelope. No ominous vines marred the outside, so perhaps it was nothing out of the ordinary. I slid my finger beneath the wax seal and opened the letter to find Thea's familiar script scrolling across the page.

Jessa,

I've had word that Mr. Fuller means to call at half past eleven. His message hints he has the item I requested. I'd very much like you to join me, if you can. My footman will await your response.

Fondest regards,
Thea

I lowered the letter to my lap. "Aunt Caris, Mrs. Darrington has invited me to call this morning."

"I suppose you must go, but why don't you take Dreda with you?"

I glanced at Dreda. "Do you mind?"

"Not at all."

I hurried to the drawing room to scribble a reply, then took a moment to write a note to Mr. Burke, informing him in veiled terms of the latest development. I pressed the seal into the wax with a bit too much force. Though I could take direct action on behalf of the missing, in the matter of Ainslie's bargain, I had little recourse. It chafed to simply watch and wait for some misstep on the part of her bargain-holder or for the results of Riven's endeavors to bear fruit, to become something I could act on. Yet what other choice did I have? I capped the ink bottle and returned it to the secretary.

In truth, one threat at a time was more than enough to confront, though I hoped Mr. Fuller didn't mean to issue a threat, but rather offer an answer. That hope carried me through the next few hours, which I used to finalize my report on Kilmere, so I could turn it over to Thea when I called today.

Finally, the time came for departure. As we rattled along in the carriage, I considered what to tell Dreda. Her insights had proven helpful, and if I gave her a task to occupy her at

Crestridge Court, it would keep her from being exposed unaware to whatever item the Collector meant to deliver—as well as from harm if this proved some sort of snare. Yet the choice should be hers. I pulled my leather folio closer. "How much do you want to be involved in the investigation at hand?"

"As much as you'll allow me." Her gaze met mine, her expression earnest and intent. "I may have little enough to offer, but I'd still like to help."

"Good, because Thea invited me today so we could meet with a Collector. He means to bring her an item that could be connected to the disappearing individuals—and he may well have used one of the guild's drivers to bring him. Will you explore that avenue? I'd like to know what others think of him—and the Collectors in general—and this seems an excellent opportunity."

She clasped her hands in her lap. "If he's brought a driver, that would be to our advantage. They're prone to gossiping among themselves in the long hours waiting."

"Just have a care. Anyone who associates with the Collectors might not adhere to the niceties of society."

"Don't worry. When I was fae-touched, no one except the Sisters—and you—believed me worthy of the niceties of society. I expect I'll manage just fine."

When we arrived at Thea's house, the butler granted permission for Dreda to retire belowstairs, then ushered me into a morning room decorated in shades of mauve and gold. Unlike in the drawing room, nothing of her antiquarian interests filtered into this space; instead, family portraits lined the wall across from silk-curtained windows, and costly vases spilled over with bouquets of fresh flowers.

Thea herself was ensconced on a settee surrounded with lace-frilled pillows, a table with a full tea tray situated alongside. She wore a deeper gray gown that hinted of mourning and shaded her eyes darker. Yet she offered me her customary smile. "Do you approve of our stage?"

"I think it well-suited to the task at hand."

She inclined her head. "One must always be ready to disarm an opponent if needed, and when one has no great strength, the appearance of weakness can be a weapon at hand."

"I've become very aware of that fact." Yet sometimes it did not give advantage enough. I settled into an oval-backed chair with delicately scrolled legs, and Jade tucked herself next to me.

"Perhaps one day you shall tell me how you've learned that lesson. I'm not Ibbie, but I'm quite capable of listening when needed."

"I'm certain you are." I offered my portfolio to her. "I was hoping you'd review my report on Kilmere and pass it on if you approve. Mr. Redgrave had wanted to look at it as well."

"I'll share it with him also. Am I right in thinking you'd rather avoid further questions from him?"

I nodded as the butler glided back into the room, accompanied by Mr. Fuller, who sauntered in like one confident of his success.

"Oh, Mr. Fuller. I was pleased to receive your message, very pleased indeed." Thea's hand fluttered about the tea tray. "Won't you take some tea? Or do you prefer a cool beverage?"

"I'd prefer to stick to business." He frowned slightly at me. "During which the strictest confidence should be maintained. We did not discuss the presence of a companion."

Thea blinked up at him. "Surely you understand that with age comes greater need? I rarely go anywhere without a companion. But you may be sure that I trust her to hear of all my dealings—she's the soul of discretion."

The scar on his face tightened, but evidently, the desire to preserve his deal won out, and he withdrew a wrapped parcel from his leather case, along with a request for a sum that nearly made me choke. How had Lianne come by a statuette, if this was the cost?

"Oh my." Thea's hand went to the lace at the neck of her gown. "I must confess I'd not expected it to be quite so costly . . . You are certain this remedy will suit?"

"I can make no promises. Only if you don't want it, there are others that'll take all I have to offer."

"Well, yes, quite understandable . . . Might I see the item in question first?"

He unwrapped the parcel and revealed its contents—a small bone-colored statuette. It didn't spark Other in a discernible way, and yet it didn't seem to belong to our world either.

The fur on Jade's neck ruffled. *It smells of pain and death. And something else . . . but I cannot discern it above the stench.*

The statuette's garments were crafted with elegant detail, but its face was hollow-eyed, twisted as if in some torment, the vividness of it all unsettling. It was ugly, as Miss Chevon had said, yet somehow I could not look away. Why would anyone welcome such a thing?

Mr. Fuller folded the brown paper back around it. "It's what's inside the statuette that'll lift your spirits whenever melancholy comes upon you. Just twist off the head for access."

Why use the statuette as a delivery mechanism? Could it somehow dampen the Other nature of whatever rested within, so it could better avoid detection? The hollow eyes of the statuette seemed to bore into mine. *If you smell death, could it contain some sort of poison? Though I cannot imagine a poison raising the spirits of those who consumed it . . .*

Jade's ears twitched. *It's not the smell of something toxic, but rather like something that is dead.*

The skin on the back of my neck prickled. *In either case, the question remains. How can such a substance raise the spirits of those who consume it? Unless it's meant to slowly kill, and the elevated spirits are merely the precursor to a sudden decline?*

If that's true, then why bother bringing the afflicted to the Otherworld at all? Fae enjoy toying with live mortals, not dead.

I pulled her closer. *What if the fae revealed to these individuals that they were dying and presented themselves as saviors? Under such circumstances, the mortals could be made to agree to a good many unwise things. Or perhaps that's not it at all. Perhaps they go to the Otherworld for more of whatever substance the statuette holds.*

I wrenched my attention back to the conversation between Thea and Mr. Fuller.

"Most ingenious." Thea tapped her fingers on the edge of her chair, as if she considered. "And this remedy has no ill effects?"

"None reported."

"Well then, I'll take it." She lifted a small money chest and emptied part of its contents into a small leather purse. Whatever she'd claimed about the required sum, she'd been prepared.

He surveyed its contents, then handed off the statuette. "A pleasure."

When he departed, I released the breath I'd held. "Whatever he said, I'm convinced the substance within this statue isn't safe to consume, possibly not even to come in contact with."

What if the mere act of opening it released some harmful working or substance? I fought the urge to snatch it from Thea.

"I've no doubt you're right." Every vestige of the fluttering uncertainty she'd displayed with Mr. Fuller vanished as Thea examined the object. "It's strange, no doubt. But I cannot shake the feeling I've seen something similar before."

I leaned forward. "Where?"

"I cannot recall. It doesn't match the styles of any past era of Byren, nor does it appear of modern make. Yet something about it . . ." She sat motionless, as though reviewing all her vast years of antiquarian knowledge. Then she pressed to her feet. "Perhaps I'll find what I need in the study."

I trailed her into the study, where she began to rummage about in drawers and boxes, riffling through age-darkened papers, gazette clippings, and sketches. "It cannot have been since I took up residence in Avons. I would remember. Then where?"

As she appeared to be speaking primarily to herself, I remained quiet, hoping the memory or scrap of evidence would surface. At last, she held a letter aloft.

"Ah, here's the proof. I'd begun to think I'd imagined it." She tilted it toward me so I could see the drawing tucked inside, a simple sketch of a small statue. While not identical to the one Mr. Fuller brought us today, it had a strong resemblance. "I knew it seemed somehow familiar. Years ago, a fellow of the society came upon a collection of statuettes in the ruins of a far northern settlement and wrote to me of his findings. A thief made off with them in the night before I arrived to see them, and only a few sketches remained. At the time I was most put out, but I hadn't thought about it long since."

An obscure ruin tucked away in the far north? Statuettes that had been stolen—or perhaps they'd vanished by Other means? Unease rooted deep in my chest. Did this ruined settlement in any way resemble Kilmere? I'd wanted to believe Kilmere the only such fae stronghold, but I had no proof. Might high fae have constructed more outposts as they attempted to conquer our world—if they'd indeed ever set out to do so?

Thea set the statuette on the table. "The light relic of Mr. Redgrave's was clearly Other in nature, and I'll admit I'd hoped this would be the same. It would have made it easier to force action."

I stared into its twisted face. "Perhaps the accumulation of small oddities will be enough to sway opinion. The fact that it was brought by a Collector will strongly hint of Other origin."

"Perhaps. But I fear it will not be enough." She shook her head. "We shall summon Lord Blackburn and your stratesman at once and see what we can make of it."

"I cannot stay. My family expects me this afternoon, and besides, I think we should wait. There's someone else who should examine it first, in order to verify its safety."

"And who is this mysterious stranger?"

"An expert in Otherworldly affairs. Mr. Burke has worked with him before, and he can further vouch for his credibility."

She shifted forward, rustling the lace cushions. "You've never mentioned him."

"He prefers not to draw attention to his knowledge, and it's not my right to involve him without his consent. But if you'll allow me to bring the statuette to him—"

"Out of the question. If there's some danger attached to it, I don't want it to become attached to *you*."

"What of your own well-being?"

"If a risk must be taken, I'd rather my own life than yours."

"And what if I feel the same?"

Her milkweed-floss brows lowered. "Then you'll have to accept that I purchased the item, and it now belongs to me."

I could think of a good many arguments that might sway her, but all of them involved truths I could not expose—and her stubbornness matched my own. Without a compelling reason, she'd not surrender the statuette. I rocked back, a sigh escaping. "You won't . . . open it, will you?"

"Certainly not. I don't have a death wish," she said tartly. "I have a strongbox belowstairs that will keep it safe for now."

"Then I'll make every effort to return soon." Oh, how tempting it was to exact a promise from Thea. But that would bind her in bargain unwitting. Where did one draw the line?

Jade, will you ask Risha to tell Riven we have the statuette? She's to be clear the message is for informational purposes only, not a request for immediate assistance. However much I might desire his insight, we couldn't afford for the precarious balance within his court to be overset.

I took my leave from Thea, then slipped to the entry, where the butler departed to fetch Dreda. She soon joined me, and together we descended the sovstone stairs to the footwalk. Once within the carriage, she angled toward me. "Was your errand satisfactory?"

"Yes and no. We've obtained an object that I believe links to the missing persons, but we still have little understanding of its purpose."

"But it is . . . Other?"

"It appears so."

Her chin quivered slightly. "Then I'm glad you're the one keeping watch over it."

I'd be considerably more at ease if I *was* the one keeping

watch over it, yet I'd have only wrested it from Thea by force or glamour—neither of which were acceptable options.

Our carriage rolled away from Crestridge Court and the fae object it now held, and with difficulty, I refrained from casting a glance over my shoulder. "Were you able to discover anything about the Collector?"

"You were right—he did have one of the guild drivers bring him." Dreda's hand went to her bonnet. "After you left me with the butler, I said I wished to nip out for a bit of fresh air, and while out of doors, I found the wind blew my hat away."

I eyed the gently swaying tree limbs beyond the carriage windows, which stirred with the mildest of breezes. "Is that so?"

"Indeed." Her hazel eyes warmed. "He was gracious enough to help me fetch it, and he turned out to be fairly chatty, in his way. His breath rather smelled of brandy, so I'm certain that loosened his tongue."

"And did he say anything worth noting?"

"After a time, he said he's beginning to think they don't pay him enough to work for the Collectors." Dreda tucked her reticule beneath her arm. "It seems he thought when he took the position that any oddities would be endured by the Collectors alone, when they ventured into the Otherworld, but he's noticed 'things that shouldn't be about.' He hinted that items remain within the guild that should not. I also gathered that the Collectors very much have rivalries with one another, and he doesn't favor Mr. Fuller, though the man has had more successful trips than most."

"I suppose it's not surprising that they each seek to best the other. They've only a short time to make their mark." And most wouldn't—but would instead die in the attempt. Perhaps when Mr. Wells had warned against Mr. Fuller, he hadn't been seeking to protect Thea's well-being, but to discredit his fellow Collector for his own gain? Whatever the case, between the statuette and the driver's report, it was abundantly clear that the Collectors weren't turning over all they gathered to the Alchemist's Guild as they were paid, contracted, and bound by law to do.

"He said something else, too, at the end." Faint lines of tension radiated about her eyes. "He asked if I worked for Mrs. Darrington. When I said I was employed by the Caldwell family, he gave me an odd look. Then he got quiet."

I shifted uncomfortably against the hard leather bench. Had rumors spread as far as the Collectors? How would they? Surely none of our actions were of interest to them. Yet there was the matter of the sunset-haired watcher . . . I shook myself. I'd enough troubles without borrowing more. We'd received a key with which we might unlock the mystery of the missing. For now, that would have to be enough.

CHAPTER 40

Dreda and I returned home to find Aunt Melisina waiting. As soon as we stepped through the door, she took charge, hurrying Lovell, my sisters, Dreda, and me into our carriage, while she, Father, Aunt Caris, and an abundance of picnic supplies were delegated to her own. True to her word, she hadn't attempted to invite any eligible young gentlemen, nor had she brought along her usual cadre of servants to execute the affair. Uncle Milton was conspicuously absent, which boded well for the peace of the day. It seemed it would be as she promised—a quiet, intimate family picnic.

Yet I felt unsettled and out-of-kilter, unable to shake the image of the statuette or the sensation that we'd missed something important. As we traversed the city, Lovell and my sisters bantered about the newest play at the Holland Theater, and I listened with half an ear, the rest of my attention fixed on the melodies of the plants we passed.

They all held sprightly tones, no hint of anything ominous, but when we halted at a crossroads, the shadows of the lamp-posts at the corners seemed to stretch long, almost as if they reached for us, and a distinct dampish scent tinged the air, though the day remained cloudless and fair.

I pulled Jade into my lap. *There* is *something . . .*

I know.

Was it cause for concern? We'd seen shadows yesterday, and they'd fled at the slightest provocation. Perhaps this was merely another test.

Risha perched on my shoulder, her lights pulsing with deeper tones, and the conversation drifted about me like leaves caught on the wind as I strained to place this vague impression of Other. We clattered on over cobbled stones, and the ephemeral sensation faded.

Lovell nudged me. "Why so gloomy, Jess?"

"It's nothing." I dredged up a smile. "Tell me about the place Aunt Melisina has chosen for our picnic."

"It's on private land not far outside Avons, apparently quite picturesque and remote—she's convinced we need a reprieve from the city."

She wasn't wrong, only we needed a reprieve from a great deal more. Still, it was further proof of her sincerity—she did not favor natural scenery, but rather those settings which lent themselves to seeing and being seen.

After a few hours in the carriage, we halted at the edge of an expansive woodland, through which a small trail cut. Lovell nodded toward the path. "We'll walk from here."

Descending from the carriage, I inhaled the scents of warm earth and blossoming flowers. The whisper of leaves in the breeze kissed my senses as I followed my family down the path until we reached a small glade near a brook, which burbled merrily in the sunlight.

Two footmen, heavily laden, had accompanied us, and now they deposited their loads beneath a spreading chestnut in the center of the glade, then retreated down the path to wait with the carriages, which were well out of sight.

Stone outcroppings behind us fell away to the even grassy expanse along the water. Beneath the trees on all sides, bluebell and fern clustered and countless tangled blackberry brambles flourished, laden with dark, jewellike berries, their sweet, earthy scent pervading the glen—in all an idyllic scene. Only I could not enjoy it as I should, my senses continually straining for anything out of the ordinary, any hint of a shift in the rich melodies of the forest.

I found nothing.

Perhaps I needed this respite more than I knew, if I spooked at every shadow. Aunt Melisina directed the spreading of the blankets and unfolding of small stools, and I swiftly busied my hands to keep my mind from conjuring phantasms.

Jade's ears pricked. *You're not one to imagine things. Perhaps I should take a look about.*

It would ease my mind, but take care.

I always do. She vanished among the trees.

The others discussed our charming surroundings as I watched for Jade's return.

After perhaps a quarter hour, she sauntered back, halting at my feet. *I'll admit the area offers a number of excellent spots to lie in wait—there's a cave beyond in the cropping of rocks, and plenty of hidden areas among the trees. Yet I found nothing, no sign of stalkers past or present.*

Lovell snatched up an empty basket. "There's nothing for it. I'll have to pick some of those berries. We cannot ignore such bounty."

He moved toward a tangle of blackberries beneath a spreading elm, and I leaned against the chestnut. *Thank you for checking. I suppose I've allowed my emotions undue sway—*

With a sudden intense snap, Other shattered my senses. A passing rent the air beneath the elm, the scents of damp and must drenching the glade. And a monstrous creature with inky fur and four slitted eyes charged through it, sniffing the air. Shadows longer than its body stretched before it.

A bau.

The world tilted about me; my pulse surged into my throat. It mustn't bite anyone, mustn't tangle anyone in its shadows, or they would die.

Lovell whirled to face the creature. It flung him against the trunk of the elm with a sickening snap. Its shadows darted toward him.

The shrieks behind me faded as I flung my senses wide, connecting with the elm. Its pulse became mine, my limbs—its limbs—sweeping down to cradle him.

The bau slashed at the tilted branches, and they shuddered, thickening until they formed a veritable fortress around Lovell. The bau snorted.

Its red-brown eyes locked on us. And it snarled, revealing razor-sharp teeth.

A wild thrum rose in my veins to match the songs of the forest. I must keep it away; nothing else mattered. I dug my hands into the bark of the spreading chestnut and opened my senses wide to every nearby plant, their vibrant strength pouring through my body as my desires mingled with theirs.

The world beyond grayed.

Then winked from sight altogether.

Root and branch bent and swayed and wove, a glorious dance I perceived only in hues of Other. A riot of reddish-black and green swirled in the distance, its song barbed and fierce—there, this one I needed.

The blackberry surged forth, twining about the bau, who was now a shadow-form threaded with power, its essence laid bare. It lumbered forward to meet the swirl of green and gold that charged the air. The song of the brambles deepened about me, overtaking every other melody as our strength mingled.

Oh. How glorious, this rich golden strength that fueled riotous untamed growth, as swift as summer sunbeams. Vines shot forward, sharp-as-sword thorns lengthened, brambles tangled with bau and—

There's another one behind. Dimly, Jade's words pierced the green-gold haze. *I'll go, if you loosen the cage.*

Don't. Behind, what was behind? A protective thrum surged from a stand of oak, and swift as thought, its massive roots surfaced to snatch another shadow-threaded creature, pulling it down deep beneath the earth.

The vibrant song and light burned through every limb, exposing the essence of every living thing that surrounded the glade. Each beat of my heart pulsed this life through my veins, all-consuming, bough and bramble swirling around me—

A sharp pain pierced my ankle. *Jessa! Listen to me. You must withdraw.*

Melodies surged across my senses, nearly drowning her voice. *Withdraw from what?*

Her growl rumbled in my ears. *Open your eyes.*

I blinked, and a different world snapped into focus. I was no longer braced against the chestnut; I'd collapsed to the ground, soil staining my gown and blood beaded at my ankle where Jade had sunk her claws in. How long had she sought to claim my attention before resorting to drawing blood? I struggled to my feet, unsteady. Swirls of green-gold still limned the immense cage of tangled branch and root about us, so dense that no bau could ever hope to pierce it. It hemmed me in with my family . . .

My family.

What had I done?

Bile burned the back of my throat as I turned, slowly. I didn't want to look at them, but I must. Oh, I must.

They huddled at the far edge of the tangled cage. Aunt Caris sobbed, and Aunt Melisina stood motionless, her face white and stricken. Father murmured something inaudible, his arms locked about my sisters. Ada buried her head in his shoulder, and Ainslie pressed a trembling hand to her lips.

They were afraid.

And not just of the bau.

Shuddering, I turned away. Across the glade, the tangle of blackberry briars had become immense, a snare of swordlike thorns descending to pierce the body of the bau from every side. It had ceased to struggle, and its black blood dripped down to stain the carpet of mingled grass and moss below.

I'd killed it.

And my family had watched it all unfold.

Unbearable pressure built in my chest. The nearest boughs swept down to wrap about my shoulders, and the entire cage shuddered, tightening around us.

It is as in Withern. You must calm yourself before you can calm them.

My pulse drummed relentlessly at my temples. *But my family, they're looking at me like . . . like . . .*

Exercising your power to such a degree has burned away some of your mortal glamour. Not all, but enough for hints of Other to peek through.

I swallowed against a rising swell of bitterness. Ordinary, I must appear ordinary—somehow.

There. That's better.

Dreda detached herself from the huddle and moved toward my side, her face pale but composed. "I believe we're safe now, Miss Jessa. Will you release us?"

How could she be so calm, when everyone else regarded me like I represented a greater threat than the bau? And why wouldn't they, given what they'd witnessed? I shrank back, and the branches tangled closer about us, blackberry vines weaving their way through, blotting out the sky overhead.

There must be a way out, a way back to how things were, a way to—

Jessa.

Glamour. *I . . . I could glamour them. Make them forget. We could go back to the way things were.*

That's not what you want, not truly. Bid the plants disperse. With a low rumble, Jade transformed into true-form, her bulk blotting the horrified faces of my family from view. *Do it now.*

I buried my face in her fur, inhaling the sweet-grass scent and absorbing her warmth, matching my ragged breaths to her even ones and opening my soul just the slightest to the melodies once more.

With each breath, I sent a soothing impression of peace and safety, images of calm and order. And when at last I opened my eyes, branch and root, vine and thorn had all returned to their proper places, leaving only the broken body of the bau—and Lovell.

On unsteady legs, I moved toward him.

"Don't . . . hurt him." Aunt Melisina's voice emerged choked, small and frightened in a way I'd never heard from her.

If she'd driven one of the great thorns through my chest, it would have hurt less. I stumbled across the uneven ground and sank down at his side. "Lovell, are you well?"

A gentle hand rested on my shoulder. It was Ada, and Ainslie appeared just behind her.

Lovell gave a muffled moan, and his eyes blinked open.

"Can you hear me?"

"I hear." He stared at us blearily. "But why are the three of you hovering over me like it's my funeral?"

"Because it very nearly was!" Ainslie's voice broke. "If Jessa hadn't—"

"There were bau," Ada said. It seemed she'd recognized them too, doubtless thanks to Mother's tales. "One threw you against the tree."

Lovell tried to move, then groaned. "That explains why I feel as though I've been run down by a coach with a full team of horses." His gaze drifted to Jade, and a strangled sound escaped. "How hard did I hit my head?"

Behind us, the others approached cautiously, and I drew back to allow them space.

My aunts bent over Lovell, and Father turned to me, his face a terrible blank. "Who are you?"

I flinched. I wouldn't cry, not now. "I'm your daughter, as I have ever been."

"But you . . . the trees. Your face . . ."

Aunt Melisina, keeping a wary distance, stepped up and clutched his arm. "Not now, Alden. We must go home at once, where we can discuss this in privacy and determine what's to be done."

"If you'd like, I shall ask the footmen to lend us aid," Dreda said softly.

"Better get the drivers too. Not sure how steady on my feet I'll be." Lovell drew a labored breath. "Then someone can explain to me why there's bau and a giant tiger-creature and—other things."

Dreda nodded and slipped down the path. I glanced at the broken body of the bau, and my stomach churned. Something must be done with it before she returned with the servants.

I'll drag it to the cave. We can hide the body there until Riven's able to examine it. Jade moved toward the bau, then looked back over her shoulder. *You did what you had to do. The bau would have slaughtered them in moments, then dragged their bodies off to the caverns to feast for days.*

I rubbed my chest, but could not dispel the dreadful tightness within. *I always thought bau the worst sort of monster, but I . . . I disposed of two of them. Myself. What does that make me?*

High fae, which you have known.

And I knew something else. Bau couldn't open passings, which meant high fae were involved in this attack somehow. Jade was right; we needed Riven. Yet he'd already promised to return to Avons as soon as he could. I could expect no more.

Jade sank her teeth into the body of the bau and dragged it toward the stony outcropping. When she returned to my side, she shrank back into cat form.

Lovell gave a low whistle. "Did you know, Jess?"

"I knew."

A silence settled over the glade as he leaned back, his face set with lines of pain. And I turned away. It was easier to detach, to examine the clearing, than to consider my family—and what might come next. While I'd restored the plants, the earth was disturbed, distorted and torn, bearing testament to the battle that had taken place here.

It would be difficult to explain to the servants; indeed, when Dreda returned with them, they murmured uneasily.

I hobbled forward. "As you see, we experienced a quaking of the earth, and my cousin was injured. He'll need assistance back to the carriage."

As would I. As the rich green power ebbed, it seemed to take all my strength with it, and I felt as though I'd run for a week on end, every muscle weary and strained.

Ada moved toward me, but Aunt Caris caught her hand. "Stay close please, my dear."

Ada's breath caught, but I gave her a small nod. If matters unfolded as I feared, I did not want to drag her down with me. I braced against the bole of the elm, collecting my strength.

And Dreda approached. "You may lean on me, if you wish."

Her kindness tightened my throat and pricked at my eyes. Mutely, I accepted her hand, and she looped her arm through mine. Why wasn't she afraid? I choked down the question as we made our way down the path, one unsteady step after another.

In one moment, I'd fractured my family and shattered the only safe haven that remained. How would I face what must come?

CHAPTER 41

The dying rays of the sun slanted through the windows of the carriage, staining the floor with tones of rust and shadow. Though they spilled across my face and into my lap, they brought no warmth. A peculiar numbness had settled into my chest, the sudden lack of sensation that sometimes follows a particularly deep wound.

Because I was alone, except for Jade and a scattered assortment of picnic supplies. When we'd returned to the carriages, Aunt Melisina had silently bidden the rest to join her, and I'd made no protest.

How could I?

I'd become what all mortals feared; therefore they feared me. A dull aching sensation settled behind my eyes as we jostled over one dip after another in the rutted lane. Each divot in the road drove home the truth—what I'd dreaded had come upon me, and no escape remained.

I'd failed to meet the expectations of my family, the standards of the mortal world—failed also to meet the fae expectations Riven had set forth, the ones that dictated I sever every mortal tie. Now I might lose everything. The numbness spread deeper, rooting through my limbs, binding me in place.

Perhaps I didn't belong to this world anymore, but surely there was a way I could *appear* to do so—that I could remain and satisfy its conventions without forsaking my fae nature. Or had any chance of that vanished when I exposed the truth to my family? Would they report it, as they should? Mr. Ludne would require no convincing—he'd leap at the chance to lock me away.

In truth, I'd no notion how they'd respond. The horror etched into their features could prompt any number of responses, none of them in my favor.

So where did that leave me? Could I convince them I hadn't truly changed, whatever affinities I'd displayed? I couldn't think how, because I *had* changed—and in ways that might compel them to cast me out without the opportunity to prove myself. Yet if I couldn't do so, I might lose them all forever. I leaned my head against the back of the carriage bench. Beyond the glass, shadowed trees bent and swayed.

Jade rested her head on my lap. *Jessa—*

I don't want to discuss it. Because if I did, it would become real, this prospect that I'd destroyed my world beyond repair. *What we need to do is find out who is responsible for the attack. They failed, which means they might try again.*

Had they failed? What if this had simply been another test, a machination by which either outcome meant a victory for the tester—as it would result either in our deaths or proof positive of my abilities and the fracturing of my family. The bargain-holder *had* appeared to take interest in our family beyond just Ainslie; certainly, she'd watched us closely enough to know details of our deeds. The scenery outside blurred before my eyes.

When he was at liberty to come, Riven might be able to trace the source of the attack. But he might also use the attack—and my family's response—as evidence to support his argument that I should sever any connection to them. My stomach hollowed. If I must be presented with more evidence that I'd disappointed all those I valued—oh, it would be unbearable.

Jade lifted her head. *Perhaps he will react differently than you expect.*

He's very certain of his view.

Well, I hope you're wrong.

Why?

Because I sent Risha for Riven shortly after we entered the carriage.

I shot upright, catching my arm on the doorhandle. *You what?*

I was . . . worried for you.

Before I could press further, insist that she somehow fetch Risha back—how had I not noticed her absence?—the light of passing seared the interior of the carriage, and Riven filled the seat across from me, the rich light about him driving back the lingering shadows.

"I didn't know Jade sent Risha until just now—I didn't mean to bother you."

"I thought we were past that." His words held a slight edge.

And I shrank back. "It's just . . . I thought you must remain at court." I studied the floor of the carriage, where a few scattered leaves attested to the foliage I'd disturbed back in the clearing. "I didn't want to cause further trouble."

"You didn't. I told the king about the attack. He concurred it was necessary to trace its source, if possible. As long as I return for the conclusion of the second ceremony at dawn, it will cause no problems."

"You . . . told the king?"

"My abrupt departure from an event he'd bidden me to attend would have drawn too much attention otherwise. But he now has a vested interest in your situation—I leveraged that to buy time." His gaze swept my body. "Were you injured?"

"I'm fine."

"Your family?"

"They're unharmed. In body, at least." Some part of me wanted to pour out my emotions, but if I did, if he used them as proof I must abandon this world . . . I could summon no argument against it, not now. I wrapped my arms about my chest.

Distraction was the better course. "I'd like to make sure it stays that way by finding answers about who was behind the attack."

"Your carriage is about an hour away from Avons. It gives us time enough." Yet he made no move to depart, the weight of his scrutiny impossible to escape in this confined space.

I shifted uncomfortably. "I suppose we should depart."

With a slight nod, he drew me through a passing that deposited us just in front of the cave holding the body of the bau. For all Risha's flighty nature, she'd given him very precise information about my location and the site of the attack. I followed Jade and Riven around the cropping of rock to where a crevice descended into a natural cave, one shrouded in a sort of perpetual night. Loose rubble scraped underfoot, and I moved inward with care.

Once inside, Riven set gleaming fae-lights at intervals around the space, and their glow outlined the bulk of the bau. It was thrice as large as Riven's formidable frame, and its ridged head crowned a body rent with many wounds.

Wounds I'd inflicted when I sent swordlike thorns to pierce its body time and again as it struggled against its bonds. Never mind that it had been a monster bent on killing my family. I'd destroyed it. My stomach roiled as the foul stench of the creature rose up to choke me.

Riven moved toward me, blocking my view of the bau. "Go get some air. I can examine the body without assistance."

I retreated to the edge of the cave and drew in several long breaths redolent with the scents of blackberry, moss, and damp earth. With effort, I blocked the image of the torn body from my mind, the sounds of shuffling from my ears.

After a few moments, Riven emerged from the cave and sent light dancing in brilliant spirals across the glade. The illumination turned the disturbances I'd left in the earth into dark, furrowed shadows. "When I said practice your affinities, I wasn't speaking of such a large-scale endeavor. Your family is fortunate that you were present."

The cool of the evening pricked at the exposed skin along my arms. "I rather think they feel otherwise."

"Then they're fools." Riven's brows lowered. "Do you want to talk about what happened?"

"Not particularly." If I did, my fragile control would surely come undone.

He folded his arms across his chest and turned to regard the glade. Silence stretched between us, and the fae-lights flickered.

Jade perched at my feet. *I don't think your answer pleased him.*

It should have done. I rubbed my breastbone, trying to dispel the ache beneath it. *He's always telling me not to feel, not to display my emotions. I'm doing my best to heed the advice.*

Perhaps he only intended it to apply to your interactions with others—not him.

Then it seems I'm destined to disappoint him, as I have everyone else. The tangle of expectations tightened about me as inexorably as the blackberry brambles had the bau—and every bit as painfully.

Riven faced me once more, the shades of dusk shadowing his features. "There were two passings, one on either side of the glen. Bau cannot create them, which means a high fae was involved with this attack, one strong enough to open multiple passings in swift succession without having to emerge through either themselves. If they'd come through, even for a moment, they'd have left some trace. Not only were they careful in how they opened the passings, they also exercised caution in their dealings with the bau. The remaining body bore no compulsion working, though there were some dead nightspire leaves tangled in its fur."

"A sign that it was Ainslie's bargain-holder?"

"Or that we're meant to think so."

I rubbed my temples. "Whoever it was, how did they force the bau to agree? They don't seem like creatures of reason."

"The fae would have negotiated with them, not a difficult task, given the prospect of defenseless prey. It's an offer almost any bau would welcome."

Then they could think, could reason—which made it much worse than if they were mindless monsters. I swallowed hard. "Who might have gained from such an attack? The fae who holds Ainslie's bargain wouldn't want her dead."

"Unless it was a consequence for her defiance. But I agree, that's unlikely. Someone instigated this and likely observed the attack through the open passing—the impression it left is far greater than one opened only long enough to discharge the bau. If it was the bargain-holder, she may have meant to intervene if events did not unfold as she desired."

"Which means that this was some sort of test? Or could it be something else altogether? Could this relate to the statuette we uncovered, an attempt to conceal whatever evidence it contains?"

"I'm inclined to the first theory, but we've no proof. Either one is possible."

"And we've no reason to suppose something similar won't happen again." Had I been the cause of all this, or did it connect to the binding mark or the missing? Either way, my entire family was vulnerable—even more so if they cast me out.

Riven drew the coils of light back to himself. "We can find no more here. What do you intend to do?"

"Go home, I suppose." I twisted the folds of my skirt around my fingers. "They're discussing what to do with me."

He moved closer, his light washing over me. "You're not at the mercy of their decisions—you can choose as you please."

"I can choose for myself, yes, but not for them. Relationship that's glamoured or coerced in any way isn't true relationship." Even to my own ears, my voice sounded strained. "I must simply accept that they may not get past this."

"And have you accepted it?" His voice was quiet and far gentler than usual.

Blight and rot. It wasn't fair that he remained so perceptive even with the working in place—nor that he offered kindness, whatever his expectations of me. It eroded the numbness, allowing pain to pierce my chest, a sensation so sharp that it nearly stole my breath. "No—but I will not be the first to walk away."

He rubbed a hand across his jaw. "Then perhaps I should accompany you."

The tangle in my chest loosened. If I didn't have to face them alone . . . "It's unlikely to be a pleasant conversation."

He shrugged. "I didn't imagine otherwise."

The call of a nightjar echoed in the distance, and I collected my courage. "In what capacity are you offering? As a representative of the king who must report to him?"

The fae-lights turned from pale ivory to something deeper, like burnished gold. "My duty ends with a report on the attack itself. My offer is that of a friend."

A weight as substantial as the frame of a bau lifted. "Then I would be . . . more than grateful. But perhaps we should not arrive together."

"You still mean to observe the proprieties of this world?"

"If I'm to have any chance of swaying them, I must. We don't yet know what this attack was meant to accomplish, and I'll do whatever it takes to stay, at least until they're no longer at risk."

He inclined his head. "Then you should delay your return home, at least by an hour. Allow their conversation to play out with Risha to observe and report back. If you're present upon their arrival, they might react in the heat of the moment in a way that is—less than desirable."

My mind filled in the details. If they sought to lock me in my bedchamber or send at once for the authorities . . . The mournful rasp of the nightjar mingled with the rush in my ears.

He continued, "If you intend to put yourself at their mercy, at least retain the strategic advantage where you can."

"Very well. I'll instruct the driver to stop at a park."

To agree to set watch on my family went against every instinct, but then, my instincts had betrayed me to them, possibly destroying our relationship forever. I'd grant that if I was to have any chance of mending the breach, I'd need every advantage I could gain. But would it be enough?

CHAPTER 42

Once in the park, I collapsed beneath a spreading alder, exhaustion overtaking me. Riven wrapped his glamour about us, but fortunately refrained from further discussion. I leaned against the trunk of the tree, watching the play of golden light against the night-dark branches and choking down the fears that sought to consume me.

Jade perched on my chest, warm and immovable, and after what felt an interminable time, Risha fluttered down to perch on the grass alongside us. I pressed away from the alder. "What's happening?"

Her light pulsed an erratic beat. "First, a great upset at driver for leaving you. Then the arrival of the physician for cousin, after that much mortal emotion. Sisters went to bedchamber to argue about what you wanted them to say or not say. Elders argued about if you are Jessa or something else, and if Jessa, how to help you be ordinary Jessa, and where you are and what they should do."

The boughs overhead rustled. "Did they mention the Vigil?"

"Your aunt Caris did, said they might be able to help. Your father said no, anything but that."

Would he carry the day though? When it came to emotionally fraught situations, he almost always deferred to his sisters. And if he didn't believe I was truly his daughter, what reason would he have to defend me?

"They worry. Talk of a search, but cannot agree on how to do even that. I judged it time to return."

I stood, my legs pinpricking as the blood rushed through them. "Riven, will you take me to the gardens? I'd like to try to speak to Ada and Ainslie before the rest."

"Yes. Then I'll call at the front, if you wish."

I nodded, and it was done. After Riven left, I slipped in the back door and ascended the stairs to my sisters' bedchamber.

When I stepped into the room, Ada rushed toward me. "Thank goodness, you're safe. We were so worried."

Ainslie hovered alongside. "Where have you been?"

"I was examining the scene of the attack with Riven."

Ada drew back. "And did you learn anything?"

"Very little. He confirmed that a high fae instigated the attacks and enlisted the bau. There's some hint that the responsible fae was Ainslie's bargain-holder—but that could also be a misdirect."

"This wretched bargain." Ainslie dug her nails into the binding mark, streaking red among the silver. "It seems I'm destined to endanger everyone else's life along with my own."

"Don't say that—the matter is far from settled."

She shook her head. "I've never seen Father and our aunts like this. Whatever comes of the bargain, the attack has done damage beyond measure."

My throat tightened. "In the carriage, did they hint at what they mean to do about me?"

"They said almost nothing. I suppose they meant to save it for the privacy of home." Ada's eyes brimmed with tears. "Oh, Jessa, I'm sorry. It's dreadfully unfair that you should be treated so, when we all share the same blood. We should go confess the whole—"

"Not yet." Not until I knew what they meant to do. I lifted Jade to my chest and buried my cold fingers in her thick fur.

Ainslie paced the room. "Between the three of us, surely we can make them see reason."

"Can we? You knew the truth, and yet you were afraid."

"Yes, we were. The bau . . . It was all so sudden, and you seemed so very altered. You looked . . . I cannot explain it."

"I know." I'd seen such a change before in Riven and Lord West, and I'd every notion of how frightening the alteration could be, even when it was just a hint of fae nature bleeding through, rather than a full transformation.

"I think all along the idea of being fae felt like an abstraction, but seeing you that way made it so very real. I never dreamed that's what it meant." Ada reached out and gripped my hand. "But I'm sorry that we made you feel as though we . . . no longer supported you."

"As am I," Ainslie said.

"You want nothing to do with your fae nature."

She moved to my other side and wrapped her arm about my shoulders. "But it doesn't mean I want nothing to do with you. Whatever you choose, we'll always be sisters."

I couldn't allow myself to relax into her embrace, not if I wished to retain control of my emotions. "We need to talk to Father and our aunts, before they act in a way that cannot be reversed."

They nodded, and together we descended the stairs. Elevated voices echoed down the corridor, Aunt Melisina's strident tones rising above the rest. "Whatever the case, we cannot simply allow her to wander the streets of Avons at this hour, alone and unprotected. Think of what might become of her."

"Begging pardon for my boldness, Lady Stanford." Uncharacteristic firmness marked Dreda's words. "But I believe Miss Jessa has demonstrated she's quite capable of protecting herself. If the bau did not harm her, I don't think a common footpad will."

"When I want the opinion of the hired help, I'll ask for it,"

Aunt Melisina snapped. "I intend to ensure her safe return so we may get to the bottom of this, which means there's nothing for it but to try to conduct some sort of discreet search."

Because she wanted to make sure I was well or because she wished to hush up the situation? I stepped into the room. "I am thankful for your concern, but please refrain from addressing Dreda in such a fashion. She's far more than hired help."

Aunt Melisina sputtered slightly, the color washing from her face, while Aunt Caris shrank back. She motioned for Ada and Ainslie to join her, and they took up chairs next to her while I remained stationed near the door.

"Jess." Lovell, who was ensconced on the settee, struggled to push himself up. "Where have you been? We thought—"

"I required some time to think, and I believed all of you did as well."

Before they could reply, Riven released the glamour shrouding him and stepped into the doorway, allowing my family to catch sight of him.

Aunt Melisina's hand flew to her throat. "Lord Riven, I didn't realize you'd called. Holden should have—I'm afraid we must request you return another time. We have family matters to discuss."

Riven halted less than an arm's length away, close enough that the scent of sun-drenched fir swept over me. He arched a brow at her. "It isn't convenient for me to return later. You may carry on."

"This is a private affair—"

"He knows, Aunt Melisina."

She inhaled sharply. "You mean to say you've hidden appalling things from your family and taken a near stranger into your confidence? You risked bringing ruin upon us all and—"

"Mother, that's enough." Lovell spoke with unfamiliar sharpness. "Jess, why did you tell him and not us?"

"Lord Riven figured it out, and he's been . . . helping me to try to find the truth of the matter. Dealing with these sorts of affairs is his line of work."

"And you didn't think we'd try to help?" Furrows etched deeper along his mouth, which was drawn tight with pain.

"I didn't know how you would feel or what you would think." My voice held a ragged edge. Calm, I must keep calm, else the whole situation would descend into chaos. I forced myself to settle into a chair and fold my hands in my lap. "I hardly knew what to think myself. And it seemed an unfair burden to place upon you."

"Not a burden. We needed to know." He drew a labored breath. "Whatever it is, we can figure it out. Solve the problem."

Evidently, Aunt Melisina felt the moment had come to retake control. Her lips pinched in a tight line, and she turned to Father. "Alden, do you truly intend the chaperone should stay for this?"

"She was present in the glade, so perhaps it's for the best." Father blinked at me through his spectacles, appearing altogether lost.

Aunt Melisina pivoted to face Dreda. "If you mean to remain, you shall not speak of what's transpired to anyone, or I shall see you never find employment in Byren again."

"You need make no such demands." Though pale enough that her freckles stood out stark, Dreda kept her voice steady. "If you want to know the truth as badly as you claim, I will give you some. I met Miss Jessa when she saved me from being plagued by an Otherworldly creature. I've kept her secrets since I first met her, as she's kept mine, and I'd no more turn her over to the Vigil than chop off my right hand. Can you say the same, any of you?"

Aunt Melisina staggered back as though Dreda had struck her, and Aunt Caris regarded her with brimming eyes. "We only thought, perhaps, that we should consult someone about Jessa's . . . situation. The Vigil is a natural choice. Who else would know what to do?"

The slightest storm charge pricked at the air, and Riven angled toward Aunt Caris. "Why should you need to consult someone?"

Her hand fluttered to the lace at her throat, now bramble snagged and bedraggled. "You were not there, Lord Riven. Jessa . . . She was not herself. Her actions in the clearing . . ."

"Were Other in nature? As Jessa said, I'm aware." His eyes glittered, shards of gold piercing the green. Yet he kept his Other nature deeply veiled.

She plucked nervously at the fraying threads. "I would not go so far as to say—"

Aunt Melisina spread her hands. "What else could they be, sister? It was no natural ability. Jessa, it's clear Other has corrupted you somehow, but don't worry, we will find a way to remedy the situation."

"What if there is no way to help?" I couldn't speak above a whisper. "What if this—what you saw—is what I am? What if it will never change?"

She faltered, her gaze lowering. If they feared me—and I could not blame them for doing so, after such a shocking and unexpected display of my Other nature—I couldn't remain here, whether or not they meant to turn me over to the Vigil. Jade leapt upon my lap, and I pulled her close. "If . . . if you don't want me to stay, I can remove to Wyncourt for the evening, while you consider what you must do."

"Pish, child. Of course you're not to leave." Aunt Melisina frowned. "But we have questions, things we must understand."

Father pushed up his spectacles. "In the clearing you said you were—still yourself. But no mortal can wield such powers. Unless perhaps aided by alchemy." Hope tinged his voice. "You've visited the guild—"

"It's not alchemy. I'll do my best to explain." The blackness beyond the windows concealed the garden from view, but their songs surged through the glass, bolstering me. "When I was a child, Father, we spoke of the aberrations I experienced. You attributed them to grief over Mother's death and told me I must learn to conceal them."

"I remember." His hands plucked at the fringe on the pillow

beside him, as if by ordering the jumbled tassels he could sort the disordered emotions of the room.

"Over time, it became evident that what I perceived was not a grief-born aberration, but something else altogether." I rested my chin on Jade's head. "The full account is far too long to give now, but the truth is that . . . I'm fae."

"Pish! That's impossible." Yet Aunt Melisina's voice held an uncharacteristic quaver.

Aunt Caris sank back into her chair, pale and colorless. "Alden, this is beyond us all. Perhaps we'd best send her to Caldwell House for a time, while we sort the matter and get the help she needs. I know you're opposed to the Vigil—"

"They make everything worse." His voice was hoarse.

"But a claim of this sort—we cannot possibly keep her here, not until we've gotten to the truth of the matter."

"Aunt Caris, I've told you the truth. I know it's difficult to believe, but—"

"My niece is not fae. Such a thing cannot be, that mortals and fae, that they . . ." Her voice broke. "Either you're mistaken and in need of our help—or you're not Jessa, and you've stolen her somehow."

My vision blurred, and words deserted me. In the silence, the tick of the mantel clock sounded unbearably loud.

And the storm charge to the air strengthened, a gathering pressure that built in the corners of the room. "Do you doubt the evidence you've witnessed?" Riven asked.

"Lord Riven, it isn't proper for you to be here for this discussion. I know you intended to court Jessa, but the situation has changed, and—"

"My interests in the matter have not." His voice was dangerously low. "I intend to remain."

Both my aunts attempted to speak at once.

"Quiet." Diamond sparks of light, concealed by glamour from mortal eyes, but brilliant and hard-edged to my own, shimmered about him. Though nothing in his demeanor hinted at a fae nature, he appeared every inch a mortal lord, imperious and commanding. "It's time for you to listen. The Jessa you've always known is the same one that stands before you now, as fae. And you should be thankful for it, else you'd already lack several other members of this family. Lovell would be dead at the hands of the Crimson Tattoo Killer if Jessa hadn't gone to the Otherworld and ended the life of the killer before he could return to claim Lovell."

A shock seemed to electrify the room.

This wasn't what I wanted. "Lord Riven—"

"Ada would be dead too, if Jessa hadn't fashioned a cure for the venom she received—which wasn't that of a serpent, but a basilisk. Like most of Byren, you're unaware of the forces arrayed against you—it's fortunate for you that Jessa *is* fae, and that she has your interests in mind."

"Riven, please." No one chastised me for dropping the proper *lord*; perhaps they no longer dared.

"If they are to make a decision, it should not be in ignorance." He braced his hands on his hips, turning to regard them. "This world is in danger. Jessa serves as evidence that there's more at work than you understand. Do not be swift to reject the few allies you possess. Seek rather to know your true enemy and so preserve that which matters."

Jade nuzzled my chin. *He says to remind you that you wished to stay near, whatever it took. This is what it takes—another fear, greater than the first.*

Perhaps Riven was right, but if they accepted me only because I might somehow protect them, because they feared something else more—I clutched Jade closer. He'd exposed far more than I ever wanted them to see or know, yet I couldn't deny he'd changed the mood in the room. They were afraid, but the fear was no longer directed at me, rather to the great unknown.

"I've long believed that Other encroaches, but this . . ." Father shook his head.

"Lord Riven says you serve as evidence of the presence of

Other." Lovell scrubbed his hand across his jaw. "But I still don't understand. If you aren't a changeling, then what?"

Once spoken, the truth could never be taken back—and it would steal from Father the memories he cherished. My stomach twisted. "There's much I still don't understand, but I've learned that high fae struggle to have children, and therefore have a practice of coercing mortal women to bear them. I thought at first perhaps that's what happened to Mother, that a fae . . . forced himself upon her, and I was the result." Sharp gasps punctuated my words, but I did not stop, could not stop. "Since then, I have uncovered evidence to the contrary. Rather, I am fae because Mother was."

All the life vanished from Father's eyes, like a flame snuffed from a candle, leaving only a guttering wick. He did not move, did not speak, did not question. Only sat.

Aunt Melisina appeared shaken. "But fae . . . surely they do not dally with mortals?"

"Unfortunately, they do."

"Then Ada and Ainslie . . ."

"Yes, Aunt." Ada spoke soft and low.

Unnaturally bright spots of color blossomed on Aunt Caris's pale cheeks, and she clutched at Aunt Melisina's arm like one who sought deliverance from drowning. "What are we to do?"

"We can forsake our fae nature, if we choose," Ainslie said. "Become fully mortal once more."

"Why didn't someone say that in the first place? That's excellent." Aunt Melisina straightened, shaking off Aunt Caris's hold. "This affair can soon be mended. Renounce whatever you need to, and we can go back to life as usual. It makes no sense how such a thing can be, yet nothing about the Otherworld follows order or reason. We must simply count our blessings that a way out remains."

She could not possibly think we'd return to life as usual under any circumstance—but perhaps she fought to cling to normalcy as desperately as I had. Father still sat motionless, his hands pressed to his chest as though he bled out from a mortal wound, and Aunt Caris was trembling like a leaf caught in a tempest.

The shards of light about Riven sharpened further. "And if Jessa does not desire to become mortal?"

"Why in the Crossings wouldn't she?"

Before Riven could deliver whatever remark he intended—and it would doubtless be scathing—I leaned forward. "It's not that simple. As Riven indicated, there's a great deal more at work here, some of which relates to the attack today. May I share, Ainslie?"

She nodded.

"Ainslie is bound by bargain to a high fae. If we cannot free her, she may well lose her life. And if I forsake my fae nature, I lose any ability to offer aid."

If I had made this confession before today, it was likely they would have consigned me to the Institutions or at least to a physician's care—it sounded like utter madness. But they'd witnessed the bau materialize, witnessed Jade's transformation and my own affinities. Now they'd little choice but to believe.

Dreda looked pale—of all of them, she best understood what it was to be afflicted by fae. Aunt Melisina sat motionless, and silent tears trickled down Aunt Caris's face, while Ada and Ainslie remained silent, tension evident in every line of their bodies. As for Father, he gave no sign of life, no indication my words pierced the deep fog that had fallen over him. Could he find his footing again, after this blow?

I made a tentative movement toward him. "Father, are you well?"

He just shook his head, slowly, slowly.

And Aunt Melisina straightened, schooling her features to their usual calm mask. "It is evident we will reach no reasonable conclusion tonight, we're all far too wrung out. Caris, if you don't mind me ordering a guest room prepared, I'll remain here to tend Lovell."

Lovell. I'd not once considered the extent of his injuries. I turned toward him. "What did the physician say?"

"A few cracked ribs, some bruising." He started to wave his hand, then appeared to think better of it. "Nothing to worry about."

"That is *not* what he said." Aunt Melisina's lips firmed. "He said on no account is Lovell to be moved for several days, because he may have received injuries we cannot see. He's to rest and allow himself to recover." She tucked a blanket about him. "As for the rest—we can discuss matters further in the morning, and I'm sure we'll come up with a sensible plan. Jessa, I trust you'll stay put until then?"

"I promise I'll be here in the morning."

Whatever might come.

CHAPTER 43

Ivy surrounded me, brushing my face, singing softly of peace and safety, drawing me toward wakefulness. I sat upright in bed, and it rustled around me, vibrant and aware. How?

Early morning light bathed the deep green with soft gold and ivory. Somehow I'd drawn the ivy through the window during the night. It had twined around the latch and pulled it open, then woven a cocoon of sorts about me, its leaves overlaying my bedchamber, another irrevocable sign that my Other nature strengthened. I gently brushed it from my face. When I'd retired last night, I expected to remain awake for hours, sifting through every nuance of conversation, every inflection of voice and expression. Yet I'd collapsed instead into deep slumber, and no wonder, with the ivy whispering soothing melodies in my ears as I slept. The lattice of vines rustled with contentment, as though satisfied with a job well completed.

I pulled my knees to my chest. What was to be done? After the conversation with my family, Riven and I had spoken briefly in the garden, just long enough to agree that we would meet at Wyncourt the following morning, after I'd fetched the statuette from Thea and he'd satisfied his duties at court. Though it might have nothing to do with the bau attack, it didn't seem prudent to store it in her home—nor was Riven willing to examine it with her present. Yet I didn't think I could escape the house without another fraught conversation.

Perhaps I could break the fast before the rest of the family rose, never mind that it would only postpone the inevitable. I twined my fingers through the ivy, bidding it return to its proper place. Coil by coil, it withdrew, the final strand pulling the window shut behind it.

Jade stretched, her front paws kneading the bedcovers. *You're developing more precision.*

But at what cost? Never mind that either—I didn't want to think on it too long. I stroked the starflower patch on Jade's chest, then hurried through my ablutions before descending the stairs. Ordinarily, the dining room would have been empty at this hour, but when I stepped over the threshold, Aunt Caris, Aunt Melisina, and Father abruptly stopped talking.

None of them looked at me, and an uncomfortable silence descended. The backs of my eyes pricked—no, not now. I pulled the numbness of the day before about me like a blanket. Perhaps if I did so long enough, I would deaden the pain once and for all.

Finally, Aunt Melisina cleared her throat. "Come in, Jessa. Don't dally in the doorway."

Appetite vanishing, I settled into my usual seat, and Jade perched in the chair next to me. Aunt Caris blotted her lips with a napkin, then offered a quiet greeting. Father said nothing.

"We've been talking." Aunt Melisina poured a cup of tea and handed it to me. "This situation must be remedied, but of course not at the expense of any of your lives."

"Were there an easy solution, I assure you we'd have taken it already."

She passed the sugar. "By we, you mean you and Lord Riven?"

"Yes, along with Ada and Ainslie."

Father bestirred himself at last. "Who is Lord Riven,

precisely? He seemed undisturbed by circumstances that would trouble the calmest of men."

Riven had respected my wishes; I must also respect his and keep his fae nature a secret, however little I wished to offer further half-truths. "He's an investigator for the king, and he has a great deal of experience in dealing with Otherworldly matters."

"How fortunate." Aunt Melisina selected a pastry from the tray before her. "Perhaps matters may not be as bleak as we feared. We shall find a path forward, make no mistake. Once this situation is dealt with, you may still make a good match and secure your future. Charles is already taken with Ainslie, so if we can simply keep this affair quiet, it may all turn out fine in the end, once you've embraced your mortal nature and these . . . distressing events have passed into distant memory."

Aunt Caris murmured agreement.

And I crumbled a scone into dust. After all the revelations of last night, my aunts were still thinking about seeing my sisters and me well-wed?

It is the way of the mortal world. You know that.

Jade was right. It was the way of this world, and it was the way of my aunts to cope with matters beyond their ken—by trying to rebuild the family I'd shattered. They could imagine no better or safer future for me, and they took hope in the fact I was not so far gone as to make that impossible. Perhaps I should be encouraged that they'd not given up on me altogether— though it seemed their approval hinged on my forsaking my fae nature as soon as I possibly could. I brushed the crumbs from my fingers.

"Aunt Melisina, I . . . appreciate your desire to help." I'd rather confront another bau than say what I must. "But it's no longer for you to decide what becomes of me. If you feel I must leave, then of course, I'll respect your wishes. But if I stay, I require liberty to manage the situation as I see best. Any discussion of my fae nature must wait. And if I'm to deal with the matter at hand of Ainslie and the bargain, I must run several errands this morning."

In the silence that followed, my pulse roared.

Aunt Melisina returned her cup to its saucer with a decided clink. "Whatever your purpose, you should take Miss Twells. Appearances must be maintained while matters are sorted—"

"I don't mean to burn any bridges in this world, but there are other ways of concealing my movements to satisfy convention." With difficulty, I steadied my voice. "This time I'll not be taking Miss Twells, though I'm thankful for the assistance she's offered."

Aunt Melisina sniffed, but she made no further protest. Aunt Caris shook her head sadly. "It seems we cannot stop you, only hope you'll see sense in time."

I never thought I'd long for her clucking and worrying, her demands for propriety to be heeded—oh, I was being ridiculous. I swallowed a large sip of tea, and it scalded my throat.

"Where do you intend to go?" Father arranged the food on his plate in straight lines.

"To call on Mrs. Darrington, then to Wyncourt."

He slowly straightened. "Those creatures, the bau . . . if you're roaming Avons, are you likely to meet more of them?"

"I don't think so, but I'll be careful."

He blinked rapidly. "All along, I thought I was protecting you all by seeking answers about Kensa's death. And I had everything wrong."

"Not everything—"

"Everything that mattered." His shoulders drew inward. "Will you take the carriage at least?"

"If you wish it." I wanted to offer comfort, but did not know if it would be welcome—and I could endure the atmosphere of the room no longer. I fled with Jade clasped to my chest and Risha drifting alongside. While we waited by the door for the driver to bring the carriage, I inhaled the scents of sun-warmed stone and the sweet-orange solution used to scour the steps.

A rich golden sun adorned the bowl of blue sky overhead and glinted off the sovstone about me, the vibrant raiment of summer that graced Avons painful in its brilliance—and somehow *wrong*. I wished instead for leaden skies, for gathered fog and shadows with which to cloak myself, but the world about me stubbornly refused to join my mourning.

Risha dipped closer. "Are you angry?"

"About what?"

"I went for Riven as Jade ordered. I should not answer to another, only to you."

"Then why did you go?"

"Because I worried also, and I thought the Lord Arbiter would help."

I plucked a withered leaf from the potted astilbe growing alongside the door. "You have a will and a good mind and the ability to make choices for yourself. I'll confess, I'd not have chosen to send for Riven in the moment, but I'm not angry."

"Sad then? Something is wrong." She fluttered before my face, inspecting me. "But sad mortals cry and talk much about feelings. Before you talked; now you don't."

I let the leaf drift away. "There's nothing to discuss."

Jade chuffed. *How long will you tell yourself that?*

As long as I must. I cannot allow my emotions to consume me, or I'll fail to do what I must.

A middle ground might exist.

I could see none. The yawning chasm of pain and confusion and the expectations I dashed on every turn wished to swallow me. And the only thing that kept me from sinking into the abyss was the net I wove of theory and fact about the bargain and the bau and the missing. It was far easier to focus on those things than to consider what my family might eventually demand, so after I entered the carriage, I fixed my mind on how to obtain the statuette.

When I entered Thea's drawing room, she offered a warm welcome, her manner easy and familiar, not stilted as my family's had become. Here I was accepted, but only because she was blind to the truth. I fixed a smile on my face, but even so, her eyes narrowed.

"You look dreadful, Jessa. Are you quite well?"

"My family and I were attacked yesterday by bau."

She drew in a sharp breath. "Here in Avons?"

"Out in the countryside. It might link to the matter of the statuette. Thea, please, let me take it to Wyncourt." Despite my best efforts, my voice frayed. "The individual who can help does not wish to be known, but has agreed to meet me there to examine it—and then keep it safe, far from Avons. I cannot say more, not yet, but I'm asking you to trust me that this is the course that must be taken."

"You ask a good deal." Her gaze drifted beyond me to the fragmented map she'd pieced together, now whole within a gilded frame. "Ibbie trusted you implicitly, and you've given me no reason to do otherwise. If the statuette will not be in your keeping, where it might endanger you, then yes, take it. But I want a full report as soon as may be."

She accepted my word, even as I betrayed her trust. The figurines on the mantel stared down in silent condemnation. "Of course."

Thea sent her butler for the strongbox, then, once he departed, she withdrew the statuette and tucked it into a leather satchel. "Stay safe, and don't give me cause to regret this."

Mutely, I accepted the satchel, a chill seeping into my flesh. I couldn't escape to the haven of Wyncourt swiftly enough. When the carriage at last halted before the demesne, its sprawling expanse reached out as if in welcome, its soft honey and ivory tones warm in the sunlight.

I hurried up the stairs, and Danvers opened the door for me. "Miss Jessa! It's a pleasure to see you."

"Likewise." I moved into the entry, and spice-sweet air tugged at my skirts and caressed my face as Wyncourt made its pleasure known.

He gave a slight bow. "May we assist you in any way?"

"No, thank you, I'll just be spending some time in the study." With that, I swept into the too-tidy room, now devoid of the life and clutter that Ibbie had brought to it. Even her desk stood in stately order. I ran my fingers across its polished surface. If she were here, what would she say to all this?

I'd only a heartbeat to consider before Riven appeared. Though he couldn't have slept between the demands of his court and his swift return to Avons, his eyes remained bright and alert, his attire as immaculate as ever. "You have the item?"

I withdrew the statuette from my reticule and handed it to him, the smooth, cold ivory sending a spider-skittering sensation up my arm.

Riven accepted it, grim lines creasing his face. He gripped the body, then reached for the head. Did he mean to open it here and now? I tensed, and Wyncourt bristled about me, its defenses responding to my emotions.

With a swift motion, he twisted away the top of the figurine, revealing a glittering powder within. A metallic, earthy odor wafted from it.

Wyncourt creaked and groaned, Risha darted behind me, and Jade rumbled low in her chest. I instinctively drew back. "Do you know what it is?"

"Pyske-dust." Riven clapped the head back on the statuette, his jaw set. "Both the production and use of it violate the laws of our world."

"Is it anything like the jewel of blood that Mr. Heard gave me?" A pyske had once crafted that pendant from its own blood, forming a powerful object of protection, the loss of which I still regretted.

"Not in the way you're thinking. Every element within the body of a pyske holds great power. Some things, like the blood used to forge that jewel, can be given willingly, and these they craft with their own workings."

I gripped the edge of the desk. "But this?"

"It's pyske bone." His mouth tightened. "To procure it, pyske must be killed, then their bones removed, dried, and ground into the powder you see."

"That's . . ." The room spun slightly, and I sank onto the

chaise, bereft of words. "Since it's from your world, how can mortals consume it without dying?"

"What's stored here has been highly adulterated with materials from this world and woven with workings to encourage the mortal body to accept it. Very little actual pyske bone remains, else it would have destroyed the recipients. Someone formulated this with great care. My guess is they experimented for a long time on disposable mortals to find the exact level of tolerance."

I pressed my fingers to my lips. A small, warm breeze gusted about me, as though Wyncourt sought to console. But no consolation could erase the brutal truth.

"The formulation allowed the mortals to survive, but consuming it would have changed them—and they'd find the substance highly addictive." He perched the statuette on the desk, and its twisted features mocked me.

"Then that alone might have compelled them to travel to the Otherworld. Perhaps that was the role of the Collectors, to provide the initial supply, then tell them they must go through the passing to obtain more?" Even as I spoke, I found myself unsatisfied. It was an unchancy plan, and one that revealed far more knowledge of the Otherworld than fae were inclined to grant mortals. I must be missing something.

"The Collectors may be responsible for the initial distribution, but I find it very unlikely they know what they're doing or that they're involved in suggesting mortals venture into the Otherworld. That would rouse too many suspicions, and this fae has been discreet. Besides, it's not necessary. The pyske-dust alone could prove a sufficient lure. Consuming it would leave the recipients incredibly vulnerable to the liminal realm—and to any suggestions provided there. The fae responsible could simply issue a command and force them to the Otherworld. In their susceptible state, they'd be almost powerless to resist."

"Which would allow this fae to remain untraceable."

"Yes. But the plan has its own risks. As I said, its production, use, and possession violate our laws."

Whatever the cruelty of the fae, at least they drew the line at mass murder for the production of illicit substances. "So why take the risk? What do they want so many mortals for?"

"None of the prospects are good. However, it's particularly troubling that whoever has claimed them isn't flaunting their new possessions."

"Why troubling?"

"There aren't many unapproved uses of mortals. Those that are—you wouldn't want to consider them."

Did he speak of the transformation of mortals to monsters? Or was that an approved usage of the vulnerable? "Do you think—"

"*There* you are." Ainslie burst into the room, Ada close on her heels. "Aunt Melisina informed us that you'd gone to call on Mrs. Darrington and to Wyncourt, but we missed you at Mrs. Darrington's, and we hoped to catch you here—oh."

She blanched, her gaze fixed on the statuette Riven held, then she slowly sank to the floor, her skirts pooling about her.

Ada's breath caught. "Ainslie? What's wrong?"

"She's remembering." Riven's features sharpened.

I shivered slightly. Now that her memories had surfaced, he could compel her to speak truth—as he had Lord Blackburn and Mocvar. If I understood rightly, because Ainslie was fae, he needed no permission from her. I wanted to plead with him to refrain, but we required the truth, Ainslie most of all. So I steeled myself for what must come.

Sparks of light flared about Riven as he strode toward Ainslie. "Tell me what you recall."

Her shoulders scooped inward. "She bound me to do it, and I wanted to stop, I knew . . . I could tell that it was hurting them, in those few moments where I could think, could remember, just long enough until the deed was done and the memory gone. But I couldn't stop, I can't stop . . . not now, not ever. Not till she's done."

The pressure in the air tightened my chest, and the watchfulness of Wyncourt prickled my skin. It did not wholly approve of Riven's exercise of power within its walls, and it stood wary vigil.

Ada moved toward Ainslie, but Riven checked her with a sharp gesture of his hand. "What was your bargain?"

"I can't . . . It's too hard."

The scent of storm swirled through the air, and the light about Riven formed jagged spears. "You will."

She remembered, so why was she resisting? Had she been ordered not to confess? Ada started forward, and I caught her arm. "Wait."

Ainslie spoke, her voice strangled. "I am to give the dust to society members who . . . who struggle, to tell them it will lift their spirits. I must hand over the pyske-dust to one each month, more if I can avoid attracting notice—no one must see or know. I had to wait until spring to begin. That's what she said. Every few weeks, there was a new statuette, I think . . . It all tumbles together so."

Ada was trembling in my arms, and I felt as though brambles snarled in my chest. The fae who held Ainslie's bargain, who'd taken pleasure in tormenting her, was also the one claiming the missing mortals. I'd hoped to find some link, felt it existed, feared it did not—but this? Why, *why* would Ainslie have ever agreed to such a dreadful thing?

"What were you offered in exchange?" Compulsion deepened his voice.

Wyncourt bristled, and I pressed my hands flat against the wall, the workings springing vibrant into my mind, prepared to defend should this power turn against me. "Allow him," I murmured. "Lord Riven has my blessing."

Though I did not know how much longer I could endure seeing Ainslie so. She rocked back and forth, her hands pressed to her temples. "I don't . . . I can't remember."

"You can. And you will speak."

The unbearable weight of compulsion saturated the air, until even I felt the urge to confess something, anything to relieve the sense of pressure. Ada pressed her lips together, her lashes damp.

"She said she needed help." The words wrenched from Ainslie. "She asked if I would help her. When I said yes, she made the mark. She gave nothing, only took and took . . ." She wrapped her arms around her knees, burying her head in them.

Ada collapsed next to her, looking up at Riven. "Please stop. She can take no more."

Amber blades of light swept over Ainslie, then Riven nodded. "She knows nothing else."

"You've hurt her." Ada's voice shook.

"She'll recover. It's unpleasant, but a truth compulsion doesn't damage like entering the mindscape—as long as she can recall of her own accord, she can speak without lasting harm." Riven's voice held no inflection. "I imagine she was glamoured to forget, and if she somehow remembered, to hold her peace— thus the pain as her mind struggled to reconcile it all. Very little was left to chance. Doubtless the glamour would have held had the statuette not triggered her memory in our presence. At the time of the bargain, her bargain-holder could not have possibly predicted the presence of an arbiter to force the truth to surface."

I sank down next to Ainslie, gently rubbing her cold hands. "But how could a bargain be formed if nothing was offered in exchange?"

"If Ainslie agreed to an unspecified request for help, she bound herself unaware. Someone crafted the situation with care to appeal to her generous nature, which suggests she was specifi- cally targeted, and if the right wording was used, she might have received nothing in exchange."

"And that would be deemed a bargain?"

"If she swore to help without setting any terms or limits, yes." Riven angled away, his jaw tight. "I cannot explain why, but the way this unfolded indicates the bargain-holder knew she was fae."

If this bargain-holder knew of our heritage, even before we did—what did that mean? My pulse throbbed unsteadily at the base of my throat. "And the Collector . . . was he also bound by bargain?"

"Very likely. Now that we know, the matter will be simple enough to confirm. More care would have to be taken with forming those bargains with mortals, but not much more, given the Collectors forsake much of their protections by venturing into the Otherworld and stealing from it," Riven said. "I imagine your Collector is not the only one, given the number who have vanished. The fae in question is taking care—limiting how many at a time are claimed, making patterns more difficult to detect."

That meant in order to stem the tide of stolen mortals, we had to not only break Ainslie's bargain but the rest of the bargains the fae lady held. And what of the mortals she'd taken? Could they be restored, or had they already suffered an irreversible fate? The magnitude of the situation rooted me in place alongside Ainslie.

"Send for tea for your sisters." Riven's gaze swept over Ainslie. "I want a word in private."

As did I. Because I could see only one possible way forward. Until this discovery, we'd had avenues to explore in this world. But now that we'd uncovered the purpose of her bargain, as well as her connection to the missing persons, Byren had nothing more to offer. With what we'd gained along the way, we could finally venture into the Otherworld without walking blind. We knew that the bargain-holder belonged to the Court of Dusk, and given that she'd sent a plant from the royal gardens, she likely held a high position. Furthermore, she possessed a strong liminal affinity, and I'd experienced a sense of her workings through the nightspire. Could I recognize them again, if I encountered them? Regardless, we now had some chance of identifying her, and I must try. I pressed to my feet. "Ada, why don't you and Ainslie retire to the drawing room? I'll send for refreshments as Riven suggested. And perhaps some brandy as well."

She nodded and helped Ainslie up while I went to give Danvers instruction. When I returned to Riven, I'd marshaled my thoughts and prepared for the argument that would surely follow. "I don't think we can progress any further in this world, not with what we've learned. And we can't afford to wait indefinitely to find the bargain-holder—Ainslie doesn't have that kind of time."

"I agree."

I'd anticipated debate, not acquiescence. I collapsed into the chaise, and the stiff pillows behind me rustled. "Then you've no objection to me venturing into the Otherworld?"

"My previous objection was to you striking out blind and without the proper preparation. It's still a tremendous risk, but now a calculated one, perhaps even a necessity, since this involves the Court of Dusk. I may enter, but I'm constrained by the terms between our courts to refrain from using my abilities as arbiter to force truth from its denizens. Only their own arbiter may make such demands." Riven took the chair across from me, stretching out his legs. "I thought it might come to this, so I've made arrangements with Nikol—found a way for both of us to enter the Court of Dusk, one that will cover for your lack of connection and experience with the Otherworld."

My breath caught. "Nikol? I thought the Courts of Silver and Dusk were at odds."

"They are. Their relations have been strained ever since the Court of Silver tried to annex the Court of Dusk during the reign of King Arven. That forced the current king into alliance with our court for protection."

The convoluted fae politics made my temples throb. "If that's the case, then how could he offer assistance?"

"In actuality, it made him perfectly positioned to do so without raising suspicion. Nikol serves as the queen's chief huntsman. That means a great many things, but one of them is that he's responsible for the arrangement of the high summer hunt, a traditional ceremony that occurs in the Court of Silver each year." He leaned back. "To create a new, challenging experience each year for decades on end is no easy task. I offered to secure the Court of Dusk as a hunting ground and their elusive shadow-drakes as quarry."

"And that benefits Nikol because it's an unusual experience for the members of his court?"

"Yes, and because it successfully opens relations between the two courts once more, both of which have gained him high marks with his queen. She believes he's negotiated all this on her behalf."

"But that cannot please your king."

"On the contrary." The green of his eyes brightened. "It gives us an excellent chance for surveillance, because one of the terms I suggested to the Court of Dusk is that they require an equal number of seats in the hunt—five of which they'd grant to the Court of Gold. My king has agreed that you and I may take two of them."

Doubtless, that would displease many fae. Did it mean I'd stirred enmity even before showing my face? I could cast no aspersions on the plan, but a flutter of uncertainty worked through my chest. "What advantage does that give your court?"

"It gives my king a chance to study you through whatever proxies he sends. And it allows me to observe all the highest-ranking members of the Court of Silver—an intelligence opportunity that hasn't come our way in a long time." A small spark of light danced between his fingers. "Furthermore, it is tradition that the Court of Silver queen grants the winner of the hunt a boon. For her to owe a favor to either the Courts of Dusk or Gold would be a tremendous advantage—naturally, she will set limits, but each faction will play to win."

My head spun. "And you just . . . knew they'd agree?"

"It was a bit more complicated than that, but yes. Each stands to gain enough to take a risk." He gave a slight shrug. "Knowing what each party in play desires and offering it to them gives one tremendous leverage. Still, it could have come to nothing. Such things are always touchy, and I didn't want you to rely on an event that might not come to pass—or might never be needed."

I stared unseeing at the mantel clock, its slow tick overloud in the silence. That he'd orchestrated all this . . . "How long did it take for you to arrange this?"

"I've been working on it since the nightspire arrived."

He'd spoken at times about laying plans, about business to attend to in his world, but I never dreamt it was to this extent. "Riven, I . . . we owe you more than it's ever possible to repay."

All expression vanished from his face. "No debts. This satisfies my king as well. If someone has found a way to siphon mortals into the Court of Dusk, he wants to know."

"Even so, thank you." I tilted my head. "But what if I had not wished to go?"

"I didn't deem that likely. I found the odds much higher that you'd try to strike out before arrangements had been made." He studied me, as if weighing his words. "I'd prefer to leave at once, but it will be a few more days before fae start to gather for the hunt. It might be just as well, because there's something we must discuss beforehand—"

The door creaked open, and Ada slipped in. "Ainslie is in considerable distress, now that she's realized what she's done. She's determined she must confess to the Magistry, and she won't listen to reason. Oh, Jessa, if she tells them, they'll surely seek to confine her."

"More likely they'd turn her over to the Vigil." I crossed to the doorway. "If she must speak to someone, it should be Mr. Burke."

"Then we must act swiftly. She's already sent for Mr. Redgrave, saying she must speak with him before she goes to the Magister."

Whatever Riven desired to say would have to wait. I hurried after Ada, and he kept pace with his long, steady stride.

Ainslie sat motionless in a chair, her eyes wide and tormented. "Don't try to dissuade me, Jessa. This can't go on—*I* can't go on luring people to their deaths. I've remembered now, but what if the bargain drives it from my mind again? What if I cannot stop myself—"

"You can't stop it." Riven filled the doorway behind me. "If you resist, the binding will kill you, assuming you have the fortitude to withstand the compulsion. Almost no one does. For a bargain binds your will as well as your deeds."

She raised her chin. "Then so be it. I won't send anyone else to the Otherworld to die."

"Ainslie, no." Ada clutched at her, as if she could forcibly keep her from harm.

A bargain was binding, but perhaps . . . "Could there be a way for Ainslie to fulfill the letter of the bargain, but not the spirit, as Dreda did with Lord West?"

Riven nodded slowly. "It's possible. It would be easier if we knew the precise wording. The fae who holds the bargain has been very careful in all her actions so far. There may be no loophole."

"Then let me buy her time." Ada straightened. "She only has to give the pyske-dust to one individual each month. Next time, she must give it to me."

Ainslie shook her head. "Absolutely not."

"We need to give Jessa and Riven a chance to find the fae in question and fix this," Ada said. "If I know what I'm taking, it lessens the danger."

"But we cannot be sure. And I cannot be responsible for your death or enslavement—I cannot." Ainslie's breath shuddered.

"You need to remove sentiment from the equation. Ada's plan is sensible." The calmness of Riven's voice cut through the rising emotion in the room. "It's unlikely a quantity was specified in the bargain, only that you ensured they took some. For most mortals that would be enough to ensnare them. However, Ada is fae, and if she takes only a grain, it will do very little."

"Besides which, if Lianne was the last one you gave pyske-dust to, we have some time left," Ada said.

And Ainslie's involvement explained how Lianne had been able to "afford" it. Doubtless, she'd just given it to her, compelled to fulfill the bargain the best she could under our watch, which was why Lianne didn't fit the profile of the rest.

"Riven and I were working on a plan." Before I could elaborate, footsteps approached. Riven shrouded himself in glamour as Danvers entered the room.

"Mr. and Miss Redgrave have arrived. Do you wish to see them here?"

"Show them to the morning room. We'll join them shortly." I rubbed my aching temples. Before things got entirely out of hand and Ainslie insisted on marching down to the Magistry, I needed to act. "And Danvers, please send an urgent message to Mr. Burke of the Avons Magistry requesting that he come to Wyncourt as soon as possible."

"Very good, Miss Jessa. Is the footman to await a response?"

"That won't be necessary." If I knew anything about Mr. Burke, he'd come the moment he could disentangle from his duties.

As soon as Danvers left, Ada crossed her arms. "Ainslie, if you tell Mr. Redgrave this, he may feel obliged to take it to the Vigil—the true Vigil."

"If he did, it would be no more than I deserved." Her voice held a brittle quality.

"But you didn't enter the bargain willingly or for your own gain—you were deceived," I said. "You believed you were helping someone vulnerable."

"It doesn't matter, the result is the same. And I cannot keep Char—Mr. Redgrave waiting." Though she spoke with confidence, her lips trembled.

How would the Redgraves respond to this—a clear sign one of us had done harm to the mortals of Avons? I could not say, but I knew one thing for certain. If he meant to take her to the Vigil, I'd not stand by and watch.

CHAPTER 44

By the time we all trooped into the morning room, Wyncourt no longer bristled, but had subsided into a sort of wary stillness about the Redgraves. They sat beneath arched windows, fair and still, as if graven from ivory themselves.

When Ainslie appeared in the doorway, Mr. Redgrave's breath caught. He stood as if by instinct and took a half step forward. It must have taken considerable effort not to close the distance between them entirely.

"I wasn't expecting to meet an entire coalition." His attempt at a light tone fell flat, since concern emanated from every line of his body.

Though she tried to keep a steady voice, Ainslie couldn't conceal the tears shimmering in her eyes. "Forgive the audience, I felt I needed my sisters."

"And Lord Riven?" He lifted a brow.

"He's trying to help in the matter of my bargain." Her breath shuddered. "And that's why I asked you and Elodie to come as well, that and—I understand from Jessa that your family is investigating the matter of the missing individuals."

He nodded.

"Well, it seems we can . . . shed some light on the matter." Her usual articulate nature deserted her, and she faltered through the story of her bargain, the responsible fae, and how it linked to the missing people and their fate.

All the while, Elodie sat still as a china doll, the light from the window spilling over her pale features, while Mr. Redgrave's hands tightened to fists at his side.

At last, Ainslie straightened. "Whatever the cost, I swear that I will not give the pyske-dust to another innocent. But the harm I've done can't be undone, which is why I mean to go to the Magistry to confess. After what's passed between us, I felt you deserved to know first."

Mr. Redgrave just shook his head. Then, despite the impropriety, he crossed the room and pulled her into his arms. Ainslie gave a little gasp and buried her face in his chest.

Ada looked at me in question, and I nodded. He was what Ainslie needed right now—and what were proprieties compared to all she faced?

When he drew away a moment later, his features were set. "Going to the Magistry is ill-advised. They'll pull in the Everstone Vigil, and nothing you say will be heeded. You'll be subjected to—it will mean your death, because they'll keep you in circumstances that make it impossible for you to fulfill your bargain." A fierce light kindled in his eyes. "I want your word you won't go."

"How can I give it? I'm responsible for who knows how many missing."

"I have advised her to speak with Mr. Burke of the Magistry before taking this further." I stepped forward. "He can be trusted to advise on the situation."

"That's wise."

Ainslie shook her head. "You don't understand—"

"I understand that what you've done wasn't of your own free will. You're a victim as much as the rest."

"The same could be said of the basilisk that preyed in Withern." Ainslie's voice was choked. "Yet her life was forfeit."

"You haven't killed these people. As yet, no one knows what's become of them."

Elodie stirred and pressed to her feet. "Charles, we must speak."

Mr. Redgrave looked as if he might protest, but at last he turned to me. "Miss Jessa, is there somewhere we might talk in private?"

I tugged at the bellpull. "Danvers will show you to the drawing room."

Danvers soon fetched them, and when they disappeared through the doorway, I hurried to an interior wall. Right or wrong, I had to hear what they said, understand what they meant to do about Ainslie. I tugged off my gloves and brushed my fingers across the plastered surface. "Please, let me see."

The wall before me fell away, revealing a passage beyond, much like the one I'd used in the study long ago when I'd eavesdropped on Riven and Nikol. Such had been the shocks of the day that neither of my sisters so much as blinked. Without explanation, I entered the passageway, and the wall closed behind me. I moved toward the drawing room, and when I reached where I judged it to be, Wyncourt opened a small translucent pane in the wall.

I pressed aside the guilt I felt over eavesdropping—this was Ainslie's life at stake—and leaned forward for a better vantage.

Elodie had discarded her social mask—the sort of light, blank prettiness favored among young ladies—and she paced the room with an energetic step. "You mean to stand by Ainslie through this?"

"As I told her, she's as much a victim as the rest." Mr. Redgrave's jaw tightened. "What could be more in keeping with our creed than protecting her?"

"She has fae blood, Charles—and our vows are to protect mortals *from* fae. There are those in our family who will refuse to look past her heritage, even aside from the matter of her bargain."

"She might have fae blood, but she's been raised in this

world, and only just learned of her own nature. How does she truly differ from us?"

"How can you ask that? You witnessed what Jessa can do, and she only learned the truth shortly before Ainslie. Her situation makes it clear fae abilities could emerge at any time. And we've no understanding of what the repercussions might be—if such things erode mortal sensibilities over time." Elodie halted in front of Mr. Redgrave. "Will Ainslie be immortal? Would she remain tied to you, young and strong, while you age and eventually die? Have you considered any of this?"

"Day and night." He blew out a breath. "She confided in me that there's a way for her to embrace her mortal nature, but she cannot while bound in bargain."

"And you think, if freed, she'll follow through?"

"I don't know." He raked a hand through his hair. "But perhaps it's time to consider that fae might not always be the enemy."

"As Ceolman did? He trusted enough to go to his death thinking he'd secured freedom for mortals, and then fae twisted even that to their own ends."

Mr. Redgrave pinched the bridge of his nose. "Ainslie isn't like that—nor is Jessa, for that matter."

"Even if that's true—and I very much want to believe it so—we've lost so much fighting the Otherworld. It won't be easy for the rest of the family to let go of that. And if it comes to light that Ainslie participated in the dispersion of the pyske-dust—as it may, since they'll thoroughly investigate her the moment you announce your intentions—then she will appear to them like all the rest."

"Then what do you suggest? That we abandon her to her fate? Or turn her over to the First?" He flung the words like stones.

She sighed. "Whatever the family might say, I don't think we should turn her in. I agree that she needs our help, if possible, whatever trouble it might cause. But it would be safer for you if you put the prospect of a future with her from your mind."

She was right. If his interest in Ainslie earned Mr. Redgrave the enmity of his family and in turn brought Ainslie to the attention of the true Vigil, then both of them took a risk in pursuing a relationship rather than cutting ties.

"Whatever her heritage or the nature of the bargain binding her, I cannot imagine life without her," Charles said.

"But why? Why Ainslie? I'll grant she's remarkably beautiful—perhaps it's her fae blood—but plenty of other beauties would be glad to join their lives with a Redgrave. I've watched them make it known to you often enough."

"I know better than to choose only for beauty. You know that." His mouth crooked into a grin. "Even were I so thick-headed, Mother would ring a peal over me for such foolishness."

"I know. But I need to hear you say it, need to know *why*."

"Must love have a reason?" He attempted a light tone, but deeper emotion bled into his voice. It couldn't be an easy thing to discuss with one's sister.

"It must, when it requires skirting the very edges of our vows to support it."

"To think that some gentlemen live life without their sisters prying into all their affairs."

Elodie folded her arms. "*Charles*."

"I'll grant it's a valid question, under the circumstances. I assure you I've thought long and hard about what I owe the family—and what is owed Ainslie." His gaze became contemplative. "Grandfather has told me time and again, 'Marry someone you'd trust to hold your back when the fang-wolves circle.' I know Ainslie would, even without proper combat training. I watched her in Withern, when Ada was hurt and Jessa was missing. She stayed solid, supported her aunts, and helped hold her family together. Though she fits within society, she's *more*."

This was private, personal—I shouldn't listen, yet I couldn't afford not to. It was clear now that Mr. Redgrave meant to support Ainslie, but Elodie . . . her intentions were murkier.

He let out a breath. "Lest you accuse me of willfully seeing only what I want to see, I offer further proof. I told her my theories about Bradon, or the best I could around our constraints. Most women would have come over with the vapors—at least those that seem to buzz around most incessantly—but she had a great deal of insight. Offered to help too, despite her own situation, which I didn't know at the time. I could go on, but you understand the gist. She's what I always hoped to find, but had begun to doubt I would."

"Oh, Charles." Elodie spoke whisper-soft. "This won't be an easy path."

"No good thing is easily won, but I've no intention of giving up."

"You never do. It's one of the reasons you've always been the best of brothers and champions." A slight wistfulness tinged her voice. "And I know you'll do no less for Ainslie, now that she's won your heart."

Mr. Redgrave dropped an arm around her shoulder. "Perhaps you should return to Redgrave Hall. Then you can disclaim all knowledge of my actions. Whatever trouble comes, it should land on me alone."

"If you are in this, then I am also. I only wished to know the extent to which you'd considered your steps—this isn't a risk to be taken with blind emotion. But now that I know you've thought it through, I promise I'll support whatever stratagem you devise." She offered a smile that wavered slightly at the edges. "Sisters can be useful assets, don't you know?"

He released her, a grin crinkling the corners of his eyes. "The very best."

"Even so, we cannot let her carry out the bargain."

"She would rather die than do so." He rapped his walking stick against his leg. "That's what worries me."

"Then we must find a better path. It sounds as if Jessa already seeks one. I suppose we should rejoin the rest and hear what they intend to do."

I withdrew, hurrying back through the concealed passage to the morning room. Mr. Redgrave understood Ainslie far more than I'd given him credit for, and he'd responded with both reason and . . . love. That Elodie supported him in this spoke well of the bond between them—and well for Ainslie, if Riven and I must leave soon. Yet could the two of them alone be expected to resist the considerable force of the Redgrave family and the Vigil they'd kept hidden for centuries?

I entered the morning room, sealing the passage once more, then I let my hands fall to my sides, exhaustion weighing my limbs. I'd no time to inform my sisters of what I'd heard, for the Redgraves returned to the room, Danvers on their heels. "Mr. Burke has arrived, Miss Caldwell. Did you wish to see him now or when your other guests have gone?"

He'd come quicker than I anticipated. I traced a finger along the ridges of the chairback in front of me, considering.

Ainslie's shoulders tensed. "I don't want to wait any longer."

"Very well. Danvers, please show Mr. Burke in."

"You don't face this alone," Mr. Redgrave said quietly. He moved closer to her until less than a handbreadth separated them, and when she tilted her face to look up at him, the emotion in her eyes stole my breath.

The moment was broken when Mr. Burke strode through the door. His sharp gaze scanned the room. "What happened?"

Ainslie stepped forward, her hands twisting in her skirts. "I'm responsible for the missing people."

Another stratesman might well have taken this abrupt confession as the chance to cover themselves in glory by seizing upon the solution to a case plaguing the kingdom. But Mr. Burke merely motioned for her to sit down, then took the chair across from her. "I have difficulty seeing how this could be your sole responsibility. Perhaps you should give an account from the beginning."

Mr. Redgrave took up a station behind her chair, and Ainslie struggled to begin her confession once more, the words jumbling in her fatigue.

"Would you like me to share?" She shouldn't have to repeat so painful a tale. When she nodded, I continued, "It began when we identified what the statuette contained—pyske-dust."

Mr. Burke listened with focused intent, asking the occasional astute question. When I completed the tale, he turned to Ainslie. "I concur with the assessment you've been victimized, yet there's no denying your actions—however unwilling—have caused harm. Since you've come forth with vital information, you can be considered an informant, which means any involvement of yours in these crimes will be absolved."

"And if I don't want to be absolved?" Sorrow shaded her eyes darker.

"Then I would suggest you take some time to consider the matter further," Mr. Burke said. "In any case, I refuse to take you to the Magistry. Things are . . . not well there."

I tensed. "What do you mean?"

"When the Crimson Tattoo Killer preyed upon Avons, we were told to act as if it were a natural matter, even when it became apparent it was anything but." The lines about his eyes deepened. "We're in the same situation again, only worse. The Vigil fears the clout carried by the families of those who've disappeared recently. There's tremendous pressure to produce a natural explanation for these disappearances. I think they'd simply claim Ainslie's confession was a product of fae-touch and madness causing her to invent tales. She'd be locked away, and they'd continue to hide the truth."

"Then we must present them with a case so solid they cannot deny it." As I spoke, I began formulating a plan.

"We need more than that. If we bring unassailable proof, the Vigil might well suggest that those who have been bound in the bargain *should* forfeit their lives to stem the tide of stolen mortals, ignoring the fact that this fae will only claim others to work her purposes."

Riven broke in at last. "Then the mortal authorities should be told nothing."

"I'd very much like to argue the point, but I'm afraid I cannot." Mr. Burke looked as if the admission pained him.

A faint smile lifted Riven's lips. "Sensible of you."

"Sensible, perhaps, but I can only justify keeping this

concealed if there's a clear path toward breaking these bargains and keeping mortals safe."

"Mr. Burke, might you join forces with the Redgraves and Lord Blackburn to find the Collectors who are bound in bargain? If they can be identified and surveilled at all times, then the pyske-dust can be seized from the individuals who receive it, before they consume anything." Jade settled on my feet, her purr indicative of approval. "Lord Blackburn desires to understand and thwart the incursion of Other into our world, and I'm certain he'd pour considerable resources toward solving the problem—and my father and Mrs. Darrington have been working with him in an attempt to make a case for the king."

"We're not without resources either," Mr. Redgrave said. "And we'd like nothing more than to lend support to this cause."

"It seems I'm to be plagued with civilians on every side," Mr. Burke muttered.

"You'll need help if you mean to cover all the territories in question." Riven surveyed Mr. Burke and the Redgraves. "If you can locate the bargain-bound mortals, it will stem the tide for a time, perhaps even provoke the responsible fae into riskier action."

Mr. Burke steepled his fingers. "Even were we to locate all the bound Collectors, what's to stop this fae from simply forming new bargains and carrying on with her plan?"

"Me." Riven stood, his presence imposing. "And Jessa. We'll be leaving for the Otherworld in a few days to attempt to locate the bargain-holder."

Ainslie's breath caught, and Ada shook her head. "Oh, Jessa, surely not."

"I always felt it would come to this—you know I must go."

They both subsided. Doubtless they wanted to argue, but what more was there to say? Elodie and Mr. Redgrave made no protest, though Mr. Redgrave looked sidelong at Riven. Since they didn't know Riven was fae, they'd naturally question his choice, rather than my own.

Mr. Burke's eyes took on a stormy hue. "Miss Ada, Miss

Ainslie—you've abandoned your arguments very swiftly. Do you approve of a plan that so endangers your sister?"

"We believe she has the right to choose as she will." Ada twisted Mother's ring.

"You'd readily let her go to her death, simply because she chooses to do so?"

"She will . . . have Lord Riven." Ada faltered beneath Mr. Burke's intent gaze. "He will keep her from harm, surely."

"Will he? Has he vowed it?"

She lowered her eyes. "I don't believe so, but—"

"You care a great deal for your sister, yet you make only a token protest to her departure to the Otherworld, an excursion from which any mortal is unlikely to return alive." He was as determined as a hound of the Hunt. "Why is that?"

"Mr. Burke, kindly cease interrogating my sister. She's not a suspect." I swallowed the bitterness at the back of my throat. "If you have questions, direct them toward me."

"Very well." A frown sharpened his features. "Will you and Lord Riven step into the gardens?"

CHAPTER 45

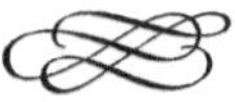

In silence, I led the way to the gardens. Doubtless Mr. Burke wanted to speak about Riven's nature and our previous excursion in the Otherworld without betraying me to my family or taking a risk that the servants would overhear. But if he guessed the truth about me . . . Of everyone in my life, he was best positioned to do so, given all of the Otherworld he'd experienced.

I stopped beneath the sweeping branches of a maple and turned to regard him.

Before I could speak, Mr. Burke's brows drew into dark slashes. "Do either of you care to explain what's really going on?"

The sunlight about Riven gleamed deeper gold, further defining the planes of his face. "You're owed no explanation."

"Because I'm mortal, and therefore undeserving of the truth?" Mr. Burke shot the words back with force.

"That's not what he meant." The tension in the air stifled me, despite the breeze wafting through the garden. I fumbled for a path through the precarious situation. "As for answers, I'm only doing what I must. I cannot abandon Ainslie to this bargain—she won't survive it."

"I understand why you feel compelled to go, since her life

hangs in the balance. It's the behavior of the rest that doesn't add up. No one else seems to find your decision to waltz into the Otherworld in the least extraordinary."

Like the kestrel he often resembled, Mr. Burke wasn't to be deterred from seeking out his quarry—in this case the truth. My stomach twisted.

And he pressed his point. "You and your sisters are close, yet they accept a decision that amounts to a death sentence with very little display of emotion. You were fortunate to escape the Otherworld unscathed the first time. You cannot trust your luck to hold. Nor can you persuade me that Ainslie would trade your life for hers. So why did she agree?"

"They know Riven will accompany me—"

"In itself, that's not enough. Unless Riven is bound by bargain to bring you back unharmed. Ada didn't seem to think so. Is he?"

The air seemed to chill about Riven, the pressure dropping as it might before a sudden tempest. I just shook my head. Somehow, I needed to dissuade Mr. Burke from pursuing this before the storm broke.

"Last time you kept your true purpose hidden from your family because you knew they'd forbid it." His eyes darkened. "Now you not only disclose it plainly before your sisters, but also the Redgraves, relative strangers who somehow also display no shock at the notion."

Above me, the maple leaves shivered. I should have exercised more care. But how? In order to entrust him with the investigation in this world, we'd had to reveal our plan to journey to the other one. I fumbled for an explanation. "It's different now that my family . . . they understand my sentiments."

He slashed his hand downward. "Sentiments be hanged. I'd like the truth."

Something inside me sank. These suspicions, now raised, wouldn't be assuaged without robbing him of his memories, glamouring him—or confessing the truth.

Sparks of light sprang into dazzling array about us, jagged as bolts of lightning, and Riven folded his arms across his chest. "Jessa doesn't answer to you—or anyone else. Why are you so concerned with her affairs? She's made her choice. Now make yours. Do you mean to uphold the mortal end of the investigation or not?"

"Not without answers." The set of his jaw indicated he'd not be moved. "I've conducted a sufficient number of investigations to know when someone's trying to conceal something of import."

He knew only because Riven had respected my wishes and hadn't glamoured him to dissuade him from pursuing this line of inquiry. My throat tightened further, and the branches of the maple quivered, its song laced with new, discordant notes. "Mr. Burke, please—it doesn't matter."

He eyed the maple, and something shifted in his face. "Tell me this. Was it good fortune that the Otherworld didn't harm you, when you traveled alone and unwarded? Or was it something more?"

Jade bristled, and the light about Riven sharpened further. I stepped back, bumping against a low-hanging limb, which I gripped as if it were a lifeline. "I . . . I think you know the answer."

"There've been oddities about you all along. I attributed them to Riven. To some protection or working he'd placed upon you. But you were the source." His voice was low, his features taut. "You're fae, aren't you?"

My voice abandoned me, so I simply nodded. The pressure dropped further, Other charging the air unbearably. *Jade, please ask Riven not to interfere.*

Done. She leapt upon the limb next to me and glowered at Mr. Burke.

"Then what? You've spent all these years conducting a charade? Or you've stolen the true Jessa Caldwell and assumed her life?"

"It's not like that—"

"Were you bored? Did you find it entertaining to play the

part of a naive mortal caught in the toils of the Otherworld, all the while mocking us behind our backs?" His anger held a cutting edge. "I feared for your life, risked a great deal because I trusted what you said was true. But it was all a game to you."

Jade growled. *Perhaps Riven* should *be allowed to interfere.*

"You know me better than that."

"I thought I did." He looked at me like one might something foul washed up on the river shore. "Now it's clear I didn't know you at all. Not if you're the threat Avons needs to be protected against."

"I swear that all I've done—all I am doing—is to protect the mortal world." My hands tightened about the limb, and translucent drops of sap wept from the bark, scattering on the grass below. "If you'd just let me explain—"

"So you can glamour me into believing more lies? I think not."

"I've never—"

"Never used glamour?" His jaw clenched. "Do you expect me to believe that?"

No, I didn't, nor could I rightly make any such claim. The tears of the maple dotted my muslin. *Stop, please stop.*

"I thought not." His gaze swept over me as I imagined it might one tried and convicted. "What about the Redgraves? Clearly, they know. Why didn't they report it?"

"I have a bargain with them." The confession seemed to scald my lips—it would confirm everything he now believed. "It binds them not to communicate my true nature to anyone."

"I see. Then you are like the rest." His voice was frigid now. "Will you constrain me the same way?"

"She won't need to." Evidently, Riven deemed the time for noninterference had come to an end. The slightest hint of his fae nature shone through, darkening his eyes and honing his features. "Because you'll answer to me if you do. You'll not speak to anyone of Jessa's nature as it wouldn't be good for your health. Is that understood?"

"Don't worry. You've made quite clear the cost of crossing fae." Bitterness laced his tone.

"Not clear enough, I think," Riven said. "Given the insults you feel free to hurl."

"Riven, please." This situation was one step away from imploding—and that would endanger everyone. We still required Mr. Burke's help in the mortal world, which meant I must somehow keep to the matter at hand, no matter my feelings. I released my grip on the maple, my hands chafed from its bark. "None of this changes the situation we face. Riven and I will be departing soon, which should relieve your mind, but the mortals here will remain vulnerable unless you find the Collectors as I proposed. Do you still want me to arrange for a meeting between Lord Blackburn, Mrs. Darrington, Father, and the others?"

"It seems I have no alternative. Send me the details once it's arranged." Without another word, he marched back into the house.

And I remained rooted beneath the maple, unable to trust myself to move or speak. Would any of the relationships that mattered to me survive the truth? I couldn't bear considering what would happen if Mrs. Darrington found out or Lord Blackburn. Perhaps they'd seek to haul me before the king, exhibit A on the incursion of Other into Avons. Unless, of course, I compelled them otherwise—confirming I was what everyone deemed fae. Jade wove herself between my legs, and I scooped her up, burying my face in her fur.

"You should have taken control of the situation." Riven's voice was devoid of emotion. "His anger—and his convictions—make his knowledge a risk."

"He feels betrayed, and I cannot blame him."

"Then you're allowing emotion to blind you." Riven flicked a finger, and the sparks of light scattered. "If you don't have the stomach for it, then let me take his memories. As it stands, he's a danger. He's the sort to decide his own life doesn't matter, if it's for the greater good."

"He doesn't deserve to have his memories stripped from him just for figuring out the truth." Jade draped herself about my neck, her breath warm at my ear.

"Then you're willing to let him expose you to the world?"

I swallowed my fear. "I think he'll keep quiet, at least until we've managed the matter of the bargain-holder, since it's in the best interests of the mortals of Byren. He must see that, else he'd never have agreed to work with Lord Blackburn and the others. I just wish I could have explained."

Riven inclined his head slightly. "Why? Do you care so much for his good opinion?"

"I counted him a friend, and I don't possess them in such abundance that I easily discount the loss." I looked away, attempting to brush the dark droplets of sap from my gown.

"Is that all?"

"It doesn't matter. All that matters now is keeping Ainslie safe."

But how much more would it cost?

RAGGED AND WORN, my sisters and I departed Wyncourt and made our way back home. Once there, I pled fatigue and excused myself from the family meal. Aunt Caris made no move to stop me, and indeed, few enough would gather at the table. Father remained immured in his study, and Aunt Melisina appeared only long enough to fetch a tray for Lovell.

I collected my sketching basket, then retreated to my bedchamber. With an unsteady hand, I penned missives to Lord Blackburn and Mrs. Darrington, requesting an audience on the morrow regarding a matter of some urgency. It was best to leave the details open to interpretation. Once I received replies, I would try to speak with Father.

And then I must inform Mr. Burke.

A soft step on the stairs drew me from my unpleasant thoughts. Not Aunt Caris—the steps were too tentative to be hers. A quiet knock sounded at the door, and I opened it to reveal Dreda.

She lifted a carved rosewood tray, laden with food. "I thought you might be hungry."

She wasn't angry like Mr. Burke, nor frightened like Aunt Caris, nor anything but Dreda—steady and loyal. I stepped aside to let her in. "Thank you . . . for everything."

Her brow furrowing slightly, she set the tray on the table. "I've done very little."

"You've done more than you know." The rich scents of the food turned my stomach. "Though I confess I don't understand—why aren't you upset?"

She perched on the nearest chair. "When I saw you protect us, back in the glade, everything that had happened since I met you made sense. It was more a relief than anything to finally understand." Her hazel eyes met mine. "I've no reason to feel kindly toward fae, but you've only ever protected me as you could. It doesn't matter to me that you're fae—you're still *you*. And knowing that you're fae, it only means you've more power to protect us, that we're safer than before."

My heart pulsed a ragged rhythm. If only my family could believe that. If only *I* could believe that. "Few share your sentiments."

"Did something else happen today?"

"Mr. Burke pieced matters together. He's . . . very angry."

"Can't imagine anyone pulls the wool over his eyes often, much less someone he trusts as he did you. As for your aunts and father, their world has been upended. Give them time, and I believe they'll come round." Her lips firmed. "Your family loves you."

"They love what they believed I was. Whether they'll love what I am remains to be seen."

"Oh, Miss Jessa." She sank down beside me and pulled me into her arms. "It will be well. You'll see."

Her gentleness undid me, and the tears I'd restrained since

the bau attack surfaced, a flood impossible to hold back. With steady arms, she held me as I cried.

And for a moment at least, I wasn't alone.

CHAPTER 46

When the tears finally subsided, bone-deep exhaustion set in. Yet tomorrow's arrangements must be completed before I could surrender to sleep. A flurry of notes carried by footmen finalized the meeting of the mortal coalition at Wyncourt tomorrow afternoon.

Risha happily carried an exchange between Riven and me, apprising him of the plans. It concluded with a message from Riven to expect him first thing in the morning with the not-at-all-ominous addendum that we still had several things to discuss.

The final note came from Mr. Burke, and it stood out for the complete absence of all social niceties: *I'll be there.*

I crumpled it in my hand, then turned to find Ada and Ainslie standing like spectres in my doorway, pale and hollow-eyed. Ada surveyed me with concern. "What was that?"

In faltering words, I confessed that Mr. Burke had learned the truth—and his response to the knowledge.

Ada frowned. "I thought Mr. Burke was a good man. The way he lent aid when you were missing showed a quick mind and sound character. And Ainslie said he supported our aunts with the utmost kindness after I was poisoned. But this . . ."

"He struggles, and I cannot altogether blame him." Not

when I'd wrestled mightily with all the facets of the Otherworld's involvement in my own life. "I wish he'd listen, but he fears I'll deceive him."

Ainslie moved to my side, her dressing gown rustling. "Then I suppose we should exercise care around him."

"For now, yes." Wearily, I removed my stained muslin and donned a nightgown. When I emerged from behind the dressing screen Ada had perched on the edge of the bed, Ainslie alongside her.

"About your decision to go to the Otherworld . . ." Ainslie fidgeted with her dressing gown. "I feel as though I'm asking you to pay the price for my folly."

"You didn't ask, and you weren't foolish. You couldn't possibly have known that your agreement to help a seemingly vulnerable old woman would pull you into an unbreakable bargain." I settled alongside her. "If our situations were reversed, you would go for me."

"Of course I would, but . . . it's hard to be the one who requires help."

I was acquainted with that sentiment all too well. "You may require it, but you can also offer it. There's much here you can do to help protect the vulnerable. Among other things, I think you and Lovell should start work on a series of articles—exposés on the Otherworld. If the king cannot be prompted to act, we might require another tactic."

"You're right. I must hope for the best and make the most of the knowledge I now have. If all else fails, I shall certainly make the fae regret she chose me." Her eyes sparked. "And I'll do my utmost to make sure there's a way for the truth to be revealed."

"Good."

"Could we join you tonight?" Ada asked. "I'd feel better if we were all together."

"Given the circumstances, I would as well." In a matter of minutes, we were nestled beneath the bedcovers, but it took considerable time before I drifted to sleep.

In the small hours of the morning, something whispered across the floor, rousing me. *Do you hear that?*

Jade's ears pricked forward, but her fur remained unruffled. *It's the nisi.*

Silently, Morwen clambered up onto the bedside table, then leaned over and tapped Ada on the shoulder.

She startled upright. "What's wrong?"

"Someone watches my house." Morwen crossed her arms, her ears bristling. "Pried at the windows, he did, but they stung him good. I saw to that. Now he stands and watches."

Ada snatched up her dressing gown. "Will you show us?"

By this time, Ainslie had roused also, and the three of us tiptoed down the stairs. We approached the front window, and I willed us to draw no notice.

There.

In the street outside our house stood Mr. Ludne and another figure, taller and angled in such a way that his face remained concealed.

Risha glared at him through the glass. "I knew I should have burned out his eyes."

Jade's tail twitched. *There's still time.*

Better we find out his purpose. I turned to Morwen. "Did either of these men enter the gardens?"

"Iron-stick man, yes. Poking, prodding, causing trouble."

We watched in silence as they conversed a moment longer, then retired to a carriage at the end of the row. When it vanished around the corner, I leaned against the cool window glass, watching the flicker of the gaslights in the street. However little I might wish it, I needed to check the gardens to ensure Mr. Ludne hadn't left any more fae—or alchemical—devices. With Jade prowling at my side, I slipped into the garden.

Though I spent more than an hour, I unearthed nothing, much to my dismay. The presence of a listening stone or some other such device would have given his visit a purpose. Its absence suggested that Mr. Ludne and his companion sought something specific, that he'd gained some knowledge that he needed evidence to support. But how could he have done so? Had Aunt Caris spoken to him, against Father's wishes?

The soft call of an owl sent a chill shivering down the back of my neck. Whatever the reason, his boldness grew, and that boded poorly for us all. If he discovered the truth, it could cost us everything.

∼

THOUGH WE RETURNED to bed after I examined the gardens, slumber came only in fragmented snatches, broken by dreams of my sudden arrest—sometimes by Mr. Ludne, others by Mr. Burke. Every time I awoke to a tempest-tossed heartbeat; every time sleep took longer to return. When the sky brightened to silvery gray, I abandoned the attempt to rest altogether and instead lay watching the dawn paint the ceiling in hues of rose and gold. For a few days more, I'd have the privilege of waking in this familiar bedchamber, surrounded by my family. And then what? The Otherworld would offer no warm welcome, only danger and hostility.

Jade climbed onto my chest, her weight stealing my breath. *Are you having second thoughts?*

Yes, but I cannot afford them.

When my sisters stirred, I hastened through my morning toilette before going out to the gardens. I filled an arched watering can from the fountain and busied myself among the plants until the familiar power of a passing sparked along my skin.

As was often the case, Riven didn't bother with pleasantries, only strode into the glasshouse as if he owned it. "We have three days to prepare you for the Court of Dusk—perhaps less, if we receive an early summons."

"We?"

"Of necessity, Nikol will be involved." Riven leaned against the glasshouse table. "You require information on the hunt, and he requires assurance that you're prepared for what you'll face.

487

We'll be meeting him later this morning in the Dythe Mountains."

I nearly dropped the watering can. "Why so far?"

"Distance makes no difference when we travel by passing, and it's best that we're far removed from prying eyes while you practice."

I set the can on the bench with a thunk. "Practice what?"

"You'll see." He pressed upright. "Will you come? We have matters to attend before he arrives."

I nodded, and he drew us through a passing, the vivid, multihued light and the shift in pressure disorienting. When he brought us into a small vale tucked between tremendous spires, I gripped the nearest boulder to steady myself. A small stream trickled among the rocks, and a riotous array of wildflowers dotted the expanse before us—fireweed, blue flax, bitterroot, and countless others, their songs thrilling with sweet, wild notes.

When Aunt Caris and I had traveled to Milburn, I'd glimpsed the Dythe Mountains in the distance, but nothing had prepared me for being surrounded by this breathtaking crown of mountains, their black peaks glinting silver in the morning light, where snow still touched the pinnacles. Before their vastness, we were small indeed.

I turned to find Riven watching me, his gaze intent. "Before Nikol arrives, there's something we must discuss."

Had he chosen this spot because he meant for me to attempt some particularly destructive or dramatic use of my fae abilities? The heated song of the fireweed surged in my ears. "Do you intend that I practice my affinities?"

"It would be advisable, yes. But that's not why we're here." He drew a small mirror from the fae pocket, as he had once before. "You cannot enter the Otherworld appearing as you do now. It will mark you as prey. You have to master your glamour, abandon this mortal guise."

I accepted the mirror, its scrolled metal cold to the touch, yet I refused to glance at its reflective surface. When my glamour had partially eroded during the bau attack, it had turned my family away from me—and Riven meant me to forsake it altogether. What would happen if I appeared before them as full fae? Something twisted unpleasantly in my chest. "I don't think I can."

"Look in the mirror. It will help build the connection between the attempt and the outcome. It's commonly used when first learning to don glamours, so it should work in reverse."

My fingers tightened around the mirror. I didn't want it to work, didn't want to watch my features change, become something Other. "Riven, I don't . . . I'm not ready."

"Unless you release the glamour, I can't take you to the Court of Dusk. It will undermine everything we seek to achieve." His shoulders tensed. "Do you still find the notion of being fae so abhorrent?"

Jade leapt upon the outcropping next to me, and I rested my hand on her back to steady myself. "It's not that."

"Then what?" He assessed me, as if seeking to perceive the emotions his working had blocked.

I set the mirror carefully on the rock alongside me. "Everything familiar is slipping from my grasp, no matter how hard I try to hold to it." And if I did this, I'd feel as though I'd in some way lost myself, my old self, and I'd no notion what the new self was or would become. My throat closed about the words.

"There's no room for sentiment in this decision."

"I can't simply stop feeling."

"I suggest you find a way. In this venture, life and death hang in the balance. Will you do what's required?"

The air between us seemed to hold a lightning charge, and I couldn't find my voice. Then, just beyond the nearest outcropping of rock, a sudden silvery flare snapped, breaking the tense silence, and Nikol stepped into the valley. He hadn't bothered to don a mortal glamour, and his dark beauty mirrored the mountains surrounding us, as I imagined they might look on a winter night, the silver-white of moon and star juxtaposed with the imposing ink-black of the stone.

I stepped back into the shadow of the tall rock.

And Riven pivoted to face him with an expression that would have withered an ancient oak. "You weren't due for another hour."

"What can I say? I'm eager to get started." Nikol rubbed his hands together. "Besides, looking at the two of you, it seems I've come at an interesting moment. What are we discussing?"

"Nothing that requires your presence. You may return later."

"After I've come all this way?" He flashed a silvery smile toward me. "What do you say, Jessa—shall I stay?"

Right now, Nikol represented a reprieve, and I seized upon it. "It seems a shame for you to leave. Riven and I can talk later."

Riven shook his head, but did not countermand my words.

"Excellent." With a swirl of shadow about him, Nikol leaned forward. "For a fae, you still look very mortal."

Riven gave a slight growl. "You're here to discuss the hunt, not Jessa's glamour."

"Was that the matter under discussion?" He tilted his head. "It doesn't seem to have been very effectual."

"Stay on task."

"As you wish." His uncanny silver eyes fixed on me. "What do you know of fae hunts?"

I braced myself against the large rock pillar at my back. "I've heard tales of the Wild Hunt, but beyond that, I know very little."

"Ah. The Wild Hunt is a very different event than the one you'll be joining. It's led by an ancient being—not high fae. He's flanked by his equally powerful and dangerous consort and lethal hounds." Nikol flicked his fingers, and shadow-hounds danced across the rocks before us. "Fortunately for this world, he's been kept constrained from crossing for quite some time."

Because of the protections in place of which no one could speak? The cold of the rock seeped through my thin summer muslin.

"His hunt is a wild, bestial affair. The queen's high summer hunt might be viewed as its opposite. Rather than a means to sate bloodlust and collect tithes, the queen's hunt is all about abiding by the rules of court and thereby gaining power and prestige." The shadow-hounds leapt at me and then vanished. "Take care you never compare the two—the Wild Hunt is viewed as an uncouth remnant of the ancient past, and if you liken them, you'll be seen as ignorant at best and willfully insulting at worst."

"I'll be careful." Of Nikol, as much as what he warned against. I sought a steady voice. "What else should I expect?"

"You'll find all those of stature within my court—they consider the high summer hunt an antidote to one of our greatest enemies: boredom. Furthermore, it provides an opportunity to display one's affinities to greatest advantage, therefore it's not to be missed."

"I see."

"I don't think you do." His shadow stretched long on the rocky soil behind him, shading the fireweed. It shivered ever so slightly, though no breeze stirred in the valley. "But you'll understand soon enough. The high summer hunt isn't about taking lives, but rather making a conquest according to the terms of the hunt, which change each year. Thanks to Riven's efforts, this time we'll seek to capture a shadow-drake and claim a vial of its blood while it still lives."

Jade's lips drew back, exposing a hint of fang. *Shadow-drakes are sentient beings, and the bloodletting leaves them vulnerable. A swift death would be more of a mercy.*

I shuddered. *Fortunately, I don't have to actually participate in this hunt, only appear to do so.* But was that condoning such deeds?

Nikol continued, "To conquer without killing—particularly the sorts of monsters that we seek—is a more difficult task than simple slaughter. It demonstrates a higher mastery of affinity and weaponry alike. The first to accomplish the task wins a boon from the queen."

"Surely it's not an open-ended favor?"

He shook his head. "No monarch would leave herself so vulnerable. This time she offers a relic. I cannot disclose its nature to you, as you're not of my court, but suffice to say I think you'd find it of interest."

"Is there anything else you can say?"

His lips turned up slightly. "I'm obliged to warn you of the dangers the hunt entails—not only from the shadow-drakes but also the snares I'll be setting and sabotage from your fellow hunters. They're not allowed to deliberately kill their opponents, but beyond that? All bets are off."

Sabotage I could do nothing about, except try to avoid drawing attention. If I didn't appear likely to emerge the victor, then surely no one would attempt to thwart me. But traps on the hunting grounds . . . "What sort of snares are set?"

"If I told you, it would take away all the fun." He gave a casual shrug. "Besides, as master of the hunt, I'm sworn to secrecy. Can't go giving anyone an advantage."

"Even with any number of advantages, I imagine I'll be outclassed."

"I wouldn't make such confessions elsewhere." He stepped closer. "One thing more—you'll also have to swear to the rules of the hunt, which are binding. Violation means death."

I spun toward Riven. "Why exactly is this our choice of entry into the court?"

"Because it will attract all fae from the Court of Dusk with sufficient power to have conceivably bound Ainslie and claimed the mortals." Despite Nikol's presence, Riven retained his glamour, his features familiar and comforting, whatever the power beneath the veil. "Regardless of the risks, it's the most likely to give us a substantive number of leads within a day or two. And given the nature of the event, you're less likely to draw notice. Attention will be elsewhere."

It all sounded very reasonable, and yet . . . "If I'm without a court alliance, won't I draw suspicion no matter how much activity surrounds the hunt?"

"Not under the circumstances." The sharp cry of an eagle echoed off distant peaks. "We've laid the groundwork to suggest you're from a remote and rather obscure court—the Court of

Roses, known for its strong botanical affinities. I doubt we could pull it off long-term, but it will suffice for the duration of the hunt."

"But if fae cannot . . . if we cannot lie, then how are we to sell such a tale?"

"Not being able to tell a direct lie just means you require a more creative structuring of the truth to achieve your ends." Again, Nikol offered his easy smile, one I was beginning to think as much a mask as any glamour fae had ever donned. "But never fear, we've taken care of it. All you have to do is play the part. The story will explain some of your ignorance, and as for the rest, keep as quiet as possible."

Though I was the one who'd wanted to go to the Otherworld in search of Ainslie's bargain-holder from the beginning, I now felt as if I was being swept along by a river in flood stage. I dug my fingers into the rock, and it chafed, even through my gloves.

Riven shifted. "You'll be attending as a guest of the Court of Gold, under my supervision. Courts have an obligation to provide novel experiences to those who are formal visitors, so no one will question our choice to bring you. It will all hang together, but only if you can pass for an ordinary fae—and I don't speak of your glamour alone." His voice held no inflection, leaving me to guess at his feelings about it all. "You cannot appear troubled or surprised by anything you witness. You'll see things you won't like, and you'll have to keep quiet, hide your feelings. I need your word you'll follow through."

My word. Would that bind me? Very likely. In this case, I knew Riven sought my protection—and Ainslie's and that of our entire mission. Even so, the silver-capped peaks seemed to close in about us. "You're asking for a bargain?"

"Not a bargain, just a guarantee. If you fail in this, the repercussions will be—greater than you imagine."

Nikol arched his dark brows. "It's a sworn bargain, or I'm out. You might be willing to take her word, but I'm as much at risk as either of you."

If Nikol pulled out his court, then the plan would fall apart

—and the time required to cobble together another one could prove fatal to Ainslie and the others involved. I trusted Riven not to take advantage of any bargain between us, yet I shrank from the notion of binding my emotions and will to anyone in such fashion. What might the repercussions be?

Riven said something sharp in the fae tongue, and Nikol parried, each evidently adamant about their stance. At last, Riven inclined his head toward me. "Your word will do."

Nikol didn't look pleased, but he gave no further argument. And I'd learned something new—not every agreement between fae *must* be a bargain. That might be the default, but it could be specified otherwise. "Very well, then I give it."

I stroked Jade between her ears. *Was I right to so swear?*

I believe so. You can't hope to change fae customs overnight. Such things take time, if they ever occur. You must hold to your purpose.

I know. Only what would I witness? And what was my responsibility for it?

"It seems my work here is done, for now." Nikol buffed his fingers against his embroidered silk jacket. "But I require proof before we depart."

Proof of what? Uneasiness whispered across my skin.

Riven nodded. "You'll have it." When Nikol vanished, he turned to me, his expression implacable. "We're not done with our earlier conversation."

I pressed my lips together tightly. If I could deflect long enough, perhaps we would be—I needed time and space to consider what must be done. "If I remove the glamour . . . can it be replaced? I can't wander Avons appearing fae."

"Once you master it, you'll be able to remove and assume it at will—the threads of it should feel very familiar to you by now, far more than that of your true self. Therefore, removing it will be the more difficult task." He sent sparks of light racing across the mirror, drawing my eye back to it. "That's why I brought you somewhere remote, to practice without distraction."

I averted my gaze. "But if someone placed the glamour on me for my protection, surely removing it is a risk."

"Everything about the choice to enter the Otherworld means risk." He folded his arms across his chest, as immovable as the mountains surrounding us. "And you're stalling."

My stomach churned as if I'd swallowed a purgative dose of bitterroot. "But if we understood why, if . . . if you entered my mindscape, perhaps you could find out the truth of how I came by it—"

"No." He stared at the stone outcroppings, his jaw tight. "It's in no way worth the risk—that knowledge won't change the outcome, unless there's a circumstance in which you'd reconsider your decision to go after the bargain-holder."

"There's not, but—"

"You have no idea what you'd endure. Don't ever suggest it again."

His clipped tone stung. Of all the things I'd expected, a flat refusal wasn't one of them.

From her perch on the rock, Jade nuzzled my shoulder. *It's clear he doesn't want to be responsible for the damage entering your mindscape would likely cause. And I much approve of his view.*

I let out a breath. At one time, I'd believed that all fae were unconcerned with causing injury to mortals, but I'd abandoned the notion when it came to Riven. In his position, I wouldn't have wanted to risk it either. It had been a poor attempt to stall. I sank onto the cleft of the rock behind me and drew my knees up to my chest. "I'm sorry, I shouldn't have asked that of you. I know I can't appear in the Otherworld looking mortal, but . . . I can't do this, not yet."

"Little time remains." He lifted the mirror from the rock. "But you're right in one thing. If you cannot resolve to do this, you will fail. Your affinities respond to your intentions—not just your will but your deeper desires. In time that can be overcome, but it takes much experience and proper training. You won't be able to forsake the glamour unless you want to do so. Take the day, find a way to prepare yourself. We'll speak of it again tomorrow."

The notes of the bitterroot strengthened, sharp and cutting, drowning out the gentler melodies of the other flowers. Though Riven wasn't forcing the issue, at least not yet, his disapproval was clear—he'd become yet another to add to the substantial list of those I'd disappointed.

CHAPTER 47

The following morning I sat motionless on the bench of the glasshouse, staring at my wavering reflection in the translucent wall panels. The meeting at Wyncourt the previous afternoon had ensured all our allies understood the nature of the situation and established the specifics of what they would do in our absence, though Mr. Burke's profound distrust remained clear. Now, only one obstacle to departure remained—my mortal glamour. I'd tried to shed it last night before I retired, but my face in the mirror remained pale and terrified . . . and wholly unaltered. What if I couldn't manage it?

Our plan hinged on me unlocking this metaphorical door, and I could not seem to find the key. Every time I considered it, fear choked me. The conflict between will and desire had betrayed me more than once into glamouring others against my own resolve, and now it seemed it was to betray me again, because no amount of reasoning with myself had brought about change. I turned away from my faint reflection in the glasshouse wall.

Jade, who'd been grooming herself in a sun patch, stopped to regard me. *Condemning your failures is no path to success.*

Then what is?

Before she could reply, the power of passing surged across my senses. It didn't hold the familiar sense of sun and storm that accompanied Riven; instead it was silver-bright and rather cold—Nikol. He filled the door of the glasshouse, the scents of starlight and shadow swirling about him, and I clutched the basket of herbs to my chest like a shield. "Nikol. I wasn't expecting you."

"The best guests are often the unexpected ones." He flashed his bright smile. "Besides, I'm here on commission. Riven said you need further preparation for the hunt, but he's engaged with court business this morning. We can't afford to lose time while he's entangled with his affairs, so I'll attend your preparation until he returns."

"And Riven . . . agreed to this?"

"He suggested it."

I'd already failed to meet Riven's expectations in the matter of my glamour; I'd not do so again by shrinking back from this task—not when he'd risked so much to set this plan in motion. I placed my basket on the worktable. "Very well. What are we to do?"

"Go to Enderly for a bit of privacy first. Unless you prefer to remain here?"

I didn't trust Nikol to exercise as much care with my family as Riven did, so the sooner we removed from home, the better. Enderly was close enough that we could take a carriage or a passing. I brushed a scrap of leaf from my arm. "How do you intend to travel?"

"By passing. But I'll warn you, I possess no liminal affinity, and I only have a portable prism, which means we'll have to be in contact for it to bring us out together." He lifted a silver chain that rested beneath his jacket, revealing a star-shaped prism no wider than a gardenia blossom.

"It's much smaller than the one Uros brought."

"The sort of prism Uros stole is used to move large groups—they're usually stationed in set positions. This is meant for individual use, but it will do for two or three in a pinch. If you want your companions to come along, make sure they're touching you."

He was being remarkably generous with information, whereas before he'd been stinting, willing only to offer answers in exchange for a bargain. Did he consider us on the same side, now that we shared a purpose? The sweet orange murmured low in my ears. "And we're only going to Enderly?"

"I give my word I'll take you nowhere else." As the sun spilled through the passing prism, a silvery-hued spectrum of light blossomed on the floor in front of us, forming the rough outline of a door. "I think you should practice your affinities in the Otherworld, but Riven disagrees. Thinks it will attract too much notice. Perhaps he's right. Regardless, he suggested Enderly was a suitable locale—a place to demonstrate what might be expected on the hunt, where there are few mortals to observe."

Though I sorted his words, I could find no loophole in them. "Very well. Let's go."

With Jade draped on my shoulders and Risha perched on her back, I accepted Nikol's arm, and the passing tugged us all through, this time a disconcerting tangle of cold and light and shadow, as if I tumbled through a night sky. When the forest of Enderly materialized, Nikol released me, taking several paces forward.

As I caught my balance, tremendous coils of shadow snapped in place around me, binding me hand and foot, while others plucked Jade from my shoulders. She shifted into true-form but was chained in place with her own shadow-bindings. Above me, Risha fluttered helplessly, snared in a dark-threaded web.

We were well and truly trapped.

A bitter, metallic taste flooded my mouth, and my pulse surged. Jade growled, and Risha's wings dimmed to an alarming pallor.

I struggled against the bindings, and they bit into my skin. "You're hurting Risha. Release her at once."

"She'll survive, at least as long as you comply." Nikol plucked a dagger from its sheath and idly polished it on his sleeve. "No one is getting released until you do as I bid."

"This isn't about preparation, is it?"

"Oh, I assure you it is. You're getting a first-class lesson on fae snares and the price that must be paid to free oneself from them—in this case, mastery of your concealment glamour." He motioned behind him to a mirror that hung suspended by shadow from the nearest fir.

All this just to compel me to act? Had Riven abandoned me to Nikol because I refused to try? Surely not. Still, I shrank back. "If you just release me—"

"I think not." He tucked his dagger away. "Riven won't force the issue, nor does he want you bound to him in a way that would constrain your will—facts I find both interesting and irksome. Fortunately for the success of our mission, I have no such compunctions."

"Then Riven didn't send you."

"Depends on what you mean by that. He doesn't know I'm here." Nikol shrugged. "However, he *did* once suggest that I teach you about fae snares before the hunt—and comment on Enderly as a likely location."

From these facts, Nikol had skillfully woven his web of deception, just as he'd suggested to me the day before. I pulled against the strands of shadow, and they tightened about me mercilessly. My breath caught. "Why are you doing this?"

"Your success means my success. But your failure also means my failure—which is unacceptable. Riven may be willing to gamble with his fate, but I hold my life more dear. You're the weak link in this plan, and I won't allow you to remain a liability. You'll master your glamour, and you'll do it before I release you and your companions."

"It isn't that simple—"

"Unlike Damir, I know what moves you." His gaze settled on Jade and Risha. "If you don't comply, your companions will pay the price."

I'd no doubt he meant what he said. A peculiar shivery numbness spread from everywhere the shadows bound me, chilling me deep within, and the resonant song of the firs thrummed deep and low in my ears. "I thought you were Riven's friend. Will he condone your actions?"

"Fae don't have friends. Not in the way you're thinking. And I don't risk my life for anyone." His silvery eyes brightened. "No more delays. Remove your glamour."

"I don't know how."

"Then I suggest you learn quickly." His lips quirked upward. "Allow me to demonstrate what it will cost if you do not. I believe you're familiar with shadowmancy, but a little motivation never hurts."

Swift as the strike of a snake, a shadow spiraled up my arm. This one burned as it traveled, the pain searing. The dark stain split into dozens of threads that raced toward my shoulder, each filament flaring ice-hot until I could no longer control my arm. I choked back a cry.

He was right. I had experienced this before—with Lord West. Did this power belong to all in the Court of Silver? My vision blacked slightly, and I swallowed against the bitterness at the back of my throat. This wasn't the same. When I first dealt with Lord West, I'd no notion of how to defend myself, I'd been forced to try to hide any hint of what I'd thought of as faults within. Now I flung my senses wide, drawing in the songs of the plants around me and pushing back the pain. Strands of color wove through each living thing in the forest about me, swaying just at the edge of my vision.

Nikol stepped closer, a mocking smile playing about his lips. "*Kit-isne* are strong. Yours won't suffer lasting damage from shadowmancy. Can't say the same for the sylph, not for certain." He shrugged, his eyes glinting. "I suppose you could always get another replacement."

Like fire, the vibrant strength of the firs behind me burned through my veins, rich and deep and evergreen, and the world about me blurred. "You will *not* hurt her."

He bent low and whispered in my ear, "Then stop me."

Any barrier between me and the forest eroded, the strands of innate power in each plant vibrant and exposed, ready to be wielded. Yet I hesitated. If it came to open combat, Nikol would win. This time, concession meant victory—but how? I inhaled the resinous fragrance of the fir, the sun-warmed leaves of the chestnut trees, the distant spice-sweet scent of the goldhearts, and my mind cleared.

Flecks of light bright as sun shining through spring leaves hovered in the air about us, limning every bough and blossom, and the songs of the plants surged into my senses, drowning out all else. In the glade with my family, I'd begun to erode my glamour. How?

A sudden spike of pain from Jade crossed from her mind to mine, a low growl torn from her throat. Nikol was hurting her.

There was no more time to think, only to act.

I claimed the part of me that *wanted* to be fae—whatever it cost—so I could shelter Jade and Risha and all those I loved. And my breath caught as I perceived a shimmering mist on my own form, entwined with runes translucent as wraiths—it was part of me, but not the truest part. Rather, it served as a veil to conceal, a comfortable place to hide. It wove beyond the surface, into muscle and sinew.

Yet I ripped it away with a single ruthless gesture.

Oh, *oh*. Though the removal wrenched, strands of green and gold rushed in to replace the shroud of glamour. It felt as if all my life I'd breathed only enough air to survive, but now a surfeit swirled about me, filling my limbs, enervating every part of me, as if I were a flower burst from an unbearably constraining bud. The shadows binding me in place unraveled, and I stumbled forward. Risha tumbled down, and I snatched her up, tucking her against my chest. Then I pivoted to face Nikol, the branches of the nearest fir bristling about me sharp as swords.

He smiled. "I knew you could manage, if properly motivated."

Everything in me yearned to strike at him. Perhaps he

expected it, even desired it, for he held shadows coiled about him like wyvern. I sensed he'd delight in a skirmish, and I wished nothing less than to give him greater satisfaction than he'd already gained. When I made no move to lash out, he clamped his hand about my right arm and spun me toward the mirror he'd hung. "Take a good look."

My reflection left me cold. Who did I perceive? The woman looking back at me possessed the finely sculpted features of the fae—features that lacked any mortal softness, faultless in their symmetry and beauty. Starlike flecks of green shot through the blue of my eyes, which now held something uncanny, something Other, and hints of gold glossed my skin, wove within the dark curls of my hair.

My chest tightened. How I wanted to hide from what I saw, from Nikol's cold gaze that beheld far too much. Yet he did not release me.

"This is who you are; this is who you must remain in the Otherworld. Don't forget it."

I distrusted my voice, so I just nodded. He spoke of the Otherworld, but how could I ever work with him in the Court of Dusk after he'd threatened Jade and Risha?

"I'll release your *kit-isne* if she swears not to attack." Nikol relinquished his hold on my arm. "It would be a shame to have to take her life. She'd be helpful on the high summer hunt."

If he releases me, I'll tear his heart out or die trying.

Please, Jade, you know you cannot. We need him for now, and you've told me yourself, kit-isne *cannot stand against high fae. Just give him your word. Then this will be over.*

You'll let him get away with it?

I walked into the trap he laid; this is the price required. I'm only sorry you had a part in paying it.

Jade snarled at Nikol. *I'll not strike out at you today. But perhaps another time, when you don't see me coming.*

He only laughed. "I advise against it, if you want to remain around to protect your mistress."

The shadows binding Jade released. She stalked to my side,

her tail wrapping around me, and glared at Nikol. I rested my right hand on her head. My left arm still throbbed, mottled with bruises and something far darker, a shadow that lingered beneath the surface of my skin, driving pain with each pulse of my heart.

Undeterred by Jade's presence, he brushed a bit of dirt off my sleeve. "It's nothing personal. I hope you understand."

"Keep your hands to yourself." I stepped out of his reach. "And remove the rest of your shadows, at once."

"As you wish." He flicked his fingers, and the shadows beneath my skin vanished; only the bruises remained. "But I suggest you adjust your perspective."

"You suggest this means nothing." I frowned at him. "Yet you attacked and threatened two individuals dear to me—that feels *very* personal."

"Well, it's not. It's a matter of business, and you'd best get used to it if you intend to spend any amount of time in the Otherworld." He tilted his head. "Consider this a lesson from a 'friend,' if you will. A lesson from one who bore enmity toward you would be much more painful, I assure you."

"Are you suggesting that this sort of thing is acceptable in the Otherworld?"

"I'm suggesting that in the Otherworld, as you call it, those with power make the rules." His voice now held a distinct edge. "One must learn to defend oneself and make strategic alliances and bargains—or else face the consequences."

CHAPTER 48

In a swirl of shadow, Nikol restored us to the glasshouse. It appeared just as it always did—bright and cheerful and homely—yet it no longer brought the familiar comfort, for every surface offered faint glimpses of my reflection, reminders that I was not of this world. I did not belong, no matter how I desired it.

Nikol tipped his head to me. "I'd say it was a pleasure, but I expect you don't agree."

Without waiting for a response, he vanished. And I tucked myself in the depths of the glasshouse. Before my family or one of the servants saw me, I must restore my mortal appearance. I removed my gloves, placing them on the gardening table, then brushed the fingers of my uninjured hand across the glossy leaves of a gardenia, its steadiness lending strength.

When I'd crafted the glamour for the garden, it had involved seeing what should have been but was no longer. The matter of my own glamour was similar—it involved what could have been, if I'd chosen to be mortal, and what I *had* been, in years past. I closed my eyes, fixing in my mind the image of my old features, the ones I'd seen in the mirror countless times over the course of my life, sensing the prick of Other about me.

Then, like the cool kiss of an autumn breeze, the glamour descended. This time, when I opened my eyes, I could still perceive the shimmering mist that had hidden itself from me before—and it rested on the surface of my skin only, as if I'd uprooted the deeper layers for good. I released the gardenia. *Do I look as I should?*

Yes. Jade leapt onto the table alongside me. *I can't imagine Riven will let himself be delayed long, since as far as he knows, you still cannot alter your appearance. When he comes, what do you intend to say about Nikol?*

Nothing.

If you prove you can remove your glamour, he'll want some explanation. Even were you minded to deceive him, his affinities allow him to perceive falsehood. Do you truly think you can keep this hidden?

I traced my fingers along the mottled bruises of my arm, which ran all the way down to my fingertips. *I'll tell him Nikol helped me see things in a new way.*

And you think he'll be satisfied?

What would you have me do? I cannot run to Riven every time I have some Otherworldly interaction that distresses me. Even the fragrance of the gardenia failed to steady my pulse. *It's not his responsibility to intervene or offer protection.*

Jade rumbled, her eyes like green embers. *Yet he has offered to assist.*

With the matter of Ainslie and the bargains, but even his patience must have some limits. And I can see no favorable outcome from telling him the whole. I snatched up the shawl hanging from a peg near the door. I'd left it there for chilly evenings working among the plants; now it would serve to hide Nikol's deeds. I draped it around my shoulders so it concealed my bruised arm. When I returned to the house, I'd treat my injury with amelior salve and no one would be the wiser. *It's not something I should expect Riven to involve himself with. Our friendship has placed burdens enough on him—I've taken far more than I've given.*

I disagree.

I tugged the shawl closer. *Can you deny what Nikol said, that this is the way the Otherworld works?*

Her tail twitched. *No. But that does not mean it should be this way.*

Many things in both worlds are not as they should be. But in this situation, the fault lies with me.

How so?

I should have been more cautious with Nikol, shouldn't have allowed him to escort us anywhere, whatever he said about Riven's wishes. Most of all, I . . . I should have found a way to keep him from hurting you. I'm sorry I did not.

She nuzzled my chin. *Jessa, he's the queen's hunter—and he got that position by skill and wit. You did what you could as swiftly as you could.*

Perhaps, but though she offered absolution, the pain of my failures pricked like stinging nettles. I turned to Risha. "Are you well? Do you feel any lingering influence from the shadows?"

"Well now." Her wings flared bright as she surged upward. "No worries."

The inflection of her words made her sound just like Asrina. They had been hatch-sisters, so it was not unexpected, but the sound twisted like rose briars around my heart. When Lord West had threatened, I hadn't been able to keep Asrina safe, and today, I'd failed to perceive Nikol's intent, leaving us all at his mercy. When we entered the Otherworld, with all its inherent threats, how could I hope to keep Risha from harm? "I'm glad you're fine now, but I might not be able to protect you in the future. However much I might wish it, I'm not certain I can defend you against other high fae. You're under no obligation to remain, nor is Kiran. You could return to your flight and—"

Her wing gently brushed my cheek. "I stay."

I sank onto the bench, my eyes sliding shut. Though I'd failed her, she trusted me, as did Jade. And I would learn whatever was necessary to prove worthy of that trust. I didn't want to concede to Nikol in anything, but it most likely *would* necessitate strategic alliances and bargains and a far greater understanding of my own affinities, all of which intimidated me. Yet what choice remained? If my actions drew attention, making those connected with me vulnerable, I must also find a way to protect them—to make it clear they could not be targeted to get to me. The light of passing gleamed in the corner of the glasshouse, this time heralding Riven's arrival. When he stepped through, I pressed to my feet, forcing a smile.

His eyes narrowed. "What happened?"

Even with the working in place, he was uncannily perceptive. Since I did not wish to discuss Nikol, I'd better distract him by offering something else. "I've learned how to shed my glamour."

His brows lifted. "Will you demonstrate?"

I gave a tiny nod. Though it still required focus, this time releasing the glamour felt like taking a deep breath after loosening overtight stays—a far more natural form and function. When I looked up, I found Riven's attention fixed on me, his gaze tracing my altered features. "Did I miss something?"

"Not at all. You look . . ." His voice lowered, and he took a small step back. "As you should. Yesterday, you opposed any attempt to remove your glamour. What changed?"

I fought the urge to restore my mortal guise. "I had a conversation with Nikol."

Something flickered in his eyes. "What did he say?"

"Among other things, he pointed out my unwillingness to embrace my true nature might harm others. He was right, just as you were."

"I see." A gathering pressure in the air rustled the leaves of the plants between us. "And that's all?"

I murmured something noncommittal.

And Jade sauntered forward. *That* is *what he said. But you might find what he did of greater interest.*

Jade!

Riven stilled. "What did he do?"

You've known him long enough that you must be aware of his proclivity for rough play. So why allow him near Jessa? Unless you agree with his methods?

"What methods are those?" His voice was a low, dangerous rumble.

Jade, this isn't helping. I thought we agreed we wouldn't say anything—

We agreed you did not wish to speak of it, but we discussed nothing of what I might or might not want to say.

"Jessa?"

Riven wasn't going to yield—but nor was I, no matter how Jade sought to interfere. I lifted my chin. "I suggest we stick to the matter at hand—I can now remove my glamour, which means we no longer have an obstacle to entering the Otherworld."

"And I'd like to know how precisely that end was achieved." His arms folded across his chest, his shoulders straining at the silken jacket that gave him the veneer of a mortal gentleman.

I faltered.

His gaze swept over me, catching on the shawl I clutched close despite the heat of the afternoon. With a single fluid motion, he crossed the space between us and plucked it away. Golden light spiraled up my arm even as I tried to tuck it within the folds of my skirts. And the sense of an impending cloudburst thickened the air, tightening in my chest and shivering among the leaves of the plants.

His jaw tightened. "What happened?"

When I didn't speak, Jade chuffed. *What do you think? He took advantage of Jessa's trust in you to gain some for himself, then drew us into a snare. He threatened Risha and me to force Jessa to act.*

Some of Riven's glamour eroded, and his fae features bled through, sharp-edged and limned in light, hinting at the vast power pooled beneath.

"There was no . . . lasting harm done." If one did not count the painful reminder of my own limitations and the awareness that I'd much to learn, both about my own affinities and the ways of the Otherworld, in order to protect those under my care. I snatched up Jade. *Stop provoking Riven.*

Because her words did provoke him, that much was clear, even if I didn't fully understand why. If one stripped out all emotion from the affair, Nikol had taken logical steps to force my hand, so Riven should have been pleased. Yet he was not. Perhaps he disliked the interference, though it had achieved his ends.

The light about him sharpened. "Then why keep it concealed?"

With difficulty, I steadied my voice. "I thought it would distract from our purpose, since in the end, it's all worked out."

"Has it?" His voice held no emotion, offered no hint as to his thoughts, yet the sense of pressure increased. "Why did you go with him?"

"He told me that . . . you wanted me to," I said softly.

"Did he?" The green of his eyes darkened to near black, a night-shrouded forest of fir. "Then perhaps it's a good reminder —don't trust anyone."

"I'll be more cautious in the future, but you won't . . . say anything to him?"

His gaze lingered on my bruised arm, and he stepped closer. "Did he threaten you to purchase your silence?"

"No, I just think it's better to leave the matter alone. This plan hinges on our ability to work together. If Nikol decides to withdraw his court . . ."

Riven returned the shawl to me, his eyes still ominously shadowed. "Words won't be necessary. Nor will he withdraw his court."

Somehow his statements didn't reassure. It was clear he'd his own thoughts on the situation that he did not intend to divulge. Yet I couldn't reasonably press further. I wrapped the silken fabric about myself. "Nikol said you had business in the Other-world. I assume some part of that was true?"

"Yes." He remained silent a moment, and the pressure in the air gradually ebbed. "I was addressing a few outstanding issues—one of which is your incomprehension of the fae tongue."

Behind me, the gardenia quivered. How had I not considered this hurdle? I'd been so fixed on Ainslie and my family . . . "How can I possibly remedy that in the time that remains?"

"It's simple enough. I called on a pyske who is influential among her kind. When I informed her of our discovery of pyske-dust and our desire to find the one responsible for distributing it, she was happy to help."

"How?"

He withdrew a small jeweled vial from his pocket. "By providing this. It's pyske-crafted, and if applied to your ears and tongue each week, it will allow you to both understand and speak our language. It won't give you true mastery, but as your mind grows accustomed to processing it, it will help the words come more readily when you truly learn it later."

"Do I want to know what it's made of?"

"Probably not." A small smile quirked his lips. "Yet there's nothing else that would be as effective."

However little I might like it, this potion had been given with the desire that Riven and I put an end to exploitation of pyske and mortal alike—and I could think of no other way to gain the ability required in so short a time. I accepted the vial, the glass cold to my touch. "Very well."

"You'll also need this." He pulled from his pocket a golden chain on which a small sunburst prism hung.

It reminded me of the passing prism Nikol possessed. Riven didn't require one to travel between worlds, so evidently he'd acquired it for me—at what cost? "I can't take such a gift."

"Consider it a loan. One that will enable you to flee if the situation requires. Circumstances could arise where it's essential for survival."

"I—thank you." As Riven passed it to me, rainbow light spilled across the floor. "How do I use it?"

"You'll need to let light pass through it. Think of the light as a key unlocking a door. If you cannot find a natural source—

sun, moon, or star—than you will have to use a fae-light. It would be to your benefit to learn to craft them."

"But what if my affinities don't permit me to do so?"

"All high fae can, just as all can cast glamour. If the fae in question possesses no light affinity, it changes the way they're drawn and limits their function—but you'll be able to manage something."

Since I'd seen Riven conjure a variety of fae-lights, that must mean he did have a light affinity. I checked the multitude of questions that sprang to my lips. He'd already made it clear that he'd spoken as much as he was able on the matter of affinities.

"There's one final element you'll require to blend in—fae attire. I've arranged for a trunk of clothing to be delivered to the Court of Dusk along with mine." He handed me a small satchel I'd not noticed before. "You'll need to wear the clothes within when we depart."

I clutched the buttery-soft satchel to my chest. "Most gentlemen in our world aren't accustomed with the finer points of ladies' fashions."

"I had assistance."

Who else had he brought into the scheme? Lady Avis, perhaps? The king trusted her and supported this endeavor, so it was conceivable he'd involved her.

Riven closed the space between us, assessing me. "Do you still want to go through with this?"

No. I checked the swiftly blossoming word and forced myself to straighten. "I see no other path forward."

"Then make ready. Our timeline has moved up. The king has extended invitations to a select group of guests from the Court of Silver to enjoy his hospitality before the feast that launches the hunt. He's further extended this invitation to include the two of us, which means we'll need to leave earlier than planned."

"How soon?"

"Tonight."

My breath hitched. This would bring us one step closer to

finding Ainslie's bargain-holder, which I desired above all else. But as for the Otherworld itself . . . I wasn't ready.

CHAPTER 49

When Riven left, I lingered in the glasshouse. I didn't have time to waste, yet I'd rather do almost anything than confess my plan to my family. Even so, I refused to leave under the guise of a cover story, not when there was a chance I might never return. With the stakes as they were, I couldn't ask permission, but nor would I conceal my purpose and allow them to think I'd abandoned the family.

Slowly, I made my way to my compounding room, where I collected the amelior salve. As I smoothed it down my arm, the skin warmed, and a rich floral fragrance wafted about me, chasing away the pain and fading the blue-black bruises to a faint mottled yellow one would have to strain to perceive. Which meant I had no further excuse to postpone the conversation with Father.

I tucked the jar back into place, then ascended the stairs. At the far end of the corridor, I glimpsed Holden showing a gentleman out. It wasn't an ordinary at-home day, so who had called? As the door closed, I hurried forward. "Who was that?"

"Ah, Miss Jessa." He gave a stiff nod. "It was a Collector wishing to speak with you. I wasn't aware you'd come home."

"I was in the gardens." Though I hurried forward to wrench

open the door, I only caught a glimpse of the man as he entered his carriage. But the reddish hair beneath his hat suggested it was Mr. Wells, the Collector who'd warned me against allowing Thea to take the pyske-dust. What had he wanted? I checked the urge to dash after him. If I did, I'd draw just the sort of attention I needed to avoid. Instead, I snapped the door shut. "Did he give any reason for his call?"

"No, but I've seen him about a few times before, or rather, the boy Dryden has—he seems to notice everything." He hesitated. "He gave his name as Mr. Wells, and he was most insistent that he be allowed to wait for you, but in the end, he abandoned the attempt. Said he had business to attend to."

The back of my neck prickled. Why had Holden let him in at all? Ordinarily under such circumstances, he would have sent the man away. "Where did he wait?"

"In the drawing room."

"If he returns, and I'm not present, please ask him to speak to Ada or Ainslie instead. And on no account are you to leave him unattended."

"Very good, miss."

I fidgeted with the clasp of the satchel I held. "Is Father home?"

"He's in his study."

"Thank you." Before I spoke with him, I must examine the drawing room. I swiftly reviewed the chamber, but found nothing amiss, nor did Jade. If he'd left no Otherworldly or alchemical devices, what had been his aim? I could follow up on it no further now, not if I meant to address Father, so I changed course for the study, a murmur of conversation emanating from beyond the closed door.

Then, as usual, Aunt Melisina's voice rang out above the rest. "Fae or not, we cannot simply allow them to face these dangers—"

"Mother, it's not a question of what should or should not be allowed—we're far beyond that. The fae won't just stop their games because you demand they do so, nor will they readily release Ainslie from the bargain, if any of our lore holds true."

"Besides, perhaps they . . . perhaps Jessa does not want us to interfere." Aunt Caris spoke in soft, faltering tones.

Though I'd far rather have addressed Father alone—in his current state, he'd have leveled little protest—perhaps this was for the best. I took a deep breath and opened the door.

My aunts startled, slight hints of guilt in their expressions, while Father scarcely stirred. Lovell started to rise, but I shook my head. "Please, just rest." I perched on the edge of the chair closest to the door, where I might flee if required. "I've come with some news about Ainslie's situation."

Lovell sat at attention. "A chance to free her?"

"Yes, but it's not without its risks." It was perhaps best to omit the information about the pyske-dust and the missing individuals—Father already knew, and it would only stir fear in my aunts. I fixed my gaze on the scrolled rug beneath my feet. "A lead on the fae who holds her bargain has emerged, and I intend to go to the Otherworld to seek her out."

A murmur of protest arose from my aunts, and Lovell shook his head. "That's madness. I know you've gone once before, but to tempt fate by returning to confront a high fae who has nothing to gain by releasing Ainslie—how can you hope to succeed, even if you do find her?"

"By figuring out what she wants and offering a more compelling bargain." Though I couldn't fathom what would be more compelling than a steady supply of mortals, I had to believe we could find *something*. "But first, we must identify her."

"Who is this *we*?" Lovell asked. "Do Ada and Ainslie also mean to go?"

"They'll remain here. Lord Riven intends to accompany me."

Aunt Melisina shook her head. "Is he afflicted with the same madness?"

"I assure you he's of sound mind." I folded my hands in my lap, studying the faint traces of bruising that remained.

"I'll have Jade to protect me as well. It is not as mad as it seems."

Though I spoke to reassure them, I'd no such confidence. Leaving aside the dangers of the hunt, I had very limited understanding of my affinities and less training in their use. If I made a misstep and revealed the truth of my circumstances . . . My hands tightened.

"It seems you've made up your mind, so there's nothing more to be said." Aunt Melisina's lips tightened into a frown. "But for the record, I don't approve."

"I realize it's a breach in propriety to travel with Lord Riven, but—"

"I'm not talking about that, but rather your choice to risk your life!" Her sharp voice held a brittle edge. "You might be fae, but their world has never been your home. You don't know its ways, its cruelties. None of us do."

I'd rehearsed countless possible reactions, but not once had I anticipated genuine concern from Aunt Melisina. My eyes pricked. "That may be true. Yet this offers our best chance at safety, in the end."

"If you must go, then I . . . I'm thankful Lord Riven means to go with you." For the first time since the attack in the clearing, Aunt Caris truly looked at me, a softness in her eyes. "I'm glad you won't be alone, and I take heart knowing that he brought you back safely before."

"And . . . do you desire my return?" I'd not meant to speak the words; they simply spilled out.

Her lips parted slightly. "How can you think otherwise?"

"Because of what you said after the attack." I could not take back the hasty words, and perhaps I did not want to—I could not leave without knowing the worst. "You didn't want me near Ada and Ainslie, as though you thought I might hurt them, perhaps hurt you. That cannot be a comfortable feeling, in your own home."

"The power you displayed, those creatures we saw . . . I'll not pretend I didn't have my fears." Her lips trembled. "And then, I was shocked at my own blindness. I'll grant I thought the notion of fae blood impossible at first, but then I began to think of all that passed before, all the ways I pressed you to act as expected, and I realized I'd failed you by making you feel you could not trust me in this. By proving myself unworthy of trust, when it came to it. Because I *was* afraid. But there's something truer than fear, and it's love. My fears are my own, and I must work on them, but . . . it's impossible for me to stop loving you, my dear."

A translucent wash blurred the room, and damp gathered beneath my lashes.

"Let's not become maudlin." Aunt Melisina sniffed. "You will return, and we'll sort everything out. We need consider nothing more now."

Aunt Caris reached for me, her fingers warm as she clasped my hand. "I've always thought I could protect you girls and make sure you enjoyed happy futures, if I just watched over you closely enough. Now . . . I know I can do very little." Her grip tightened. "Just promise me you'll come back."

"I'll do everything within my power to return."

All this time, Father had remained silent. Now he stirred. "Is this truly what you want—to risk the Otherworld?"

What I wanted didn't matter, nor could I even discern my own desires through the storms within my soul. I clasped Jade close. "Rather, it's what I must do."

"If anyone goes, it should rightly be me." He adjusted his spectacles. "It is my responsibility to protect all of you. Yet I must face the painful truth that you're far better equipped for this excursion, that I would only be a liability."

"And you're needed here, for the matters we discussed with Lord Blackburn—and to help Ada and Ainslie seek the truth about Mother."

"I think it's time I began to accept that all I believed about our marriage was false." He scrubbed a hand over his face. "I've spent these past days thinking it over. I never understood why she chose me, why she fell in love with me. She had beauty, wealth, independence—all rare for a lady in our world. She could have wed anyone she pleased or remained at liberty to do whatever she desired. Instead, she married me. So I must conclude there was some fae stratagem involved, one I cannot yet perceive."

"Oh, Alden," Aunt Caris murmured.

I couldn't promise that everything he'd shared with Mother was real. Only, I wanted to believe it, and the evidence suggested there was far more at work in her life than we understood. I sank down in front of him and waited for his eyes to meet mine. "I can think of a good many reasons she might have chosen to marry you, not least of which is that you're *real*. You've never hidden behind glamour or subterfuge or courtly manners, all the while waiting to strike the weak and vulnerable. Your love for her was true, and it has been faithful even after death. I've no doubt she knew its measure while she lived. If all she required was a mortal marriage, she could have chosen anyone, as you said. But she wanted you."

"Thank you, Jessa. But it's better for me to accept that she needed me for a purpose. It is the only reason fae approach mortals."

"Perhaps that's often true, but not always. Mother might have been an exception, and I mean to find the truth. Don't give up hope, not yet."

He lifted a hand to my cheek. "You're so like her."

Did that mean my presence brought pain? I hesitated, uncertain what to say.

"If it is worth anything, I hope . . . I want you to know that you have my love." He swallowed. "I know I haven't always been the father you needed, but I never want you to doubt that."

Then he stood and shuffled from the room, leaving us in fraught silence. The truths revealed had brought so much pain. Would the full truth, if I could ever uncover it, mend what had broken—or shatter it beyond repair?

~

AFTER I WITHDREW from my aunts and Lovell, I sought Ada and Ainslie, who held counsel with Dreda in the morning room. Confessing my imminent departure to the three of them came easier, since they were already aware of my intent, and they joined me in my bedchamber to help me prepare.

Ainslie secured the door behind her. "Are you certain you trust Lord Riven's arrangements?"

"I do. He's gone to a great deal of trouble to situate matters." Beyond the window glass, the song of the oak murmured an invitation to come within the shelter of its protective boughs and stay.

"Even so, it's difficult to think of you beyond reach." Ada wrapped her arms about her middle.

"If something truly went awry, I could send Risha." Though there would be nothing they could do to help, at least they'd know—no, I refused to think in such a way. Straightening my shoulders, I placed the satchel on the bed.

Ainslie tilted her head at it. "Does that hold some sort of secret weapon?"

"I wish it did. Rather, it's what Riven says I must wear, if I'm to blend in."

Dreda moved to my side. "If you wish, we can help you dress. It's little enough to offer, but perhaps it will help."

"I'd welcome the assistance. I don't quite know what to expect." I opened the satchel, revealing exquisite material. Threads of silver shot through a backdrop of sapphire blue, the fabric light and flowing and wholly unfamiliar. As I lifted the garment from the satchel, the blue deepened to indigo with ripples of dusky purple, and the silvery threads shimmered like stars in the expanse of the skirt. The satchel held a separate bodice that tapered to a V—one long enough to suggest the waistline would hit my natural waist, rather than beneath the bust, as was mortal convention.

Ainslie eyed the garments with clear intrigue. "Why bother with a separate bodice and skirt, I wonder?"

Jade lifted her head. *A bodice may also be worn with what you would call trousers, making it more versatile.*

Ainslie started, while Ada peered curiously at Jade. She'd never deigned to speak into their minds before. Yet both were becoming more impervious to the unexpected turns of Other, and Ainslie turned to Jade.

"That's acceptable for fae ladies to wear?" She fingered the fabric, which shimmered brighter at her touch.

On suitable occasions—not court events, but those like the hunt or any more active affair.

I examined the long, trailing skirt more closely and discovered capacious pockets, which I immediately tested with a small bundle of sketching pencils. By some fae glamour worked into the fabric, when I tucked an item within the pocket, it created no unsightly bulge on the outside. However, they were not fae pockets of the sort which Riven possessed—they did have firm limits according to the size of their design.

I shook myself and returned the pencils to their proper place. However much my mind wished to distract me from what was to come, I couldn't afford to spend time speculating on the whys and hows of fae attire, nor how desirable it would be to possess a true fae pocket. I gathered the clothing into my arms, then ducked behind the dressing screen to change into the undergarments, which were as unfamiliar as the outerwear. Fortunately, they were simple in structure and perfectly fitted for both support and comfort. My sisters and Dreda helped me sort the bodice and skirt, along with the elaborate jeweled belt that I donned last of all.

I'd tucked the passing prism within the satchel for concealment, and now I drew it out again, its brilliant array of color playing across the aged wood floor. Its fine clasp interwove with the chain so tightly that I could scarcely find it, let alone unfasten it. Harder still was attempting to reclasp it, once I'd placed the chain about my neck.

"Let me help." Ada stepped forward.

Even her nimble fingers struggled, but at last she secured it. I performed a final examination of the satchel, and I brushed against something hard at the bottom—a dagger with an elaborate jeweled hilt and sheath that complemented the dress. It bristled with ominous beauty. *Jade?*

It's meant to be worn openly. Attach it to the belt.

Its jewels chilled as I fastened it in place. And though I maintained my mortal glamour, I couldn't deny the overall effect was dazzling.

Ada swept her hands along the sides, smoothing the material, though it fell naturally into graceful lines. "You're certain this is meant for travel?"

"That's what Riven said."

Her brow furrowed slightly. "And he procured these?"

"He had help." And I hoped by help, he'd meant someone else had managed the situation altogether, because otherwise, it felt a great deal too . . . intimate for comfort.

"Well, whoever picked these has excellent taste." Ainslie forced a note of cheer into her voice. "If this is the sort of attire they favor in the Otherworld, then perhaps I *should* go after all."

"Oh, Jessa." Ada blinked rapidly, as though to dispel tears. "I wish you weren't going—or that we could go too."

I squeezed her hand. "I know."

Suddenly, Morwen popped her head out from beneath the bed, then scurried over to my side. She drew her fingers along the silken material of my gown, her eyes very bright. "Mortal fabrics not the same."

"Perhaps I'll have the opportunity to bring you some fae ones, when I return. But . . . that man you saw in the night, if he or anyone else ever seeks to plant devices about the house, will you remove them? And tell Ada at once?"

"Shall do, yes." Her pink head snapped toward the window, as if she suspected Mr. Ludne of lurking in the gardens even now. Then she turned back toward me. "What of the man with sunset hair?"

"The one who was here today?"

"Yes. He walked through the house."

I straightened. "You mean he didn't remain in the drawing room."

"No. Was my sleep time, so I did not know until he tangled with *triva*. It woke me, then I looked. Was near study of your father, left traces up the stairs and down."

The earlier prickling unease returned with a vengeance. "What is *triva*?"

"A working to trace the unwanted, those not of the house." Her curls bobbed. "Did not place on main level, because those not of house come often there. But up, yes."

"I'm glad you did." I sank onto the bed, my skirts pooling about me and my fears knotting in my stomach. What had Mr. Wells wanted? He could have no good purpose—the least dangerous one I could conceive was that he'd sought to claim the statuette, knowing Mr. Fuller had sold it to Thea. Perhaps he'd tried Crestridge Court first before seeking me here.

I should ask Thea—no, I wouldn't have a chance, because my time in this world had run out. The knot tightened. I didn't want to leave my family exposed to the Vigil and Mr. Ludne and anyone else who might seek to exploit them, yet I'd no choice but to trust my sisters—and even Mr. Burke—to keep watch. Whatever enmity he bore me, I believed he'd take seriously his duty to protect my mortal family.

Yet even he could not stand against the Vigil, if they came in force. I stared at the dusky expanse of my skirt splashed against the very mortal bedquilt. It would be easier to face the unknown dangers of the Otherworld if I knew my family would be safe. I lifted my gaze to my sisters. "Please be careful—"

"We will. Try not to think about us. You cannot be all places at once," Ada said.

I forced a smile. "I wish that was a fae affinity."

"We'll manage, Miss Jessa, never you worry." Dreda stood between Ada and Ainslie, and I'd no doubt she'd remain with them as long as she had breath.

"Thank you, all of you, for everything." I glanced out the window at the lowering sun. "I don't know when precisely Riven means to come, but I think it's best we say goodbye now, so we can do it without an audience."

Ainslie's embrace came quick and fierce, Ada's gentle and soothing, Dreda's steady and strong—and when they left, a void opened. Ignoring the discomfort, I stripped away my mortal glamour, then paced the chamber restlessly.

I couldn't just remain here waiting, but nor could I appear elsewhere like this. I rummaged in my bedside table for my sketchbook, but I couldn't find it. Perhaps I'd left it downstairs, but I certainly couldn't venture in search of it now.

In any case, I no longer had time, for a diamond-bright passing opened, revealing Riven. His gaze swept over me and lingered for a moment, glimmers of gold appearing in the green of his eyes. "Are you ready?"

I nodded. And like a summer tempest, the light of passing swept around us, drawing me into the unknown.

CHAPTER 50

We emerged in a forest of ancient trees shrouded with moss and fern. For a single suspended moment, the chorus of their voices broke over me like a wave across the shore, then the rich, wild sensation of Other followed in their wake, the essence of every living thing distilled into a bright, vibrant force that burned through my veins.

Every one of my senses wakened fully; every part of me *lived*. From the smallest spindled moss to the most towering of trees, the melodies of each plant surged through my senses, vivid and resonant. Perhaps shedding my mortal glamour had expanded my capacity, for I found I could absorb it all without drowning.

Yet still I staggered beneath the intensity, the vividness of shape and color, the layers of scent and sight. The melodies swelled about me, deepening and strengthening as I embraced them, until they became all-consuming. The outward appearance of the blossoms and boughs about me faded, revealing bright threads of power within each one—the *essence* Riven had referred to, perhaps? I closed my eyes, recalling the gently arched branches in my mind that filtered the raw intensity of sensation before, and they sprang to life once more, absorbing and dampening the onslaught.

I drew one deep breath, then another, the fierce, sweet fragrance of the Otherworld swirling about me, laced with the deep, earthy notes of the forest. When I dared look about me again, I found my vision had resolved. Seven trees encircled us, staggering in size, their bases larger than many a villager's cottage, their smooth bark a deep copper-purple banded with palest ivory lenticels, reminiscent of the rising sun. They spoke their name in bell-like tones—*evernesse.* In the very center of the ring they formed, a natural spring bubbled up into a pool so clear that the colorful pebbles along the bottom stood out in vivid array.

I turned to Riven, and my breath caught. No trace of his mortal glamour remained, and his beauty rivaled that of the wild forest about us. Jade gently nudged my shoulder, drawing me back to myself. Sometime since our arrival, she had shifted to true-form, and I leaned against her bulk, her immense presence grounding me. "Where are we?"

"In my court." The green in his eyes mirrored the vibrant leaves of the evernesse above. "I thought you might favor this place—also that you'd require a moment to orient yourself to this world before plunging into the Court of Dusk."

"It's perfect." If all of the Otherworld offered the welcome of this venerable forest, then I'd be hard-pressed to stay away. I traced the lines of the lenticels in the smooth bark before me, the life of the evernesse pulsing vibrant and strong beneath.

"It serves another purpose as well. We need a trail from the Court of Gold in case someone attempts to trace our point of origin."

I stepped away from the tree. "You think someone might go to such lengths?"

"Not unless we trigger suspicion." The lowering rays of the sun caught on the leaves of the evernesse and cast shadows across the planes of Riven's face. "Every fae who travels to the king's seat at Beresstone from another court must first pass an interview conducted by the arbiter of the Court of Dusk, Lady Ulrika. In theory, she's limited to three questions, but since you're entirely unknown, she'll try to take her time with you."

My heart pulsed unsteadily, as did the fern fronds at my feet. "She shares your ability to perceive emotion?"

"All arbiters possess that ability. Take care in what you say. The working I placed on you is keyed to me—it will offer you no protection from her affinities."

"Then does it even matter what I say, when she can perceive my fears?" The scents of the forest pressed heavy on me.

"Your instincts are sound. You'll know what to say to her, if she presses." Yet his eyes shaded darker. "Unless she catches you trying to deceive her, she's bound only to use the very mildest of compulsions—she won't be able to force answers. Keep your replies to one word, if possible. If she presses, don't deny any emotion you possess, but rather consider which emotions you might cause to burn more brightly than others."

"If she discovers deception, what then?"

"Then you will be treated as an enemy." He folded his arms. "Don't allow that to happen."

"Will your presence make any difference?"

"Given our alliance and the relative frequency of my appearance in her court, I won't be questioned at all. You'll most likely speak to her alone."

The soft murmur of the spring and the gentle stirring of the tree limbs above invited me to forget my purpose—to remain here where I was safe and sheltered. I shook off the desire. "What else should I know?"

"Far more than we have time to address, if we took weeks on end." Riven eyed the sun, which perched on the rim of the earth, scarcely visible through the thick foliage of the forest surrounding us. "Of most immediate relevance, their day begins shortly before twilight and stretches through the night hours. They won't expect guests to fully adhere to their way of life, yet court events and certainly the hunt will reflect it. It's why we wait until near dusk to arrive, as a nod to their customs. Try to last until dawn before you retire, if you can."

In my current state, sleep was the furthest thing from my mind. "I don't think that will be a problem."

"Good. You should take time to explore the common areas open to the public this evening—the libraries, gardens, great halls, and so forth. I'll be interested to learn who approaches you."

"You think the bargain-holder might seek me out?"

"She's shown interest in observing you, and it would lend savor to her games. But whether she does or not, it offers you a chance to begin accumulating gossip. Members of the court will speak more freely around you than they will me."

My shoulders tightened. "Then . . . you don't mean to accompany me?"

"It's best if we're not overmuch in company." Something tense coiled within him as well, furthering my unease. "Jade's presence, her unusual bond with you, will give others pause. Likely make them attribute you with greater power than you yet possess. Though she'll draw attention, she'll also be excellent backup. If you discover something noteworthy, then seek me. Otherwise, it's better that our connection appears a more distant, official one."

"I see."

He angled away. "If you feel prepared, we should depart— we don't want to lose our window."

I didn't, but then, I never would, not given what I must face, not with the ancient forest whispering invitations for me to dwell here and learn its secrets for ages on end. I closed my ears to its alluring melodies and locked my fears deep in my chest. "I'm ready, whenever you wish to go."

Once more, a passing charged the air about us, this time pulling me through to a small island in the middle of a river so vast that I could scarcely make out its far side. Before us, imposing obsidian mountains loomed, and about us wove layers of workings, thick and consuming.

Yet the power rolling from Riven was stronger still. He'd altered yet again, this time in some intangible way. He was walled off, remote and untouchable and . . . frightening. For the first time, I could imagine him holding another fae captive by affinity alone, choking out life with a wave of controlled, inexorable power. I shivered, my skin pebbling as if touched by frost.

I'd glimpsed Riven the fae lord several times, but now I beheld him as arbiter, and . . . I could not reconcile these other forms with his familiar one. The roar of the river against the stone surged into my ears, and my throat tightened.

I forced my gaze away. Twilight had settled across the landscape, pooling shadows among the stones, and the sky above held hues of coral and charcoal along with smudges of purple. The rays of the setting sun caught in the magnificent series of waterfalls that spilled down the mountain, and both were woven into a demesne of immense proportion that started halfway up the mountain and towered above the peak in sharp spires. The falls spilled around and through magnificent arches, and great covered walkways and immense windows faced the western sky.

Riven had said liminal affinities ran strong in this court. Had the king chosen this location for its duality of nature—water kissing stone, mountain reaching sky, and the demesne occupying the space where all of them joined? Regardless, the effect was one of both power and beauty—and I could have gazed upon it for hours.

Yet Riven strode forward without a single glance at the demesne. "This way."

He moved toward a polished stone tower that shot knifelike toward the sky, all sharp lines and angles. It was no natural formation, but rather a fae construct. Did someone dwell within? Or was it the port of entry to the demesne? Without offering explanation, Riven sauntered through the arched doorway, and with Jade alongside, I kept pace the best I could, trying to conceal my utter disorientation.

Within the tower, fae-lights illumined a circular chamber, the walls and floor carrying intricate patterns in varied colors of stone—and workings that bristled with implicit threat. If we were intruders, I'd little doubt the stones themselves would rise against us. Across the space, an imposing woman with ash-pale hair and eyes the shade of bluestars addressed another fae, her low tones just indistinct enough that I could not make out her words, nor the replies the fae lord offered. A closer inspection indicated that a glamour muffled the sound.

Riven stood motionless, as if carved from stone himself, and I attempted to imitate his stillness as I waited next to him. I couldn't afford to appear as if I gawked, so however much I wished to inspect every detail of the chamber, I allowed myself only to take in what rested in my line of sight—a row of arched windows, latticed along the top with finely scrolled stone in celestial patterns.

"Lord Riven." The fae lady stalked toward us. "It seems we are destined to have the pleasure of your company more often than we're accustomed to."

He simply inclined his head. "Lady Ulrika."

"You may go. I've no need of you, only your companion."

Though I did not possess their ability to perceive emotions, her words held a distinct edge of hostility. I rested my hand on Jade's shoulder. *She seems to dislike Riven.*

Her court owes fealty to his—it's reason enough for some resentment.

"I'm required to accompany Lady Jessa." Riven sounded almost bored. "I'll wait outside. Send her to me when you're through."

"The steward can attend her."

"That won't be necessary. Unlike some, I don't pawn off my responsibilities."

Her features tightened. In some way, it had been a jab. Apparently, they were very much not in accord. "Suit yourself."

Riven offered a clipped nod, then returned the way we'd come, soon vanishing through the doorway. I forced all my thoughts toward a placid admiration of the architecture and away from the wrench of loss I experienced when he departed. However unsettling the transformation in him, he was the one certain thing in this treacherous place. But I could not afford to expose any such sentiments before Lady Ulrika.

"Lady Jessa." Her cool gaze settled on me, and she crooked a long, slim finger, the nail of which bore some sort of crimson polish. "Come."

I followed her to a bench positioned below two particularly brilliant fae-lights. Beneath their radiance, not even the slightest shift in expression could be concealed. Her power crashed over me with the force of a storm tide, carrying with it a near-irresistible urge to start talking, to confess every hidden thing stored in my soul. This was a mild compulsion?

"Please sit."

I perched on the edge of the unyielding bench, yet she remained towering over me—as if I needed a reminder of the differential in power between us. I drew a deep breath, considering what Aunt Caris had said about love being stronger than fear, clinging to that love for Ainslie, for Ada, for all my family, and allowing it to wash away any emotions that might betray me to this arbiter.

She tapped her fingers idly against her leg. "Do you bear any malice against King Alastor or his court?"

"No."

"Will you seek to murder King Alastor or any other member of his court during your stay?"

What in the Crossings? My fingers curled about the edge of the polished bench. "No."

"Will you adhere to the laws of our court?"

"Yes."

I'd answered the three questions Riven had spoken of, and yet her gaze sharpened. "You appear uneasy. What is it you fear?"

"You cannot tell me I'm the only one to feel discomfort in the presence of an arbiter." I folded my hands in my lap, taking care to keep strict truth in each statement and fighting the growing urge to spill my soul. "I prefer that my emotions remain my own."

"So you say." She assessed me. "Yet you appeared quite at

ease with Lord Riven. One might even say you trust him implicitly. Why is that?"

"We've reached an understanding." Blight and rot. The words had escaped before I could stop them.

"Between your courts or personally?" Her words drove like thorns into my flesh.

I drew the melodies of the rowan that bloomed beyond the door toward myself and managed to remain silent. Surely fae would divulge no more than required.

She leaned forward, and the deep scent of ebony wafted about me, along with something sharper and more metallic. "Has he taken you to his bed, then? Perhaps as part of a bargain in exchange for protection?"

A knife blade of shock severed the melody of the rowan, and my pulse surged in my ears. I should reply, say something, anything, yet words deserted me.

"I see that's not the case." Her lips curved in a satisfied smile. "I'd not heard he had such proclivities, but it doesn't hurt to inquire. One never knows what might be learned."

If she'd meant to overset my emotions, she'd succeeded. How could she possibly think—

It's not the insult it would be in the mortal world. Some high fae adhere to the old ways, others have a more . . . liberal mindset. She seeks an explanation, and it's one of few that would make sense from her perspective.

"If not due to some intimate attachment, then why do you extend trust?"

"I fail to see what relevance this has to my sojourn in your court." I extended my senses beyond the rowan to the stately river birches that pillared the water's edge, their songs hedging my mind. I would say no more.

"As you say, it has no relevance to your stay here. The choice to answer or not is yours. Just as the choice to trust is, however unwise it might be."

Though she offered an escape, her discomfiting power pressed down upon me, and again I choked down the urge to confess details of how Riven and I had met, what had passed between us . . . I sank deeper into the greening strength of the birch, the bright vitality of the rowan, and the cool comfort of the river rushes. And I allowed the silence to stretch.

At last, she inclined her head toward Jade. "If you've no desire to speak of Lord Riven, perhaps you'd care to tell how you came to be bonded with a *kit-isne*? It's been some time since we've had one within Beresstone, longer still since I've heard of one bonded with fae. In the rare situations they choose to accept such a bond, they ordinarily choose one of particular renown."

None of these were questions I was bound to answer, else she would have forced me with the sort of compulsion impossible to resist, instead of the undercurrent of pressure she'd brought to bear. Yet a refusal to answer might suggest I'd something to hide, particularly since I'd already refused to discuss my relationship with Riven. I hesitated. On the balance, withholding information seemed the safer choice, more in keeping with what I knew of fae. "You've asked your questions, Lady Arbiter. Have my answers satisfied?"

"You have satisfied the requirements, for now." Still, Lady Ulrika regarded me closely until another fae lady moved through the doorway, her presence drawing attention. Lady Ulrika waved a hand toward me. "You may rejoin Lord Riven whenever you please."

I didn't linger, in case she changed her mind, nor did I run from the chamber as I desired to do; instead, I kept my pace to a slow glide. Riven lounged on a bench just outside the door, appearing utterly at his ease. When I emerged from the building, he stood, no hint of warmth or welcome in his features—I might as well have been a parcel he was sent to fetch. My chest tightened.

He wove a concealment glamour around us, one far sharper-edged than those he'd used in the mortal world. The diamond shards of light shimmering within it bristled a warning.

I tilted my head. "Will it seem odd that we're keeping our conversation concealed?"

"Not at all." He gave a slight shrug. "It's the only way to be assured of a private conversation in such proximity of the king's seat. You'll find they're used with great frequency, even in private spaces."

"I see." I took that as a warning that any conversation might be overheard, no matter how empty the space about me *appeared*.

"I take it Lady Ulrika was satisfied." He strode toward the edge of the river, his pace measured, and I fell in alongside him.

"Perhaps not satisfied, but willing to allow my departure at least. She seemed particularly interested in the fact that I do not fear you." I fidgeted with the jeweled belt—I'd no intention of confessing her more sordid suggestions.

"I'm not surprised."

"What relevance could it have to our stay here?"

"I suspect it had personal relevance, rather than professional." His tone remained devoid of emotion. "Lady Ulrika is relatively new to her position. It takes time to grow . . . accustomed to the role. She struggles."

I'd disliked Lady Ulrika on sight for the threat she represented and the enmity she clearly bore Riven. Yet what must it be like to occupy such a role?

Perhaps Riven read something of my sentiments in my features, for he stopped short, his expression forbidding. "Whatever you may feel for her situation, do not trust her. Your ends and hers stand in opposition, and she could swiftly undo all our plans."

"I understand."

"Good. The king's demesne isn't to be entered lightly. Protocol dictates we enter the passing chamber only upon our arrival, lest it be taken as an invasion. The grounds and gardens are also acceptable points from which to come and go, after that point," he said. "A servant will meet us in the passing chamber and escort us to our quarters. We'll likely be placed at some distance from each other. They prefer to separate acquaintances in such fashion, so as to more easily take note of how often they seek each other out."

How was I to begin to navigate this unfamiliar territory? In the mortal world, I'd used my knowledge of convention and human nature to assess the individuals I encountered; here I feared I might make tremendous blunders simply for lack of understanding. I swallowed the urge to ask for some word of reassurance. For what could be offered?

I'd give a great deal to return to the mortal world, even for a moment, to my family and to Riven as he ordinarily was . . . Only which one was true?

He halted at the edge of the river, then we passed into an immense and striking room on the ground level of the demesne —which was in fact elevated hundreds of feet from the river below. Layers of Other pervaded the chamber, both the hostile living awareness that I'd come to associate with a demesne and something more, a starlike scent and presence, cold and ancient and all-powerful. It swirled around me, catching in my chest, weighing, judging, measuring. And then it released, and I could move again, though it still infused every ell of this space.

Above us, an arched ceiling upon which stars danced in vibrant array was held in place by spiraled beams of stone. What sort of working fueled this living display? I'd little time to consider, for two willowy men approached us, not high fae, certainly, but some other unknown entity. Their skin held brown-green tones, their hair resembled river rushes, and their arms and legs were reedy.

One bowed low before Riven. "Lord Arbiter, will you allow me to show you to your chambers?"

With a nod, Riven followed him, leaving me alone once more—and feeling wholly unmoored. The other servant halted before me. "Lady Jessa, this way, if you please."

I shouldn't appear awed by all I beheld, yet I *was*. Every turn revealed some new splendor, the workings woven through every part of the demesne complex beyond my comprehension. In the end, I fixed my gaze on the back of the willowy man as he led the way to my bedchamber, one far more expansive than I'd expected.

As I stepped inside, the room enveloped me. I'd entered a living celestial scene, a vibrant moonrise that spilled from the ceiling down over the walls, light pooling on the floor in shimmering coils. I brushed my fingers across the wall, seeking the reality beyond perception, and I met the smoothest of stones, a living canvas upon which this scene etched itself, as vibrant as if I stood on the riverbank beholding the splendors of a full summer moon.

The floor beneath my feet seemed to crunch like river rock as I moved deeper into the space. A large circular bed occupied the center of the room, piled high with pillows and silken coverlets, and if I strained, I could perceive the outlines of various furniture along the walls.

Jade sprang upon the bed. *If you move toward them, they should resolve into more solid form.*

I closed my eyes to block out the dazzling array. How easily I could lose myself in the intrigue of Other—and become distracted from my true purpose.

Jade nudged me. *Someone's at the door.*

A moment later, a soft knock sounded. I opened the door to find a servant similar in appearance to the one who'd escorted me to my chamber. She stood with an empty tray in her reedlike hands.

I stepped back to allow her entrance, and she set the tray on a table—which had originally appeared like a rock formation within the liminal tableau of my chamber—then lowered her head. "What would please you for fast-breaking?"

Fast-breaking? Of course, dusk was to this court what dawn was to the mortal world, and now they prepared for their "day." I hesitated. "I would like to try that which is most favored in your court."

Her expression didn't alter, but she reached into the satchel at her side and withdrew ivory dishes with lace-woven edges.

Then she brought forth an assortment of food, arranging it in a picturesque array. Evidently, the satchel was a sort of fae pocket, but how the food maintained form and temperature was beyond my understanding.

She stepped back and folded her hands. "May I attend you in any other way?"

I checked the impulse to offer thanks. "No. That will be all."

Her motions as graceful as the sway of a river reed, she slipped from the room, and I surveyed the meal set before me, a brilliant display of color and texture, from the delicate star-shaped pastries to the sculpted arrangements of smoked meat and fish. Even the fruits held gleaming jewel tones. A tall fluted goblet held a liquid that shifted color as I lifted the glass, and it tasted as one might imagine light would, vibrant and invigorating.

Jade and I shared the delicacies before us, a full world of flavor represented in the collection of smoked meats, sweet-tart fruits, and impossibly light pastries. It was far more than sufficient for the two of us, and at last, I brushed my hands, moving to the looking glass to freshen up.

Surprisingly, I didn't appear much the worse for my travels. Only a few stray curls needed restraining. At this point, I could delay no further—it was past time to follow through on Riven's suggestions. *Any notion where we should begin?*

Jade licked a paw and swiped it over her face, smoothing her fur. *Risha will know more. She has greater experience within court.*

I turned to Risha, who'd perched within the beams of the liminal moon. "Bright one, where would you recommend I start?"

Her light took on a rosy hue, as if she was pleased to be asked. "I have already exchanged messages with Court of Dusk sylphs. They say many will visit the queen's Chamber of Stars at this hour."

"Very well." I'd rather seek the library Riven had mentioned, yet if I wished to become familiar with the court, I must display myself before its members. Whatever the risks of exploring the Court of Dusk, I'd gain nothing if I hid within my chambers.

Only what would I find when I ventured forth?

CHAPTER 51

When I secured the door behind me, it blazed with a bright emblem, one woven of thorns and roses and complicated runes. I rested a hand on Jade's shoulder. *Do you know its purpose?*

It looks like a sigil—all courts have them. Perhaps it belongs to the Court of Roses, from where you're meant to hail?

If that's what it signifies, any passerby could readily locate me. No one else here comes from that court.

A rumble of displeasure sounded in her chest. *If you are not strong enough to defend yourself, you are not worthy of defense—to go by fae logic. They'd think nothing of leaving you exposed.*

As I examined the sigil, a willowy woman appeared, similar in bearing to the man who'd escorted me to my bedchamber. She swept toward me, her skirt trailing diaphanous behind her like a swell of massed cordifolia. "May I assist you?"

"I'd like to visit the Chamber of Stars."

"If you'll follow me, I will take you."

She led me through a maze of corridors woven with layers of illusion that left my senses reeling, each unfolding passage more elaborate than the last as we left the guest wing and entered the public spaces of the demesne. Risha bobbed at my shoulder, and Jade padded alongside, their familiar companionship reassuring in this vast foreign place. We ascended a staircase crafted of some sort of shimmering substance and emerged into an immense chamber with a translucent roof that exposed the glorious night sky above. A pool, its surface still and dark, stretched across the center of the room, reflecting back the magnificent starscape. On the shadowed walls, fae-lights resembling stars in the heavens clustered thickly, giving the illusion that we moved through a celestial space.

The beauty alone overwhelmed my senses, but it paled in comparison to the mingled power flooding the space. There might have been a hundred or more fae scattered across the immense chamber, most conversing in small groups of two or three. Yet a closer look revealed an undercurrent of tension—either detached rivalry or cold disdain bristled from nearly every interaction. Did the tension arise because two rival courts mingled, each seeking to gain advantage over the other? Or was this just ordinary fae behavior?

Never mind that now—if I continued to linger on the threshold, I'd draw unwanted attention. With Jade at my side, I glided into the room, feigning calm I did not feel. To distract myself, I glanced up. The translucent roof above our heads acted with telescopic effect, bringing the jeweled constellations above into sharp clarity, as if I'd journeyed far closer to the heavens. Oh, if only Father could catch a glimpse of this display . . .

"First time in the chamber?" The resonant voice sounded far too close for comfort, and the scents of smoke and shadow enveloped me.

I wrenched my gaze away from the sky to find an imposing fae lord standing across from me, conducting a candid assessment of my person. I fought the urge to step back. "Why do you ask?"

"Because you're clearly taken with the spectacle." He moved closer still, the midnight-blue fabric of his jacket shimmering with undercurrents of silver, his raven-dark hair unbound and worn long. "If you'd spent all your days in this court, it would have become commonplace."

I rested a hand on Jade's shoulder, her presence reassuring. "Or perhaps I'm simply an admirer of the heavens and the continual alterations therein."

"Perhaps." His dark-as-night eyes considered me. "Yet I prefer fact to speculation. To that end, I propose a bargain."

He offered no pleasantries, just moved straight to his purpose, unconcerned with any potential offense. Who was he? He must be from the Court of Silver, else he'd have known for sure this wasn't my home. In any case, the sense of power rolling from him exceeded the others gathered in the room. Whatever his identity, this wasn't a lord to toy with, nor deny. "What sort of bargain?"

"You answer two questions, and I'll answer two in turn." With a faint crackle, a crimson-tinged glamour sealed our conversation from any listeners. "No limits."

"Putting a bargain before an introduction seems rather out of order."

A flare of interest kindled in his eyes. "You don't know who I am?"

Only a few moments in the chamber, and I'd made my first misstep. Evidently, he was of sufficient prominence that I *should* have been able to identify him. "I'm afraid not."

His lips tilted into a fierce, glinting sort of smile, one best suited to the creatures that stalked the night. "Then I am correct. You are Lady Jessa of the Court of Roses."

"I am Lady Jessa, yes. And you?"

The scent of burning cedar laced the air, warming the space between us. "Is that one of your questions?"

"As yet, I've agreed to no bargain." And I was already weary of being on my guard, of the chance one treacherous word would bind me to danger.

Jade yawned as if bored by the proceedings, in the process showing off her gleaming white fangs. *Risha says this is Prince Sable of the Court of Silver. Queen Astra's son.*

Bless Risha, her initiative, and her sylph sources. "But I'm pleased to make your acquaintance, Prince Sable."

"I see whatever lack of knowledge has resulted from the isolation of your court, you're not without your sources." The scents of smoke and cedar strengthened. "Now, for my questions."

He wasn't going to accept a denial. What would happen if I offended one of his standing? Alternately, what weakness would it suggest if I agreed? I needed to take back some measure of control. "As you observed, this is my first visit to the Chamber of Stars, and I should like to view it. Shall we walk and discuss the matter?"

"After you." He waved me onward. Though the glamour remained, it faded to a near-translucent state that allowed full appreciation of our surroundings. In a way I suspected might be characteristic of fae, he didn't attempt to make light conversation, only waited for my answer to his demand.

We approached the edge of the pool, Jade ensuring her body always remained between us. *You won't find many willing to part with information without some sort of exchange. I believe if you were here from the Court of Roses, you would desire this bargain. But not necessarily on his terms.*

Very well. I fixed my gaze on the reflected stars. "I will answer your two questions, but only if you grant me three in return."

"Done." Swift as a kindled spark, the binding wove about my arm, a shade of copper reminiscent of flame. "Now, tell me. What was your purpose in leaving your court?"

"To see to the interests of my family."

"Your family, not your court." One brow arched slightly. "I wonder what your monarch might say about that. Perhaps she will tolerate it, if you form an advantageous enough alliance."

"It is my hope to do so." I could confess as much without lying, although my notion of an advantageous alliance no doubt differed a great deal from what he had in mind.

"And what court do you most desire to forge ties with?"

This, then, was his true question. Had he approached me of his own accord, or did Queen Astra have interest in connecting with my supposed court of origin? "As of now, I have no decided preference. I'm open to all possibilities."

Again, that sharp smile slashed his face. "Excellent. What of your questions?"

I inhaled the cool evening air, which was as fresh and clear as though we truly strolled out of doors. Small wonder he'd granted three questions, when the direction of them might prove as insightful as my answers to his own. Though I yearned to pursue matters related to our inquiry, I'd best not leap to that and betray undue interest. "If an alliance were to form between the Court of Roses and the Court of Dusk, what terms might be required?"

"I cannot speak on behalf of my queen. However, she would accept an audience with you."

Which meant she certainly desired this alliance. Just how well had Nikol and Riven crafted my fictitious background that someone so powerful took an interest—and how much trouble would it cause if the truth were revealed? I allowed the silence to stretch a moment, silvery clouds drifting to obscure the moon above. If I represented a court, what else might I ask? Dared I hint at an interest in mortal experimentation? "And if I had interest in acquiring a group of mortals, with whom would you recommend I speak?"

"In my court or this one?"

"Both. I prefer to keep my options open."

"In this court, I hear rumor that Lady Maeve has excellent sources and will deal, if given sufficient incentive. As will Lord Corbin, if my conversation with him was any indication." The shimmering pool reflected cold light across his features. "In my own, Lord Rowan has some cultivated lines, but you will have to visit our court if you wish to treat with him. He has chosen to abstain from the hunt."

How convenient that he put forth the name of an inaccessible individual when it came to his own court. However, my true interest was in the Court of Dusk, and the names he mentioned offered possible prospects. I tilted my head, choosing a different path, in hopes that it would obscure my true interests. "You understand I must make all my decisions with care. Any alliance must offer something not readily attainable otherwise."

The ember-edged shadows about him deepened. "Naturally."

"In light of that, I would like to know—what advantage does Queen Astra intend to take of the changing balance between worlds?"

"It seems your court has not removed themselves from broader affairs as much as they wish us to believe."

"It is better to keep one's purpose to oneself until such time disclosure brings gain."

"And is now such a time?"

"Perhaps." I shrugged slightly. "My question remains."

"Then know Queen Astra takes great interest in this . . . changing balance, as you call it. The outcome will shape the future." He assessed me once more. "But then, you know that, else your court would not break their long silence."

My chest tightened. I'd *not* known that the fae courts viewed affairs between worlds in such light. Furthermore, his words hinted that Queen Astra observed and meant to take advantage of the alterations, not that she'd instigated the shift. Riven had said the same of his own king, while also suggesting that someone sought to force a conflict between worlds. To what end?

A soft chime echoed through the chamber. Evidently, it signaled something to Prince Sable. "I'm due for Convocation. Should you wish to continue our conversation later, you'll find my chambers in the western ascent."

I offered a slight, noncommittal nod. Did he intend to measure my interest in a court alliance, or did he mean something more? Fae had their own social mores, which made it impossible for me to decipher. In any case, the proper bounds between lord and lady in no way resembled those with which I was familiar. When he withdrew his glamour and strode from the chamber, I forced myself to continue strolling along the pool's edge.

Two ladies approached from the opposite direction, absorbed in conversation. They didn't bother with any sort of concealment glamour, so either they wished to be overheard or viewed their discussion as inconsequential. Perhaps, to other fae it was. But given how little I knew about this world, even the most trivial of matters intrigued.

"Do you supply the moon doves for the fight tomorrow?" The first speaker, a lithe fae adorned in a raiment of ivory that offset her dark features, brushed along the edge of the pool.

"A number of them, yes."

"Then the king has chosen another to share the responsibility?"

"I suggested it." The second lady glided along, smooth and expressionless. "I'd little time to prepare, and I must retain a sufficient number as breeders for next year."

Fight?

Jade's tail bristled slightly. *The Courts of Silver and Dusk favor moon dove fights as entertainment, and they wager quite a bit on the results.*

The ivory-clad fae shook her head slightly. "I imagine the recent strictures on the use of youngling sylphs as bait hasn't made training them easier."

Risha's wings darkened.

And Jade rumbled low. *Risha says it's not a kindness; rather, they rely on sylphs to perform many mundane tasks and cannot let their numbers drop too far.*

It must be very difficult for her to hear their deaths discussed so lightly. My chest tightened further as I rounded the far side of the pool. One of the unusual-looking servants scurried out in front of me, rushing toward a sequestered nook where a fae lord and lady sat conversing.

The servant bowed low before them. "My apologies for the delay."

The fae lady leaned forward, murmuring something I could not decipher. Then a crackling cloud of energy enveloped the servant, who collapsed writhing to the floor.

Instinctively, I moved forward, and Jade checked me. *Do not intervene. You need to move on.*

Yet I couldn't wrench my gaze from the sight of the helpless low fae, trapped in anguish.

She won't be killed. No one would dare kill the royal servants without the king's permission. Still, the glow of Jade's eyes had dimmed.

Yet this is acceptable?

For failure to perform as expected, yes.

Just as I began to form unchancy plans to create a distraction, the crackling cloud faded, and the low fae collapsed to the floor. The fae lady ignored her, continuing her conversation with the lord as the servant crawled away.

Somehow, I forced myself onward, passing through pooled shadows to the other side of the expanse. I might have gained some insight from my conversation with Prince Sable, yet if another fae approached, I feared my raw emotions would bleed through—and I could lose far more than I'd gained. Even now, my neck prickled as if someone had watched and taken note of my response.

Perhaps a strategic withdrawal?

Better that than to reveal the truth. I glided from the Chamber of Stars, doing my best to make it appear a purposeful errand rather than an overwhelmed flight. Never mind the importance of engaging other fae, I required the chance to regain composure before I betrayed myself.

Yet returning to my chambers felt too great a concession to defeat. Perhaps the library? If we were to seek a shadow-drake, I needed to understand its nature, so the time wouldn't be wasted —and the quiet among the stacks would offer a welcome reprieve.

After we wandered through the corridors for a time, Jade caught scent of the library. We passed through a vaulted great hall, which ended in double doors at least four times my height, and as we approached, they swung open, revealing an immense tower beyond.

Across from the door stretched a stunning expanse of glass— a single impossibly large panel without seam or joint. It offered an unhindered view of a magnificent waterfall beyond, its spray turned to pale silver in the moonlight. Along the bottom of the window curved a scene of the setting sun, and when I craned my neck to perceive the top, I glimpsed stonework that captured the rising moon. The rest of the curved walls contained endless shelves of books, among which sylphs darted, their lights shaded with purple and ivory.

Jade's ears pricked forward slightly. *They're star sylphs, a kin to Risha's kind, and they dwell mostly in the Courts of Dusk and Silver. She says they act as librarians.*

A collection this enormous must require a great many. I tilted my head further to behold the expanse. We stood at the base of the tower, and above us stretched level after level of books, connected by spiraled stone stairways that resembled cascading falls.

At once, the tension in my shoulders eased. Though this held many differences from the libraries in the mortal world, the familiar scents of leather and parchment soothed. Among paper and ink, I could collect information in peace—and without drawing undue attention. I moved forward. The space was so vast that I didn't register the other fae occupying it at first, but soon their presences pricked into my awareness, each carrying very different sensations. Bolstered by the peace of my environment, I recalled to myself the river birch standing like sentinels at the water's edge, and as their melodies filtered into my awareness, they drove back the imposing sense of power emanating from the fae scattered through the library. So armed, I ascended the first stairwell and chose a book at random from the shelf. Its pages were blank. I returned the book and selected another; it also contained an empty expanse. *What am I missing?*

I don't know, but I'll inquire of Risha. After a moment, Jade turned toward me. *She says many books bear glamours that make them unreadable to those outside the court that possesses them. Fae hold the belief that knowledge is power, and they have no intention of sharing it freely.*

That was unfortunate, but what might be common knowledge to the average fae could still offer a great deal of revelation to me. As I replaced the second book, a bitter purple-tinged scent wafted through the air. I glanced over my shoulder, seeking the source.

And I found nothing.

I attempted to press the scent from my awareness, but it thickened until it became almost choking, despite the fact that no other fae occupied this level. When I'd wrestled with the nightspire in the gardens, this smell had hung heavy in the air. Was it something common to the Court of Dusk—from which the nightspire sprang—or could it relate to Ainslie's bargain-holder in particular?

Can you trace its source?

Jade chuffed. *It seems to come from everywhere and nowhere at once. Perhaps it does belong to the court or reflects some affinity exercised within it.*

That was a reasonable explanation, far more than the notion that the bargain-holder might expose herself with such immediacy, yet the deep fragrance pricked unease down my spine. Since I didn't possess the ability to trace it back to its source—whether it was innocuous or malevolent—I held to my course, meandering down rows of translucent shelves as though I surveyed the books.

The scent faded, and I did my best to press it from my mind. Threat or not, all I could do was remain watchful and carry out my original purpose. *Jade, can you ask Risha where we might seek information on shadow-drakes?*

Yes. Jade pivoted toward Risha. *She says she shall find out.*

Risha fluttered over to another sylph, conversing for a moment before returning to my side. "This way."

We ascended two more levels, then Risha's light shimmered over a book whose spine read: *A Concise History of the Wilderfell and Its Inhabitants.* I plucked it from the shelf, and to my relief, found ornate script scrolling across the pages. Though shelves rimmed the tower walls, chairs were dotted at intervals along the balustrade. I chose the nearest one, and Jade situated herself alongside, her body shielding mine, her gaze watchful. I skipped to the section on shadow-drakes, and Risha perched on my shoulder, reading along with me.

Though pyske and shadow-drakes couldn't be more different, it seemed they both possessed innately magical bodies, which made them desirable targets. In the case of the shadow-drakes, their blood was a deadly, untraceable poison. Once fashioned by fae, it could mimic the symptoms of any other poison and would act when bidden, either immediately or after a delay. I didn't want to consider what damage it could do in the hands of a fae monarch—or any individual bent on malice, fae or mortal.

But why would King Alastor allow the Court of Silver queen to take such a lethal prize?

Likely he claims some portion as a tithe.

Wonderful. That meant after the hunt, both monarchs would have added another lethal weapon to their arsenals. I forced myself away from speculation of the harm that might be done and back to the book.

Once bled, the shadow-drake would lose strength for a time, which would likely doom it to destruction, either by other creatures eager to seize its territory or low fae seeking to utilize other elements from its body. If it sensed defeat, it might choose to take its own life, rather than endure the pain of being forcibly bled and the slow death that might follow.

This is the vulnerability you referenced, why you said a hunt to the death would be kinder.

Yes. Jade's ears shifted back. *In this case, it's not an act of mercy to refrain from taking a life, but rather a display of prowess without care for the suffering that will follow.*

I stared at the silvery falls beyond the window for some time before returning to the pages before me, which now addressed the history of how the shadow-drakes had come to occupy the Wilderfell Forest. The narrative suggested that when shadow-drakes had greater numbers, they'd allied themselves with the Court of Dusk and had willingly given their blood. This sacrifice did them no harm—it was the force used to claim their blood unwilling that left them weak, rather than the loss of blood itself. They did this in exchange for a peaceable dwelling within the forest, which offered safe nesting grounds for their young amid the nightsward they required to line their nests. But the fae had deceived them as to what they'd do with the blood, and when the shadow-drakes learned the truth, relations had been severed and enmity had sprung up between them.

Why must things be so . . . broken? I snapped the book shut and shoved it back onto the shelf, my stomach roiling. Was there ever an instance of fae as a collective showing mercy? Or did they always take advantage of their power to amass still more?

You cannot dwell on it now. Jade stood. *Risha says there's a*

*book on the top level that talks about the abilities of the shadow-
drake, what you might encounter on the hunt.*

I drew a deep breath, attempting to refocus on the matter at
hand. *Then I suppose I should take a look.*

Perhaps I'd chance upon someone with whom I might
converse, because for all my awareness of the other fae occupying
this space, I'd yet to encounter one.

As I ascended the final stairwell, a dusky-purple shadow
swirled across my path. It coiled in a distinct pattern on the
steps ahead—one that resembled nightspire leaves and vines. I
swallowed against a choking coppery taste.

Somewhere in this vast space, the bargain-holder must lurk,
must watch and wait for my reaction. Would she mount a direct
assault? If so, how could I hope to deflect it? I was sealed off
from any direct connection with plants—and I didn't imagine
the king would favor a breach of his walls even if I possessed the
power to accomplish such a deed.

Could I borrow the properties of the plants from a distance?
Somehow, the bargain-holder had pulled elements of the nightspire into this place, though the plant itself didn't exist within
these walls. Even now, its song echoed in my ears, carrying a
sense of malice and hunger.

At once, the nightspire shadows split into a dozen fragments,
then each one formed a full-size plant, these shadowspire vines
spiraling toward me. My pulse throbbed at the base of my neck.
No more time for deliberation.

I flung my senses as wide as I could, the songs of the living
things beyond the demesne surging into my senses. Many of
them responded to the bidding of another, those within the
king's gardens, but . . .

There.

On the far bank of the river, something familiar sprang from
the ground—a tangle of reddish-black and green, sharp and
thorned and full of summer life. My battle with the bau had
imprinted the essence of the blackberry brambles on my senses,

and I pulled it to myself until it danced vibrant among the shadows, holding them at bay.

Then a woman stepped from behind one of the pillars, her form as upright and unyielding as mountain ash. When my gaze met hers, I staggered back. Something about her was utterly *wrong*, the flat pallor of her ashen eyes, the dark sheen of her hair, the sharpness of her smile. It was not the face of one inclined to negotiation, nor even reason. A bitterness emanated from her, and it rooted me in place, my limbs frosting over, my hold on the distant brambles faltering.

Jade stalked forward with a growl, and the woman vanished. My breath shuddered. I was beyond my depth. *Ask Risha to go for Riven and tell him the bargain-holder was just here— perhaps enough remains to trace her path.*

A moment later, Risha winked from sight, and I struggled to hold my connection across the distance to the twining brambles —their living presence the only thing holding the shadows that she'd left at bay. Just a moment now, and I could release them . . .

Yet Risha returned without Riven, and the sense of frost sank deeper.

Jade rumbled low. *Riven's closeted with King Alastor, no sylphs permitted in.*

The bargain-holder must have known that—just as she'd known me, just as she taunted my lack of knowledge, my comparative weakness. My temples throbbed. I needed to go, but where? To the gardens, where I might mount some more meaningful defense? Or would that be too isolated a locale? In any case, I must abandon the stairs, as their vantage was wholly unprotected.

I darted up the remaining steps. The window didn't stretch to the topmost level; instead, a series of spiraled alcoves occupied the space between shelves. Before I could choose a course of action, the bargain-holder appeared again, the shadowspire about her holding a familiar echo of power. The coppery taste in my mouth strengthened, bitter and astringent. She toyed with me, and I'd little means of defense.

Acting on instinct, I ducked within the nearest alcove. And someone spoke behind me.

"Mind your step."

I spun around and found a fae lady enthroned on the cushioned arch that formed the back of the alcove. Her unbound hair flowed down her back like a river of silver, one that matched the shimmering falls beyond the room, and her eyes held the brightness of the moon outside—along with some of its uncanny age. Both formed a striking contrast to her bronzed skin.

I hesitated. "Forgive me, I hope I'm not disturbing you."

"Not at all." Her brows lifted ever so slightly. "I think, rather, someone seeks to disturb you?"

It was pointless to deny it, if she'd witnessed the skirmish on the stairs and the woman who'd taunted me. So I simply nodded.

"Then why not join me? You won't be disturbed here, and it shall relieve the boredom of my wait."

"I . . . appreciate the invitation." I situated myself on the far side of the arch, where I might keep watch on her and the opening, before which the shadows danced.

One snaked forward, only to wink from sight as soon as it crossed into the alcove. Somehow the lady had dispelled it, though she hadn't as much as twitched a finger. Most of the fae I'd encountered so far carried a distinct feeling about them, their affinities or some aspect of their nature bleeding through in a discernible way, yet from her I felt only a sense of a vast ancient distance that left me out-of-kilter—but then, almost everything in this court gave me that sensation.

She regarded me unblinking, making no attempt to hide her scrutiny. "Which court do you hail from?"

"I come by way of the Court of Gold, though it is not my home."

"And where is your home?"

"Far from here," I said softly.

"Then you must be the one sent from the Court of Roses. Lady Jessa?"

"News spreads quickly, I see."

"Only that which is worthy of note. I don't often trouble to keep abreast of court affairs, but others—they have reason to find out everything they can about those who visit our court. And they talk."

Jade settled at my feet, filling the alcove, her bulk reassuring. "You know my name, but I don't know yours."

"I go by Talis." She leaned forward slightly, her gown rustling. "What do you make of our court?"

"I have seen little of it so far."

"And you've come first to the library." Her moon-bright eyes fixed on my face. "Why?"

"I meant to collect information on the shadow-drakes. I've never encountered one, and I prefer to understand what I must face."

A soft laugh escaped her. "Then you have come to the wrong court. That which seeks to claim you here you'll never see coming. It's the nature of things that dwell in the between-spaces, and it's as true of shadow-drakes as the rest."

Did she offer a warning or a threat? "That may be true, but I find the quest for understanding a worthy one, regardless."

"Spoken like one of few years." Her lips tightened. "I don't imagine anything but experience will change your mind. I was young once, and curious about many things—and I had the misfortune to pass that trait to my daughter."

"Why do you deem it a misfortune?"

"It led to her needless death." The words lifted some sort of veil, offering a glimpse of a chasm of endless grief behind her eyes. Then the lines of her face smoothed out into an impassive mask. "Take care your curiosity does not lead you astray."

What could I possibly say to that? Perhaps a change of subject was in order. I smoothed nonexistent wrinkles from my skirt. "Do you mean to participate in the hunt?"

"The hunt." Her voice was soft, almost contemplative. "It offers the chance of gain and the certainty of loss. It's what will be lost that I find of greatest interest."

Her words arrested me. Most fae I'd encountered considered how they might gain power, not what might be lost in doing so. What made her different? Before I could press the point, we were interrupted by two fae lords cresting the stairs, their conversation echoing in the cavernous space. "You believe the rumors about Lady Maeve true?"

Swifter than I could draw breath, Talis wrapped a glamour about us, one shaded with purple and charcoal hues of dusk. Clearly, she wanted to hide our presence—and I'd no desire to earn enmity without cause, so I kept quiet.

The slighter of the two lords shrugged. "It's difficult to believe she'd take such a risk. Memories of the war haven't faded so far, and King Alastor would take a dim view of our court being the first to revive the ghoul project, whatever the motive. It holds too strong a tie to Ascent philosophy for comfort."

"Yet between her affinities and those of her husband, they possess most of what's required. They'd need to bring only one other into the scheme, two at the most, if they wished to expedite matters."

I folded my hands on my lap to still their trembling. I'd the strangest sense I witnessed a piece of formal theater being enacted for—whose benefit?

"I don't doubt Lady Maeve's abilities. Rather, I question if she'd risk acting against the wishes of King Alastor."

"A better question might be what does he truly desire? Of course, he must publicly declaim any such practices, but if other courts experiment once more, should ours abstain?"

"There's no clear evidence as to the deeds of the other courts, not yet. And he'd not wish to be the first to stir wrath."

Why would crafting ghouls bring down the wrath of the other courts? And what in the Crossings was Ascent philosophy? He'd mentioned the war—was it our Forgotten War? Or did I take far too great a leap?

The first lord shrugged as they passed our alcove. "Perhaps someone should address the matter with him, test the waters."

"His mood might be favorable, once the hunt has reached a successful conclusion."

With that, their conversation shifted to the hunt, and they passed from sight. Talis followed their departure with her gaze, then she released the glamour. "Well, that was entertaining."

"They meant us to hear?"

"Undoubtedly."

"Then why did you bother to conceal our presence?"

"The charade must be carried on, ever and always." Again, a soft, melodious laugh escaped her. "Being from such an isolated situation, you're doubtless unfamiliar with all the players of our court, so perhaps you do not appreciate this bit of acting. These lords are quite young, and from lesser families. Naturally, they cannot be seen to bring an accusation against Lady Maeve themselves. Yet if they just *happen* to be overheard, and that information just happens to be carried back to the king—well, it could raise an investigation into Maeve's affairs. If the investigation proves the rumors true, and the king does not in fact support her endeavors, he'll act, which could leave a vacuum of power for them to fill, particularly if they're poised to take advantage of it. I'll grant it wasn't an overly polished delivery, but that will come with practice."

"And this Lady Maeve? Do you think it likely she'd undertake such an endeavor?" Prince Sable had provided her name as a source from whom to acquire mortals. If she had interest in crafting ghouls, it could explain her desire to claim so many. Tension coiled in my chest. Was she the one who'd taunted me mere moments ago?

"She's arrogant. Always boasting of the magnificence of her gardens, making spectacles for the pleasure of the king." Her mouth twisted.

The hint of emotion Talis displayed suggested she might be provoked to speak further, if I pursued this line of inquiry. "Are her gardens truly so spectacular?"

"If you appreciate overblown dramatics, I suppose. I'll grant she possesses affinities strong enough to craft something outstanding, but she's far too concerned with court politics and power to connect with her plants as they deserve." Scorn laced her voice.

Wait, did Talis also possess an affinity for plants? "You speak as one with experience."

"If that's your way of asking if I share her botanical affinity, then yes, I do. Yet our experience in no way compares." The sense of power gathering beyond some sort of intangible barrier strengthened. "I established my gardens long before she emerged from her mother's womb. I have no need to prove them the greater. They simply are, because I do what's required to keep them that way."

Questions bubbled within about what it meant to have a botanical affinity and how to properly nurture it. Yet I could not afford to betray so much of my own ignorance, nor could I afford to trust anyone within this court, even though the bargain-holder had already chosen to reveal herself. I could afford no distraction until I'd identified her—and kept myself from her coils.

Talis stirred, like one rousing from a dream. "I have another appointment."

It was a not-so-veiled order for departure. Yet where should I go? If I departed for a remote area of the gardens, could I draw out the bargain-holder? It would be folly without more information. If it came to open confrontation, if she lashed out before I could engage and attempt to gain understanding, it was unlikely I'd survive the assault long enough to negotiate Ainslie's freedom.

No, I needed to find an avenue of retreat until I could speak to Riven. Yet her shadows still writhed in wait, dark and ominous, a signal that she did not mean to surrender her advantage.

How could I find a path to safety?

CHAPTER 53

Though I wrapped myself in the protective life of the blackberry vines as I departed the alcove, the shadowspire lashed at me relentlessly, and my control frayed at the edges. How long could I continue to maintain the connection? Pulling the essence of the brambles through the thick workings of the demesne left me unsteady, and already the chamber grayed at the edges.

At the base of the tower, I hesitated. Where should I go? Perhaps if I returned to the deeper regions of the demesne—the private spaces that held the guest bedchambers—it would cut her off from the outside world, the source from which she drew the shadowed form of the nightspire.

My attention locked on the bramble song, I rested one hand on Jade's shoulder and allowed her to lead as I pressed back the assault of the shadow-plants. Yet the vivid illusory images on the walls disoriented me further; where the celestial scenes spilled across the floor, they obscured the path chosen by the shadowspire. One of its coils broke through and lashed my ankle, sharp and venomous.

I tripped.

And Jade caught me. She rumbled low in her chest. *We need to hurry.*

Though my ankle throbbed more each moment, I quickened my pace. As we delved deeper into the mountain, I lost the distant songs of the blackberry brambles. Yet it seemed my theory held some truth, for the shadowspire had withered and vanished also. I stumbled to a halt, gritting my teeth against the persistent, searing pain that crept up my leg. Was this an injury like the ones Lord West and Nikol had inflicted, or had the shadowspire carried something worse? I had some salve tucked in my pocket, if I could only situate myself to use it.

I forced myself onward until I reached the rose-and-thorn sigil that marked my door. Then I hesitated. What if the bargain-holder had only made a momentary retreat? Riven wasn't reachable, but I could search for Nikol. He had a vested interest in the success of this venture . . . Yet he'd not hesitated to hurt Risha and Jade for his own ends. Perhaps he'd see my removal as a simplification of his life, since he viewed me as a liability. He'd achieved what he wanted, as Riven had negotiated the hunt on his behalf—now I was the only unchancy element that remained. My head pulsed in time with my ankle. *What do you think, Jade?*

Risha and I already discussed the matter, while you saw to our protection. Were Nikol at liberty, we'd deem it worth the attempt—but he's also with the king.

Though I was truly without high fae allies—even dubious ones, for the moment—I still had Jade, and with her at my side, I could endure facing a great deal. *Thank you.*

I limped into the bedchamber and collapsed on the bed, drawing the salve from my pocket. I smoothed it over the vining bruises on my ankle, but they took a considerable time to fade. Even when all outward signs vanished, a throbbing ache remained. Had the shadowspire done some harm beyond the edge of my perception?

My thoughts scattered as intense exhaustion took hold. I needed to capture an image of the bargain-holder for Riven. If only I'd dared to bring a sketchbook . . . Did fae use sketch-books . . . They were rather mundane . . . Nikol had drawn with shadow once . . .

I woke abruptly, a metallic taste coating my tongue and my ears buzzing with something very like the sound of angry bees. I pressed upright, yet could not perceive the moonscape that adorned the walls nor Jade nor anything beyond a thick veil of shadow.

I turned.

And my heart leapt.

There was the bargain-holder. She sat on the left arch of the bed, close enough to touch, her ashen gaze locked on me. I couldn't sense Risha or Jade or anything beyond the bed and the bargain-holder and a void beyond. This time, there was no escape. I held on to the tiny spark of anger in my chest, the only thing keeping me from drowning in fear. "What have you done with Jade and Risha?"

She twitched a finger. "Wrong question."

A bitter purplish scent surged into the air around us, and I struggled to connect to any sense of life beyond this shadowed sphere. "Have you come to kill me?"

"No. No, no, no." Her voice took on an eerie, singsong lilt. "Why should I? I just came to talk, to tell you how it will be and to look at you as you are now—untouched by loss."

Even as she spoke, vivid images of Mother and Ibbie etched themselves on the canvas of my mind, opening up a well of grief. "No one is untouched by loss."

"You think you know sorrow, but you know nothing. What-ever has been taken from you, you've always remained surrounded by those you love. But what happens when they're *all* gone? Bereavement and desolation. But you cannot show anyone how you feel, oh no."

My stomach roiled, and I swallowed the rising nausea. She had Ainslie, only Ainslie . . . and this wasn't real, oh, please, it *couldn't* be real. "What do you want?"

"Do you think you can unlock my desires? None among the

living can grant them, least of all you." Her pointed finger jabbed toward me. "I could grant *your* desire, but I don't want to. You will not find me again, though you seek. But I'll be watching."

"If you'll just listen—"

"The die is cast, the game is begun. Now I wait, always and ever wait. And I will see your loss become complete." With those words, she began to fade, first her limbs, and then her torso, and last of all her dead ashen eyes vanishing from sight.

Yet her disappearance didn't dispel the darkness. An uncanny chill crept along my limbs, seeping to my very core, and I couldn't stop shivering. Somehow I must return to my world, to my family. What had she done in my absence? Could she have forced more bargains? I snatched at the passing prism around my neck.

No. Riven had said I couldn't just open a passing anywhere in the demesne, and if I went straight from here to there, I might well put a target on my family, if anyone took notice. Perhaps she *meant* to compel me to such an act; perhaps that was what would cause me to lose everything.

I swung my feet over the edge of the bed, into the pooled blackness, and slowly, it ebbed away. Jade. Where was she? She'd been right here when I'd fallen asleep. Why couldn't I see her? How could she just—

There.

Across the room, she paced, her tail lashing. When the last bit of the haze lifted, she sprang toward me, leaping upon the bed so that the whole of it shook, her body twining around mine. *I slept, then you were gone, so wholly vanished I couldn't sense you, even from afar. Could not reach your mind. I thought . . .*

Her massive frame shuddered, and I nestled against her fur, her heart drumming fast and unsteady where my head rested against her chest. My own still thrummed unevenly to match. Risha fluttered down to perch on my shoulder, her warm light spilling over us both.

And I struggled to gain some clarity of thought. The

bargain-holder meant to display her mastery of the situation, and she had, but perhaps she'd given us something in the process. Now that I'd seen her, surely we could identify her, could find her again, no matter what she'd said. But if she had no willingness to renegotiate a bargain, if she meant to keep herself concealed and watch whatever she'd planned unfold—no, I refused to accept it.

In any case, I could do nothing if I remained cloistered here. Now that she'd spoken to me, I didn't think she meant another direct assault. She'd tested, taunted, and delivered her parting shot. And if I was wrong and she had something else in mind, she'd proven she could find me here as well as anywhere else. What then?

The gardens. I needed the gardens. Never mind that the plants within were bound up in the power of the demesne; they still represented a haven.

Jade lifted her head. *Risha, will you ask a servant to bring sketching materials and directions to a quiet garden? And seek Riven again. If there's any way to reach him . . .*

Risha flared upright. "If such a way existed, I'd have used it already. You think I wish my lady to suffer?"

"I know." I stroked her velvety wing. "You've never once neglected your duties, bright one."

A slight hint of rose threaded through her blue light. "I shall go."

In short order, a willowy woman appeared in the doorway, offering a silvery sheaf of paper and an ink pen. It wasn't what I would have chosen. My fingers ached for charcoals, for dark shades with which to capture her shadowed features, the hints of madness and triumph and something else . . . grief, perhaps? But it didn't matter. I needed only an image sufficient to depict her features to Riven, and as soon as the servant showed me to a small garden tucked among the clefts of rock, the picture poured from me in vivid, emotion-tinged darkness.

I sank to the ground and leaned against a birch, utterly spent. Sharp-edged stars glittered in the distant heavens, and this hidden garden reflected back their detached beauty. Whoever crafted it had fashioned it to hold all the enchantment of night, with blossoms shaded white or ivory and tree leaves silver-bright or pale alabaster. In the darkness, they reflected the light of moon and star, dazzling the eye. Their harmonies filled the space about me, yet failed to calm my racing thoughts.

What now? Did the king mean to release Riven from his counsel chamber tonight? If he did not, would the bargain-holder's trail become too faint to track? From Riven's description, her trace would remain in the Otherworld for weeks, but she'd seemed so certain we'd not find her . . .

At last, Riven strode around a towering oleander, every inch the emotionless fae lord. "Risha said you encountered the bargain-holder."

Though his glamour concealed us, his words remained detached, as if he did not care what had passed in his absence. And in that moment, I realized how much I'd hoped he would come as a friend—not a fae arbiter—and offer companionship rather than this cold distance. I choked down the desire and thrust the finished sketch at him. "Please tell me you know who she is."

A fae-light sprang to life, illumining my drawing, then Riven shook his head. "Whoever this is, she's not part of any court I know. Definitely not the Courts of Silver or Dusk."

"That's impossible. She's *here*—I just saw her, and the night-spire, it came from the king's garden in the first place." My words jumbled, and I sought to steady my voice, to smooth the ragged edges of emotion. "Could she have glamoured her appearance?"

"Perhaps. Did you sense one?"

"No, but I was not at my best." Starting with the shadowspire on the steps and moving onward, I told of my encounter with Talis and the fae lords who'd mentioned Lady Maeve, then the pursuit of the bargain-holder. When I described pulling the essence of the blackberry brambles into the demesne his eyes flickered, then they shadowed when I told of the encounter in my bedchamber. Had I disappointed him with my failure to anticipate her movements? To gain anything of significance from our encounters? Lady Ulrika or Talis—or any of the others in this court, for that matter—would surely have known how to check her power. Ghostly pain spiraled up my leg once more and sparked an ache deep inside.

Coils of light spilled from Riven. "May I?"

I nodded, and golden warmth surged through my body, driving back the lingering pain in my ankle and the cold fear that had gripped me since I'd encountered the bargain-holder.

"She left a trace of liminal power in your body, small but enough to demonstrate she could have done far more. There's something about it . . ." The light vanished, leaving me oddly bereft. "Jessa, are you certain you want to go through with this?"

"I can't draw back now."

"I could craft a story to cover for your removal from court, if needed."

"And then what?" The bargain-holder would still have Ainslie in her coils, and it sounded as if she meant to come for the rest of my family as well. The birch leaves overhead rustled. "She knew me, knew things beyond what the average individual would, things she must have taken time to learn. Ainslie didn't fit her pattern of Collectors, which suggests she sought her for a reason, that perhaps she bears some sort of personal enmity toward my family. There is no way back, only forward."

"I concur that there's something more at work here. I expected she'd seek you out in some subtle way, not expose herself so readily." His jaw tightened. "I should have given you some sort of ward, no matter the risk."

"Why would it be a risk?"

Riven just shook his head.

And Jade regarded us with glowing eyes. *He cannot be seen to be overly invested in your situation or survival, beyond in whatever way his king would dictate. A friendship between you would not fit the narrative.*

Why, *why* must everything be so complicated? Why must

fae bury emotion between so many layers that it might as well not exist, concealing their true selves—or deadening them—so that none should gain an advantage over them? I couldn't afford to think about it now, nor to waste what little time we had discussing the matter further. The songs of the birch spilled over me, and I straightened. "The way she approached me flies in the face of all our dealings with her thus far. She seemed unsound of mind, nothing like the cautious, strategic fae who unfolded a plan with care and cunning over many months."

"How so?"

"Her cadence of speech was odd, and she appeared obsessed with the notion of watching me lose everything that matters." I rubbed my hands along my chilled arms. "Could her peculiarity of speech indicate she's come from another court?"

"The high fae courts share a common language, so that in itself doesn't hint at her origin. That she betrayed so much emotion does hint at instability." He moved closer. "It could be a partnership; if so, your encounter indicates the hold of the more levelheaded member weakens."

This was familiar territory, the exchange of ideas and examination of various angles oddly comforting, however detached Riven might appear. "So you think she's just the outward face of the partnership, rather than the mind behind it? That Lady Maeve or someone else has employed or partnered with the woman I encountered?"

"If her power mirrors the one you encountered in the nightspire, yet her behavior does not—it's certainly suggestive." His contemplative gaze rested on the distant rock face. "The woman you encountered couldn't have entered the court uninvited, which means at the very least she's a guest of someone powerful enough to conceal her presence. I'm familiar with all those of consequence in this court, including Lady Maeve. She'd have sufficient ability to hide a conspirator, if it suited her."

"Before I went to the library, I encountered Prince Sable in the queen's Chamber of Stars. When I suggested I might have interest in acquiring a group of mortals, he provided her name, along with that of Lord Corbin."

He shot me a swift glance of appraisal, but did not press for details. "I can look into Corbin, but unless three or more individuals have allied, Maeve's our most promising lead," Riven said. "Your botanical affinity provided an opportunity to . . . casually inquire of the king about the various gardens in the court. I hinted you might be inclined to stay after the hunt, and that I might encourage it, if my own stay were extended. Though he'd prefer to see me go, he'd also welcome an opportunity to further a connection to the Court of Roses, so he was pleased to suggest a possible itinerary. The Court of Dusk isn't known for its botanical affinities, and it turns out that only three possess such power in any significant measure—Ladies Maeve and Talis and Lord Revilon. Corbin's not among them."

"If it's a partnership between the individual I encountered and someone of botanical affinity, I suppose we can't discount any one of them, not even Talis." Though I'd sensed nothing in her suggesting she'd involved herself in such a plot, nor that she even possessed any particular interest in me. "Still, more fae could be involved."

"Which is why I'll test the waters with Corbin. But in absence of a clearer lead, we should first seek Maeve in Silvwind. We have time before morning breaks."

"You mean to go now?"

"We can't afford a delay, not with the bargain-holder's erratic actions."

"But will Lady Maeve find my interest in her gardens suspect? It's common in the mortal world to take such tours, but I did not imagine it here."

"Think of it more as a request that cannot be openly declined without suggesting fear or something to hide. It offers a chance to know one's rivals—and an opportunity to bargain, should you see something you desire."

"And Silvwind is her demesne?"

"The demesne rests within the heart of the estate; we will

visit the public manor and gardens." The moonlight sharpened his features. "Except for very specific circumstances, few fae will enter the demesne of another, fewer still will extend an invitation—Damir, in his arrogance, being a rare exception. The seat of the monarch is different, because of his bonds to the land and the court itself. She'll invite us into the manor, but no farther."

I tucked that notion away to explore later, tracing my fingers against the smooth bark of the birch. "Apart from her possible involvement in the missing mortal scheme, do you think there's any veracity to what the lords said about the ghouls?"

"I don't know. But I intend to find out, if I can." The glamour around us took on umber tones. "Such an accusation is no light matter, but without evidence the treaty between courts has been betrayed, I cannot act in my arbiter capacity here—at least not without King Alastor's permission. And if he's sanctioning this scheme, he certainly won't grant it."

"Which means?"

"That I'll do what I can with the access I'm granted." He lifted his shoulders. "Maeve will say very little in my presence, particularly if she has something to hide. If I offer an escape from my company by suggesting she take you to tour the gardens, she should be amenable."

"And she'll just leave you to explore?"

"No, I expect she'll assign some unfortunate underling in her household to 'make me comfortable.' She won't want me to linger long, even under supervision, so take advantage of your opportunity."

With that, he pulled us into a passing. I was almost growing accustomed to the surge of power and the disorienting alteration in pressure, and this time, I only needed to steady myself on Jade briefly after our arrival at Silvwind. Stately queenswood trees surrounded an ethereal manor, which appeared to belong to the gardens surrounding it, as it was crafted from some sort of material that reflected the surrounding plants.

Riven sent a spark of light dancing against a niche alongside the door—the fae version of a calling card, perhaps? The spark gleamed brighter, and after a moment, the door swung open. A starry trail whorled across the floor, halting a few ells away as if it waited for us.

Jade's ears pricked. *Riven says we are to follow it.*

The ever-unfurling path concluded in an octagonal chamber with windows on seven of the eight sides, each pane of glass offering a vantage of the lush foliage beyond. In the center, a round sofa offered a view of every side of the room. A woman standing at the central window turned, her hair upswept into a dark spiral, her eyes an unsettling shade of mauve. The scent about her held notes of moonflower and freshwater pearl, and her beauty was every bit as shimmering and detached. "Lord Arbiter." She evinced no flicker of interest in my presence; her attention remained fixed on Riven. "What brings you to my door?"

"I'm afraid that's my responsibility." I offered a small smile. "I've heard you have some rare specimens in your gardens, and I wished to see them while I visited your court."

I'd hoped no one, fae or mortal, would be immune to the opportunity to display their passion and have it appreciated, but it appeared Lady Maeve might be the exception. I could detect no softening of her perfect features; they remained as aloof as the stars above. "I'm afraid, Lord Arbiter, you've caught me at an inconvenient time, since I prepare to remove to Beresstone before dawn. Yet for your guest, I could perhaps spare a few moments."

She managed to make it appear she conferred a great favor upon Riven, as well as convey my insignificance—evidently, I didn't even warrant a direct reply.

Riven simply arched a brow. "You must do as you please. We can always return another time."

With that simple pronouncement, he'd disclaimed any hint of debt she might have implied and managed to threaten an undesirable consequence.

Jade chuffed softly. *Very satisfactory.*

Lady Maeve gave him a cool smile. "That won't be necessary.

Perhaps, Lord Arbiter, you'll allow my steward to see to your refreshment? I cannot imagine my gardens hold interest for you."

Riven settled onto the sofa, despite the lack of invitation, lounging against the arched central back. "As you say."

She summoned a servant, then turned to me. "Lady Jessa, I presume?"

"Yes."

"This way." One of the immense windows swung open like a door, and she stepped through.

Together, we entered something more magnificent than a garden. In my world, it might have been called a wilderness, yet clear order bound the riotous array of plants into a harmonious whole. All the botanical life within these gardens thrummed with high fae power, each growing thing held in a form of thrall. Some were joyfully bound, much as the plants I'd worked with before responded with delight to my bidding as our purposes mingled. Others echoed with discordant notes, as if constrained against their will and inclination. The back of my neck pricked. I tried to take comfort in the fact that events had unfolded as Riven had predicted so far, yet I'd no way to anticipate what might come next.

And now that we'd left Riven behind, her unsettling mauve eyes rested upon me in a calculating way. "Is there something you find of . . . particular interest?"

Her personality and demeanor radiated the sort of restrained power I'd expected to find in the bargain-holder. Was she the one we sought? My skirts brushed against low blooms. "I have great interest in all you cultivate, and I'd like to see what you consider your most spectacular work."

"So you shall." She beckoned me forward, leading the way down a fae-lit path. "It is said that long ago one of our court mastered the art of fusing mortals with botanical life."

My mouth went dry. "To what end?"

"A novelty. The captive mortals adorned the tree like blossoms. That account has always intrigued me, and it prompted me to some experimentation of my own."

I nearly stumbled over a stone. Could this scheme to claim mortals have its origin in something as simple as a desire to exceed some past legend? If so, would she divulge it so freely? Certainly, she seemed to watch me with care, as if weighing the effect of each word.

We rounded a bend and entered a clearing occupied by a single massive tree. Its heavy limbs willowed downward, each adorned with enormous ivory blossoms that were kindled with light like that of the stars. My breath caught. At the heart of each intricate bloom, a sylph occupied the place a pistil would ordinarily belong, the petals having become a cage. In some way, they were bound, the two disparate elements having become one.

"I found the notion of mortals rather clumsy for such a purpose—they're not at all to scale, besides which, there are many greater uses to which one can put them." She gestured toward the laden limbs. "Sylphs, on the other hand, I possess in abundance. Their life fuels the flowers and illumines them from within, keeps the blooms from ever fading. This tree has been in full blossom for two decades."

I stood unable to move, as if I shared their grim fate. The blue in Risha's wings darkened to near black, and beneath my hand, Jade's muscles coiled tight. Couldn't Maeve hear the groan of the tree beneath its unnatural load? Or did she simply not care?

After such long bondage, only one sylph still struggled against its coils—the rest slumped within their satiny prisons, scarcely stirring. My eyes stung. I'd given my word to Riven that I'd not denounce what I found deplorable, but the fragile threads of control remaining to me wavered—and I did not trust my voice. *Tell Risha I'm sorry. So sorry.*

I'd fled the Chamber of Stars, but I'd not fail this time. To hide my face, I stepped closer to the horrifying tree, pretending to admire the handiwork. "How very remarkable." I'd withhold the remarks I felt due, if I could manage. "I take it that it's not only your gardens you wish to . . . bring to new heights, but mortals as well?"

"Who doesn't, in this hour? So many delightful possibilities are on the cusp of presenting themselves." The light of the imprisoned sylphs spilled over the lily-pale skin of Maeve's face, giving it an eerie glow. "Of course, your court has been rather behind in such matters."

"Perhaps we wish to change that."

"Then you have much work ahead." She glided back toward the path. "I'm afraid I must return to my duties—and restore you to the Lord Arbiter."

"What a shame." If I didn't cast some sort of lure, I'd lose the moment. She was interested in the experimentation done with mortals in the past—perhaps that gave me an entrance. I pivoted to face her. "I'd heard rumor you were forward-thinking. In light of that, I thought you'd take interest in the work once done at Kilmere. Of course, I might have misheard."

If she'd watched me, she'd know I owned Kilmere and therefore could share information on it. If not, the hint still might be enough to spark her interest.

And it seemed it had. Though her features didn't shift, the spindled seabright along the path bristled to attention. "I'd not heard the Court of Roses had any part in that affair."

I'd no notion of what they'd done in centuries past, and of course, if she did hold some part of the bargain, she'd be aware I wasn't from that court, which would make this statement only pretense. I tilted my head. "It's the present and future that concern me at the moment. I've recently had opportunity to examine the fortress, and its power has in no way diminished." Though its nature had wholly changed. "Of course, if you wish to know what I witnessed there, it will come with a price."

"Naturally. But perhaps this is not the choicest of moments to speak of such a thing. It's better for such negotiations to be unhurried," she said. "When the hunt concludes, perhaps you might come and stay at Silvwind a few days, if it pleases you—and if you can detach from your current company."

Did she seek unhurried conversation or to snare me in her demesne without Riven, where I'd be at her mercy? Beyond the borders of her gardens, wild oaks murmured low, their songs stilling the turmoil within. I couldn't know her intent for certain, but I couldn't afford to close the door. "My court might be displeased if I openly spurned the hospitality the Court of Gold has offered."

"I shall trust in your ingenuity to achieve your desired end—if you wish to continue our conversation."

"I'm certain something can be arranged." If she *was* the second person in this partnership, then perhaps she would bargain, no matter how unwilling the ashen-eyed woman appeared. Or perhaps she too toyed with me.

As we departed the clearing, the wind played through the large ivory blossoms overhead, swaying the sylphs along with the flowers. I'd no means by which to force her hand, yet the notion of the stolen mortals enduring such a fate—or worse—twisted like briars in my chest.

How much time did they have?

CHAPTER 54

Ghouls haunted my dreams that night—or morning, rather—interspersed with images of the ever-blooming sylph tree and dead ashen eyes. When I jolted awake, a faint bitter scent pervaded the air. I'd sleep no more.

Yet deep within the mountain and swathed in layers of workings, I'd little sense of how much time had passed. I crossed the room to a curved dressing table, which took on a more distinct form as I approached. On it, I found a small timepiece, its face a complicated mandala in shades of dusky blue. Though it lacked numerals, the relative position of its silvery hands indicated the hour neared sunset.

Tonight, King Alastor would hold a feast, and we'd have further opportunity to watch Lady Maeve and perhaps ask discreet questions of those assembled. Riven and I had discussed Maeve upon our return to Beresstone shortly before dawn and had left the matter unresolved, though what he'd gathered from the steward left him certain she did pursue what he'd termed *forbidden knowledge*, whether or not it had proceeded as far as attempting to craft ghouls.

He'd left with my drawing of the bargain-holder, saying he'd a source who owed him an answer, and he meant to use it to collect information. If we knew who she was, would it offer some means by which to trace her? Her certainty that we could not made it difficult to cling to hope.

Yet perhaps we did not need her, if we could identify the other one involved.

Jade stretched across the floor. *If it is a partnership, perhaps we can leverage one against the other.*

If we can understand how they came together and what each stands to gain. And if we were not mistaken in our assumptions. *But I can do nothing if I don't prepare for this feast.*

Jade lifted her head, sniffing at the air. *The wardrobe is there, behind the moon.*

Indeed, one of the mottled patches on the surface of the illusory moon concealed a small knob, and when I twisted it, a surprisingly vast wardrobe revealed itself. It wasn't a piece of furniture, but rather a space carved from the stone of the wall itself, and one that contained a multitude of choices. Riven had told me he'd procured clothing, but I'd not expected the vast richness before me, an assortment of items that dazzled the eye. Some of the gowns had rows of tiny jeweled buttons down the back, others had multiple components that appeared to belong together, but I could not discern their assembly. Still others were separate bodices and skirts, like the one I'd worn thus far.

Did fae employ lady's maids? If not, I was destined for trouble, because I didn't see a way to don the more elaborate gowns myself—and tonight would be an occasion when I couldn't afford even the smallest slip. Improper attire would certainly undo all my efforts.

A forceful rap at the door drew me from my musings. I'd grown used to sensing the approach of high fae, knowing who neared before I saw the individual. Yet something within the demesne—perhaps simply the overwhelming sense of its workings and the pervasive presence of the king—dampened my ability to receive. When I bent my senses toward the door, the familiar feeling of Riven's presence washed over me, and I hurried to open it.

He strode into the room and secured the door behind him, something in the lines of his body bespeaking tension. "Corbin isn't behind the scheme—or if he is, he's far beyond our reach. He's served this past year in an ambassadorial role in the land of the Dracai."

"Then Lady Maeve remains the most likely candidate."

Riven gave a clipped nod. "But there's something more. I spoke to my source about the woman you drew. He recognized her, but said she's dead."

I stumbled back a step. "It was truth?"

"Truth as he believed it."

That was impossible. I'd seen her—her shadows had left a mark, the implacable power behind them unmistakable. "She can't be dead."

"According to the lord, she died centuries ago. He would speak no more, nor could I press him once he'd discharged his debt. Not in this court."

"Did he tell you who she was?"

"He could say only that she was one of those the king decreed should remain nameless."

Riven had chosen his words with care, suggesting he brushed against the edge of his geas. "Can you explain what that means?"

"No."

Rubbing my hands along my arms, I paced the room. "Well, he must be mistaken."

"Or you saw what someone wanted you to see. But a glamour wouldn't convey the sense of power you perceived— that's unique to the individual. It could be covered or concealed, not falsified." Riven remained still, clearly considering, though as usual, he voiced almost nothing of his speculation. "Did Jade see her also?"

Yes. She was real.

"And she matched the image Jessa drew?"

Yes, though the second time, we were separated. I did not see her then, nor Jessa.

"You think perhaps I had an experience like Ainslie's?"

"I'd wondered, but it's highly unusual for a liminal suggestion to influence more than one individual. Of necessity, they're tailored to their target—and it's the thoughts and feelings of said target that shapes what's experienced. If Jade saw her, and her perception matched yours, then I'm inclined to think she's in some way real."

"What if she was believed dead, but has been hiding elsewhere all this time?" It would certainly explain her confidence that we'd never find her.

"It's conceivable. Though a great deal of care was taken to ensure that those deemed nameless were truly . . . eliminated. If she appeared within any court after the war, she would have been traced." His shoulders tightened. "And if somehow she took to the liminal realm and concealed herself there, by now she'd be truly mad. It's not a place to linger."

The door creaked open, and I jumped. Instead of the ashen eyes I half-expected, bright silver ones met mine, and Nikol flashed a smile. "Am I interrupting?"

"What is it you want?" Riven's voice was terser than usual.

Nikol ignored him. "My queen has sent you a gift for the feast tonight." He lifted a small box that appeared crafted of solid starlight, cold and shimmering.

With care, I accepted it. Instead of the chill I expected, it held surprising warmth, and the light swirled as if it responded to my touch. I opened the box to discover a necklace that mortal queens would have envied—unfamiliar translucent jewels shot through with fiery, ever-shifting hues, cascaded down a silvery chain like a starfall. "I don't understand."

Nor could I dream of accepting it. To incur a debt to a monarch set as a rival to Riven's king would be a disaster in the making, particularly since his king had already taken interest in my situation. If it appeared that I was open to an alliance with the queen—that could only draw wrath. I snapped the box shut.

Nikol extended me a note. "Perhaps this missive from Queen Astra will explain."

On a fine silver leaf, a bold hand had inscribed in black ink:

To Lady Jessa of the Court of Roses,

I trust you'll accept this small gift as a token of welcome to the hunt. Rest assured, it incurs no debt, except that of a brief discussion before you depart the Court of Dusk.

Astra

Beneath her elaborately scrolled signature twined what must be the sigil of the Court of Silver, which pulsed with living threads of starlight. I extended the letter to Riven. "Is it safe to accept this?"

"One would think you didn't trust me," Nikol said.

I folded my arms. "I'd have to be remarkably obtuse to do so."

He placed a hand on his chest as if I'd dealt him a blow. "I'd protest, but perhaps it's a sign you're finally learning. It's about time."

Riven frowned at Nikol, then glanced over the message. "She's making it plain the gift comes without cost. Given your relative positions, you'd be expected to grant an audience at her request, even apart from this gift. If you don't accept, you'll insult her hospitality."

"Yet it's far more than a token."

"Of course it is. Starfire gems are much coveted." Nikol tapped the edge of the box. "She believes you represent a connection to a court that has long shunned any relations with others. If she can gain goodwill, it is to her advantage in terms of possible future alliance."

Despite my feelings toward Nikol, a slight twinge of worry tightened my chest. "And if she finds out about the deceit?"

"Perhaps I spoke too soon. It seems you're *not* learning—

never point out that what someone has done on your behalf puts them in a precarious position."

"While I'm reluctant to agree with Nikol, I must. And there's no reason for concern in this case. If the truth comes out, I'll be the one blamed—a Court of Gold scheme to undermine her," Riven said. "As it stands, she doesn't want my court to steal an advantage, if there's one to be had. And to thwart us would give her pleasure, even if she gained nothing else."

Nikol inclined his head. "Precisely."

Whatever the slight animosity I'd sensed from Riven when Nikol appeared—perhaps due to his interference in the matter of my glamour—this had taken true cooperation on their parts to pull off and a degree of trust between them. For the first time it occurred to me just how peculiar their friendship was. Despite Nikol's disclaimer after he'd snared me, and Riven's insistence on the formality of debts and bargains in their dealings, some deeper understanding existed between them—that much was clear. How had such a thing come to pass between rival courts? I shook off the speculation. "So it incurs no debt because it's a bribe?"

"That's about the sum of it," Nikol said.

"And . . . it's not like the bracelet Lord West gave me?"

Riven lifted the lid and surveyed the necklace. "She hasn't tampered with it. It's a risk that almost certainly wouldn't pay off. If I raised the issue—and I would have, if she'd tried anything, in order to cast her in a bad light—then the gift would have the opposite effect from the one intended."

The shifting pattern of light on the floor matched the jumble of thoughts within. I once thought I desired to understand more of fae machinations; now I wanted nothing more than to retreat to the relative order of my own world. I brushed a finger along the starfire jewels. In that moment, I yearned for my sisters, Aunt Caris, even Lianne—they would have exclaimed over the beauty of the piece, helped me dress and situate it properly. Neither Riven nor Nikol would be of any use in the matter, but perhaps they could tell me what to expect at least. "Can you advise me on how to dress for the feast? I looked over the wardrobe, and many of the gowns appeared too complicated to put on alone."

Silver light danced in Nikol's eyes. "Perhaps I can make amends by offering assistance."

Warmth crept up my neck, and Riven shot Nikol a withering look. "Out."

He held up his hands. "Not before I secure permission to escort Jessa to dinner."

Jade glared at him, her disapproval of the suggestion evident. Why would he offer such a thing? He'd made it plain how he felt about my presence. I tilted my head. "The last time I went with you, you led me into a trap. Do you intend a repeat performance?"

"Not this time." The shadows behind Nikol deepened. "It will please my queen, and it would not look well if you and Riven were always in one another's company."

"Why?"

Riven moved between us. "It would appear that the Court of Gold intends to force an alliance, rather than allow you to engage with the high-standing members of other courts—as you would naturally do, to determine what's most to your advantage."

Though I'd rather attend the meal alone than with Nikol, his presence would provide an element of protection. I pulled the box to my chest. "Very well."

Riven inclined his head. "You have what you came for. I see no reason for you to linger."

"Nor do I." Again, a slight amusement seemed to dance in his eyes. "I'll return in an hour."

When Nikol departed, Riven crossed to the wardrobe, withdrawing an emerald-green gown. "A river wylding will be assigned to attend you. She should arrive soon. You'll want to wear this, and she'll help you with whatever's required." He hesitated. "Before she comes, I suggest you conceal your passing prism somewhere safe. It's better for the wylding to remain unaware you possess it. While they don't have a malicious nature, they don't share the spirit and binding of an oalan. Any passing fae could press information from them."

"Is that a concern?"

"It's always preferable to hold information in reserve. And were it known you relied on a passing prism, someone would only have to steal it—or have it stolen—to leave you at a significant disadvantage." He draped the gown over the bed, and its golden embroidery caught the light.

"I see." My hand stole to the chain, which I'd thus far kept tucked beneath the neckline of my gown. However, the one Riven had chosen for tonight would not permit such concealment—and Queen Astra would expect her own gift to be on display.

"Make sure you find somewhere to keep it on your person, once you're dressed for dinner," he said.

Blessedly, all fae gowns possessed pockets, so after I changed, I'd tuck it deep inside of one where none would take note. I fumbled with the fine clasp of the necklace once again. Oh, what I would give to have Ada here now. At the last, the chain itself tangled with a wayward curl, and I surrendered. Looking up, I found Riven watching me, an unreadable expression on his face. "Will you help?"

"If that's what you wish," he said quietly. "Turn around."

I spun so he could reach the clasp, and as he picked up the chain, a sort of sparking warmth traveled down my neck, following the brush of his fingers. My breath caught. What was wrong with me?

I could feel color rising to my face as he gently worked the clasp open, and when it released, he swept the loose curl back in place, his touch almost a caress. My thoughts jumbled, and I turned swiftly. He dropped the prism into my hands, and at once I became aware we stood far closer than was proper.

The expressionless fae arbiter had vanished. Riven's eyes sparked with some indecipherable emotion, and the sweet, distant notes of trillium and wild rose threaded the stillness between us.

Then he stepped back abruptly. "It's growing late. I'll see to it that someone comes and assists you."

My fingers closed about the sunburst prism in my palm, and it warmed in response, yet I could not find my voice.

He halted before the door. "Are you comfortable attending the meal with Nikol?"

"I . . ." I fumbled for the right words. "Not entirely, but then I've not been comfortable with anything since my arrival. I suppose it comes hand in hand with the choice."

He inclined his head, impassive mask restored once more, and vanished through the doorway. And I collapsed on the bed, attempting to regain equilibrium. Surely I refined far too much on a small matter—in this world, such proximity between ladies and gentlemen happened all the time, and I'd best become accustomed to it.

The next hour slipped away with surprising speed. As Riven had promised, one of the willowy fae-folk soon arrived to assist me, and she sorted the layers of clothing with a surprisingly deft touch. When I'd finished dressing, I regarded myself in the glass —and someone wholly unfamiliar looked back. Even if I'd grown accustomed to my fae appearance, my attire alone would have disconcerted.

A long, sweeping gown of emerald green formed the base of the outfit, the skirt threaded with gold-embroidered roses and thorns. Atop that, the river wylding had secured something foreign in every way—a sort of cross between armor and adornment crafted of a metal that resembled near-weightless gold. This scrolled metallic bodice dipped in at my waist and swept down along my hips, while a high-necked silken cape caressed my arms and trailed down my back. Where the neck of the cape met the bodice of the gown, it formed a diamond expanse of skin at my breastbone. There the starfire jewels burned bright, taking on shades of gold that complemented the gown. In the mortal world, such attire would have overwhelmed; here, it belonged—in a way I did not.

I turned from the mirror and dismissed the river wylding, choking down the instinctive thanks that rose to my lips—I couldn't afford trouble.

Risha fluttered down onto the dressing table, her flight unsteady, her light dim. "You're missing one thing."

"Never mind that—are you well?"

"Well enough. But you must take what's on the bed."

I turned to behold three roses of solid light as brilliant as the summer sun. "Oh, Risha . . . where did you find these?"

"I didn't find them, made them of sun essence. Worked on them while wylding worked on you."

Jade's eyes glowed. *It's a rare gift, one that costs a great deal.*

I cupped my hands around her tiny form. "Then I thank you for the gift and sacrifice, lovely one."

I might indebt myself to her by my words, but in this case, I no longer cared. For the first time, I believed that Risha remained because she *wished* to—that she made an offering of friendship, not one of service or obligation.

Her wings fluttered, small blue flames rippling across them. "You are my lady now. I'd not have you appear only with the adornments of another court."

I lifted the magnificent roses, then hesitated. I didn't belong to the Court of Roses, so how could I adopt it as a symbol?

You may not belong to the Court of Roses, but the roses belong to you. They're part of your heritage as fae, the blood that runs through your veins and binds you to all plants. Jade nuzzled my shoulder. *Further, they're a symbol of love given—I've never heard of a sylph voluntarily making such an offering to high fae.*

For that reason alone, I couldn't reject them. I secured the magnificent roses in the elaborate upsweep of curls the river wylding had achieved. If nothing else, I'd wear them for Risha . . . in the hope I could somehow keep her safe, along with the rest who were so vulnerable. But as I swept from the room to meet Nikol, my ankle twinged, a reminder of my recent failure. If I couldn't even defend myself against a minor assault, how could I hope to free Ainslie and the rest?

CHAPTER 55

On Nikol's arm, I swept up endless stairs. Our proximity disconcerted as much as my surroundings, the sharp wash of shadow about him too reminiscent of his snare for comfort. Yet on this occasion, we were in accord —and that made him far less a threat than the others assembled. Jade shadowed us from behind, while Risha had remained in the bedchamber. According to both her and Jade, her presence would not be expected on such an occasion. High fae summoned sylphs when needed, yet another skill I'd not acquired.

Nikol's glamour deepened around us. "Have you encountered a fae monarch before?"

"Of course not." I hesitated. "Why do you ask?"

"You'll see. Just follow my lead."

The stairs ascended to a smooth circular expanse carved from the very pinnacle of the mountain. Only Nikol's presence kept me from staggering to a halt as the immense power of the monarchs assembled on the dais crashed over me. I could not wrench my gaze from the king, who seemed to embody his court —his hair the deep blue shade of the sky at dusk, his eyes holding the multitude of hues stars possessed in this world. His consort provided his perfect counterpart, matching his beauty but in reverse, her hair a brilliant silvery shade and her eyes dark as ebony. She sat at his right, Queen Astra at his left, but here in his own demesne, King Alastor burned brightest. His starlike scent I recognized at once as the one that pervaded the demesne —clear and bright and ancient. As for Queen Astra, though she clearly kept her power restrained in his halls, her ruthless beauty remained unchecked. If his form held the ever-changing allure of dusk, hers possessed the dark and deadly beauty of night, the aroma of winter-blooming jasmine and shadowed stone charging the air about her. Whether by some subtle compulsion or the draw of their innate power, every sinew in my body urged me to collapse at their feet.

Jessa.

Jade's voice recalled me to my senses, and I tightened my grip on Nikol's arm, following the lines of fae who bowed before the dais that seated the monarchs. Despite their majesty, the fae did not offer low, humble bows such as mortals were expected to give their kings, but instead the slightest of inclines that acknowledged they must submit to a sovereign while still maintaining their own claim to power. Somehow, I managed to imitate their behavior, rather than prostrate myself.

Obeisance granted, the hold of the monarchs ebbed slightly, and I found myself able to survey my surroundings. Beyond the dais, along the back arc of the circle, stretched a low balustrade revealing endless gardens beyond. In front of the balustrade, tables arched around the smooth central expanse, which ended in a sheer drop to the river valley below. From this vantage, the beauty of the court spread out before us, painted with the vibrant hues of the setting sun. Faint stars scattered across the rose-and-dusk shaded sky—we'd come at the liminal hour.

And in this spectacular setting, fae mingled rather like mortals would at a ball, each one more glittering in beauty than the last. The decadent attire Riven had selected had clearly been the proper choice. Anything less, and I would have appeared as out of place as I felt. Without thought, I found myself searching the space for him—I would have given a great deal to have him at my side, rather than Nikol.

But he had yet to appear.

I recognized only a few individuals among the crowd gathered—Lady Maeve and Prince Sable among them. Conversation thrummed about me. Evidently, the first order of business wasn't dining but mingling. Nikol plucked two glasses from a nearby pedestal and offered me one. The liquid inside gleamed with some sort of inner light, and it held a bright, wintry scent. When I took a cautious sip, it seemed to spark within my mouth. *What is this?*

Jade sniffed. *Mirwen. It carries essence of winter star—I'd not overindulge.*

Perhaps some of my sentiments about the strength of the beverage made escape, for Nikol's lips quirked upward. "Would you like to try something else instead?"

I shook my head. I'd rather pretend to sip at the mirwen then be forced to imbibe something even more pungent. Though I might be fae, I was in no way accustomed to the potency of their beverages.

"Very well." He took a long draft from his own glass. "Riven said you'd like to speak to Lord Revilon. He's the one near the west terrace, and as it happens, he was one of those most outspoken against the notion of allowing my court here for the hunt. Shouldn't take much to provoke him into conversation, if we play our hand right."

I questioned the veracity of anything Nikol said; however, his words appeared straightforward, and I did want to speak to Lord Revilon, so I nodded. "I assume an ordinary introduction is out of the question?"

"Where's the fun in that?" His uncanny eyes sparkled. "Besides, you want him inclined to favor you. A little bit of conflict will achieve just the right touch." As he spoke, he maneuvered me toward Lord Revilon, then leaned closer to speak low in my ear. "If you make it out of this court alive, I'll come to call upon you—I'd like you to make some introductions for me. Perhaps there's an enterprising young woman who'd like to provide me a child."

A tide of heat swirled up my chest, and I snatched my arm away from him. "You presume a great deal."

The fae lord turned, his bearing as stately as a towering elm. "You will find that characteristic in all your dealings with the Court of Silver. It is their nature."

Some of my anger faded when I realized he'd meant to provoke me in front of Lord Revilon. Yet we'd have words later —just to make sure.

A smirk twisted Nikol's lips. "If you intend to persuade Lady Jessa that your court is any different, then I shall be the first to inform her of your past dealings."

Lord Revilon drew himself rigidly upright to address me. "Perhaps you'd prefer more pleasant company, Lady Jessa?"

"Alas, I'm not always at liberty to follow my preferences." I frowned slightly at Nikol. "I've been obliged to accept an escort this evening. I'm sure you understand."

Lord Revilon unbent enough to offer a slight nod.

"Yet I'm pleased we have an opportunity to speak with you, since I hear you have gardens worth viewing. And I must confess some curiosity after Lady Maeve showed me her rather unusual sylph tree. Do you seek to cultivate such novelties as well?"

"What you deem a novelty might also be viewed as an unnecessary corruption of otherwise pure essence." The last bit of light filtering over the horizon caught on the silvered embroidery of his jacket. "Maeve and I hold very different views. If her gardens please you, it's likely mine will not."

Though he swathed his sentiments in noncommittal fae-speech, it seemed unlikely that he pursued mortal experimentation. Would he have some other reason to claim so many? "I would not say my sentiment was pleasure. However, I find it wise to be informed on all views—and I'm certain I would find your gardens intriguing."

Before he could reply, Lady Talis appeared on the expansive dining floor, her bearing regal and distant, as if she meant to move through the space without engaging anyone in it. Yet when she passed by, she offered me a small nod.

"You are acquainted with Lady Talis?" A note of surprise laced Revilon's voice.

Perhaps under ordinary circumstances, fae would not share such information freely, but I wanted him to speak of Talis, so I must offer something. "After a fashion. We happened to meet in the library."

"Then she's ventured out twice in as many days. How remarkable."

"She's reclusive then?"

"More than reclusive. I cannot recall the last time she left her demesne. Yet we've not invited another court into our own in centuries—it seems that's drawn her forth." A speculative gleam entered his eyes. "You will excuse me."

"Of course." If her very presence drew note, it was unlikely she'd ventured forth long enough to make a secret alliance—and by her own words, her garden alone concerned her, not the politics and power maneuvers of court. In that, I sympathized with her. When Revilon removed himself, I turned to Nikol. "What do you know of his dealings?"

"Despite appearances, Revilon's shrewd and slippery. And there's no love lost between him and Maeve." Nikol swathed us in glamour as we spoke, yet through its shadowy folds, another fae lord caught my eye. "Though I'm only beginning to orient myself to the dynamics of this court, I've little doubt he'd be pleased to outmaneuver her."

Nikol's words faded as I examined the profile of the fae lord who spoke with Lady Maeve and the man at her side, presumably her husband. Something about the angle of his jaw was unsettlingly familiar, and when he turned, my breath caught. "Who is that?"

"Damir's son—Evander. They look rather alike, don't they?"

Sudden cold pierced me. Was there any way he could have learned about my involvement in his father's death? Had Lord West confided anything in him of our dealings? Nikol didn't know the whole matter either, so I must tread with care. "His father was not fond of me, since I kept Kilmere from him. Does Evander share his sentiments?"

"Not to my knowledge."

I angled away from Evander, regarding the expanse of the court stretched before me. It was natural that he'd be present. Riven had said all the Court of Silver high fae of standing would attend the hunt, yet I'd not given it a second thought. Heedless of the way it seared my throat, I drank deeply of the mirwen, its heady sensation burning away some of the chill within.

Nikol assessed me narrowly, then plucked the glass from my hand, giving it to a wylding who passed by. "Of course, I don't know every detail of your dealings with Damir. In their convening, Riven gave our arbiter facts which were judged true. But I will say this—rumor has it Evander seeks to find out what led to the kill, what prompted the basilisk to strike. Information Riven could not be expected to provide."

My stomach roiled. "Surely it's not so very strange that a creature kept in such bondage would lash out at its captor?"

"Evander thinks otherwise. But then, he's the sort to believe it's a privilege to be enslaved to one of such a great family." Bitterness tinged Nikol's words. "Just like his father."

"Did you know Lord—Damir?"

"I knew him well enough to be certain his removal improved our court." His tone remained cool. "Even my queen did not grieve his absence overmuch. He ever struggled to bend the knee."

"I see." From our vantage, I could perceive a set of stairs that angled up from the west terrace to a sort of pavilion forged from stone. So skillful was the craft and well-woven the botanical life through it that from a distance it appeared merely a spire of the mountain. I seized it as an excuse to remove from the reminder of Damir and the past. "Perhaps we could go look at the pavilion?"

"Contemplating escape already?" A smile flashed across his

face. "Or perhaps you just can't resist the chance to steal away for a moment together?"

"I'd rather a moment alone with a wyvern." The blunt words slipped out before I could collect them. Perhaps the Otherworld already had its way with me, for ladies of the mortal world certainly did not speak so freely.

But Nikol only laughed and gestured me forward. "Then carry on."

On the stairs, he encountered a fae lord who engaged him with some question of the hunt, and I took advantage of his occupation to slip into the shadowy pavilion. Its cool quiet enveloped me. Yet something else pricked against my awareness, a sense of vast ancient distance. Talis?

Had she shared my desire for escape, perhaps? As I moved to the far side of the pavilion, she came into view, sheltered beneath one of its pillars. She appeared weary, faint lines radiating from her moon-bright eyes as she regarded the brilliant gathering of fae stretched out over the stone expanse. Watching her, I'd the sense of one suffering under an unbearable weight.

And it gave me courage to approach. "Are you well?"

"Such events are not to my taste." Her rich voice held notes of restrained emotion. "Yet one does not ignore the bidding of the king. It always ends poorly."

Her words made it clear she'd come against her own inclination. Perhaps I wasn't wholly out of the ordinary among fae in preferring the solace of my gardens to the glitter of society events in which one must perform to an exacting standard. Never mind that the standard varied a great deal between mortal and fae worlds, the pressure to perform remained.

"And you?" Her silvery brows arched as she regarded me. "Does our court meet your expectations?"

If I were from the Court of Roses, how would I answer? The vines spilling over the pillars rustled softly. However at ease her confession made me feel, I should still exercise care. "I have found my stay satisfactory so far."

"I wonder very much if that will be your sentiment when all

events have unfolded." Starlight caught in her silvery hair. "Have you participated in a hunt of this nature before?"

She'd worded that neatly enough to make evasion challenging. "I'm not fond of such excursions. I prefer the quiet of the gardens."

"In that, we are alike." Her voice dropped low. "In what else, I wonder? I suppose time shall tell all."

"Lady Jessa?" Nikol approached.

After an imperious nod of greeting, Talis withdrew. I pasted on a smile and turned toward Nikol, wishing I might have sheltered with her longer. Of all the fae I'd encountered so far in the Court of Dusk, she was the only one I would have liked to speak to further, both to better understand the glimpses of pain I caught and how she'd navigated this world as one who did not take interest in its politics and power maneuvering. Yet none of those could I discuss before Nikol.

Though I could perceive no bells, a deep tolling sound rang over the mountaintop, and as one, fae moved toward the dining tables.

Nikol offered his arm. "It's time we rejoined the company."

As we descended, I caught a glimpse of Riven alongside King Alastor, and some of the tension left my shoulders. Nikol maneuvered us through the throng and to a table, positioning me at the end, which meant I'd no one to the left of me—a welcome reprieve. As we waited for the rest to assemble, I turned to him. "What you said before we spoke to Lord Revilon—"

"Don't worry. I've no interest in acquiring a child by force or bargain. It's just that the suggestion was a sure way to spark genuine anger—Lord Revilon is too shrewd to be taken in by pretense."

Which meant I was entirely too predictable on the matter of protecting mortals. But what was the alternative? Riven's gaze swept over us, sharp and assessing, before moving on down the line of assembled fae.

Nikol nodded in his direction. "It seems I'm being watched to ensure I adhere to proper behavior."

"And do you intend to?"

His silver eyes gleamed. "Given the trouble that followed the last time I had the pleasure of your company alone, it seems prudent. For now."

The last time we'd been alone was when he'd tormented Jade and Risha to force the abandonment of my glamour. I lifted my glass and took a sip to hide my face. Just what had happened between him and Riven afterward? Whatever it was, they'd put it aside sufficiently to work together on this scheme, as Riven had promised. Perhaps such moves and countermoves, actions and consequences, were all an expected part of fae court life and did not lead to the fallout they might in mortal relationships. Or perhaps they were simply better at hiding it.

Once all the gathered fae were seated, blooming floral centerpieces and plates with elaborately styled food appeared before us. With difficulty, I schooled my features. Did the king have the power to bring objects through passings on their own? Or had he used some other mechanism altogether? Whatever the underlying process, the effect was spectacular. As the feast began, concealment glamours wove and dissipated at regular intervals around the tables—and none seemed to attract undue attention. At the center of my plate spiraled a star of some sort of meat adorned with a bright vermilion sauce. Tentatively, I tasted it, and flavor exploded on my tongue, layer after layer of warm spice unfolding. Like the fermented beverage Nikol had procured for me, I found it almost overwhelming, yet at the same time, these flavors brought a sense of surprising comfort.

Dusk deepened around us, and fae-lights sprang up radiant about the tables. Just as I began to think I might manage to make it through the evening without significant mishap, a small group of mortals appeared in the center of the floor. My food took on the taste of ash in my mouth, and my body tensed as I surveyed their features. None of them matched the descriptions of the missing, but could they truly be unconnected?

Beneath the table's edge, Nikol snatched my wrist, his hold tight as a manacle, and a concealment glamour thickened the air about us. "Before you do something you'll regret, know that none of these are the ones you seek. They were brought into court for this event—I watched their arrival yesterday."

"Nevertheless, they suffer."

"It's not your concern. Unless you mean to abandon the ones you set out to save." He released his grip.

Nikol's words held no perceptible twist of deception, but still, it was possible the supplier of these mortals was connected to the one I sought. "Who brought them?"

"Lady Maeve's husband."

Soft strains of music drifted through the air, and the glassy-eyed figures began to dance in an impossibly fast and intricate pattern that no mortal could conceive or maintain for long without fatiguing. I felt as though the weight of the mountain itself descended on my chest.

Riven had said nothing of this, though he must have known. Why?

Jade stood like a statue behind my chair, and her warm breath swept over my neck. *Perhaps because he's already investigated the matter and knew you'd be hard-pressed not to interfere.*

I could imagine it. I stole a glance at Riven, who now occupied a position near the monarchs. He spoke with Lady Ulrika and spared not a single glance at the suffering mortals. I turned my gaze to my plate, the very beauty of the arranged fruits repugnant. So much care had been taken with meaningless things and so little with precious lives.

Of course, to fae, mortal lives weren't precious. Riven had once said fae regarded them as insects crawling upon the earth, here today and gone tomorrow. In which case, why should they care?

When I glanced up again, I found Lady Maeve's attention fixed on me. Had my face betrayed my feelings? I forced myself to take a bite of spiced plum, though it soured on my tongue. All about me, fae feasted and conversed, some watching the antics of the dancers with the sort of vague amusement with which mortals might regard frolicking puppies—but without the concern most mortals had for their pets.

Sweat now sheened their faces, and one of the ladies stumbled. Her ankle dangled at a peculiar angle, and her face twisted in agony, yet still she danced. I clenched my hands in my lap. If this torturous dance continued, they would eventually die. How could I sit here and do nothing, when they were no different from those we'd come to free?

You must hold your course.

My throat tightened. *I don't know if I can.*

You gave your word.

I had, and though I hadn't bound myself in bargain, Riven had accepted my promise in good faith. How could I justify breaking it? I could conceive of no way to help them, yet how could I fail to act? If that were Ainslie bound to this floor, condemned to dance to her death . . .

With a smooth motion, Nikol stood. "King Alastor, if the mortals might be retired, I have a gift to present on behalf of my queen in recognition of your hospitality."

The king flicked his fingers, and the mortals vanished as if the ether swallowed them. It *must* be some sort of passing that he opened, though it appeared to operate under different rules than those I'd observed until now. *Can you tell where they were taken?*

I can still catch their scent. I believe they've been removed to somewhere in the gardens behind us.

Nikol beckoned to someone standing in the shadows along the balustrade. "At the bidding of Queen Astra, I snared a breeding pair of firebirds. May they adorn your court for centuries to come."

River wyldings wheeled in an immense cage that contained glorious feathery beings, their plumage holding every hue of flame. Their tail feathers streamed behind them like rivers of fire, their eyes were glowing embers set in fierce faces, and their powerful frames could have carried off a full-grown man with little effort. I pressed my lips together. They were wild and magnificent, in no way made for captivity.

Within the Court of Gold, firebirds are always given liberty, as they represent the glory of day. Naturally, the Court of Silver holds the opposite view. Their natural habitat does not extend as far as the Court of Dusk, which makes this a fitting gift.

"They are a fine pair." King Alastor's voice resonated in the evening air, yet his expression didn't reveal the slightest flicker of gratitude, merely approval of a worthy offering.

"With your permission, I shall key their bindings to you," Nikol said.

"Granted."

Something flickered in the air around the cage—a reconfiguring of the workings that bound the firebirds?—and then Nikol left my side and unlocked the cage. A vast web of shadow about him kept the firebirds from assaulting the assembly and drove them to the air. Once they launched from the mountain, a radiant array of fire poured from them, kindling the night sky with brilliant light and creating a magnificent display. The binding Nikol referenced must have constrained them from flying far, for they stopped short every time they drew near the rim of the river.

Yet he didn't attend to their flight, now that he'd entrusted them to the king; rather, he watched me. Unless I missed my guess, he'd chosen to intervene to keep me from betraying myself—and by extension, him. Though he didn't possess Riven's abilities, he was astute. I supposed neither of them could have ascended to their current positions without a perceptive nature, and the requisite power required, of course. For my part, I simply wanted to lose myself in the garden—not the hundreds of acres stretching behind us, but the small homely garden on Camden Row. What was happening there, in my absence? Beneath my glittering finery, my chest tightened.

Nikol took his seat next to me once more, and the interminable meal continued, courses appearing and disappearing at set intervals, until at last, an impossibly light and airy confection appeared. It held more layers of flavor than I'd ever dreamt could exist in one dish. "Is this the end?"

"Yes, it's a simple hunt feast, so it's much abbreviated. Most will attend the moon dove fight next."

If I had to endure another moment of senseless cruelty, I might shatter. I dragged the tines of my fork through the glittering confection before me. "And if I don't wish to do so?"

"Some will retire to private negotiations or events, so your removal won't draw undue attention. Not like any indication of disapproval would."

This concession was all I required. As soon as the monarchs rose, I made my escape into the garden, instinctively turning away from the areas where fae clustered and moving toward the quieter regions where the king might have sequestered the mortals. Nikol might claim they'd nothing to do with the missing I sought, but I needed to be sure—whatever the risk.

CHAPTER 56

The paths through the garden weren't of crushed stone or shell or brick or any of the items that the mortal world used, but rather a smooth, luminous substance that cast a gentle glow—just the perfect amount to enhance the beauty of the floral beds bordering them.

These gardens promised a world of enchantment, and some part of me yearned to sink into it. Yet it held a world of cruelty, for somewhere in its depths the imprisoned mortals were concealed. *Can you trace their scent?*

Jade halted next to me. *Yes, but is it wise? You cannot act on their behalf.*

I just . . . need to see their situation and, if I can, learn how they were lured here or if they've seen other mortals.

And if they're hurt or in immediate peril?

I . . . I don't know.

She chuffed. *Well, we should ask Risha to join us before we venture any farther. Depending on what we encounter, we may need her.*

I agree. Please do. The bargain-holder had seemed to indicate I would not see her again, but she might well change her mind —and if she did, I wanted to be able to reach Riven. So we waited in a secluded niche surrounded by a variety of plants, all of which bore white blossoms in varying shapes and sizes and most of which did not belong to the mortal world, though they willingly whispered their names to me as I trailed my fingers across their soft petals—*mistwynd, inevine, silverblade, nightsward.*

When Risha appeared, she and I followed Jade deeper into the garden until we reached a glade where a prison of woven trees held the mortals. No provision appeared to have been made for them, and they huddled together inside, a shivering, forlorn heap of humanity. I wrapped my arms around my stomach, the cold metal overlaying my bodice digging into my skin.

If this was how fae regarded mortals, how could anything between our worlds ever change? And if whatever protections had existed were now eroding . . . how could humans hope to survive? Instinctively, I reached toward the trees that bound them, but they might as well have been constructed of adamant —they remained unyielding and unresponsive, bound to the will of another.

Perhaps it had been a mistake to come, to further witness suffering I could not hope to alleviate. A chill breeze tugged at the edges of my gown. If I approached and questioned them, as I'd hoped, and one of them mentioned my presence to their captors . . . what then? Was it worth the risk? However much it wrenched me to think of abandoning them, perhaps I should wait and talk to Riven first—whenever I might manage.

As I wavered, a short, rather thick figure appeared, and I shrank back into the shrubbery at the very edge of the glade, willing her to take no note of my presence. When she approached the cage, silvery moonlight spilled over her face, revealing mortal features, delicate and beautiful in a human way. She withdrew something from the folds of her cloak, and as it fell back, it revealed the source of her swollen frame—she was heavy with child.

Nausea churned within.

She passed bits of food through the small gaps in the woven

trees that imprisoned the mortals, and one of the men roused from his stupor enough to offer thanks. He struggled to his feet. "How came you here? Did you cross?"

"Not 'cause I wished it. Only my mistress, her cows escaped, and she would have had my hide if I didn't return them, and they'd crossed over, and so did I to fetch them, and I thought if I was quickish, I could return, but I never did because . . . he found me."

The man's gaze lowered, and he recoiled. "Now what? You carry the spawn of one of these evil creatures?"

"You think I had any choice? Fighting their will is useless." Her lips trembled. "In time, you'll see. Either you serve a purpose or they use you till you die—or both."

"I won't accept it." His voice echoed through the clearing.

"Hush. No one knows I'm here. You think they care how long you live?" The faint call of some unfamiliar bird echoed in the distance, and she jumped. "I must go."

She hurried down the path toward me, and before rational thought could take hold, I stepped forward. Her eyes widened, and she sank to the ground before me, an ungainly motion that made me fear she'd topple.

"Please, my lady, I didn't see you. I meant no disrespect."

I stood rooted in place as she bowed trembling before me. This was *wrong.* The desire to embrace my cast-off mortal glamour welled within me, along with the need to reassure her that she was not alone. With a desperate wrench, I tamped it down, keeping my fae features intact. I reached for her. "It cannot be good for your condition to remain on the ground."

However reluctant, she took my hand, hers cold and tremulous within my own. Her palms bore a series of thin scars, so evenly placed that I'd no doubt they were deliberately inflicted. My heart twisted within my chest. If I could not reveal myself as an ally, I must gain information on her plight another way—as much as it pained me. Perhaps then I'd see my way clear to help. "I saw you speaking with the captives, giving them food."

Her face became paler than a paperwhite peony, her eyes dark and wide as those of a startled doe.

"I require information. Should you see your way to providing it, I'll also see my way to keeping silent about your presence here." The words tasted bitter on my lips, but I pressed on. "Whose child do you carry?"

"Lord Revilon."

Revilon. I'd passed cordial conversation with him, thinking he'd not trifle with mortals as Maeve did, and all the while—I swallowed against the burning in my throat. "And does this lord hold other mortals?"

"No, my lady. He claimed me because he sought to increase his family."

I bit my lip. If Riven hadn't intervened when I almost bargained with Mocvar, I would have shared her plight—and even now, I could still feel the sickening terror that revelation had brought, just as I saw it written in the pale, wretched features before me. And it crushed the very air from my lungs. I couldn't do this, couldn't walk away from this suffering, this injustice.

Jade stalked between us. *You need to leave her, before your attention draws notice.*

How can I turn my back on her?

There are those in your world who suffer, yet you do not try to help everyone.

I clenched my hands so tightly the nails dug into my skin. *Perhaps not, but I've always sought to aid those who have come into my path.*

Equally, you always think before you act. Consider the cost of this choice.

She was right that I'd always sought caution as I walked the delicate dance between worlds, fearing the cost of a misstep. And I'd given my word to draw no attention to my views. Was there a way I could keep it and yet spare her? My hand drifted to the passing prism Riven had given me, which I'd tucked deep into a pocket so I could bear the starfire jewels about my neck.

We were in the gardens, not the demesne proper, so could I take her through it without drawing notice? Bring her to Kilmere and bid the stronghold to hide her from any who would seek her? It had the power to do so, I'd little doubt of that. "If you could keep the baby, would you desire it?"

"My lord has already informed me I will not be kept as a nursemaid, but sent to bear another. I serve at his pleasure." Her eyes appeared almost vacant. "It's useless to consider otherwise."

She should not have to endure the anguish of surrendering her child, much less a repeat of the assaults that led to her condition. The passing prism warmed beneath my fingers. If I lifted it, moonbeams would shine through. We were far distant from the main party, and I sensed no nearby fae. Perhaps we would draw no notice. I'd promised not to expose myself, not to speak out against what I found deplorable—but not to avoid helping if I could without endangering our purpose. I edged closer. "But if there was a way—"

The pressure in the air about us dropped, and Riven appeared amid knife-sharp shards of light. I stumbled back. I'd witnessed the storm charge of his power before, but this was different; there was something detached and forbidding and cold about him, like lightning limned by frost, were such a thing possible.

The woman collapsed once more, but he ignored her, snapping a thick concealment glamour about us. The air crackled with the force of it, and I froze in place. How had he come—

Oh.

Risha fluttered near his shoulder, her wings blazing bright. Whatever friendship I thought existed between us, she clearly held her loyalty to Riven higher.

He closed the distance between us, his leather boots crunching against stone. "It's time you returned to the demesne, Lady Jessa."

"But I—"

He glanced down at the woman with the sort of dispassionate distaste one might a toad on the path. "Mortal, return to your master. At once."

She flinched.

So did I.

With difficulty, she struggled to her feet, but he made no move to help. Then she scurried away, leaving me to face Riven.

"She needs our help and—"

"You gave your word." His glamour about us strengthened, the power thicker than a summer storm. "I told you that you would witness things that you found deplorable and you would have to shut your eyes to it or abandon your mission. You agreed. You cannot help her."

"I've kept my word not to expose my sentiments before the court, but surely we can offer aid where there are none to take note?"

"If you imagine you can take the child of a fae lord without attracting notice—or that King Alastor does not feel any passing within range of his demesne—you're much mistaken." The edge to his words cut deep.

And I faltered. Perhaps I had deceived myself in my desire to lend aid, but I couldn't confess it—because that would mean it was right to turn a blind eye to this suffering, an unbearable conclusion. The musky smell of damp earth and the bitter scent of black nightshade mingled to choke me. "There must be some way."

"She's not your concern."

Like fine chains, coils of light wove about me, then vanished. Though I tried to step back, I found I could not increase the distance between us. "What have you done?"

His eyes were the shade of a wintry fir forest. "What is required. I'll escort you to your room. It's time you retired for the evening."

"I can't just abandon her—"

"You will." His voice dropped ominously low.

And my breath caught. The branches overhead lashed the

night sky, as if in response to my pain. No, that wasn't right—these weren't bound to me. "Riven, I—"

"It's time to go." He spun and walked away, the invisible cords of power leaving me no choice but to follow him down an unfamiliar path and beneath the arch of weeping cypress.

A rumble emanated from Jade, but she padded next to me without attempting to interfere, and as for Risha, she concealed herself next to Riven. In silence, we traversed the seemingly endless path, not back to the mountaintop where we'd dined, but a different trail that descended to a small terrace. A painful tightness constricted my chest beneath its golden prison. Not since the moment we'd first met had I been so aware of my own vulnerability in his presence. I'd told him I trusted him, but I'd not thought he'd use his affinities to force me to his bidding, nor realized how little effort it would take for him to do so.

The stone of the mountain closed in around me as we entered the demesne proper. Clearly, I'd gone beyond inspiring disappointment and had succeeded in sparking anger . . . and my own churned to meet it, a veritable tempest of emotion that lacked both order and reason, but rose hot and choking and painful, pricking at my eyes and tightening my throat. After what felt an eternity, we stopped before the rose-and-thorn sigiled door.

"I'll come for you when the court rises tomorrow afternoon." His voice held no trace of emotion, only an implicit command to remain in my bedchamber until he returned.

I took a step back, bumping into the unyielding wall behind me. "I'd rather you not—if that matters."

My voice emerged unsteady.

And for a moment, he made no reply. Then he turned away. "As it pleases you. We gather for the hunt an hour before twilight. See to it that you're there."

At last, the power binding me released. I stumbled through the door, securing it behind me—not that it would make a difference if Riven or anyone else desired to enter. My vision blurring, I fumbled with the clasp of my cape and sliced my finger on its sharp edge.

Withering frost, I couldn't even manage my own apparel. A bead of blood dripped onto the shimmering fabric of my gown, followed by another.

Jade gently nuzzled my cheek, and my chest tightened. *Did you tell Risha to go for Riven?*

No. She sat back, regarding me with her steady green gaze. *But I don't disagree with her choice.*

I thought you were on my side.

I am, which is why I support her decision.

And Riven's actions? I swiped my stinging hand against my gown, heedless of the streak of blood it left.

I don't approve of his high-handedness, but I sympathize with his desire to see you to safety.

I hardly think that's what was going on. I wrenched at the sun flowers in my hair, but they tangled in the strands and refused to release, much like the emotions in my chest, one impossibly snarled with the other. I collapsed on the bed, forsaking my attempts to shed the detestable fae garb, and buried my face in the pillow. Was I angry at Riven—or angry at the cruelty of the fae in general and my own sense of powerlessness in the face of it, a feeling which had driven me toward rash action? I drew a shuddering breath, unable to restrain my tears any longer.

After a time, Risha crept up on my damp pillow. "You are upset I went for Riven?"

Yes—no. I'd no notion, not anymore. "Not angry, not when I've given you leave to choose. I understand you answer to Riven first, that your allegiance lies with his court."

"That's not why I went." Her light pulsed with tones of gray. "Nikol set a shadow on you when you entered the gardens, and I knew he watched. I saw it return to him when you approached the mortals. If Riven had not come, Nikol would have. When I reached Riven, he was there already. He told Riven to manage you—or he would."

My stomach dropped. His *management* of the situation

surely would have involved far more pain than Riven's had—I'd no doubt of his resolve to protect his interests.

"Something else I saw. The mortal wore jeweled cuff on ankle, like the bracelet Asrina said Damir gave you. Wherever she went, her lord would find her—and if she attempted to elude him, the punishment would be most severe. He would force from her whoever helped him and make them pay."

My empathy for her situation had blinded me to a true assessment of the dangers, not only those that Risha and Riven had pointed out—which I should have recognized myself—but also those that I knew more intimately, like the fact the very trees themselves could have testified against me. I buried my face in the pillow. "I almost cost us everything."

Yet even knowing that, I couldn't absolve myself of responsibility, couldn't let go of the sense that I should have done *something* for the captive mortals—though it was now painfully clear any effort would have led to disaster.

Jade padded over to the side of the bed and lowered her face till her nose kissed my forehead. *Your tender heart is one of the reasons I love you, as well as the fact that you always hope, even when others have given up. Yet sometimes those desires will lead you astray, which is why you require us also. It may be that there's still a way to gain their freedom, but not now.*

I reached up and stroked her fur, and she gave a quiet purr, which abruptly turned to a low, rumbling growl. *Someone approaches.*

CHAPTER 57

I scrubbed my hands across my face and straightened my gown, then scrambled to my feet as a soft whispering sounded outside my door. I could not reach the plants required for defense, yet I instinctively flung my senses wide and —there.

At the very edges of my awareness, tiny starprick shimmers of light, pale and ever-shifting in hue, drifted through the air like dandelion down. What was I seeing? Before I could attempt to sort the jumbled impression, it faded.

The door swung open.

Jade stalked forward, and I straightened. Whoever came through, I would not shrink back. Some part of me expected the bargain-holder, yet an unfamiliar individual entered the room, form swathed with a thick indigo cape, shot through with silver threads that dazzled the eye. A void of power and possibility swirled about the nebulous figure. It secured the door, then stood still, as if watching me.

"You've made very bold, coming here." Though this night had left me bruised and battered, I intended to expose no part of it. I lifted my chin. "What do you want?"

"I've called not because of my own desires." The low voice held feminine notes. "But to offer you what *you* want."

"And what is that?"

"Information about mortals who have gone missing."

My blood ran cold. If she'd sprung at me with a knife, it would have been less of a shock. "That's an interesting theory." Somehow, I spoke with a steady voice.

"It's no theory. I do not act unless I am sure."

If she knew my purpose here, then she could undo everything. What sort of demand might she make? I forced myself to draw a slow, steady breath, to think. It was still possible she didn't know, that she sought to force me to betray myself. Yet I felt as if I trod a path with a sheer precipice on either side.

"Don't worry. I've no intention of divulging your purpose." The silver threads shimmered bright. "Rather, I have a bargain to propose."

"What are your terms?"

"You will be first to claim the shadow-drake's blood, then you will grant me the relic Queen Astra gives you. If you do, I will tell you the identity of the one who has bargained with mortals to disperse pyske-dust on her behalf and thereby lure many into this world."

The chill drove deeper into my body, as if carried by the pallid light of the moonscape on the walls around us. She knew the truth somehow. Which meant . . . what? Was *she* the partner to the one I'd first encountered? Perhaps I'd been wrong about Lady Maeve—or perhaps this was Lady Maeve, wrapped so strongly in glamour that I could not gain a clear sense of her. If only I understood the workings of the Otherworld better, what could be accomplished and what could not. I drew myself up to my full, insubstantial height. "Are you the one responsible?"

A slight laugh rippled from beyond her veil. "A worthy question, but I hold none of these bargains nor the mortals claimed. However, I assure you that you'll never find the one who does without my intervention. I offer you not only a name, but an audience with the fae you seek—a chance to make your case, though it will likely avail you little."

She offered what I most desired. Why? Surely it wasn't out of goodwill. Could her need for this relic—of which Nikol had refused to speak—rival mine to find the missing and free Ainslie? I fought the urge to rub my throbbing temples. I'd already nearly exposed everything tonight. What if I made another mistake? "If I managed to win the relic, how would I find you?"

"If you win, I will find *you.*" Her veil fluttered about her as if stirred by some unseen breeze. "Do you accept my terms?"

"They contain no requirement that I do win, only the promise that *if* I do, you'll receive the relic and I will receive an audience with the one who holds the bargains?"

"That is correct. May I suggest that you do not have time to dally? With each day you're absent from the mortal world, those you care for become more vulnerable."

My pulse surged in my ears. She truly knew everything. How was it possible, if she wasn't one of those who held the bargains? It didn't matter; now I must control the damage. "It seems you've learned a great deal. If I enter into a bargain with you, it must include your silence on my history and my present aims."

Though she'd said she had no *intention* of sharing it, intentions could change—and they were in no way binding.

"To share that information would undermine my own goals, at least as long as we have a common purpose. But so you will believe the sincerity of my offer, I'll grant your request. My silence on your origin and the purpose of your presence shall be part of our bargain, as long as you remain in the Court of Dusk."

Then I must bargain, because if she carried whatever evidence she had before the king—I couldn't even consider the consequences. Yet how could I undertake this hunt? Seek to claim something vital from a creature that had never done me harm? But if I did not, if I failed, then I abandoned Ainslie and the bound mortals to their fate. Qualms and quandaries aside, perhaps it was ridiculous even to believe I *could* succeed if I tried —this shadow-drake was a lethal danger, and I'd never hunted so much as a rabbit before. In any case, I needed only to promise an effort to purchase her silence. "I accept your terms."

"Wise choice."

Beneath the cloak I still wore, a binding mark coiled about my upper arm, its chill sinking deep into my flesh.

"I look forward to your success."

With that, she departed, and I wrenched back my cloak to search for some hint as to the fae who'd bound me. But I found nothing. I could feel the power of the binding thrumming beneath the surface of my skin, yet no visible mark remained. I collapsed on the edge of the bed. She'd appeared and departed as swift as a winter mistral, upending everything by her passing. With her knowledge, she could have pressed for a far more damaging bargain—she could have asked for nearly anything, but she'd confined herself to this one request. Why?

I could fathom no answer, only I knew what I must do next. Whatever had passed between us, I had to tell Riven about the bargain. I'd already fractured things between us by skirting the bounds of the promise I'd given, and I didn't want to test his patience further. Yet seeking him was the sensible course, since he might be able to perceive some trace of the fae—might wish to, given that her knowledge could expose him.

Yet I'd rather walk through a field of thistles unshod than seek him again tonight.

Jade padded to my side, a pillar of strength. *I agree we need his insight. There's something wrong about all of this—not just the fae you bargained with, but also the one who appeared before.*

I leaned against her, tracing the thorns of gold on my gown with my uninjured hand. *And a great deal more.*

I would keep strictly to the matter at hand; surely he would understand. And it would be better if I went to him, in case she kept watch over my bedchamber. I turned to Risha. "Bright one, can you help me find Riven, without it appearing as though we set forth to do so?"

She perked up. "Yes, yes. Those visiting the Court of Dusk like to view the starielle that bloom at night. We should go there first, then stroll the gardens. We could happen upon him."

"He's still within the gardens, then?"

"Yes, yes."

Another time I'd ask how she was aware of his presence, how she zipped with such assurance between individuals and locations. For now, I was simply thankful. With unerring confidence, she led us to a display of starielle that would have mesmerized in other circumstances. A chorus of song rose from decadent blossoms that opened and closed in a harmonic pattern, as if they responded to the pulse of the stars in the heavens above. Yet their beauty left me untouched, as all my attention remained fixed on what had happened and what must yet come.

Risha meandered along the starielle and into a bordering path, and I followed, pretending to admire the unfolding vista. Bit by bit, she led us through labyrinthine ways into the depths of the garden, where some sort of oppressive power charged the air. She halted before what appeared to be an arena of sorts, a large rectangular area bounded on all sides by tall pillared trees. A working of a different weave than any I'd perceived before hung over it, so thick it took a moment to discern what took place within, the source of the oppressive sensation.

Within the working, Nikol and Riven, divested of their formal jackets, faced off. I halted abruptly. It wasn't some sort of formal event, for they had no audience. *What in the Crossings is happening?*

Jade gave a soft rumble. *Fae vent their energies by sparring, much as the men in your world do, only their bouts are much more dangerous; true damage may be done. Thus they take place only in querants like these, which are bounded by workings to constrain the force wielded. At set intervals, there's a cease to allow for necessary healing so the bout may continue.*

I see. It appeared the cease had come to an end, as a clash of shadow and light shook the ground about me and quavered the trees. Such was the force that I feared the querant wouldn't contain it, but surely, the king wouldn't allow sparring matches that posed a danger to his gardens. Only by bringing all my attention to bear could I sort through the tempestuous clash of power and perceive the fae forms swallowed in vivid workings, though I struggled to trace their rapid movements. A spear of light from Riven broke through a tangle of shadow, driving into Nikol's shoulder and forcing him to give some ground. At once, he spun and vanished, reappearing behind Riven.

In that heartbeat of transition, Riven glanced up, his gaze fixing on me. He held up a fist, and the shadows about Nikol winked from sight. The working around the querant drew back, and the two lords emerged, their breathing unlabored despite the intensity of the clash between them.

With lithe grace, Riven closed the distance between us, the air still sparking with residual affinities. Nikol sauntered along behind. Though I'd never expected to feel thankful for Nikol, his presence offered a welcome buffer against the bristling tension. If I kept my gaze fixed on him, I need not see the disapproval in Riven's face.

Nikol arched a brow. "I thought you'd retired."

"I had, but . . . I had an unexpected visitor. I believe both of you will have an interest in what she said."

The sense of gathering storm intensified, and Riven's glamour closed about us. "Who was it?"

"She kept fully concealed—I never saw her features. I suppose it might not have been a woman after all, but the voice sounded female."

"Does this individual bear responsibility for the blood on your gown?" His voice held a distinct chill.

"No, that was . . . nothing of consequence."

His gaze dropped to my hand. "I see."

I tucked it in the folds of my skirts. "Somehow, she knew everything, where I'd come from and the information I sought."

Nikol buffed his fingers across his shirt, a deceptively casual motion. "Any theories on how that's possible?"

"None, since she disclaimed participation in snaring the mortals. She offered a bargain—if I win the relic, she will provide access to Ainslie's bargain-holder. She seemed quite certain that we would not find the identity of the responsible party without her assistance—at least not in time. It could have been a deceit, but I could not gamble with Ainslie's life."

Riven's arms folded across his chest. "You agreed to this fae's terms?"

I gave a slight nod. "I did not know what else to do, and I saw no snare in it. If I cannot win, then I'm under no further obligation. The bargain also binds her to silence about my purpose here."

Nikol's eyes narrowed. "She offered as much?"

"Rather, she conceded at my request, and I cannot think why. She should have pressed her advantage much harder than she did."

The shadows surrounding Nikol deepened. "I don't like it."

"Nor do I." Riven strode forward. "Let me see the binding mark."

"She left no visible mark."

Nikol gave a soft whistle. "You're certain?"

I drew back the folds of my cloak, exposing my upper arm. "Unless you perceive something I cannot."

Riven set a warm spiral of golden light where the binding mark should have been. "Can you still feel the mark?"

"Yes." The light withdrew, and my skin chilled.

"Whatever the constraint of your bargain, it's now paramount that you win the boon. No one should have so much insight into our purpose—finding her now is equally important to locating the bargain-holder."

"I thought perhaps you could trace her."

"Within the demesne, it's Lady Ulrika's right to do so—and

I don't think you want to explain yourself to her. It would expose far too much."

My heart sank. This sharp curtailing of any affinities besides those belonging to the king and his arbiter explained why Riven had said fae preferred to avoid the demesne of another.

Riven pivoted toward Nikol. "To avoid any appearance of collusion, I suggest you depart while we discuss strategy."

"Where's the fun in that?" The shadows behind him danced. "I could craft better snares if I listened to your plan."

"Nikol." A hint of a growl laced his words.

"Very well, I'm going." He spread his hands, then vanished into the shadows beneath the trees.

Uncertainty knotted like bindweed within my stomach and spread its invasive vines, tangling through my body until every muscle coiled tight. I nearly pleaded with him to return, simply so I would not have to face Riven alone—though he gave no sign he recalled what had passed between us earlier this evening. Perhaps it had been inconsequential to him, but it *wasn't* . . . at least, not to me. I kept my gaze on the twist of scarlet-and-gray fern at my feet. However unwelcome it might be to endure further reproach, I couldn't just leave matters this way. "Riven, I owe you an apology—"

"You owe nothing." His voice held the unyielding note of stone. "We have business to attend and no further time to waste."

I pressed my uninjured hand into the elm behind me, its rough bark digging into my skin. If possible, it seemed my attempt to make amends had worsened the situation. Clearly, he didn't want to broach what had passed between us. The low melody of the ferns throbbed in my temples. If I looked at him, I'd surely betray far more of my feelings than I intended, so I instead regarded the maze of roots before me, the paths they drove through the fern.

"Since you're unfamiliar with the hunt, I'd intended that we only appear to pursue the shadow-drake together. Now it seems we will have to join the actual hunt." His words were clipped.

"As long as I renounce any claim to the prize, it will not hinder your bargain. Yet you'll have to draw the blood yourself. Are you willing?"

"It seems I have no choice." The bindweed within twisted tighter. I didn't know how I would manage, couldn't endure the thought, but I couldn't fail Ainslie—nor Riven—again.

"Finding our quarry won't be an easy task. Shadow-drakes can join actual shadow, their bodies becoming incorporeal in the process—which means they no longer hold any trace of their essence. It makes them almost impossible to track."

"Then how—"

"Certain subtle signs can betray them. In this, the Courts of Silver and Dusk have an edge, as the shadow arts run strong in them. Yet even they will struggle."

Would his arbiter affinities—the ability to discern truth from deceit—aid in our quest? I wanted to ask, yet didn't want to prolong the uncomfortable interview further.

"The Wilderfell Forest itself possesses significant power, all unbound—that will give you some advantage, as few of them have the affinities to put it to use," he said. "It will be an effectual weapon against the shadow-drake when located. To fulfill the terms of your bargain, you'll have to help snare it."

"I understand." Silence stretched between us, discomposing me further, and I struggled to hold together the fraying edges of my emotions.

"Dawn approaches in an hour. The court will retire soon." Riven hesitated. "Will you return to your chambers alone, or do you desire company?"

Blight and rot. The formality of the words, the undercurrent of tension they held, caught painfully in my chest. Though he'd attempted to bury it beneath a strict rehearsal of the facts, matters weren't right between us. How many more friendships was I destined to lose? For Mr. Burke and much of my family, I was too fae. For Riven, I was far too mortal. And as for myself . . . I no longer knew what I was. My hands tightened, and the motion reopened my injury. Hot blood pooled in my palm once more.

"I can find my way back," I said softly. "I won't . . . make any detours."

"That's not what I—" He cut off abruptly, fell silent for another moment. "You'd best go. Sleep if you can. You'll need your strength for the hunt."

In a great glade beyond the demesne, a throng gathered. At the center of the clearing stood an enormous passing prism, and the light emanating from it held a world of color all its own, cool tones of silver and blue and midnight black. The reddish light of the setting sun seemed to bathe the rest of the scene in blood. I shuddered. Was shadow-drake blood red? Or was it dark like the ichor that had spilled from the bau? If we were successful, I'd find out. And if we failed . . . then I'd doom Ainslie and the others held captive.

Such thoughts had plagued me all morning, until at last I'd fallen into a restive sleep. I'd woken only an hour before the hunt was meant to begin—just enough time to ready myself with the aid of the river wylding. If this hunt were operated by individuals of sense, we'd not wait until nightfall to seek a dangerous predator who concealed itself in shadows, but then, this wasn't meant to be a display of reason but of prowess.

And anyone who witnessed the assembled fae would have no doubt of their prowess. The glade held enough power to destroy the entire kingdom of Byren in the blink of an eye, leaving naught but desolation.

Riven appeared at my side, the storm charge of his presence

drowning my awareness of all the rest. He gave the slightest incline of his head by way of greeting. "Since I have promised my king you'll return to your home intact, you shall remain with me for the duration of the hunt."

Doubtless he spoke for the benefit of those who might overhear, for he'd not bothered with a concealment glamour. Yet the cold detachment in his words stung. How much of it was an act for the surrounding audience—and how much did it reflect his true feelings? It didn't matter now, only I must summon the proper response. If I *were* from the Court of Roses, would I resent this interference? Most likely. I lifted a shoulder. "I suppose I have no choice in the matter."

"None whatever."

"Then you'd best see that we take the prize."

"I intend nothing less."

A hush fell over the clearing as Queen Astra glided forward and took up position to the left of the passing prism. King Alastor appeared on her right side, stately and magnificent. His voice rang out over the assembly. "The shadow-drakes have long since claimed Wilderfell Forest as their refuge, and it's past time they pay the debt they incurred. Tonight, our courts will collect, will remind them that they enjoy the Wilderfell only by the gracious hospitality of the fae."

He nodded to Queen Astra, and she stepped forward. "May good fortune favor the strongest of you, and may your strength and skill secure the prize. The passing prism will scatter you to different locations within the forest. You are to remain in place until the horn of the hunt sounds, then you shall proceed as you see fit. Each of you must take the hunt oath before you pass."

In an orderly fashion, as though they lined up for a dinner party, fae approached Nikol, swore the hunt oath, then proceeded through the passing prism, vanishing one by one—or occasionally in pairs.

Will you ask Riven why some others have chosen to work in tandem?

Jade bobbed her head. *They are familial pairs. By agreement, the boon will belong to the elder or stronger of the two; the other is simply expected to contribute to the success of their family line.*

I see. No time remained to consider what else I might expect —we'd reached Nikol.

He regarded us with an aloof detachment. "The terms of the hunt are as follows. You may use whatever means you please to remove your opponents from play, but you must leave them alive. If you fall into a snare, you must pay the penalty to escape, and if you use your affinities to gain release instead, you'll forfeit your place in the hunt. You agree not to kill the shadow-drake, but take its blood while it yet lives. And you accept the risk of death by snare, shadow-drake, or any of the other monsters released into the wood. Do you swear?"

"I so swear," Riven said.

With difficulty, I echoed his words, and a silvery-bright binding mark formed on my arm. Then, alongside Riven, Jade, and Risha, I strode into the light of the passing prism, and it swept us away from the clearing and into the Wilderfell. Towering trees surrounded us, ancient and wild, their songs and all the others in this vast wood fierce and unyielding, tamed by no working. Layers of scent threaded through the forest— greening moss and decaying leaves and quickening sap—all deep, earthy, living aromas. Far overhead a dusky canopy stretched, leaves kindled to flame by the last rays of the setting sun.

Beneath the gnarled limbs of the old-growth trees, deep shadows massed, impenetrable and disorienting, yet far less daunting than the trees themselves. This was their domain, and we were intruders in it. A certain hostility edged their melodies, an anger toward those who sought to penetrate their depths without offering any sort of veneration. I braced myself against the trunk of the queenswood that towered overhead, and oh— the potent song that surged across my senses drowned out every other melody, threatening to consume body and soul.

I snatched my hand away. Though the songs of the forest invited me to sink into their depths, it would be far more prudent to rely on Riven's skill for tracking rather than succumbing to their allure—at least until I'd oriented myself further. We waited in uncomfortable silence until a thrilling horn echoed through the forest.

"This way." Riven bore off to the left, down a scarcely visible path. He used no fae-light to illumine our way, but rather appeared to rely on his fae senses to navigate—and I kept as close as I could.

As we moved farther into the forest, night deepened about us, and Riven continued onward at a steady pace. Though I knew fae were scattered all through the Wilderfell, I sensed nothing of their presence. Did they cloak themselves in concealment for the hunt, or did Riven deliberately steer us clear? Given that we endured no assault, I suspected the latter.

He seemed confident in his pursuit, yet some part of me wished it would fail. Wished that some other party would find a shadow-drake first, that I would not have to wrestle between one life and another. My foot caught on a fallen log, and I stumbled, catching myself on Jade's shoulder.

If you face the shadow-drake, you'll have no room for such doubts. For they will not hesitate to strike.

I know.

With each step, my will to remain detached from the forest faded. Its wild melodies seeped into my very veins, and the outer world faded as the essence of every living thing about me surged to the forefront. Against these brilliant strands of color, a spiderweb of shadow stood out stark and black between two towering oaks.

I stumbled to a halt. Riven also stood motionless, watching and wary. I blinked, struggling to order my senses. It wasn't a web, but rather an opening to—where? A choking stench emanated from it, and my stomach tightened.

Riven stepped in front of me just as immense shadowy creatures poured forth from the depths—a dozen and more. Like chain lightning, a brilliant bolt from Riven passed from one monstrous form to another, and they all collapsed in a smoldering heap. He stalked past them, glancing over his shoulder. "Mind your step."

That was all? These creatures were larger and more formidable than the fang-wolves we'd faced in Kilmere, and only now did I realize just how much restraint he'd exercised to fight them, using only strength that mimicked mortals'—in order to spare Withern from Kilmere's wrath. I edged around the enormous corpses until I reached Riven's side. "That was . . . efficient."

He shrugged. "We couldn't afford a delay to deal with them individually, yet efficiency comes with its own price. The light will have revealed our position, if anyone cared to take note."

As ever, he appeared entirely unruffled. How many decades —or centuries—did it take to face an unexpected attack without even an elevation in pulse? I struggled to steady my own as we moved through a dense patch of towering sword fern. A whisper of warning passed its fronds, sending a spider-skitter sensation down my spine. What now?

A low, keening sound of distress echoed in my ears. It didn't belong to the forest; rather, it was . . . human? Could the fae have pressed mortals into service for the hunt, perhaps as a lure for the shadow-drakes? I strained to peer into the depths of the forest, my vision shifting between ordinary and Other perception. Gossamer wisps of fog wafted through the black-and-silver night, and a familiar wild-rose scent drifted on the breeze. My throat closed.

Ainslie.

My pulse thrummed at the base of my jaw. The bargain-holder had warned me I would lose everything; the mysterious fae had further hinted if I didn't act soon, it would be too late. What if I'd already missed my chance? What if Ainslie had been drawn here against her will? She'd have no hope of survival. I darted through thick brush toward the scent of rose. Wait—

Do you smell it?

Yes. Let me go first—if she's here, I'll find her. Jade surged into the lead.

And Riven kept pace at my side. "What is it?"

Jade halted abruptly, the fur at her ruff raised, and I nearly crashed into her. "I'm not certain, but I think . . ."

There.

A woman stumbled along, her movements far too uncertain and unsteady to belong to any fae. Then she lost her balance, or the earth about her became unbalanced, and she vanished into a void, crying out in a voice I'd known since birth. It raked painfully across my senses, and a sudden roar in my ears drowned out all else.

It *was* Ainslie.

I bolted toward her.

"Wait!" Riven leapt after me, caught my arm.

Yet it was too late. My leg snared in a shadow-working, and the earth opened to claim us—just as it had Ainslie moments before.

CHAPTER 59

We plummeted down into the dark. I met rocky earth with enough force to bruise flesh and drive the breath from my lungs. I gasped, struggling to gain sufficient air to form words. "Riven. Ainslie."

Even as I choked her name, the earth beneath us shifted. Pillars of stone shot up, closing in, forcing us to our feet until at last we stood in a narrow shaft, rather like an upright grave, unable to move. If I moved forward just a fraction of a step, I'd collide with Riven. The scents of old earth and wild rose pervaded the air, but the sun-and-storm fragrance that hung rich about Riven pressed them back, holding at bay the terror that snapped at the edges of my awareness.

Because I'd been imprisoned in such tight quarters once before, entombed in rock that Lord West had bidden, and my body remembered. Just as it recalled the shadows dancing across stone, like the ones that drew around us. My breath shallowed as remembered pain ghosted across my limbs.

A pang of fear from above pierced my heart—Jade. She clawed at unyielding earth. *I cannot break through.*

Don't try, it would only violate the terms of the hunt if you did. We're all right.

Only I didn't feel so, no matter how I tried to convince myself of the truth. Lord West was dead. He didn't stand on the other side of the stone, ready to inflict torment, to threaten those I loved. This time, I was with Riven. On some level, that brought comfort, yet I'd already angered him with the incident of the mortal woman, and he must be even more frustrated that I'd led us straight into a trap. Was Ainslie snared somewhere else, or had it all been an illusion? I should have waited, should have made sure, rather than allow my fears for her to prompt unchecked reaction.

My chest tightened further, each breath labored, each lungful of air insufficient. The thick sigiled workings of the snare wavered before my eyes. If Riven hadn't already regretted his decision to offer help, he surely must now. I welcomed the thick darkness about us, for I didn't want to see the censure that must lurk in his gaze, to be reminded yet again that I'd failed.

I became aware Riven was speaking, a low rumble I couldn't distinguish beyond the rush of my pulse.

A brilliant fae-light kindled next to me, its warmth and vibrance caressing my face. Then a concealment glamour wrapped about us, offering a small buffer from the shadow-worked stone.

"I saw Ainslie, heard her. Is she near?"

"She's not here; she never was. I would have sensed her if she were nearby. You witnessed a snare crafted specifically for you."

"What do you mean?" The cold stone dug into my back, and I couldn't stop shivering, couldn't properly order my thoughts.

"I mean that Nikol understands your inclinations, and he designed this just for you. He excels at crafting mimics—it's one of the many reasons he so swiftly ascended to his position." Despite the circumstances, Riven's voice remained calm. "He knew Ainslie would be a plausible victim and that you'd do anything to save her—that her presence would move you from reason to reaction."

My eyes slid shut. Foolish, *foolish*. Was that why he'd also chosen this particular trap to confine us, one meant to remind me of what Lord West had done? Wait—he shouldn't know anything about that.

Riven continued, "It was designed to trigger you specifically, which is why I perceived nothing. Though I'm certain he hoped I'd follow, and he'd take us both. If it's any comfort, many older and far more experienced fae will fall to his snares over the course of the hunt."

"Still, I should have waited, shouldn't have let emotion drive me." I wanted nothing more than to escape, to hide from my endless succession of missteps. "You've made that quite plain."

"So I have." The words held an edge.

Somehow, I'd misspoken again. No matter how I might wish it, I'd not be able to avoid whatever condemnation he meant to offer.

His hand wrapped gently about my wrist, where my pulse beat ragged. "I don't need to perceive your emotions to know you're afraid. Why?"

"We're trapped in a fae snare." I lowered my gaze to his boots. "Isn't that reason enough?"

An uncomfortable silence followed.

At last Riven spoke, his voice low. "Is it the snare you object to or my presence?"

I faltered. "Why would I object to your presence?"

"You tell me," he said softly. "Since last night in the gardens, you've not once looked at me. You've avoided all unnecessary contact. Did I—are you afraid of me?"

"What?" Shock drove back fear. I tilted my head up to meet his gaze—and found not the anger I'd expected, but shadows that hinted at pain. "Why would you think that?"

"Most fae are, for all they seek to conceal it. And I did force your hand. I sought the best path out of the situation, and I thought it would be easier if you didn't have to choose to abandon her. Perhaps I was wrong." He studied my face. "I'm . . . not accustomed to being unable to read emotions and reactions."

It was an advantage he'd voluntarily surrendered for my comfort. My eyes stung. "I was only afraid that I'd destroyed any trust between us. You were so angry."

"I wasn't angry. I was—if you'd taken the woman and child from court, I couldn't have protected you from Lord Revilon. It would have been his right to challenge you, and you could not have hoped to stop him. He would have meted out whatever fate he saw fit. And his version of justice would have been brutal."

My chest tightened. "And it would have endangered everything you worked toward as well. I know you took a great deal of risk—"

He shook his head. "I always leave an out. If you were exposed by Revilon, the Court of Gold would have escaped with its reputation intact. I wouldn't have undertaken this plan unless I had a way to preserve the appearance of my integrity and that of my court, no matter which way things unfolded. But I couldn't have spared you."

"I know. Afterward, I considered all the ways it could have gone wrong. Reason tells me you were right to intervene, but my heart still says it's so dreadfully wrong. In other circumstances, that could have been Ada or Ainslie . . . or me, trapped and suffering, with no one to help. I can't just . . . I don't know how to stop feeling, to see these things and ignore them, knowing I could act."

"Kel's teeth," he muttered. "I know."

"But you wouldn't accept my apology." If I must endure this uncomfortable conversation, I was determined to have the whole unpleasantness exposed. "Why didn't you let me try to mend matters?"

"Fae, as a rule, do not apologize." The light flickered across the sharp planes of his face. "Those I've received have begun as yours did, implying a debt owed. They were unwilling offerings meant to appease."

Because said fae feared what would happen if they did not. Finally, his earlier question began to make more sense.

"I meant what I said before. You owe no debt." He surveyed my features as if he sought to discern what might yet remain hidden. "I intervened as I did because the situation had to be handled swiftly—and in a way that satisfied Nikol."

"Risha told me he watched as I met the mortal woman."

"Not only that. He also monitored to ensure he was satisfied with the resolution."

That meant he'd sent one of his shadows with Riven, and Riven had accepted it to prevent him from exposing the whole. That explained a great deal.

Yet the caution about Riven suggested he struggled to believe the assurance I'd offered. I hesitated. When he'd placed the working he'd said it would conceal my emotions, unless I chose to reveal them. Could I? I drew myself back to the moment when the sigils had traced across my skin, bending my awareness to where they even now pulsed within, willing them to release, ever so slightly—just for this moment, so he would understand my fears were not of him, that I meant what I said.

His pupils dilated, the darkness devouring the brilliant green of his eyes. "Jessa. Do you know what you're doing?"

"Yes. Making sure you understand. You trusted me to keep my word, and I truly believed I was in that moment—but if you'd not come, I might well have broken the spirit of it, if not the technical vow. And I'm sorry. My apology was only ever because I regretted breaking any trust between us. Never because I feared what you would do if I did not try to make peace."

"You haven't broken trust. Not ever." His voice was gentle and a touch ragged at the edges. "Yet if you feel you need forgiveness, you have it."

The effort of altering the working exhausted me, and I released my hold, allowing it to fall back into place. We'd reached an understanding, and for now, that was enough. At my back, the rocks shifted again. A sharp shard pressed into my shoulder, pricking at the place Lord West had driven stone through my body. I flinched.

It took all my effort not to throw myself at Riven to escape.

If I gave way, the stone might only tighten further, crushing us in this tomb . . . I was shivering again.

"What's wrong?"

"Everything about this—it's very like when Lord West tormented me near Kilmere. When he killed Asrina. I know it's not the same, but . . ."

I could not escape the relentless assault of memories, nor the treacherous response of my body. "How did Nikol know?"

Riven traced light down my arm, the warmth of it driving back the cold, questing fear. "I mean to have that answer out of him later. Meanwhile, we will pay the forfeit and gain our release."

"What sort of forfeit will be demanded?"

"Something unpleasant, but not as unpleasant as remaining imprisoned till someone manages to apprehend a shadow-drake." He withdrew the glamour and spoke as if to the air. "What is the forfeit?"

A flowing script appeared on the stone alongside us: *In exchange for freedom, a hidden truth must be spoken.*

"It seems Nikol did intend to snare us both." His expression had become forbidding. "If I'd requested the forfeit earlier, we might have already gained our freedom."

Because of the relatively forthright discussion between us? Would such small truths be enough? Or would something more painful be required? The bruises that scored my side throbbed. Riven never divulged deeper truths, which meant if we wanted release, I'd have to dredge up something painful, something hidden, and expose it, become even more vulnerable than I already felt. I shifted my weight from one foot to the other. "Will Nikol hear?"

"No. The working is self-sustained, though for it to adjudge truth he would have had to pull the Court of Silver arbiter into crafting it."

My shoulders tightened. "Since it's my fault that we've fallen into this snare, I suppose I must speak—"

"No. Not this time."

A sort of crackling tension filled the air between us, stealing my breath. "Riven—"

"Let me do this." The fae-light darkened, black stars dancing in its depths.

And I waited through the cold stillness that followed, waited as pressure built in the air around us, waited for some hint of what might come.

"The mortal family I killed—they were my family. My blood." No emotion tinged his words, yet something in his eyes —a sort of shattered-glass look—cut to my soul.

I couldn't move, couldn't breathe. The thick workings around us uncoiled, and stairs unfurled to the forest above, its rich songs swirling into the space between us. His confession had been sufficient to gain our release, yet his glamour still enclosed us, binding out any intruder. Did he mean to say more?

"My parents wanted to gain another child. After several decades, they wearied of waiting. My mother procured a mortal woman to bear her a child by my father. As some do, they chose to keep this woman as my nursemaid. In such capacity, she served until my father decided her mortal ways had influenced me too greatly. So he killed her."

Pain sharp as a sword pierced my chest. How could such a thing be endured?

"By our law, it was his right, for her infractions." He might as well have recited from said ancient law, for all the emotion that filled his words. "I should have let that end matters, but I . . . missed her. So I went to the mortal world in search of her kin. My kin. I convinced myself it would bring them peace to know she'd died, rather than hoping someday she'd be restored to them."

The cold of the stone seeped through my garments, crept toward my heart. "You were young—"

"Old enough to know better. I knew the nature of my father. Knew the danger I could bring upon my mortal kin." His hands tightened at his sides. "Yet I chose to satisfy my own desires. I never told them of our blood tie, yet still they welcomed me warmly, despite the pain my news brought. They made me like family, and I visited for years."

That explained why he'd a far greater understanding of mortal sentiment and convention than most fae I'd encountered. Everything in me dreaded what must come next—because I already knew this story had a tragic ending.

"When I came to visit one day, I found them dead, their bodies disfigured. My father's sigil marked the doorframe of their house, his message to me. Their passage was not a peaceful one—he'd made sure they suffered greatly. If I'd learned from the death of my mother, they would have passed quiet lives in peace and safety. Instead, I killed them because I did not have the resolve to distance myself."

Bile burned the back of my throat, and I swallowed hard. He hadn't killed them by his own hand, yet he'd spoken it as truth, because to him it *was* true. This must be why he'd been so adamant that I must detach from my own family. My lips trembled. "It wasn't your—"

"Don't say it."

Between one beat of my heart and the next, I glimpsed a hint of the emotion he kept concealed beneath the ruthless mask of a fae lord, a hidden pain that cut unbearably deep. "Riven, if you'll just—"

"It is past." His words were clipped, the mask restored. "And it's time we moved on."

How could he confess all that and then lock it away as if it had no significance? Accept no comfort? I studied his expressionless features, and a sudden certainty overtook me. What so often came across as lack of emotion was, in fact, a surfeit of it, buried deep. Hidden in order that he might survive. What did it cost to exercise such control?

I reached out and rested my hand on his arm, fighting the urge to fully close the distance between us. "It's not so simple. Feelings cannot be excised just because we wish it."

He became impossibly still, and a sort of sparking warmth

filled the air between us, driving back the chill of stone and night.

"Jessa, I . . ." Then he gave a slight shake of his head and moved away from me into the newly opened passage, his shoulders straight as he stalked up the stairs that had formed, all lithe, menacing grace. "This way."

And I followed him into the unknown.

CHAPTER 60

When we emerged from the snare, the pale wash of the moon and the cold, multihued light of the stars struggled to pierce the dense foliage before us. Nevertheless, their ethereal light gave the Wilderfell a distinctly Other appearance, even apart from the potency of life that surged through every leaf and limb. Riven marched into the darkness, scarcely leaving time for me to clasp my arms around Jade's neck and reassure her of my well-being, even as I considered the trust he had extended while we were snared belowground. However he'd closed himself off afterward, he'd offered far more than required to free us. And I would not discount the offering, even if he seemed determined to do so.

I pressed a swift kiss to the top of Jade's head, then hurried after Riven. Risha fluttered to perch on my shoulder. Though her light pulsed warm, it could not drive away the cold sent to the very core of my soul by the calculating cruelty that he had recounted. With the power fae held, they could easily justify acting however they wished, exerting their will over others—and once one began, where did it end? What couldn't be excused? I stumbled over a stone. By taking active part in this hunt, I was becoming party to a similar cruelty—accepting that the only way to achieve my goal was to take the life of another, never mind that my desire was to spare those I loved. Many deeds could be justified in such a way.

My steps slowed. I'd had no peace about my aim to bleed the shadow-drake from the time I'd agreed, but I'd allowed my fear of losing Ainslie, my need to keep the knowledge of my purpose secret, to sway me to this bargain. But it wasn't too late; I could still make a choice—not to abandon Ainslie, but to try to forge another way.

Riven might disapprove, but we'd reached understanding on a great deal already; surely we could work through this also. I hurried to catch up to him, my mind racing with how best to present a convincing argument for the idea that took shape in my mind. How long might I have? "Are we anywhere close?"

"Quite close, I believe. Since I possess none of the shadow arts, I must rely on the very faint and occasional touch of liminal they impart in their incorporeal form—when they are shadow and yet not." He tugged a branch out of the way so I could walk beneath it. "But we have something else to concern us."

My breath hitched. "What now?"

"For some time, a company of fae have trailed us—at first from a great distance. But they took advantage of our time in the snare to close the gap."

"Why?"

"I imagine they seek to ensure the Court of Gold makes no honorable showing in this hunt. It wouldn't surprise me if similar parties sought to thwart the others from my court. They won't want the relic to leave their own court."

"They wouldn't attempt a direct attack . . . would they?"

"Why not? They have numbers on their side, and I'm bound by the rules of the hunt not to kill them, which means forced restraint."

"You're very calm about this." And I . . . was decidedly not. Now that I sought their trace, the trees about me murmured of the presence of nearby fae, seven lords and ladies come to halt our progress.

"It's to be expected, but I want you out of the way when they come."

"I can't leave you to—"

"You will." He halted, light sparking about him, driving back the shadows. "All evidence suggests we're getting close to a shadow-drake, so they must be dealt with now. You've never faced fae in open combat, never received proper training. If you remain, there's too great a chance you'll sustain serious injury, which will force you to forfeit the prize. So you'll find somewhere to shelter and let me deal with them—if not for your own sake, for Ainslie's."

I might have argued further but for those words—and for the fact he was correct, I'd no equipping for direct battle. My glimpse of Nikol and Riven sparring had assured me of that. "Very well."

A wall of shadow approached. "Follow the line of rowan to the crevasse beyond. I'll find you once they're dealt with."

"But—"

"Go."

As I drew the boughs of the rowan to conceal our passing, I couldn't resist the urge to look back over my shoulder. A blinding collision of power seared my eyes, Riven's form towering dark amid the brilliant flare of light. He was powerful, even as fae reckoned it, but there were many of them and—

Jade nudged my back. *And he needs no distraction.*

If I'd bound myself to a court, I might be a help rather than a distraction—yet this brief sojourn within the Otherworld assured me I wanted nothing less. *I wish you could teach me.*

As you have neither fangs nor claws, I'm afraid I can offer little instruction.

We passed beyond the line of rowan to a deep seam in the earth, which offered concealment. With care, I descended the crumbling slope of stone, and when I reached the bottom, I collapsed onto an old stump, its broad surface large enough to hold ten of me. Even at this distance, tremors from the battle shuddered through the old wood. I wrapped my arms about myself. I'd given my word to leave Riven to manage the fae; now I'd make it worth the risk taken. I'd allowed Riven to lead us this far, because his skill and experience made it the logical choice, but he might not disentangle from the other fae in time for us to seek the shadow-drake together. And it might be more willing to listen if I came without him. Many of the low fae I'd encountered did not hold the same values as the high. Some, of course, equaled their cruelty, while others, like the sylphs and basilisks, valued such things as familial bonds and honor. I'd have to hope the shadow-drake was among the latter.

What do you intend?

That we try to search ourselves. Riven can find me anywhere within the Wilderfell, he's demonstrated as much long ago.

She padded to my side, her sweet-grass scent wafting over me. *And you would face one without Riven?*

For what I have in mind, Riven won't be required.

You think of the lore book.

Yes. It said if they give their blood willingly, it won't result in death—that it's the forcible claiming of their power that inflicts harm.

Jessa . . . Her eyes glowed like green lanterns in the dark. *The enmity between shadow-drake and fae runs deep. It may be impossible to even gain an audience.*

I dug my hands into the decaying wood. *Even so, I must try.*

And if your efforts to make peace fail, are you prepared to defend yourself?

If I must. But could I, against a creature of such strength? Jade, at least, had knowledge of battle, if she'd lend it . . . *I won't ask this of you, unless you're willing.*

You know I'll always stand at your side. I've faced such predators before.

As when she'd lost her first bond-mate to a rock drake attack. Perhaps that explained her bristling tension. I stroked the starflower patch on her chest. *Then we are agreed?*

A breath gusted from her. *Yes.*

What now? If I opened myself indiscriminately to the life of the forest, it would overwhelm me. And even if I did, I doubted the plants could distinguish between shadows and the shadow-form of the creature we sought.

A cry of pain shattered the night, and I sprang to my feet, my body tensing. What was happening? Why had I agreed to go—

Because you each must do the task for which you're fitted. You must trust that Riven knows what he's about.

I drew a deep breath. He did, which meant I must focus. How could I find the shadow-drake? The lore book had suggested they'd sought refuge in the Wilderfell Forest in part because it offered a safe nesting ground for their young among the nightsward. I'd encountered it in the king's garden—could I discern its song among the rest?

Uncertainty gripped me. So much could go wrong, but . . . if I could find a nest, surely a parent would lurk somewhere nearby, and if we approached, it was likely they'd reveal themselves, rather than leave their young exposed.

I closed my eyes, tamping down all my fears, and listened. In the distance, toward the edge of the crevasse, the deep, resonant thrum of the nightsward resounded, a determination to protect and shelter edging its melody. Small wonder the shadow-drakes forged their nest from its living limbs. With Jade and Risha at my side, I ascended the far side of the crevasse, where a large nightsward mounded beneath a tree. It crested at the height of my head, where it spilled over into a multitude of vines, its large velvety leaves rustling at my approach.

I ran my fingers across one of its thick, rambling shoots, the image of a shadow-drake nest fixed in my mind as the book had depicted it—and I bent my thoughts toward discovering one such nest.

An eager quiver raced through the nightsward, and images flooded my mind fast and furious, that of a sinuous, stately shadow-drake weaving nightsward and silvan branches into an immense nest and tending her eggs with gentle solicitude, the ceaseless vigil she kept, despite her weariness.

Will you take me?

One of its vines tugged at my legs, then began to race across the ground.

Slower, please.

At a more sedate pace, the vine crept over the rocky edges of the crevasse, waiting as I navigated with difficulty the treacherous path. I stumbled as the rocks shifted beneath my feet, scraping my arm as I caught myself against a particularly jagged stone, and at the last, I surrendered wholly to my Other senses, allowing Jade and the song of the nightsward to navigate me along the unchancy path. Once free of the crevasse, it led us though a dense tangle of brambles, the strands of which withdrew as I passed to make way for me, and then further, through towering stands of trees. For a considerable time, I followed the lead of the questing vine, trusting it to guide me across unfamiliar ground. Jade prowled alongside me, her stalwart presence a protection. More than once, I glimpsed the kindled eyes of some creature in the shadowed forest, but each time, a growl from her quelled their advance. Still, how long before we stumbled across something yearning for a battle, something that wouldn't be deterred by a warning? I rested my hand on the ruff of her neck, taking solace in her presence. Even so, the farther we moved from anything recognizable and the denser the forest became around us, the more I questioned my decision.

Riven had said we drew near to the shadow-drake, but perhaps he'd been mistaken. Or perhaps I'd miscommunicated my purpose to the nightsward, and it simply drew me to the heart of the Wilderfell. Nevertheless, I followed it deeper into the forest until it reached a clearing made by a fallen queenswood. The gap her immense form left in the canopy allowed moonlight to spill silver-bright over the fern and nightsward that blanketed the forest floor. Once more, the vine tugged at my ankle, and I moved to the far side of the hollow, still unable to perceive any sign of a shadow-drake—

Oh.

My vision shifted to another vantage, which revealed a living nest of nightsward and shadow cradled in the branches of an enormous silvan tree. Within its depths rested three dark eggs, each one the size of my body. No shadow-drake coiled about it, but if what I'd witnessed was truth, she stood guard somewhere near.

Jade paced restively in the clearing. *If you mean to go through with this, the safest place to negotiate with the creature is from within the nest. There she will not attack indiscriminately, for fear of injuring her own offspring.*

Before I could second-guess my choice, I rested my hand on the nearest silvan tree, and its branches swept down to lift me high. My mouth went dry as they deposited me into the nest.

For a hiss sounded from above. Shadows wafted about me, cold and chill, and the hollow plunged into abject darkness, all light of moon and star blotted out. I lifted my gaze, straining to perceive what lurked within these shades.

There.

Impossibly inky shadows streamed from enormous wings as the beast soared down from the treetops, its eyes glowing like brilliant blue stars.

I'd found the shadow-drake—or rather, it had found me.

CHAPTER 61

Star-blue flares danced down its neck like flame, and a stream of shadow spouted toward me. I drew the nightsward about me like a shield, and somehow, it held the shadows at bay. "Wait. I've only come to talk."

"Fae are ever treacherous. Why should I believe you?" The shadow-drake vanished, yet her sibilant words echoed above my head.

"Because I've not come to hurt you but—"

"All within this court have heard tell of the hunt. If you don't attack outright, it's only because you seek to lay a hidden snare." She hissed, the sound seeming to come from beneath every shadowed branch at once. "Oh, yes, I've heard the truth. You must not kill me yourself, only bind me and divest me of my blood. My power. Then leave me for others to torment."

"That's not my purpose."

"So you say as you hide among my young."

"I wish them no harm either." I shifted, and the nest crackled beneath me. "Give me your word that you'll listen to what I have to say, and I'll meet you in the hollow below."

Shadows whispered in the silence, carrying the bitter scent of venom and malice. "I'll grant your request. Though I warn you—you'll come to regret it."

I pressed my hand to the smooth silvan bark, and once more, the sweeping boughs wrapped about me, depositing me on the ground. Every nerve pricked with awareness as I awaited the appearance of the shadow-drake, the song of the nightsward bristling about me.

And from the shadows pooled beneath a craggy oak, her sinuous form emerged, lithe and majestic. If I were properly fae, I'd gather all the power I could summon to greet her, an implicit threat to force her to listen. Perhaps she expected it; certainly, the lines of her body held a tense wariness. In my mind, she hadn't been anywhere near so imposing, and my resolve faltered. No, I would see this through, as I'd planned. I strode to meet her, and then . . . I knelt before her, divesting myself of whatever small advantage I might possess.

And she stiffened, her hood flaring. "Why do you bow?"

"Because I want you to know I truly mean no harm."

"You are a fool if you expect me to believe any such claim. You may not belong to this court, but you're ready enough to partake in their ancient wrongs." A tower of shadow rose behind her. "And you will not leave this clearing alive. I will claim your life and that of any other fae who seeks the blood of my kind—or give my own trying."

Her shadows snaked forward, writhing cold against my skin, tightening like shackles about my legs. Jade quivered, prepared to strike, and I fought down a sudden throb of green-gold life pulsing beneath my breastbone, the quickening urge to mount a defense. Threats and humility could not exist together, and I'd chosen my path before I came. I met her eyes. "You gave your word to listen."

"And I shall honor it—after the manner of your kind."

"Then you'll join your wrongs to theirs and commit murder for your convenience?"

Her tail lashed, bowling over several saplings. "It's not

murder if you stand and defend yourself. Or are you too weak to do so?"

"Do you believe strength is found in inflicting one's will on others? Or the power one can summon in battle? Because I think otherwise." My voice dropped low. "I saw the tenderness with which you crafted your nest, how you kept watch over it, how you're willing to risk your life in its defense, even now. And I think you know that however much the fae claim it to be a weakness, there's a far greater strength found in love."

Her sides heaved—anger? Consideration? Then her great head lowered toward mine, its hood flared wide.

Jade tensed.

Wait.

Her fangs flashed white, but she stilled, glowering at the shadow-drake. *She's too close. I won't be able to reach her if she strikes, not in time.*

I know. Please, Jade.

The scents of musk and ancient ember washed over me as she sniffed my head. Then she rocked back, her shadows releasing me. "You are fae, it is unmistakable. Yet you talk like shadow-kin. I will hear your explanation of this and more. Why have you come?"

On unsteady legs, I pressed upright. *If anyone else approaches, I need to know.* Because I meant to expose a great deal. Even if I'd fully mastered a concealment glamour, any exercise of affinity in her presence might undo whatever progress we'd made.

I'll keep watch.

With Jade steady at my side, I spilled the story to the shadow-drake, her fanged maw only a handbreadth from my face, her form towering above me as she absorbed my quiet words. When I fell silent, she did not fill the void with commentary of her own, only stood still, her gaze fixed on her nest. And something flickered in the depths of her star-bright eyes. She exhaled a silver cloud, her head lowering once more toward mine —and Jade leapt toward the clearing's edge, her lips baring into a snarl.

Someone has stepped through a passing, very near. Her scent . . . It's Lady Maeve.

The shadow-drake stiffened. And every plant about the clearing—from the smallest spindled moss to the tallest silvan tree—bristled to attention, their songs surging defiant through my mind, the world washing away as their essences rose to the surface, a glorious riot of color and sound. At my side, the shadow-drake flickered—but she did not vanish.

Why didn't she flee, adopt her incorporeal form?

I sank deeper into my Other senses. Every shadow, as far as I could perceive, was now limned with silver, bound to Lady Maeve. They no longer offered shelter.

The shadow-drake's immense chest swelled as she prepared her defense. Jade moved into position at my other side; Risha tucked herself within the trunk of the fallen queenswood.

And Lady Maeve materialized in the clearing. "Most impressive work for one without shadow arts. You are to be congratulated, Lady Jessa. But the night belongs to our court. I suggest you remove yourself and concede defeat." Then her brow furrowed. "But not before telling me—what kind of mesmerism have you worked on the creature to keep her bound to you with no working?"

"That's no concern of yours." Why was she wasting time in conversation? Why didn't she launch her attack? Should I? *Will I give her some advantage if I strike first?*

Almost certainly, since you don't have the element of surprise. The longer this plays out, the better. Riven may yet come.

Maeve sauntered forward, stopping a wary distance from the trees that bounded the edge of the clearing. Though her plant affinity must far outstrip mine, she made no attempt to wrest them from my control. "You do not wish to disclose your secrets, naturally. Yet I could put such an affinity to use. It seems you have more to offer than I thought."

My shoulders tightened. Vines of green-gold swirled about my feet, and I sank deeper into the connection with every living thing about me, their desires mingling with mine in a way that was becoming familiar. "If you wish to negotiate in the future, then you'll leave the shadow-drake to me now."

Lady Maeve laughed. "You might be a useful ally, but the relic shall certainly be—and it will cost me nothing. Step aside or pay the price."

"No. She belongs to me." As if the words sealed some sort of bond between us, a fierce protectiveness surged within me. I couldn't hope to keep her from Lady Maeve, not truly, but I could perhaps give her a chance to escape.

"Suit yourself." If possible, the darkness about her deepened, a growing pressure that betrayed her intent to strike. "Perhaps I shall claim another prize—that of the young she conceals."

In an instant, the shadow-drake sprang for her nest. Beneath Maeve's control, the darkness shattered into a thousand pieces, each hurling forth like a spear. Swift as thought, a tremendous explosion of nightsward and silvan trees sprang to meet the shards as I bid, surrounding the shadow-drake and her young with an impenetrable barrier. Yet how long would it hold?

Maeve's shadow-workings tangled with the vivid green and gold of my own, and I felt their assault in the core of my being, as if they raked sharp talons along my flesh.

Jade vanished. *Keep her distracted.*

Keep her distracted? I was hard-pressed simply to survive; I sank beneath the weight of her workings and my own. The bladelike notes of the nightsward sliced the air, meeting the bright fury of the silvan trees and the more distant barbed cry of hawthorn brambles . . . Their vigor far outstripped my own, rioting in my veins with almost unbearable force.

Then something collided with my back, a jumbled impression of an immense spider-shadow passing from Jade's mind to my own. The working sank fangs deep into the base of my back, stilling my limbs with paralyzing pain. Instinctively, I pulled the essence of the nightsward into my frame till pale green sigils danced beneath my skin—and it pressed the pain to the blackening edges of my awareness.

But my workings about the shadow-drake and her nest

faltered. Even so, Maeve did not seek to wrest control of the plants, but rather stabbed sharp blades of shadow through them. A brilliant blue flame licked out from behind the hedge, driving back the infiltrating shadows, giving me just enough time to draw the edges of the weave together again as the world spun about me, everything blurring into a jumble of confusion. Something venomous licked out from the shadow-fangs, and a bitter taste flooded my mouth. I twined lush jasmine vines about the spider-form on my back, seeking to dislodge the monstrous working, but in vain. Venom burned up my spine, the flicker of blue flame and shadow and green-gold danced beneath the trees, and I fought to keep hold of reality.

Where was Jade?

There.

Swifter than my eye could fully trace, she sprang on Lady Maeve, hunger for her blood pulsing through our connection, her fangs sinking deep into Lady Maeve's side. She staggered to the side, then stabbed two swords of shadow into Jade in rapid succession, driving her back.

And I stumbled as if she'd pierced my own flesh. I couldn't lose Jade.

Yet I couldn't so much as move her direction, my own limbs faltering, the immense weight of power charging through the clearing binding me in place. I was failing, just as the bargain-holder had assured me I would, my hold on the workings faltering beneath the pain that pulsed from my core to every limb. I couldn't sense Jade anymore, nor Risha, nor anything besides the flames coursing within and the silver-bright flare of the trees and the metallic taste flooding my mouth. Above it all, the sudden brilliant charge of a summer tempest broke over my exposed senses.

Riven.

Everything came to a crashing halt as he strode through the trees. "Come now, Maeve." He spoke in a relaxed drawl more suited to a ballroom than a battleground. "Give it up."

The shadow-fangs sank deeper into my back, and hot spirals

of pain cascaded downward. All I had to do was hold the workings around the shadow-drake, around her nest, around Jade—and Riven would manage Maeve. Already, she withdrew some of her workings from the assault, gathering them around her as she faced Riven, her features wary and watchful.

"I'm not the one who must withdraw." An unseen wind stirred the brush about her. "I hold Lady Jessa in a working that will sever her spine before you can touch me. She has a great deal of raw power, but very little experience, it seems. I wonder very much that she was sent on such an errand as this—but perhaps that explains why you were given watch. Doubtless your king does not want to give an account to the Court of Roses for permanent damage done to his guest."

"Nor will he." His eyes burned bright gold. "Are you so certain of your position?"

"Of course, my workings are without flaw."

"It is as you say." His gaze swept over me. "But there are things you do not know."

Jade's voice broke into my awareness, tinged with pain. *Riven says, if you are willing, draw on his power.*

What?

As you did in Kilmere.

I recalled the sense of reaching for him, the connection between us that had altered my perception of the workings beyond us and guided my purpose in Kilmere, opened the well of his knowledge and power to me. Then we'd made physical contact, but here in the Otherworld, he was unshielded by any mortal glamour and his presence burned like the sun when I opened toward it, filling all the space about me. As soon as I opened my soul to his, a vast ocean of power swept over me, along with understanding of every thread of the shadow-spider Lady Maeve had bound to my body.

Much as silver had infiltrated the shadows of the clearing, golden light now illuminated every line of my body, and I drove shards of light into the heart of her working, unraveling its weave. The shadow-spider vanished into motes of black, and instantly, a brilliant working wrapped around Lady Maeve, pulling her through what appeared to be a mirror of light that opened at her feet.

Then Riven severed the connection between the two of us, and I stumbled. His hands closed about my arms, tugging me to my feet. Though the spider working had vanished, some deep, weakening pain lingered, and I could not force my legs to hold me. And yet . . . "Jade."

Coming. She limped into the clearing, and my heart wrenched.

You're hurt.

No more than you.

A fist seemed to tighten about my heart. *But I brought you into this. If I hadn't—*

It will be well.

I looked up at Riven. "Lady Maeve? Will she return?"

"She'll find herself back at Silvwind, bound tightly enough that it will take her the rest of the night to free herself."

His hold on my arms tightened. "The working is gone, but its venom remains. We need to get it out." Bright embers of light raced across my skin, vanishing beneath the surface, burning away the traces of her working.

I pressed my lips together to restrain a cry—the remedy was nearly as painful as the affliction.

"Like half the gathering before we left for the hunt, she heard me communicate my commission from the king to keep you safe. She must have been surprised to find you alone, but no doubt she expected me to show up at some point, so she took precautions in the workings she used. If I'd forced her through the passing while her working remained attached to you, it would have crushed you as she intended. Same if I'd forced it to release from the outside. It needed to come from you. She must have waited, taking your measure until she was confident you could not free yourself before she deployed the working. She was careful—just not careful enough. But then she could never have accounted for such a variable."

The light continued to drive the venom from my veins, and my legs steadied. "Will she realize what I . . . what we did?"

"If she considers it, she'll soon persuade herself it could not be. It is . . . not done. She'd never believe that you'd allow anyone the chance to claim your affinities, let alone the arbiter of another court." He released his hold. "It's far more likely she'll think I gave you a ward that activated at my presence. After all, why wouldn't I want you to suffer a bit first—to bring home the debt owed?"

The twist to his words assured me he only echoed fae sentiment. And I straightened. "Well, I cannot help but be thankful that her precautions were insufficient. And that you came when you did."

"While we're on the subject of precautions—I sent you away for your safety." His words held more than a hint of growl. "Not so you could throw yourself at the feet of a shadow-drake."

"I thought you sent me away so our mission would succeed," I said softly. I wasn't above using his own words against him, if needed.

His gaze held mine. "Both can be true."

I scrambled for some other defense. "How did you know what I meant to do?"

"Jade took it upon herself to keep me apprised, when you found the shadow-drake." Riven nodded toward her as she lowered herself into the bracken at my feet. "Fortunately for you, she's a great deal concerned with your safety."

She chuffed, but the sound was strained. *It is a job more suited for a whole cohort of* kit-isne.

Yet none would compare to you. I knelt next to her, stroking her fur. "In any case, I've failed. Jade told me I might, but I hoped otherwise."

Riven arched a brow. "Are you sure?"

Beyond him, inside the working of nightsward and green-gold sigils that somehow still held, the shadow-drake inspected her nest. With effort, I untangled the weaving, watching her as she examined each egg, her silvery breath drifting about them.

Then she turned to regard me, a challenge in her eyes. "You said I was yours."

"I didn't mean you were mine in the sense that I thought I had some right to you, only that . . ." What had I meant? "I wanted to keep you safe, if I could."

"Yours to protect—that is not a charge fae ordinarily accept." Her hood flared as she examined Riven. "But this seems a night for exceptions. Because this one, he protects you."

"I—yes." Though I didn't fully understand his reasons, he'd intervened on my behalf time and again.

"You interest me." She dropped down from the silvan tree, the ground quivering slightly beneath her. "Yet I would learn what happens if I decline your request."

"If you do, then Lord Riven and I depart. And the hunt continues, but we—we no longer participate." I swallowed hard. She still didn't believe, still sought for some way I meant to deceive and betray. And how could I blame her, with all that had passed between fae and shadow-drakes in the past?

Her ember-tinged breath wafted about us. "I wish to know one thing more: what account those in your power give of you. You will allow them a private audience with me."

"Only if you swear their safety—and truly swear this time."

She exhaled. "I swear upon the name of Alathor, the first of the great shadow-drakes, I shall not harm the child of the sun or the *kit-isne*."

I turned to Jade, pain still evident in the lines of her body, and Risha, who'd crept from beneath the fallen tree. "Are you willing?"

"Yes, yes." Risha's light flared bright.

Always.

I didn't deserve their friendship, but I was grateful beyond words for it. The shadow-drake swathed them all in a thick fog, and I fought the urge to pace the clearing, tangling my fingers in a thick pocket of nightsward.

Riven turned to me. "To be perfectly clear, my comment

that you lacked experience in open conflict with fae did not mean you should seek one to challenge."

"That wasn't my plan."

"No." His eyes shadowed. "But you did intend to throw yourself on the mercy of a creature who hates fae."

"That's true. I was never at peace with the terms of the bargain, but . . . after what we discussed in the snare, I just couldn't carry it through in the way we'd planned. I thought we'd have time to form a new plan, and then . . ."

"The Court of Silver party waylaid us."

"Yes."

Whatever he might have said, the shadow-drake interrupted as she appeared once more with Jade and Risha. "I have decided to grant your request. And I have healed your *kit-isne* as well."

How?

By spitting on my wound. It is not a method I would choose, but I must admit it worked.

So their blood injured, and their saliva healed? Did the fae know about this? If not, I wasn't about to announce it.

"You may have my blood." Her hood lowered. "But it will not be given to the fae lord. You must take it, must know its cost, must use it with honor, as your companions vow you will."

"Thank you."

Riven shook his head.

And star-blue flared along her neck once more. "You thank me?"

"Yes, because it is deserved for your sacrifice."

Her muzzle brushed my forehead. "I will remember."

Which meant I might owe a debt, but—it was only right. I plucked the dagger from the belt about my waist, my hand closing around its cold hilt. She was willing, yet something in me still shrank from the task, from the notion of driving the blade deep through thick hide into flesh.

"You still hesitate?" Her gaze traveled toward Riven. "You have a job before you."

He muttered something that sounded very like agreement.

Then she regarded me. "If you don't mean for another to die tonight, you must take the offering."

I tightened my grip, then with strength I'd not realized I possessed—courtesy of my fae blood?—I drove the blade into her leg.

A shudder passed over her immense frame, but she remained silent. Riven handed me a small empty vial, doubtless drawn from the ever-useful fae pocket. Thick bluish blood dropped slowly into the bottle, where it cast a faint glow reminiscent of her flame. I restored the jeweled stopper.

"Do you have another bottle?" she said.

Riven stepped forward. "Yes."

"Then you are to collect more. And keep this one."

"But—"

"You have conceded you owe me."

With the force of her eye upon me, I could scarcely disclaim it. "Yes."

"Then do as I ask."

I held the second bottle beneath the steady drip of blood, and when it filled, I tucked both vials in my pocket, then dared to rest my hand on her neck. "It seems wrong to leave you injured."

"This sort of injury won't trouble me long." She licked the wound, and it stopped dripping. "I'll heal best among my kind."

Riven inclined his head toward her. "We will remove from this place before I summon the queen's hunter, so your nest will remain unmolested. With your permission, I'll also put a concealment glamour on it to ensure it remains safe."

"It is well." With that, she dissipated into shadow.

CHAPTER 62

After he removed us from the clearing through a passing, Riven sent a sigiled flare of light far above the canopy of trees. And I sank onto a low-hanging branch, Jade resting her immense head on my feet, where I could stroke the patch between her ears. "Now what?"

"We wait for Nikol."

I leaned against the bole of the tree, and it cradled my weary body. We'd come so far—and it should have felt like a victory, but in reality this was only another step taken toward something darker and more dangerous.

A vine rustled across the forest floor, as though it sought me of its own accord . . . and when it crept into the circle cast by Riven's fae-light, I recoiled. I'd recognize those purple-black leaves anywhere; they'd haunted my thoughts often enough. Nightspire sought me once again, though the song reverberating from this one was altogether different than the plant I'd encountered before. It bore no workings, and its serpentine coils rose rampant, wafting in the air about me, not blood-hungry, but questing, curious, and so very strong.

I hesitated. Riven had once said that by nature nightspire

was designed for assault, but could the situation be more nuanced? What if that was the purpose to which fae bent its strength, rather than its natural intent? I reached forward and stroked its leaves, taking care to avoid the sharp thorns. It bristled with wary attention, ready to claim its territory, yes, but not indiscriminately. Its murmur suggested it sensed my affinity and had come to investigate, yet it had not attempted to strike. Which meant what?

Perhaps that its relentless nature was its own, but the twisted malice of the one sent to me before belonged to another. This one lacked the silver threading which had marked the workings of the bargain-holder, and also the sense of hunger for blood and destruction. If its strength could be bent to attack, couldn't it also be bent to protect?

At the end of the vine clustered dusky-purple seedpods, and I suggested to the nightspire if it would release them into my keeping, it would find a new place to flourish. The nightspire offered no resistance as I gently tugged them loose. Perhaps sometime I'd find out what its nature was *meant* to be.

For now, I'd much left to face.

Success with the shadow-drake meant only the privilege of facing the canny, powerful fae who held Ainslie's binding. With her, there'd be no appealing to mercy, not when she'd made it clear she wanted to see me suffer loss. My brief skirmish with Maeve assured me that in unrestrained combat, where no rules limited the exercise of affinities, I'd meet my end swiftly. Which left what? Not emotion or power, but some attempt to reason and negotiate, which would work far better if I'd any notion of what she desired. And before that, I must appear before Queen Astra . . .

I looked up to find Riven watching me closely. "Are you still in pain?"

"Not pain exactly . . . I just feel as weary as if I've scaled a mountain. Or perhaps, more accurately, like one descended to crush me."

"That's to be expected. The natural healing ability fae possess, along with what we can draw from our affinities, means we can take a great deal of damage. But still, the unaccustomed power you expended and the effort you exerted to heal will have taken their toll. Don't let on, if you can avoid it."

Because any sign of weakness would make me a greater target. I sighed softly as I tucked the nightspire seeds deep into my pocket, then brought up something that had nagged me since the confrontation with Maeve. "Why didn't Lady Maeve try to take control of the plants in the clearing? It would have left me defenseless."

"She'd no way of knowing that. If she had, doubtless she would have taken the time. But you might have possessed a number of other affinities, and I have observed your connection with plants is . . . unusually strong. If you already held them before her arrival, using another affinity to attack was wiser than wasting time trying to break your hold."

I couldn't deny the sense of her strategy, as her shadow-working had nearly done permanent damage. If Riven hadn't come when he did, the outcome would have been far less favorable. "Will you appear before Queen Astra with me?"

"It's unlikely that she'll welcome my presence."

"But—"

In a flare of silver, Nikol materialized. He sauntered toward us. "Did you succeed?"

In answer, I drew out the vial of poison blood, its faint blue glow belying its true nature.

He gave a soft laugh. "That will cause considerable upset."

"With your queen?" I closed my hand around the bottle. "Will she be angry that it wasn't one of your court to claim the boon?"

"She'd prefer one of ours emerge triumphant. As would I. But given the way the hunt has unfolded so far—this is preferable to the alternative of forgoing the blood prize altogether."

"What do you mean?"

"That the shadow-drakes have shown unexpected resolve.

Two were captured before you snared yours, but both took their own lives before their blood could be claimed. It seems that they covenanted together to embrace death rather than have their power taken by force." His silvery eyes caught the moonlight. "Which makes me quite curious as to your success."

Riven arched a brow. "And yet, you've no need for that knowledge."

"Granted." A small smile played about Nikol's lips. "Yet this is where your part ends and mine begins. Whatever your role in the capture, you know you'll not be welcome before the queen. Unless you've changed your mind and mean the prize to go to your credit?"

"Even if I desired it, I had no part in the capture of the shadow-drake, so I could make no claim."

"The plot thickens." Shadows danced about Nikol as he surveyed me. "And you still insist on depriving me of this tale?"

"I expect you'll survive," Riven said dryly. Then without further inflection, he added, "However, I cannot speak to your odds if Jessa doesn't emerge from the queen's chambers unharmed."

Why would he suggest any concern? Though I supposed Nikol already knew he'd a vested interest in the outcome of these negotiations . . .

"One would think you mistrusted my queen."

"An accurate assessment."

"Then know this—she has interest in Jessa also. She'll not burn any bridges."

Riven inclined his head slightly.

So that's what he'd been after—a confirmation of the queen's intent as it concerned me, most likely how her interests might threaten those of his king. Before the conversation could devolve further, I pressed to my feet. "Then perhaps we should delay no longer?"

"Agreed." Nikol lifted the passing prism, varied shades of silver spilling across the bracken before us. "If you'll come along, Lady Jessa?"

Though reluctant, I accepted his arm. Risha perched on my shoulder, and I rested one hand on Jade's head, then a tide of shadowy power brought us into an antechamber adorned with dazzling illusions and equally dazzling realities. No one could mistake it for anything but the queen's quarters, for though she occupied King Alastor's demesne, the pervasive scents of winter-blooming jasmine and ancient stone dominated the space, along with the uniquely overwhelming sense of Other I'd only experienced in the presence of the monarchs, as if some part of the Otherworld itself was distilled within their bodies.

We swept toward double doors at the end, but I slowed halfway. "Will she expect me in a more presentable state?" I wore hunt attire, a fitted bodice and the trousers that had so intrigued Ainslie—and both were worse for wear.

"Those sorts of pretensions are for mortal courts." Nikol gestured for me to move forward. "We have our own, and your current appearance suits them well."

Under other circumstances, I'd say that was a politic way of stating I looked dreadful, but Nikol would want to satisfy his queen, so I'd accept it as truth. Shoulders tight, I followed him into Queen Astra's temporary audience chamber. Though I braced myself, my knees still threatened to buckle when I entered the room, and Jade's ears flattened.

"I hear the Court of Roses carries the day. An intriguing outcome." Her voice was low and resonant, threaded with the detachment of the starry heavens. "Yet not an altogether disappointing one."

What was I meant to say to that? Lack of experience made discretion a better choice than speech—after all, even fools could be believed wise, if they kept silent.

Her ebony eyes swept my frame. "You have something for me, I believe."

I offered a small nod. "If I may approach?"

"You may."

Determination steeling my spine and driving back fatigue, I

glided over to her. With a small bow, as I'd observed the other fae adopt, I presented the vial of blood.

A spiral of shadow etched the outside as her silver-hued nails closed about it. "Well done."

The words of approval did *not* warm; in fact, they held a calculating edge that left me unsettled.

"And now, I offer the promised boon." She flicked her fingers, and a servant approached with a small sealed casket, no bigger than a man's fist.

What did it hold? I could scarcely open it to examine its contents—that would suggest a lack of trust in the queen's integrity. Still, what power did this relic possess? And what might my bargain-holder do with it? I gave a small nod. "I am pleased to accept."

"And will your court share your pleasure?" she asked.

"I cannot say. I speak only for myself."

"A suitably cautious answer." Her fingers curled around the vial of poison. "You have lately accepted the hospitality of the Court of Gold—has your decision been made?"

What decision? With effort, I stopped myself from fidgeting beneath the weight of her gaze. "I've made no final decisions."

Not about any of the multitude of things that oppressed me.

Her lips curved upward. "Then perhaps a visit to our court will interest you also."

One didn't decline a monarch's invitation, at least not outright. I kept my face as expressionless as I could manage. "Perhaps so."

She stood, her gown falling in graceful lines about her powerful form. "King Alastor awaits, so I shall summon you later to make arrangements. Nikol will see you out."

I murmured my assent, and Nikol escorted me into the antechamber. Evidently, Queen Astra had made a swift departure, for any sense of her presence faded, leaving only her lingering scent.

"That went well," he said.

"You don't have to sound so surprised." And then I stumbled

over the edge of the rug—perhaps I'd spoken too soon. So much for not revealing my exhaustion.

Unexpectedly, Nikol reached out to steady me, a thick glamour wrapping about us. "One should be even more wary of an apparently satisfied monarch than an openly wrathful one. Keep that in mind."

"That's not comforting."

"It's not meant to be." Almost imperceptibly, his features tightened.

And I halted. "Nikol, you're quite certain this hasn't caused trouble—"

He held up a finger. "That's not how any of this works. Because if I tell you yes, then you owe me something. Is that what you want?"

"No." I released a shuddering breath. "I just want to be able to express concern like an ordinary person without it being twisted into some dreadful thing."

"Well, you can't—not if you want to survive." His veneer of careless humor vanished, exposing a sharp-edged anger. "For all our power, fae don't have liberty to live as we choose. We, all of us, are bound in some way to whoever is stronger, whoever has waited and watched for some opportunity to seize an advantage over us—and we seek to do the same in our turn."

There was a certain bitter twist to his words that suggested he chafed beneath whatever bound him. Yet I doubted very much if he'd make any confidences about it. I clutched the casket to my chest. "That's not exactly a glowing endorsement for joining a court."

"Make your alliances well, and you'll be shielded from the worst fates." The shadows about him sharpened. "But perhaps you know that, since you've worked to keep Riven close. How much has that cost you?"

"It's not like that." I shouldn't have said it; I knew as much the moment the words left my lips. He'd slipped under my guard by exposing a hint of his own pain.

"Then what is it like?"

"I suggest you ask Riven, if you want to know." Then I moved past him, ducking through the doorway to yet another antechamber, this one leading to the central corridor beyond. And he let me go.

But before I could escape the queen's chamber, another concealment glamour wrapped about me—and the fae I'd bargained with appeared, cloaked and veiled as before. How had she found her way into the queen's private chambers, which were warded against intruders—unless she had far more power than I'd known or the two had some understanding between them? Or she . . . *was* the queen. No, that made no sense, because if she was the queen, she'd not need the relic she'd already had in her own possession . . . I'd been too long in the Otherworld, and my exhausted mind was now conjuring peculiar explanations, each one more complicated and confusing than the last. With difficulty, I straightened. "I have what you requested."

"I know." The silvery threads on her cloak brightened. "Now we shall fulfill our bargain. I've made arrangements for you to meet the fae you seek at the east gate of the Beternys Labyrinth in a quarter hour. She'll hear you out, though I think you'll find very little satisfaction in your interview."

"And if I bring a companion?"

"Bring whom you please. It will make no difference."

The casket chilled my fingers as I handed it over to her. "Then why are you doing this?"

"To suit my own ends. But I will offer a word of advice at no cost—losses are inevitable. Sometimes you must retreat and accept what cannot be recovered, then later seek out your opportunity for vengeance."

Somehow her statement hurt all the more for the dispassionate tone it was delivered in. My hands tightened. "And have you taken your own advice?"

"I have, in fact." Her voice was thoughtful. "And it's beginning to pay off quite well."

"Yet what does vengeance accomplish?" My stomach twisted. "It cannot bring back those lost, cannot heal grief."

"You must rid yourself of such weaknesses as love and sorrow. And if you will not accept this counsel, you must endure the consequences. In reminding you that you're not obliged to appear at this meeting, that you yet have opportunity to retreat, I have given what aid I can. The choice is yours." The air about her stirred, then she slipped through a side door and vanished into the depths of the demesne.

Jade peered after her. *She troubles me.*

She troubles me also. I cannot think why she'd take the time to offer counsel as she did, unless she wishes to control the outcome for her own gain. Yet what could she gain if I don't face the bargain-holder? I rubbed my temples. *Of course, it could all be a deception.*

I shook myself. I'd no time to consider it further—we'd only a quarter hour to reach the labyrinth, and I had no intention of facing this fae without Riven, still less of taking the counsel given. I hurried in the direction of my bedchamber, but Riven intersected my path as soon as I entered the central corridor beyond the queen's chambers.

He muttered a curse. "She already approached you."

"Yes. We're to meet the bargain-holder in a quarter of an hour outside Beternys Labyrinth."

"Beternys Labyrinth?" His eyes narrowed.

"You know it?"

"It's part of Talis's demesne. There are rumors about it, but no one's been inside for centuries, not since—certain events in our past."

My mouth went dry. I didn't want to consider her having some hand in this. "Do you think she's the one we seek? If so, she'd have had to conceal her movements even from her own court. Revilon said she doesn't leave her demesne."

"Either she's involved on some level or it's an elaborate misdirect. Both are equally likely."

My thoughts spun in spirals. "If it *is* Talis, do we have any leverage?"

"No—from all I know of her, she has no interest in life

beyond her gardens, which are enclosed by the labyrinth." His voice was grim, and it left me altogether unsettled.

It was one thing to ignore the mystery woman's warning, but if Riven was concerned . . . What if the bargain-holder wouldn't relinquish her claims?

Cold to the core, I buried my hands in Jade's fur as her words drifted back to me: *I will see your loss become complete.*

The labyrinth towered before us, twisted trees that stretched taller than the Cloister spires of Avons, every limb permeated with power. Fae workings had lent yew and blackthorn strength and stature far beyond that accorded to their ordinary forms. By the light of the moon, they bristled with hostility, casting sharp shadows on the grassy expanse upon which we stood. Talis had forged immense gnarled trunks and woven thorn-tangled branches into an impenetrable hedge, one branded with sigils of silver and deep purple.

Their form and essence echoed the power I'd first encountered in the nightspire, and a dusky-purple scent arose from the tangle, tinged with something bitter that hollowed my stomach. We'd come to the right place. Before us, the gate—a shadow-form etched in the center of a single enormous yew bole—swung open.

And Talis emerged.

A burnt, metallic taste coated my tongue, as mingled pain and fury burned through every line of my body. Was she the cause of all this suffering? Or was her presence just another feint and the power shrouding the labyrinth a glamour meant to deceive? My chest tightened as if nightspire bound it, yet I forced myself to choke out the question, "Are you the one who used pyske-dust to draw mortals into your snares?"

"Yes. I am." She crossed the distance between us, her gown rustling softly, her features serene. "I hold your sister in my hands and many others besides. What do you mean to do about it?"

My stomach churned, and the bitter taste intensified. Though we'd only conversed twice, she'd engaged my sympathies by revealing hints of her own pain, exploiting my desire to believe I wasn't wholly out of place among the fae. I'd thought perhaps we shared some common ground, even wished to know her better, and all along she'd held Ainslie captive. How could I have missed this? My whole body shook.

And Riven interposed himself between us. "As you have confessed to the use of pyske-dust, the matter is simple. You will appear before your king to face his justice."

Thick bindings of light wrapped around her legs, halting her advance, and she mounted no defense. But her lips tilted upward slightly. "Before you act, Lord Arbiter, you will listen. Hurt me, and you will hurt all those bound to me. Kill me, and the mortals won't be freed. Rather, those tainted by pyske-dust will all die at once—and those bound in bargain will find their bargains passed to those I've chosen to inherit them. If I go before the king and pay the price, they will as well. They are bound to me, pain for pain, death for death. You are not obliged to King Alastor as you would be to your own monarch, so you need not report my breach if you choose otherwise. You're under no oath to him. Of course, if you have no purpose for the mortals in question, then by all means—take me. But you cannot end this game without my consent."

Blight and rot.

The sharp rustle of wind in the blackthorn mocked my helplessness. And my chest tightened. She knew what the mortals meant to me, knew we'd come to gain their freedom—and she wielded her knowledge as a weapon to cut away any advantage we might try to claim.

Yet Riven didn't appear surprised; perhaps he'd expected something of the sort. He dissolved the coils of light binding Talis. "You wanted this audience. This part of the game. Why?"

"That's between me and Lady Jessa." Freed from her bonds, she continued her advance, halting less than an arm's length from me. "As it happens, Lady Jessa, you remind me a great deal of myself when I was young. Your affinities are only beginning to bud, of course, but there's so much potential."

So not every sentiment she'd expressed had been false—somehow she truly believed we had a likeness. My heart thudded against the metal lacing my bodice. "So you decided to torment me?"

"All the torments you endure you inflict upon yourself." She drew a silvery nail down my cheek, a sort of clawed caress that left my skin crawling. "You could walk away at any time."

"So you say. Give me one reason to believe you."

She regarded me with features of ageless beauty, yet something merciless peered from behind them, an unnerving hint that this mattered in ways I failed to understand. None of it made sense. The woman I'd encountered before, the one I'd believed to be the bargain-holder, had watched and waited and stalked us . . . Why now would Talis say I could walk away? What was the connection between the two? I couldn't continue to navigate this situation blindly; I needed to understand. "You say you hold these bargains. If so, then who did I see in my bedchamber? It was her power I felt before, in the mortal world, but now . . ."

Now it rolled from the labyrinth beyond Talis, yet all I could read in her was the same vast distance I'd sensed in our first encounter.

"Your lack of knowledge of our world truly must be remedied." Something shifted in the air about her, and a glamour I'd not perceived before released. Her true essence flowed into the air about us—the bitter dusk fragrance of the labyrinth was her own, and it mingled with the distant void of starlight and the malicious hunger of the nightspire. How had I missed it?

It wasn't a glamour, Riven says.

If not a glamour, then how had she kept her power so deeply veiled?

Her silver nails flashed in the moonlight. "The power is mine, but I may lend it to my constructions as I see fit. Perhaps the Lord Arbiter would have recognized my craft had he encountered it, though the last recorded liminal figment was long before his time. You were stalked by what could have been—what would have been, if my daughter had not died."

I staggered back. Riven's source had said the woman was dead, and it seemed he was correct. All along I'd sensed Talis's power emanating through a construct of her dead daughter. Bile burned the back of my throat. She'd used the figment to chase me to herself in the library, to torment me while she held herself at a distance, watching through the eyes of the one she'd lost. The one she'd loved yet could not mourn. *You cannot show anyone how you feel, oh no.* That's what the figment had said.

And Talis, she'd said the charade must be carried on, ever and always. So she'd spoken as she'd conducted one before my eyes—and I'd remained blind to it. Small wonder she'd been so confident in her victory, confident I'd not find the liminal figment—because apart from her, it didn't exist.

At my side, Jade bristled. *Riven asks you to step with care. He says she's right, liminal figments haven't been seen in centuries—and with good reason. They require a great fracturing of the mind. Not many have the capacity to split off some portion of themselves, tie it to the liminal realm, and still remain functional. And he says it requires drawing the power from somewhere . . . something that's stuck between.*

My mind raced through our previous interactions. In the form of her daughter, she'd spoken of loss, devastation, and bereavement. In her own, far more rational form, she'd appeared as unfeeling and detached as the rest of the fae. Yet even then, she'd spoken of loss. This then was the crux of the matter, her daughter who had died—the form she'd chosen to wield as a weapon, the woman the king had decreed was to be nameless and forgotten. Why? What had happened? If I'd any hope of taking ground, I needed to understand, needed to prod her to speech. "Would your daughter have wished to be remembered in such fashion? A construct wearing her face and wielding your power?"

"Does it matter? She had liberty to choose, and she chose destruction. Now I shall recall her as I wish. For the memory is all that remains." The silver hair that trailed down her back shimmered with moonlight, and her features remained cold—as if the mention of her daughter meant nothing.

Yet the words the liminal figment had spoken, those tinged with madness and great sorrow, those were Talis's words, and in some fashion must reflect another self, one she kept concealed beneath the impassive fae mask.

"Now you also have the opportunity to decide your path. I offer you a choice."

"What sort of choice?" My throat tightened around the words. Her liminal figment had wanted to watch me lose everything; she wasn't interested in some impersonal, distant triumph.

Her moon-bright eyes latched on to me. "You believe you can save those you love, if only you risk enough—that you can be spared loss. Well, I intend to offer you the opportunity to prove it. If you successfully pass through my labyrinth, I will answer all your questions about the nature of the bargain and the source of the pyske-dust, even why your sister was chosen—but there's one condition. You must successfully traverse the labyrinth, and you must do it alone, without your collection of companions. I think you'll find there are no loopholes in the bargain I've constructed, but you're welcome to try to find them, should you succeed in reaching the other side."

"Why should I accept such an unfavorable bargain?" I didn't know what the labyrinth held, but it was clear she believed it impossible that I would emerge. I twined my hands in Jade's fur. "If I pass through the labyrinth, I want the mortals freed—all of them."

"And yet my terms remain. Do you imagine another option

exists? My death will not free those you care about, nor am I interested in any inducement you might offer. They are what I want, what I require."

I remained rooted in place, the blood rushing in my ears. She understood me to a disconcerting degree. How long had she watched; how much did she perceive? Certainly enough to offer this outrageous bargain with confidence I wouldn't turn away from any chance to gain their liberty, however small.

"This, then, is your choice." The detachment she'd presented was eroding, a hint of hunger creeping into her gaze. "It's the only one that remains. Which loss will you accept? Will you cast aside your life along with theirs? Or will you embrace the truth that there's no sparing them?"

The bitterness in the air stung my skin, burned in my throat. If I agreed, if I made it through, if I entered the demesne proper, perhaps I could discern a path to free them.

If . . . if . . . if . . .

What now? The moment I stepped through that gate, I'd be wholly in her power—but if I chose to turn her down, I'd leave Ainslie and all the other mortals in her clutches forever. My stomach roiled. Could there be another way? Something I'd missed. If only I could talk to Riven.

As though he intuited my thoughts, he stepped forward. "You may consider this an affair between you and Jessa alone, but I have a vested interest in this situation. She and I have an agreement concerning my aid in finding you and the mortals you've enthralled that predates any bargain you may now make. Not to mention my duty to my king."

She tilted her head. "Then I very much hope you don't mind losing whatever bargain-price you've exacted. I don't expect you'll see her again, once I'm through."

He arched a brow. "Then you'll grant I have a right to discuss the matter before she enters any agreement with you?"

"Certainly." She waved a hand. "Take all the time you like."

How could she appear so poised and in control yet also be the one whose power and emotion fueled the raw, slightly mad liminal figment of her deceased daughter? Which was truer? Or had they both become equally real? And why did she bother to offer me this choice? What did she stand to gain? She must seek some additional advantage, or she'd never have allowed things to unfold this far.

Riven strode away from the labyrinth until we sheltered beneath an age-knotted cypress. His glamour rolled over us like a thunderclap, blotting away the outside world. "You're not going into the labyrinth."

I choked down the immediate retort that rose to my lips, forcing a calm I did not feel. "Can you see another choice? It's either abandon Ainslie to Talis—to say nothing of all the others —or try to make it through."

"And if you do, then what? She guaranteed you nothing, except the exact terms of her bargains—and she will have left nothing to chance." He raked a hand through his hair. "Talis isn't like Damir. She's been watching. She knows *you*. Whatever she has in mind for you to face, it will hit where you're vulnerable. There's a reason she wants this, and you'd be a fool to deliver yourself into her hands."

"Then tell me there's another way, and I'll gladly take it."

"Sometimes the only choice is to walk away. Accept there's no path to victory."

"You suggest that I accept Ainslie's death?" I whispered.

The light cast by the glamour sharpened his unyielding features. "If Ainslie were standing here now, would she send you to die—or accept her own fate?"

Of course Ainslie would try to dissuade me. She was convinced that she deserved whatever came, never mind that she'd been coerced into a bargain that she'd no chance of resisting. Yet in Talis's grasp, her death was more certain than my own. She'd resolved not to fulfill the terms of her bargain. How much longer could she skirt the edges of her oath before Talis visited her wrath? With Ibbie, I'd failed, but now I knew so much more—and I still had a chance of saving Ainslie, of avoiding the unbearable grief of love lost.

The starflowers beneath my feet blurred into a mass of white, their mournful songs filling my ears. Some part of me wanted to ask Riven if he would have made the decision he demanded of me, if he'd been presented any chance to preserve his mortal family. Yet I'd not use something revealed in trust as a weapon to leverage my argument. If he knew of no other alternative, aside from allowing Talis her way, then the path forward was clear. I lifted my chin. "What Ainslie would say doesn't matter. I'm going into the labyrinth."

"Are you?" Sharp shards of light cut the air between us, and gold flared in his eyes—did he consider taking the choice from me?

"Unless you mean to stop me by force." He'd not hesitated to do so in the matter of the mortal woman in the gardens, but this . . . Beneath our feet, the carpet of starflowers dimmed.

In a single glittering flare, the light shards about Riven vanished. And he said quietly, "The choice is yours."

The cypress boughs overhead seemed to exhale with relief, and I could breathe again. "Then I would like your help, to learn what I might face. But I understand if you want no part in it, given I cannot accept your counsel. If you want to walk away—"

"I'm not going anywhere. If you intend to do this, you're right, you'll need some idea of what's to come. But you also need to ensure it's in some way worth the risk." Whatever he felt about my decision, he'd become once more the fae lord—decisive, emotionless, and focused on the facts at hand. "She won't agree to release the captives, but there's an alternative concession you can demand. Tell her that if you make it through the labyrinth, she must allow you the right of outrance afterward, the stakes being freedom for the mortals. I don't think she'll be able to resist. It would be a matter of pride and intrigue both."

"The right of outrance?"

"It's one of the oldest forms of fae challenge—it's not a match of strengths and affinities, but rather a game that can take any form the challenged one dictates, usually some sort of puzzle of wits. The Court of Dusk at one time relied on it exclusively to arbitrate difficulties, and I think it will appeal to her. As you're the challenger, she'll have the liberty to set the terms, but then she's already dictating them. Further insist that I arbitrate all your dealings to ascertain the challenge is conducted by the rules, in those exact words. She wishes to isolate you, and this will assure that if—when—you make it through the labyrinth, she'll have to grant me access to the demesne. She'll still be able to set the terms, but it gives you a better chance of freeing her captives than relying on some loophole in her bargain."

A small ember of hope flared. It was something, more than I'd had before—yet she still must agree. And I had to make it through the labyrinth first. "And what of the labyrinth itself?"

"Physical threats will exist along with those of a more ephemeral nature. You cannot hesitate to protect yourself." He tapped the dagger at my waist. "I'd offer you a sword, but given your lack of training, it's more likely to be a liability. Still, you need to be prepared to use a physical weapon—whatever plants that exist within the labyrinth will be bound tightly to Talis."

"I know what's at stake." Not just for me, but for those she held captive. "I'll do what I must."

"Even if the being in question wears the face of someone you love?" His words pierced deep.

Could I drive a dagger into a being that appeared to be Ainslie? Or Ada? I shivered as a worse thought took root. "What if it *is* someone I love? What if Talis has already brought Ainslie here or . . . snared someone else, and I can't tell the difference? The liminal figment, she said I'd lose them all—"

"Don't let Talis get into your head. It's what she wants. Your fears will make you more vulnerable. She's holding immense liminal power in the fabric of the labyrinth. I've never seen anything quite like it."

"What does that mean?"

"You had the tiniest taste of liminal suggestion when Damir planted constructs to fuel your nightmare. But this—the way she's crafted the labyrinth, you might as well be walking the liminal realm itself. There's a reason fae just pass through, that a certain level of experience with liminal power must be gained before you try to form a passing. The liminal realm shows realities and half-realities and realities that may be, sometimes those that were and are no longer. If you accept a possibility it presents as real, it will become real—or rather, as able to do damage to you as if it were."

"I . . . I don't understand."

"Say you perceive a shadow-drake within the labyrinth. It's not there, but it could be." The glamour about us deepened. "Your belief that it does exist will bring a real and dangerous being into the liminal space of the labyrinth, one that wasn't actually present before."

I rubbed my hands along my chilled arms. "So you're saying she'll have real dangers placed throughout the labyrinth, and if I ignore them, they could kill me, while others I must ignore lest they become real and also kill me."

"That's the gist of it." His jaw tightened. "It will present prospects and possibilities, exploit your fears, and seize on that within you that's in a liminal state."

The cold seeped deeper. "Then how will I know what is true?"

"Do your best to anchor yourself to something you know is real—if nothing else, the love you have for your family."

"I thought you believed that a weakness."

"It *is* a weakness, a vulnerability which Talis exploits even as we speak." The pressure in the air increased, throbbing in my chest. "But it's also something true—it's a part of you that nothing else has shaken. So hold to it."

And if it wasn't enough . . . if I failed in this . . . I couldn't trust myself to voice the question, so I simply nodded.

"One thing more." His voice dropped low. "If you're willing, I want a bargain."

"Why?"

"The liminal realm and the multitude of prospects it presents can easily overwhelm, acting as a sort of paralytic. So I want your word you'll not give up—you will fight until you come out on the other side. Swear it by bargain, and it might give you an edge."

If I surrendered to emotion now, I'd never regain my composure. So I strove for a light tone. "And what do you offer in return for my vow?"

His gaze lingered on my face, his eyes becoming impossibly dark. "Whatever you want."

The air left my lungs, and all rational thought fled as the scent of sun-drenched forest drove back the bitter dark of the labyrinth. I drew an unsteady breath. "Riven, I . . ." My pulse thrummed, drowning out the songs of the starflowers. Yet somehow, I spoke. "That hardly seems a fair exchange."

"I don't possess friends in such abundance to easily discount the loss," he said softly, echoing my words from what felt a lifetime ago.

And for the first time I wrenched myself from the morass of my own fear to consider—impossible as it might seem—that he could have fears of his own. For all that he appeared the detached fae lord, I knew it wasn't true—he'd lost a great deal, most likely more than he'd confessed. If he were the one entering the labyrinth, I'd . . . not have nearly the equilibrium he'd displayed. "Then I accept."

A brilliant binding mark wove about my arm, its warmth dispelling the cold of fear. He stepped back, increasing the distance between us. "Talis waits."

And so did Jade. In silence, she perched at the edge of the glamour that stood between us and Talis, motionless as a statue. "I just need one moment." I hurried to Jade and knelt before her, looking up into her eyes. *You've said nothing. It's unlike you.*

Because it's not right that you should go without me. Kit-isne *do not separate from their bond-mates.*

Yet Talis will not grant me any sort of boon, certainly not a companion to help me along the way.

A deep rumble shuddered from her. *I know.*

What then?

I would sacrifice any other life before yours.

I felt as though an immense tangle of roots tightened about my chest. She wanted me to abandon this course. If those closest to me were adamant that I should turn back . . . What if I was making a mistake? The starflowers shuddered about me.

Her breath swept warm across my face. *But you must go.*

You don't want me to.

No, but—I know you. If you turned back now, if you didn't try, it would kill your soul. Perhaps in time your body. Just . . . come back to me.

I flung my arms around her neck, clinging to her tightly, her ragged breathing matching mine.

Then Riven spoke. "If you are still resolved, it should be delayed no longer."

I scrambled to my feet, blinking away the mist that obscured my sight. "I'm ready."

Talis stood unmoving before the shadow-gate, her form blending with that of the labyrinth. "Well, Lord Arbiter, did you succeed in dissuading your charge?"

"I did not." He shrugged. "It seems your assessment was correct."

"How disappointing for you." A fierce jubilance rustled through the yew and blackthorn beyond her, betraying perhaps more than she intended. She *hungered* for me to enter this labyrinth; it mattered to her beyond all sense and reason.

Why? If I understood that, I might have the key to unlock everything. But my sudden certainty that she desperately wanted this gave me confidence to present Riven's request. She might not be willing to offer the mortals' freedom, but she needed me to enter the labyrinth, needed me to accept her bargain—she wouldn't decline this. "However, Lord Riven offered other counsel that I have accepted—a condition on which the whole hinges. If I make it through the labyrinth, you'll grant me the right of outrance."

"Outrance." Her lips curved, and the ashen-eyed form flickered into existence behind her. "The Lord Arbiter has a great deal of faith in you, if he believes you'll live long enough to offer such a challenge."

I fixed my gaze on the liminal figment—and she dissolved from sight. A chill scurried down my back. "As protection for his investment in the situation, he has insisted that he arbitrate all our dealings to ascertain the challenge is conducted by the rules."

"I would expect no less. You appeal to a very old tradition, and I shall accept. Survive the labyrinth, and I will answer your questions and accept outrance for the lives of your mortals. Winner take all." She nodded slowly. "Yes, it is the perfect conclusion to this affair, should it be needed. I thank you, Lord Arbiter, for the suggestion. And I invite you to wait within my demesne for the outcome. I give my word that my demesne shall behave—I've no more desire for a war between courts than you. It might prove destructive to my gardens." She shifted to examine Jade. "The *kit-isne* may come also. When her mistress dies, I will have use for her."

Jade bristled. *If my mistress dies, I will spend my life to claim yours.*

"That would be a great folly. Perhaps you will use this time to reconsider." She turned to Riven. "Lord Arbiter?"

He gave an expressionless nod. "I accept the invitation."

"Then we proceed." A cold smile unfurled across her face. She waved a hand, and the shadow-gate opened, its appearance like the fanged maw of some great beast.

I pressed my hand to Jade's head. Then I stepped through the gap.

CHAPTER 64

The gate closed behind me, and I stood in the immense trunk of the yew, caught between the labyrinth before me and those I cared about behind. The foliage wove tight above the maze, a living boundary that blotted out stars and moon and any scrap of light from the outside world. It wasn't the dead darkness I'd experienced entombed beneath the earth, but rather a living, rustling, velvet-dusky darkness, filled with the threatening voices of hostile plants. Nothing else existed except for this deep purple-black void. Even my connection with Jade had been severed the moment I stepped through the gate.

Then a fae-light, not of my conjuring, sprang into existence at my shoulder, its silvery hue marking it as belonging to Talis. Perhaps she wished me to see what I must endure.

It cast a cold, glaring light over the dark plants that hemmed me in. Could I reach them? Though I sought a connection, they rejected my claim, a vine-like tendril lashing with stinging force into the gateway, drawing blood across the back of my hand. It clamored for more—more pain, more blood, more suffering.

And I shrank back. This way was closed to me, as Riven had suggested. Talis held the plants in such thrall that I couldn't hope to reach them. But I wouldn't make any progress if I remained in the gateway; I must venture into the labyrinth.

Alone.

The word seemed to take on a life of its own, a wrenching, breath-snatching thing. Wrapping my fingers about the cold hilt of the dagger, I strode into the labyrinth proper—and a vast, ancient sorrow crashed over me, so strong that it forced me to my knees.

Someone reached for me, and a gentle hand lifted my chin. I looked up and beheld . . . Ibbie. The silvery fae-light caught in the strands of white woven into her cinnamon-brown hair, and she regarded me with such tenderness that every fiber of my being yearned for her to be real.

She stroked my face. "My dearest Jessa."

"Ibbie." I breathed out the word.

"Did you know that, at the end, I would have given anything to see you one more time?" Her features became gaunt. "Instead, there was only *him*. Only fear. Only death."

Even as she spoke, her face altered, the life and vitality draining away until only a desiccated husk remained, frozen in a rictus of torment. The world about me darkened, the fae-light dimming, the haunting melodies of the hedge pressing in.

With difficulty, I blocked their songs. Yet I couldn't avert my gaze from the broken form before me. It wasn't real, and yet . . . this was how she'd died, tormented and afraid. And I hadn't stopped it, hadn't been there for her.

Cold and aching and desolate, grief stole into my bones. If I embraced my fae nature, this would be my reality. One by one, I'd watch those I loved die, whether to some brutal end or simply the ravages of time, while I would endure . . . alone. No, I couldn't think about it, not now.

I tore my attention from the corpse and forced my numbing limbs into motion. The path behind me fell into darkness; the narrow way before me flickered with eerie shadow. And two paces ahead, the liminal figment materialized.

"You failed her, you know." Her lips twisted into a smile.

"Just as you will fail the rest. It's the inevitable end. Loss and sorrow."

"And what of love?"

Her ashen eyes paled. "It fails too. It makes you vulnerable. If you do not love, you cannot lose. Will you protect yourself? It's not too late."

"My course is set." But my pulse thrummed at the base of my jaw. Could she help in some way? Talis had given me little to work with, but this part of her was unpredictable, given to madness. Perhaps she could help me understand; perhaps by understanding I could find a way through. "Will you tell me why I'm here?"

"You haven't guessed?" An off-key laugh escaped her. "I suppose not. And *she* wouldn't say, wouldn't like to show any weakness."

"Talis, you mean?"

"Yes."

"But you are . . . part of her."

"Not here, oh no." Her hands pressed to the sides of her head. "Out there, I do as she bids. Within the demesne, she doesn't like to admit it . . . but she's beginning to lose control. Here I am her, but also myself."

"Then you can choose. Will you tell me?"

"She didn't come for me when I sought the Court of Ascent. Didn't try to change my mind." The words erupted from the figment, edged with bitterness. "She knew what the king would do, knew his edicts, but she didn't try to save me. And I died. It was the right choice to heed the king, the right choice, oh yes, so she's told herself over and again. She couldn't have spared me even if she tried, I chose my course, she would have only died too, so she says in her own mind, as she puts on a smile and pretends I meant . . . nothing."

"What does that have to do with me?" Despite my efforts, my voice shook.

"You have to take the test and you have to fail, because if you don't, it means she was wrong. Wrong, wrong, all along."

Her eerie singsong voice echoed down the rustling passage. "It means if she'd gone soon enough, risked enough, perhaps I would be alive. And we'd work and play within the gardens as we ever did. She never believed the view fae hold of family, not truly. I loved her, and she loved me. But she didn't even *try*."

I was shaking, and I couldn't steady myself. What pain had Talis endured to drive her to this?

"You, though. You try and try, but it will all be the same in the end." Her ashen eyes locked on mine. "Because you'll be dead too. Maybe before you lose them all, maybe after. But you will fail. You will taste pain again and again, and I will watch until you have nothing left. Until you are nothing. Then she will be proven right."

She vanished. And I felt as though the blackthorn boughs unfurled within, their thorns slashing as they went, leaving me raw and exposed. This was madness, beginning to end. Fae couldn't show grief, nor guilt, nor any emotion that might suggest weakness, therefore Talis had buried hers so deeply that it had taken on a life of its own. Even her love she'd felt compelled to keep hidden, and when she could find no way to conceal it and act—she'd left her daughter to her fate.

Perhaps Talis had been right that no matter what she'd done she couldn't have saved her daughter. I knew nothing about the circumstances, but in her own soul, she must doubt it—else she'd never have tied all this to me, as if my failure to save those I loved would bring her peace. How many centuries had this tormented her, while she pretended to feel no sorrow?

The bitter purple scent coated my lungs, tightened my chest. This labyrinth was hers, a construct born of loss and suffering, a maze impossible to emerge from alone.

As she'd left me.

As she felt herself?

Perhaps, but I could dwell on it no longer—even now, my limbs stiffened, as if the sorrows sought to bind me in place. If I didn't start moving, perhaps they would. So I ventured farther into the maze, trying to keep a proper count of each turn I took.

And the air about me chilled. Thick cobwebs gathered along the edges of the labyrinth and stretched like gossamer ropes above my head.

A dry, creaking laugh echoed about me. Then a hook-clawed foot appeared around the corner ahead, followed by a spindle-jointed leg. Not real. It wasn't real. Uros was dead, the rest of the auvok permanently imprisoned. Yet if I looked on it much longer, it might become so. Though it took all the will I could summon, I closed my eyes, and I walked past, my skin tingling, as I braced for a venomous strike.

But none came.

I passed through a dense patch of bitter cold, then it ebbed, and I dared open my eyes. Another sharp corner twisted the labyrinth back on itself, yet no other way opened—either I must retreat or see what it held in store. I advanced into an unexpectedly open expanse. In its center, a fountain rushed. Dark stones took shape beneath my feet, and stars danced beneath the foliage above.

Mother stood alongside the fountain, quiet and watchful. She didn't pace or show any sign of restlessness, only held herself as if waiting—for what? A fae-light flared at her side. No, that wasn't right, she'd forsaken her fae nature. Hadn't she?

It wasn't Mother, of course . . . yet Riven had said sometimes the liminal realm gave glimpses at what once was but was now no longer. Could this be one such? Could I learn something of her fate, if only I watched?

Despite myself, I crept closer.

A cloaked form approached her, so nebulous I couldn't perceive its nature, its features swathed beyond recognition. Yet Mother appeared to know it, for she went very pale.

I strained to better perceive the figure, which suddenly wheeled to face me. Red eyes burned in a monstrous face. And it sprang upon me, its hands closing about my throat, clawed fingers impossibly strong.

My fingers brushed the hilt of my dagger, but before I could strike, the creature flung me against the fountain. I crashed into the stone with bruising force.

It snarled. Then it bounded across the gap.

This time I was ready, the dagger clenched in my fist. When its hands tightened about me, I stabbed the dagger deep into its side.

It didn't flinch.

Its grip about my throat tightened.

And I threw all my strength behind the dagger, driving it into the creature's chest. With a sickening twist, it pierced muscle and sinew. My hand trembled—I didn't want to kill, didn't want to become *this*.

The figure collapsed alongside me. And Mother's eyes looked at me from its face. "I died because of you."

Then vines spiraled about her body, dragging it away. It wasn't Mother, hadn't ever been Mother, but I'd killed something, and its blood was hot and silvery across my hands. It slicked the blade of my dagger, its stench choking me. What if she'd spoken truth?

As the prospect took root, the dagger slipped from my grasp. *Had* I caused her death, in some way beyond my knowledge or ability to recall? A fog obscured my vision, then closed in about me, thick as a mourning shroud, holding image after image of Mother.

In them, I lost myself.

Yet something burned bright on my arm, almost painful in its intensity, a vivid golden light that drove back the shroud about me. I drew a shuddering breath. What was past I could not change, but I'd sworn to fight for the future, for those I loved. Riven had said I must anchor myself in something true. And what could be truer than that? Of those things that would remain for eternity, the greatest was love. Never mind what the fae said, the ties of family and friendship lent strength—and the binding mark on my arm, one forged by compassion, proved it.

After retrieving the dagger, I pressed to my feet and swished my hands along with the blade in the fountain, the bright spirals of blood washing away in the dark water, then forced myself back onto the path. I forged on until I reached an immense open circle. From it, paths spiked out at even intervals. Which should I choose?

The sound of weeping filtered into my ears, and something warm and wet splashed on my cheek, the top of my head, my bare arms.

Tears?

No . . .

They were crimson, not clear—drops of blood.

Despite myself, I looked up. And then froze. Above each path, the blackthorn boughs had impaled bodies; they hung twisted and broken. I pressed my lips together to choke down a cry, forcing myself to stop, to consider. Unlike the other apparitions I'd encountered within the labyrinth, these mortal figures might well be the ones stolen, the ones I sought. Riven had said Talis required fuel for her labyrinth. Was this her purpose for the mortals she'd snared? Did they power her workings?

The weeping strengthened, drawing my gaze to the farthest point, where a woman struggled. Though the thorns pierced her body like the others, she yet lived. And she raised a trembling hand toward me. "Please, help."

Blight and rot.

Was she real, stolen from our world as a source of the power Talis required? Or a construct meant to deceive? In this case, both held an equal chance of being true—and it was impossible to discern the difference. How could I risk leaving a living soul to such torments? No, if I must err, let it be on the side of sparing lives. Resolve hardening, I darted across the expanse and halted beneath her imprisoned form. The fae-light glistened over tearstained features that I recognized from her portrait—Lady Chevon.

Though she was impaled above my head, she wasn't so high that I couldn't climb the hedge to free her. If I was quick enough, could I outpace the workings? It was a vain hope; nevertheless, my hands closed about the branches, seeking purchase between the thorns. I ascended one ell, then two, before the barbed fury of the blackthorn assaulted me. A branch lashed out, closing about my arm. Its thorns pierced unbearably deep, binding me in place.

No, no.

I just had to go a little farther, and I'd reach her. I strained my fingers, and my left hand brushed hers.

"Don't leave me here, please don't leave me."

The thorns dug deeper, the pain so sharp that the leaves before me blurred and blacked at the edges. Still, I flung my senses wide, seeking any opening in their songs, any means of connection by which I might break the hold Talis exerted.

Instead, their grief and rage poured into me. New branches sprang from the hedge, their barbs slashing at my core, thorns seeking purchase. If I didn't free myself, I would die. Where was their essence? Another bough of blackthorn lashed out, ripping the edge of my bodice, and faint blue light spilled from the exposed pocket.

The poison.

Would it work? With my free hand, I wrenched the top from the bottle, then I flung the liquid into the mass that tangled below me. And when the poison spilled upon the blackthorn-and-yew prison, the branches writhed, shriveling, their hold failing.

I plummeted down to the labyrinth floor, the breath driven from my lungs, my body broken and bruised. I couldn't move my pierced right arm, and my ribs throbbed unbearably, every ragged breath an agony.

Above me, the bodies still dangled, their torment my own. Lady Chevon writhed in place. "Please, please . . . make it stop."

Withering frost, I couldn't save her, nor any of the others that might be imprisoned here. Couldn't summon the strength to climb again, couldn't thwart the malevolent trees, no matter what I wished. My stomach twisted, and bile rose, choking, in my throat.

And still, their blood wept . . . mourning, always mourning, always suffering. Rivulets of crimson swept about me; a copper-bright stench permeated the darkness.

The mind that had crafted this prison of torment held Ainslie. What if she'd been taken already? What if her body adorned one of the labyrinth walls even now? No, no. I couldn't think it, couldn't add fuel to the vast web of possibility woven through this labyrinth of death.

The triumphant blood-sated notes of the blackthorn rang in my ears. I needed to *move*, needed to seek some path forward, but my body refused to pay heed, crushed beneath the oppressive grief bound within every line of the maze. I tasted it on my lips, all salt and metal and purple bitterness. This was no cold, distant sorrow; it was the raw, brilliant fire of grief searing through every limb, of love severed before its time, of things lost that could never be restored—

No, that wasn't right.

Nothing was beyond restoration. Even death wasn't the final word. The gold light of my binding pulsed bright, and I dug my hands into the soil beneath me, sodden with blood and tears—mine?—then pressed upright.

Jessa. Can you hear me?

Yes. My heart leapt. Had Jade found some way to reach through the workings cutting off the labyrinth from the world beyond? The sound of her voice drove back some measure of pain, cleared my thoughts. With my left hand pressed to my ribs, I struggled to my feet. *Where are you?*

I'm coming to you. Riven found a way. He pointed out a weakness in Talis's wording, and she'd no choice but to let me in. Jade emerged from the passage across from me, the starflower patch on her chest a beacon of hope amid the blood-choked darkness.

Her sweet-grass scent pressed back my despair, and—wait, *think*. I wanted so badly for this to be true, but was it? If Jade had reached me, she represented my best hope of surviving the labyrinth, and I hers—we couldn't afford to be separated by my fears. But if she had not . . .

I played Talis's words again through my mind, seeking some

fault or weakness that Riven could have exploited, and came up with nothing. Yet this Jade knew my thoughts. If she were somehow a creature of the liminal realm, how could she perceive them? I limped one step toward her, then stumbled to a halt. *Did* she perceive my thoughts? Or did she merely expound upon her original point, providing information she imagined I'd request? The burning grief subsided, along with the bright ember of hope, leaving me cold and empty. *Jade, wait. Don't come any closer, not yet.*

She shook a drop of blood from her head. *Together we stand a better chance.*

If you're Jade, then stop and wait for me to come to you.

She padded steadily onward through the purple-black gloom. *You're hurt. You can lean on me.*

Please, no. My uninjured hand curled about the hilt of the dagger. Whatever I faced, whatever had come for me, it wasn't Jade. But it *was* real, for I'd accepted her, believed she'd come to me, believed she could find a way—and now she stalked toward me, the perfect predator, prepared to destroy.

I edged back, the scents of blood and pain deepening about me once more. The leaves overhead rustled, mocking my weakness. "I know you're not Jade. It's time you went back to whatever realm you came from."

My voice shook.

And Not-Jade stalked closer. *I swore a vow to protect you, and I mean to keep it.*

Whatever she said, she meant to attack, I could read it in every line of her body. The strength that had protected me could now easily destroy. I'd access to none of my affinity within the maze, unless I risked the nightspire—which was sure to stir the fury of blackthorn and yew. But what choice did I have? Even hale and whole, I'd little hope of success against Jade without my affinities. So I snatched the dagger with my left hand and forced my right to collect one of the nightspire seedpods, though it sent blackening pain through my body.

And she sprang.

CHAPTER 65

I released the seeds, and they fell into the soil beneath me, green-gold sigils flaring about them. And the nightspire surged upward, an impenetrable wall that bristled with resolve to protect, to assault any who tried to penetrate its defenses. In response, the fury of the labyrinth roared in my ears, the notes of the blackthorn and yew an attack that sent me staggering.

Ancient roots surged to the surface, upsetting the earth beneath my feet, swarming around the nightspire—which fought valiantly to stave them off. Though it refused to surrender, it would soon be overtaken. And Not-Jade stalked the edge of the boundary, waiting for the moment the nightspire failed.

The moment I failed.

The nightspire vines faltered, and I snatched up another seedpod, scattering them. *You were made for this.*

But perhaps I was not.

A virulent yew root rent a gap in the tangle of nightspire. And the gap revealed Jade's face. Her green eyes glowed bright, yet held a world of sorrow. *I'm sorry. I have no choice.*

What? My hold on the nightspire faltered, and Not-Jade

hurled herself forward with a power that broke the weakened vines. Her body tangled with mine; her claws scored my side. With one last desperate surge, I tangled the nightspire vines around her frame, pouring all my remaining strength into them.

Thorns shot out like swords, pierced her in a dozen places, bound her in place. The light ebbed from her eyes, and her body went limp. My own eyes blinded with tears, my side slicked with fresh blood, I struggled from beneath her dying, thorn-torn frame. *It's not Jade. Not Jade.*

But she *looked* like Jade, perfect in every line and whisker. How could it be, if she was not?

Jessa. Her eyes met mine, and her voice whispered through my mind, soft and gentle. *You made the right choice. If it was my life or yours—I'd always choose yours.*

Then the glow left her eyes.

The songs of the yew and blackthorn were drowned by the furious rush of blood in my ears, by a grief that threatened to rend my chest. What had I done? No, it wasn't Jade, it couldn't be Jade. But why would Not-Jade say such a thing? Unless I'd been horribly, horribly wrong. What if this *was* Jade? What if somehow Talis forced her into this? Or somehow bound the lives of Jade and Not-Jade together?

I bent over her broken body. Surely I'd know. Surely some sign of the truth must remain, something to assuage this terrible fear that sank its talons deep. Cruel and victorious, the blackthorn thrilled overhead. Its roots wrenched away vast swaths of earth about me until Not-Jade and I were moored on an island of barren land. Death hemmed me in on every side, cut off any avenue of escape. And still, I couldn't tell, didn't know . . .

I collapsed against her body, my blood mingling with hers, and I wept until I was hollow, every emotion wrenched from within and exposed, my strength utterly spent. At last, I lifted my gaze.

And she was there.

The liminal figment hovered in the void beyond. Her eager

eyes feasted upon the sight of Not-Jade's body, absorbed my grief. She inhaled as though it held a sweet savor.

Then she vanished once more.

An eerie silence descended into the darkness. The fae-light offered only the smallest of beacons; it lit no path before me, because none remained. Why had I thought I could do this? I wasn't fae enough to survive this world nor mortal enough for my own, yet still I'd striven to satisfy the conventions of both worlds, only to fail utterly in each. When I'd believed I had no choice, I'd accepted my fae nature, but ever since Riven had told me I could choose, an unbearable weight had descended. Everyone I cared about had a view on the matter, my family desiring nothing more than a total abandonment of my fae nature and Riven counseling the opposite altogether—a severing of mortal ties and all sentiment. And I'd wanted to please them all, as if in so doing, I could keep myself from the pain of losing that which I held dear.

Instead, my heart had remained torn and divided, betraying me into the worst sort of pain. If I didn't care for them, none of it would have mattered. The figment was right in one thing: if I'd not loved, I would not now suffer this crushing weight of loss.

Was that why Talis had crafted the figment? Because some part of her yearned for love and connection, but a greater part feared the pain? A construct you controlled would never hurt you. She'd never reject your true self, never abandon you, never fall victim to the misfortunes of life, never choose a dangerous path that led unto death. Perhaps she'd offer a sort of companionship, a semblance of affection. Yet without the ability to choose, it could never be love.

True love only came with vulnerability and the willingness to accept the soul-crushing anguish of loss. The prospect of great joy presented itself only alongside the risk of great pain. My bruised ribs throbbed, and I buried my face in Not-Jade's fur.

For so long, I'd feared that pain. I'd wanted to make the

right choices, wanted to please everyone, wanted to find some certainty that if I just chose the best path, I could control the outcome—I could protect myself from losing all I loved.

Yet there were no such guarantees. Not unless I walled myself away as Talis had done, existing in an isolated world in which I controlled every part, even the figments of those I loved, in which I bent all my power to protecting my own heart, heedless of the damage it did to all others.

I shivered, the coldness of Jade-not-Jade seeping into my flesh even as my blood seeped into her fur. If Jade had chosen to give her life for mine, if I'd been the one to take it, I didn't know how I'd survive. Oh, I had to believe she still lived . . . but if it turned out I was wrong, what then? Would I claim her love hadn't been worth the pain it exacted?

In no world could that be true. Her love was a thing of beauty, worthy of honor, worthy of the cost. Yet if I remained divided within myself, my love colored by fear, I couldn't honor it as I should. In considering my future, I'd not allowed myself to truly consider what I desired to do, only how I might satisfy those I loved so they wouldn't turn their backs on me. If I pursued that end, I took away both their ability to choose and my own.

What *did* I desire? I didn't want to forsake my fae nature or to abandon the feelings fae scorned as mortal weakness. I didn't know how it was possible to hold true to both sides of myself, when each world frowned on the mores of the other. It might well result in the losses I feared. I might find myself without a home in any world.

Yet I must try.

In the end, Jade had released me to choose, as had Riven, when he could have readily taken the choice from me. They'd done what Talis would not. She'd never release control of her demesne and the false life she conjured within it, nor could I take it from her by force—she was far stronger than I. She'd had centuries over which to learn and hone her powers, and to fae that meant everything. Yet perhaps it wasn't what was needed.

If I didn't seek to protect myself, didn't strive to conjure whatever strength I could to stave off the pain of loss, what might I perceive? Once more, I allowed my gaze to sweep over the bristling trees and vines that comprised the labyrinth, where love had become twisted into bitter sorrow and control. Yet there was more.

My breath caught.

Within the living walls of the labyrinth, between bough and sigil, sparkled fragments of power that appeared like milkweed down limned with starlight. Was this what the essence of the liminal realm looked like? I'd glimpsed a hint of it before, within Beresstone, yet this didn't tease the edge of my senses, but rather exploded into it, vivid and gleaming. Much of it was bound to the labyrinth itself, woven into its workings, but some floated free, scattered and shimmering with possibility, waiting to coalesce from drifting seeds of potential into a new reality, one that belonged neither to one world or the other.

But to truths that superseded them both.

I slipped my hand into my pocket and withdrew the last of the nightspire seeds. They nestled in my bloodstained palm, and I invited the star-down liminal power to settle over them, to draw forth deeper truth into reality.

If grief goes hand in hand with love, so does joy. If death, then resurrection. You are the other half of the labyrinth; you belong here. And in the end, you endure.

The seeds glowed bright with starry power. When I released them, they sank into the bloodstained soil, and then they shot upward, erupting with glorious life—no longer nightspire, but something new, something that shared its fierce determination but also burst with exuberant joy.

These star-vines bore dusky-purple leaves shot through with green and gold and the bright starlight of liminal possibility. I urged their roots to go deep, to quest for the light of moon and star beyond the borders, and they raced joyously to twine with the yew and the blackthorn—which recognized the star-vines as one of their own. The star-vines rioted ever upward, leaving no part of the labyrinth untouched, twining with their kin-not-kin until they became one. Their glow suffused the circular chamber I stood in, and when they touched the tormented forms imprisoned above, they vanished.

Far in the distance, one radiant vine broke through the edge of the labyrinth. And its release promised my own.

CHAPTER 66

In response to my request, the star-vines twined together to build a thick bridge between the earthen island I occupied and the remainder of the labyrinth. It represented the only path out, the only way to free the captives Talis held. Even so, I struggled to force my body into motion. The bleeding had stopped, but my ribs still throbbed, and my side and arm steadily pulsed pain.

A tendril of star-vine popped up and caressed my cheek, and another twisted about my waist, careful to avoid the gashes left by Not-Jade and the blackthorn. Together, we stepped onto the bridge, the star-vine acting as a guide, bringing steadiness to my faltering steps. Its joyous melody wove through the bitter notes of the blackthorn and yew, softening them until they became hostile no longer, their mourning twined with bright notes of hope. This melody kept me putting one foot in front of the other, despite my dread of what I'd encounter when I emerged. Though I yearned to escape the twisted confines of the labyrinth, my release meant I'd face Talis once more.

And she still held every advantage.

The boughs overhead murmured as I passed, and my steps

slowed further. Beyond my reluctance to confront Talis and whatever horrors she had in store, another potential reality loomed, one I dreaded even more.

Jade.

Or her absence forever.

The scent of drying blood on my skin tightened my throat. Would she be waiting with Riven or not? As long as I remained in the labyrinth, I could convince myself she lived. Yet if I emerged and did not find her . . .

I shuddered. It was unfathomable. I could not think it—not yet, and please the Infinite, not ever.

I stumbled around a corner, and a clear, fresh breeze swirled about me, carrying the sweet fragrance of a multitude of blossoms. Did I near the labyrinth's edge at last? The need for truth, despite what it might cost, seized me. I hurried forward, though the pace sent pain burning down my limbs.

Moonlight streamed through an arch in the immense yew, much like the gate I'd passed through to enter the maze. Dared I trust its reality? I limped forward as the star-vine filled my mind with bright images of spectral gardens and a pale, stately house veiled with ethereal flowers—the demesne. I stepped into the arch, and the sight lent by the star-vine became my own— gardens vaster and more starkly beautiful than any I'd ever beheld.

A line of stately queenswood led from the labyrinth to the garden proper, and beneath their spreading boughs, the purple panicles of love-lies-bleeding spilled over teardrop lily of the valley and brushed the tops of black eversword. Where the tree-lined path entered the garden, sheer white shrouds wafted from still taller and more ancient trees, dusky-dark shadows pooling beneath them. Starlike fae-lights were positioned at just the right intervals to shimmer through the shrouds, diffusing light across branches and blossoms to breathtaking effect. Their fragrances suffused the night air.

And yet . . . nothing truly *lived*.

For as I stepped forward, the songs of the plants assaulted

my senses with a jumble of pain and confusion. Oh, *oh*. Somehow, she'd bound each plant in a sort of stasis, where it existed yet never changed, never grew. Each living thing was held in a sort of eternal prison that demanded it occupy its designated place in this picture of perfection. About every working, every line and filament of every plant, star-down fragments of liminal power drifted. If I understood Riven right, for it to pervade the Otherworld to such an extent meant something was drawing it here. What?

Answers wouldn't come if I held back, nor would I gain anything from delaying our confrontation. So I drew myself painfully upright—and strode from the labyrinth. When I stepped beneath the queenswoods, a familiar form bounded toward me, dark and starry at once.

Jade.

The hollow sensation within at once filled with a glorious, heady relief, so strong that it seemed the branches of the trees above swayed with its force. When she halted before me, I wrapped my arms around her neck, clinging to her as if she might disappear at any moment. But she did not. She was real, so beautifully, wonderfully real.

My Jessa. Her warm sweet-grass scent washed over me. *What did she do to you?*

I thought . . . I was so terribly afraid I'd killed you. I drew back, and she pressed her nose to my forehead in a sort of gentle kiss that washed away some of the labyrinth's horror. *There was a Not-Jade and . . .*

Words failed me.

She rumbled soft and low. *Later, you shall tell me all. For now, be wary. The hostility of the demesne grew the longer you remained in the labyrinth. I could not endure that woman's presence any longer, so I emerged to wait for you. I have told Risha and Riven of your appearance.*

Even as she spoke, Risha materialized next to us, her light burning with the brightest of blues. She landed on my shoulder and nestled in, her wings fluttering warm and soft across my cheek. I brushed my finger across the top of her head in turn. *Where is Riven?*

He waits with Talis, watches her. But I do not think she'll delay.

Beyond Jade, in the distance, something shifted in the trees. A figure in a silver-laced cloak stood, watching. The fae I'd bargained with . . . how had she come here? What was the connection between her and Talis? Was she here to ensure all the terms of the bargain were fulfilled and she'd no outstanding obligation? I could imagine such a condition, a demand for access to the demesne in order to ensure a satisfactory conclusion, but still . . .

She vanished deeper into the garden, and I pressed to my feet as Talis and Riven emerged from the manor. They stopped at the far end of the queenswood path, and Talis crooked a finger, beckoning me onward.

Though reluctant to concede to any of her demands, I didn't want to antagonize her unnecessarily. The situation held danger enough already. So I limped down the path, Jade bearing some portion of my weight. When I reached its end, the unmistakable workings of a demesne crackled into my awareness, similar to those within the labyrinth, but stronger still. Such was her might that she'd extended the demesne beyond her dwelling and into the garden, for this space held the ancient, disquieting awareness that I'd encountered in each demesne I'd had the misfortune to enter—save Wyncourt, whose warmth welcomed.

The labyrinth had been her construct, but *this* was the seat of her power, threaded through with iron strands of control. Nothing in it existed outside her will, her desire. Though I dared not take my gaze from Talis, the brightness of Riven's presence bolstered me, driving back the oppressive might of the demesne. As for Talis herself, she no longer kept any hint of her power veiled. It burned with cold hatred, and her silvery eyes held hints of ash, of the deadness found within the figment.

Any words of conciliation died on my lips.

She glided forward, her features a cool, blank void. "Do you imagine you've accomplished something with your display in the labyrinth?"

How could I respond without inflaming the situation further? "Rather, I think I've learned. I'd hoped we could talk about—"

"Hope." Her ever so slightly off-key laugh chilled me. "Child, don't you know hope always betrays?"

"Not always." I took a half step forward. "I know you mourn your daughter, but—"

Dusky-purple sigils darkened about us, staining the earth beneath our feet, thrumming with anger. "If you mention my daughter, I shall strike your *kit-isne* dead."

However deep Talis tried to lock her emotions, they bled into the demesne about us, not to be denied. Starlight glistened off suddenly dew-studded grass, as if the very ground wept. And though the threat to Jade reminded me of all she'd done, all the torments she'd inflicted on Ainslie and the others, some part of me still ached for her grief. "It doesn't have to be this way."

"It will be as I say. You have no part in dictating the terms." Her face held the detachment of the stars overhead, but her eyes, oh they burned. "Ask your questions. And then I will end this."

Riven strode between us, his bearing calm and confident. "You owe me, and I mean to collect on our wager before this goes any further."

"Cutting your losses after all, Lord Arbiter?"

He lifted a shoulder. "That's one way to look at it."

He made a wager with her?

On you surviving the labyrinth. A rumbling purr issued from Jade. *She was quite put out.*

Though he'd not wanted me to enter the labyrinth, he'd nevertheless held faith that I'd emerge, however unfavorable the odds. My eyes pricked.

"Very well. Lady Jessa, make no mistake, this delay gains you nothing." She stalked toward the manor house, her silvery hair trailing behind her like a burial shroud.

The moment she left, Riven wrapped us in glamour. Though

he still wore the mask of an impassive fae lord, his eyes held the glorious light of a sunrise. Bright coils danced along my skin, warming, strengthening. "We won't have long. Talis is fracturing. Her emotions are nearly beyond her ability to control, her mind long strained by division. That will not make her less dangerous, but more so." His gaze swept my injuries. "Can you manage?"

"I can do what I must." Or so I hoped.

He withdrew something from his fae pocket. "Drink this, at least. It will help."

Without hesitation, I opened the small bottle and swallowed the whole dose. It burned and soothed at the same time, driving back the pain, clearing my thoughts. "Thank you."

"It would be better if you could see a fae healer, but we don't have that luxury." He took the empty bottle, tucked it back into the pocket, then assessed me once more. "You feel for Talis. Why?"

"Because I've seen what she's lost. How she's broken herself to try to hide her pain."

"She hates that more than all the rest. Whatever enmity she bore you before, after what you said, it's gone past all reason—if reason ever existed." His jaw tightened. "She'll do anything to ensure your defeat."

"She thinks it will bring her peace," I said softly. "But it cannot—only facing the reality of her loss will."

"She's had centuries to fortify herself against that. I don't think she'll relent. Not now. But your time in the labyrinth had some use besides revealing another of your affinities."

"Another . . . what?"

"You have a liminal affinity." He nodded toward the labyrinth, where the star-vines mingled with blackthorn and yew. "I'd wondered before, but those vines you forged within the labyrinth confirmed it. You'd not have perceived liminal power —let alone been able to wield it—otherwise. It will bear discussion later."

Whatever the odds against me, he didn't suggest later might not come, only equipped me the best he could.

"While I waited with Talis, I became more aware of her views. By observation, she's gained some understanding of you, but it's not as thorough as I first thought. She has some substantial gaps in her perception, things so far removed from her nature that she struggles to grasp them. Perhaps that will cause her to overlook a precaution that should be taken in the terms of outrance." His gaze lingered on the labyrinth. "But I won't be able to directly advise you or interfere in any way."

Yet he was trying to tell me something. "I understand." But I did not. What did Talis have in mind?

"Should you succeed, there will be equal reason for caution." The light about us flared brighter. "It would be better if this took place outside her demesne."

"But she's not likely to agree to that, is she?"

"No. After what you did in the labyrinth, she won't surrender any advantage. The demesne will greatly constrain any ability to use your affinities within it. Certainly, it will prevent you from wielding them in any way against Talis—or any way that might be deemed a bid for control. If you choose to wield them, exercise great care." He hesitated. "There's something else too. She's spent centuries weaving liminal power around this place in a way that makes it impossible to open a passing within the demesne."

Though he might not be able to advise on outrance, he was telling me a great deal. As ever, Riven had layers of purpose in what he did. His wager with Talis had bought us precious time —but no more remained, for she glided back toward us, handing a gossamer-wrapped parcel to Riven. Then her attention locked on me. "Ask what you will."

I struggled to order my thoughts, to judge what might hold importance. "Where did you acquire the pyske-dust?"

"From another fae who kept his or her identity concealed. It would have been greatly to that one's disadvantage to allow anyone to perceive the slightest identifying factor, and since I did not want to compromise my supply, I made sure not to seek any trace. It was a profitable business for us both, and I meant it to continue."

"And this fae supplied you with pyske-dust in exchange for . . . what?"

"An object of power acquired during the war." The stately silvan behind her swayed.

"For what purpose?"

"I was not told."

Nor was this line of questioning likely to help me free those ensnared. I shifted, trying not to wince. "Were all those you bargained with Collectors, aside from Ainslie?"

"Yes."

"Then why did you choose her?"

"That was one other noteworthy aspect of my bargain for the pyske-dust—I must make sure that you or one of your sisters was among the bound. Ainslie happened to be the one I encountered first." She shrugged. "But soon, well, you all became of interest."

Or obsession, as the figment had suggested. But that wasn't the worst of it. If someone else had orchestrated all of this, someone whose identity remained hidden—what did that mean? Did someone else seek to eliminate us? If so, why use such an indirect route? Or was it instead a test to see if Ainslie was fae, see if she could resist glamour? Black eversword crept toward me, rustling maliciously, stopping just short of striking, and I forced myself not to retreat. "Did this fae specify why it must be one of us?"

"No. Nor did I ask."

"How did you snare Ainslie?"

"She was an absurdly easy mark." Behind Talis, the liminal figment took shape. "I needed only to tell Ainslie I'd lost my daughter and plead with her for assistance. At once, she agreed —no limits or conditions—to help me however I needed."

Of course Ainslie had offered help. Her sympathy would have burned bright and quick for a mother who'd lost a daughter, since she was a daughter without a mother. My hands curled tight. "And the others?"

"Collectors are easy marks, and I did not wish to be long from my gardens." She idly plucked one of the black blooms of the eversword. "It was no more complicated than that."

"And what were the terms?"

"For Ainslie, as I said, I needed to promise nothing. For the Collectors, monetary compensation sufficed. Each was required only to dose one new victim with the pyske-dust each month, starting with the onset of spring."

"Why spring?"

"The change in seasons lent the required element needed for the workings I meant to place on the mortals." The bloom withered at the edges. "The Collectors have proven themselves exceedingly effective, whereas your sister . . . she fought the bargain at every turn, even when she could not recall it."

She'd revealed little more than Ainslie had about the terms of the bargain. Certainly, I could see nothing in it to liberate the bargain-bound, let alone the mortals she'd taken for some unknown purpose. Though I couldn't be sure, I now believed those I'd seen in the labyrinth were mere liminal suggestions—however real their presence had seemed. I gripped Jade, her presence alone keeping me upright. "What of the mortals you claimed with pyske-dust? What was your purpose for them?"

"Is that your final question?"

"Yes."

"You understand once it's answered, we enter outrance."

"Yes."

"Excellent." The blossom shriveled into dust, and she cast its desiccated form onto the earth, a smile twisting her features. "I shall deliver the answer you desire, but there's something you must see first."

A translucent concealment glamour wrapped about us, then Talis looked over her shoulder, crooking a finger. "Come. Or forfeit."

I stole a glance at Riven.

He'd become utterly expressionless, only the slightest tension in his shoulders betraying a warning. Dread coiled in my stomach, wrapping tight as I followed Talis toward the heart of the garden. We passed through a dense arch of blackthorn, which then swept back to reveal an immense fountain—and something more. I froze, my blood pulsing cold and hot at once.

Oh, please, no.

CHAPTER 67

Though I blinked, their forms remained, not liminal constructs, but dreadfully real. The waters of the fountain caught and refracted brilliant silver fae-lights across the faces of Ada and Ainslie, the Redgraves alongside them and Mr. Burke slightly ahead, watchful and wary, yet clearly unable to perceive us beneath the glamour. My pulse thundered in my ears, fear and fury surging through my body in equal force. I spun toward Talis. "You had no right to bring them into this."

"I had every right. They consented. All I had to do was tell them your life was in danger and you were in need of their aid."

If she'd stabbed me, it would have been less painful than the knowledge my presence had drawn them into this snare. For now they lived, but what did she have in store?

Shadows clustered thick behind Talis, and before her, ephemeral forms twisted and writhed, specters of what might be. "Blind fools that they are, they leapt to follow me. I will admit they tried to exercise care, but they satisfied themselves with the assurance I'd not harm them."

The words might have been factual, but they weren't *true*, couldn't be true, because if she'd brought them here, she meant only their destruction. The harsh notes of the blackthorn battered against my failing defenses, and I struggled not to betray myself further.

"Had the time not been so short, I might have taken your aunts and father as well. We are playing for the lives of your mortals, after all." The liminal figment appeared amid the shadows behind Talis, a malevolent smirk twisting her features. "Welcome to outrance."

Their lives lost—it had been her obsession from the beginning. My breath came in short, unsteady bursts. I should have anticipated this sooner, should have done something, anything, to keep them safe—but how? Every muscle in my body burned with the urge to break free of her glamour, to run to them before some fell entity emerged from the depths of the demesne to claim them. But she'd said this was outrance. If I dared move before I knew the terms, I might forfeit everything—or trigger their destruction. "What are your terms?"

"I will welcome them, as I've promised, then I shall tell you the terms. You shall have your chance to speak with them, once I've answered their questions and yours—if you wish." With that, she stepped out of the glamour, which still held about the rest of us.

Flanked by Mr. Redgrave and Mr. Burke, Ainslie stepped forward to meet her. Though her face held little color, she met Talis's eyes steadily. "Where is Jessa?"

"You shall see her in due time."

"You said she's in mortal danger, and you expect us to wait until the moment when it's convenient for you to—"

"Silence." She flicked a finger, and Ainslie's voice cut off. "As it happens, there's another matter intimately connected with the dangers your sister faces. Your bargain." She stepped over to Ainslie, traced the lines on her upper arm with a silvery nail. "In case you've not already guessed, I hold it."

Ainslie's features washed paler still, and Mr. Redgrave drew an iron dagger etched with old runes.

Purple-dusk shadows flared about Talis. "Don't try, not if you want your love to live."

"You said you'd not harm us. You gave your word."

"*I* will not. But I cannot answer for my demesne. That sort of weapon here will only spark its wrath."

Indeed, the demesne bristled, its workings dark and jagged spikes that sliced the stone beneath the feet of the assembled mortals. I started forward, but Riven rested his hand on my arm. "You must wait for her to unfold the terms, unless you want to forfeit."

"They cannot see—"

"Yet they're not blind to the dangers."

I rocked back. And at last, his jaw set, Mr. Redgrave conceded, restoring the dagger to its hidden sheath. "Clearly, this is a game to you—are we not to know its rules?"

"They're not for you, oh no." A singsong lilt crept into her voice. "You've long wondered what became of the mortals you betrayed. Now you will know—if you take this path."

"And if we're not minded to follow you?" Mr. Burke asked.

"Then you will remain ignorant. And you will abandon Lady Jessa to her own ends."

Ada wove her hand through Ainslie's. "We'll go."

Elodie and Mr. Redgrave exchanged a glance, then gave small nods. And Mr. Burke fell into place between the rest and Talis, his kestrel-sharp gaze taking in every line of her figure, every ell of the garden. They started down the fountain path, and the liminal figment materialized within the glamour, her bitter scent burning the air.

"You're to follow too, answers for you, answers for them, all will lead to your end."

However much her bidding chafed, I'd no intention of letting Talis take the others out of sight, so I moved after them. Either Talis or the liminal figment sustained the glamour about us until we came at last to the heart of the garden—a breathtaking fractal pattern of living things that spiraled out farther than the eye could see. Within each echoed segment of botanical life, a pallid statue stood, liminal power spreading weblike from its base.

Tension radiated from Riven. "This is how she sustains the whole."

What did he read in the workings that strangled the garden, the statues themselves? How did they connect with the liminal realm? I could not ask, not before the figment. She moved us relentlessly onward, until we stood at the base of the nearest statue, a small woman whose features twisted in anguish.

And then I knew.

I skimmed my fingers across the stone of her skirts—she was polished smooth, like marble, but warm, and when I rested my hand upon her chest, the pulse of a beating heart met my fingertips. Those mortals shown in the labyrinth had been an illusion, but their torment hinted at the reality of these mortals, taken and snared between. My heart beat erratic against the wall of my chest, and I couldn't stop trembling. Was Lianne one of these, her bright cheery soul trapped in agony?

Ainslie trembled too, in a way evident even at this distance —perhaps she'd been shown this before and memory had returned. Or perhaps she simply feared the truth. Mr. Redgrave gently gripped her elbow, steadying her, while Ada clutched her other hand.

Elodie turned to Talis. Whatever she felt, she kept extraordinarily calm—bless the Redgrave equanimity. "What is it you want us to see?"

"My collection of statues, of course. They are those taken from your world, those whom Ainslie and the Collectors betrayed into my hand."

"And you've killed them to . . . decorate your gardens?" Elodie's voice shook.

"Oh, child. I haven't killed them. That would have availed nothing. They're neither fully living, nor fully dead, rather ever caught between. They feel, they hunger, they thirst, and yet their desires will never find fulfillment." Her lips tilted upward. "Fascinating, don't you agree? They're one of my greatest achievements."

The garden blurred before me, and I steadied myself on Jade, whose whole body bristled with the desire to attack.

"They have been silenced, but for you, I shall offer proof." The sigils about the statues rippled, and the garden echoed with their tormented cries.

Ainslie crumpled, only Mr. Redgrave's firm grasp keeping her upright. She buried her head in his shoulder, and Ada stood motionless alongside, silvery tears staining her cheeks. "Make it stop."

"As you wish." Her gaze swept the assembly as if she sought to absorb their pain. "For them, it will never end. But of course, I would not wish *you* to be uncomfortable."

Mr. Burke said nothing, yet fury rolled from him in near tangible waves.

"What then?" Mr. Redgrave's voice held the edge of iron. "You brought us here to torment Ainslie further?"

"That was not my purpose. No, the truth is that Jessa has bought you a chance to redeem these mortal souls—at great cost, I might add. Quite frankly, I did not expect her to do so." Her features tightened slightly. "Of course, it's up to you if you wish to pay the remaining price. She's purchased you only the opportunity to do so."

Ainslie pressed upright. "What is it? I'll do—"

"Stop," Mr. Redgrave said sharply. "Do not bind yourself unwitting." He nodded toward Talis. "We would hear your terms."

"Very well. As it stands now, a . . . very generous application of blood will free them from their condition. There are a great many of them, and a mere drop won't do. I'm given to understand you mortals are the sentimental sort, so unless you wish Ainslie to spend her life's blood, I suggest that you all volunteer along with her." A dusting of liminal power coated her words, lending each suggestion great emotional force. "Of course, if you want her to die, if you believe that's a just penalty for her deeds, that's on your head. I merely present you some of the options."

"Why?" Mr. Burke stepped forward. "It's clear that you want these mortals. You went to great lengths to attain them. Why would you offer us a means to purchase their freedom?"

"As I said, I am bound to do so. I must also warn you that despite all her efforts on your behalf, Jessa will try to dissuade you from this course. It's unfortunate, but she will be compelled to do so—else she'll forfeit everything. If you free the statues, you will also free her tongue."

"Why issue a warning?"

"It pleases me." Talis tilted her head, and the fae-lights caught in her silvery hair and deadening eyes. "I've begun to make a study of mortals, and I'm . . . interested to see how emotions overtake reason to make mortals take wild risks. For all her fae blood, Jessa has a great deal of mortal sentimentality— and it has certainly driven her to unwise lengths. I wonder if you share this weakness. Or if you expect her to undertake the risks all alone?"

They appeared battered, all of them, shocked and disoriented and confused—as was no doubt Talis's aim. I swallowed my rising fear. Why was she telling them this, planting these ideas? She'd woven a bewildering jumble of half-truths to create the deepest sort of lie. To what end?

"You have a limited window in which to act. If you've not redeemed the mortals before dawn, I'm afraid their condition will be permanent. Yet you must wait for your sister. That much I've vowed to her."

How long did we have till dawn?

An hour, at the most. Jade glowered at Talis.

Ignoring her, Talis passed through the glamour, her stride graceful as ever. Yet something about her had altered. Her skin appeared almost translucent, her eyes wavering in color as though they shifted from the ashen shade of the figment and her own bright silver, an effect wholly unsettling.

"You wish for the terms of outrance, and they are as follows.

It will take place within the bounds of the demesne. If any of the mortals act to free the statues by the application of blood, you lose. And so do they. As I'm held to my words, the statues will be released—into the liberty of death—and these five shall be my first new ones, the start of a collection even more powerful than the last, as I've refined my technique these past months. Their blood shall bind them." She lifted slim shoulders. "Naturally, you're bound not to reveal the terms of outrance nor speak of what passed between us before our arrival. You must find some other way to dissuade them, if you're to succeed."

This, this was her end. The revelation spread like strangle-root through my chest, all tangled pain and choking fear, stealing breath and thought alike. I turned away from her dead, triumphant eyes toward Riven's living brilliance, my throat unbearably tight. "Is this permissible?"

"Yes. Talis informed me in advance of the terms she intended to set for outrance. It is all in keeping with our law." His voice held no inflection. "Outrance has few limitations. It cannot be a physical battle or duel of affinities—and a path must exist for the challenger to achieve victory. Otherwise, the challenged sets the terms."

I struggled to straighten my weary body, to meet Talis's mocking gaze. "Under what conditions will I win the outrance?"

"If we reach dawn, and they have not applied their blood to the statues, then the victory is yours," she said. "You may speak with them now, though perhaps you will not want them to see you as you are—you may well lose them when they perceive your full fae nature."

I would reveal myself if it meant their safety, and yet Talis had done all she could to undermine any argument I might make. Ainslie wanted nothing more than to undo the harm she'd unwillingly caused, and Talis knew that. If I could not reveal the truth, what possible inducement could dissuade her?

"Well? Do you wish to address them?"

"Yes." No. My stomach twisted. Exposing my affinities before my family had been difficult enough, but this? I forced myself to step beyond the glamour, Jade a steady presence at my side.

Ainslie flinched, as though struck, and Ada's hand went to her lips, while Mr. Burke edged in front of the ladies, as if he thought I intended harm. As for Mr. Redgrave and Elodie, they remained motionless, rooted as if by shock. Their reactions were shards of glass dug into an open wound. I'd taken such care to keep anyone in the mortal world from seeing me unglamoured, and now this—before Talis, no less. I longed to shrink back into the shrubbery, yet I held still, waiting.

Mr. Burke advanced, his fingers skimming the hilt of his sword. "How do we know you're Jessa and not some other fae who has altered form?"

Would donning my mortal glamour help or make the situation worse? I had to try. I gathered the familiar threads of my mortal glamour, pulling it over myself for one moment, two, then releasing it again. "You covered for me in the matter of the basilisk. And Uros. And my first excursion into the Otherworld. I am now as I was then."

Something flickered in his eyes, and he released his hold on his sword. As one, Ada and Ainslie drew shuddering breaths, exchanging glances that held volumes.

Then Ainslie approached, hesitantly, her fingers skimming along the tears in my bodice, the blood staining my garments. "This . . . was for me?"

"Not you only."

"I'm sorry. I should have been the one to suffer, if it was required." Her lips trembled. "I have to end this. And I will, now that there's a way."

"Not like this."

She shook her head. "We were warned that you must try to dissuade us, but Jessa, I cannot let this suffering continue."

"I know, but this isn't the way."

"Can you deny it will liberate them?"

"No, but—"

Tears shimmered in her eyes. "Can you say, truly, that you wouldn't sacrifice them to spare me?"

"I'm saying there's more at work here. And I'm asking you to trust me."

"But how can we know you truly mean what you say?" Ada whispered. "Talis said you were bound to dissuade us from this course. Perhaps you'd say otherwise if you could speak freely. How are we to know?"

Everything in me wanted to tell her the full truth, but if I did, I'd forfeit everything. According to the terms of outrance, some path to victory must exist. What was I missing?

My shoulders tightened. If I glamoured away their knowledge of the blood sacrifice and compelled them to leave the Otherworld through a passing, Ainslie would be safe. They all would. However little I desired it, I could set the terms, control their futures, and bind them to my will. It would mean they'd be beyond Talis's reach, and they'd forgive me in time.

Perhaps.

If they remained whole after I'd forced their wills and erased their memories. Yet compared to an eternity of torment trapped within the form of a statue . . .

Blight and rot.

My shoulders dropped. Why had they come? I wouldn't have thought it of Mr. Burke, given the strain between us, but if Talis had told my sisters I was in mortal danger and implied their presence could save my life, they would risk themselves. Where Ainslie went, so also Mr. Redgrave, and with Mr. Redgrave, Elodie. And where mortals trod in danger, Mr. Burke would follow, regardless of his other sentiments.

"Jessa?" Worry radiated from Ada.

"Wait, please." I choked out the words. Somehow I needed to find a way to give them the knowledge I held, but Talis had stripped me of my voice, invalidating anything I might say, any attempt to reach them.

"We can't afford to wait." Strain frayed Ainslie's voice. "We must act."

Yet Mr. Burke watched me closely. "When making life-or-death decisions, it's best not to rush."

Mr. Redgrave and Mr. Burke began to debate the situation, while Talis watched, her eyes dark and eager. She'd left open only one path I could perceive: take control and violate their wills. Yet given the way she'd manipulated circumstances from the beginning, I'd no doubt if I seized this means of attaining victory, somehow I'd play into her hands. And regardless, I wasn't willing to strip them of their choices, their memories, their will.

What then?

I couldn't reveal the terms of the outrance, nor could I . . . what were her exact words? I couldn't speak of what had passed before. She must know the revelation of our earlier interactions and of the labyrinth itself would change their decision. Without that information, how could I sway them? Riven had taken pains to say the gaps in her knowledge of mortals and of me would leave a potential weakness in her plan.

Oh . . .

A possibility unfurled before me, ephemeral as the flowers that spilled over the base of the statues. Could I use the liminal realm to *show* them our earlier dealings?

Fae loved to craft their words to control the narrative and the outcome, so Talis had taken that option from me. But if I was willing to reveal the unadulterated whole of what had transpired—the reality of what I was, my mistakes and flaws, the weaknesses fae abhorred and the strengths mortals feared, I could give them the understanding that would empower them to choose.

Ainslie moved closer to the statues, and Ada snatched her hand, holding her back. My breath caught. Some part of me still shrank from the notion of such exposure, but in the labyrinth, I'd resolved to embrace elements of both my fae and mortal natures and to forsake such fears. Now, it was time to follow through. I closed the distance between us. "Part of what Talis said is true—I am constrained regarding what I may speak. Yet more than anything, I want you to understand the nature of the situation so you have true liberty to choose."

Even as I spoke, I attended to the bright song of the star-vine, the joy of love that made it worth the pain. I invited star-down motes of power toward myself, fixing the dizzying array of potential prospects in my mind. They brightened, shifting their pattern to swirl about me. I couldn't interfere with the workings of the demesne nor the plants Talis had bound to her will, but so much liminal power drifted through the air that she couldn't possibly bind it all. I beckoned to it, then breathed it in, allowing it to filter through my senses, my memories, everything that the liminal elements woven through the labyrinth had witnessed. And then, I released it outward, carrying all that imagery, all that pain, all the events of the labyrinth and those before, when I chose to enter it, willing the essence of the liminal realm to reveal what had been in order that it might shape what still could be.

Vivid images sparked against the backdrop of the garden, swirling around us in full immersive life, like a moving picture, one that revealed all the horrors of the labyrinth, each encounter there, my failures and weaknesses—and the words the liminal figment had spoken about Talis's purpose, her pain. When the images vanished, a deep silence descended. For the space of a single heartbeat, even the songs of the labyrinth and the garden ceased before roaring back into the void, swirling across my exposed senses in a way that almost drove me to my knees.

Jade pressed herself against me, her bulk bolstering me. *I'm sorry that you had to endure that alone.*

I chose it, and I don't regret the path. I rested my hand on her head.

For the first time, Ada ventured to my side, tucking her warm hand into my cold one. "Oh, Jessa." Her words choked, and she could say no more.

But Mr. Redgrave stepped into the gap. "Ainslie—you cannot go near the statues."

"But fae cannot lie. She's said they'll be freed." Ainslie wrapped her arms tight about herself.

"And you have confidence, after that?" Mr. Burke assessed me, then turned to regard the statues. "I'm no longer certain it's a liberty that they want any part of—nor that worse won't befall them afterward."

Relief nearly dizzied me. He was shrewd; they all were perceptive in their own ways, they'd just needed more to go on, something to cut away the shroud of deceit Talis had woven about them, something to break her emotional hold and reveal the truth of her cunning and her nature.

Ada cast a wary glance at Talis. "You know they're right. What we saw, it changes everything. That sort of loss . . ."

Dark rage bled from Talis. I'd exposed something of her along with myself, something she'd long hidden—I'd not desired it, but she'd left me no other room to maneuver. Her form flickered, and star-down power clustered around her, ever darkening.

Sharp sparks of light gathered around Riven. What would happen if he set himself to resist her within her demesne?

"We don't have to understand all that passed before—we've seen enough to know that we cannot trust this course," Ada said.

Ainslie pressed her lips together, then crossed to my side. "You know how much this matters to me. That I cannot live with the knowledge I've doomed them."

"I do."

"And yet still you counsel me not to give my blood?"

"Yes."

"Then I . . . I will trust you. You would not have gone to such lengths for nothing." A shudder passed over her whole body. "The statues stay."

The moment the words passed her lips, the world about us shattered.

CHAPTER 68

Dark trees broke loose from the ground about us, becoming monstrous, their roots lashing toward Ainslie and the others. Shadow-workings closed in, the entire garden now a maelstrom of assault, held back only by the power pouring from Riven. In vain, I reached for the storm of liminal star-down, already torn between two immensely powerful beings—

And then the earth beneath my feet fell away. Jade snatched at my skirts, and together, we plummeted downward. Yet we did not hit stone nor earth; a web of shadow snared us, lowering us to the floor.

Thick cords bound me to a pillar, Jade alongside. They bit into my flesh, cold and bitter, spiraling pain upward. I flung myself against them, but I could gain no release. Nothing down here lived, and only a few distant motes of star-down danced along the vaulted ceiling far above. Where were we?

I forced myself to stop. To look.

We'd been drawn beneath the ground and bound to one of the fluted columns that supported the arches above. In front of us, a rune-etched sarcophagus towered, atop it a female figure of stone. Talis's daughter? Beyond the sarcophagus, a tremendous blue-white flame was suspended in midair, flickering uncannily as with an awareness of its own. Nothing fueled this fire; it simply burned cold, casting its light over the carvings on the coffin, shadowing the features of the stone figure on top. I strained against my bonds, managing to shift just enough to perceive a small row of additional sarcophagi on either side.

We were in a crypt.

Did Talis mean to imprison me down here, binding me to her grief? Or use me in place of the mortals outrance had liberated? A quiver started deep within. Bound here, I'd so little ability to mount any sort of defense—and above, the mortals remained vulnerable, even with Riven to protect them. *I'm sorry I brought you into this.*

No apologizing. I have chosen, no regrets.

A bitter dusk scent swept over the crypt. In a swirl of shadow, Talis emerged from behind the sarcophagus. She stalked toward me. "It would have been better for you if you'd lost outrance. Then perhaps the arbiter would have whisked you away. But since you won, you have to die. Failure is the inevitable outcome of risking your life for another, failure and loss."

My heart sank. She had to make me fail—or else face her own reality. Was there any way I could still reach her? "Will you tell me one thing first? Your daughter has been dead all these years. Why did you wait until now to act?"

"Tell her, yes, then she will see." The singsong voice of the figment spilled from Talis's lips. "It's always hopeless, your sorrow will be her sorrow—soon, very soon. When all she loves is gone."

"Yes. Yes. I will tell her. Then she will understand." Now Talis spoke in an ordinary fashion, as if unaware another voice had emerged from her mouth. She drew closer still, her presence an oppressive force. "When my daughter died, I had to pretend satisfaction. To my court, she was nameless, a traitor, her death cause for celebration. If I did not share this sentiment, then I too betrayed my monarch."

From all I understood, fae never embraced mourning; rather, they viewed it as an outward expression of the weakness of love. But this—to expect a mother to celebrate the death of her child —it was cruel. Yet any sympathy might only inflame her further, so I kept silent, waiting, searching for any avenue of escape.

"For long, I hid my mourning, tending to the gardens she'd loved. I kept them always just as they were on the day she was said to have died. But then I considered. After the war, her body was not found. Nor was she among those bound in the Netherworld. I wondered if perhaps she'd succeeded in hiding herself after all. That she'd thought better of her vows to the Court of Ascent, after their victory no longer seemed assured." Her skin became more translucent still, her bones dark shadows beneath it, her eyes ashen. "I didn't try to reach her during the war, couldn't take such a risk. But enough time had passed, I deemed, that no one would suspect. I thought I could find her if I explored the liminal realm long enough—or find the truth, at least. So I kept myself always there. Or here in the demesne, building an impenetrable fortress in case she should ever be found."

I shivered, and the bonds cut deeper into my skin. Talis was slipping, and with it, my chances of reaching her, of reasoning with her. From far above, sounds like that of deep thunder rolled and rumbled.

"He brings the storm, but it does not matter, oh no." She tipped her head back. "Nor will he come to save you, not this time. He's far too busy above."

Cold sweat dripped down my back. There must be a way out, but I could not see it.

"Where was I . . . oh, yes. Her body was found, what remained of it, after all these long centuries. And I had to craft a new plan. The pyske-dust fae was oh so helpful." Her voice became that of the figment once more, low and singsong. "I could not lose her, could not grieve her, had to get her back. And the mortals enabled me to reclaim some part of her. Do you really think I would give that up?"

The ground about us shook as if gripped by an immense quake, and dust filtered down from the ceiling. Sigils flared along the pillars, marching down into darkness.

Her lips curled into a venomous smile. "Riven is strong, oh yes, the strongest fae arbiter in the courts. But even he will be hard-pressed. Century upon century, working upon working, I've built these defenses. In my demesne, he's at his weakest—and I'm at my strongest. He'll see it soon enough. And he won't protect your mortals. No, he'll abandon them all in the end, remove himself, slip away to the labyrinth, open a passing. To watch over such fragile creatures, no—it would make an escape impossible."

I lifted my chin. "He won't abandon them." Even as I spoke the words, I knew their truth.

A snarl escaped her throat, the last vestiges of the composed fae lady slipping away. "Admit your defeat. Admit it's all futile, every effort you've made. He'll leave them in my hands, and once you are dead, I shall return to your world and claim the rest of your family one by one. There will be none left to stop me because your body will be here, cold and alone, just like my Sinael. And that is all you need to know."

The figment's eyes peered out from hers. I couldn't reach her, couldn't reason with her—she was too far gone. My mouth went dry. What remained?

A blade appeared in her hand, darkly shadowed, and she closed the distance between us. My throat closed, every muscle tightening as I strained for the distant motes of power.

So few, so far.

So impossible to reach.

Jade lunged against her bonds. A strange sense of an opening void of power and possibility charged the air. And hot fear pulsed in my temples, blurred my vision.

Talis lifted the blade. "To know you've lost is enough. I will make it a quick death, I can be merciful, yes, no need for a slow and painful—"

Her words cut off with a gasp and gurgle of blood. Crimson

blossomed like a rose against the shimmering silver fabric of her gown, and then a clawed hand passed through her chest, wrenching out her heart. Her body collapsed, and my bindings fell away.

I heaved great ragged breaths, my stomach churning. I lived. I *lived*, against all sense and reason. And Talis did not. How?

A figure in an indigo-and-silver cape emerged from a glamour, holding the heart with a claw-gloved hand. Hers was the figure I'd glimpsed when I emerged from the labyrinth, the source of the nebulous power I'd sensed as Talis approached. She'd kept herself on hand all this time, but why? The room spun about me; only the pillar at my back held me upright. Why would the fae who'd bargained with me for the relic I'd won from Astra intervene on my behalf? Or perhaps she had not. Perhaps she'd only taken advantage of the upheaval in the demesne to slip in and settle her own score. Would she seek to claim my life next?

I couldn't just stand here. I needed to move, to act. Yet my shadow-bruised limbs refused to respond. "Who are you?" My voice sounded distant and unsteady to my own ears.

Jade stalked between us, the fur on her neck rising.

"No need for that, *kit-isne*. As for you, Lady Jessa, have you not guessed?" With her unbloodied hand, she pulled back her veil, revealing the gray-eyed, dark-haired fae who'd claimed friendship with Mother. "Or do you have so many fae willing to kill for you that you doubt my identity?"

I swayed, bracing myself against the pillar. "You . . . How?"

"I told you I'd be watching, and I would help if I could." She glided closer, the silver threads in her cloak gleaming. "As for the logistics, I made sure Talis would welcome me as a guest for a few days by offering her a bargain she couldn't refuse. I suspected if you made it this far, she'd not let you live, and I meant to be nearby to intervene. When Talis opened the crypt, I was prepared. And, of course, she was hard-pressed, her attentions divided between the Lord Arbiter and you—and her own shattering mind."

"If you meant to help me all along, why did you force me to get the shadow-drake blood and the relic? You could have simply offered your information and an introduction whenever you wished."

"Of course I *could* have." Her laugh rippled the dead air of the crypt. "But I'm not that altruistic. Have you forgotten I'm fae? We don't do anything without some gain. I expected that with sufficient motivation you could win me the boon, and we'd both gain something."

Fatigue and pain clouded my thoughts, and I clung to the only clear one that emerged from the haze—she sought to gain, so would she use the offered aid to entangle me further? With difficulty, I straightened. "I see. As I did not request your aid with Talis, you'll grant no debt has been incurred."

"You are learning, little one. Kensa would be pleased." Her low, melodious voice wrapped about me. "I'll concede you've incurred no debt, despite the fact I spared your life."

"May I have your name?" Since I was bound not to speak of her, a name could do her no harm.

"You may call me Divna." She tilted her head. "As the Lord Arbiter no longer attends to the defense of the mortals and Talis can no longer exert her control over the demesne, I expect he'll break through the workings on the crypt in short order. It's unfortunate—I would have liked to speak to you more. Another time, perhaps."

She drew her veil back over her face and vanished with Talis's heart still in her hand. Only a spattering of blood marked where she'd stood. Then the vaulted ceiling above my head ripped away as if it were parchment rather than ancient stone, allowing broken, fragmented songs to spill their anguish into the crypt. Unbearable pressure flooded the room, and golden sigils flared about me.

A bright-edged passing brought Riven into the cold space, his light enveloping me with an intensity that stole my breath. He stalked forward, his eyes shadowed the deepest of greens. "What did she do to you?"

"Not what she desired. I'll be fine."

"I thought—" He cut off abruptly. Though his power still burned bright, the storm charge about us slowly ebbed, the shards of light turning softer. Then he shook his head. "You're an extraordinarily difficult individual to keep alive."

"I don't expect you to—"

"I know." His voice was low, resonant.

And a different kind of pressure built in my chest. In a way, it had been easier when I'd feared he didn't concern himself with the fates of others—at least easier than realizing I'd caused him some measure of the worry I experienced for Ainslie and the others. When I'd extended an invitation to friendship, I'd not realized how greatly it would be to his disadvantage. The jagged notes from the garden above sliced into my soul, and I drew a slow breath. "You weren't wrong. Talis meant to kill me, but someone took her life first."

"Who?" He pivoted to survey her body.

As before, when I attempted to talk of Divna, my throat closed about the words.

His arbiter mask dropped into place, an intense focus behind it. "The fae who holds your geas was responsible?"

Somehow I managed a nod, though the motion sent a spike of pain through my chest, one that matched the broken melodies above.

"I would ask why, but as you cannot answer, it seems an exercise in futility." He paced the scene, surveying the blood, the crumpled body, perhaps traces of Other I could not perceive.

"My geas-holder took Talis's heart. Why?" The geas permitted me to say that much, perhaps because the missing heart was self-evident.

"At best, as a sort of grim trophy. At worst, an intent to operate far outside the bounds of fae law. This fae might have spared your life, but you cannot extend any trust." He bent to inspect Talis's body more closely. "I have no right to pursue your geas-holder, not without Lady Ulrika. I'll have to send for her and report what has happened. Given Talis's reputation, her attempt to kill you won't come as a surprise."

I looked away from Talis's bloodstained chest and sank down on the base of the pillar, my legs no longer willing to offer support. "And I suppose . . . it can't be helped?"

"It cannot. But I'll speak with her first. What happened should be of little consequence. We're here at the invitation of the king. If Talis was foolish enough to attempt to take my life —or yours—then her death is due penalty for her actions. But Ulrika won't miss the opportunity to press you, and I cannot step in too quickly without it seeming as if you have something to hide."

What was one more fae who wished to inflict pain? "I understand." Despite my resolve, my voice shook.

His gaze swept my body, and he took a half step closer. "It doesn't have to be right away. Take a moment first."

"What about Ada and Ainslie and . . . the others?"

"Since Talis had to fulfill the terms of her bargain, Ainslie's binding is broken. That will be true of the Collectors as well. The statues have been freed, though doubtless she'd have sought to bind them once more after your death." His jaw tightened. "I should have kept her from claiming you."

"How? You already protected our lives from assault on every side. And I had some chance of defending myself, the others none."

He inclined his head, but made no further concession.

With each passing moment, the remnants of my strength faded. "I think perhaps you should send for Lady Ulrika. If I must face her, I'd rather it be while I can still stand."

Assuming I still could.

"Take this." He handed me another fae-drink, then dispatched Risha for Lady Ulrika. All emotion washed from his features, and he stalked toward the body, where he stood vigil, arms folded, face expressionless.

In a swirl of ebony and silver, Lady Ulrika appeared, her gaze fixing at once on Riven and Talis crumpled at his feet. "What now? Did you kill her?"

"No. Nor did Lady Jessa."

"Then what?"

He lifted his shoulders. "It began when Lady Jessa expressed interest in her collection of mortals."

"I see. Lady Maeve indicated to me that the Court of Roses had interest in mortal experimentation."

Riven inclined his head, his features impassive. "Talis agreed to part with her current collection if Lady Jessa bested her in outrance, but when Lady Jessa succeeded, it shattered whatever remained of her sanity. She attacked me along with the assembled mortals, then pulled Lady Jessa into the crypt, where she intended to murder her."

Lady Ulrika tapped her crimson-tinted nails against her black skirt. "Then you claim Lady Jessa acted in self-protection?"

"No, another fae appeared and took Talis's life while she was distracted by Lady Jessa."

"That may be the account you've received, but I will have her truths directly." She shifted her attention to me at last. "What happened in the crypt?"

A near-irresistible urge to speak seized me, and I struggled to control what emerged. "Lady Talis spoke of her daughter, her loss. How she wanted to find a way to bring some part of her back—and she spent much of her time in the liminal realm to that end."

Her body stiffened slightly. "You're certain?"

"Her words were impossible to mistake." Just as the urge to confess all was near impossible to choke down. The far-distant flicker of the star-vines pulsed into my awareness, and I straightened. "She didn't expect me to succeed with outrance. When I did, she brought me here to kill me where Lord Riven could not interfere."

Ulrika raised a brow. "If she'd succeeded, I'd imagine that would have caused a great deal of trouble in your court, Lord Arbiter."

"And yours." His voice was silky smooth. "King Talon would look dimly on such hospitality, given the treaty between us. Nor would he relish answering to the Court of Roses."

"Then I suppose we must consider her death our good fortune." Yet even as she spoke, some portion of her power wrapped around me, tight and constricting. "What do you know about the fae who killed Talis?"

"I . . . very little."

"Yet said fae left you alive. Why?"

Her friendship with Mother. The words burned on my tongue, yet with equal force the geas choked me. "It was not said."

"You shall describe this individual."

Her power tightened about me till I felt as one caught between hammer and anvil, geas and suggestion battering at me from either side. "I cannot."

"Enough." Riven strode between us. "I've already determined the fae bound her in geas. She will not be able to speak, and you've no grounds to shatter her mind to uncover the truth. If you want the identity of the one who killed Talis, then track her yourself—as is your duty."

"A geas. I'll grant that changes things. Very well. We are through, Lady Jessa."

Would she have heeded the dictates of fae law if Riven had not been present or twisted them to suit her own ends? Fortunately, I'd not have to find out.

Lady Ulrika sent ebony shadows chasing over Talis's broken form, and I averted my eyes. Whatever she'd done, I could take no joy in her bitter end. Then she turned to Riven. "Will you return to Beresstone?"

"Not yet. Perhaps not at all. After this, Lady Jessa may well have had enough of the Court of Dusk, and I'm obliged to return her intact to her people," Riven said. "We remain only long enough to collect the mortals included as part of the bargain, though the way Talis used them, they may not survive."

"And if I have further questions after I've traced the fae and examined the demesne?"

"If required, we will convene."

When she'd vanished, leaving only a metallic tang to the air, I wrapped my arms around myself. "What you said about the mortals not surviving . . ."

"Was mostly for Lady Ulrika's benefit, but they're in poor condition. Their survival is by no means guaranteed."

Stone scattered overhead, and I flinched involuntarily. Ada and Ainslie peered over the edge of the crypt, their features strained. "Jessa?"

Riven frowned up at them. "I told you to stay put. There are too many remaining workings you might trigger."

Ainslie ignored him, leaning precariously over the edge. "Jessa, are you all right?"

"I'm fine."

Riven gave a slight growl. In the span of a single heartbeat, he'd brought them down through a passing. "I didn't save you from the demesne to have you break your neck the moment I turn my back."

"You cannot possibly think we could wait any longer to see Jessa was safe." Ada offered him a soft smile. "But for your actions, you have our thanks."

He drew a sharp breath, and I held up a hand to forestall a lecture on the dangers of her offering. "I'm fine—but what of the others?"

"They wait in the gardens."

"Not for much longer, if your presence here is any indication," Riven muttered. "I'll bring them into the crypt to wait while I secure a path to the edge of the labyrinth. The freed mortals I've put in a sort of sleep. They'll need attention, but not here."

He vanished, yet when a passing next opened, it discharged only Elodie. "Charles and Mr. Burke insisted on standing watch over the mortals, and Lord Riven has gone to make a way out."

"Are you well?"

"Well enough. Just a bit bruised and battered, and given it felt the world was ending about us, that's a marvel." She glanced between us. "I'll give you your privacy. Who knows when I'll have another chance to properly study the Otherworld?"

With that, she moved to examine the carvings of the crypt, and Ada and Ainslie wrapped their arms about me. Ainslie squeezed painfully tight, and I gasped as it sent searing pain across my bruised ribs.

She drew back slightly. "Sorry. It's just that . . ."

"We thought you were dead. When we came, and then again, when the land itself attacked and you disappeared . . ." Ada's lips trembled. "We feared the worst."

"It's over now." Though I struggled to believe my own words.

"Can you speak now of what would have happened, if we'd given our blood to free the mortals?" Ainslie asked.

I allowed the story to spill out, jumbled and disorderly, and as it unfolded, they grew paler still.

"We came so very close to death." Ainslie stared unseeing into the dark corners of the crypt. "I cannot quite fathom we're safe."

Then Elodie gave a sudden cry, and I spun to seek her. She'd gone to inspect the central sarcophagus, then beyond it to the blue flame.

I limped toward her. "Are you hurt?"

"I only wanted to try to understand the nature of the fire, then I thought I saw something just beyond the flame—I suppose it was only a residual glamour, but it startled me." She pressed her hand to her chest, as though it pained her.

"Were you burned?"

She shook her head. "Truly, I'm fine. Only I feel a bit foolish. I thought . . . That is, our family has spent generations preparing to confront Other. Yet I've hardly made a good showing."

"You've survived the Otherworld and traversing a fae demesne. I don't think anyone would deem you a fool. And you came. Whatever your reasons, I'm grateful."

"If I'd understood, perhaps I would have faltered. All that we think we know about fae, and none of it prepared me. Yet I cannot regret it, if only for the realization it's brought of how little we know." Hesitantly, her eyes met mine. "You really are fae."

"Yes."

"Some part of me didn't fully believe it—or at least, didn't understand what it truly meant." The lightening sky above cast her features in shades of gray. "And seeing you like this . . . it is a great deal to take in."

Whatever else she might have said, Riven's arrival interrupted. He'd brought Mr. Burke and Mr. Redgrave, and Elodie's attention turned to her brother. "What is your judgment of the mortals?"

He shook his head. "They're not well. If returned to our world in such a state, they'd soon be claimed by the Institutions, assuming they survived. It's possible the First could shelter them, but we'd have to explain a great deal that's better left unsaid."

"Then what can be done?"

Mr. Burke inspected the crypt. "Perhaps we'd better discuss it when we've removed to safety."

Riven shook his head. "Some analysis must be made before they're returned to the mortal world, and not just because of the dangers of your Vigil."

"What then?" Mr. Redgrave watched Riven closely as he spoke. "It seems to me you're a danger far greater than any they face in our world. All the more so for your deceit."

Oh.

They'd not known Riven was fae before this. Mr. Redgrave made very bold with his accusation, given what he'd seen Riven do, given that at any moment he could strip the knowledge from them. Would he?

"It is true. I could destroy them this moment, if I desired. And you alongside." The air crackled between them. "Either you make me the same vow you did Jessa—never to communicate it to anyone—or I shall be forced to take the knowledge from you."

Mr. Redgrave held his gaze—what had possessed him to challenge Riven? "Not much of a choice."

"No. I'm not as generous of nature as Jessa."

Elodie rested a hand on Mr. Redgrave's arm. "Nevertheless, we agree."

"She cannot speak for you. Do you consent?"

Mr. Redgrave gave a stiff nod.

"Good. You are so bound." Then he continued, "As for the mortals, I need to assess them—to determine what sort of workings Talis placed on them."

"Could they cause lasting damage?" Ainslie's voice faltered.

"It's possible. I'm more concerned with their consumption of pyske-dust. If mortals consume fae food and drink, assuming it doesn't kill them, they'll never peacefully make their home in the mortal world again—the craving for the essence of the Otherworld will drive them mad," Riven said. "Despite its cultivation for mortal usage, the pyske-dust may have done the same. It depends on how much they took."

Ainslie twisted her hands in her skirts. "If they did, what then? Are they doomed to live in the Otherworld forever, captives to whatever fae snares them next?"

"By fae law, they belong to Jessa now." Riven glanced at me. "It's her mercy and protection they'll rely on."

What in the Crossings? The bargain had been only to liberate them from Talis, not somehow transfer her claim to me. I scarcely felt like a bulwark of protection—more like a storm-battered sapling. The weight of their collective gazes descended upon me, and I bowed beneath it.

"So they are bound to Jessa's bidding, no matter what that might be?" Mr. Burke's kestrel-sharp assessment brought an echo of his earlier question: *will I have to protect them from you?*

"Yes. Talis had legal rights over them, and the bargain gave them to Jessa."

"Can't she just release them?" Elodie eyed me uncertainly. "That is . . . you don't want to keep them?"

"Certainly not."

"Releasing them would be the worst thing she could do," Riven said. "You don't understand the condition they're in. They're incredibly vulnerable to Other."

A swell of voices rose, as Mr. Burke and Mr. Redgrave each began to champion various notions, Elodie chiming in. The weight of conflicting expectations, fae and mortal convention, descended heavily upon my shoulders once more. All I wanted was to hide in my familiar bedchamber at home, bury myself beneath the covers, and hear Aunt Caris's gentle voice as she came to make sure I was well . . . But the time for that had come to an end.

My chest tightened. Never mind what the others expected; what did the injured mortals need? Riven was right that they required some protection. How could I offer it to them? I'd scarcely survived my encounter with Talis alive and that only due to the intervention of another. How could I care for a cadre of vulnerable mortals?

All I knew was that I wanted to find a way, to give them a chance to heal, were it possible. Perhaps their lives and suffering could serve more than one purpose. If we could restore them and they testified to what they'd endured, it would be a story difficult to silence, given their positions in society. Whether or not the king wished to listen, he'd have little choice. Yet for their testimony to hold authority, they'd need to be clear of mind, not the broken beings Riven had lulled into slumber. If I could offer a safe haven, perhaps they could be restored, and Byren strengthened along with them. Voices rose about me, and I stepped forward. "Please, stop."

Everyone fell silent.

Ada gently wrapped her arm around me, and I rested my head on her shoulder, just for a moment absorbing the very mortal gesture of comfort.

"What do you mean to do?" Mr. Redgrave asked.

"Whatever lies in my power, small though it may be. I agree with all the points raised. They cannot stay in the Otherworld, because I have no home or alliances here. They cannot be released in the mortal world as they are, since the Vigil will be only too glad to seize them and because they may no longer be fit for it. Therefore they must go somewhere that's neither—or both."

Riven nodded slowly. "You think of Kilmere."

"Yes."

"The only appropriate housing that remains is belowground. If they recover enough to understand their situation, they'll have questions."

"I know, yet I can think of no other alternative. Do you think it will serve?"

A smile lit his eyes. "It will."

"But they cannot be left within Kilmere alone, can they?" Ada glanced above, where the sky brightened with the first hints of dawn. "Who will see to their care?"

"I have a notion of whom to ask, but we should remove them before Lady Ulrika returns," I said. "Any further discussion can happen within the ruins."

CHAPTER 69

After my first encounter with Kilmere, I never would have dreamed that it would offer a welcome refuge, but when Riven brought us just outside its walls, relief swelled within me, all the stronger when we crossed the boundary and entered the ruin proper. Its moss-covered stones and old-growth trees, its unyielding strength and fierce determination now represented protection rather than predation.

The salt air of the sea mingled with the lush greenery thriving within Kilmere's crumbling walls. Though the ruin did not offer the warm welcome of Wyncourt, its living awareness nevertheless offered acknowledgment, awaited direction. As I made my way toward the central keep, the others trailed after me. I'd never found any living quarters within Kilmere, nor had I ever had time to seek them. I'd been far too busy fighting for my life. Yet given the fae who'd dwelt here in times past, they must exist—unless the bedchambers had all been aboveground and had succumbed to age.

When we passed beneath the arched doorway, I touched the stone, and it warmed. I murmured a request for living quarters, and an image of the corridors below impressed itself on my mind. "This way."

As one, we descended down the smooth, broad stairs, the mortals Talis had held carried on palanquins fashioned of light that moved as Riven directed—fortunately, for otherwise we'd never have managed their number. We soon reached the octagonal chamber from which passages spoked outward. Kilmere directed me through the third opening, and we soon found ourselves in a sprawling wing given over to bedchambers.

Those that must have belonged to the fae lords and ladies were stately, their furnishings of striking beauty, yet they were unsuited to our purpose. When I said as much, Kilmere urged me onward, down a smaller passage. I pushed open a door to reveal a long chamber with many beds, perhaps used to house lesser beings in centuries past, but now well-suited for a temporary hospital of sorts. The palanquins deposited each mortal into a bed, the ladies in one large chamber and the gentlemen in another we discovered across the hall.

Once the mortals were settled, Ainslie gave a slight shudder. "I'm thankful that this offers a refuge for them, yet I must confess I'd prefer to be aboveground."

"As would I," Elodie said.

Mr. Redgrave and Mr. Burke exchanged glances. "Perhaps we should all go."

They departed, but Riven and I halted in the corridor between the two hospital chambers.

"It will take time to examine each individually," Riven said. "Time we can't afford right now. I must return to court. Rumors of what happened will already have reached the king."

"Can they be kept in slumber?"

"For another day or two. I'll shore up the workings before I go." His brows drew in. "But you need to understand that what's happened in the Court of Dusk changes things. The king will—"

Perhaps having realized we didn't follow, Mr. Burke returned. He stopped at the end of the corridor, tension radiating from him. "Jessa, I'd like a word."

My pulse picked up. If he meant to press the point of the

danger I represented to this world, I was ill fit for the conversation in my current condition.

Riven frowned at him. "Perhaps she's not inclined to grant you an audience."

"Perhaps you should allow her to answer for herself."

The tension between them caught in my chest. We were all frayed and weary. If it exploded into open conflict . . . I moved toward Mr. Burke. "If you wish to talk, I'm willing to listen."

He inclined his head. "Aboveground, if you will."

"Very well."

In silence, we ascended the stairs, while Riven retreated into the hospital chambers, doubtless to attend the workings. What had he meant to say? I didn't know which conversation I was more reluctant to endure.

Mr. Burke halted before a low crumbling wall that looked out over the ruin. "It seems this plan to restore the mortals relies a good deal on Riven's goodwill, unless you possess the power to assess the damage done them."

"I don't, at least not to my knowledge."

"Do you think he'll help?"

"I haven't asked him, but I believe he means to."

"Good. I intend to stay in Withern for a time. I can get another week's leave, and—"

"Why do you intend to stay?" I refused to allow this conversation to continue as if things were well between us—as if he hadn't hurled accusation of the basest deceits. If he still felt that way, I needed to know. "Because you want to be sure I won't hurt them?"

"What? No." He braced his hands on the wall, looking out over the tumbled stone expanse. And the silence stretched between us.

"Our last conversation—I handled things badly. I owe you an apology."

"You spoke only what you believed of me."

"Yet I should have taken time to listen to your account. To

weigh and analyze the facts. If I had, I would have soon realized there was more to the story."

The sprightly song of the goldleaf basil teased at my senses, along with its sharp, vivid scent. "And . . . how is it that you understand now?"

He finally turned toward me. "After you departed for the Otherworld, I received a call from your sister."

"Ainslie called on the Magistry?" Aunt Caris would have been overset if she'd learned of it.

"No, it was Ada—and she visited my home. Despite still recovering from his injuries, your cousin Lovell somehow procured my address and brought her, then gave us a private audience."

To Aunt Caris, that would be even worse—no lady *ever* called on a gentleman. And Ada had always shied away from conflict. It seemed our circumstances were starting to change us all. "What did she say?"

A reluctant smile tugged his lips. "She informed me in no uncertain terms that my behavior was deplorable."

The ferns at my feet shot to attention. "I cannot imagine Ada using those words."

"She did not. Rather, she offered the gentlest of reproaches, which made it worse. Because everything she said was true." He rubbed his jaw. "She told me she'd not thought me the sort of man who leapt to conclusions before collecting all the facts. Who'd abandon a friend so readily."

"You did think I'd betrayed you—and Byren."

"You're not supposed to let me off easily." His lips quirked. "I should have listened to what you had to say, rather than immediately leveling accusation. Making assumptions. This is your chance to castigate me properly for my failings."

"Life is far too short for that." As I'd been vividly reminded. If the mysterious fae hadn't arrived when she did, I'd be buried in the crypt along with Talis's daughter—assuming she'd no worse purpose for my body. I shivered. "And I value your friendship. I always have, even when I had to hold back parts of the truth."

"As I do yours." He studied me. "What we witnessed of that labyrinth—"

Though the rays of the sun bathed us, the mere mention of its name seemed to cast a shadow over the expanse before us. "Let's not discuss it."

"As you wish. Yet it forced me to consider my own losses and fears. How they've . . . informed my actions." He sounded unusually hesitant. Whatever he meant to say, it wasn't easy for him. "To me, you represented a chance to make a past failure right. That's not to say I didn't come to respect you and value your friendship in time, but that's what you meant at first. From the moment I met you, you reminded me of my sister. Like you, she'd listen to input, then quietly go on her own way, doing as she felt right."

"You speak of her as if she's gone."

"She is. Her death is the reason I joined the Magistry." His hands tightened about the stones. "I failed her, but I thought I could keep you safe, despite the fact you seemed determined to rush into danger at every turn. Though as it turned out, you never needed protection."

"I wish that were true. I'm only just beginning to learn how to use my affinities, and when we met, I didn't understand them at all."

"And yet already you have the power to destroy mortals, if you wish." His eyes shadowed. "When that became clear, when I realized you were fae, I thought I'd allowed sentiment to overtake duty, to blind me to the truth. Else how could I have missed your nature so long? I'd failed my sworn oaths by not only overlooking a threat, but also allowing you into Magistry investigations. Even so, I couldn't bring myself to report you to the Vigil."

I skimmed my fingers across the lichen growing along the stones, and it brightened. "You know that's part of the reason I never spoke of my nature. I didn't want you or any of the others to have to face that conflict."

"And what was the other part?" His gaze rested upon me, uncomfortably perceptive.

"I feared how everyone would react, if they knew. Feared losing all that mattered to me."

"And I lent credence to those fears."

"Not you only. My family struggles. And somehow I must find my way, when I properly belong to neither world."

"I can offer no counsel, other than to suggest you take your time to decide."

"It . . . it doesn't feel as though I'll have that time. The Vigil already watches me and my family, and my actions have also drawn Otherworldly attention." What had Riven been about to say? New fears pricked at my weary mind, thornlike. "Both will endanger my family—yet I cannot bring myself to walk away."

"Nor should you. Not without allowing your family some voice in the decision of what risks they want to take."

"Riven believes I should cut all ties without their input."

"I have observed that most fae don't value family bonds." He kept his voice carefully neutral.

"That's true, but . . ."

"Is he pressing you to act against your will?"

"No. It's simply that I do not see my way clear." A crumbling wall now framed Elodie and Ada. They strolled beneath the rowans, talking with an ease that would have been unthinkable in former Kilmere. Though I'd no notion where Ainslie had gone, I imagined Mr. Redgrave looked after her. For now, they were safe, but ultimately, they were all so very vulnerable. "I have no right to ask, but if I cannot—will you look after my family?"

"You have my word."

"That means a great deal." The distant roar of the surf swept over me, carrying exhaustion in its wake. "If you don't mind . . . I just need a moment."

Mr. Burke nodded. "I'll join the others."

As soon as he left, I sank down in the shadow of the wall, resting my head against its cool strength.

Jade wrapped herself around me, warm and comforting. *Whatever comes, we will take it one step at a time. Together.*

Then she rested her immense head in my lap, and I stroked it. The distant murmur of voices caught my ear. One of them Ainslie, perhaps? As I pressed back into the stone of Kilmere, I murmured, "Is she well?"

And Kilmere opened a view before me of Mr. Redgrave and Ainslie standing at the seawall, soft morning light playing about them. She surveyed the distant horizon, but Mr. Redgrave didn't once glance at the sea—he only watched Ainslie. "You're free now."

"I can scarcely believe it. I was so afraid for so long, and now . . . now I feel as though I'm in a dream, a beautiful one that's burst in after an endless nightmare." Ainslie's hand stole to the place the binding mark had once etched across her skin. "To think that I have a future, that I have liberty to choose—it feels like an unfathomable privilege."

"And what will you do with that privilege?"

"I'd rather hoped to discuss it with you," she said softly.

He gently touched her cheek, lifting her chin until her gaze met his . . .

And I wrenched away from the stone. Whatever would pass between them, it was not for other eyes to witness. Yet their tenderness stirred my own longing for a sure future, for such a confident love. Theirs had been a complicated path, but mine . . . I could not even begin to understand the rules that might govern it. If fae family life was structured around power, did they even allow for the prospect of love, or was it all about strategic alliance?

I pressed the thoughts aside, but a deep ache settled in my chest. Now that Ainslie had been freed from the bargain, she'd sever her fae nature. I'd no doubt of it. Even were it not for her love for Mr. Redgrave, she'd no desire to embrace whatever affinities might be locked within her. And everything in me longed to persuade her otherwise, despite my resolve to support her choice.

Because it meant her life would end.

And mine would not.

Riven ascended the stairs. His gaze landed upon me at once, and he crossed to my side, wrapping a concealment glamour about us, then sank down next to me. With a sharp look, he assessed me. "What did Burke say?"

I traced the lines of a dragon-head fern with one finger. "He apologized for his earlier reaction and mended things between us."

"Then what troubles you?"

"Those things that are lost, and those that will never be the same again." My voice came out shakier than I'd hoped.

"You've chosen to embrace your fae nature."

"Yes. Not because I must, but because it is what I desire. When I use my affinities I feel as though I'm truly myself, truly alive. But I cannot be fae . . . as it is understood to be. And I fear what that means."

"I know, but you will have to learn. Or pay the price."

"Why? What happened to Talis—it might never have taken place if she'd even once been met with compassion for her loss, had someone to mourn with her over her daughter."

"Perhaps. Yet this has been the way of the courts since—for some time. It's unlikely to change. And any sign of emotion, any hint of weakness will be exploited."

"Yet you stayed." The dragon-head fern tinged gold beneath my touch. "You could have left us, cut your losses, but you accepted the weakness—if you wish to call it that—that came with the choice to protect mortals, rather than abandon them to the demesne."

"Against all sound judgment," he muttered.

"Do you regret it?"

He remained silent a long moment. "What I did could be justified as protecting my court's investment in you and the relations between the Courts of Gold and Roses. That's the story that will be carried by Lady Ulrika to her king. If it could not have been spun in such a way, then any protection I offered would have soon made each of you targets. It would have availed nothing, in the end."

The words stabbed deep, and I turned away. "You must also carry a tale to your king. What will you tell him?"

"The portion of the truth he must know. Your survival of the labyrinth and outrance, the affinities you're developing." Sparks flared about Riven. "As I've said, he takes an interest. He's exercised patience, because he stood to gain. I'm not certain how much longer he will wait. You can leverage Lady Avis for a delay, as we discussed. But sooner or later, he'll demand your appearance in court."

"Can he demand it if I'm not one of his subjects?"

"As of now, you are unallied and unprotected. He can do as he pleases. For a time, alliances will be courted. Then there's a risk they'll be forced. Unbound fae most often meet with death —or wish for it, once all the interested parties have taken advantage of their vulnerable position."

Riven had never softened the truth when talking with me, even when I wished he would. The ferns quivered, and I released my hold. Whatever I'd said to Mr. Burke, I'd hoped for time to consider—time to find a way to keep a home in this world. How much time remained? And what did a court alliance mean? I tilted my head to study him. "Then you suggest I ally with your court?"

"I suggest you choose mine or another. Each would have its own complications."

A very fae answer. Would the complications mean a requirement that I hold fae convention? What would be demanded of me? I pulled my knees to my chest, resting my head on them. "I don't think I can do this."

"You're more capable than you know."

"Not of pretending I don't care. Not of watching mortals

suffer. Not of seeing my family at risk." I leaned back against the cradle of stone, the songs of the ancient trees thickening the air about me. "Would joining a court offer them any protection?"

His jaw tensed. "No. They'll have the best chance if it's believed you care nothing for them—that they're castoffs from an old life, discarded the moment you recognized your true nature."

"Whatever I do now, at least one person besides you will know that's not true."

"You're thinking of what Talis said, that the fae who supplied her with the pyske-dust ordered her to ensnare you or one of your sisters."

"Yes. I cannot fathom the reason for their interest in us, and I fear the steps they'll take next, now that the bargain has been broken. Clearly, this individual doesn't even adhere to fae law, which bodes poorly for their ultimate purpose." Talis had manipulated many situations, but this unknown fae had controlled her . . . and how much more?

"That's not the only cause for concern. The individual who holds your geas presents equal danger. To have found you, to have killed Talis in such a fashion—your geas-holder is strong."

Yet Divna had suggested she was one of the weaker fae. A deceit meant to gain my sympathy? Or something else that I couldn't yet understand? Could I somehow hint that the geas-holder and the one who'd demanded Astra's relic were the same? When I tried to speak, pain seared my body.

A slight frown tugged at Riven's lips. "Perhaps we should abandon the matter of the geas-holder for now."

"Can a geas ever be broken?"

"Like a bargain, it requires the agreement of the one who holds it."

Which wasn't likely. My mind drifted back to all that had happened before Divna arrived. "I've wondered—what would have happened if I'd glamoured the others not to use their blood on the statues. I couldn't fathom Talis leaving such an easy path to victory, but I couldn't see how she could gain from it either."

"Nor did she. She expected you to exert control as a fae would over the situation, all the more so because she'd seen your determination. So she set a working that would have shattered their minds at the smallest glamour or compulsion. The force of it would have killed them."

I pulled in a shuddering breath. Small wonder I'd perceived concern in Riven, because he'd known that I'd struggled to control my glamour in the past. As Ainslie said, we'd come so very close . . . And with the revelation, I needed some distraction, lest *I* shattered. "When she bound me in the crypt, Talis said you'd brought the storm. What did she mean?"

He hesitated, then perhaps recognizing my need to shift the conversation, conceded. "In this case, she meant a literal one. When ether is wielded in a specific way, it brings a storm. It's an incredibly destructive power, therefore only useful in specific circumstances."

I stared at him, reminded of how little I still knew of his nature and his role.

Before I could inquire further, he shifted the subject. "Whom do you mean to enlist to keep watch over the mortals?"

"I'd thought of Dreda, if she's willing. She's perfectly suited to the task—her loyal nature and sympathy for those afflicted by Other would stand her in good stead. She wouldn't be able to manage alone, but she could make a beginning—and I have a feeling some among the Sisters of Verity would help."

"They'll require more than just mortal aid for recovery. Are you willing to bind those who serve here to silence?"

"If they consent." I examined the towering wall of the keep, softened by the light of the glamour. "I suppose it's time we returned to Avons."

"Yet you cannot go back to your family looking like you've been in a war with wyvern and lost."

Even were it not for the bloodstains, I still wore fae clothing. Could I glamour it away? I wasn't sure I'd mastered it sufficiently yet to extend beyond my person and into my attire, but perhaps . . . I tilted my head. "I don't suppose you have a gown hidden in your pocket?"

"No, but I have one in yours."

"Mine?"

He withdrew the gossamer-wrapped package Talis had given him. "You may thank Talis for this—or rather, your own success in the labyrinth."

"You wagered for a fae pocket?"

"You seemed to have an interest in them. I thought it fitting that she'd be forced to provide one." He studied me. "Will it be too painful a reminder?"

"No." I clutched the package to my chest. "Perhaps a bit, but more than a reminder of pain, it will be one of hope."

"There's one thing more. After you encountered the woman in the garden, the one who said she belonged to Lord Revilon, I made inquiries about her. She was compelled to go into the gardens and tend the mortals, but to pretend she came in secret."

"By whom?"

"That is unclear. If there'd been more time, the inquiries might have borne more fruit. But it's evident someone sought to assess you, to see how you would react to the appearance of a vulnerable mortal thrall."

Despite the growing warmth of the day, a chill traced down my back. "Who might have such an interest?"

"Unfortunately, there are many possible parties at this point. You've exposed yourself in very public ways before the Courts of Silver and Dusk. Though you've returned to this world, you'll need to remain wary."

I nodded. "May I ask one thing more?"

A small smile played about his lips. "If I said no, would you refrain?"

This time, I'd no doubt of the levity of his words, and despite the seriousness of the matter, I couldn't restrain a twitch of my own lips. "If you, Lord Arbiter, made such a dictate, I'd certainly oblige."

He laughed, the richness of the sound sparking joy. "If ever once you heeded all my *dictates*, I'd know you were overtaken by a mesmir."

Perhaps we'd both overcome certain fears, if we could jest about his position as arbiter rather than worrying it would sever the relationship between us. "It would make your life easier."

"Easier isn't better." He looked as if he were going to say something more, then he lifted his shoulders. "What did you wish to ask?"

I sobered. "If somehow I came by knowledge of the location of the dawn-dagger, would you recommend claiming it or leaving it lie?"

"If you happened to stumble across such information, I'd suggest you claim it at once. Before you left Kilmere, even. You'll require any advantage you can get."

"I'll keep that in mind."

Distant calls seeped through the glamour—Ada and Ainslie sought me. Riven stood, extending his hand to help me to my feet. When I took it, his fingers closed around mine for the briefest moment, his grip warm and steady . . . and far too welcome. "Keep the passing prism for now. It will be sufficient to return you to Avons, and later here. The mortals will be in a sustained slumber for two days. If I cannot return before then, you'll have to tend them the best you can."

Uneasiness crept down my spine. "Do you anticipate trouble?"

"It's always a possibility."

The nonanswer almost certainly meant yes. "Riven, I . . ." How could I possibly express all I felt? "I know you don't want gratitude. But had you not stayed with us at the demesne—"

"Jessa. No debts, not now."

I hesitated. Did he mean his king might use an implied debt to Riven to snare me? "Very well."

The light of passing gathered about him, and I fought the urge to ask him to stay, the absurd fear that if he left, I might not see him again. Perhaps the labyrinth and the crypt and all the dark notes of grief still preyed upon my mind to an extent.

"I'll return when I can." With that, he vanished.

And I drew myself upright. He *would* return, and meantime, we'd a great deal to do, starting back in Avons . . . and whatever choices my family might make when I revealed the truth.

CHAPTER 70

After we returned the Redgraves and Mr. Burke to their respective homes, I brought Ada and Ainslie into the glasshouse, where we could collect ourselves before facing the rest of the family.

"I've never been so glad to see home." Ainslie ran her hand across the wall of the glasshouse, then turned to me. "What do you think we should tell them?"

"The truth, though perhaps without some of the darker details? They need to understand both what happened and the ongoing risks of my . . . our natures." Whatever Riven might say, I couldn't take the choice from them, couldn't just sever ties and leave without a word of explanation.

"Even if you tell them, I'm not certain they'll understand." Ada brushed at a dark stain on her skirt. "Until I entered the Otherworld, I don't think I did, not truly."

"Still, I must try." Within Kilmere, I'd changed into mortal garments and tidied my appearance, even restored my mortal glamour, before fetching the dawn-dagger and tucking all my fae items into the fae pocket, which I'd secured beneath my clothes. To any mortal, I'd appear ordinary, but still . . . The weight of exhaustion descending on me nearly swept me from my feet.

"Will you go in first? I'd like a moment alone before all the questions that will come."

"I think you need more than that." Ada gave a slight frown. "How long has it been since you slept? You look exhausted."

"I'm not sure. My time in the Court of Dusk felt like one endless night."

"Then you need more than a moment."

"Perhaps, but . . ." How could I explain the unease that still plagued me? "It will do."

Ainslie eyed me. "You won't leave, will you?"

"Not now. I give you my word." The sweet orange brushed my shoulder, gently reassuring. "Yet it seems you might, in the not-so-distant future. I assume things between you and Mr. Redgrave went well."

A delicate rose hue crept into her face. "They did. He's warned me we'll face challenges from his family, but given what he risked in the Otherworld for me . . . it hardly compares."

Ada twined her fingers through Ainslie's. "And whatever comes, you will not face it alone. I'm very glad."

"As am I." No matter the ache our impending separation might cause.

"He's the one good that has come of all this—well, that and beginning to learn the truth, no matter how painful." Ainslie glanced ruefully down at her garments. "We'll try to slip in without drawing notice. We'd benefit from a bit of tidying first ourselves before any conversation, and perhaps it's best we all address them together."

As they retreated into the house, I entered the garden proper —and though its beauty paled in comparison to those I'd seen in the Otherworld, every familiar bough and blossom whispered a welcome, surrounding me with a gentle protectiveness. I moved toward the side of the oak that faced away from the house and sank down beneath it, the sun bathing my face. Ivy wrapped around my limbs, the song of the oak thrummed in my ears, and the greening strength of the plants poured into my veins, each pulse washing away some measure of fatigue. Was this why fae didn't require as much sleep as mortals? Because their affinities allowed another way to fill the void?

In any case, as their strength became my own, I reflected on what might come. We'd succeeded in freeing those Talis had taken, but they remained vulnerable, as did Byren. Unless we could restore those she'd stolen or find some other way of proving the truth of our claims, it would remain so. Would I be able to stay in this world and offer aid? Or would my family prefer that I remove myself and the danger I represented? Some sort of middle ground must exist. Could I take up residence else-where in Byren—in Wyncourt or even Kilmere, perhaps? But no, unless I wished to scandalize all of Avons and bring further scrutiny to my family, that would never do, at least until I came of age. It would be unthinkable by mortal standards, unless my family came with me and the decision appeared to come from Father. And if they removed with me, I'd expose to any Other interested parties my desire to remain connected with them. What then? I sighed.

In lesser-form, Jade climbed into my lap. *I'm not certain anyone can answer that.*

Yet Riven seems so sure of the course I must take. I smoothed her fur. *His father murdered his mortal family.*

She chuffed. *That . . . explains a few things.*

Yet things between our worlds are different now—Other encroaches and will continue to do so. The mortals need help, need to understand what they face.

And you do not want to dwell in the Otherworld.

I tugged her closer. *Were it all like that glorious forest Riven took me to first, I might welcome it—provided I could still main-tain a relationship with my family. But it's not. It's bloodthirsty and cruel. An unfeeling nature is a point of pride, not shame. And that doesn't even begin to address the endless stratagems, politics, and doublespeak.* An image of the sylph tree seemed to dance before me, and I closed my eyes against it. *It was difficult enough for a few days. Any longer, and I don't know how I could endure it. Yet I cannot deny it holds a great deal of information I require.*

Though the references made to the Court of Ascent and the war had left me with more questions than answers. Whatever had taken place had brought sharp division among fae and had done a great deal of damage within the courts. Could it possibly be the same as our Forgotten War? If so, then most of my assumptions about the matter were incorrect. For how could mortals have done such damage to fae? In any case, I felt quite certain both the court and the war were among the topics forbidden by geas. *Am I right?*

A breath gusted from Jade. *Unfortunately.*

Perhaps if I spent more time in the Otherworld, I'd have greater opportunity to learn by chance, information let slip in a context the geas couldn't bind. But at what cost?

Jade tensed in my lap. *The boy is near.*

Of course he is. Had he sensed the use of my affinities somehow? I opened my eyes. "How long were you watching me?"

He stumbled back. "Didn't see nothing."

Clearly, it was an untruth, as even now ivy coiled about my limbs. Yet I'd chosen to embrace this nature, and perhaps . . . perhaps he needed the truth. At my urging, the ivy spiraled past me and brushed the hair from his eyes. "Now you have seen something. And I don't think it's the first time that you've experienced the inexplicable."

He shuddered, his dark eyes pained. "Shouldn't have shown me. Why did you?"

"Because when I was your age, I would have given the world to have someone tell me that I wasn't fae-touched and in danger of going mad." Then perhaps I would not have lost so many years to fear; perhaps I might have started to uncover the truth sooner.

"Can't say that about me. Don't know."

"We don't know, not yet, but we can find out." I pressed to my feet. "I think perhaps you know more than you're willing to say."

"I know the Vigil'd give good money to learn the truth of you." His dark eyes glittered.

On the face of it, his words sounded like a threat. But I did not think he meant them as such. He was testing me, much like the wary animals he tamed tested him. So I kept my voice calm. "I cannot deny it. Do you mean to share the truth with them?"

"Don't hold with the Vigil, but that toff that belongs to them has been sniffing round. Offering the servants money for information about you and when you'll return from your travels."

My breath caught, and the branches of the oak overhead shuddered. "I see."

He peered at me from under his shaggy hair. "Set my dog on him when I saw him yestereve. He ran off like his trousers were afire."

"I'm grateful for your intervention. But we digress from the point—will you tell me what you've experienced?"

"Why should you care about what happened to me?"

"Because I care about all the peculiarities that are happening in Byren."

"Guess you got your own." He looked between me and the plants, then scuffed his boot in the grass. "I always had a puny heart. Caused more problems the more I grew. Then one day some men came. They told my da they'd a procedure as would fix it, so he agreed. They promised it was safe. Said it would be over and done before long, then I'd be home. But when I woke, they didn't let me go, not though a full moon had passed and more. Didn't let my family see me neither." He rubbed his chest. "It hurt like all the furies, and I thought I would die, only I didn't. Don't know how. But things started happening, things I didn't understand. Then my da, he broke in, and he found the truth of the matter. They'd put something Other inside me, and they meant to keep me to see what would happen. He tried to get me out, and he kilt the man who done it, and then they hanged him for it. He made me swear not to say why he kilt the man or the Vigil would take me—or if not, the toff who'd paid for the work sure enough would."

My heart drummed against my bruised ribs, and yet that

pain paled before his. "Oh, Dryden." I rested a hand on his shoulder. "I'm so very sorry."

"You . . . you believe me?"

"Of course I do." My shoulders knotted. His story echoed what I'd once read of alchemists experimenting on children. And to see what he'd endured, how it had broken his family . . . My hands clenched into fists.

His body shook. "Wasn't right, what they did, but wasn't in my power to fight back."

I fought for a steady tone. "Is that when you began to connect with animals?"

"Aye. Always liked them, but 'twas after that they seemed to take an unnatural listening to me, and I to them. Except that one." He motioned to Jade.

"I'm afraid her allegiance is elsewhere."

He nodded. "'Twas her liking of you that made me think perhaps you were different from ordinary folk."

"I'm glad you decided to trust me, because I believe we can get to the truth of what happened to you. The arts that made you what you are were forgotten long ago, and though alchemy has revived, this should not have—let alone been practiced on you against your will." It didn't follow a logical progression. This ability had belonged to the pinnacle of their practice, and its sudden emergence beyond the current art suggested someone was behind this. But who and why?

The crunch of footsteps against crushed stone set us both on alert, then Dreda appeared through the foliage. "Dryden, here's your—oh, Miss Jessa. You're back and safe!"

She dropped the basket and flung her arms about me, and I leaned into her embrace. Dryden quietly collected it and vanished into the mews with his dog and rabbits on his heels.

"When your sisters told me you were in danger and they must go after you, I feared I'd never see any of you again. And I wished I'd insisted on going with them, no matter what they said. It would have been better than not knowing . . . believing the worst." She regarded me, eyes wide. "But no matter; you're back now. And unharmed?"

"I took no lasting damage." And my time beneath the oak, coupled with the fae-drink Riven had given me and my innate ability to heal as fae, had done a great deal to restore my body already.

"Did you find the lost ones?"

"Yes, but it's proven a complicated matter." One that felt distant and unreal in this homely, sunshine-kissed garden. "If you're willing, I'd like your assistance with it, perhaps along with Sister Margery and some of the others who can be trusted." I unfolded the tale of what we'd found and the condition of the mortals housed in Kilmere. "Would you consider taking a position as a caregiver, temporarily?"

Her hazel eyes brightened. "I'd like the chance to help them as you once helped me. I know in small part what they must feel, though my situation wasn't as dire."

"Then you wouldn't be afraid to enter a fae stronghold and live there for a time?"

"Not if you tell me it's safe."

"It has become so."

She inclined her head. "But what will you do about a chaperone?"

"Despite what my aunts feel, I no longer require a chaperone." It wasn't something I'd ever expected to grieve, and yet . . . "Perhaps their views shall change, when they learn what I intend."

"And what is that?"

"To embrace my fae nature." I skimmed my hands across the ivy. "But that discussion should rightly take place with my family."

Her gaze lowered. "Then I will let you go to them."

"I'd rather you come, if you're willing." I looped my arm through hers. "You're one of us now."

The brilliance of the smile she offered in return lifted my flagging spirits. Together, we slipped into the house and collected Ada and Ainslie from their bedchamber, then descended to the morning room, where Aunt Caris, Aunt Melisina, Father, and Lovell were gathered. When we stepped through the door, chaos ensued. Everyone sprang to their feet, and a jumble of conversation met my ears.

"Why didn't Holden—"

"How did you—"

"You're safe, thank the Infinite—"

"What happened—"

Ainslie held up both hands. "One at a time, and we will answer all your questions."

"First this." Aunt Caris bustled across the room and scooped us all into her arms. "I thought I might never be able to do this again, though I prayed . . ."

Her voice broke, and I tightened my grip around her. Whatever her fears, her love had overcome them. Even Aunt Melisina dabbed at her eyes with a lacy handkerchief.

Lovell moved toward us, leaning heavily on his walking stick. "What happened?"

I drew a deep breath and then gave as concise and devoid-of-danger account as I could manage while still speaking the truth. Even so, they appeared almost bruised by the recounting, and Aunt Caris studied us with some anxiety.

"But you are unharmed?" she asked.

Ada patted her shoulder. "We're well enough, thanks to Jessa and Lord Riven."

"And Lianne?"

"She was . . . much harmed." The memory of her still form brought a stab of pain. "But I hope she can be restored and return here, if she wishes."

"Then it's a job well done and fortunately over." Aunt Melisina whisked her handkerchief from sight. "Now you can abandon this fae nonsense altogether, and we can—"

"No. Aunt Melisina, I know you mean well, but the truth is that I don't want to surrender my fae nature. It's part of me, and losing it would feel like losing some vital part of my soul. Something of what I was made to be."

My statement drew all the air from the room. Aunt Melisina sat motionless, and Aunt Caris's lips trembled. And Father . . . he gripped the tome he'd been holding as though he were a drowning man, and it was his only support.

At last, he stood and crossed the room to stand in front of me. "There's much I still don't know, might never know. But I do know this. Fae or mortal, you'll always be my daughter. It may not matter to you, not anymore, but I couldn't ask for a better one—all three of you, you're just as you should be."

A sob tightened my chest, and I choked it down, wrapping my arms around him and resting just for a moment. "It matters," I murmured.

He patted my back, then turned to embrace Ada and Ainslie as well.

Yet Aunt Caris still fidgeted with her lace handkerchief. "My dear, I still don't understand how you can desire such a thing. It's so dangerous and—"

"I know. But can you accept it?"

She let her hands drop into her lap. "If it's what you truly want."

"It is."

Lovell cleared his throat. "Does that mean all of you intend to embrace your fae heritage?"

"No, I have already chosen otherwise. I will remain mortal." Ainslie's eyes glistened. "I've never felt as Jessa does—my fae nature doesn't call to me as it does to her. Perhaps it would have been different if it hadn't been bound and stifled all these years, but I cannot change what is past, and when I consider the future—I want one here, in this world. I can't deny the thought of being mortal in the face of Otherworldly threats frightens me, and I know our world will face trouble, but I want nothing more than to work to protect it, hopefully alongside Mr. Redgrave. And I think perhaps I *can* help in some measure, because of the knowledge I've been given."

Aunt Caris turned to Ada, trembling. "And you?"

She twisted her hands in her skirts. "I don't know, not yet."

A small hope sparked to life within—perhaps I'd not be wholly alone. I'd expected her to follow suit with Ainslie, for the two of them had never separated from one another.

Ainslie must have shared that expectation, for she inhaled sharply. But she didn't try to speak any word of influence over Ada, unlike our aunts. They earnestly attempted to make her see reason, each argument twisting a knife blade a bit deeper in my chest. Beyond the window glass, the boughs of the maple tossed restlessly. I'd not even confessed the danger my presence would be yet . . . nor could I get a word in edgewise.

Only Holden's appearance brought a momentary lull. "Mr. Ludne. He will not wait."

Indeed, he appeared on Holden's heels, all sharp satisfaction and bristling unpleasantness, his ward-pendant pricking against my awareness with a flesh-crawling sensation.

Father snapped to his feet, his body tight. "What is the meaning of this?"

His winterberry eyes gleamed with cold pleasure as he withdrew a folded paper from his pocket. "I have an order to bring Miss Jessa to the Everstone Institution, signed by the First and the Magister."

I stumbled back, and the room grayed at the edges, his voice becoming distant and indistinct. Assuming the ward-pendant didn't interfere with its workings, I could escape him readily through the passing prism. But at what cost? My family would remain vulnerable, accused of rendering me aid against the edict of the king and Vigil—and my sudden disappearance would make their plight far worse. Could I somehow collect them all first? A passing prism required physical contact between us, and they were scattered through the room . . . and such a deed would destroy any chance they had of a future. Their innocence must be proven, must be protected.

Jade growled. *I could snap his neck.*

Then what? My entire family comes under suspicion of murder?

I'd braced for fae to strike, but not this. I'd thought I had time, but now even that had been taken from me.

"It's clear you are an utter fool." Aunt Melisina favored him with a frigid glare. "You cannot go about leveling false accusations against young ladies of quality, much less hauling them off to an Institution, whatever the faraddidles you've concocted for your superiors. When my husband learns of this—"

"He'll disavow all connection to her, most like." A fanatical light burned in his eyes. "I've received a very creditable eyewitness report of unnatural dealings, and that on top of my own observations and the evidence turned over." From a leather satchel, he withdrew my missing sketchbook. "This alone is reason enough for condemnation. Whatever front Miss Jessa puts on, it's clear her fae-touch runs deep. Her removal is for her safety, as well as your own."

Though the sight sent ice through my veins, I refused to reply, to acknowledge it belonged to me. Who had handed it over to him? One of the servants? My stomach churned. Holden had disapproved of my flouting convention—would he have gone so far? Or what of the sunset-haired man Morwen had seen go upstairs? Never mind, it didn't matter how he'd obtained it, not now. Only that I found a path to free my family from suspicion.

He tucked the sketchbook back under his arm. "Needless to say, I wouldn't expect to see her again. Not for a very long time, at least. Cases like this don't often take to rehabilitation."

Aunt Caris gave a muffled sob, Father stood white with fury, and Lovell gripped his walking stick as if he might strike the man down, despite his condition.

"If you don't come along quietly, Miss Jessa, I'm permitted to bring in your family to ensure your compliance." Mr. Ludne gripped his own walking stick, the iron raven-head handle chilling me even at this distance. "As of now, the case can be made that they knew nothing of your fae-touch. However, I'm by no means convinced—and I have authority to bring them all in for however long it takes to force the truth."

We could send for Riven.

No. If he leaves his court right now, the consequences could be unpleasant for everyone. And his presence will not fix this. I could glamour Mr. Ludne as readily as Riven could, but that's not what's required.

I drew myself up to my full height. "You've gone to a great deal of effort to carry out your grudge, but such dramatics won't be necessary."

"Jessa, no." Ainslie anchored one side and Ada the other. "You can't do this."

"I must." Despite what I'd told Jade, a furious urge to glamour him rose up in me. But he'd taken this to the highest authorities in Byren—the Magister and the First of the Vigil. I required another path to secure safety for my family. I turned to Mr. Ludne. "All I require is your word that if I go with you to the Institution, you'll leave my family alone. You will *never* approach any one of them again, and you will ensure they're left out of the investigation."

"Done."

The power of the bargain seared the air between us. I'd no doubt he didn't intend to keep his word—the slight smirk on his lips betrayed him. But it didn't matter. He was bound, and since he was the instigator and accuser, it would purchase their safety. His word would hold him—he'd have to leave my family alone, even fight for their innocence. They'd not suffer for my choices, and once I arrived at the Institution, fulfilling my end of the bargain, I could as swiftly depart.

I don't know what kind of wards they have. You and Risha should follow outside the carriage; we will meet outside the Institution. I don't want you to come to harm.

I'm not leaving you.

I hesitated. *Very well. I'd rather have you with me. Risha can remain without, and you can convey anything necessary to her.*

Mr. Ludne seized my arm with a bruising grip, and his ward-pendant sparked a greater pain. Jade rumbled low, following at my feet.

With sudden ferocity, Mr. Ludne kicked her away. "The beast stays. Deal with her, or I will."

Jade snarled.

And Ada hurried toward her, an act of true courage.

A swell of fury surged within me, and vines lashed at the windowpanes, awaiting my bid to strike—but no, I'd given my word. I'd bound myself, and I'd do it again to ensure my family had shelter from the repercussions of my choices. They'd done nothing wrong, and I'd never let them suffer on my behalf. *Just follow, as closely as you can. I'll meet you outside the Institution, then we can decide what must come next.*

His grip implacable, Mr. Ludne marched me out of the house. Once we were beyond its walls, the faintest prickle of Other broke through the haze caused by the ward-pendant. That wasn't right—did he keep some other fae device on his person? In the carriage? I pulled the star-bright songs of the white poplars to myself, seeking a barrier against the ward, searching for the source of Other. Yet before I could sort the jumbled impressions, he opened the carriage door and shoved me inside. As I stumbled across the threshold, a fae working closed about me.

And the world vanished.

AFTERWORD

Want a peek into Jade's mind? Read on from her perspective in the bonus scene.

go.sarahchislon.com/bos-bonus

Jessa's story continues in *Mirror of Argent,* which releases fall 2025. Pre-order now so you don't miss it!

go.sarahchislon.com/moa

ACKNOWLEDGMENTS

Every time I write a book, I embark on a journey along with my characters—and though writing is a solitary pursuit, I'm privileged to share parts of the creative process with truly wonderful people. As always, I want to offer the biggest thanks to my husband, CJ. Your delight in my stories and your continual encouragement and support make all this possible. Thank you, my love.

I'm also fortunate to work with some very skilled and lovely people in the production of these books. To Lauren Donovan, Kara Aisenbrey, and Deborah O'Carroll—I couldn't ask for a better editorial team. I'm more thankful than words can say for the passion and skill you bring to your work and the love you have for this series. And to Lena Yang—this may be my favorite cover yet. Thank you all!

I'm also deeply grateful to the family and friends who offer encouragement and support (all the more to those who don't ordinarily read fantasy)!

Although they're not yet old enough to read this series, my amazing daughters still cheer me on, exclaiming over cover design and story art and asking all sorts of questions about the creative process. In turn, they excitedly share their own story ideas, which I have the privilege of seeing them learn to put to the page. My girls, I'm so thankful I get to be your mama.

And always and forever, I'm most grateful to my Maker for the gift of life and the ability to create.

ABOUT THE AUTHOR

Sarah Chislon lives in Virginia with her husband and three daughters. When she's not writing, she's homeschooling her children and running a web development business with her husband. As an avid reader and a lifelong story-weaver, she delights in creating fantastic worlds and exploring them alongside her characters.

For more information on her books, visit her website sarahchislon.com—or sign up for her newsletter to receive updates and free bonus content.

facebook.com/sarahchislon

instagram.com/sarahchislon

bookbub.com/profile/sarah-chislon

www.ingramcontent.com/pod-product-compliance
Lightning Source LLC
Chambersburg PA
CBHW022248310726
48973CB00001B/6